For the Trekkers

GLOSSARY

Airyanãm (Avestan) Noble, heroic.

Aspis (Classical Greek) A large round shield, deeply dished, commonly carried by Greek (but not Macedonian) *hoplites*.

Baqca (Siberian) Shaman, mage, dream-shaper.

Chiton (Classical Greek) A garment like a tunic, made from a single piece of fabric folded in half and pinned down the side, then pinned again at the neck and shoulders and belted above the hips. A men's *chiton* might be worn long or short. Worn very short, or made of a small piece of cloth, it was sometimes called a 'chitoniskos'. Our guess is that most *chitons* were made from a piece of cloth roughly 60 × 90 inches, and then belted or roped to fit, long or short. Pins, pleating, and belting could be simple or elaborate. Most of these garments would, in Greece, have been made of wool. In the East, linen might have been preferred.

Chlamys (Classical Greek) A garment like a cloak, made from a single piece of fabric woven tightly and perhaps even boiled. The *chlamys* was usually pinned at the neck and worn as a cloak, but could also be thrown over the shoulder and pinned under the right or left arm and worn as a garment. Free men are sometimes shown naked with a *chlamys*, but rarely shown in a *chiton* without a *chlamys* – the *chlamys*, not the *chiton*, was the essential garment, or so it appears. Men and women both wear the *chlamys*, although differently. Again, a 60 × 90 piece of cloth seems to drape correctly and have the right lines and length.

Daimon (Classical Greek) Spirit.

Ephebe (Classical Greek) A new *hoplite*; a young man just training to join the forces of his city.

Epilektoi (Classical Greek) The chosen men of the city or of the *phalanx*; elite soldiers.

Eudaimia (Classical Greek) Well-being. Literally, 'well-spirited'. See *daimon*, above.

Gamelia (Classical Greek) A Greek holiday.

Gorytos (Classical Greek and possibly Scythian) The open-topped quiver carried by the Scythians, often highly decorated.

Himation (Classical Greek) A heavy garment consisting of a single piece of cloth at least 120 inches long by 60 inches wide, draped over the body and one shoulder, worn by both men and women.

Hipparch (Classical Greek) The commander of the cavalry.

Hippeis (Classical Greek) Militarily, the cavalry of a Greek army. Generally, the cavalry class, synonymous with 'knights'. Usually the richest men in a city.

Hoplite (Classical Greek) A Greek soldier, the heavy infantry who carry an *aspis* (the big round shield) and fight in the *phalanx*. They represent the middle class of free men in most cities, and while sometimes they seem like medieval knights in their outlook, they are also like town militia, and made up of craftsmen and small farmers. In the early Classical period, a man with as little as twelve acres under cultivation could be expected to own the *aspis* and serve as a *hoplite*.

Hoplomachos (Classical Greek) A man who taught fighting in armour.

Hyperetes (Classical Greek) The *Hipparch*'s trumpeter, servant, or supporter. Perhaps a sort of NCO.

Kithara (Classical Greek) A musical instrument like a lyre.

Kline (Classical Greek) A couch or bed on which Hellenic men and women took meals and perhaps slept, as well.

Kopis (Classical Greek) A bent bladed knife or sword, rather like a modern Ghurka kukri. They appear commonly in Greek art, and even some small eating knives were apparently made to this pattern.

Machaira (Classical Greek) The heavy Greek cavalry sword, longer and stronger than the short infantry sword. Meant to give a longer reach on horseback, and not useful in the *phalanx*. The word could also be used for any knife.

Parasang (Classical Greek from Persian) About thirty *stades*. See below.

Phalanx (Classical Greek) The infantry formation used by Greek *hoplites* in warfare, eight to ten deep and as wide as circumstance allowed. Greek commanders experimented with deeper and shallower formations, but the *phalanx* was solid and very difficult to break, presenting the enemy with a veritable wall of spear points and shields, whether the Macedonian style with pikes or the Greek style with spears. Also, *phalanx* can refer to the body of fighting men. A Macedonian *phalanx* was deeper, with longer spears called *sarissas* that we assume to be like the pikes used in more recent times. Members of a *phalanx*, especially a Macedonian *phalanx*, are sometimes called *Phalangites*.

Phylarch (Classical Greek) The commander of one file of *hoplites*. Could be as many as sixteen men.

Porne (Classical Greek) A prostitute.

Pous (Classical Greek) About one foot.

Prodromoi (Classical Greek) Scouts; those who run before or run first.

Psiloi (Classical Greek) Light infantry skirmishers, usually men with bows and slings, or perhaps javelins, or even thrown rocks. In Greek city-state warfare, the *psiloi* were supplied by the poorest free men, those who could not afford the financial burden of *hoplite* armour and daily training in the gymnasium.

Sastar (Avestan) Tyrannical. A tyrant.

Stade (Classical Greek) About 1/8 of a mile. The distance run in a 'stadium'. 178 meters. Sometimes written as *Stadia* or *Stades* by me. Thirty *Stadia* make a *Parasang*.

Taxies (Classical Greek) The sections of a Macedonian *phalanx*. Can refer to any group, but often used as a 'company' or a 'battalion'. My *taxeis* has between 500 and 2,000 men, depending on losses and detachments. Roughly synonymous with *phalanx* above, although a *phalanx* may be composed of a dozen *taxeis* in a great battle.

Xiphos (Classical Greek) A straight-bladed infantry sword, usually carried by *hoplites* or *psiloi*. Classical Greek art, especially red-figure ware, shows many *hoplites* wearing them, but only a handful have been recovered and there's much debate about the shape and use. They seem very like a Roman gladius.

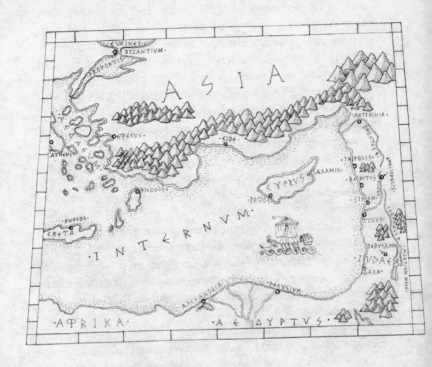

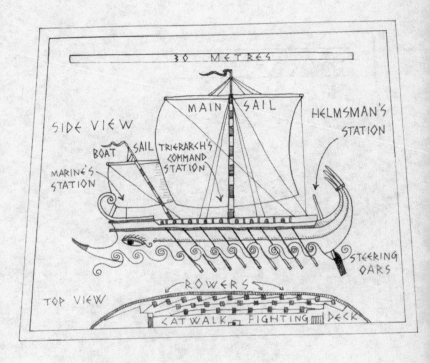

30 METRES

SIDE VIEW

MAIN SAIL

HELMSMAN'S STATION

BOAT SAIL TRIERARCH'S COMMAND STATION

MARINE'S STATION

STEERING OARS

ROWERS

TOP VIEW

CATWALK FIGHTING DECK

The kurgan of Kineas rose above the delta of the Tanais River like one of the pyramids of distant Aegypt rendered in turf. At the top, a plinth of Parian marble winked white in the sun.

At the foot of the kurgan, where the spring-brown Tanais washed against the muddy beach, stood Srayanka, who had been Kineas's wife. Behind her waited a thirty-oared open boat, the stern firmly set in the mud, awaiting her pleasure while she hugged her children again – Melitta, who at twelve was already the image of her mother, and Satyrus, who was her twin and yet showed his father more, in his hips and shoulders and around his mouth. A mouth that was quivering with suppressed tears. Satyrus hugged his mother again and then Melitta took his hand and they stood on the beach with Philokles, their tutor.

'Mind you let them away from their scrolls and dead poets,' Srayanka said. 'Take them riding. Fishing. Too much writing kills the spirit.'

'Reading trains the mind as athletics trains the body,' Philokles intoned automatically. He slurred the word 'athletics'.

'I should only be gone five days. One ugly task, and we're off to the sea of grass for the summer. What have I forgotten?' Srayanka looked at Satyrus, who remembered things.

'You've told us *everything*,' Melitta said.

'The new athletics coach from Corinth should arrive any day,' Srayanka said. 'See that he is well received.'

'I know,' Philokles said. He was no more drunk than usual, and resented her repeated instructions with the ease of ancient habit.

'We all know,' Melitta said.

Satyrus would have liked to speak, but it took all his effort not to cry. He hated being separated from his mother. But he gathered his wits, took a deep breath and said, 'I want to go in the boat.'

I

Srayanka smiled at him, because Satyrus loved boats and the sea the way his sister loved horses and the sea of grass. 'Soon, my dear. Soon you can command my boat.' She looked out over the water. 'But not this trip.'

Satyrus trembled with the effort of suppressing his reaction. But he smiled at her, and she smiled back, pleased that her son was learning to command himself.

And then, despite her misgivings, Srayanka walked down the beach and up the boarding plank into the boat.

They took two days to sail to the gap in the long sandbanks that defined the Bay of Salmon, and another day to make their way through the passages between the temporary islands to the Euxine. Once they were clear of the last treacherous mudbank, they coasted along the shore, camping in the open for the night and then rowing slowly along the beach before Heron's city of Pantecapaeum, looking for the rendezvous.

It was one of those days people remember when they remember being happy – the sky as deep and blue as it could be, the spring sun lighting the green grass as it rolled away to the horizon, the sea a perfect azure reflecting the bowl of heaven, and the crisp golden beach neatly contrasting the black mud of the fields to the south and west. In autumn, they would be full of grain – the grain that made the Euxine rich.

Srayanka sat in the stern of the open boat with a handful of her best warriors and Ataelus, a Sakje tribesman from the east who had been her husband's scout. He was more than a scout now – his clan numbered in excess of six hundred riders.

A mixture of Greeks and local Maeotae – farmers, like the Sindi further west – rowed the boat. Srayanka smiled to watch them row together, because the mixture of the three races represented her not-quite-a-kingdom on the Tanais River. Today, she was going to land near Pantecapaeum to seal her status with a treaty – a Greek concept, but well within her understanding – that would ensure the safety of her shipping and her farmers and her children.

It was all very different from the way of her childhood, she thought, as her face warmed in the sun. As a spear-maiden, she had ridden the sea of grass. When angered, she had made war. When her enemies were stronger than she, she had ridden away into the grass and vanished. Kineas and his dream of a kingdom on the Euxine had changed all that. Now she had thousands of farmers to protect and hundreds of Greek colonists and traders. *Hostages.* She could no longer ride away.

Well up the beach, as far as a good horse would go in two hundred heartbeats, she could see the man with whom she had come to treat – Heron, the tyrant of Pantecapaeum. Like Ataelus, Heron had been one of her husband's men a dozen years ago. Not one of her favourites, but the bonds held. Heron intended to make himself the king of the Euxine, and much as that thought offended her, acknowledging him would cost her no horses, as the old Sakje saying went.

She chuckled.

Ataelus gave her one of his broad smiles. It was easy – and foolish – to take those smiles for a lack of ready wit. Ataelus was just one of those men who found much to smile at. 'For being happy?' Ataelus asked. Fifteen years of living around Greeks and his Greek had never improved.

'We're going to make Heron the ghan of the Inner Sea,' she said in Sakje. In that language, her contempt was obvious – that she, who openly wore the sword of Cyrus and might end her days as queen of all the Sakje on the sea of grass, should bend the knee to some Greek boy with a mere city at his beck and call.

'For calling him Eumeles,' Ataelus said with a shrug – in Greek. 'Eumeles, not Heron.'

Srayanka watched the beach grow nearer and shook her head. 'I can't bring myself to like him,' she said.

Ataelus shrugged, the most Greek thing he did. He was wearing a heavy over-robe of Qin silk worked in gold. Under it he had a harness of bronze and horn scales. Despite his small stature, he looked like what he was – a cheerful warlord. 'Want to change your mind?' he asked, finally speaking in Sakje.

She shook her head. She could see Heron – Eumeles – standing a little in front of his guard, two dozen mercenaries. He was showy, dressed in purple and gold, with red sandals and a fancy sword. Another man stood just behind him – a stranger, but his position said he was almost as important as Heron. The second man was not remarkable in his dress, in his size, in any way. He had nondescript hair and was of middling height. But the fact that he stood so near Heron caused her to narrow her eyes.

'Who is he?' she asked in Sakje. No need to go into details with Ataelus.

Ataelus moved his chin the breadth of a finger, but the gesture said that he, too, had never seen the man before.

Srayanka smiled at her captain – nothing so grand as a navarch, as the Greeks called their boat commanders. 'Put us ashore here,' she said. 'We'll walk a little.'

Ataelus grinned at her caution.

The bow of the open boat hissed and grumbled as he passed over the waves in the shallow water and then made a firm *crunch* as they ran up the sand. The men in the bow jumped free of the boat and dragged the light hull up the beach an armspan, and then the rest of the rowers were out, and the keel was dragged free of the water. Only then did the Sakje – none of them remotely resembling a sailor – jump down on to the sand. Two of Srayanka's warriors touched the sand and then their brows.

Srayanka watched Heron, just a few dozen horse-lengths away. 'Relaunch the boat,' she said in Greek. 'Ready to sail in a moment.'

Ataelus raised an eyebrow.

'Humour an old woman,' Srayanka said. She checked her *gorytos*, the bow case that every warrior wore all the time, her fingers touching the bow and the arrows, the knife strapped to the back of the case, and the sword of Cyrus at her waist.

All the Sakje mimicked her. The warriors looked at her and at Ataelus.

'I'm a fool,' she said. 'Let's get this done.' *For my children*, she thought. She liked her life – she had no real need to be queen of all the Sakje, nor even to displace her former enemy Marthax. She wanted to enjoy the rest of her life. One bend of her knee, and all she had worked for was safe.

She did not want to bend her knee. *Oh, husband of my heart.*

We defeated Iskander, and now I bend the knee to a fool.

Walking in sand was messy and undignified, and she wished she'd overcome her fears and her contempt and landed the boat at Heron's feet. *Eumeles' feet*, she thought. The scarecrow. The useless boy. A nonentity who pretended to be her husband's heir.

And then she was there – a horse-length from the tall, thin man in the purple cloak. She bowed to him.

'She is beautiful,' the man behind Heron said. His accent was Athenian, and she thought of Kineas. He seemed startled by her.

'All yours,' Heron said. He turned his back and vanished through his guards.

Betrayal. She knew it in an instant.

She got her *akinakes* – the sword of Cyrus, as long as her arm and wickedly sharp – in her hand before the guards could cross the sand. *What a fool, to use that gesture to warn me of his betrayal*, she thought, and the cool jade of the sword of Cyrus steadied her. She grabbed the first heavy spear thrust at her and jerked it, and then reached over the man's big, round shield to sink the point into his neck.

A blow in her side, but the armour under her robe turned the point, and she spun, but they had already closed around her and they weren't taking chances. She went down almost to the ground and swung her short sword *up* under a shield and the man screamed as he went down and she was into his place – a blow against her back, and another, and pain so sharp. She felt her vision tunnel and the strength going from her legs, but the *other* man was there, and she fell at him. She had lost control of her muscles before her sword slashed across the bridge of his nose and his blood fountained across her back. She saw their feet – some bare and some heavily sandalled.

'Fucking *whore*!' the Athenian screamed.

She smiled, even though dark was coming down and she knew just what that meant.

The solid sound of an arrow going home in flesh – the complex sound of the head punching through the guard's white leather *thorax* – would have made her smile again, except

5

that she was too far down the dark path for that. *Ataelus,* she thought. *Alive, and hence shooting. Save my children, Ataelus.*

Then shouts. Feet pounding. The Athenian cursing, sounding like a man with a bad cold.

Cold – every part of her cold. *Lying awake in her wagon on the sea of grass, naked to invite Kineas to play, but cold – and then the warmth, the reward as he came into her bed, warm and the smell of man and horse and dirty bronze that he wore like perfume.*

'Don't blame me,' Heron said. 'I gave her to you. You fucked it up.'

'She cut off my *d-d-dose!*' the Athenian groaned.

'Nonsense. Most of it is still there. I've sent for my healer. Now, what do you want – her head?' Heron was impatient. She formulated her curse on him, and spat it out, syllable by syllable, like the last drops of honey dripping from a jar, as the darkness came down. And she could still hear.

'Fuck you.' The Athenian managed to sound as if he had a spine.

'Any more insults and I'll tell Lord Cassander you died in the fighting. Am I clear? Good. My healer will see to your nose and then I will attempt to rectify *your* mistake before it costs me more money and more time.' Heron sounded as he always did – superior.

'You mbissed the little Scyth and dhow his boat's got away,' the Athenian said. The shock of his wound was wearing off. 'You were the fool who gave us away. Burder mbe and Cassander will come for *you!*'

'If you are an example of Cassander's might, I have just backed the wrong horse,' Heron said. 'Give my regards to the Lady Olympias. Remember – I am to be king of the Euxine. This was the price. Am I clear?' A pause. 'She was supposed to bring the brats. Where the fuck are they? I need them dead.'

'Fuck you,' the Athenian spat.

Srayanka was losing interest. The cold was going – she could feel his warm feet against hers, and she could smell the scent of old bronze and oil and horse – and a little male sweat.

As always, Kineas's touch relaxed her, and she flowed away.

PART I

FORGING

1

316 BC

The sand of the palaestra was cool under his cheek, but the weight of his new trainer crushed the air from his lungs.

'You have a good physique for a boy,' the athlete said. He rolled off his prospective pupil and offered him a hand. 'But any time you offer a test of strength to a *man*, he'll beat you.'

The new coach had the shoulders of a bull. He stood a head taller than his twelve-year-old student, and he was wider – deep of chest, and with the sort of muscles that decorated heroic vases. His name was Theron, and he had competed for the laurel at Nemea and at Olympia and lost – narrowly – at both. He had come a long way to be the boy's coach, and he made it clear that he wanted to see what he was getting.

What he was getting was a slim figure with the muscles of a boy – an athletic boy, but he had neither weight nor breadth. He was handsome enough, with a shock of dark brown hair and wide-spaced eyes. His body was well enough formed, his nose as yet unbroken, and he had not yet sprouted the hair of adolescence.

The boy grasped his teacher's hand and popped to his feet. He gave a petulant smile and rubbed his hip. His shins were decorated with bruises, the brown blotches so regular that his mother said that he looked as if he was wearing Scythian trousers. 'I'll have you someday,' he said. Then he relented and grinned, wondering if that was too brash.

Theron shook his head. 'You've speed and talent, boy, but that chest of yours will never have the width to put my head in the sand.'

The boy bowed, a natural movement devoid of servility. 'As you say,' he said. He didn't mean it, and his attitude came out clearly in his delivery. In fact, there was a tinge of mockery to the sentence. He glanced at his tutor, another big man, who reclined under the stoa of pillars.

The athlete's resentment showed in his suddenly red face.

The boy's sister, perched in the cool arch under the colonnade, laughed.

The new coach – the prospective coach – spun. 'Girl!' he said. 'You are not allowed in the palaestra.' He inclined his head. 'Young mistress.' He moved a hand to cover his privates.

The males were both naked.

The 'young mistress' rose from her concealment. 'I disagree,' she said. She was wearing a man's *chiton* over her slim hips and long legs. She was also twelve years old, with the first sign of her mother's deep breasts and with large and adult eyes of no particular colour. 'My mother will insist, if you like. I, too, wish to learn to fight the Greek way.'

Theron, a born athlete who had travelled three thousand stades across the Euxine to take a contract that would make him a wealthy man in Corinth for the rest of his life, stood his ground. 'It is unseemly for women to take part in athletics,' he began.

'Spartan women take part in all the games,' the girl said. 'My tutor tells me so.' Her eyes flicked to the big man reclining under the colonnade.

'When he's sober,' her brother added. He picked up a strigil and began to scrape the sand off his backside. 'And he says women run at Nemea. You competed at Nemea, did you not, Theron?'

Theron looked from one to another, and a slow smile caught at the corners of his mouth. But while the boy was watching the smile, he reached out one hand at the end of a giant arm and grabbed the boy, rotated him and tripped him over an extended foot, pinning him in the sand. 'In the palaestra, I am *master*,' he said. 'Your sister should *not* be here. When she returns from making her treaty, I will speak to your lady mother about the women's events – I would be happy to teach a child with such long limbs to run. But not *pankration*. Pankration is for men. It is for killing.'

The girl nodded. It was clear from her posture that she was nodding from courtesy, not in agreement. 'My mother has killed fifty men,' the girl said. 'You?' She nodded before he could answer. 'I'll expect a daily lesson from you, then,' she said to the recumbent form of her twin brother. 'It will be good for you to teach me. You'll have every lesson twice.'

'Master, may I get up now?' the boy asked.

Theron leaped to his feet and again extended his arm. 'Of course.' He turned his back on the girl and confronted his new pupil. 'Does your sister watch you train?' he asked.

The boy laughed. 'She trains with me,' he said. 'Master.'

Theron shook his head. 'Not until I have spoken to your lady mother. Young mistress, please leave the palaestra.'

The girl nodded again, a slow gesture that was identical to her brother's nod. 'We will speak of this again,' she said. She rose to her feet with muscled grace, showing none of the coltishness of her age, and walked out of the arches, heading to the baths. She paused at the archway. 'You should call us by our names,' she said. 'That is the policy of my mother, and it is a good one. I am not the mistress here, any more than you are master. I am Melitta. My brother there is Satyrus. We are the children of Kineas of Athens and the Lady Srayanka. Our family fought at Marathon against the Medes and on the sea of grass against Darius. My father was descended from Herakles, and my mother from Artemis.' She bowed her head. 'The only mistress here is my mother, and she has no master.'

Theron didn't know many twelve-year-old girls in Corinth who could stare him down. She hadn't blinked since she had begun to talk. 'I understand that your father is dead,' he said.

The girl – Melitta – gave him a long look. 'We will speak of this again,' she said, and went into the baths.

Theron turned back to his proper charge – Satyrus. 'I said three falls,' he said. He glanced over his shoulder as if to make sure that the girl was gone.

'Was that one fall, or two?' the boy asked. There was no wickedness to his question. He meant it just as he asked it. 'Master?' he added, a little late. *Have to watch that if I want to keep him*, Satyrus thought to himself.

Theron swung his arms. 'That was one fall,' he said. 'Are you ready?'

The boy took up his stance. He was confident in his postures – his tutor knew the pankration well enough to teach a boy. Theron stood without moving, and Satyrus held his stance for as long as it took him to draw twenty breaths and release them slowly. He held it well, his hands high, weight well distributed, left foot forward and ready to kick. Theron began to circle and Satyrus circled with him, carefully keeping his distance. He had misjudged Theron's immense reach the last time. Now he was careful.

Theron lunged in, moving from his left foot to his right and reaching with his arms. The boy blocked one of his reaching arms and kicked hard at his knee, but Theron moved a fraction and took the kick on the side of his leg. He grunted.

'Good kick,' he said as he backed away.

Satyrus flashed a grin and moved in to attack, spun on his front foot and kicked again.

Theron grabbed for the leg – he had expected another kick – and grasped air. The second kick was a feint.

Satyrus whipped the kicking foot around, spinning his centre of gravity. He closed, grabbing Theron's extended hand with both of his own and throwing his weight to rotate the arm.

Theron's other arm shot out and grappled the boy's shoulders, pulling at him, grasping for a hold to turn the boy's body and take the weight off his arm.

Satyrus was too small to resist that grapple long. Desperate, he bit the older man's left bicep, drawing blood.

Theron shouted and punched him in the head and Satyrus's whole body moved with the strength of the blow, but he set his jaw and tried to hold his grip on the sweat-slick muscles of his opponent's arm. Pressed almost ear to chest, he could hear Theron's heartbeat racing as he sank to one knee under the pressure of the boy's attack on his shoulder joint.

Theron's second blow to his head broke his hold, and Satyrus fell bonelessly to the sand. It wasn't that he decided to relinquish his hold – the strength just flowed away from his limbs. He wondered if he was going to die, as men did in the *Iliad* when the strength left their limbs. His vision tunnelled and the palaestra began to go away. But he could still hear. He heard the big Corinthian get to his feet, his hands brushing away the sand. He heard the sound of someone clapping.

'Good thing that you won,' came the voice of his tutor. He sounded drunk and sarcastic. 'Embarrassing to lose to a new pupil. Knocking him unconscious will probably teach him a lesson, too.'

The new coach sounded upset when he replied. 'I never meant to hit him so hard,' he said. 'Apollo – I'm bleeding like a sacrifice.' He shifted his weight. Satyrus could hear everything. He could hear the sound of the man breathing. 'I regret that,' he said.

The tutor rose unsteadily, his feet scraping loose sand on the marble floor as he stumbled, every grain giving its own sound to Satyrus's ears. Then he crossed the sand. Satyrus heard the uneven sound of his footsteps, even on the sand, heard him fetch a canteen from the far wall and felt the cold water hit his face as he sprinkled the contents liberally. Satyrus felt his eyelids flutter of their own volition, and light came to his eyes like a bolt of pain.

'Ugh,' Satyrus said.

He tried to sit up, and after a few heartbeats he managed the trick, only to fall on all fours and vomit up his barley porridge. He still had some of Theron's blood on his mouth.

Theron knelt at his side. 'Can you understand me?' he asked.

'Yes,' Satyrus replied. 'Master.'

Theron nodded. 'You scared me,' he said. He shrugged. 'I applaud you. That any boy could scare me like that is, in itself, a kind of victory. I will take you seriously. Now promise me that you will not bite or gouge in a contest. It is against the rules.'

'Not in Sparta,' said the tutor. He wiped the boy's mouth with his chiton.

Theron sat back on his heels, his puzzlement plain on his face. It was clear from his expression that he couldn't decide if the tutor was a peer or a slave. He had a paunch and his hair was thinning on top, and he was clearly drunk – functional, the way many hard-drinking slaves went through life, but drunk nonetheless.

The room was spinning around Satyrus, and he was in no mood to help the new man. Besides, if he couldn't see that the pins of his tutor's chiton were gold, he was a fool.

The drunkard leaned forward. 'You going to live, boy?' he asked. The smell of sour wine washed over Satyrus, and he retched again. When he was done, he extended a hand to his tutor.

'Yes, master,' Satyrus replied. He had no trouble calling the drunkard 'master'.

But Theron had obviously not risen to be a champion by underestimating his opponents. 'You are a Spartan,' he said to the tutor.

The other man nodded. 'I *was* a Spartan,' he said. 'Now I am a gentleman of Tanais.' The Spartan's wit dripped with self-mockery.

'Theron of Corinth,' the athlete said, extending his hand.

'Philokles,' the other man said, accepting Theron's hand. Theron made a face suggesting that the Spartan had quite a grip for a drunk.

The two big men watched each other for a few heartbeats. Theron grinned. Philokles smiled slightly.

'Can I get up now?' the boy asked. He rubbed his temple. 'Everything is moving around,' he said.

Theron pressed with his thumb at the impact point, his heart pounding, and he showed his relief with a sigh when he found nothing moving under the pressure while the boy tried to hold his head still against the pain. 'No more fighting today,' he said. 'And no afternoon nap. Sleeping after a heavy blow is dangerous.'

Philokles nodded at the Corinthian. 'You've read the Hermetics?'

Theron nodded. He raised an eyebrow at the tutor, whose smile broadened.

'I feel better,' the boy said. Lies. But the lies of virtue. 'Let's have a third fall.'

'No,' Theron said.

'Let's go fishing,' Philokles said. 'A pleasant way to spend a spring day. Aesop would approve, and Xenophon wrote a book on it.' The Spartan rose to his feet. 'I'll find some lines and some wine. Meet me at the stables before the sun is at the zenith.'

He bowed.

Satyrus returned the bow, a little unsteady. He went across the sand under his own power and headed for the baths.

'Do you fish?' he heard Philokles say. His ears were ringing and it was all he could do to walk without putting his hands on the columns for support, but he had done other things as hard.

'My father was a fisherman,' Theron said.

'I'll take that to mean no,' he heard Philokles say, and then he was safe within the steamy warmth of the archway.

The town of Tanais was the same age as the twins, the newest town on the Euxine Sea, far up the Bay of Salmon. The new settlements spread up the north bank for almost a parasang, with Greek farms interspersed with the heavy stone buildings of the Maeotae farmers native to the valley where the wheat grew like a carpet of gold. Much of the mouth of the river was covered in small wooden wharves and hurdles for drying fish – the famous produce of the Bay of Salmon, the foundation of the fish sauce that every Athenian gourmand craved.

Between the salmon and the wheat, the town was already rich.

The town itself was a small affair centred on a temple to Nike and the accompanying baths and palaestra of a much grander town, built in wood on stone foundations and decorated in the latest fashion. The ivory and gilt statue of the goddess was the dedication of two of the town's most prominent founders: Diodorus, a soldier of fortune currently far to the south in service to Eumenes the Cardian, and Leon the Numidian, one of the Euxine's principal merchants. Their names appeared on the founding stones of the temple and the palaestra, on the stone *stele* to the dead of the town and on the marble plinth at the corner of the new law court. Leon owned the warehouses at the edge of the water, and the stone wharves, and his contributions had dredged the harbour and raised the breakwater that had turned a chain of tiny islands into an impregnable defence against the Euxine's occasional winter storms.

The Lady Srayanka, the mother of the twins, was not a Greek woman. Her name appeared on no dedications. No founding stone had her initials, and none of her weapons were dedicated at the altar of Nike, but her hand was visible all along the river. As ruler – queen, some said – of all the Eastern Assagatje, it was her word that kept the settlement free from the predations of the tribes of the sea of grass, and her warriors that made the town independent of the labyrinthine politics of the nascent kingdom of the Bosporus to the west. In her name, the Sindi and the Maeotae farmers lived in safety along the river valley. Her horsemen and the *hippeis* of the town kept the bandits away from the high ground between the Tanais and the distant Rha, so that merchants like Leon could bring their precious cargoes from the Hyrkanian Sea far to the east – and farther, from Seres itself, and Qin.

Satyrus was her son, and Melitta her daughter. They walked through their town, hand in hand, to the stables built in their father's name, in the hippodrome where their father's friend Coenus still drilled the remainder of the men who had followed their father east in his fabled war with Alexander. Most of them were away in the south with Diodorus, on campaign, as mercenaries.

'How's your head now?' Melitta asked.

Satyrus blinked. 'For some reason,' he said slowly, 'it's worse in the sun.'

They entered the hippodrome – a building that was new and well-built and out of all proportion to the number of cavalrymen that the town actually supported. Satyrus gritted his teeth against the ache in his head as they crossed the sand, and squeezed his sister's hand until she grunted in pain.

'Sorry,' he said.

They passed the line of columns at the edge of the stables – wooden columns, but carefully painted to look like marble – and the smell of horses enveloped them.

16

Pelton, an old freed slave of Leon's, greeted them. 'The gods prosper you, twins,' he said. 'Master Philokles took a mule. That new feller – too big for a mule – he took a horse.'

Twins was something like a title in Tanais. Melitta nodded. 'I'll take Bion,' she said. Bion was a Sakje charger, bigger than a Greek pony, like a warhorse scaled for a tall girl. She called the beast 'Bion' because the gelding *was* her life. Happy or sad, angry or elated, she dealt with the rigours of life by riding. Twice now, she had gone with her mother to the summer pasture of the Assagatje, riding with the maidens while her brother learned philosophy and law in faraway Athens. Her horse was her answer to most things.

Satyrus walked down the line of stalls until he reached the end, where his father's charger cropped barley straw with the contentment of a retired warhorse. 'Care to go for a ride?' he asked the giant. Thalassa was a mare – but a mare of heroic proportions. She raised her head and nuzzled him for a treat until he produced a carrot. Then she chewed the delicacy with a finicky patience, tossing her head.

'You want to go?' he asked again. 'I think the answer is yes.'

The former slave laughed. 'When has the answer ever been no? Eh? Tell me that!' He stepped in and put a bridle on the old mare in a single motion, his lower hand putting the bit into her mouth without so much as a jingle of the bronze against her teeth.

Melitta put her palms flat on her horse's back and sprang on to her in one go. 'Pelton, do you ever wonder why you were a slave?' she asked.

Pelton looked at her for the time it took an insect to cross a leaf. 'Nope,' he said. 'Will of the gods, mostly, I expect.' He plucked a piece of grass and put it in his mouth.

'Could happen to anyone, couldn't it?'

'Sister!' Satyrus didn't always appreciate his sister's approach to the world – a blunt approach, to say the least.

She looked down at him from her horse. 'Well, Leon owned him. And Leon was a slave. So Leon should know better.'

'Better than what?' Satyrus asked. He liked to think that

he was already a man – a man who understood things. One of the things he understood was that you didn't tease slaves about their slavery.

'Better than to own people,' she said.

Satyrus rolled his eyes. He led Thalassa out of the stable, her heavy hooves ringing on the cobblestone floor and sending *pings* of echo off the whitewashed walls to penetrate his brain and increase his headache. He led her around to the mounting step and climbed on to her, sitting well back, as a boy can on a big horse. He adjusted his gorytos and then leaned over to his sister. He could see Philokles down by the gate, arguing with Theron. 'It's not nice to talk to slaves about slavery.'

'Why not?' Melitta asked. 'Pelton was a slave. Who else would I ask? You?'

Satyrus made the sound that brothers make all over the world, and tapped Thalassa's sides with his bare heels, and the mare surged into motion. Satyrus could feel her power – even at the age of seventeen, she was a big animal with power and spirit, the veteran of a dozen battles. When he was on her back, he could imagine that he was his father at the Jaxartes River, about to crush Alexander.

Pelton emerged from the stable with a scruffy straw hat clutched in his fist. 'This'll help, male twin.' Satyrus wheeled the mare in a neat curve and snatched the hat and pulled it on. The shade of the broad brim was like a healing balm.

'All the gods bless you, Pelton!' Satyrus said.

'And you, twins!' the former slave called.

'My sister means no harm,' Satyrus said.

Pelton smiled. 'Hope she never has to find out for herself,' he said, before he went back into the stables.

Theron and Philokles were arguing about the nature of the soul as Satyrus and Melitta passed the bronze equestrian statue of their father that stood at the edge of the agora, his hand raised, pointing east, as if he had just ridden from the hippodrome. There was another statue to him in Olbia, where he already had semi-divine status as a hero who had overthrown the tyrant, and the Sakje still sacrificed horses to him at the kurgan on the coast.

In Athens, on the other hand, many men spoke ill of their father, and a year ago Satyrus had attended the legal proceedings that had finally revoked his father's conviction for treason, making Satyrus a citizen and returning his grandfather's fortune. Which had only served to prove what every twelve-year-old knows by heart: the world is far more complicated than it appeared when you were ten.

'Surely Plato argues the point convincingly,' Theron began, as if he'd already made this argument and was still awaiting some acknowledgement.

Philokles had a leather bag over his shoulder. He tapped his mule into motion. Theron was mounted on a tall horse, one of the town's cavalry chargers, and he towered over the Spartan, but he had to thump the horse's sides to get him into motion. In a few surges of the charger's hindquarters it was clear that the Corinthian wasn't much of a rider.

Melitta was looking at the eastern horizon as if following her dead father's hand. The town sat on a bluff, and she could see a parasang, thirty full stades, or more in the early afternoon sun. 'Is that smoke?' she asked.

Philokles looked under his hand, and so did Satyrus.

'I expect they're clearing new fields,' Satyrus said. He regretted his tone almost at once – hectoring his sister with a display of knowledge when he didn't actually know what he was talking about. *I must outgrow that,* he thought.

She glanced at him and gave him half a smile, as if she could hear every word of his interior dialogue. 'Leon's still away,' she said, indicating the empty wharves as they rode through the gates.

'Leon the Numidian is our richest citizen,' Philokles said to Theron, who was more interested in mastering his horse than in the town's social life. 'Married to a barbarian. Wonderful horseman. A well-rounded man, for all that he started life as a slave.'

'Even in Corinth I've heard of your Leon,' Theron said. 'Whoa!'

'It will do you no good to lose your temper at a horse,' Melitta said. She laid a hand on Theron's bridle and stroked his gelding's neck and the horse calmed. 'That's quite a squadron for this time of year,' she said, pointing out to sea.

Satyrus looked. At first he saw nothing, but after a moment he could see a line of sails just nicking the edge of the world, three or four hours out in the bay. 'Triremes,' he said, because the sails were matching sizes. Closer in, a pentekonter raced for the beach under full oars.

'Is that mama's boat?' Satyrus asked. He was relieved to see it.

'Early for our mother,' Melitta said. But she smiled. They both wanted her home.

Theron glanced at her and looked away, changing weight and sitting too far back on his horse. The horse sensed his inattention and decided to be rid of him. He half-reared and then shot forward and Theron landed on the road like a sack of barley. The gelding raced away.

'Oof,' he said. Then he lay still.

Satyrus put a hand on his borrowed straw hat and leaned forward, the change of his weight enough to push Thalassa into a gallop, and he raced across a field of new emmer wheat that rolled away to the east, broken only by boundary walls and the line of the road. He caught the gelding easily, turned Thalassa under the offending horse's nose and caught his dangling reins. 'Come on, Hermes,' he said. Hermes was a gelding who missed his prick and tended to take it out on his riders. Satyrus stood up on Thalassa's back and jumped on to the gelding, pulled the reins and began speaking a litany of nonsense to him. The gelding turned and trotted back to the group, and Thalassa followed along, riderless but obedient.

When he was within range of her voice, Melitta called out, 'Can you handle him?' just to annoy her brother, who responded by prodding the gelding to a gallop and racing through the middle of them, scattering dust and almost riding his new coach down.

'Sorry!' he said. By way of apology, he handed the Corinthian the reins to his father's warhorse. 'Master Theron, this is the smartest horse who ever lived. She's the mother of half the cavalry horses on this side of the Euxine and she's still the toughest thing on four legs. Just don't sit so far back on her rump.'

The athlete made a poor showing of mounting the tall horse without a step, but he got up on his fourth try. Melitta didn't hide her laughter. Theron glared at her, and then at Philokles.

'Is this the order you maintain, master tutor?' he asked.

Satyrus caught his sister's eye, and they rode a little apart. Close enough to listen – far enough to give the appearance of privacy.

'If you mean Plato's views of the soul as he – rather mean-spiritedly, I might add – puts them in the mouth of Socrates, I'd say that they're interesting, but scarcely irrefutable,' Philokles said.

'You dislike *Plato*?' Theron asked.

'I dislike a sophist whose underlying theme is that he's smarter than his audience. Name me one dialogue where Plato is bested by a student.' Philokles wasn't looking at Theron but at Satyrus, who shook his head and smiled, because no such dialogue existed.

Theron shrugged. 'I doubt such a thing happened,' he said.

Philokles laughed. 'Their father studied with Plato until he died. I'm afraid that his tales of his former teacher have left an indelible impression.' The Spartan smiled. 'I prefer Simonides or Heraklitus!'

'That posturer? He only worked for money!' Theron sounded outraged.

Satyrus and Melitta grinned at each other, because Philokles said that their father had said that Plato was a *pompous ass*, which was an image so droll as to evoke giggles even here.

Theron looked at the children. 'They're both quite intelligent,' he said. It didn't sound like a question.

Philokles nodded. 'Is breeding people any different from breeding horses?' he asked. 'Their sire was a brilliant soldier and an educated man – a decent athlete as well, third or fourth in the hundred-and-ninth Olympiad.'

'Really?' Theron asked. 'What event?'

'Boxing,' the Spartan replied. 'Boys' boxing. He never competed as a man.'

'Why not?' Theron asked. Any boy who could make the top tier would have been a front-runner as a man.

'War,' Philokles said. 'We had quite a bit of it, back then.'

'No shortage now,' Theron said.

'At any rate, the mother's no different. You'll see when she's back from Pantecapaeum. She's not the beauty she used to be, but she's a first-rate tactician, she gives a fine speech for a barbarian and she's a brilliant athlete.' Philokles looked out over the fields and smiled to himself.

'She's a runner?' Theron asked. Running was virtually the only sport open to Greek women.

Philokles' smile became a grin. 'She's an archer – a mounted archer. Perhaps the finest on the sea of grass. And a pretty fair swordswoman.'

Theron nodded. 'I see. Hence the daughter.' He glanced at Melitta. Satyrus watched his eyes.

The Spartan nodded. 'Just so,' he said.

It took them an hour to ride to the fishing spot, a small bluff at a curve in the Tanais where rushing water from the Spring of Niobe (a local nymph) tumbled down the hillside to swell the river. The spring water ran all year, clear and cold, and small trout congregated in the deep pools just above the confluence.

The twins dismounted immediately, tethered their horses amidst the lush grass, hung their bows on their saddlecloths and went upstream, bronze knives in hand, to cut rods. When they were satisfied with what they had, they came back. Philokles was laying the horsehair lines out in the goat-cropped grass at the edge of the stream. Then the Spartan deftly attached bronze hooks decorated with red thread and hackles the colour of a bay horse.

'I've never seen anyone fish like this,' Theron said.

'Come!' Melitta said, taking his hand. He seemed shy of the contact, but he went with her willingly.

'Don't scare the fish,' she said in a whisper, and went down on all fours to crawl up the big rock that separated them from the stream. She was up the rock in a moment, just her head showing to the fish. She raised an arm carefully, and when the

Corinthian was in place beside her, she pointed. 'See the trout?' she asked.

Theron watched for the time it would take him to fight a bout, following her pointing finger, breathing carefully. 'I see it,' he said.

She was conscious of the warmth of a grown man next to her on the rock. *Something to be aware of*, she thought. 'Watch,' she said. *Different from lying next to my brother*.

Time passed. She was conscious that he must be bored, annoyed at the passing insects for failing at their duties. But at last a fly slowly came down, one of the big brown flies that the fish loved. It trailed across the water, its abdomen brushing the surface from time to time. Melitta assumed that it was laying eggs – eggs so tiny she couldn't see them, although she had watched this dance many times.

Her brother crawled up the rock on her left side. 'Any luck? Oh!' he exclaimed, as one of the pool's residents powered up from the dark at the bottom of the pool and took the big insect right off the surface of the water and rolled away in a red-orange flash, leaving a growing circle of ripples in its wake.

Melitta grinned in delight, slipping back down the rock and clapping her hands. 'See?' she asked, or rather demanded.

Theron's grin was lopsided and far friendlier than either of the children had seen from him yet. 'I do see. This isn't fishing with nets – it is fishing with insects!'

'Not real insects,' Satyrus said. 'For some reason, even if you catch them, the fish won't take them. But if you tie some feathers to a hook ...' He pointed at the rods of young cornel that Philokles had rigged. The dogwood sticks were the height of a grown man, and the horsehair lines were the same length.

'And if you dabble the bug on the surface like the real ones ...' Melitta added.

'Then sometimes – bang! – you get a big fish. They strike like a bolt from Zeus.' Satyrus took one of the rods eagerly. Melitta grabbed another and untied her sandals.

'I'm going upstream,' she said.

Philokles nodded. 'I'll go with the young lady.' He followed her. He seemed sober now, and Satyrus thought that his tutor was as happy as he'd ever seen him. Perhaps he needed company. Adult company. The thought saddened the boy a little. He wanted to *be* adult company, but he loved the big Spartan, drink and all, and if Theron of Corinth made him happy, so be it.

Satyrus went back to the rock, pondering the Corinthian and his odd reactions to his sister. He moved carefully up the rock, brought his dogwood rod level with his shoulders and flipped the hook over his head. The feathered hook sank through the still air and landed lightly on the water, the feather of the hackle resting on the surface tension.

After a heartbeat, Satyrus gave the gentlest of tugs and the bug skittered across the surface. He took a breath and repeated the motion.

Nothing. He sighed softly and popped the fly back off the water and over his shoulder, the hook arcing through the air and tiny drops of water brushing his skin. Using just his wrist, he flicked the hook back on to the water, took a breath and skipped the fly.

The movement of the fish was so fast that only long afternoons spent at this pastime enabled the boy to pull the hook *just right* and he had a fish the length of his arm pulling at the end of his rod. He raised the rod and dropped the fish on the cropped grass behind the rock. 'Will you take it off?' he asked Theron, who wasn't fishing but just watching.

The big man knelt in the grass and took the hook from the fish's mouth. He bashed the fish on a rock, then pulled out a bronze knife and gutted the fish in two strokes.

'You've done this before,' Satyrus said accusingly.

Theron smiled. 'I've never seen anyone use a fly like that,' he said. 'But my father had a fishing boat. Cleaning fish is the same everywhere, I'd wager.'

Satyrus held out his rod. 'Want to try?' he asked.

Theron rinsed his hands in a side pool and reached out for the rod. 'I'd love to.'

'Why don't you like my sister?' Satyrus asked as the Corinthian flicked his hook on to the water.

'I don't dislike your sister,' the man answered. 'Do you know that in Hellas, women do not go fishing with their brothers?'

Satyrus could see a rider across the stream. He was a couple of stades away and he was moving so fast that he raised dust.

'I've been to Athens,' Satyrus said proudly. 'The girls all had to stay at home.'

'Exactly,' Theron said.

'I thought it was stupid,' Satyrus added. 'I think that's Coenus!' he said, sliding back off the rock.

'Who's Coenus?' Theron asked politely. A fish chose that moment to hit his lure, and despite his inexperience, he jerked the rod and he hooked his prey – a trout at least as long as his forearm.

'Well done!' Satyrus exclaimed with all the enthusiasm of his age. He reached out and unhooked the trout, a big male with a heavy jaw and some fat on his backbone. The big fish had swallowed the hook, and Satyrus pulled carefully at the horsehair line, trying to retrieve the hook – fish hooks were precious.

'He's riding hard,' Theron said.

Satyrus got bloody fingers on the shaft of the hook and pulled, and the hook ripped free of the cartilage, and the big fish spasmed and vomited blood. Satyrus reversed his bronze knife and killed the fish with a practised blow. Then he laid it on the grass and gutted it. 'Coenus was one of my father's companions,' he said as he worked. 'He's quite old – older than you. He married a Persian, and keeps the temple of Artemis down the valley. He's a great hunter. His son is at school in Athens.' The boy smiled. 'Xeno is my best friend. Besides my sister, I mean. I wish he was here.' More soberly, 'Coenus says that a tutor is no substitute for Athens.'

'He's riding fast,' Theron said, still perched on the fishing rock.

Satyrus raised his head as he dropped the two fish into the net bag he wore. 'He is,' he said. 'Will you excuse me?'

'There are other riders behind him,' Theron said, rising to his feet. Something in the posture of the riders disturbed him.

'Get the horses,' Satyrus said. 'I'm going down to the road. Get the horses and the others.'

Theron hesitated, and Satyrus looked back. 'Move,' he said. 'Coenus is bleeding. Something is wrong.'

The Corinthian chose to obey. He jogged off up the trail along the stream.

2

Satyrus ran downstream until he came to where the big oak trees overhung the road. He climbed down into the road. He could hear the rhythm of Coenus's gallop. He stood in the middle of the road.

'Coenus!' he shouted.

If Philokles and Theron were big men, Coenus was bigger, and middle age had not diminished his size. A life of constant exercise kept him fit. He was clutching his left side, and blood flowed freely down his belly.

'What are you *doing* here, boy?' he croaked. 'By the light of my goddess's eyes!' He was holding his horse with his knees, despite the wound in his side.

Satyrus had his knife on a cord over his shoulder. He pulled it over his head, opened the brooch that held the shoulder of his chiton and stepped out of the garment. 'Bandage your side,' he said, tossing him the garment. 'What happened?'

'We're attacked!' Coenus said. He turned his head at the sound of hoof beats.

'They're well behind you,' Satyrus said. He was suddenly afraid. 'Attacked?'

'Sauromatae,' Coenus said. He used Satyrus's chiton as a pad to staunch the blood, and Satyrus stood on tiptoes to help him tie it as tightly as possible. Satyrus found that his hands were trembling and his senses heightened, so that he could hear his sister calling out and Philokles answering.

'Quick, boy,' Coenus said. 'Who is with you?'

'Philokles, my sister and Theron,' he answered. 'The new athletics coach.'

Coenus looked over his shoulder. The rise of the bluff on their left blocked any sight of his pursuers. 'We have to get to town,' he said. He grabbed Satyrus's hand. 'Thanks, boy,' he said gruffly.

Satyrus grinned, despite his nerves.

The hoof beats were getting closer.

'Ares and Aphrodite,' Coenus muttered. 'They're on us.' He turned his horse and drew his sword one-handed, a crook-bladed *kopis*.

Two men on ponies cantered around the bend in the road. They were barbarians and their horses were painted red. One raised a bow and shot, despite the range. His arrow fell short. They pressed their horses into a gallop and both loosed arrows together.

Satyrus ran off the road into the trees. He was unarmed and nothing but a target, and he was scared. Coenus sat still in the middle of the road. He looked tired and angry. He glanced once at Satyrus, and then put his knees to his horse and she responded with a leap into a canter.

The next two arrows flew over his head.

Behind the screen of trees, Satyrus could see his sister on Bion, the Sakje horse flying along the broken ground at the edge of the water and then leaping the stream like a deer.

Philokles emerged from the cover of the oaks with their horses in his fist. 'Satyrus!' he called.

Satyrus ran out on to the road and sprinted for his tutor.

Coenus's horse took an arrow and gave a shrill cry and then plunged into one of his attackers, and Coenus's arm went up in the classic overarm cut and came down like an axe cutting wood, and the unarmoured man was literally cut from the saddle, the blade ripping from the curve of his neck all the way into his breast, but the blow was too strong and the horses were moving too fast and Coenus lost his blade. He tried to turn his horse, but the mare was spent from a long gallop and wounded, and she didn't want to turn.

Coenus's other assailant had troubles of his own, as he'd kept his bow to hand too long and had dropped an arrow in the road. He froze in indecision as Coenus flashed past him, and he never saw the arrow that took him in the belly.

Satyrus ignored Philokles and vaulted on to Thalassa's back. His tutor was screaming at him to run. He ignored the Spartan and turned his horse down the road to where Coenus's horse was in the process of collapse, exhaustion and wounds having done her in. His sister's arrow had saved Coenus, and the Sauromatae warrior sat his horse in the middle of the road, both hands wrapped around the shaft of the arrow, screaming in agony and yet still mounted.

More Sauromatae came around the curve at the far end of the valley, drawn by the screams.

'Satyrus, run!' Philokles shouted again.

Satyrus had a secure seat. Thalassa moved under him, and he reached down and secured his gorytos and tied the girdle around his waist as he rode. He tried to ignore the shaking of his hands. He couldn't hear anything but the beat of his horse's hooves like the thudding of his heart, and he had a lump of bronze at the base of his throat. He was *afraid*.

Melitta was not afraid. She was on the road, fitting an arrow to her bow. She shot, and the men on the road moved, most of them pushing their horses to the verge or even in among the trees.

Satyrus didn't draw his bow. Instead, he used his knees to line Thalassa up with Coenus, who was kneeling in the road.

'Coenus!' he yelled. His voice was shrill but it carried, and his father's friend looked up. Then his face changed as if he was making a hard decision – and he stood up, clutching his side.

Melitta shot again. She had a light bow, and now that the surprise of her having a bow at all was lost, the Sauromatae were shooting back – strong men with men's bows. She backed her horse down the road. She shot again, arching her back as she shot to get the most from her bow.

Satyrus reached down and held an arm out to Coenus. The pain showed like a scar on the big man's face, and his lips were more white than red, and it was close – no matter how heroic, a twelve-year-old cannot haul a warrior on to the back of a charger. But Coenus found the strength from somewhere and got a leg over, almost tumbling his saviour on to the road, and then Thalassa sensed some change of weight and she was turning, moving away.

Philokles was up on Hermes, with the coach behind him. As soon as he saw his students in retreat, he turned his own horse and pressed him to a gallop, and they were away down the road.

The five of them galloped back along the river road for two stades without slowing, until Bion picked up a stone in his hoof and Melitta had to pick it clear as the men watched the road behind them. Thalassa never flagged, nor did her head go down at the halt. Instead, she looked around, as if aware that fighting was next. Then she raised her head higher, straining at the reins, and gave a cry.

Satyrus had a pounding head and the weight of a grown man who was in pain on his back, and Thalassa's fidgets were nothing but increased complication until he realized what she was seeing.

'By the Father of the Gods,' he said, pointing.

Coenus, slumped in agony, raised his head. 'Oh, Gods,' he said, and his head went down again.

Philokles held up a hand. 'Hoof beats!' he said.

Melitta vaulted on to Bion's back. She had her bow in her hand in a moment.

There was a column of smoke rising to the west – from the town. Melitta watched it the way a child watches the death of a loved one – unable to take her eyes away.

Satyrus felt the strength of the fight – the *daimon*, some men called it – leave his limbs, and he felt as weak as he had when Theron hit him in the palaestra. 'Perhaps it is just a house fire,' he said, but he didn't believe his own words.

Melitta's voice broke as she spoke, but no tears came. 'Raiders,' she said. 'The ships I saw!'

Philokles didn't sound drunk when he spoke. 'We must get across the river,' he said.

There were Sauromatae riders coming around the last bend. They were approaching carefully this time, and there were a dozen of them.

'We should take refuge in the shrine,' Melitta said.

Philokles was watching the riders. 'This – this was planned.' He shook his head. 'There will be no refuge in temples, children. All these men have come to kill *you*.'

Satyrus sucked in a breath.

Melitta sat straighter. 'Well,' she said, and her eyes were bright with unshed tears, 'we will have to give them a surprise then.'

Satyrus wished that he'd said such a thing.

'That's the spirit,' Philokles said. He got down from his horse and stood bare-handed on the ground. 'Can you children shoot one of the riders as close to me as possible? I need a spear.'

Theron looked around at them. 'What are you doing?' he asked.

The riders were nocking arrows.

'Walk away,' Philokles said to Theron, who remained on the horse they had shared. 'Leave us and live.'

Theron shook his head. 'You three are going to fight all those horsemen?' He grinned. He looked from one to another, his grin growing, and he slid from his horse. 'I'm in.'

Satyrus had to smile at the athlete's declaration. He drew his own bow and struggled to string it with the weight of Coenus hanging on his back.

Theron reached up and took the wounded man. He set him gently on the ground.

Philokles went down on both knees in the road, picked up a handful of dust and rubbed it in his hair. He raised his arms. 'Furies!' he cried. 'Those who guard the most sacred of oaths! I must break my vow.'

Theron looked at Satyrus. 'What vow?' he asked.

Melitta was watching the horsemen. 'Mother says he vowed never to draw the blood of another man,' she said. 'Watch out!'

Satyrus got his bow strung and fitted an arrow as the first dozen came from their foes. There were too many arrows to avoid, and his heart almost stopped in terror as the flight came in. Time stretched as the arrows fell, and then they were past.

None of the arrows hit a target. Now he was down low on Thalassa's neck and Melitta was with him, the two horses kicking up dust as they sped right at the Sauromatae, and again he could hear nothing but Thalassa's hoof beats. This was a sport the children knew, although they had never played it for real. They left their tutor kneeling in the road, looking like a fool or a mime in a play.

The Sauromatae were not good archers. They had slim bows of wood and not the recurved bows backed in sinew and horn that the Sakje used, and they relied too much on their spears and armour up close, or so Satyrus's mother said. All her comments floated through his brain as Thalassa's hooves pounded along the grass at the verge of the road, a slow rhythm that marked out what might be the last moments of his life.

Melitta, the better archer of the twins, loosed her first arrow and turned away, guiding Bion with her knees as the big gelding curved away to the right.

Satyrus held his course until he saw the Sauromatae raise their bows, and then he loosed – a clumsy shot, wrecked by speed and fear, so that the arrow went high and was lost. But he was close enough that his shot had the same effect on some of the Sauromatae.

Not all, though. Thalassa lost the flow of her gallop as he turned her, and the rhythm of her run changed. When he looked back, she had an arrow in her rump.

He turned her back, head on to their enemies and now, suddenly, close. He had an arrow on the string, the horn nock sliding home between his fingers, fear a few yards behind him but catching up – they were big men, and the closest one had a ferocious grin. He had dropped his bow in favour of a long spear.

'Artemis!' the boy shouted, more a shriek of fear than a war cry, and loosed. He couldn't breathe, almost couldn't keep his knees tight on Thalassa's broad back. He was so *afraid*.

His arrow knew no fear. The man with the grin took the arrow in the middle of his torso, right through his rawhide armour. He went down over his horse's rump, and Satyrus could breathe. He leaned hard to the left and Thalassa was still there for him, skimming the ground in great strides and yet managing to turn away from the barbarians. The man he'd hit screamed soundlessly, his mouth round and red and his rotting teeth black, and all Satyrus could hear were hoof beats.

Satyrus reached across his body for an arrow, half drew one and dropped it. He felt for another. *One more,* he thought. *I'll shoot one more and that will be enough.* He got the fletching

32

of another arrow in his fingers and pulled the arrow clear. He leaned back, got the arrow on the bow and the nock on the string and put his charger's head back at the enemy.

Another one was down, and a third man was clutching an arrow in his bicep and screaming – rage and fear and pain all together as a pair of children flayed his raiding party. But the flow of the fight had carried the Sauromatae up the road, almost to where Coenus lay in the grass and Philokles knelt. The Sauromatae ignored them.

Thalassa missed another stride and almost went down. She slowed sharply.

I'm dead, Satyrus thought. He rose on his knees and shot the way Ataelus the Sakje taught, from the top of his mount's rhythm. His arrow went deep into the gut of a young Sauromatae. He drew another arrow as they turned towards him. He had started on a better horse, but she was tired and old and had carried a heavy burden for several stades, and despite her heart she couldn't keep the pace for ever.

Lita shot again. They were ignoring her, and she shot the horse of a man near Coenus so that the man was thrown right over his horse's head. He rolled once in the road and tried to get up.

Satyrus shot at a man in red with a golden helmet, and the arrow glanced off the man's scale cuirass of bronze.

Philokles rose from his knees. He stepped up to the man who had just been thrown by his wounded horse. Philokles killed him with a vicious kick to the neck. The man's spine snapped and the sound carried across the vale. Then Philokles bent and picked up the man's long spear.

The action on the road and the snap of their comrade's spine drew attention away from Satyrus. The second of hesitation saved his life, and Thalassa powered through a gap in the circle closing around him and he shot one man from so close that he could see every detail of the shock of pain that hit him, could see the spray of sweat from the man's hair as his head whipped around and the burgeoning fountain of blood emerging from the man's throat where the arrow had gone in.

Tyche. The best shot of his life. He turned Thalassa again, ready for her heart to give out in the next stride, but while she was moving he was alive. He made for the road, because the flow of the battle had left it the emptiest part of the battlefield.

Melitta shot again, and missed, but he watched them dart away from the point of her aim, gaining him another few strides.

Thalassa crossed the road close to Philokles. Dust and sweat streaked the Spartan's face like an actor's mask of tragedy. Satyrus twisted in his seat and shot straight back and missed the man behind him, even though the range was just a few horse-lengths. But in his peripheral vision he saw the man duck, and then saw Philokles rip him from his horse with a spear point through the face, gaffing his jaw the way Maeotae farmers took the big salmon.

Philokles' kill broke the Sauromatae. It was not just that they were taking heavy casualties – it was the manner in which Philokles' victim died, his head almost ripped from his body. The other Sauromatae flinched away, abandoning their wounded, and galloped off down the road.

In heartbeats, the drone of the spring insects and the calls of a raven were the only sounds to be heard over the panting of men and beasts and the murmuring of a wounded Sauromatae boy with an arrow in his guts, calling for his mother. Satyrus thought that it would have been nice not to understand his thick Sakje. It might have been nice to think that the boy, just a few summers older than Lita, might live, but no one lived with an arrow in the guts.

I did that, he thought.

'We have to get across the river,' Philokles said, as if nothing had happened.

'Please motherohpleaseohhhhh,' said the boy in the tall grass.

It wasn't a boy. Satyrus was close enough to know that his target was a maiden archer, one of their young women. '*Please! Ohmotherohhh—*' she said.

Satyrus looked away, afraid of what the girl in the grass meant about life and death, afraid of himself. Thalassa trembled between his thighs. He raised his eyes and met Philokles' look.

'*Please!*' the girl begged.

'War is glorious,' Philokles said. 'Do you want me to kill her? Another death will hardly add to the stain on *my* soul.' His voice was without tone – the voice of a god, or a madman.

Satyrus looked at his sister. She was retching in the grass, her head down. Bion was wrinkling his lips in equine distaste.

'They're forming up for another try,' Theron observed. He was looting the downed Sauromatae. He had a sword, a back-curved Greek kopis.

Satyrus drew an arrow from his quiver and rode over to the girl. She was rocking back and forth, arms crossed over the blood. Her face was white and her hair was full of sweat and dust. She had some gold plaques on her clothes. Somebody's daughter. This close, she didn't look any older than he was. *Take her quickly, huntress*, he thought.

He was curiously far away, watching himself prepare to kill a helpless girl his own age, and his hands didn't tremble much. The range was close.

He shot her.

He meant the arrow to go into her brain, but the shaking of his hands or the flexing of the shaft put it in her mouth. She shuddered, and made a choking sound, and then vomited blood like the fish.

Like the fish.

Her whole body spasmed again, and then she lay still. He watched her soul leave her body, watched her eyes become the eyes of a corpse.

It was like being hit in the head by Theron. He couldn't see much. He sat on his horse, and he heard the Sauromatae charge, and he heard his name called, but he couldn't control his limbs. So he sat and watched the dead girl.

Time was an odd thing, because this time yesterday she had been alive, but she would never be alive again.

Philokles shouted his name.

Lita shouted his name.

And then there was just the grass in the breeze, and the sound of the insects, and the ravens calling.

*

'You with us, boy?' Philokles asked. He poured a mouthful of wine into his mouth.

Satyrus spluttered and shook and swallowed some the wine the wrong way.

They were still in the fields by the road, and Satyrus was lying on the ground. His head hurt, but he didn't have a wound on him. 'What happened?'

Theron's face appeared. 'You killed the girl. Then you fainted.' Theron's sword arm was red to the elbow.

For the second time that day, Satyrus tried to get to his feet and threw up instead. He lay back and Theron gave him another mouthful of Philokles' wine, while the Spartan collected horses and gear with Melitta.

'Can you ride?' he asked when he came back.

'I'm sorry,' Satyrus said. He was deeply ashamed.

'Never mind sorry, boy. Can you ride?' Philokles held his shoulders.

Satyrus nodded and sat up slowly.

Thalassa was bareback now. The arrow was gone from her rump.

'We have a lot of horses now,' Philokles said.

'Ares,' Satyrus said. 'You killed them all?'

'No,' Philokles said. 'Everyone helped.'

Theron grinned, and then put his smile away as no one else seemed to think that winning the fight was something to be happy about.

'There'll be more, almost immediately. We have to get across the river,' Philokles said. 'All these people – they're Upazan's people. The man in the gold helmet had his badge, the antlers.' He shook his head, clearly leaving some thought unspoken. 'Get mounted.'

Satyrus had never heard Philokles sound like this. He knew that it was because he had shown fear, had fainted. He got on to a dead man's horse and hung his head, hot tears burning in his eyes.

'I'm sorry,' he said.

'I'm sorry too, boy,' Philokles said. 'We'll have to swim the river. Thalassa probably won't make it.'

Coenus gave a groan. He was tied roughly to a Sauromatae pony, and the red war paint was staining his chiton. 'Leave me,' he said.

'Fuck that, you big Megaran snob,' Philokles said. He put a gentle hand on Coenus's shoulder.

They were all mounted, and Philokles led them straight across the fields to the point. At the edge of the water, they could see all the way up the bluff to the town. Flames licked from above the wall, and there was fire in the gate like the mouth of a giant forge. There were men in armour up the hill, several stades away.

More horsemen were coming.

'Now or never,' Philokles said. 'Theron, can you swim?'

Theron laughed and rode his steed recklessly into the river, which was four stades wide at its narrowest point. It was spring, and the current raced by them, as they were on the outward edge of the curve beneath the town where the river ran fastest.

Satyrus might have hesitated, more afraid now of showing fear than of being afraid, but his horse followed its herd-leader and leaped into the muddy water. The animal bearing Coenus went in next, and in the time it took an eagle to catch a salmon, they were a line of heads swimming for their lives.

Melitta swam like a Nereid, and Bion, though tired, kicked along beneath her. But Coenus struggled just to keep his head above water and his horse wasn't much better. Without really thinking about the risks, Satyrus released his horse to make its own way and swam across the flow to Coenus, but he mistook the current, spun around and got kicked in the gut. In a heartbeat he was under the muddy brown water, sinking away from the noise, still exhaling. He got a fist tangled in something – hair – and suddenly his whole body jerked as he was towed forward. His eyes saw light and he pulled harder and his head came out of the water and he breathed – *ahhh* – and he was moving fast, his right hand wrapped in Thalassa's mane. Her head was up, and despite her wounds and his weight she was powering through the water. He breathed again, choked and sprayed water and snot from his nose.

Thalassa was turning, ignoring his struggles as she swam

closer to Coenus. Coenus was coughing, his face out of the water but his horse sinking away under him.

There were arrows falling from the sky. It took Satyrus a few heartbeats to realize that they were being shot at from the bank. He could hear a man shouting in the Sauromatae dialect for volunteers to go into the water and finish them off. He didn't turn his head to look. His whole concentration was on Coenus. He was close – closer – he reached out a hand and tried to pull the man up, but he was twelve and Coenus was the biggest man he knew.

Then Philokles was up with him, and Theron, swimming alone without a horse, and they cut Coenus free before he drowned himself and his horse. Theron pushed the Megaran's head and shoulders into Satyrus's arms and he pulled hard, eliciting a low scream of pain from the big man. And then they were swimming.

Satyrus looked up and found that they were halfway across. But the current had moved them, and they were no longer at the narrows. He set his shoulders and concentrated on keeping Coenus alive.

Time passed slowly. His shoulder hurt, and every other moment he thought that the dying man might drag him into the water. He was afraid for Thalassa, who made harsh noises though her mouth and nostrils, coughs and hacks almost as if the horse was attempting to curse.

There were leaves and logs in the river, deadwood floated away by the spring rains in the high ground to the east, and once a dead sheep, bloated and stinking, passed them as they swam on. The point was so far behind them that even from his perpsective just above the surface, Satyrus could see the Bay of Salmon widening away. They were almost as far from the other shore as they had been when they slipped into the water. Even with the powerful aide of the horse swimming beneath him, even with his arms wrapped around her neck, Satyrus was tired.

Coenus was a dead weight. Satyrus thought that the man's cold body still had life in it, and he passed several minutes trying to find a sign of breath. He wasn't sure. When he looked up, the stone farmhouse that marked the end of the Maeotae territory was in sight.

He looked around for Melitta, and she was right there at his side, holding on to Bion with one hand and pushing against Coenus with the other, swimming strongly but with lines on her face like an adult. Their eyes met. She gave a push, probably all she had strength for, and Coenus went a finger-breadth higher on Thalassa's proud back.

'Poseidon, Lord of Horses,' Satyrus said.

She swam more strongly, and Satyrus tried to sing the hymn, and Melitta joined in, two thin voices singing, whole words left out as the singers struggled to breathe, but Thalassa seemed to relish it, and her ears went up, and she moved faster. The stone house on the shore was closer.

'I think – he's – dead,' Lita panted.

Satyrus thought of the dead girl. He shook his head.

Thalassa's legs kicked hard. They were half a stade from shore, but suddenly she rose out of the water, stumbled, scrambled and pushed, and she was walking. Satyrus could see the drowned meadow beneath her hooves, the mud billowing away from her steps in brown-black clouds. She managed a few long strides and then she slipped and fell and they all went down in a splash, Coenus and Satyrus underneath, but Satyrus had his toes wrapped in her saddlecloth and when she came up in deeper water he was still clinging to her and he had Coenus wedged with desperate strength against her side.

Theron was there, and Philokles, pushing against his sides, and Melitta with an arm around Coenus's neck, holding his head clear of the water. He wasn't dead yet, because he was spluttering.

The marshy bank was just a few long strides away. Melitta let go of Coenus and she and Bion were first up on to the bank, followed by two unridden horses. Then Thalassa pushed herself up, one giant lunge to plant her hind feet on the mud and a struggling leap almost straight up, with the weight of a boy and a big man, and she was up, front feet scrambling over the edge. Satyrus lost his seat and slid free to fall on grass, and Coenus fell on top of him in a tangle and moaned.

Philokles and Theron climbed the bank under their own power. Satyrus had been kicked at the end and he lay, just breathing, with waves of pain running from his right thigh to his brain. Theron lay breathing beside him. Philokles dragged himself to his feet. He went to Hermes, the big gelding, and pulled the Sauromatae spear from the horse's saddlecloth where he had bundled it with the gear of the other men they had killed.

Satyrus rolled over, ignoring the pain, determined not to be afraid this time. He looked for his other horse, and she was gone – lost in the river. So much for dry bowstrings. He pulled his bow out of his gorytos, which was still full of water. All his arrows were soaked and his bow felt odd, whipping in his hand, the bindings wet through.

Strapped to the outside of his gorytos was the short, sharp steel akinakes that Ataelus had given him. He drew it. It was no longer than his forearm, a pitiful weapon against a grown Sauromatae warrior coming up the bank. He stumbled to the edge.

There were four riders in the water, and they had had as hard a swim as he had. They were not armoured. Most had cast their helmets aside and only their heads and the heads of their horses came above the water. The Sauromatae didn't even seem to know where they were. They let their horses swim them to shore, and the first horse touched the mud at the same spot where Thalassa had touched, scrambled in the shallows and then swam the last few lengths to the bank.

Philokles leaned over the edge and killed the lead man while his horse gathered itself for the scramble up the bank – a single punch of his spear.

The other Sauromatae milled around a few horse-lengths from shore, calling to one and other.

'Come and die,' Philokles yelled. 'Did Upazan send you?'

The barbarian warriors swam their horses back to the drowned meadow and got their legs under them. Then the one with gold in his hair shouted back. 'Let us ashore and we swear not to harm you!'

They were only a few horse-lengths apart. It was an easy

bow shot – but no one had a bow that would function. Satyrus, exhausted, managed a laugh.

'Did Upazan send you?' Philokles called again.

'Yes!' the barbarian returned.

'Then you can swim back to him,' Philokles called. He stepped away from the edge. He sank on his haunches and looked at the children and Theron. 'We can't let them up the bank,' he said. 'I can't go on much longer.'

Theron looked around. 'I can,' he said. 'Who has a javelin?' The water was drying from his body. He looked like a god.

Philokles went to Hermes, moving like an old man, and took a javelin out of the kit strapped to the gelding. He walked with an unaccustomed heaviness.

Theron looked them all over. 'We won't get far,' he said. 'That house will have to shelter us.'

'We can only stay a few hours,' Philokles said. 'Sooner or later they'll send a ship.' He gave the athlete the javelin.

Theron unbound his hair and took the leather thong, wrapped it twice around the spear and made a loop. Then he tied the loop off. He appeared unhurried. He walked to the bank, measuring off his strides, right out to the edge and then back. After three times, he hefted the javelin, well out of sight of the barbarians. 'I assume that if I kill one, the other two will charge us,' he said.

Philokles was silent. He took a deep breath and stood, the big spear in his fists. 'Do the thing,' he said.

Theron ran three steps, skipped once and threw the javelin. It flew like a thunderbolt and hit one of the barbarians so hard that it went a third of its length through his body before he fell into the water.

'Nice throw,' Philokles said.

The other two came forward. They were brave, and they knew they had no choice, so they urged their horses forward across the last stretch and up the muddy bank. The first man came up just where Thalassa had come up and died there, spitted on Philokles' spear. The second man's horse took him further upstream to an easier climb, and he made it up the bank. His horse had spirit, and he turned the animal and went straight for Philokles. He got his own spear out and up and parried Philokles' butt-spike – the Spartan was just getting the weapon clear of his kill.

He might have had Philokles then, except that Melitta got under his horse with her knife and ripped at his booted leg, slashing what she could reach, desperate to save the Spartan.

Satyrus didn't feel as if he was in control of his own body, because he didn't recall pushing his body into panicked attack, but he was suddenly cutting at the rider with his akinakes, the blade locked against the other man's long iron sword. Satyrus saw his blade skip over the bigger weapon and cut the man's tattooed bicep, and then Theron was there, cutting with his kopis in big, overhand cuts like a slave hewing wood, and they swarmed the man until he was dead.

When he was down, his cries stilled, they looked at each other, covered in blood. Theron made a sound like a fox's cry, choked grief or rage, and they all looked away at once.

Satyrus saw movement in the corner of his eye and he turned to see Thalassa give a little skip, almost rearing. She tossed her hooves at the heavens, and then she toppled and fell.

Philokles walked over to her, a hand stretched before him in supplication. He put a hand on her withers, and then on her head. He shook his head.

'Her heart went,' he said.

'Poseidon, Lord of Horses, take her to you,' Satyrus said, and burst into sobs, heavy, wrenching sobs of a kind he hadn't cried for people. And Melitta fell across him crying. They went to the horse, patting her head ineffectually and weeping.

'We need to eat,' Philokles said. His voice had a dead quality to it, as if he wasn't letting himself think about his words. 'There'll be another pursuit as soon as they find a way to cross the river.'

Melitta shuddered. 'I thought we were safe,' she said, and immediately sensed the illogic in her words.

'You'll never be safe again,' Philokles said. 'Get your packs and follow me.'

All they had was their fishing kit, and they had it on their shoulders quickly. Satyrus stood looking at Thalassa in the grass. 'We should burn her or bury her,' he said.

'We should, but we can't. I'm heading for that house.' The Spartan pointed at a distant stone house – a Maeotae farmhouse, perhaps the farthest along the shore.

The yard was empty and the man didn't want to raise the bar on his door. Philokles threatened him from the yard until he complied, and the twins were afraid of Philokles' rage. Melitta and her brother had exchanged looks of horror. Yesterday, they had had the love of these farmers. Now they couldn't trust the man whose roof gave them shelter.

'Hey!' the man called, scared, as Theron scooped sausage from the rafters.

'We need to eat,' Theron said.

'We have fish!' Satyrus said, and Theron managed a smile.

'We do, at that,' he said. He and Satyrus each had a fish in their soaking leather bags, and the fish were no worse for their swim in the Tanais. Theron broiled them on the hearth and shared the fish with the farmer. It didn't make him love them any more, but he shared some sour wine, and they were quickly asleep.

Theron woke them at the edge of dawn, a heavy hand on their heads, and pulled them stumbling into the cold spring morning past the terrified farmer.

'Boat on the water,' he said. 'Time to go.'

Out on the swollen river, they could just see the flash of oars as a pentekonter rowed steadily against the current. The boat wasn't making much headway, but it was coming. The first rays of the sun were pink and red.

Their horses were all lame, the riders equally spent despite ten hours of sleep, and they had to walk slowly away from the stone house. Theron had a bag of sausages and he handed everyone a link – heavy garlic and spice, overpowering in the morning.

Or so we thought. Melitta pondered her brother's sullen silence. He seemed ashamed, when he should be proud. He had fought well.

I put two in the grass myself, she thought. *My mother will be proud, and I will not go to Hades without slaves.* Then she thought of her father's horse – a tangible link to the man she knew only through her mother and Philokles and Coenus's stories. Dead. She frowned away a new bout of tears.

As they crossed the farmyard to fetch the horses, she saw a rough bundle on the manure pile. She had to turn her head away, and her eyes met Philokles'. 'Is that …' She paused, 'Coenus?' she asked quietly, so that her brother wouldn't hear.

'You think I'd leave Coenus on a manure heap?' Philokles asked, and didn't meet her eye. He wasn't sober – she could tell – and there was something wrong with him.

Melitta made bright small talk to hide the corpse from her brother. She knew who was on the manure pile. The farmer wasn't going to betray them, because Theron or Philokles had killed him.

Coenus, on the other hand, had lived through the night. He was stiff, but his wounds had stopped bleeding, and he had the farmer's whole store of linen wrapped around his torso. He was in better shape than Philokles, who could barely walk.

They made less than ten stades in the first hour, and if it hadn't been for Theron's muscles, they might have done worse.

Melitta watched her tutor sink into the same kind of sullenness that affected her brother, and finally she spoke up. 'Where are we going?' she asked.

'Heraklea,' Philokles said.

That was a quarter of the way around the Euxine. 'That will take weeks!' Melitta said.

Philokles stumbled to a stop. 'Look, girl,' he said. 'Yesterday, we were attacked by Upazan. Galleys out of Pantecapaeum sacked the town. What does that tell you?'

'Pantecapaeum is an ally!' Melitta cried. Her brother raised his head.

'Mother was going to Pantecapaeum,' he said. 'To renew the treaty with Eumeles.'

'And now you will be hunted,' Philokles said. 'Upazan and Eumeles have made a deal.' He shook his head, utter weariness

44

getting the better of his good sense. 'All we can do is run.'

Melitta's nails bit into the palms of her hands. 'What of mama?' she demanded. 'She's not dead? She's not dead!' She grabbed her brother's hand, and he gripped it as if she was a sword.

'She's not dead!' the boy shouted.

Philokles and Theron kept walking, and Coenus raised his head, shook it and looked away.

'Maybe not,' the old soldier said.

None of them spoke for a long time. After a while the sun tried to rise on a grey day, and then it began to rain.

Coenus's head came up. 'Rain,' he said. 'Cover our tracks – cover our scent.' He looked at Philokles and drew a deep breath, although they could see that it hurt him. 'Now you have a chance.'

Philokles stood on the road in the rain for as long as it takes a good smith to shoe a horse. Then he said, 'We need to get off the road.'

Coenus nodded. 'Cross-country until you have to cross the river,' he agreed.

Theron shook his head. 'We must be ahead of the news – no one else could have swum the river.'

Coenus's eyes came up. He was having trouble breathing and his eyes were dull, but he got his head up and he pointed his walking staff at Theron. 'Listen, boy,' he said. 'Eumeles needs these children *dead*. His whole fucking attack on our town is for *nothing* if the children live. He'll be across this morning, if he has to swim himself. He'll flood this side of the river with soldiers – men he trusts.'

Theron swished his walking staff in irritation. 'This is *not* the sort of expedition I signed on for.'

But then he saw something in Philokles that changed his mind. Melitta saw him start. *He doesn't want to end up like the farmer.* She'd never seen Philokles the tutor – Philokles the drunk – like this.

He was scary.

He looked them over and gave a smile – a half-smile, almost of contempt. 'Cross-country it is. Follow me.'

They walked all day, leading their horses. The rain continued, and they crossed muddy fields and walked through dripping woods. Melitta was tired in an hour, and exhausted before they sat under an oak and ate more garlic sausage. Coenus could barely walk. Her brother met her eye and shook his head, but they were too tired to talk. After they had eaten the sausage, they walked again. As darkness began to settle, Philokles and Theron began to take turns carrying Coenus, and then they stopped in a stand of ash and cut poles and made a stretcher out of his *chlamys* and walked on again, carrying him between them. None of the horses was fit to ride.

In the evening, they came to a village. Theron went in alone, and came out dejected. 'Men were here this morning,' he said. 'They took all the horses and killed some men.' He shrugged. 'I took this,' he said, and held out a clay pot the size of his hand. 'I tried to pay, but everyone ran off.'

They made a camp above the town. None of them had a fire kit, and everything was wet through, and Theron couldn't get a fire started. He looked at Philokles. 'You're the old soldier,' he said.

'I get fire started by telling a slave to light one,' Philokles shot back.

'Fine pair of bandits you two will make,' Coenus muttered. He sat in the dark, shredding bark between his fingers for a long time – so long that Melitta fell asleep, and she awoke to the warm kiss of golden fire on her face.

'He did it with a stick!' Satyrus said with delight. They gazed at the fire for a while, listening to their bellies rumble, and then they were asleep.

In the morning, they cut north again at Coenus's urging, into wilder country farther from the river and the shore of the Euxine. Bion had recovered and Philokles and Theron got Coenus up on her, and they made better time. Theron ran down a rabbit and they stopped in the hollow of a hilltop and made fire – quickly, because Coenus had shown them how to wrap coals and embers in wet leaves to carry with them. Rabbit soup in Theron's clay pot – nothing to eat it with, so that Melitta burned her lips drinking it straight from the pot – and roast rabbit cooked on a green branch used as a spit. Melitta grew used to taking direction from Coenus as he lay on a pile of cut boughs, protected from the rain only by their one spare cloak, which had belonged to one of the dead Sauromatae.

After the meal they were all better, even Coenus. They slept a little, collected embers and walked on. That night they slept in deep woods, soaked to the skin but warmed by a big fire. In the morning, Coenus was well enough to look over the horses and frown.

'The two steppe ponies are well enough. And Bion is healthy. But we're killing the other two – they're too well bred for this life. We should kill them for meat or trade them to a farmer.'

'For meat!' Satyrus asked, his eyes wide. 'Our horses? Hermes!'

Coenus grunted and sat, suddenly and without ceremony. 'Son, there are *no rules* now. We can't get attached to anything. Including each other.' He looked at Philokles. 'I'm slowing you, brother.'

Philokles shrugged. 'Yes, you are. On the other hand, without your knowledge of hunting and living rough, the children might already be dead – or I'd be driven to taking chances.' He looked down the hill. 'As it is, we've made time. We're only a day or so from the ford at Thatis.'

Coenus smiled grimly. 'I'll try and stay useful, then.'

Philokles grunted. 'See that you do. Otherwise – well, I suppose you'd make a good roast.'

Theron turned away from Philokles' laughter and Coenus's grunts. 'You Spartan *bastard*!' Coenus spat. 'You make it all hurt more!'

'They're *joking*,' Satyrus said.

Theron shook his head. 'They're – not like anyone I've ever known,' he said. 'I thought that I was tough.'

3

The plain of Thatis was an endless succession of rich brown streams, swollen with the rain. Maeotae farmers tilled the mud in silence, and only a handful even raised their eyes to watch them if they were forced to come into a village. It was all so dull that they were almost captured owing to simple inattention. They were walking along the wooded edge of a field of wheat when Coenus raised his head.

'I smell horses,' he said.

'Ares!' Philokles whispered.

Just across the hedge, in the next field, were a dozen horsemen, led by a tall man in a red cloak with a livid scar on his face. Two dismounted soldiers were beating a peasant. Scar-face watched with an impatience that carried over a stade of broken ground.

Melitta's heart went from a dead stop to a gallop.

'Just keep walking,' Philokles said.

Theron didn't know much about horses, and he walked off, but Satyrus jumped in front of Coenus's mount and got his hands on Bion's nose. 'There, honey,' he said in Sakje. 'There, there, my darling.' He looked up at Coenus, who gave him a nod.

They walked along the edge of the field until they came to a path going off up the ridge, deeper into the woods.

'What were they doing?' Melitta asked.

'Nothing good,' Philokles spat. 'Keep moving.' He grunted. 'Thank the gods they missed us.'

They climbed the ridge, apparently without being spotted, but when they reached the open meadow at the top, they could see horsemen across the meadow, working the field carefully despite the pouring rain. Another group of horsemen was in the trees below them – they saw the second group as soon as they stopped.

'Think they've seen us?' Philokles asked.

Coenus shook his head, his lips almost white. 'We must be

leaving tracks. Or some poor peasant saw us and talked. But they don't know where we are – not exactly. If they did, they'd be on us.'

They watched for another minute from the cover of the trees. Melitta could see six of the enemy horsemen, all big men on chargers – Greeks, not Sauromatae. The lead man had a face with a red wound across it, and it looked as if his nose had been cut off. Even a hundred horse-lengths away, it looked horrible.

'Off the trail and up the next ridge,' Coenus said. 'Fast as we can. We're heartbeats from being caught. If they see us, we're done.'

Up until then, Melitta had thought that the going couldn't get any harder – constant rain, endless trudging along, no food to speak of.

None of it had prepared her for walking across country instead of walking on trails. Every branch caught at her. Every weed, every plant growing from the forest floor tore at her leggings and her tunic. Her boots filled with things that cut her feet, and Philokles wouldn't stop. They came to a stream, swollen from days of rain, and no one offered her a hand – the water came up to her belly, and proved to her that she hadn't actually *been* wet until then.

'Don't move,' Philokles said.

She was halfway up the muddy bank, one sodden boot on a rock and the other still in the stream, when the order came.

Satyrus was in the stream.

Without turning her head, she could see that well upstream, half a stade or more, a man on a horse had just emerged from the thick brush of the valley and was looking right at them.

'Do not move,' Philokles said, quite clearly, at her side.

He was moving.

So was Satyrus. Without a splash, her brother lowered himself into the water and vanished.

Melitta turned her head, as the Sakje taught, because nothing gives the human form away to a pursuer like the face. She pressed herself into the bank and tried to ignore the cold of the water on her left leg. It would be worse for Satyrus, who was now fully immersed.

She could feel the enemy's hoof beats through the earth. He was riding along the verge of the stream.

Beside her, Philokles began to pray quietly, first to Artemis and Hera, and then to all the gods. She joined him.

The hoof beats stopped suddenly, and she heard a splash.

'By the Maiden!' Coenus said. His voice sounded as loud as a trumpet.

Melitta looked upstream, and saw a horse thrashing in the deep water of the next long pool above the ford.

'The bank collapsed under him,' Philokles said. 'Stay still!'

The horse thrashed again, and then the rider emerged on the bank, just a few horse-lengths away. He was cursing in fluent Greek. He was an officer – his breastplate showed fine workmanship.

'Dhat you, Lucius?' called a voice from where they'd come. A voice that couldn't be more than ten horse-lengths away, and sounded as if it had a horrendous cold.

'Yes!' Lucius shouted, his voice betraying his annoyance. 'My fucking horse put me in the drink.' He stood on the bank and wrung out his cloak. 'That you, Stratokles?'

'Yes!' The man addressed as Stratokles was closer. 'More tracks!' He emerged as he was calling out, walking into the grey light and the rain just as Lucius came up the bank to meet him. They were perhaps three horse-lengths away, and a long peal of thunder rolled across the hilltops and echoed from the valleys.

Only the overhang of the bank and the thin greenery of a single bush stood between Melitta and her pursuers.

Thunder barked overhead, and a lightning flash followed close, the *bang* almost intimate.

'Fuck Eumeles, and fuck this. What tracks?' Lucius demanded. 'No one's paying me enough to do this shit. If Zeus throws one of those bolts at me—'

'Look!' Stratokles said. His voice was thick, and even without moving her head, Melitta could see that he was the man with a wound on his face.

'Whatever. One horse. Maybe two. We're looking for six men – isn't that right? And a pair of children?'

Lightning struck again, just as close, and a gust of wind tore through the trees.

'They aren't moving in this crap. *I* can't move in this crap.' Lucius looked around. 'There are bandits here, and I don't really want to find them. They'll fight back! And this storm is going to flood this stream. Let's get moving.'

'The peasants said—' Stratokles began.

'Screw the peasants, my lord! Listen, that fool you caught last night – he'd say anything. You wouldn't let that creepy Sicilian torture him – well, good on you, lord, but sometimes it is the way. We asked the question ten times before he answered. If he'd known, he'd have told us right away.' Lucius snorted. 'Give me a hand up.'

There was a squelching noise.

'Anything down there?' came a call from up the hill. Melitta could hear the jangling of bridles and all the music of a troop of horses.

The rain came down, heavier than ever, and Stratokles pulled his wool cloak up over his head. 'Fuck the weather,' he said. 'We'll never get a scent. And I'm not all that sure we saw a hoof print. Everything fills with water as soon as – bah. To Hades with it. Let's go back.'

'Let's find a rich peasant and kick him out of his house,' Lucius said.

'Ndothing down here!' Stratokles called. 'Sound the rally.' He put a hand to his nose and shook his head.

Then Melitta could hear the sound of a horn being blown, three calls repeated over and over. She clung to her patch of bank and shivered, moving as little as possible. She couldn't feel her leg.

Time passed. She had time to wonder if she could do any lasting harm to her leg by leaving it numb, and to watch a fish swimming in the current and wonder if she could become a fish, and she had time to wonder how Coenus was doing, and then Philokles' hands reached down, grabbed her shoulders and lifted her clear of the stream.

'Sometimes the gods are with us,' he said. 'Where's your brother?'

'Somewhere in the water,' she managed to choke out, and then she collapsed against Bion, who nuzzled her.

Theron dragged Satyrus out of the water where he had taken cover in a bed of reeds, downstream at the bend. He couldn't walk.

'We can't build a fire,' Theron said.

Philokles grabbed her shoulder. 'Walk,' he ordered.

Melitta hated to be weak, but she couldn't make her limbs move. 'Can't,' she said. Satyrus just shook his head.

'Crawl then,' Coenus said. 'It'll get you warm.'

So they did. It was a new low, crawling through the wet woods, feet filthy, hair sodden, but it soon restored enough warmth for them to stand, then walk. Satyrus used one of the Sauromatae ponies to keep him erect for a while, and they walked on. Melitta had lost one of her Sakje boots, so sodden that it lost all shape and fell off her foot. After another stade, she found that she was dragging it by the laces – she was so tired that she hadn't noticed until it got caught in some undergrowth.

'How are you?' she asked her brother.

'Fine,' he said, and gave her a smile. That smile was worth a great deal. She drew some energy from it.

'I thought you were dead!' she whispered fiercely.

'Me too!' he said back, and they both smiled, and then it was better.

But Coenus was worse. He began to cough, and to tremble. Immersion was the last thing he'd needed, and now he was gaining in heat what the rest of them lost, and starting to mumble.

'We need to get him into a bed,' Theron said. 'I could use one, too.'

Philokles nodded. They went over the top of the ridge, and then down towards the cook fires of another village.

'They didn't follow us over the ridge,' Theron offered as an opinion.

Philokles shrugged. 'I'm about to risk our lives on it,' he said.

They came down on to the muddy road just short of a small plank bridge. Theron went across first, looking at the ground and then at the far tree line before motioning the rest of them to follow him.

The village was so small that they were through it while Coenus was still muttering an internal debate as to whether to steal the town's single horse. A wealthy peasant watched them ride by from the shelter of his stone house. No one spoke to them.

Theron turned aside and asked the wealthy peasant for lodging. The man went inside and they heard him drop the bar on his door.

'Every one of these bastards will remember us,' Philokles spat. 'Peasants. Like helots. Sell you for a drachma.'

Theron wolfed down warm bread stolen from a farmyard, passing pieces to the children and to Coenus, who ate it ravenously. Other than the bread, they gained nothing from the town. Just beyond was the next river, and the ferry, and then they had to stop and wait for half an hour in the endless rain while Philokles checked it out.

Sure enough, there was a party of cavalry keeping watch on the ferry. Philokles spotted them when their sentry got restless and dismounted in the trees to relieve himself.

'Now what?' Melitta asked.

'We're already wet,' Philokles said. 'We ride upstream and cross with the horses.'

It took them the rest of the day, and they made camp in a tiny clearing between two stones with ancient carving, just at nightfall. Their fire was weak and wet, and smoked constantly, so that it was difficult to sit close enough to get warm, and they had nothing to eat but the last of the bread.

It was the longest night Melitta could remember. Thunder came, and lightning, and whenever it flashed, she woke – if she was sleeping at all – to find her brother's eyes locked on hers. The night stretched on and on – long enough for her to have an ugly dream about her mother, and another about Coenus, caught by wolves and eaten, and then the sky was grey in the east and the ground was pale enough to see to walk.

'Nothing to keep us here,' Philokles said.

Theron sat on his haunches, his fingers clenched until the knuckles were white on his walking stick. 'We need food.'

'Any ideas?' Philokles asked. 'If not, keep walking.'

When the sun was high in the sky, somewhere beyond the endless grey clouds, they reached another swollen stream.

'I don't think this is the Hypanis,' Philokles said, shaking his head. 'Ares, I have no idea where we are. I hope I haven't got you going in circles.'

'No,' Coenus muttered. 'Not circles.'

Every time they awoke, Melitta expected Coenus to be dead. But so far, he wasn't.

'Not circles,' he said. 'Not Hypanis, either.'

They crossed with the horses, again, all wet to the bone as every person had to swim some of the distance with one hand on a pony.

'The horses are failing,' Philokles said when they were done. He was wearing his chlamys like a giant chiton, pinned at the shoulders. It made him look even bigger.

'We need a house,' Theron said. 'I don't think Coenus will make another night in the open.'

'I doubt we're ahead of the bastard's cordon,' Philokles said. 'We'll never escape them if we spend a night in a town.'

'Maybe they're past us,' Theron argued. 'They can't be everywhere.'

'You just want to sleep in a bed,' Philokles accused.

'Is that so bad?' Theron asked. 'I'd like a cup of wine, too.'

It was Coenus's fever that convinced Philokles to risk a night in a house. He walked down the trail and found a farmer's field, and exchanged a few words with the man, and he came back to them where they waited in the trees.

'I like him. He's the village headman, and I think he can be trusted.' Philokles looked at Coenus. 'We need to get out of the rain.'

'Don't take the risk on my account,' Coenus muttered. Theron ignored him and nodded.

The farmer, called Gardan the Blue for his bright blue eyes, was friendly, and his wife welcomed the twins as if they brought her house good fortune. They sat together in the main room of the house, swathed in dry wool and warm for the first time in five days, enjoying a meal of goat and lentils and barley bread. They ate like hungry wolves.

Melitta assumed that they would buy fresh horses from the extensive string she had seen in the paddocks, concealed in a stand of woods away from the road. She waited for Philokles to mention it, and when he didn't, she nudged him.

'If we buy their horses, we can make better time,' she said.

Philokles looked at her with ill-concealed sorrow. 'I have the gold from the men we killed, and our gear,' he said. He nodded in the direction of the farmer. 'We can't give him a fair price for his horses. Not and have the money to take a ship.'

Neither of the twins had given a thought to the sea. 'But where will we get a ship?' Melitta asked.

Philokles looked around at the farmer, smiled grimly and shook his head at the children. 'Quiet. He's a good man, and I don't want to have to kill him to keep you alive. Understand?'

They went to bed without another word.

In the morning, the farmer walked them to the edge of the road. He bowed to the twins. 'Young master? Young mistress? May I speak freely?'

Satyrus nodded. 'You are a free farmer,' he said seriously. 'You can say anything that you want.'

Gardan tugged at his beard. 'You're on the run,' he said. He looked at Philokles. 'You don't have a clean garment among you.'

Philokles nodded, looked around and then said, 'It's true. The Sauromatae attacked the city with help from Eumeles. Soon enough, some of them will come down this road looking for us.' He shrugged. 'I recommend that you be helpful to them.'

The farmer nodded. He rubbed his beard. He was a short man, swarthy as many of the Maeotae were, although he had the blue eyes of a Hellene and jet-black hair from the age of heroes. 'My uncle fought with Marthax at the Ford of the River God,' he said. 'We remember your father.' He tugged his beard again. 'I know what happened at the town,' he said slowly. He looked at Philokles. 'Been two patrols through, both Sauromatae. Farmers round here don't take kindly to such people. A man was killed.' He shrugged and pointed at the heavy bow that rested on pegs over the door. 'They may come back to burn us out, and then again they may not,' he said with something like satisfaction. Then he seemed to gather himself. 'I'm chattering. What I mean to say is, no one in this steading will give you away. Nor any of our neighbours. We know who you are. And there's five good geldings down the road in a pasture. No one's watching them.' He smiled. 'I'll tell the next barbarian that the last barbarian stole them.'

His wife came out of her door into the yard, a bag of feed in her hand. 'There's clean fabric and wool blankets,' she said.

Philokles didn't answer. Instead he looked at the twins. 'This is a lesson,' he said. 'I have told you of Solon and Lycurgus, and I have read to you from Plato and from other men who account themselves wise. But this is the lesson – that good returns good and evil returns evil. These people have saved our lives because your father was a good man, and your mother has ruled fairly and well. Remember.'

Satyrus nodded soberly. 'I will remember.' He extended a hand to the farmer, who clasped it.

Melitta rode forward a few steps. 'When I am queen,' she said, 'I will return this favour a hundredfold.' She kissed the wife and clasped hands with the man.

The horses were just where the farmer had said, and three of them had bundles tied to their backs.

'When you are queen?' Satyrus asked.

Melitta shrugged. 'It is a role, brother. We are exiles. Perhaps we will return. Those people just gave us all of their profit from a year of farming – the whole generation of their horses, the wool from their sheep – there's linen here that was grown as flax in Aegypt and paid for with the wheat. They gave it all in one open-handed gesture, like heroes – because of who we are.' She shrugged. 'They are more like heroes than we are.'

Satyrus spent too much time gulping against sobs. Now he did it again. They rode through the rain in silence.

Philokles was quiet too.

'Why are *you* crying?' Satyrus asked.

Philokles met his eyes, not even trying to hide the tears. 'All we built,' he said heavily. 'A decade of war to create peace. Gone.' He took a rasping breath. 'You have no idea what was given to gain this land and the peace it deserves.' He shrugged. 'Leave them Hermes and the other horse – they're good beasts, and then Gardan won't be at such a loss.'

Satyrus nodded. He took his tack off Hermes and put it on the strange gelding, and then whispered to the old cavalry horse for a bit. He looked sheepish when he was done.

'Mama says Pater always talked to his horses,' he said defensively. Then he gave a wry smile. 'At least Hermes will survive this adventure, if we don't.'

'We're doing pretty well, I think, given the odds,' Theron said. With a meal in him and a dry chiton, he was a new man.

'Our father gave his life for this country,' Melitta said.

'Not just your father, my dear.' Philokles managed a smile. 'A great many men, and no few women.' He looked back into the rain, and his smile faded, and he seemed to be watching something else, somewhere else. 'I hate the gods,' he said.

Coenus shook his head. 'I hate impiety,' he said. 'It's foolish for a man to hate the gods.'

'Someone's feeling better,' Theron said.

Five fresh horses made all the difference. They rode hard, but the horses were changed regularly. The blankets and clean clothes and the gold pins they were wearing made them look prosperous instead of desperate, although the wiser elders on the road wondered quietly why they were out in the rain at all, or moving at such speed.

They were eight more days from the Hypanis River, and as they trotted over the rain-sodden landscape, Melitta knew that she couldn't have walked the whole way. And Coenus – despite his fevered wound, was better for the saddle and for sleeping dry. Gardan the Blue had packed them a heavy wool blanket, carefully felted, as big as the roof of a small house – the work of four or five women for a whole winter. It made a waterproof shelter.

They were in better shape when they came down the last slope to the Hypanis, a small party with packhorses and good clothes and enough rest to make good decisions.

'I'm afraid of the ferry,' Melitta heard Philokles say to Theron and Coenus. He sent Theron ahead, but Theron came back with the news that, aside from outrageous rates, the ferry was safe.

'We've ridden clear,' Philokles said. He shrugged. 'They have so much ground to cover – Eumeles can't be everywhere.'

Theron bargained with the ferryman the way a slave bargains for fish in the agora, hectoring the man and threatening to swim the river himself on horseback until the man conceded, a copper obol at a time, and finally they were crossing with their whole train for a single silver owl. Coenus watched in silent disapproval, but his fever was so high that he couldn't contribute much. His face said that they should be above such things.

The rain stopped while they watched the brown Hypanis flow past their broad raft. It took the effort of the ferryman, both his sons and Theron to wrestle the unwieldy thing against the current, and they had to make two trips, because the rush of water prevented the horses from swimming well.

Philokles paid down a second silver owl without being asked, and the ferryman bit it with a knowing smile.

'You overpaid,' Theron said.

'He risked his boat for us,' Philokles said. 'And no one will follow us for a day or so.'

Theron pursed his lips. 'Why?' he asked. 'The river will go down if the rain stops.'

Coenus roused himself. 'The river will go *up* for another day, as the water comes down from the hills.' He pointed at the loom of the mountains to the east and south, where the foothills of the Caucasus were visible even in the clouds.

'And I put a cut in the pull rope,' Philokles said with a shrug. When Theron glared, Philokles shrugged again. 'I paid for the rope. And he was an arse-cunt.'

*

They were another day riding to the sea at Gorgippia, a small town that owed allegiance to no one. The town existed to make fish sauce for the Athens market and not much else, and the smell hit them ten stades away. In the harbour, vats of fish guts gave vent to a stench so strong that the twins gagged and breathed through their mouths.

'Poseidon!' Melitta swore. 'I can taste it on my tongue!'

Satyrus was glad to see her make a joke. It had been a quiet ride.

Philokles was on edge from the moment they entered the town, but there were no boats in the harbour except local fishing craft, and after some careful probing in wine shops, he grew more confident.

'No one has been here,' he said. He shook his head. 'Eumeles may have given up.'

Coenus was gasping like a man suffocating. Philokles remounted and supported his friend. 'He needs cool baths and a doctor,' he said.

Normally, a party of gentlemen would look for the richest house and try to arrange guest-friendship. Normally, the children of the Lady Srayanka would have had no trouble finding lodging. But Philokles didn't want to show his hand yet. He took them to the best of the waterfront wine shops and paid a few obols for some beds in a wooden barn behind the drying sheds. The straw was clean, and the smell of animals was refreshing compared to the overpowering odour of rotting fish.

Coenus went to sleep the moment he was off his horse.

'That is a tough man,' Theron said.

'He thinks he's a pompous aristocrat, though,' Philokles said. He had a clean, wet linen towel, and he wiped the Megaran's face. 'He's far gone, Theron.'

Theron put his head down on the bigger man's chest and listened, and then felt this wrists. 'We need to change his bandages,' he said. 'I doubt that there's much that a doctor can do that we can't,' he said to Philokles. Eight days of rain and silent children had caused them to pool their knowledge about many things, and they had each other's measure.

Coenus didn't wake up as the two men and the twins rolled him over, sat him up and unwrapped the bandages. The cut that went high across his ribs looked better, with new pink flesh along the dark red line of the scab.

The lower cut that had, as best they knew, not quite penetrated his guts, was infected along its whole length, the skin inflamed above and below the line of the wound and two long tendrils of angry red tissue like the trailing legs of a squid. There was pus at the ends of the wound.

Theron put his head down and smelled the wound, and shook his head. 'Wet and dry and wet and dry for eight days? It's a miracle that he lives. Apollo's arrow is doing him more damage than the original wound – the infection is deeper than when we crossed the ferry. Send the children to make a sacrifice to the golden archer, and let you and I do what we must do.'

Satyrus knew, even as a queen's son, when he was being dismissed so that adults could do adult things. He bowed and caught his sister's hand. 'We'll find a temple,' he said.

They walked out of the barn into the first sun they'd seen since the fight at the river. Hand in hand, they walked along the smooth pebbles of the beach that gave the town its existence. If it hadn't been for the smell of fish, the place would have been pleasant. As it was, it was like Tartarus.

'The smell will kill him,' Melitta said. 'I've read it – it is a miasma, and it will choke his lungs.'

'Let us go and make a sacrifice,' Satyrus said.

Melitta nodded, head high to hide tears. Then she said, 'Do you believe in gods, brother?'

Satyrus glanced at her and squeezed her hand. 'Lita, I know things are bad – but the gods—'

She pulled at his hand. 'Why would gods be so childish?' she asked. 'Satyrus, what if Mama is dead? Have you thought about it? If she is dead – it is all gone. Everything. Our whole lives.'

Satyrus sat on a wooden fish trap. He pulled her down next to him. Then he put his head in his hands. 'I think about it all the time – round and round inside my head.'

She nodded. 'I think Mama is dead.' She looked out to sea.

'There's been something missing – something gone—' She lost her battle with tears and subsided into his shoulder.

Satyrus wept with her, clinging to her. They wept for a few minutes, until the tears had no point, and then they both stopped, as if on cue.

'Coenus is still alive,' Satyrus said.

'Our father's friend,' Melitta added. They got up together. Hand in hand, eyes red, they walked up the shingle towards the town, such as it was.

Behind them, a long triangular sail cut the horizon.

They found the Temple of Herakles two stades outside of town, on a small bluff that looked over the bay and seemed free of the smell. It was the only temple that the town had, and the priestess was old and nearly blind, but she had a dozen attendants and a pair of healthy slaves. She received them on the portico of the temple, seated on a heavy wooden chair. Her attendants gathered around her, sitting on the steps.

Satyrus thought that she looked friendly, but she scared him too. It was Melitta who first gathered the courage to speak.

'We need to make sacrifice for a friend who is sick,' Melitta said. They were still holding hands, and they bowed together.

'Come here, child,' said the crone, raising her head to look at them around her cataracts. 'Handsome children. Polite. But unclean. You are both unclean. At your age!' She sniffed.

Satyrus bowed his head. 'Unclean, despoina?'

She gripped his right hand in hers, and he felt the bite of her nails in his palm. She raised it to her nostrils. 'I can smell blood even through the fish sauce, boy. You killed. You have not cleaned yourself. And your sister – she too has killed.' She raised her head again, and smoke from the temple brazier behind her rose in a fantastic curl behind her head like a sign from the god.

Satyrus made the satyr's head sign with his left hand to avert misfortune. 'How may I become clean?' he asked.

She tugged at his hand. 'You are a gentleman, I can see that. Where are you from?'

He didn't want to resist her tug. He looked into her eyes,

but the cataracts made them hard to read. He felt a rush of fear. 'We – we come from Tanais,' he said.

'Ahh,' she said, as if satisfied. 'And how do a pair of children come to me soaked in blood?'

'Men tried to kill us,' Melitta said. 'Bandits. We shot them with bows.'

'One of them was a girl,' Satyrus said, the words coming from deep within him. 'I shot her to end her pain. She had an arrow in her guts and she begged—' He sobbed. He could see her sweat-filled hair.

The priestess nodded. 'Life-taking is a nasty business,' she said. 'Horrible for children.' She turned to her attendants. 'Bathe the boy for the ritual. Then bathe the girl.' To Satyrus, she said, 'When you are clean, you may sacrifice a black kid – each – and I will say the prayer lest some uncleanness cling to you.' She looked unseeing out over the bay. 'Where is your friend?' she asked.

'Friend?' asked Satyrus, who was still thinking of the girl he'd killed. He wondered if her face would ever leave him.

'You have a friend who is sick, yes?' the priestess asked. Her voice rasped like the sound of a woman scraping cheese with a grater. 'This temple also serves Artemis and Apollo. Did you not know?'

'We did not,' Melitta said. She saw now the statue of her patron goddess among the Greeks, a young woman with a bow. She bowed deeply to the priestess. 'We have a sick friend in town.'

The priestess nodded. 'The men in the trireme are searching for you. You will be safe here, and nothing is more important than that we make you clean. I will send a slave to your friends. They must come here.'

Satyrus turned and for the first time saw the trireme coming into the harbour under sail.

Coenus came up the bluff in a litter while the trireme was performing the laborious task of turning around under oars and backing her stern on to the beach. She was full of men – Satyrus could see the warm wink of sun on bronze on her deck. Philokles put the horses in a stand of oaks behind the temple.

'You bet your life on an old priestess,' he said.

Satyrus stared at the marble under his feet. 'You didn't lie to the people in the wine shop.'

Philokles nodded. 'I didn't tell them the truth, either. They assumed that we were small merchants from up the coast, and I let them think it.' He shrugged. 'It doesn't matter. The navarch on that fucking trireme will be on to us in twenty questions.'

Theron dumped a heavy wool bag inside the precincts of the temple. 'Are we asking sanctuary? Or running?'

The old priestess emerged, supported by the larger of her two slaves. 'The children are bathing to be clean in the eye of the gods,' she said, 'a process that would benefit you too, oath-breaker.' Then she pointed at Coenus with a talon-like finger. 'Take him to the sanctuary. We will not give him up, nor will those dogs from Pantecapaeum have him. The rest of you should ride as soon as you are clean. He'll only slow you.'

Philokles bowed. 'As you will, holy one. Why do you help us?'

She shook her head in annoyance. 'I can tell the difference between good and evil. Can't you?'

'Then you know why I broke my oath,' Philokles said.

'I?' she asked. 'The gods know. I am a foolish old woman who loves to see brave men do worthy deeds. Why did you break your oath?'

'To save these children,' Philokles said.

'Is that the only oath you've broken?' she asked, and Philokles winced.

She turned. 'The girl is bathed and clean,' she said. 'Come, boy.'

He followed the old woman into the sanctuary, which was sumptuous beyond anything in Tanais, with walls picked out in coloured scenes showing the triumph of Herakles, the birth, the trials of Leto and more than he could easily take in. There was a statue of Apollo as a young archer, in bright orange bronze, his eyes and hair gold, and his bow of bronze shooting a golden arrow. In the centre of the sanctuary was a pool. The water moved and bubbled. Above the pool stood a great statue of Herakles, nude except for a lion skin, standing in the first guard position of the pankration. The sight of the statue made the hair stand up on the back of Satyrus's neck, and he smelled wet fur, a heady, bitter smell like a cat. Or a lion skin.

'This is the pool of the god,' she said. 'It was here before there was a temple. We do not let just any traveller enter this pool. Remember as you go in that Herakles was a man, but by his deeds he became a god.'

An attendant took his chiton, unpinned the pins and threw the garment into the fire that burned on the altar. He dropped the brooches – not his best pair, but solid silver – into a bowl on the altar, and the fire on the altar flared and smoked.

'The god accepts your offering and your state,' the priestess said. 'Into the water with you.'

Satyrus thought that his sister had just done this. He wondered why he hadn't seen her.

Strong hands grasped him and he hit the water and was under it in a moment. The water was warmer than blood and bubbled fiercely, fizzing around his limbs and with bubbles rising between his legs and up his chest. He rose to the surface and took a breath, eyes tightly closed, and somebody placed a hand on his head. 'Pray,' he was commanded, and the hand pressed him down into the pool.

He could hear the voice counting above him. The bubbles continued to rise around him and he was on the edge of panic, his hair rising in the water and his skin scoured and his breath stopped so that coloured flashes came before his eyes, and still the hand pressed on his head. The pool was too small for him to stretch his arms. He was trapped.

'Pray!' the voice said.

Lord of the sun, golden archer, he began. What was he praying for? He wanted to live! Not drown!

Coenus.

Golden archer, take your shaft from the side of my friend Coenus, he prayed. *And forgive me for killing that girl. I only did it because – she begged – I couldn't stand her pain!*

But what if she, too, could have been healed?

Lion killer, hero, make me brave! He prayed fervently, and an image of the golden statue of the god at pankration filled his mind.

The hand on his head released him and he shot up from the pool, then the temple slaves pulled him on to the marble and a towel began to rub him vigorously.

'Did you hear the god?' the old woman asked.

'No,' Satyrus said. *Or perhaps I did.*

The woman nodded. 'That's as well. Your sister did.' She held something under his nose, something with a strong scent. Like hot metal. 'You are clean. Do you know how to sacrifice an animal?'

Satyrus, who had sacrificed for his family since he was six, was tempted to make a childish retort, but he bit it back. 'Yes,' he said.

'Good,' she said. The slave led him out of the back of the sanctuary, to an altar at the top of wooden steps that led down to the oak woods. His sister was drying her hair.

An attendant – a young priest, he thought – handed him a blade – a narrow blade of stone with a gold-wire handle. 'It is very sharp,' he whispered. 'And as old as the stars.'

Satyrus took it. The kid was tethered to the altar. Satyrus put a hand on the young beast's head and asked its forgiveness. He raised his eyes to the sky and cut its throat in one pull, stepping clear of the fountain of blood.

The attendants caught the animal and slaughtered it with the precision of long practice.

'Well done,' the priestess said. 'Now go. I will look to your friend.'

Satyrus went down the steps, wiping the blood from his left hand on the grass at the bottom.

Melitta mounted first and tossed her wet hair over her shoulders. Her eyes were sparkling. 'There are gods!' she said.

Satyrus got up on the horse he had named Platon for its broad haunches. 'I know,' he said.

Philokles had the train of spare horses in motion.

'Where are we going?' Satyrus asked Theron.

The athlete shook his head. 'Philokles got a tip in town,' he said.

'We're going to Bata,' Philokles said. 'We'll be there tonight if we ride hard. There's a Heraklean merchant in the harbour, if he hasn't left yet. If he has, we ride for the mountains. We can't come back here.'

'What if the marines follow us?' Satyrus asked as they jogged along, already moving at a trot and screened from the beach by the trees.

'They'd need horses,' Philokles said. He smiled grimly. Then he shook his head. 'Don't ask,' he said to Theron.

There was a ship waiting off the beach in Bata, stone anchor deep in the mud and waiting for twenty more jars of Bata's salmon roe in oil before unfolding his wings for Heraklea. The ship had seemed like a gift from the gods; the more so when they sailed down the coast to Sinope without the sight of a trireme. Satyrus and his sister were too tired to examine the gift, or question it, and the ship ran south with a fair wind and the gentle hand of Moira to guide it.

Five days out of Bata, Melitta had her first sight of Heraklea in the last full light of the sun, and the marble of the public buildings shone like coral in jewellery or well-burnished bronze, pale orange in the setting sun, and gold and bronze sparkled from statuary and adornments. Heraklea was as rich as Sinope or Pantecapaeum or Olbia. Richer than Athens. The tyrant, Dionysius, was not a friend of their mother's, or their city. But nor was he a friend of Eumeles of Pantecapaeum. He was a friend of his own power, and Philokles said they had no other choices.

'Tanais might have looked like that in twenty years,' Melitta said.

'Tanais is a blackened corpse,' Satyrus said, his mood dark.

Melitta took his hands, and together they stood against the rail of the merchant ship as she heeled into the evening breeze and thrust her way across the waves to Heraklea. 'You need to take life for what it is,' she said. 'Look!' She waved her arm like an actor. 'Beauty! Enjoy it!'

'You need to stop pretending to be an all-wise priestess,' he shot back. 'Our mother is dead and our city is lost. Do you realize that we could be enslaved? That any man on those wharves with the strength to take us could kill us or sell us? We could be pleasuring customers in a brothel before another sun sets. Do you get that?'

She nodded. 'I get it, brother.' She looked at Theron and Philokles, who were rolling dice in the cover of an awning. 'I think they will protect us, and I think the gods will see us right.'

'The gods help those who help themselves,' Satyrus said.

'Then get off your arse and start helping,' Melitta said. 'Killing that girl is the best day's work you ever did. Stop moping like a little boy. You are a king in exile. Start acting like one.' She looked over the side. 'You must follow my lead in this. I know what I'm doing.'

Satyrus watched the wharves. Melitta had assumed that the sea would cure him – the sea that he loved, where he went on his summers to sail on Uncle Leon's ships and learn the ropes. This voyage, he hadn't even watched the sailors rig the sail.

'Fine,' Satyrus said.

The angry silence that followed lasted them until the ship's side scraped along a stone jetty, and then again until they were standing in the dust and ordure of the Heraklean waterfront.

Philokles had spent some time with the captain of the merchant ship throughout the voyage – keeping him sweet, or so Theron said. As they approached the wharves, Philokles took the man aside on the platform where the steersman conned the ship. When they were done talking, Philokles came down the gangplank with a worried look. Theron was trying to unload the horses with the help of the deck crew. They had kept the three best horses from the farmer, and Melitta's Bion. The rest of the horses had been sold at Bata, where they had got a good price. Shipping the horses had cost more than shipping the people – but Philokles had told the twins that without horses, they were too vulnerable.

Bion hadn't liked being swayed aboard in a sling, and now he didn't like walking down the gangplank, resisting every step, showing his teeth and acting like a mule. Melitta had to coax him on to dry land with a hastily purchased honey and sesame confection.

'Stupid horse,' she said fondly.

Satyrus ignored her. He stood with his back against his own horse and his arms crossed.

Philokles tugged at his beard. 'I have to take a risk,' he said. He was not quite sober – in fact, he had drunk steadily once they were on board.

Theron shrugged. 'It's been all risk since I joined this crew,' he said.

'Why do you stay?' Melitta asked. She was drawing looks from passers-by on the wharves, as a young woman of good family out in the public eye. In fact, she was a young woman of good family who was out in public wearing a short chiton with a scarlet *chitoniskos* over it and she was wrangling horses. She got a great deal of attention.

Theron smiled. 'The company's good,' he said. 'And I'm not bored.'

Philokles gave them all a crooked smile. 'This is not the place to have this conversation,' he said. 'Let's go.'

Satyrus got on to his horse with a wriggle and a push. Melitta did her usual acrobatic vault, and every head on the street turned.

'You have to stop doing that in public,' Theron said. 'Girls don't ride. They certainly don't ride astride. They don't vault on to horses, and they don't do acrobatics.'

'Of course they do,' Melitta said with a toss of her head. 'I see it on Athenian plates and vases all the time.'

Theron made a choking noise that Satyrus recognized through his sullenness as ill-concealed laughter. 'Those are flute girls and *hetairai*!' he said.

Melitta shrugged. Then she turned her Artemis smile on the people around them, and some of the men smiled back.

'Where are we going?' Melitta asked.

'Leon the Numidian has a factor and warehouses here,' Philokles said.

'Uncle Leon?' Melitta asked. 'Will he be there?'

'I doubt it,' Philokles said. 'Gods, what a salvation that would be. Zeus Soter, let Leon be there.'

PART II

FORMING

4

Stratokles rode up to the wall of the barn before the Macedonian mercenary could get the girl's knees apart with his own. He had her hands pinned and he'd headbutted her to stop the screams, but she was a tough woman with a farmer's muscles and she wasn't giving up without a fight, as the Macedonian's face testified.

Stratokles slid down from his horse, pivoted on his left foot and kicked the man in the head so hard that his body made a gentle thump as it hit the stone barn.

'Who allowed this?' he asked the ring of mercenaries who had gathered to watch. 'You – you're a phylarch, aren't you?'

The man so addressed, a Sicilian from far-off Syracuse, flinched at the man with the livid red scar across his face. 'Yes,' he muttered.

'Are you aware that without these people, we'll *never* catch the fucking children?' Stratokles was furious – not just from the constant pain of his face, but from the stupidity of the men he was saddled with.

'They know where the children are!' the Macedonian spat. He sat up and retched. 'Fuck me.'

'I may, at that,' Stratokles said. He had a knife in his hand and it was pressed against the Macedonian's temple. 'Don't move around too much.'

The Sicilian phylarch shook his head. 'It's been a hard ten days, lord. The boys need some—'

'Some rape? I recommend that they practise on each other, then. Listen, you fuckwit. These people are Heron of Pantecapaeum's *citizens*.' Stratokles shook his head.

'We done worse when we took that town – Tanais. You weren't so high and mighty then.' The phylarch knew he had the rest of the men with him.

Stratokles shrugged. 'Sometimes men have to do evil deeds to attain an end. Tanais had to be sacked. It was a symbol – a symbol your master can't afford. But one day of sacking a town – an event that should have sated your urges for a little longer – does not give you the right to rape your way across the countryside.'

The phylarch shrugged. 'They all hate us anyway.'

Stratokles nodded. He sheathed his dagger, and the Macedonian breathed again. Stratokles shook his head. 'Are you surprised?' He picked the girl up. She had a broken nose, two black eyes and blood all down the front of her chiton, but she tried to resist him. He grabbed her wrists and threw her over his shoulder, then carried her around the barn to where other soldiers had the wife and the farmer himself penned in the house.

'Let me past, you idiots,' Stratokles roared. He walked up the steps to the stone house and put the girl on the floor. 'I'm sorry for what my men have done here, but her virtue is not stolen, and her nose will heal. Sooner than mine,' he said with an attempt at humour, but it fell to its death on the iron-hard faces of the farmer and his wife. She leaped to her daughter, put her arms around her and the two began to talk – fast – in the local tongue.

'We know you had the twins here – three days back? Perhaps four?' Stratokles looked at the boy, cowering against the hearth. 'I'm doing my best to restrain these animals, but it could get ugly here and I'm just one man. If you tell us what we need to know, we'll be gone the sooner. And no one needs to get hurt.'

'This is what Heron of Pantecapaeum stands for, is it?' the farmer spat.

Yes, it is, Stratokles thought to himself. Politics made strange allies – and for Stratokles, a democrat of the most rabid sort, a man of principle, dedicated to the freedom of Athens, to be forced into a yoke with the tyrant of Pantecapaeum was the richest sort of irony.

'Please,' Stratokles said. 'Help me to help you. When were they here?'

The farmer wilted. His eyes went to his son and daughter. Outside, the mercenaries were moving around with heavy footsteps, their very silence ominous.

'Three days back,' the farmer said. 'They took our horses.'

The best of the mercenaries was an Italian named Lucius, a big man with a brain who had stood by Stratokles repeatedly during the chase. Stratokles demoted the phylarch on the spot and promoted the Italian in his place. There was a lot of ugly muttering.

Stratokles rode in among them, pushing his horse right up against the Macedonians. 'Listen, children,' he said. 'I could have killed fuckwit here for mutiny and rape – but I chose to assume that his useless phylarch shared some of the blame. So you get to live.' Stratokles grinned around at the ten of them. 'If you annoy me enough, I'll just start killing the ones I find most annoying – get me? I can take all ten of you – together, apart, one at a time, any way you want it. Care to start dancing? If not, shut up and soldier.'

'You ain't our officer,' the ex-phylarch said – in a whine. 'We're paid men – mercenaries. We have our own rules.'

Stratokles' smile widened. 'I'm your officer now.' He looked around at them again – a useless assortment of boys and thugs. 'And the only rules here are mine.'

They were badly mounted, and he suspected that the children he'd been sent to kill were now better mounted, but he knew horses and they made the best time he could manage, five days across the hills and down the valleys to the Hypanis. There should have been a ferry across the swollen torrent, but instead they found an angry ferryman and a cut rope.

'Yesterday, the thieves! The fucking catamites!' the ferryman shouted.

He had a dozen or more customers camped around his stone house, waiting for the water to go down.

Stratokles looked at the river, and then at the horses and men he had with him. He was tempted to curse the gods, but he knew from experience that the gods give what they give.

'We swim,' he said.

'Fuck you,' the former phylarch said. 'I ain't swimming. They're a day ahead – downriver, into a port and gone.'

Stratokles looked at Lucius, who shrugged. 'I'd put it a nicer way,' he said. 'But the man's got a point.'

Stratokles nodded. 'Well, I'm swimming,' he said. 'Lucius, I'd appreciate it if you came. The rest of these scum aren't worth my trouble. Ride back to Heron, tell him you failed, and see what you get.'

As it was, they rested the horses overnight, ate a hot meal in the man's barn and the river was down in the morning. Even with that, though, the swim across the Hypanis was one of the scariest things Stratokles had ever done. Halfway across, when an underwater log thumped against the ribs of his horse and both of them rolled under for a moment, he thought he was done.

Oh, Athens, the shit I do for you.

But then he was up the far bank. He had brought a light rope from the ferryman, and he tied it to the big oak at the top of the bank, and the ferryman gave him a wave and a cheer.

'Service restored,' Stratokles said to Lucius, who'd also made the crossing.

'Aren't we going to wait for the lads?' Lucius asked when Stratokles rubbed his gelding down and got back up on him.

Stratokles watched the ferryman and one of his sons inching across in a light boat, using the line Stratokles had carried to keep from racing away downstream. 'It'll be all day before he gets his hawser across,' the Athenian said.

'You're the boss,' Lucius said. 'You think we can take six men all by ourselves?'

'I have to try,' Stratokles said.

'Well, I'm with you,' Lucius muttered. 'I'm a fool, but I'm with you.'

They made Bata in three more days. There was a heavy trireme beached by the stern, and Heron of Pantecapaeum was just coming up the beach when they rode their tired horses down to him.

'They got away,' Stratokles said.

Heron nodded. 'This morning. About five hours ago.' He looked at Lucius, and then back at the Athenian. 'You're a better man than I took you for. You stuck it out all the way across the countryside.'

Stratokles shrugged. 'I missed them, though.'

Heron nodded, his long nose seeming to mock the stub that Stratokles had. 'The ship they're on is a coaster bound for Heraklea,' he said. 'I can give you this ship and the marines on board. Go and kill them.'

Stratokles took a deep breath. 'I have business in Heraklea, and an agent or two,' he said. 'On the other hand, this is getting beyond my remit. I'm not your man, Heron. I'm Cassander's. And killing those children can't become an end in itself. What damage can they do you?'

Heron looked out at the ship, and shrugged. 'Just do as you are told. Or tell Cassander and your precious Athenian tyrant that unless those children die, I'm no part of his alliance and he can whistle for the grain he wants.' The tall man gave Stratokles a slight smile – more like a mockery of a smile. 'I dare say he'll find that he can spare you for a few weeks.'

Stratokles stifled the wave of resentment that threatened to escape his throat and take voice. The political daimon that ruled his thoughts – the spirit of expediency, he called his daimon – told him that Herons come and go.

The things I do for Athens, Stratokles thought. 'Introduce me to your navarch,' he said.

5

The factor's steward said that Leon was not there, and his factor, when summoned at Philokles' insistence, was none too pleased to speak with them. He was a middle-aged Heraklean merchant named Kinon, and he viewed the four mounted travellers outside his palatial house with distress and suspicion. Kinon was as wide as he was tall, and not all with fat. He wore a fortune in jewellery on his person, with a jewelled girdle and gilt sandals. Two armed slaves stood behind him, and the heavily studded gate was only opened wide enough for the three of them to stand abreast.

Kinon spoke brusquely. 'I do not expect Leon for some weeks. Indeed, I do not know if Heraklea is on his summer sailing itinerary at all. Good day to you.'

Philokles slipped down from his horse and stood in the gateway so that it was difficult to close the gate politely. 'We'll accept your hospitality anyway,' he said.

'I haven't offered my hospitality,' Kinon said.

'Leon is my guest-friend. I need the shelter of a roof, as do these children and their trainer. Are you turning me away?' Philokles seemed bigger and far more noble than usual.

Kinon looked at them. 'What proof do you bring that you are the guest-friend of my employer? Get you gone before I send for the tyrant's guard.'

Philokles shrugged. 'I helped free your master from slavery,' he said. 'He was the slave to Nicomedes of Olbia. Kineas of Athens and I—'

'Kineas? You are that Philokles, the Spartan?' Kinon took a step forward, slapping his head. Satyrus, watching, couldn't decide whether it was a theatrical gesture or a real one, or perhaps both together.

'I am Philokles, of Olbia and Tanais. These children are the children of Kineas, and a curse on you for making me say that on a public street.' Philokles didn't seem so drunk.

'Keep your curses for those who mean you harm,' Kinon said, but he turned red. 'A thousand apologies. Come in. What are such noble guests doing here with so little ceremony? Now I know that Leon would require me to show every courtesy. Could you not just have said, or sent a note?'

The armed slaves helped bring the horses into the house's business yard. The house steward was already raising his hands to heaven.

'Where shall I stable so many horses?' he asked the gods. And Melitta didn't like how his eyes lingered on her.

Kinon dismissed his worries with a wave of the hand. 'Guests are from the gods,' he said. 'So are their beasts.'

'I could not send a note because I did not wish it to be known that we were here,' Philokles said. 'My charges are in a dangerous position. Tell me the news. What is the tyrant's relationship with Pantecapaeum?'

'Eumeles, who used to be called Heron?' Kinon was pleased to be master of the situation, and pleased, now that he had guests, to show off his possessions. Two more slaves came out of the slave quarters at the back of the business yard. They took over the animals while a young girl brought wine mixed with mineral water, fizzing on the tongue. It made Satyrus think of the bath at the temple of Herakles.

'He's the one,' Philokles said. He tasted his wine and bowed, indicating his pleasure. Troops of slaves, it seemed, emerged from their quarters to take the baggage off the horses and march it into the house.

The steward reappeared. 'I have prepared rooms for them, master,' he said.

Kinon nodded, his lips pursed, until another girl appeared from the arch that led to the garden-courtyard, this one beautiful like a young Aphrodite, with wide eyes above a narrow, arched nose and lips that seemed too lush to be real. Satyrus looked at her, and her fleeting glance – slaves rarely raised their eyes – caught his in a flash of green. She smiled a little. She had a garland in her hair and five more in her arms. With her eyes down, she gave Satyrus a garland. 'My master welcomes you,' she said, and her eyes touched his again.

Satyrus blushed and took the garland. He could see every contour of her body under her simple linen chiton. All women, and all men, were naked under their garments, and almost no one except the sick wore undergarments, but this seemed to be the first time that Satyrus had ever noticed such a thing. He dropped his eyes and missed her flash of a smile.

Theron didn't. He took his wreath and grinned. 'That, sir, is a beautiful girl.'

Kinon patted her shoulder with unfeigned fondness. 'Beautiful and modest. I bought her for a brothel, but I don't think I'll ever sell her.' He gazed on her with a connoisseur's appreciation. 'There is more to life than profit.'

'Your sentiment does you great credit,' Theron said. 'What is your name, girl?'

'I am called Kallista,' she breathed.

'What could be more natural for her?' Kinon said. 'Now your Eumeles – you must know – our Dionysius hates him, as does his brother. It is very – personal. Yes?'

Philokles drank the rest of his cup of wine and handed it to a slave. 'That is the best news that I have heard today, Master Kinon.'

'There is no "Master" here,' Kinon said with courtesy. 'This is your house. May I engage you as guest-friends of my own account? The children of Kineas and Srayanka?'

Melitta's eyes flickered at her brother – *do it!* – and he stepped forward. He imitated Philokles' gesture, handing his wine cup to the air and assuming that a slave would appear to take it. It worked.

'I am Satyrus, son of Kineas of the Corvaxae of Athens and Olbia. Herakles fathered my ancestors on the Nereid who dwelt on the slopes of Gagamia in Euboea. Arimnestos of the Corvaxae led the Plataeans at Marathon and won undying honour there. Kallikrates Eusebios Corvaxae led the exiles from Plataea. He and his son gave their lives for Athens.' He reached out and took both of Kinon's hands. 'I ask your guest-friendship, Kinon of Heraklea, and I gift you with mine, and my children's.'

Kinon clasped his hands. The merchant's hands were soft

and a little moist, but his grip was firm. 'So might the heroes themselves have spoken. Indeed, for a youth, you sound more like a man of Gold than a man of Iron. I am honoured with your guest-friendship, Satyrus Eusebios of the Corvaxae.' He took a wine krater and snapped his fingers, and one of the slaves who had been carrying a sword appeared with an offering bowl. Kinon poured a libation. 'I swear to Hera, to Demeter who loves all guests, and to your ancestor Herakles that I will be your faithful host and guest.'

Satyrus pinched the libation bowl between his thumb and forefinger. 'Grey-eyed Lady of Wisdom, and the strong-armed smith who works bronze and iron, keep this man and be my surety that I will be a faithful guest and friend.'

'I feel as if I have Peleus's son, Achilles, as a guest,' Kinon said. 'From an irritation, this has become a pleasure. Please follow me to a more comfortable situation.' He led the way through the main arch, and they went from the businesslike courtyard with shed and slave quarters to a garden with roses and three colonnades. There was a fountain in the centre, and couches had been arranged on a clear space of gravel amidst the rose bushes. They were not quite in bloom, but the buds were formed.

'You are in luck,' Kinon said, as they looked at his garden. 'The roses will bloom tomorrow or the next day. How long will you stay?'

Having sworn the guest oath, Satyrus was now the centre of their host's attention. He looked at Philokles, who made a small sign with his hands.

'Just long enough to see the roses,' Satyrus said with a smile.

Kinon smiled back, a little too warmly, and Satyrus wondered if he had sent the wrong message to the man.

'I think we could all do with a bath,' Philokles said.

'Goddess!' Kinon was genuinely shocked. 'I've been remiss. Did you ride all the way here?'

Theron spoke up. 'We came on a merchantman from up the coast,' he said.

Kinon exchanged a glance with his steward, and Satyrus

wondered what it meant. 'Is that Draco Short-Legs? From Sinope?'

Philokles nodded. 'The very one. May I bore you with another question? I crave news.'

'Speak to me, sir. May I call you Philokles?'

'You may. If all your wine is as good as what you just served us, we'll be great friends. Have you heard of our friend Diodorus?'

'The captain of mercenaries? Who on the Euxine does not know the man? Indeed, I just sent him fifty new Boeotian helmets made to his order in our shops.' Kinon nodded. 'He's more than just a soldier. He's a good man of business. And his wife is a delight.'

Philokles laughed for the first time in days. 'Sappho?' He shook his head. 'She is superb.'

Diodorus had defied convention and married a hetaira. The situation was more complicated than that – Sappho had started her life as a respectable woman of Thebes, and only when the city was sacked had she been sold into harlotry. Diodorus loved her, and made her his wife. In fact, he'd gone farther, taking her into society with the same boldness with which he led a cavalry charge. And Sappho herself was intelligent, direct and plain-spoken in a way that most women were not. Younger, she had been a beauty. Now she was a mother of two daughters and she could still turn heads at a symposium.

'I think we'll be good friends,' Philokles said. 'If only we might have a bath.'

An hour later, they were back in the rose garden. Satyrus was as clean as he'd been since the Temple of Herakles, and Melitta wore an Ionic chiton, long and flowing and pinned with a set of mother-of-pearl brooches cut like Nereids.

Kinon eyed her critically. 'I purchased it for Kallista,' he said. 'But when I heard your brother speak of your ancestry, I though that you had to wear it.'

Melitta looked at him gravely. 'Has anyone ever told you that you are very like Odysseus for wisdom?' she said.

Kinon laughed. 'Ah, flattery. How I love it. That was well

said, mistress.' He waved at the couches. 'Will you recline, mistress?'

Melitta shook her head. 'A chair, I fear, host. I lack the experience to control my garments at a feast, and I would not stain Kallista's dress for anything.' She smiled at the slave girl.

'Yours, now, mistress,' Kinon said. 'I would not lend a guest a garment.'

Melitta blushed. The linen and the pins were worth more than everything she currently owned. 'Thanks,' she stammered.

Kinon arranged her chair himself and pulled Kallista by the hand. 'Will you wait on the young mistress, my beauty?' he asked, as if she were a member of the family. Raising his eyes to his guests, he said, 'I do not treat her as a slave in the privacy of my garden.'

Theron shrugged. 'I could rest my eyes on her for ever,' he said.

Satyrus would have liked to have said that. He settled for a nod.

Philokles laughed. 'This is the effect of Leon!' he said, a little too loudly. He had been drinking for an hour.

Kinon settled on to the couch opposite the Spartan. 'You understand?'

Philokles smiled. 'I am a Spartan bastard,' he said. 'I understand all too well.'

Theron took wine from a slave and leaned on his elbow. 'I would like to understand,' he said.

Kinon nodded. 'Leon began as a free man and was made a slave. When he became free, he determined to free more men. And women. We call them our "families".' He grinned self-consciously. 'I am not likely to have any other kind of family,' he said. 'I was a slave.'

'Theban?' Philokles asked.

'Ahh. The Boeotian accent.'

Philokles nodded. 'And your respect for Sappho.'

'Yes, I knew her – before.' Kinon shrugged. 'Slavery is neither the beginning nor the end of life. But Leon made me free, and put me in a position to become as rich as I am.' He shrugged. 'I will give the same gift to Kallista, when she is old enough to find a husband and not a brothel.'

Philokles spilled a libation on the gravel. 'To freedom!' he said, and slipped the krater on to the back of his hand. He drank the bowl dry and flipped the leavings across the garden with a practised flick of the wrist, so that the drops of wine rang as they struck the bronze slops urn.

'To freedom,' echoed all the other diners. More drops of wine crossed the roses, but no one else hit the urn.

'You're good,' Kinon said.

'I spend a lot of time practising,' Philokles said, his voice light.

Melitta leaned across her brother and whispered in his ear. 'Kinon is flirting with Philokles,' she said.

'Hush,' Satyrus said, shocked. He saw the slight smile on Kallista's face, and he blushed – and she blushed. Their eyes were locked, and he had to make himself look away.

His sister glanced back and forth between her brother and the slave girl. She shook her head. 'Brother,' she hissed.

He hung his head. Their mother had strict rules about servant girls – and boys.

Theron and Philokles talked with Kinon long into the night. At some point, between wine and shared anecdotes, Philokles stopped hiding their situation, and Kinon expressed immediate sympathy. They began to map out how the twins could travel, either to Athens, where Satyrus owned property that was untouchable by Eumeles of Pantecapaeum, or to Diodorus, who was, it appeared, in the field with the army of Eumenes the Cardian.

Philokles was sober enough when it came to politics, but Theron, who had drunk less, finally shook his head.

'I think I need to hear all that again,' he said, pleasantly enough.

Kinon looked at Theron as if he was a fool. Satyrus sat forward. 'Please,' he said. 'I, too, would like to understand.'

'It's all been the same since the Conqueror died,' Kinon said bitterly. 'Alexander conquered, well, damn near everything!'

He took a drink, tried to hit the bronze urn with his dregs and failed. Theron took the bowl.

Kinon shrugged at his own failure. 'When Alexander died, he left chaos. In Macedon, Antipater was regent – for Alexander, yes? And throughout the old Persian empire – Darius's empire – Alexander had left satraps. Petty kings who ruled over wide areas. Some were the old Persian satraps. Some were Greeks, or Macedonians. The system depended on a strong hand on the reins, and Alexander's hand was very strong.'

Theron took the bowl and drank the whole of it, rolled it on his wrist and his flick caught Kallista on the top of her hair. She leaped from her couch and tossed water back at him, and they all laughed. It took time to settle down again. Satyrus couldn't help but notice how transparent her linen was when wet.

'Shall I go on?' Kinon asked.

'Please,' Satyrus said. It was his turn with the bowl. He sipped carefully.

'So the army met in council – all the spearmen, and all the cavalry, and all the officers – and none of the Persians or auxiliaries. Trust me, that will make trouble in time. At any rate, Alexander left no heir – no one who could run his empire. He has two children – one by Roxane, and another by-blow by a Persian noblewoman – some say she's a common harlot, others that she is a princess.' Kinon looked around, because Philokles was smiling. 'You know her?'

'Nothing common about her,' Philokles said with a smile. 'She's – remarkable.'

'At any rate, the army vote to hand the empire to Alexander's brother, the halfwit. But he can't rule himself, much less the world. And there are rumours – still – that Antipater was about to revolt anyway, that Eumenes and Seleucus were about to divide up the world – anyway, there are ten thousand rumours. The fact is, Alexander died and there was no one in charge. So all of his generals decided to fight over the empire. Perdikkas had the army – he had been Alexander's top soldier at the moment of the conqueror's death. But Antipater had the *Macedonian* army, the army that had been kept home.'

'The army that defeated the Spartans,' Philokles said. 'Only needed odds of five to one. Useless fucks.'

Satyrus was done drinking. He'd been careful, and consumed the whole cup without spilling a drop. He laid the cup along his arm as Philokles did, and he snapped it forward – and the handle broke. The cup smashed on the marble floor. His sister gave him the look reserved for siblings who behave like idiots, and Kallista burst out laughing.

Slaves hurried to clean up the mess.

Philokles roared. 'Good shot, boy! Only, next time, hold the rim, not the handle.'

Kinon laughed like a good host. 'Another cup, Pais!' he called to the slave nearest the door.

'Bring a metal one,' Theron added.

Satyrus squirmed. Melitta decided to rescue him. 'So Antipater had an army, and Perdikkas had an army.'

Kinon nodded. 'A sober young lady. Antipater had Macedon, and Perdikkas had the rest – so it appeared. But one of Alexander's generals—'

'The best of them,' Philokles put in.

'I must agree,' Kinon said with a civil inclination of his head. A new cup appeared and was handed to Philokles. 'Ptolemy had taken Aegypt as his satrapy. He had a large Macedonian garrison and he began to recruit mercenaries.'

'Like Uncle Diodorus!' Satyrus said.

'Just like.' Philokles nodded and sipped wine.

'So Perdikkas decided to defeat Ptolemy first and take Aegypt to provide money and grain for his army. Which had been Alexander's army.' Kinon looked at Satyrus. 'Still with me?'

'Of course,' Satyrus said. 'And Perdikkas failed, got beaten and was murdered by his officers.'

'No one ever called Macedonians civilized,' Philokles said.

'Now Antigonus has the army that used to belong to Perdikkas – except for the part that Eumenes the Cardian has. Antigonus means to unseat Ptolemy. Ptolemy! The least harmful of the lot! And a good friend to Heraklea!'

'Perhaps Antigonus will lose?' Philokles said. 'I know Ptolemy. He's a subtle man.'

'You know him?' Kinon laughed again. He was drunk now. 'I am in the company of the great.'

Philokles finished the cup, flicked his wrist and his wine drop scored on the bronze rim of the urn like a bell tolling. 'I know him pretty well,' he said. 'I took him prisoner once.' He laughed, and Kinon looked shocked.

Melitta nodded. 'It's true. And my father and Philokles released him. They're guest-friends, I think. Right?'

'That's right,' Philokles said. 'That's why Diodorus is a little more than just a mercenary to Ptolemy.'

Kinon shook his head. 'You took him prisoner? In a battle? Next you'll be telling me that you knew Alexander!'

'My father did,' Satyrus said. 'But please go on. Perdikkas is dead, and Antigonus One-Eye has his army.'

'Exactly.' Kinon got the bowl and balanced it expertly while talking. 'Antigonus has the whole field army behind him, and Ptolemy won't get another miracle in the Delta. He has no soldiers to speak of now, just some military settlers and some useless Aegyptians. He won't last the season. I'll miss him – he's the only one of those Macedonian fucks who wants to build something instead of just killing.' As he drank, his Boeotian accent got thicker, and now he sounded like a character in a comedy.

Philokles shrugged. 'And Eumenes is left with the rump?'

'Less than the rump – although he's wily. Antipater had him once and he escaped.' Kinon snapped his fingers for more drink. By this point, he had Kallista sitting on a stool beneath his couch, and he played with her hair while he spoke. Melitta had already excused herself like an Athenian matron.

Philokles laughed again. 'I remember his wiles,' he said. 'He and Kineas chased each other all over Bactria.'

Kinon sighed. 'And then there's Greece, of course. Now that Antipater is gone, and we had Polyperchon as a replacement – too old, and not smart enough to live – Athens made a bid for independence back, oh, six years or so. They defeated Antipater's army and frankly they looked to overthrow the whole system. That united all the Macedonians for a while.'

Philokles shrugged. 'And Kineas's old friend Leosthenes died.'

Kinon looked knowing. 'Died – or got very sick and slipped away when the whole alliance started coming apart. There are people who claim to have seen him. But the chaos that he caused in Thrace and Greece is why One-Eye has time to move against Ptolemy – because Polyperchon is still rebuilding. The Athenians showed that the Macedonians could be beaten. And there's a new man on the stage – Antipater's son, Cassander – he's a different matter. Bad to the bone, that one – smart like a lion and rotten like an old corpse.'

Theron shook his head. 'I paid no mind to politics when I was at Corinth. It wearies me, friends. And all of you know these men – these great men – like fellow guests at a symposium. I'm going to retire, friends, secure in the knowledge that the only people of consequence I know are athletes, and none of them is much of an adornment at a dinner party.'

When he rose, he gave Satyrus a long look. Satyrus got the message. 'I thank you for hospitality and good talk, wisdom and beauty.' He slipped the last in with a look at Kallista.

Kinon nodded. 'Tomorrow we'll have a look at the agora.'

'Perhaps the palaestra?' Theron asked.

'Of course!' The host patted his stomach. 'I may remember the way there!'

And with that laugh, Satyrus stumbled off to bed. He managed to make it to the couch in his room, and then his wits turned off like a snuffed lamp.

In the morning, they threatened to stay off. Melitta came to wake him, prodding him under the ribs with her thumbs and tickling his feet until his groans turned to counter-attacks. She giggled, backing away from his couch, and he discovered that he had a splitting headache.

'Time to get up, sleepyhead,' she said.

'Oh,' he said, clutching his temples.

An older slave, heavy with muscle and black as an Athenian vase, came in and began to tidy his chamber. Satyrus wanted to get off his couch, but he couldn't quite make himself do it.

'Could you fetch us some water?' Melitta said. 'You're twelve, Satyr, not twenty. You drank far too much wine last night.'

'I don't think it was the wine,' Satyrus said plaintively. 'I think I've hurt my head, or caught a cold.'

The black slave snorted. He was only gone for a few moments and then he returned with a silver pitcher of water and a bronze cup. 'Drink up, master,' he said with a grin.

Satyrus raised his head. 'Why are you *smiling*? My head hurts!'

'Drink all the water in this pitcher,' the slave said. 'I'll get you another when you are done. Then your headache will cure itself. I promise.'

Satyrus managed to drink down two pitchers of water, and then he and Melitta made their way out into the rose garden where all the guests were reclining. Melitta watched him with a superior smile. 'More wine, brother?' she asked.

'Hard head, boy?' Philokles asked. 'Worst age for a male, Satyrus. At twelve, you are invited to behave like a man, but you can't. Best be wary of the wine.'

Theron raised an eyebrow at the Spartan, and the two men glowered at each other for a bit. 'Advice everyone could heed.'

A young male slave came in, sheathed in sweat, with a scroll. Kinon took it and opened it, his eyes scanning the page, and he frowned.

'I asked our tyrant, Dionysius, to grant us all an audience.' He rolled the scroll and scratched his chin with it. 'He has declined the honour, saying that the time for meeting is in-auspicious, which is a load of mule dung and no mistake.' He handed the scroll to the same black slave who had waited on Satyrus after he awoke. 'Zosimos, have this scraped clean and put in the stack.'

Zosimos took the scroll and vanished through the pillars of the colonnade.

Kinon glanced around, pulled out a gold toothpick and went to work on his teeth. Satyrus looked away. A female slave offered him wine, and he hastily put his hand over his cup. 'Might I have some more water?' he implored her.

She went to a sideboard and returned with a gleaming silver pitcher and a slight smile. He accepted both gratefully.

'Something is amiss,' Kinon said. 'Nonetheless, I'm sending to Diodorus by courier so that he is warned of your circumstances. I'll send a caravan with the armour – three days at the least, I'm afraid. What do you need?'

Philokles leaned forward. 'Clothes, weapons, remounts. Some cash. Kinon, I am merely being candid – pardon my bluntness.'

Kinon shook his head. 'No need to apologize. I am rich, and my friend Leon could buy and sell twenty of me, and together, your burden isn't a flyspeck. Arms and armour are easy – we make them. Why don't I have Zosimos take you to the shop? None of the gear will be silver chased or inlaid, but it is all solid and workmanlike. Take what you need or have Zosimos order it with our smith.' He rubbed his chin. 'I don't like the fact that the tyrant won't see you.' He looked around. 'Where is Tenedos?'

One of the female slaves darted into the colonnade and Tenedos, the steward, emerged, chewing on a stylus. 'Master?' he asked, very much in the tone of a man annoyed to be interrupted.

'What shipping came in today, Tenedos?' Kinon asked.

Tenedos took a breath and Satyrus thought that he hesitated. 'Pentekonter from Tomis, laden with wine, property of Isokles of Tomis. Merchantman from Athens, laden with pottery and fine woollens and some copper, property of a mixed cartel of Athenian merchants and some of our friends. The copper is ours. Military trireme, no lading.'

Kinon sat up and swung his legs over the side of his couch. 'From Pantecapaeum?' he asked.

'By way of Gorgippia and Bata, if the oar master is to be believed.' Tenedos tucked his stylus behind his ear.

Philokles swung his legs over the edge of his couch. 'Ares!' he said. He sounded tired.

Kinon shook his head. 'This is Heraklea, not some grain town on the north shore of the Euxine. We have laws here, and a good ruler, even if he is a tyrant. But they've got to him.

Tenedos, I should have told you – now I am telling you. I wish to know anything you learn of this ship, of its master and its navarch and who they visit. Understand?'

'Yes, master,' Tenedos said, sounding both competent and long-suffering.

Philokles nodded. 'If you will lend me young Zosimos, I will see to some armour. He looked at Satyrus. 'Fancy some armour and a light sword, boy?'

Satyrus was off his couch, headache forgotten, before Philokles was done speaking.

'As would I,' Melitta said.

'We're not on the sea of grass now,' Philokles said.

'Will that render me safe from assault?' she asked.

'As a woman,' Kinon started, and then reconsidered. The code of war said that women were exempt from the rigours and results, but no one fought by the code any more. The Spartans and the Athenians had killed the code in their thirty-year war, almost a hundred years before. Women caught with a defeated army were sold into slavery.

'I'll come with you,' she insisted.

Theron rolled off his couch. 'I'll come too.'

Philokles raised an eyebrow. 'We won't be able to pay you for a long time, athlete. I honour you for your loyalty, but shouldn't you be finding a new employer?'

Theron gave a wry smile. 'So anxious to be rid of me? I thought that I'd get myself a free suit of bronze. That will pay my fees for some months.'

Kinon laughed. 'I hadn't thought what taking in a pair of princes would be like. Of course! Tutors and trainers! We'll need a sophist!'

Philokles shook his head. 'I've got that covered,' he said.

Kinon laughed heartily. 'Now I've seen everything!' he said. 'A Spartan sophist!'

Philokles returned a twisted smile. 'Just so. When I can't convince a man, I kill him.'

They had to walk all the way, through the landward gate, called the Sinope gate by the locals, from stone-cobbled streets to gravel roads and then to heavily rutted dirt and mud. The armour smith's place was a dozen stades outside of town, and they went far enough to get a good picture of the life of the local helots.

Satyrus walked next to Philokles. 'That ship from Tomis?' he said.

Philokles' eyes flickered over the fields and the bent figures working them. 'I was thinking more of the trireme. What about it?'

Satyrus shrugged. 'Wasn't Isokles a good friend of my father's?' he asked. 'We'd be safe there.'

Philokles nodded and tugged his beard. 'I hadn't given that thought. You may have a point. We could probably secure passage on his ship. But what then?'

'Across Thrace to Athens,' Satyrus said.

'Right across Cassander's territory?' Philokles asked. 'Does that seem wise?'

Satyrus let his shoulders droop. 'Oh,' he said.

The armour smith had a circle of houses, almost like a small village, and a dozen sheds, each more ill-built than the last, and a slave barracks in the middle surrounded by a fence. A stream flowed through the middle of the facility, and it stank of human waste and ash. The road outside the gate was a cratered ruin from heavy cartage, and there was a dead donkey at the bottom of one of the worst pits, its body bloated and stinking.

Satyrus was shocked, and he wrinkled his nose in disgust.

Theron smiled. 'You thought that armour and weapons were made in forest glades by Hephaestos and his mortal helpers? Or inside volcanoes, perhaps?'

Melitta looked at the devastation of ten forges and all the support the forges required. As she watched, a string of donkeys, perhaps fifty of them, were driven past. Every donkey had a pair of woven basket panniers, and each one was full of charcoal. The drovers were careful to leave the road and get the whole string around the deep potholes where the dead donkey rotted. 'By the lame smith!' she said. 'This is an assault on Gaia! This is like impiety!'

Theron shook his head. 'This is a good-sized commercial

forge, mistress.' He shrugged. 'Over there,' he said, pointing at the mountains that stood like a wall on the southern horizon, 'is Bithynia and Paphlagonia. There is a war there. Armies of twenty thousand men, and every man must have a sword, a spear and a helmet – at least.' He looked at the twins. 'We have manufactories in Boeotia and in Corinth. This one isn't bad. It's just a dead animal.'

'Wait until you see a battlefield,' Philokles said.

The factor of the armour factory was a Chalcidian freedman. His face was red and his arms and legs and chiton were covered in burns, and he had no hair at all. 'Zosimos!' he said. 'A pleasure.' His voice belied his words, but he gave the black man a quick smile at the end to pull the barb.

Zosimos bowed and flashed a smile in return. 'Eutropios, I greet you, and I bring you the greetings of my master, Kinon. He asks that these men, friends of his, and of Master Leon,' Zosimos said this with a significant look, 'receive whatever armour they might need, and weapons.'

Eutropios put his hands on his hips. He had the muscles of Herakles. In fact, his upper physique was a match for Theron's. 'I thought he was too well dressed to be a new smith for me,' he said, looking at Theron. 'I hoped, though. Listen, tell your master from me that if he wants this big order to go out before the Mounikhion, he had best not be sending me any new orders. If these gentlemen,' and Eutropios bowed without much courtesy, 'take armour from the order, I'm that much worse off.'

Philokles dismounted from his horse, pulled his straw hat off his head and offered his arm to clasp. 'I'm Philokles of Tanais,' he said. 'This is Theron of Corinth, who fought the pankration last year at the Olympics.'

Eutropios nodded, the corners of his mouth turned down in appreciation. 'So – I've heard of you. And you,' he said to Philokles. 'You're the warrior.'

Philokles shrugged. 'I'm a philosopher now,' he said, 'and the tutor to these children.'

Satyrus writhed at being called a child in the presence of a master weapon smith.

'And who needs arms?' the smith asked. 'Oh, get down from your mounts – believe me, I have nothing better to do than to talk to Olympic athletes.' He turned his back on them and started walking. 'I'm sure you'll want to see the workshops. Zosimos worked for me – he can show you anything.'

'I need arms, as does Theron. And for the young ones – men are trying to kill them.' Philokles' voice changed. 'Pardon, sir, if we have interrupted your work. But I have known a number of craftsmen, and all of them work flat out. There is never a good time to visit. True? Please aid us. We will not require a tour, or much of your time. A few workmanlike items and we'll be out of your hair.'

Eutropios turned back to Philokles. 'I have no hair,' he said. 'You fight Spartan-style or Macedonian?' he asked.

'Spartan,' Philokles said. 'With an *aspis*, not one of these little Macedonian shields.'

'Now, that's lucky for you, because I have some made up. No one wants them any more, except some of the cities up north. Hoplite panoply? I have two or three to hand, from an order that never sold. Cavalry equipment? Don't even ask. Everyone is a horse soldier now. Soon enough, there won't even be any hoplites. No one wants to do any work any more – everyone wants to ride a fucking horse.' The Chalcidian grinned sourly. He led them to a heavily built stone house that held up sheds at both ends. The door was sealed shut. He took a curious tool from his belt and twisted the seal wire and opened the door for them.

Satyrus gasped. The room was a veritable treasury of Ares. Bronze helmets, bronze-faced shields and rows of swords, most with a light coat of rust on them, straight-bladed and leaf-bladed and bent-bladed, of every size. Spears stood against the wall, their blades dark with rust, their bronze *sauroteres*, or butt-spikes, brown or green with patina. 'All built for the tyrant's guard, but now he has them aping the Macedonians,' he said. 'The swords are good,' he said, as he plucked a short kopis from the floor and wiped the surface rust off on his chiton. 'Good work from home. I bought this lot from a pirate – the shipment was for Aegypt. Saves me time to have a store of them.'

Philokles nodded. 'No scabbards,' he said.

'Do I look like a scabbard maker?' the smith asked. 'Hephaestos, protect me! Are you expecting to be offered wine? Ares and Aphrodite. Zosimos, will you fetch these fine gentlemen some wine while they look at my wares and ask for fucking scabbards?'

Theron picked up a longer kopis, made in the western style with a bird-shaped hilt. It was a heavy weapon. He swung it without much effort.

'Sure you wouldn't like to do a little smithing, boy?' the smith asked. 'Shoulders like that, you won't have to worry about someone trying to kill you in the Olympics. I'll make you rich.' He laughed. 'Hermes, I'm already rich, but I can't spend it, because I can't stop working.'

'He needs Temerix,' Satyrus said to Melitta. She smiled at him, and then both of them realized that their friend, the Sindi master smith of Tanais, might well be dead, or a slave, with his eastern wife and their three sons, playmates all.

Life would seem exciting for an hour and then something would happen to remind them. Satyrus wiped his eyes and stood straight. 'Temerix is the toughest man I know,' he said. 'He would survive, and Lu is too clever to be – attacked.'

Melitta shook her head. 'And Ataelus? He must be dead. He was with mama.'

She wiped her eyes, looked around the room and spotted a small helmet with cheekpieces on the stack of helmets, mostly unrimmed Pylos helmets and a couple of Boeotians. She pulled it on and it went down over her eyes.

Philokles lifted it off her head, the bowl fitting in the palm of one of his great hands, and replaced it, rocking it gently on her hair. 'Not bad,' he said. 'We'll make you an arming cap.'

He reached into the pile and pulled out a small helmet with a bowl like a loaf of bread. 'Try that,' he said to Satyrus.

Satyrus wanted to look like Achilles, and not like some cheap foot soldier. This was a plain Boeotian, with a simple rim and no cheekpieces and no crest. He put it on his head and it sank past his temples, but it only needed padding. And a helmet of his own was better than no helmet.

'Fits,' he told Philokles.

He went to the rows of swords and came up with a short, leaf-bladed weapon the length of his forearm. Philokles approved, despite the fact that the blade was red-brown with rust.

'Just a little work,' the smith said. 'You suited?' Then he seemed to relent, relaxing visibly. 'You want to see the forge?' he said to Satyrus. He wrinkled his nose at Melitta. 'Not much for a girl to see.'

Melitta made him laugh by wrinkling her nose back. 'You need to get to know a better class of girl,' she shot back. 'Let's go.'

Theron and Philokles declined. They were trying shields. So the children followed Zosimos and Eutropios out into the smoke-filled air and then into the largest shed, built of upright rough-sawn boards on poles driven deep into the ground.

The sound was loud outside the shed, but inside it was almost overwhelming. Satyrus and Melitta had seen Temerix at work, his hammer ringing on his bronze anvil or his iron one, and they'd seen him work with one of his journeymen, Curti or Pardo, the hammers banging in turns, but this was ten anvils in a circle around a furnace whose heat struck them like fists as they entered, and the hammer blows rang like continuous thunder on a hot summer day. Every smith in the shed was working bronze, building helmets, working them up from shaped trays that were probably made in another shed, working on the bowls and turning the whole helmet slightly after each blow. Every smith had a helper, and some had two, and the pieces were constantly being reheated in the furnace before coming back to the smiths. On top of the high furnace at the centre of the room, a bronze cauldron bubbled away, adding steam to the smoke.

The twins stood, amazed. Individual workers stopped, drinking cool water from pottery canteens hanging on the walls, or watered wine from skins, or a hot drink from the bronze cauldron on top of the furnace, or rubbing their hands, or putting olive oil on a burn, but the shed continued to work as a whole, the ringing of hammers never ending.

Eutropios watched with pride. 'We're working a big order,' he shouted. 'I love it when every hammer is working.' He gave them a smile.

At the sound of the master smith's voice, many men stopped working and looked at him, so he had to wave them all back to work. 'Guests!' he shouted. Some of the smiths laughed.

'Are they slaves?' Melitta asked.

'Hard to say,' Eutropios said. 'Slaves don't always make the best craftsmen, young lady. Most of those men weren't born free. Some are working off their freedom, and others are taking a wage. None of them are getting the same wage they'd make if they had their own forge.' He shrugged. 'Every few months, a couple wander off to start a business, and I need more. I eat smiths like my forges eat charcoal.' He waved at the boys running water back and forth, or carrying nets of charcoal. 'The boys are mostly slaves. I use 'em until Kinon finds them a buyer. It's hard work, but good food and all they can eat. They go to market well fed and well muscled.'

Melitta chewed her lip.

'My sister has taken against slavery,' Satyrus said in disgust.

'When you said we could end up slaves, it made me think. What about that girl? Kallista? I'm *pretty*,' Melitta said in disgust. 'Men would look at me the way you all look at her.'

Eutropios laughed. 'Lady, that will happen anyway,' he said. 'Let me be a good host. Come this way.' He led the way to another shed, where two men worked on long wooden benches while half a dozen younger men held things.

'Whitesmiths,' Eutropios said. 'Finishers. See what they're making?' They were finishing small blades – knives shaped like swords but made the size of meat knives. 'Look at them – no black on them any more. See what Klopi here – he has the knack – see what he's got. The blade shines like a mirror. People pay money for hilts in bronze and gold – but it is the bladework and the finishing that costs the money to make. And a polish like this won't rust.' He swatted Klopi on the back. 'Nice work. Master work, in fact. Come and see me tonight.' He looked at the other blade. 'Not bad. Klopi, help him finish and show him how you got that deep lustre.'

When they emerged from the sheds, Theron and Philokles had a mule with panniers loaded with bronze and iron. 'We have a good deal of work to do ourselves,' Philokles said.

They spent the ride back to Heraklea babbling like the children they were, while their tutors made plans.

6

No sooner were they back in the courtyard of Kinon's house than Philokles set to work, borrowing labour from the house staff. He sent Zosimos out to find a leatherworker to make scabbards and belts and straps for the corslets, and he started with the shields, ripping the old leather backing off. Melitta and Satyrus were handed jars of rancid oil and scraps of linen and powdered pumice. They enthusiastically rubbed the surface rust off the blades of the swords, helped by various slaves who knew how to use the tools at hand. In minutes they were red to their elbows with rust.

Kinon came out into the working courtyard, dressed in an elegant chiton and with a heavy cloak over his left shoulder. He glanced around. 'If he's fobbed you off with a lot of old stuff—'

'I think we're entirely satisfied,' Philokles said. 'A little work won't hurt any of us,' he said with a glance at the twins.

Satyrus agreed. It felt good to be dirty – good to be doing something. He enjoyed the slow progress of his work, watching the red fall away from the steel, and then the rhythmic effort would widen the bright spot. There was a lesson there, he thought.

Melitta began to hum to herself as she worked – a Sakje song about drinking wine. Satyrus started to sing the words, and then they were both singing.

Kinon nodded. 'I have an appointment,' he said. 'Tenedos is out listening for news. I'll see you at dinner,' he added. He stopped in the gate, where Zosimos was entering with a leatherworker, the man's trade obvious from his apron and knife. 'I'm reminded of my father,' he said, looking around. 'This was the way our courtyard would be when he made ready for war, and all his clients and friends gathered to fix their kit.'

Philokles raised his head. Satyrus followed his glance and saw tears on the Theban's face, and he went back to singing.

*

Dinner was just as good as the first night, and Satyrus gazed on Kallista until his devotion was obvious to everyone there, but he couldn't keep his eyes open, and fell asleep on his couch, to his own acute embarrassment.

Melitta stayed up later, listening to the older men make plans and watching the complexities of the interplay between the men. Friendship was growing between Philokles and Theron, and something similar between Philokles and Kinon, but Kinon and Theron didn't seem to be getting along. She watched them carefully.

After the wine began to circulate quickly and the slaves were sent to bed, Kallista came and stood beside her. 'May I share your couch?' she asked.

Melitta moved aside and the older girl lay down. Melitta put an arm around her and they snuggled against each other.

'I haven't been dismissed, but Kinon won't want me listening,' the beautiful girl said. 'He's flirting with the Spartan. Why don't they just say what they want?'

Melitta peeked over the back of her couch. The men had forgotten them altogether. They were laughing in the way that Melitta associated with jokes about sex, or women. In that respect, Sakje men and Greek men were little different.

'Philokles doesn't know what he wants,' she said.

'My master wants him,' Kallista said.

Melitta held her breath a moment. 'I thought that – that is to say, it seemed. Oh dear. I thought that he loved you?'

Kallista laughed. 'First, mistress, I'm a slave – he can have me when he pleases, or send me to pleasure his guests. I've done all that. But no – in this house I've never been asked to oblige my master in any way, except to wait at table. I am an adornment. Much like the silver pitchers.'

'Oh,' Melitta said. 'Do you— Is it better? Than – obliging?'

Kallista laughed. 'How old are you, mistress?'

'Twelve,' Melitta said.

'I've had men since I was eleven,' Kallista said. 'Sometimes it's nice. Sometimes it's big, drunk men who want me on their cocks in the middle of a party.' She shrugged, turned away so that Melitta couldn't see her face. 'But I've never kindled, Aphrodite be thanked, and Kinon hasn't pushed me at a man since I went into this house. Perhaps my hymen will grow back,' she said. She rolled over carefully so that the couch didn't make a noise. 'Have you? Had a man?'

Melitta felt herself blush. 'No,' she said. 'It all looks – silly.'

The older girl chuckled. 'You don't know the half of it. And your brother? Has he?' The girl pulled her a little closer.

Melitta felt an alarm bell begin to ring softly in her head. 'Why do you ask?' she said.

'No reason,' Kallista replied. 'He's pretty enough, for his age. Men would want him – girls too.'

Melitta thought about that for a moment. 'I don't think he's given it much thought,' she said.

Kallista stiffened, then rolled away again. She lay with her back to Melitta for a little, and then rolled to her feet. 'That must be nice,' she said bitterly, and vanished into the darkness.

Melitta lay by herself for a moment, and then followed the other girl. She could hear the sound of her feet on the colonnade, and she tracked her. The older girl was crying very softly. Melitta caught up with her at the entrance to a dark room by the simple expedient of running a few steps and grabbing her shoulder.

'I'm stupid sometimes,' Melitta said.

The older girl collapsed in her arms, sobbing. Her sobs were very quiet. Melitta realized that when you were a slave, you didn't even own your sobs.

'Hey!' Melitta said. She came from a family without a great deal of patience for tears. 'I'm sorry!'

Kallista put her head on Melitta's shoulder.

Then she started kissing the nape of Melitta's neck.

Melitta froze for a moment, and then wriggled out of the other girl's embrace with all the skills that her brother had taught her. 'Hey,' she said again, the sound of her voice threatening to get louder if required.

'Oh,' Kallista said. 'I thought—'

'Aphrodite,' Melitta said.

'I'd like to be friends,' Kallista said.

'Do you always chew on your friends?' Melitta asked.

'It's fun,' the older girl breathed.

'Listen, Kallista,' Melitta said, stretching a hand out. 'I ride with the spear-maidens in the summer. I know what girls do.' She shrugged. 'Maybe we can be friends.' She pushed away from the column at her back. 'But not lovers. I'm twelve, not five – I know how all that works.'

'Do you?' the beautiful girl asked, and Melitta caught the derision.

'Well,' Melitta admitted, 'probably not.'

Kallista squeezed her hand.

Melitta felt a flutter of *something*, like a flush that spread from her chest to her groin. She let go of Kallista's hand and fled for her room, leaving Kallista laughing, or crying, behind her.

But she didn't get to sleep quickly.

Kallista was on her mind when she awoke, and as soon as she bathed she walked around to her brother's room, where he was stretching as if for the palaestra.

'You look better,' she said.

He shrugged. 'Comes and goes,' he said. 'You?'

'The same.' She sat on his sleeping couch. 'You have a thing for Kallista,' she said accusingly.

That got her brother to grin. 'I do,' he said. 'Just like our Lady Mother promised – all the feeling in the world, as if she was the only woman who had ever lived, Aphrodite incarnate.' He spoke with self-mockery, because their mother had lectured them so often on the perils of young love and the intrigues of sex.

Then he sat down next to her and they embraced, both thinking of their mother.

'Maybe Mama is all right,' Melitta said.

Satyrus held her more tightly, and she hugged him back.

'Kallista made a pass at me last night,' Melitta said.

Satyrus stiffened and then sat back. 'Oh,' he said.

'She asked me about you,' Melitta said. 'I rather like her. It's nice having a girl to talk to. But there's another face to her – something else. When she asked about you, she sounded – greedy.'

Satyrus got up and went back to doing his pankration guard positions. 'Oh, I understand,' he said. 'With my well-known riches, she thinks I'll make a good client? I think I've seen the play.'

'Yes,' Melitta said. 'I think that's just how she sees you.' She was sorry to inflict pain on her brother, but she saw her shaft sink into him. She promised her mother, alive or dead, that she'd fill that role whenever she had to – somebody in the family had to be tough. And she wasn't letting her brother get taken by a hetaira, no matter how lovely. It made her feel better.

'Ouch,' Satyrus said. He faked a kick with his left leg and then struck with his left hand, but in a flare of anger he misjudged his distance and his hand hit the plastered wall. Dust flew, and he cursed, holding his hand under his right armpit. 'Fuck,' he said.

'Satyr!' his sister admonished.

'I feel like an idiot,' he said.

'I'll withhold the obvious comment,' she said. 'Let's go and eat.'

'I need to get out of this house,' Satyrus said. 'Wine one night and slave girls the next. Save my virtue, Lita.'

'I'm doing my best,' she said.

'Weren't you tempted by her, though?' he asked. He put his hand in the water pitcher.

'No,' she lied.

They walked out together to breakfast, pancakes and honey with sesame seeds. They both ate all they were offered, and then had to bathe again because they were so sticky. Philokles laughed at them, and Melitta laughed at herself, because for all her wisdom (and she offered prayer and libation to Athena for her help the night before), she was still a little girl who ate too many pancakes.

By mid-morning, they were in the business courtyard again,

cleaning helmets under Theron's exacting direction. Philokles had a pile of horsehair.

While they worked, Philokles went over his plan. 'Tomorrow or the next day, we'll go south,' he said. 'Theron will go as the captain of the escort and I will go with him. You are just two noble children travelling under our charge. We'll be travelling through a war. I hope that we don't have to do it for long.'

Theron shook his head. 'Why don't we just take a ship for Athens?'

Philokles spoke quietly. 'Tenedos says that the marines from the trireme are watching the waterfront. I think they want us to take ship so that they can catch us out on the sea.' He looked at Satyrus. 'That's a firm "no" on the subject of going to Isokles.'

Satyrus ground away at the green-brown patina on the helmet he was cleaning for the time it took to think his way through the whole hymn to Athena. Then he said, 'How long will they hunt us?'

Philokles grunted. 'For ever,' he said. 'Until you go back and kill them and make yourself king. That's the way of it.' His eyes met Satyrus's, and Satyrus felt as if he was being asked a particularly hard philosophical question.

Satyrus looked away. Philokles seemed to be accusing him of something. Of being afraid – afraid to stand up for his rights. Or something. 'I'm tired of worrying,' he said.

Theron shook his head. 'Satyrus, the worrying has just begun.' He looked as if he meant to say more, but Zosimos came through the gate. He made his way through the armour and stood between the twins. He gave them a showy bow.

'Master Eutropios sends you these,' he said. He held out a small bundle wrapped in linen. 'He apologizes that they do not have scabbards.'

Inside the bundle were the two heavy knives, or very small swords, that they had seen the whitesmiths polishing the day before. Now they gleamed like water, and had hilts of steel and bone.

Philokles reached out. 'May I?' he asked.

Melitta handed him hers. 'Please,' she said, although she loved hers from the first touch.

'Very nice,' he said. 'Somewhere between an eating knife and a short sword.' He handed it back. 'Zosimos, would you be kind enough to take them around to the leather-working fellow?'

Satyrus stood. 'Can you carry my deep thanks and those of my sister to the smith?'

Zosimos smiled. 'Sure.' He grinned again.

There were now two armed slaves on the courtyard gate all the time. They opened the gate for Zosimos to go out, and Tenedos came in. He glared at them and went off towards the slave quarters.

'I thought he was buying us remounts?' Theron asked, after the man was gone.

'I think he disapproves of us,' Philokles said.

By late afternoon, the twins were barely able to keep polishing for sheer fatigue. Theron had given both of them a workout in the garden, and Philokles had given them a lesson in swordplay on the hard earth of the yard – basic stuff, and so much like pankration that all the footwork was the same, and most of the attacks – and then they'd been put back to work. But Satyrus raised his head to see Zosimos come into the yard past the armed slaves.

'The smith is delighted that you are so pleased,' he said. 'But you can give your compliments in person. The caravan will form up at the factory. We will leave in two days. So you should come out tomorrow evening and spend the night.'

'Thanks for your help, Zosimos,' Philokles said.

Zosimos nodded. 'I'll be coming with you. I'm to accompany the caravan out and back, and then I'm free.' He grinned. 'Except for all the legal parts.'

'Then what?' Theron asked.

'I think I'll try being a smith,' the young man said. 'Master Eutropios has been offering to train me for years. Well, since my shoulders got big, anyway.' He went away smiling.

The equipment in the courtyard was finished to Philokles' exacting requirements – the edged weapons polished and sharp, the wood shafts of the spears oiled, the heads ground and the butt-spikes gleaming like gold. He packed the helmets in leather bags, put covers on the shields and pulled the cross belt of his sword over his head. Theron did the same. They fitted, and the scabbards were careful work, leather over wood with bronze fittings. The twins' knives had the same mounts, and they put them on proudly.

'I suspect you're the only Greek woman in Heraklea with her own *xiphos*,' Theron said. 'Hail to you, grey-eyed goddess!' He put a helmet on her head.

'Stop clowning around,' Philokles said. 'I wish we could ride out to the factory right now.'

'And miss another dinner with Kinon?' Theron said, somewhat waspishly, Satyrus thought.

Philokles gave him a long look. 'You are a man of virtue, Theron.'

Theron blushed.

'Because you are a man of virtue, I have to say that some of your insinuations are womanish and unbecoming.' Philokles, when sober, was quite imposing.

Theron frowned. 'Philokles, you too are a man of virtue. But you drink too much, and lose that authority which would be yours by right. The authority to tell me that I'm womanish, for instance.'

The two men were standing.

'How much I drink is between me and the gods, Corinthian. Keep your views to yourself.' Philokles' hands bunched into fists.

'Fine words from you, Spartan. But then Spartans were always better at dishing it out than at taking it.' The Corinthian stepped up to Philokles.

Philokles moved forward, eye to eye with the athlete.

'Stop it!' Melitta said. 'Stop it! Have you forgotten that there are people in this city who seek to kill us?' She rose to her feet and looked around. 'I'm going to have a bath,' she said. 'I recommend that you *men* do the same.'

She marched out of the courtyard like a queen.

Satyrus busied himself with the last spot of verdigris on his own small helmet and wished that he was as brave and regal as his sister.

Theron glanced at Philokles. 'She told us, eh?'

Philokles nodded. 'You've heard of Kineas?'

Theron nodded.

'Now you've met him. That was him. In his daughter.'

Philokles poured a cup of rough wine from a skin that hung on the wall and spilled a libation on the ground.

'Here's to the shade of Kineas, and to his children. And to friendship with you, Theron.' Philokles drank.

Theron took the horn cup. He looked at Satyrus. 'Is it hard, having a hero and a demi-god as a father?' He gave the boy a smile. 'My father was a fisherman. Sometimes that is the easier path.' He raised the cup to Philokles, poured another libation and took an orator's stance. 'To the shade of Kineas, who sits with heroes – Arimnestos and Dion and Timoleon, Ajax and Achilles and all the men who shed their blood at windy Ilion. And to your friendship, Spartan, which means a great deal to me, whatever I say in anger. And to the twins.' He spilled wine at each pronouncement and drank in turn. Then he offered it to Satyrus.

Satyrus accepted it, wishing he could think of something noble to say. Finally he spilled a libation and said, 'I wish I was more like my father. May he be with the immortals, feasting. May you two be friends.' He took a sip, smiled self-consciously and handed it back.

The solemn moment was broken by the shouts of Melitta in the bath. She was throwing water at someone, and that someone shrieked and giggled.

They were all bathed for dinner. Kinon returned from his business just a few minutes before the couches were set.

'Tuna!' Melitta pronounced as she came in. She was beautifully dressed in an ionic chiton with silver deer as brooches – Sakje deer, made out on the sea of grass by a silversmith. She lay down on the same couch as her brother. 'Kallista says we're to have tuna, as it is our last night.'

Satyrus looked like a prince himself, in a wool chiton of white with red-orange flames rising from the hem and falling from the shoulder in a repeat pattern that baffled the eye, his garment pinned with gold at each shoulder.

'You found it on your bed?' he asked his sister.

'No, Kallista brought it to me when I finished my bath.' Melitta was unused to reclining, and she reached under her hip to smooth her dress.

Kinon grinned. 'I wanted both of you to have something beautiful to wear. Dionysius has agreed to receive you tomorrow, in public. After that, you will be safe. Indeed, I would hesitate to leave with the caravan – you will be safer here.'

'Best not spill any food on the clothes, then,' Melitta said softly.

Philokles didn't look happy. 'Much as we enjoy your hospitality,' he began, but Kinon interrupted him.

'Leon, our master, has been all the way west to the Pillars of Herakles. His business there is secret – even his trip is itself a secret. But I have had news today that he is safely returned to Syracusa, and will visit Alexandria for the summer before coming here. He will be *here* in late autumn. I have sent letters to him. I think that you must wait here. In addition, I have started the process of arranging for Satyrus to speak to the assembly in Athens. I spoke to Theogenes. He sometimes represents Athenian interests here. He suggested that you live in his house as an Athenian citizen.' Kinon took a sip of wine. 'I do not trust him that far. He has Stratokles there.'

'Who is this Stratokles?' Theron asked.

'A politician from Athens,' Kinon said. 'Just arrived two days back. On a trireme from Pantecapaeum,' he said, and paused to let the import of that statement filter through.

'He now claims to be the representative of Athens here in Heraklea. He claims vast wealth, family connections and political power.' Kinon shrugged. 'I'm not sure – but he does appear the representative of Athens. He's busy buying every cargo of grain we have to sell, and that gains him friends. I've done business with him myself. He is an extreme democrat – the sort of man who wants to give every citizen equal power. He and Leon are sometimes rivals. And he has the name of a killer. Where he goes, enemies of Athens die.'

'We'll avoid him then,' Philokles said with a smile.

'Oh no,' Kinon said. 'I don't trust him, but he has the ear of the tyrant – Demetrios of Phaleron, the tyrant of Athens, that is. And Demetrios was a friend of Phocion's, and of Kineas, your father. We need him. He can get you a passage to Athens and safety.'

'Except that he arrived here on a trireme from Pantecapaeum,' Satyrus put in, and Philokles nodded. 'Ares, what a rat's nest. I think we should stay away from this Stratokles. See what we can learn about him. In the meantime, what of Macedon, Kinon?' Philokles asked. 'Tell me where you are with respect to Polyperchon?'

Kinon held out his cup for more wine. The heavy scent of tuna in syphillium wafted in from the kitchens. Bowls of white cabbage in honey vinegar were put on the side tables that were positioned next to every diner. 'Ahh. The crux of the matter.' Kinon drank some wine. 'It is not Polyperchon, with whom we had good relations. I think you are behind on your news, my friend. Polyperchon is deposed as regent of Macedon, and Antipater's son Cassander has the reins in his hand – but behind him is that madwoman Olympias, Alexander's insane mother.'

'That is news,' Philokles said. 'You said something of it just before we went to bed. But what of Heraklea? What side is she on?'

Kinon shook his head. 'No one is on our side. Perdikkas – remember him? The first commander when Alexander died? – assigned us to the satrapy of Phrygia and refused to accept our status as a free city despite all our years. And he received all our discontents and exiles, and threatened, through his lieutenant, Eumenes the Cardian, to lay siege to the city. Then he died in Aegypt – murdered. Now Antigonus has his army and he faces off against the Cardian. Confused yet?'

'But …' Philokles said, 'you and Leon sell weapons to the Cardian!'

'No,' Kinon said. He looked over his shoulder, where Kallista was motioning for the slaves to bring in the tuna. She was more beautiful than ever, in a cross-gartered chiton of dark, crisp blue. 'No,' he said, clearly having lost the thread of what

107

he was saying. He looked away. 'No,' he said for the third time. 'We sell weapons to your Diodorus, who is a great captain and a good customer. He serves Eumenes the Cardian – for money, and with the permission and even the support of Ptolemy of Aegypt. We would prefer for Antigonus to defeat the Cardian. But we'd really prefer it if they went on fighting each other in Phrygia and left us alone.'

Satyrus felt as if his head was spinning. 'I don't understand,' he said.

Kinon tested a finger bowl of tuna for his guests and nodded vigorously. 'Superb. Tell the cook she's a genius.' He looked back at Satyrus. 'No one can understand all of it, young prince. But Heron – at Pantecapaeum – is part of this game. The big players want all the small players lined up or out of the game. Your city of Tanais threatened the kingdom of the Bosporus, and your mother was the obvious queen of all the Assagatje. That makes you children the heirs of two small empires – in two bodies, you unite the whole north of the Euxine. That means gold, grain, Sakje warriors and Greeks.' He watched for a moment as his slaves carried the tuna around the garden, showing off its size and quality, before carving steaks from it and serving them on trays.

Kinon watched it all with pride – pride in his team and pride in his table. 'The Macedonians aren't united. Antipater's death was like the end of the world for them. Antigonus is not Antipater, nor yet is Cassander – or Olympias – in charge. The Athenians are still powerful, and they will back anyone who gets the garrison out of their city – at the moment, they favour Cassander.' He shrugged. 'I think that Stratokles is working for Cassander. And Cassander needs grain from the Euxine to woo Athens. Am I making sense to you?'

Theron looked around in confusion. 'I heard all this every day in Corinth and still it made no sense to me.'

'Attica and Athens eat three times as much grain as they produce,' Kinon said. 'Men like me grow rich collecting the grain from the Euxine and selling it to Athens. Cassander needs that grain to flow to make Athens happy. He can accomplish this by supporting Eumeles of Pantecapaeum as sole king of the Bosporus. Hence, you children are in his way and need to be eliminated.'

Philokles nodded. 'I'd come to the same conclusion myself.'

Kinon continued, 'Our Leon is heavily invested in Aegypt and the new city there at Alexandria, so we are, willy-nilly, allies of Ptolemy. That sets us against Cassander, and against Antigonus sometimes and Eumenes the Cardian at other times. Cassander is power-mad, Antigonus is an excellent general and a useless ruler, Eumenes would be a great man if he weren't so addicted to proving he's a better man than any Macedonian. He really is the best general and the best man of the lot, but is a Greek and not a Macedonian – you can imagine what that means.'

Philokles gave a grim smile. 'I know,' he said.

'And he married one of Alexander's mistresses – you know that? Banugul? She had a son by Alexander, although not many people know it. A handsome boy named Herakles.'

Melitta's eyes happened to be on Kallista. She saw the slave girl's attention fix. She was listening attentively, and her eyes stole off to cross with someone else, someone standing behind Melitta. She rolled back, casually tossing her arm over her brother, and saw Tenedos, the steward, standing by a sideboard with a ewer of wine. He didn't seem aware of the conversation, and Melitta, watching, saw so many slaves come and go that she couldn't be sure.

Perhaps slaves listened all the time.

'I know Banugul,' Philokles said.

Kinon grinned. 'So you said last night! I gather there's a lot to know. Leon was fulsome in her praises. He continues to be her friend, and loans her money, and keeps track of her son.'

Even as Melitta watched, Philokles took a gulp of wine and stared off into space, lost in reminiscence. Next to her, her brother cleared his throat.

'I think that I understand it, Master Kinon. So Cassander must be allied with Heron,' he said. He was handed a gold cup by one of the slaves, and he took an appreciative sip. 'I can see how the sides will shape up – even how this will affect the Euxine.'

109

Kinon looked at the boy with respect. 'Yes, young prince. That is exactly correct. I've only had a few days to put this together, but it appears to me that Heron has offered to put the whole north of the Euxine at Cassander's disposal in exchange for a free hand.'

Melitta spoke quietly. 'Any news of our mother?' she asked.

'I fear not.' Kinon shook his head.

'Let us do honour to the meal, and banish sad thoughts,' Philokles said.

Melitta leaned over so that her chin was on Satyrus's shoulder. 'They think she's dead,' she said.

'Yes,' Satyrus whispered. The food swam before his eyes.

Melitta put her arm around him. 'It's better if she's dead, rather than a slave or worse,' she said. 'We are her children, and the children of Kineas. Make your face a mask of bronze, and start to think of our revenge.' But even as she spoke the words, her voice broke.

Satyrus sobbed first, but in a moment they were crying – not bold princes of the Euxine, but two children whose mother was probably dead. They lay together, weeping, and the other diners avoided looking at them.

Their sobs lasted through much of the tuna, and then they dried their eyes and ate. Satyrus began to build himself a mask of bronze in his mind. Philokles' new helmet had a high peak and long cheekpieces that covered his face in the front, imitating a moustache and beard and a Thracian hat. Satyrus chewed the excellent tuna and some rich salmon sauce on oysters and good, thick barley bread and thought of the armoured mask, and how it would cover his face, hide his fear. *If I cannot be brave,* he thought, *I will pretend to be brave. That is my duty.* He looked at his sister, who was obviously enjoying her food, pouring quantities of honey vinegar over the fish in a way the cook had never intended, to suit her sweet tooth, and he wondered why the gods had given *her* so much courage.

He drank several cups of wine, on purpose. Then, when the men were preparing to do some serious drinking, Satyrus got off his couch holding a krater. He walked to the middle of the garden, and the others fell silent. He was nervous – he was taking a chance, although he couldn't see just how.

'Kinon, this may be our last night as guests. Tonight I spill a libation to Zeus, master of all, who loves a man who has guests. And I offer libation to Athena, my patroness, and Herakles, my ancestor, and all the gods.' Satyrus felt just a trace of nerves, like elation. The wine covered the rest.

'Hear him,' Theron said.

'Well said,' Philokles agreed.

'And before all the gods, I offer this oath. That neither age nor weakness nor infirmity, nor the number of my enemies, nor any other power of the earth, the heavens or the underworld, will keep me – keep us, the twins – from our revenge on anyone who ordered,' his mask slipped and his voice broke, 'ordered our mother's death. They will die. We will rule the Bosporus. They will rue the day they chose to start this war.'

Philokles watched him with sad eyes. 'Alas, boy, such an oath, once sworn, carries power. Even now, the Furies listen, and they move the strands of fate. What joy did you just forfeit? What doom have you created?'

Melitta rose and went to stand by her brother. 'I stand beside my brother in this oath. We care nothing for the consequences, dear tutor. We will have revenge. Eumeles who was Heron will die. Upazan will die. Cassander of Macedon will die. Every hand against us – to the end of the game—'

'Stop!' Theron begged. 'By the gods, will you children stop before the gods punish you first?'

Melitta appeared to be filled with fire. Her face caught the last of the sun, the deer on her arms twinkled like stars and her dress was an unearthly white. 'We will stop for nothing,' she said. Her words sounded oracular. A gust of wind swept through the garden, moving the roses and making the torches flare into great gouts of flame.

Kallista clapped her hands. 'The gods hear you, Melitta!' she said, and then looked embarrassed at her own temerity.

Philokles glanced at Theron on the next couch. 'You sure you want to stay with these children?' he asked. There was no irony to his question.

Theron sighed. 'I feel the weight of doom,' he said. 'Until this moment, I was the son of a fisherman.'

'Now you are the ally of the twins,' Philokles said.

Kinon shook his head. 'Swearing revenge is all very well for my rose garden,' he said. 'But keep that to yourself in front of Dionysius. He plays this game. He plays it well. He out-manoeuvred Alexander and he has kept us free of Perdikkas and now Cassander. Don't make him send you away – because he will not harbour you if you endanger his policy.'

'What is he like?' Philokles asked.

'He's the fattest man you'll ever meet,' Kinon said. 'And perhaps the most brilliant and ruthless. Some say he is the soul of Dionysius of Syracusa come again. He's his brother's heir and no mistake. And he is not afraid of anything.'

Theron drank his wine down. 'For all that, he's a tyrant,' he said. 'I'm a man of Corinth. Timoleon overthrew that Dionysius of Syracusa.'

Kinon looked around. 'We do not say such things in Heraklea.'

Theron shrugged. '*You* may not say such things,' he said. 'I am a man of Corinth, the city of tyrant-slayers.'

Philokles glared at the athlete. 'Perhaps we should call it the city of poor guests, mmm? Think again, Theron. This man has given us gifts we cannot repay, and how do we return them? With rudeness?'

Instead of becoming angry, Theron winced. 'My apologies, host. Philokles is correct.'

They spoke more about politics, and Satyrus watched Kallista as she sat by her master.

'We should go to bed, if we have to be princes for the tyrant in the morning,' Melitta said.

Satyrus nodded and yawned, eager to be an adult and without the strength to be one. 'Bed,' he said. Kallista smiled at him, and he smiled back. He would never see her again – it all seemed so unfair. But he rose and said his good-nights, and thanked Kinon with his sister for his spotless hospitality, which made the man smile.

He stumbled on the smooth marble of the colonnade, and

he didn't even undo the brooches on his chiton, but merely peeled it over his head and handed it to yet another slave and slipped on to his sleeping couch. The spring air had a touch of chill and he pulled his Thracian cloak – carefully cleaned by the staff – over himself, and he was asleep.

7

Satyrus woke instantly to a sound in his room. The room was dark, with the doorway illuminated by the light coming from the courtyard and filtering down the colonnade. Something moved across the doorway and Satyrus was alert, his heart beating hard.

'It's just me,' Kallista said from the middle of the room.

Satyrus's heart didn't beat any the slower, although for different reasons.

She slid on to his couch, found the Thracian cloak and wriggled under it, and her breasts brushed against his chest. She giggled, put a hand between his legs and put her mouth unerringly over his.

He was caught between fear, excitement and an odd anger – this was *not* the way he wanted Kallista. If he wanted her at all. And yet, he did – as his erection testified.

She put a hand on his chest and pinched one of his nipples *hard*, the way his nurse had done when she was angry, but while the pressure was the same, the result was different. She took one of his hands and placed it on her breast – *ahhh* – a smoothness and softness that was almost unbelievable, a sort of Olympian perfection. His cock leaped to attention under her smooth hand. She laughed.

In the courtyard, a man screamed '*Alarm!*' and there was a crash, like a log hitting a wall. The whole building shook.

'Aaaagghh!' the same voice screamed. Satyrus knew that scream – a man with death in his guts. His erection vanished and his mind moved fast and he was off the couch in the dark, hand sweeping the wall until he found his sword hanging on its baldric from a peg. He put the belt over his head and grabbed the cloak off the bed.

'What in Hades are you doing?' Kallista said.

'Aaaagh—' The next scream was cut off suddenly, and then there was another crash and a cheer – a terrible sound, and then running feet. Satyrus threw the cloak over his arm and went to the doorway, brushing the curtain aside.

There was a man in the colonnade with a weapon. He wore a helmet that glinted in the distant light of the garden, and he was less than an arm-length away, a big shadow against the stygian dark of the corridor.

'Get some light in here!' the man shouted, his voice filling the corridor. 'Follow me!'

Satyrus wanted to hesitate, but before the fear could catch him he cut low, just as Philokles had shown him again and again, his left hand stretched forward with the wrapped cloak to block a counter-blow. And the man caught his movement and his weapon came down into the wool cloak, numbing his arm, but his sword went behind the man's greave and as Satyrus recovered he pressed the cut, ripping the tendon at the back of the leg just as he'd been taught.

The man went down in a tangle of bronze and limbs and Satyrus stepped clear just as the man voiced his pain. 'Aiyyee! Ares! Gods, I'm cut! Aiyyyeee! Ah ah ah!'

They're wearing armour, Satyrus thought, and then the fear caught him and he stood paralysed. He tried to open his mouth, tried to call.

'Satyrus!' his sister shouted. 'Wake up! We're under attack!'

His limbs loosed and he almost fell and then he moved clumsily, stumbling like a drunkard. 'I'm here!' he called.

'There they are!' a man's voice shouted, and there were torches in the colonnade, light flickering off the thrashing man on the floor. Satyrus got past him, abandoning Kallista, and he was beside his sister.

'Run,' he said.

'Where?' she asked him. Their portion of the colonnade led to a blank wall at the corner of the property. In light, there was a mural of more pillars painted there to give the suggestion of space.

'Ares,' he cursed. 'Athena aid us!'

The men with torches came to their comrade and there was commotion and cursing. 'Hamstrung!' one voice said. 'I'll kill the bastard! Kleon will never walk again!'

'Just kill everwud you fide,' another voice said. He ripped open the curtain to the room where Satyrus had slept.

Satyrus was frozen with indecision – the right thing to do was to attack them, make a futile effort to save Kallista. He would die. But it was the virtuous thing.

He didn't want to die. He was an ungracious animal.

There was a crash in the dark and half the light went out. Satyrus crouched and pushed his sister behind him.

In the fitful torchlight, Satyrus watched Theron and Philokles, side by side, with shields on their shoulders, rip into the armoured men in the doorway. The men turned quickly – too late for the torch-bearer, who went down like a sacrifice and didn't even moan. His torch lit the scene from the ground, sputtering and burning fitfully.

The attackers fought back silently. They had swords and they knew how to use them. Philokles gave a cry and stepped back, and one of the adversaries bellowed, stepped forward and died on Philokles' sword, tricked in the dark into believing he'd hit his opponent.

Satyrus got his limbs in motion and came up behind them. Again he went low, cutting at the tendons of Theron's opponent. The man screamed like a horse and went back, straight into the boy, and Theron's back cut with his kopis took off the top of the man's head and he collapsed on Satyrus, pumping gore, so that Satyrus was trapped against the wall.

'Shit,' the last man fighting said, and died.

'There must be more of them,' Philokles panted. 'Boy? Are you all right?'

Philokles was looking into his sleeping chamber. Satyrus was trying not to puke at the warm spongy stuff all over his face. 'I'm right here,' he managed in a squeak.

Theron caught up the torch and thrust it in his face. 'I thought that man went down too fast,' he said. 'Well cut, little hoplite. Now get up. Where's your sister?'

'Watching your backs,' she said. 'There's more of them, in the other wing, and more yet in the slave quarters. I can hear them.'

The screams from the slave quarters were harrowing – several people, cries from nightmare. The other wing had the sound of rushing feet.

Theron and Philokles had time to turn around before they were hit by the rush.

'They're armed!' someone shouted, and Theron plucked up the torch and threw it over their attackers and there was no light at all, or almost none – just a flicker of light from the floor, but the attackers were backlit and Theron and Philokles fought from the darkness, nearly invisible.

Satyrus was on the floor. He could see their feet by the single flickering torch. He reached out and flicked his wrist and the blow was light, but the weight of the blade alone sliced the man's sandal and his foot, and he yelped and went down. Then another man took his place.

'Kill theb!' said a voice behind the fight. 'Gods! Do a hab to do this myself?'

'Give us some help then, Stratokles!' came a deeper voice. 'I don't see you in the front rank!'

Theron stumbled and went down on one knee. He grunted, his legs straddling Satyrus. Satyrus swung his blade as hard as he could at Theron's opponent, who took a thrust right through the arch of his foot. He gave a cry, swore and the rim of his shield came down on Satyrus's face, breaking his nose and sending him back a foot in a mist of his own blood and the metallic agony of a face wound.

Cut back cut back. Satyrus knew from wrestling and pankration that the moments after taking a wound were the most dangerous and his sword slashed empty air in front of him as he writhed blind in pain on the ground and his blood fountained down his chest. Then it caught something – a shield – and his arm rang and he skinned his knuckles, the pain almost lost in the pain from his nose.

Theron powered to his feet under his shield and Satyrus's opponent went flying back. Then Theron grunted and went down when a spear shaft hit his unprotected head, and Philokles was holding the corridor alone.

Satyrus wiped at his face and there was another bloom of pain as he tried to stand, using the wall behind him to get himself up, but his nose *hurt* and his legs didn't want to work.

He got up anyway.

Philokles was everywhere in a burst of god-sent prowess, and his sword was at their throats and at their knees and he forced them all back off the bodies.

'Get that archer in here!' called the voice that gave most of the orders – a voice that sounded as if it had the worst head cold of all time.

'Like fighting fucking Ares!' the gruff voice said.

'Charge him! Finish him!' the man in charge said.

'Charge him yourself, you ball-less fucking Athenian!' a gruff voice called out. 'You, warrior. We offer you life. Take it and go free.'

'Come here and die,' Philokles said. 'I'm killing your wounded.' From the sounds, he was doing just that. 'Who's the little fuck in the fancy helmet? Anyone you liked?'

'Fuck you! Leave him—'

'Too late. Dead now. This big mule—'

'Fuck YOU!' the Athenian voice screamed. There was a rush of feet, and then an impact like stone on stone. There were two men on Philokles.

This was the longest exchange so far. Philokles and the two enemies hammered at each other for five blows – ten blows, and Satyrus stabbed repeatedly at the other men's feet, but they were fast and had foot-guards on their sandals. Finally, gruff-voice swore and ducked back – but the smaller man forced Philokles back in a flurry of blows. The Spartan was tiring.

Then the smaller man put his shield over one of the bodies, hoisted the man, took a blow from Philokles on his own blade and backed up a step. Philokles hammered his shield. Satyrus lunged at his lower leg and was defeated by a heavy bronze greave. The man backed away again. 'Archer!' he roared.

'Anyone else?' Philokles said. 'I'll come and get you, then.'

'Archer!' the Athenian screamed again.

'Fuck this!' the gruff voice said, and there was the sound of feet moving away.

'Stand your ground!' the commander ordered. 'You – shoot him!'

'Drop,' said Melitta's voice.

Satyrus didn't have far to drop, so he obeyed.

He heard the buzz of an arrow like a drone flying fast, and it hit armour like a hammer on a gourd.

There was a thin scream, and from his new vantage point back on the floor, Satyrus could see a pair of feet in expensive sandals, stumbling. Then, by the light of the courtyard torches, he caught sight of the man – a livid scar across his face. He was lifting another big man over his shoulder, weaving and then gone into the garden.

'Nice shot, Melitta,' Philokles said. The words were sane enough, but the voice the dead timbre of a madman – but a sober madman. Fighting had burned the wine out of Philokles. 'In the dark, too.'

Satyrus had a hand on Theron. 'Theron's alive,' he said. Then, 'That was the same man we saw on the plains south of the Tanais. Scar-face.'

'Stand your ground,' Philokles said. 'We're not done yet.' He sank to one knee. 'Scar-face tagged me in the shin. Good swordsman.' He coughed and stood back up.

Melitta took her brother's hand and helped him to his feet. She had her bow in her hand.

'There's fighting by the gate,' Philokles explained. 'More fighting.'

They could hear it, and the screams of the wounded. Satyrus took a deep breath and made himself rewrap the Thracian cloak around his arm. Then he stepped forward until he was abreast of Philokles.

'Here I am,' he said. Although all his Ms sounded like Bs. Like scar-face.

'Good boy,' Philokles said. 'If they come again, just keep them from wrapping my shield for as long as you can.'

Satyrus resisted the temptation to wipe his nose. Blood was still pouring down his chest.

Melitta came up close behind them. 'I have eight arrows,' she said. 'That's all I had in my room.'

'I'm sorry I brought you here,' Philokles said. The fighting at the gate was petering out. 'Shall I – shall I kill you?'

Satyrus felt his knees tremble again and cursed himself. 'No!' he said. 'I'll die fighting.'

There. For once, he'd said what he wanted to say.

Melitta took a deep breath. 'I think—' she began.

'Hold! Put down your weapons!' came a deep voice.

Satyrus grasped his little sword tighter.

'I have forty swords and as many archers,' the voice said. 'Whoever you are, I order you to put down your weapons.'

'Zeus Soter, my lord, the fuckers have killed everyone in the place,' said a thin, rasping voice, and suddenly there were lines of torches coming in under the colonnade. Twenty feet away, a big black man in head-to-foot bronze armour filled the colonnade, as big as Philokles. He was like a man made of bronze. He looked around quickly and caught site of the three armed people in the dead end. 'You!' he shouted. A line of armed men filled the colonnade in front of him with drilled rapidity.

'Who are you?' Philokles' voice boomed.

'I am Nestor of Heraklea, the commander of the guard. Put down your weapons or die.'

'I am Philokles of Sparta, and these are the children of Kineas and Srayanka of Tanais,' he said.

'Let me see! Let me through there,' the captain said. He stepped out of the line and peered at them. 'Ares, Spartan! You must be quite the spearman. So they didn't get past you, eh?' He stepped forward. 'Ground your weapons, all of you. My orders are to take you to the tyrant if you live.'

Philokles swept out an arm and pushed both of the twins behind him.

Melitta sobbed. 'Kill me,' she said. 'I'm too scared to do it myself. *I won't be a slave!*'

Nestor heard her. 'No, lady! Stop!' He held up his hand, and the line of his soldiers paused. 'We did not do this. A rumour came to us that you were to be attacked tonight. We came in time. I have two dead men in the yard. You may live, lady – I give my word, I bring you no harm but my master's orders.'

Satyrus stood, naked, covered in blood, and afraid. He looked at Philokles, and Philokles shook his head.

'I cannot make this choice,' he said. 'I can kill men, and

discuss philosophy, but I cannot choose. It may be as he says. It may be that you will leave this place to be a slave.'

Satyrus reached back and grabbed his sister's blood-slick shoulder. 'There's no logic in it, Lita. The tyrant doesn't need us dead.'

'You wager my life in a brothel?' she asked. 'And your own?'

A dying man gave a long moan.

'We retain our arms,' Satyrus called out, his thin voice cracking as he called. 'None of you comes within a sword cut of us.'

Nestor shrugged. 'If that's what it has to be, my lord.'

Satyrus's eyes met Melitta's.

His eyes said, *I want to live.*

So did hers. 'Not if the price is too high,' she said out loud.

'I think we can do this,' he whispered. 'If not – I'll try to kill us.'

Satyrus stepped past Philokles, from the dark into the torchlight. There were bodies everywhere, and the torchlight wasn't kind. It was worse than the end of *Orestes*. 'I am Satyrus of Tanais,' he said. He bent and wiped his blade on the cloth of a dead man.

Nestor bowed. 'My lord. Will you – Ares, you're a child. Someone get a cloth!'

The worst of it was that everyone else was dead. Zosimos lay by the gate, hacked down with a heavy blade so that his head was askew from his trunk. Kinon had died in his bed, but he'd been pinned in his sheets and then hacked to pieces. Satyrus didn't see the steward's body, but he saw the blood trickling down the steps of the slave quarters like water from a spring, and he finally lost it, spewing tuna steak and barley bread into the blood while some foreign soldier held his head.

If the tyrant's guard wanted to enslave him, he wasn't doing much to resist.

'There, laddy,' the soldier said. 'Gives me the fucking willies. Poor boy.' He was patted on the head.

'Let go of my brother or I'll cut your hand off,' Melitta said. She was standing alone in a circle of soldiers, naked and covered in blood, with her akinakes in her hand. Philokles was sitting on a step, drinking wine from a skin.

'Hermes, girl! I'm helping him!' The soldier stepped back. 'Fucking Medea come to life.'

'Get her a dress,' Nestor said.

'I found another live one,' a third soldier said. He produced Kallista. She was shrieking with sobs, uncontrolled, unacted, her fists pummelling at the man who held her. She was not beautiful. She looked like the embodiment of fury.

Nestor addressed himself to Satyrus. 'May I get you some – never mind. Listen, boy. We're walking away from this. I'm taking you to the citadel. Can you hear me?'

Satyrus straightened his back. 'Something I have to do first,' he said. He walked over to the crowd of corpses where the tyrant's guard had stormed the gate. 'A torch, please.'

One of the guardsmen gave him a torch. He held it high, looking for a man with a scarred face. He didn't find one.

'Some of them got away,' Satyrus said.

Nestor shrugged. 'Not unless they can fly,' he said.

'Have you searched the whole house?' Satyrus asked.

Nestor shrugged. 'My orders are to bring you along. We'll search tomorrow.'

Satyrus was too tired to argue. 'Lead on,' he said. He held out a hand to Philokles, who got unsteadily to his feet.

They walked through the courtyard paved in corpses, out of the gate, where a thin trickle of liquid splashed out into the street's gutter and shone red in torchlight.

'Do you need to be carried?' Nestor asked Satyrus.

'No, I can walk,' he heard himself say, as if from a distance. 'Be careful of my sister.'

'No man would touch your sister,' Nestor said.

Somehow, they walked the stade along the twisting city streets, passing twice through the walls until they came to the citadel gate. Nestor gave the password and sentries grounded their spears, the butt-spikes clashing on paving stones, and then they were inside. There were paintings on the walls, and the floors were heated, and slaves appeared with bowls of water as if from the air.

And then they were in a chamber as big as a rich man's house. On the dais sat the fattest man he'd ever seen, a man as broad as he was tall. He had a shock of blond hair that stood straight up, and his eyes burned with intelligence under heavy brows.

'Welcome,' he said.

The twins were ushered to the space in front of him, and Kallista was brought to stand with them. She was utterly silent, her beauty extinguished in grief. Melitta was naked except for a soldier's cloak, and her feet glistened with blood. Satyrus was conscious of his nudity. The Thracian cloak was still around his shoulders and over his left hand. At some point he had sheathed his blade, but his hand rested on the hilt. His right ankle ached. More than ached. His face throbbed, and his nose led the chorus of pain.

Philokles loomed behind him, still carrying an aspis and a sword.

The tyrant waved at a slave. 'Get my doctor,' he said. To Philokles he said, 'You are the first armed men to enter my presence in a generation.'

Philokles seemed to be speaking from very far away. 'I think we can accept the tyrant's good intentions, Satyrus. Satyrus?'

Satyrus's eyes were resting on the face of another child, or perhaps a young woman, whose head peeked out from behind a curtain just beyond the dais. Her face was like that of a Nereid, with an upturned nose and freckles and a cloud of dark curls. Their eyes met. Having faced death and survived, Satyrus had the courage to smile at the Nereid. She smiled back.

'Satyrus?' Philokles sounded gravely concerned.

'Get my doctor!' the tyrant said.

Standing there with a smile on his face, Satyrus became conscious that he was wounded. His ankle hurt, and there was blood coming off his shin, a moist sweat on the arch of his foot. When he looked down, it came in little spurts that sparkled in the lamp light. He watched it for a moment, and then he was gone.

Melitta thought that the worst part of the whole night was waiting to see if her brother would die. It was clear from the attentions of the guards and the slaves that the tyrant had no ill intentions, and so his wound became her whole focus. She refused sleep, drank some watered wine and watched Sophokles, the Athenian surgeon, bandage his foot after giving him something that slowed, but did not stop, the bleeding.

Melitta didn't like the doctor. And, having heard what she had heard in the fight, she distrusted all Athenians.

When he was done wrapping the bandage, the man got to his feet. He rubbed the bridge of his nose.

'Will he—?' she asked.

'It is with the fates and the gods,' he said. He turned to a slave – there were four of them in the alcoves at the end of the room. The tyrant seemed to have a great many. 'Get me wine, and poppy juice,' he said. To Melitta, he said, 'You should sleep. I will give you poppy, and you will have rich dreams.'

She stepped back from him. 'I wouldn't accept it,' she said. 'I'll stay here until he awakes.'

'He has lost a great deal of blood, girl. He won't awake for a while – indeed, he'll sleep for hours. Or – he'll die.' The Athenian doctor shook his head.

'I can wait,' she said.

He put on a voice he must save for women and idiots. 'Listen, honey,' he said, putting an arm on her shoulder. 'You can't affect the outcome. You need to sleep. A little girl like you—'

She rolled out from under his hand and backed against her brother's couch. 'I've lost my mother and my kingdom and people are trying to kill me and my brother and I think I'll just stay awake beside him,' she said.

'Don't make me—' he began.

She pulled her knife out of its sheath under her arm. She adopted the stance that Philokles and Theron had been teaching her – left arm out, knife hand close to the body and low.

'You're deranged,' he said.

She nodded. 'Perhaps,' she said.

The doctor affected patience. 'Don't make me wake your guardian, girl. He'll be quite angry.'

Melitta met his eyes steadily. 'Theron? Call him.' She was too tired to be afraid. 'Better yet, why don't you go and see to Philokles?'

'Theron? The man with the blow to the head? He'll be fine.' The doctor was impatient. 'Girl, you are interfering with my work.'

She stood aside, the knife held firmly. 'Be my guest,' she said. 'I'll just watch.'

There was a chuckle from the doorway, and Nestor, the guard captain, came in. His armour was off, and he was just another big man, now wearing a handsome chiton of Tyrian purple wool. 'Let her alone, Athenian,' he said. 'She's a titan.'

The doctor sighed. 'She needs to be in bed.'

Nestor chuckled again. 'She nearly gutted one of my men. Girl, you'll get a husband faster if you wave that about less.'

'I am *not* waving it about. This is the low guard, and my hands are steady!' She wished she hadn't sounded quite so anxious.

Nestor stepped fully into the room and his grin flashed in the lamplight. 'Sheathe the weapon, my lady. As a favour. The doctor means no harm and neither do I.'

Melitta bowed. 'My pardon,' she said. She really was tired.

'A chair,' he said to the slaves.

'Where is Kallista?' Melitta asked.

'The other girl? In the slave quarters. Is she yours? I'm sorry – I took for granted she was Kinon's. Shall I ask her to attend you?' Nestor made a motion and another slave ran from the room.

'Where is Philokles?' she asked.

'In the next room, with the other man,' Nestor said.

Melitta nodded. 'When Kallista comes, I will go to bed,' she said.

Her brother lay unmoving, as pale as the Aegyptian linen on which he lay. His lower right leg was wrapped in bandages that were slowly becoming the colour of Nestor's chiton.

'He's not going to die,' she said.

Nestor met her eye. 'Good. I honoured his courage.' He was very serious.

'He doesn't think he has any courage,' Melitta said.

Nestor gave a small smile. 'Many men who appear brave suffer from the same failing,' he said. 'Sometimes they die trying to prove themselves brave when no one has ever questioned their courage,' he added.

'That's my brother,' she said proudly.

Nestor shook his head. 'Make sure you save him then,' he said to the doctor, as if he could just order such a thing.

When Kallista came, she looked more like Medusa than Helen of Troy, her make-up smeared, her eyes wild and her hair unkempt. She stepped straight into Melitta's arms. 'They killed everyone!' she said. She burst into tears.

Melitta held her while she sobbed, and then started to walk her to the door. 'Take me to my room,' she said.

'I'll take you to the women's wing,' Nestor said.

'I want to be right here,' Melitta said.

Nestor nodded. 'Very well,' he said with a yawn. With two slaves, he took her past where Philokles lay unsleeping on a couch, past Theron's snores and into a darkened room. The slaves moved about, filling the pitchers with water and wine, lighting lamps, turning down the linens on her sleeping couch.

'Shall I make up a pallet on the floor?' one of the palace slaves asked.

'If you would be so kind,' she replied. Kallista kept right on crying.

Nestor bowed. 'If my lady will permit, I, for one, intend to get a few dreams through the gate of horn before the sun rises.'

Melitta returned his bow. 'Thanks for your courtesy, sir.' She paused. 'How long has the Athenian been a doctor here?'

Nestor thought a moment. 'Not long,' he said. 'Why?'

Melitta bit back her answer, born of fatigue and unreason, she was sure. 'No matter,' she said. 'Thank you for all your help, Nestor. May the gods be with you.'

He smiled and patted her head, which she normally hated. This time, it was somewhat reassuring.

When he was gone, she waved her hands at the slaves. 'Go!' she said.

They both looked at her. Kallista continued to sob.

'Now,' she said. 'Go and attend the doctor!'

Both slaves left silently. She steered the other girl to the bed.

'It's my fault!' Kallista said through her sobs.

Melitta had suspected something like this. 'Why were you in my brother's room? At Kinon's?' she asked, and her voice was sharper than she meant.

'Tenedos told me to fuck him,' the beautiful girl sobbed. 'I was supposed to take a lamp and leave it burning outside the room!' she wailed. 'We would all be free! That's what he said!' She looked around wildly. 'And now they're all *dead*.'

Melitta got up from the couch and went to the table, where, as she expected, the doctor's poppy juice was freshly prepared by the ewer of wine. She mixed the two, filled a cup and handed it to Kallista.

'Listen, girl,' she said. 'Do you want to live?'

Kallista nodded. She sobbed and choked again.

'You are my slave. Listen! You came here with me. There's no one to say otherwise. Right?' Melitta called upon her dwindling reserves. 'We'll talk tomorrow. Drink this.'

Obediently, the older girl took the cup and drank.

'Good,' Melitta said. 'You can start by tasting my food and wine.'

The slave girl was asleep in minutes.

Melitta watched the darkness and blood behind her eyes until the sun rose.

At some point she must have slept, because she woke to the bright light of a noon sun pounding through the courtyard outside and into her room. For a long moment, she didn't know where she was. Her back hurt like fire, and she was in a chair.

Kallista was snoring in her bed, a breast bare in the reflected light, her usual beauty restored by sleep. Melitta got up and found that every muscle in her body hurt. She limped across the room and pulled a cloak over the slave girl. Then she stood in the middle of the room, rubbing her hips and buttocks.

She stretched, and remembered that her brother was dying – might already be dead. She was out of the door of her room, flying along the row of pillars. Philokles' room's door was covered by a curtain of beads that dazzled in the sun, and her brother's was tied back. There was a slave asleep in a chair with a Thracian cloak over his legs.

Satyrus was as pale as unworked clay. Her hand went to her mouth and a sob escaped her. She stepped up beside him, reached out a hand and hesitated.

As long as she didn't *know* that he was dead – the world would not end.

She put a hand on his forehead.

It was cold as ice.

She pulled it back as if it had been burned, and another sob escaped her. *I should kill myself*, she thought. *I'm really not sure that I can deal with this.* The problem was, as she realized immediately, that she didn't want to kill herself, any more than she had wanted to do so in the dark and flame of the fight.

But with her mother and brother both gone . . .

His chest moved.

The sound of his exhalation seemed to echo inside her head for some time, like the west wind in the halls of Olympus.

'Philokles!' she yelled in her joy.

She slept again and woke to softer evening shadows, with Kallista sitting by her bed, fanning her. 'Mistress?' she said, as soon as Melitta's eyes fluttered open.

'Kinon gifted you to me,' Melitta said. Her brain was running at a high speed, like a chariot rolling effortlessly on a smooth road. She could see a great many things, and one of them was that Kallista was in as much danger as the twins themselves. 'That's why you are mine. He gifted you at dinner last night. Understand? And you were in *my* room when the attack started.'

'Yes, mistress,' the other girl said. There were dark smudges under Kallista's eyes, as if she had been punched, and the whites of her eyes lacked their usual clarity, but otherwise she was unaffected.

Melitta rose on one elbow. 'Tenedos told you to go to my brother's room and leave a lamp outside?'

'Yes,' Kallista replied.

'So that his murderers could tell what room he occupied,' Melitta said.

'You must believe me, mistress. I knew nothing of what he intended.' The beautiful girl shuddered.

'You understand, Tenedos may still be alive. He needs you dead. What do you know of this Stratokles?' Melitta asked.

The older girl shook her head. 'He's Athenian. Kinon spoke of him with – contempt.' She shrugged. 'He wasn't one of our friends.'

Melitta nodded. 'Get some more slaves,' she said. 'Make up the room, bring me something to wear and fetch me Nestor.' She took one of the other girl's hands. 'Stand by me, and I'll see you free before the year is out. Fuck with me, and I'll see you dead.'

'I swear—' Kallista began.

'You'll do anything to survive,' Melitta said. She nodded, mostly to herself. 'I must not hold that against you. Let me tell you that I think you know more about this than you are telling. Now go!' She shooed the slave out of her rooms.

Melitta shrugged into a chiton, cursing the foolishness of Greek female garments. Then she ran down the hall and looked at her brother. He had a little more colour in his face, and he was still asleep. She watched his chest rise and fall for a while.

'How soon will I be shouting at you for something stupid you say to hurt my feelings?' she said aloud. 'How long before I slap you?'

'Any time now, I would think,' Philokles said. He was sitting where the slave had been sitting, and she'd missed him. Now she ran and embraced him.

'We got off easy,' he said.

'Not so easily,' she said, still hugging him.

'True enough. Kinon is dead,' he said. 'And Zosimos, whom I liked. And many other men and women. All of the Bosporan marines.'

'Marines?' she asked.

'The armed men who attacked us were mostly the marines

off the trireme.' Philokles sighed. 'Whatever god told me to kill their wounded, I feel like a murderer today. None survived. So we will never know who ordered their attack. It must have been Heron.'

'It was Stratokles, the Athenian. I heard him.' Melitta stepped away from her tutor. 'And Kallista was ordered to leave a lamp burning outside my brother's door when she went to – to make love to him.'

Philokles started. 'Ordered? By whom?'

'Tenedos – the steward.' Melitta went back to watching her brother.

Philokles was silent for several breaths. 'I must tell the tyrant,' he said. 'How do you know that Stratokles was involved? He was the man Kinon was going to use to get us to Athens!'

'I heard him. He talks like a man with a cold, because of the scar across his nose. I heard other men call him by name. And he has my arrow in him,' she said proudly.

'He may be dead in the house,' Philokles said. 'The tyrant's bodyguard were not kind.' He got to his feet, and Melitta could see that he was as stiff as she, or worse. 'Gods, I am old,' he said.

'You are a hero,' she said.

'Just a killer,' he said. 'You were a hero. Your father's daughter.'

Melitta caught his hand. 'Why do you never praise my brother like that?' she asked.

'Men don't need to be praised,' Philokles said. 'He is Kineas's son. Of course he's brave.'

Melitta shook her head. 'He thinks – I don't know. I have only his silences to go on. I think he thinks that he is a coward, and that you think the same.'

Philokles grunted. 'I was raised in a barracks,' he said. 'No one praised me. I survived.'

Melitta shook her head. 'And look how little it affected you,' she said.

Philokles paused for a second at the curtain, as if to retort, but then he thought better of it, and went out.

Kallista came with a flock of palace slaves, and her room

was cleaned and her bed made. Kallista continued a fawning devotion to her new mistress, but Melitta was very careful with the beautiful girl.

Slaves brought food, and Kallista tasted all of it. Slaves turned down her bed, and Kallista offered to share it. 'I like to sleep with someone, mistress,' she said. 'I'd be happy to warm your bed – or more.' She smiled, and the artful winsomeness was slightly offset by the fatigue and the desperation.

Melitta wasn't interested. 'On the floor, please,' she said.

She lay awake until Kallista began to snore softly. Then, right hand clutching her short sword under her blanket, she fell asleep.

Her brother was awake in the morning. His leg was infected, but the doctor seemed unconcerned and let him hobble about on it. He proved his fitness by hobbling into her room just after sunrise. His nose was still red.

'We're alive!' he said. He hugged her, gathering her in his arms where she lay, and she woke up slowly, already happy at the sound of his voice. 'I didn't even know I was wounded, Lita. Oh, I feel so – alive!'

'My muscles still hurt,' she said. 'By Artemis, goddess of all maidens, I've never been so stiff. Your skin has colour!'

'Most of it in my nose!' he laughed. 'The doctor says I'll be pale for days,' he said. 'I'm to eat all the meat I can find. The tyrant is giving us a public dinner tonight. Philokles says that Stratokles has fled the city. I saw him – noseless bastard, as if he was a leper!'

'I think you need to slow down, brother. How's Theron?' she asked, throwing her legs over the side of the bed and wriggling past her brother, whose eyes seemed to have strayed to Kallista's body. 'Did you make love to her?' Melitta asked.

Her brother shrugged. 'We started. Then the attack came.' He shivered.

'She was ordered into your bed, brother. To show the attackers where you slept.' Melitta put her fingers on his cheek. 'Remember what our mother says about slaves. She'll do anything to survive. Anything.'

Satyrus watched her. Then he looked at his sister and smiled his old 'let's go and make some trouble' smile. 'I hear everything you just said,' he admitted. 'And then I look at those feet – that leg.' He grinned. 'I just want her.'

Kallista reached out an arm, gave a snort and rolled over.

Melitta gave her brother a mock slap. 'She's mine now. Hands off.'

'Yours?'

Melitta leaned close. 'I'm telling everyone that Kinon gifted her to me at the dinner,' she whispered. 'It'll keep her alive.'

'I'd forgotten,' Satyrus said, straightening. 'Okay, she's yours. Can I have her when you're done?'

He had a satyr's smile, and Melitta's slap had some venom in it this time. She'd forgotten his broken nose, and he sat down hard. 'Ouch!' he said.

While she cosseted him she thought, *That's how long it took me.*

Satyrus was stiff too, and his ankle hurt like fire, and his nose was two sizes too big, but he was an instant favourite with the guard and he was young enough to bask in their admiration, so he wandered the citadel all day, looking at the armoury, eating in the military barracks where the tyrant quartered his most trusted guards. The guardsmen were all mercenaries, some of whom had been elite soldiers under Alexander: Hypaspists or even Argyraspids with the king of Macedon. All seemed to be named Philip or Amyntas, and all seemed to be fond of boys. He was kissed a little too often, but they said good things too, and made rough jokes. He refought his part of the action, lying on the clean floor of the barracks hall and showing how he had cut at the feet of his attackers, and they roared their appreciation.

'That's good thinking, for a boy,' one old veteran said.

'Get your head out of your arse, Philip!' another with a grey beard said. 'His da beat our sorry arses over the Jaxartes. Remember that? Kineas the Athenian! I knew your da, boy. You've got his head on your shoulders. He was a *strategos*.'

'Was he brave?' Satyrus asked, and then regretted the question.

Philip rubbed his beard. 'Not brave like Alexander,' he said. 'Don't get all soppy on me, Amyntas! Nobody was brave like the king. He was afraid of nothing.'

'He was as stupid as a mule,' Amyntas grumbled. 'That's not courage. That's tom-foolish.'

The two veterans glared at each other. To Satyrus it had the sound of an old argument.

'You remember Cleitus? Not black Cleitus, who the king killed. Remember red Cleitus? In the phalanx?' Another man with the heavy accent of Macedon came in and slung his cloak on a bed. 'He was brave.'

'He was fucking insane!' Philip said. 'I was there when he went over the wall at Tyre!'

'And you remember how thin he was? And how, no matter what he ate, it hurt his guts like fire?'

'Sure,' Amyntas said. 'He said he'd rather die than eat!'

'And remember what happened when Antigonus got him healed? He stopped fighting like he was insane. He covered up like everybody else. Right? 'Cause of how he had a reason to live, right enough.'

'What's your point, you north-country bastard?' Philip asked.

'Huh. Maybe I don't have a point. Maybe I just like the fucking sound of my own voice, eh? Whose little bum-boy is this? He's a little long in the tooth, but I'll be happy to keep him until his hair comes in.' The newcomer pinched Satyrus's cheek.

'Kineas the Athenian's son, as we saved in the fight the other night. Put two men down hisself.' Amyntas walked over. 'Not a bum-boy.'

'Fuck me,' the newcomer said. He gave a military salute. 'Pardon me, boy. No harm meant.'

'None taken,' Satyrus said, stiffly. The barracks was like another world – scary and fun and dark and light.

'Draco,' the newcomer said, holding out his hand.

'Satyrus,' he said.

'Now you've touched the hand that saved Alexander on the wall!' Philip said. 'Hah! You'll go far, boy. Draco saved the king once, in India. Didn't you, darling?'

'I was just the poor sod who was next on the ladder. He farted on me all the way to the top,' Draco agreed.

They all laughed.

Draco came with them later in the day when Satyrus accompanied Philokles to Kinon's house. The bodies were there, laid in neat, orderly rows in the courtyard where they had eaten dinner, and it was all Satyrus could do to keep his gorge from rising. But he walked up and down the rows, and then came back to where Draco stood with Nestor.

'That's all of them?' Satyrus asked.

Nestor nodded. 'In this heat, if we'd missed one, we'd know.'

Satyrus shook his head. 'Tenedos, the steward, is not there. Nor is Stratokles the Athenian, nor the first man I cut – I saw Stratokles dragging a wounded man when your lot rushed the gate.' Talking steadied him. He took a breath, and the stench hit him again, and against his will his gorge rose and he threw up.

Draco stepped adroitly aside. 'Poor lad. You'll get over it, with time.'

Draco gave him water from his canteen, and he rinsed his mouth in the street and then forced himself to confront the courtyard again. The smell was just as strong, and so were the flies. There was brown blood everywhere like a slaughterhouse or a sacrificial altar.

Satyrus had come to see the bodies, but he was also there to claim their goods before the tyrant seized what was left of the estate. Kinon had left no heirs and no will.

'Take whatever you want,' Nestor said. He turned to Draco. 'When young Satyrus has secured his party's goods, I want every one of these bodies on the wagon in the street. Do it yourselves. Then every man who was here when we stormed the place gets one pick from the man's goods. Rest goes to the boss. Clear?'

Draco nodded and winked at Satyrus. 'Sounds good to me, Captain.'

Satyrus's sandals stuck to the floor every step as he approached his quarters, and there were flies everywhere. He breathed carefully as he turned the corner. The semi-dried blood was like a red-brown carpet in the sun, stretching away to the door of his room. He closed his eyes and took a breath, and he could feel the tickle of the copper in the old blood at the back of his throat even with his eyes closed.

Sure enough, there was a lamp outside. But when he bent to check it, he could see that the wick was new-cut. It had never been lit. Had she forgotten?

There were so many layers to the puzzle that it made him feel light-headed.

He could hear Draco laughing with another man around the corner. *How do they get used to this?* he thought.

His room was better – his cloaks were on the floor where he'd thrown them. He rolled them up, collected his bags and managed to get them and his sister's gear and their new clothes and their jewellery packed and on to their horses without spewing again. His right ankle and shin now hurt with every movement, and he kept rubbing his nose like a fool, but he forced himself to walk down the far hall – where he had never gone – under some paintings of men having sex with other men, and into the receiving room. He was looking for something to take – something that would remind him of Kinon.

Draco was standing in front of a Persian wall-hanging. 'What'd you take, boy?' he asked.

'Nothing yet,' Satyrus said sheepishly.

'You'll never make a soldier if you can't loot a house. What you looking for?' the man asked.

'He had a set of gold cups,' Satyrus said. 'He was proud of them. I thought I'd take one for each of us.'

'I stand corrected, little prince. Looting comes naturally to you. Gold cups? How many?' Draco winked.

'Ought to be six,' Satyrus said. 'I'll take five.'

Draco winked. 'Glad to meet you,' he said. 'Let's look.'

The gold cups were in the heavy chest in the pantry. It was sealed. Draco shrugged and smashed the seal, and there was a treasury of heavy plate, beautifully crafted drinking ware and wine equipment.

Draco counted out five gold cups. 'Sure you don't want the rest?' he said.

Satyrus shook his head. 'You keep it,' he said.

Draco waved for another soldier. 'Thanks, my lord.' In seconds, the guardsmen were bundling the silver and gold into their cloaks.

Satyrus took the stack of cups – they nested – in the bosom of his chiton. He found Philokles loading the horses in the stable, and showed them to him.

'One's for you,' Satyrus said. 'One for Lita, one for Theron, and one for Kallista.'

'That's well thought, young man,' Philokles said.

Satyrus put a hand on his arm. 'Tenedos is not in the house,' he said.

Philokles nodded. 'I saw. Nor all the men I put down – just the marines, I'd say. It's a mystery.'

'Or this Stratokles has allies.' Satyrus felt better for saying it. 'We need to get free of this place.'

Philokles shrugged. 'That convoy of armour? It won't leave for days, now. Too many loose ends from the dead men.' He turned to go back for another load. 'I agree we need a way out of this,' he added.

When he was alone in the stable, Satyrus wrapped the cups in a blood-soaked towel and put them in his shoulder bag.

They rode up to the back of the citadel, approaching by the military road that was used only by the guard and the palace servants, because only the guard kept horses. There was a jam at the lower gate, where a train of donkeys carried game – deer, mostly – for the evening's feast.

His ankle was throbbing, and an odd depression had settled over him. There was a man right by the gate. His back was to Satyrus, and something about him was familiar.

'We should go back to regular lessons tomorrow,' Philokles said, out of nowhere.

'Fine,' Satyrus said. A black cloud of infinite dimensions had replaced the joy of being alive. Taking the gold cups made him feel like a thief.

Nestor was cursing the delay. 'What's going on at the gate? I'll whip the fools.' He turned back to them and his brow cleared. 'You are the most militant tutor I've met, sir. What do you teach? The arts of war?'

The Spartan spat. 'I'm no *hoplomachos*,' he said derisively. 'I teach philosophy. Politics.'

'Swordsmanship,' Satyrus said.

'Well, you seem a good teacher to me,' Nestor said. 'Your student held his own in a fight against men in armour.'

Philokles gave Satyrus that look which he associated with his tutor's gentle contempt.

'All I did was lie on the floor,' Satyrus said.

Nestor laughed. 'Your sister has you pegged,' he said.

Satyrus sat with his ankle throbbing for as long as it took to run a stade in armour, and then again. Somewhere in that time he had the nagging feeling that something had been forgotten. By the time the column finally shuffled forward, it had almost gone from his mind, and then, as he passed the gate, it hit him.

'Philokles!' he said. 'I saw Tenedos! With the kitchen staff at the gate!'

'Are you sure?' Philokles asked.

Satyrus wished that his ankle didn't hurt so much. 'Pretty sure,' he said.

'Who is Tenedos?' Nestor asked.

'Kinon's steward. The twins think he was involved in the attack.' Philokles was giving Satyrus an appraising look.

'Describe him,' the black man demanded.

Satyrus did his best. 'He's balding, Thracian. I'd even say he was Getae – his head is round like that. He has a slight stoop and – wispy hair.' *How did I miss that?* he asked himself.

'There's enough bald Thracian slaves in this building to glut the market,' Nestor said. 'I'll put the word out.'

'He can't be operating alone,' Philokles said. 'No slave would do anything to endanger his skin.'

They went in under a fine marble arch and turned right across the courtyard for the stables. Satyrus rode in, but Philokles had to dismount to avoid hitting his head.

Satyrus looked at their train of animals. 'Where do we put all this stuff? Will we still ride with the caravan?'

137

Philokles shook his head. 'I don't know, boy. I don't know anything any more.'

Satyrus got up and gave his tutor a hug. Philokles stiffened for a moment and then squeezed back.

'Sorry, boy. Things are – I need a drink. I *don't* need a drink. I need to get on top of this, and I'm not.'

'We need to get out of here,' Satyrus said.

'Agreed,' Philokles said.

'What if there's somebody inside? Working with Stratokles?' Satyrus said.

'Then we ought to be dead already,' Philokles said. He shook his head. 'I thought that I'd left all this behind. I was good at this once.'

Satyrus hesitated. 'What if there's someone inside but waiting for orders?'

Philokles stopped moving and turned to Satyrus so sharply that the boy was afraid the Spartan meant to hit him. It had happened, at least in the distant past. But Philokles made an odd clucking noise instead. 'That's good thinking, lad,' he said. 'And now you've seen Tenedos, we need to be on our guard. All the time.'

Philokles hailed a soldier, who got them a file of slaves to carry their gear. It was odd to be bringing bags of armour into the palace, and the slaves didn't like the weight of the loads.

Satyrus led the way, carrying his own pack and his satchel with the bloody towel full of gold cups. He was eager to give one to Melitta, and doubly eager to give one to Kallista. He climbed the steps from the working courtyard to the main floor and turned to the left, leaving the official precincts for the guest quarters and the tyrant's family space. He led his caravan of slaves up the steps of the formal entrance to the palace and past a pair of sentries, one of whom shot him a wink. Satyrus grinned. Then he went in under the bust of Herakles and followed the colonnade towards his room. The scale of the citadel and the palace dwarfed anything in Pantecapaeum or Olbia, and was far larger than anything in little Tanais. He wondered what it would be like to live with this level of opulence. Just as an example, in Tanais, the only stables had been in the public hippodrome. The tyrant of Heraklea had his own stables for his private use, and they could accommodate more animals than Tanais's public stables.

Satyrus tried to consider what this meant in terms of political power. It was the sort of thing that would please Philokles, and he began to compose a question – an intelligent question.

Then he heard his sister scream.

8

Satyrus dropped his pack and ran, despite the pain in his ankle, the shifting of his nose and the pounding of his heart. She screamed again.

He saw the Athenian doctor burst out of another curtain halfway around the courtyard and run towards his sister's room.

He reached under his arm and drew his sword. The gesture was becoming natural.

His sister screamed again and called, 'Help!'

He pushed through the curtain to her room. Melitta was full-length on the marble floor, trying to hold Kallista. Kallista was flopping on the floor, her face purple. Satyrus put his back against the wall and tried to cover every side of the room with his blade.

'Poison!' Melitta said.

Kallista was writhing as if she was in a pankration fight with an invisible opponent. The Athenian doctor burst in, followed by Philokles.

'Ahhhhhgggg!' Kallista bellowed. She had both hands at her throat. Her eyes were bulging like eggs.

The doctor cast around the room. 'What did she drink?' he barked.

Melitta pointed at a ewer of wine. 'She tasted it for me. Oh, Hera, she tasted it for me.'

The doctor smelled it. Then he put a finger in, hesitated and tasted it. He wrinkled his lips like a horse and spat.

'Fuck, she's dead,' he said bluntly. 'Poisoned. Not much I can do.'

Philokles didn't hesitate. He fell on the girl. Despite her violent struggles, he had her unable to move in seconds. Melitta rolled off. Theron came through the door with his head in a bandage.

'Help me!' Philokles growled. 'Get her legs!'

'What in Hades?' the doctor asked.

Theron got his left arm under her knees, pinned her ankles together and wrapped one great hand around them and lifted her up. Philokles kept her arms pinned.

Philokles whirled. 'You have hemp, doctor?' he demanded.

The moment her head cleared the stone floor, Philokles yelled, 'Keep her there!' at Theron. 'Hemp?' he demanded again.

The doctor shrugged. 'I'll find some,' he said, and walked out. 'Just keep her there,' he said over his shoulder.

The moment the doctor was out of the door, Philokles punched the slave girl in the stomach – a vicious blow with his whole weight behind it that made Theron stumble.

She responded with an explosive vomit all over Philokles. Some of the stuff spattered Theron and Satyrus got a gobbet in the face.

'Now look what you've done!' Melitta shouted. 'Wait for the hemp!'

Satyrus grabbed a towel, sopped it in water and wiped his own face. Then he set to cleaning Philokles.

The Spartan punched the girl again. Upside down, she flinched, her guts heaving, and puked again, a thin stream of black-purple liquid. Satyrus caught it as it passed her mouth.

He tossed the towel in a corner and grabbed another, thanking Zeus that the girls had just bathed. He turned to Theron, who was straining under the continued weight of the girl held up high.

They heard footsteps, and Nestor came in with a clash of bronze.

'Poison,' Philokles said. He stuck his hand into Kallista's mouth and made her gag.

'Hermes, god of travellers,' Nestor said, making a sign with his hand. 'Seal off this corridor!' he called outside.

'Let the doctor in!' Philokles cried, and moments later Sophokles returned. Behind him, a slave came with a brazier, a bronze bowl and a tripod.

'How did you induce vomiting?' the doctor asked. He shrugged. 'One way or another, this is it. Apollo, god of healing, and all the gods be with me.' He smiled at the slave. 'Right here. Put the tripod here. Well done. You have some bellows?'

The slave produced bellows.

'Make it hot!' the doctor said.

Kallista opened her eyes and screamed.

Sophokles threw the herb on to the brazier and a pungent smoke arose. To Satyrus, it was the scent of the sea of grass. The Sakje made little hide tents and sat in them to enjoy the smoke.

The doctor used the bellows until the smoke was rich and thick, then reversed them, sucking the smoke into the small instrument. He put it in Kallista's slack mouth and forced the smoke into her lungs. She coughed, choked and vomited again.

'Not dead yet!' Sophokles proclaimed grimly. 'Apollo, stand at my shoulder and save her!' He made more smoke and pushed the bellows deep in her throat before forcing in the smoke.

She retched and coughed, but no more bile came up.

'Let her down. The next time I need a patient held immobile, you two are my choice. Lay her on the couch. That's right.'

Satyrus was light-headed in the smoke. He could see Kallista – in her full beauty, dressed for a party – hovering just over the crumpled and stained victim on the couch, like an allegory. She seemed to smile at him.

A draught of air pushed the smoke aside, and the vision of a healthy Kallista vanished like a rainbow.

Kallista drew a deep, shuddering breath. Her whole body twitched.

'Make her drink water,' Sophokles said.

Melitta handed her brother a pitcher. 'Go to the well, draw it yourself and bring it back,' she said imperiously.

Satyrus discovered he had the acidic vomit in his hair when he ran a hand through it. He wiped his hand on his chiton – *damn, my best one, from Kinon* – and ran for the courtyard.

One of the guardsmen came with him. Satyrus looked at the man under the helmet – one of the Macedonians from the barracks. 'I'm going for water,' he said, stepping aside.

The guardsman was burdened with a heavy spear and a

shield. He was slow. Satyrus waited until he was moving and then ran down the stoa towards the stairs.

'Hey!' the man shouted. 'Wait for me, lad!'

Satyrus ignored him, cut down the slaves' stair to the main courtyard and stuck his pitcher into the water.

There were groups of slaves, mostly women, all around the fountain, chatting away. Most of them were looking at him. He looked back. When his jar was full, he got his feet under him and hoisted the jar clear of the fountain. All the slaves moved out of his way, clearing a path.

Tenedos the steward was trying to hide behind another man.

Satyrus froze. The guard had followed him down the stairs, but he was separated from Tenedos by the whole crowd of slaves. He thought that he could take the slave man to man – Tenedos was bigger and older, but it was unlikely that he had ever trained to fight. He could hear Theron saying, *Any time you offer a test of strength to a man, he'll beat you.* But he was just a slave – and Satyrus had a blade.

Of course, Kallista needed the water.

Fuck, why is life so hard? he thought. He turned his back on the slaves and set his pitcher down on the stone. He took a deep breath, whirled around and started for the man.

Tenedos moved fast, shoving a young woman flat on the floor and pushing a bigger man against the rim of the fountain as he fled. Satyrus jumped over a downed stool and saw the Macedonian guard moving fast, despite his armour, across the back of the fountain room.

Tenedos slipped through a door and was gone. Satyrus rounded the corner at full speed and raced under the eaves of the slave quarters where the women's quarters overhung the working courtyard, but there was no one there but two old slaves weaving linen chitons who shoved themselves flat against the wall as he raced past. The steward must have gone into one of the slaves' rooms – or into the kitchens.

The guard came up, panting. 'Well?'

'That's the steward from Kinon's!' Satyrus said. Seeing that his words meant nothing to the guard, he said, 'The assassin!'

143

The guard nodded sharply, put a bone whistle to his lips and blew hard, over and over. Every slave in the area immediately lay flat on the ground, and the corridors around the courtyard were full of the sound of running feet.

'We'll get him,' the man said. 'As soon as I get a squad here, my lord, you're going straight back to your chambers.'

Satyrus shook his head. 'I can identify him. He's in one of these rooms. Let's—'

The guardsman shook his head. 'Look, lad – we're protecting you. *Let us fucking protect you.*' He grinned.

Half a dozen archers appeared, big black men with ostrich plumes in their hair.

'Assassin. In one of the slave rooms.' He pointed his spear.

'Take him alive!' Satyrus shouted.

The lead archer turned. 'Perhaps,' he said with a wicked smile.

'Back to your room, my lord,' the Macedonian said. Behind him, three of the archers nocked arrows while the other three drew wicked-looking iron knives.

'Medje,' the Macedonian said. 'Your steward is doomed. Wait until they get their fucking monkeys. They can smell a man a stade away.'

Satyrus did not want to leave the chase, and he wanted to learn more about the Medje – he'd seldom seen a group of men who gave such an impression of competence. 'How will they know him?'

'If he isn't lying on the floor in the position of submission ...' The Macedonian shook his head. 'And if he is, he won't have a slave disk. Now *move.*'

Satyrus put his sword back in the scabbard and snatched up the pitcher as he passed the fountain house, angry with himself, and ran for the slave stairs.

'I saw Tenedos,' he said as he put the pitcher into Melitta's hands. It didn't seem as if anyone in the room had moved. 'He was in the working courtyard. I think he saw me watching him.'

'Did he escape?' Philokles asked. 'Why didn't you run him down?'

Satyrus thought that was unfair. 'The palace guard are after him. One of our guards made me come back.'

Nestor nodded. 'Good,' he said. 'That's a man who knows his business.'

'What on earth were you thinking, boy?' Philokles asked. 'Nestor, will you search the palace?'

Nestor grunted. 'I'm sure it is being done. And the boy did right – as did my man. Your prince has no business chasing assassins. He's the target.' He leaned out into the corridor and began to shout orders. Then he turned back to the room.

'You two will know him?' he said to Philokles. 'You and Theron come with me. I'll make up two parties. I must attend the tyrant – he'll lock the palace down.'

'We don't need the palace locked down,' Philokles said.

Nestor shook his head. 'We do. This may all be aimed at the tyrant.'

Frustrated, Satyrus glared at Philokles in the middle of the room. Melitta took the pitcher. 'Don't mope,' she said. 'Send slaves for more water.'

In a few minutes, the whole complex was flooded with soldiers. Men of the guard were at every door and most of the windows, and when a slave moved, guards would call out so that the slave's movements were watched and recorded somewhere. Every time the whistles blew, all the slaves would lie flat, their arms by their sides. It was efficient and scary.

Draco appeared at Satyrus's side. 'A man can't even get laid without your enemies fucking it up,' he said. But he gave Satyrus a grin. 'Let's go to your rooms, my lord. I've been ordered to go through them with you.'

He gave Satyrus a nod, and together they went out into the stoa, as another guardsman called out that they were moving. When they reached Satyrus's portion of the wing, they went through all of the rooms on his side, opening every chest and looking under every chair and bed and behind every drape. His thoroughness was unsettling. Satyrus had never considered that men might be *trained* to search a room.

Slaves continued to bring pitchers of water. Satyrus turned to go back to his sister's rooms.

'No more traffic,' Draco said. 'You can wait here, my lord.'

'You know me,' Satyrus said.

'Go to your room. Read the *Iliad*. Whatever. Just obey, understand?' The Macedonian mercenary was all business.

Satyrus shrugged with adolescent annoyance and went to his room. He was alone. He went to the alcove and found the scroll bag he'd seen there the day before.

Sure enough, the *Iliad*.

Satyrus slumped on the floor and tried to read about Achilles' rage, and tried not to think about the hourly process of assassination.

Achilles failed to illuminate his problem. No one in the *Iliad* faced enemies who crawled in the dark and used poison – well, except Odysseus. But the winged words had their own healing; he was lost soon enough, reading avidly.

There was shouting in the corridor, and a sound in the distance like a scream, and his head came up from his scroll. He was scared. He wondered if the next thing he'd see would be an assassin bursting through the door.

'Fuck,' he said. Without meaning to, he thought of his mother and the warmth of her infrequent embraces. And then he thought about the Sauromatae girl crying for her mother as she lay dying. His hands shook.

He backed into a corner, his brain running like a chariot drawn by maddened horses. He thought about the city and the stables and about his mother. He thought about his father, the demi-god. He thought about his sister. About Kallista. What kind of life did she lead? Would she die? Was it his fault?

Slowly, his breathing slowed. His hands stopped shaking, and he realized that he had his sword in his hand, and he was huddled in the corner of his room.

'I'm losing my wits,' he said aloud. He sheathed the sword and wiped his face and then poured water over his head and rubbed his face, hard.

'Draco?' he called out. Voice fairly steady. Of course, the man had heard him. No privacy anywhere.

'My lord?' the soldier asked.

'I'd like to go down to my sister's room,' Satyrus said.

'Prince Satyrus moving!' Draco called. 'Go ahead, my lord.'

Satyrus stepped out into the evening air and moved along the gallery to Melitta's room. When he passed the soldier, the Macedonian turned to look at him.

'Another few minutes and this'll be over,' he said in a whisper.

'Thanks,' Satyrus said. 'Lita?' he called.

'Come in!' she said, and he ducked through the curtain.

Melitta was sitting on a chair by Kallista, who was lying on the bed. She was deeply unconscious. Melitta gave a bright and entirely fake smile.

'Hello, brother,' she said.

'You all right?' he asked.

The corners of her mouth quivered a little, but her smile remained in place. 'No,' she said. 'People are trying to kill me. Us. It's different from a fight. It's horrible, Satyrus! I like people!'

Satyrus put his arms around her, happy to comfort somebody. Especially his sister, who usually comforted him. 'It's not everybody, sis. It's just a couple of idiots. If I'd been quicker on my feet, we'd be safe.'

'What are you, Achilles? Is it all on you? Are you the centre of the world? Stop all this assumption-of-responsibility crap! It's the product of too much Plato!' She put her cheek on his shoulder and squeezed. The weight of her head was grinding one of his best gold fibulae into his shoulder, but that was an occupational hazard of being a brother.

'I didn't get him, and that Macedonian made me come back here. I should have stayed at it! It makes me feel like shit.' Satyrus felt better just for saying the words out loud.

She looked up, her eyes red, and shook her head. 'Slavery doesn't make them weak, you daft weasel. Slavery makes them desperate. Promise me that when we're king and queen, we'll have no slaves.'

'Done!' he said. 'I swear it by Zeus and all the gods.'

They stood there, embracing, for some time. The shadows got longer. Kallista continued to breathe.

'I'm better,' Melitta said. 'Thanks.' She stepped away and started to rearrange her hair.

'Hey?' he said. 'What if I'm not better?'

She made a rude noise. 'Can I tell you something?' she said, her back to him.

'Probably,' he said. He was watching Kallista. In his head, he was comparing her blotched face, swollen lips, burn marks and stressed flesh to the image of beauty she had presented the first night in the rose garden. The comparison was full of lessons.

'When I thought you were dying, I was going to kill myself,' she said evenly. 'I don't think I'd want to live without you, brother.' She put a pin into her hair.

He rubbed his hand through his hair in embarrassment. 'Yeah,' he said. Another of his excellent responses.

'My lord?' Draco asked from the other side of the curtain.

'That's Draco, our sentry. Come in!' Satyrus called.

The Macedonian pushed his head through. 'We're out of here, my lord. The Medje have your man, and the dinner is on – our tyrant won't be cowed by a slave. So you're to dress.' His eyes flicked over to where Melitta sat. 'My pardon, m'lady.'

'Hold on,' Satyrus said, slipping through the curtain. 'Thanks.'

Draco grinned from under his Thracian helmet. 'No problem, m'lord.'

'What happened to "Satyrus" or "boy"?'

'Orders. You two is to be treated as visiting royals.' Draco grinned. 'Most visiting royals don't help us loot a house, o' course.'

'Can I ask a favour, Draco?'

'Sure. Ask away. I'm back off duty as soon as I get this thorax off.' He slung his shield around on his back.

'Can you find me a chiton? A nice one?' He pointed to the long streak of black vomit on his fine flame-decorated garment.

Draco grinned. 'That's easy. Hey!' he said, turning. 'Hey, Philotas! Where's that squeeze of yours?'

Another armoured man emerged from the columns on the other side of the guests' courtyard. 'She's right here, you whoreson.'

'Send her over here. The prince needs some clothes.' Draco chortled.

'So does she!' Philotas laughed. 'It might be a minute.'

Draco shrugged. 'He's a pig-dog, our Philotas. Girls love him. His cock's longer than a girl's foot.' He rolled his eyes. 'His girl is one of the wardrobe slaves. His *current* girl.'

Satyrus tried to be a man of the world. 'My mother says "no slave girls".'

'Aphrodite! Why's that?' Draco seemed shocked.

'Because they can't decide for themselves. They aren't in control of their bodies.' Satyrus managed to deliver the line well, without primness, as if he really knew what he was talking about.

Draco laughed. 'Ares, who cares?' he said. 'Willing? Unwilling?' He looked at Satyrus. 'Oh, balls. I'm sorry, boy. Don't take it like that – I'm no monster. Your mum's just a little strict for me.'

The slave girl came up, her eyes averted and her ionic chiton neat and graceful. 'Master?' she asked.

'The prince would like to know if he might get a chiton from the wardrobe,' Draco asked in an official voice. 'His best got ruined in the poison attempt.'

The slave raised her eyes and looked at his chiton. She fingered the stain. 'Never come all the way out,' she said. She brightened. 'But I have a little bitch who it'll do good to try. Can we move about, Draco?'

'Free as friggin' birds, honey,' Draco answered. 'My lord, I leave you in good hands.'

'Give me the cloth, m'lord.' She all but snapped her fingers, and Satyrus pulled it off over his head.

'Get the brooches, m'lord,' Draco said. 'Or you'll never see 'em again.'

'Don't you have somewhere you ought to be, guardsman?' the woman said to Draco. Her nimble fingers plucked the fibulae off the shoulders. 'No one in this wing would steal, m'lord. Draco is from Macedon – they're the thieves.'

Draco gave him a look that said he'd stand by his statement, and Satyrus was left standing naked with a pair of gold brooches in his hand and a sword strap over his shoulder.

Life with slaves and guards was so alien that he almost laughed aloud.

Philokles came up behind him. 'Planning to go to the dinner naked, boy?' he asked. 'The sword is a nice touch. You could be young Herakles.'

Satyrus blushed and hurried back to his room. As quickly as he could, he wriggled into a chiton.

'Best bathe. I can smell the vomit on you,' Philokles called after him, leaning in past the curtain.

'Will you go, sir?' Satyrus asked.

'I will, too. We can just squeeze it in.' Satyrus felt his tutor's hand on his shoulder, and they walked off down the gallery to the stairs.

Philokles didn't know the palace like Satyrus did now. 'This way,' he said, heading down the slaves' stair. 'It's faster!'

'No, boy,' the Spartan said. He pulled Satyrus past the slaves' stair. 'Not fair to them. You didn't grow up with slaves, but I did. They need their own places where the likes of us don't interfere. Just like soldiers. Officers don't go into soldiers' parts of camp. Bad manners.'

'Oh,' Satyrus said. They went down the public stair together. The baths were crowded because everyone had either been on duty or locked down for the afternoon. The men in the steam fell silent when Satyrus entered.

'Welcome, prince,' Nestor called out.

Satyrus blushed. He blushed more when he saw the murals on the walls. He got in the steam, and then he plunged into a cold bath deep enough to dive and swim, with a beautiful bronze woman with a fish tail at the bottom, as if swimming for the surface. When he emerged, he took a warmer bath and then went into the towel room.

'Massage?' a bored slave asked. 'You're the foreign prince, eh? In there,' he said.

Satyrus found himself on a slab between Nestor and Philokles. They were like a pair of matching statues as they reclined, waiting for masseurs – Nestor in black and Philokles in white. Philokles was not at his best – years as a tutor in a backwater had not forced him to maintain his fighting trim

– but he was not fat, either. Nestor's musculature was perfect, and he would have adorned any gymnasium in Greece.

'Boy or girl?' the towel boy asked.

'Surprise me,' Nestor said.

A heavyset man came in and set to work on Philokles. 'Soldier, sir?' he asked. 'I can always tell from the shoulders.'

Nestor laughed. 'He's a Spartan!' he said.

The masseur grunted. 'You've pulled some muscles here, sir. Best take some light exercise.'

'I'll keep that in mind,' Philokles said.

'Where's Theron?' Satyrus asked, as another man started to pummel his shoulders. Then a huge thumb was thrust roughly under his shoulder blade and it *hurt*. 'Ares!' he squeaked.

'Be nice, Glaukis – probably the first real massage the boy's ever had.' Nestor hissed between his teeth. 'They all hurt, m'lord.'

Satyrus's masseur grunted and rotated his arm as if forcing his head down in pankration.

'Oww!' Satyrus said.

The two big men laughed.

Eventually, it was over. There was a point where it started to feel good, and another point where he started to feel the glow he got from a long exercise bout.

'Oil, m'lord?' the masseur asked.

'Just a little,' Satyrus said.

The masseur helped him off the slab. 'Second curtain, m'lord.'

Satyrus headed down a corridor, barely able to walk with the absolute relaxation of his muscles. Erotic scenes involving various combinations of partners adorned the walls. Satyrus wasn't prudish and he certainly knew how it all worked – there was even less privacy in Tanais than in Heraklea – but he blushed anyway.

The second curtain gave way to a small room with a small dark-haired girl not much older than he. She helped him up on to a stool. 'Scented?' she asked. 'Cedar or lavender?'

'No scent, thanks,' he said.

She began to apply oil, her hands light but efficient.

'Anything else, master?' she asked as she began to massage the oil into his penis.

'No, thank you,' he said. No squeak at all – he was quite proud of his lack of shock.

'There you go, then,' she said with an utter indifference that made him feel he'd made the right choice.

He walked back up the main stair in a glow of well-being, *eudaimonia*, and he walked straight into his sister's room. 'How is she?' he asked.

'Goodness, you glow like a god,' Melitta said. 'She's breathing better.'

'Do you know that when they put oil on you in the baths, they offer sex acts? Do they do that in the women's baths?'

Melitta giggled. 'Yes and no,' she said. 'Let's not go into details.' She turned bright red, and they laughed.

The laughter went on.

'Go and put some clothes on, brother,' she said. 'There's a slave waiting in your room.' She made a motion with her hand. 'We're suddenly at the age where people will talk if we're together naked.'

Satyrus turned a bright red. 'Zeus Soter!' he said. 'That's disgusting!'

Melitta shrugged. 'The Macedonians do it all the time. Ask your soldier friend Draco.' Melitta gave a wicked smile – a smile that most twelve-year-old girls couldn't manage. 'Your guard friends think that's what we're doing in here.'

Satyrus vowed never to be naked around his sister again and headed off to his room.

Satyrus found the wardrobe slave waiting for him.

'Sorry to keep you waiting,' he said.

She continued to look at the floor, but she gave a small smile. 'That's polite. I had a nice rest, and I tacked the side seams. Put it on. Good – you're not dripping oil. Smudges the fabric.'

She held out a chiton, which was light wool, woven beautifully, but with a double row of purple decoration woven in. 'Himself will never wear it,' she said. 'Came with the tribute and it wouldn't go around his head, much less his body.' She smiled. 'Thank him for it when you make your bow, just so I'm covered.'

'Hestia, goddess of the hearth, watch over you. What's your name?' he asked.

'Harmone, my lord. There – you look like a prince. You need gold sandals.'

'I've never had such a thing,' Satyrus said.

Harmone laughed. 'I'm a slave, and I have four pairs,' she said. 'The world's a funny place and no mistake.' She waited at the doorway.

Waiting for a tip. Satyrus cast around the room, saw all of his kit where the slaves had dumped it – was it really just that afternoon?

'It's going to take me some time to find my purse,' he said.

'I'll wait,' she said. 'I knew you was a gent.'

Satyrus wondered what he had in his purse. 'Harmone?' he asked, as he pulled his sleeping roll off the pile. 'What's a fair tip? This isn't how I live every day.'

She rolled her eyes. 'Ten gold darics'd do me fine,' she said, and giggled. 'You're a rare 'un. An obol or two is fair for any extra service a slave does, except fucking. That's more, unless offered free.'

Satyrus's hand stopped over his satchel. He looked at her. She smiled.

She was a good ten years older than him and he wasn't *sure* she was offering, and the world was a very confusing place. He had to look away – she was licking her lips – and his down-turned eye caught a needle sticking point-first out of the flap of his satchel, just a few finger-breadths from his hand. The point of the needle was dark with something stuck to it – wax.

Or poison.

'Hades,' Satyrus breathed. He'd *heard* of poisoned needles. 'Harmone. I'll tip you later. Get Nestor!'

She caught the seriousness in his voice.

Satyrus didn't move. The discovery of the reality of poisoned needles had frozen him in place. He felt very vulnerable indeed. He tried not to think. He didn't panic, especially – he just crouched by his pack until Philokles and Theron came. Then

Nestor arrived with a file of soldiers. They told him not to move while they sent for more soldiers in heavy gear.

His sister stood in the doorway, dressed for dinner, with her hair piled on top of her head in silver pins, and chewed on her fist.

Men in heavy felt mittens pulled his gear apart. Men in heavy military sandals came in and literally carried him out of the room. He leaned his forehead against the cool smoothness of a pillar and breathed for a while as his hands and knees shook. Then he went to the door.

'Someone hand me out my sword?' he asked. Good voice. He did that well – touch of irony.

Melitta smiled.

Philokles looked stricken. And a little drunk.

'This is all my fault,' he said thickly.

'We need to get out of here,' Satyrus said. 'If Kallista can travel in a litter, I suggest we leave tonight.'

The doctor came up behind Philokles. 'That ankle of yours needs a couple of days,' he said.

'I could be dead in a couple of days,' Satyrus said. He managed to hide the bitterness.

Philokles turned to Nestor. 'I'd like to send a messenger to the smith to see if his caravan is still going. It has probably left – or been cancelled. If it has left, I'd like an escort until we catch it.'

Theron pushed in. 'I'll go,' he said.

'No, Philokles said. 'From now on, we all stay together all the time. Nestor leaves a guard on Kallista until we come back from dinner, and then we sleep in Melitta's room, and in the morning we pack our beasts at first light and ride.'

Nestor nodded. 'Pending the tyrant's permission, of course.'

Philokles nodded back. 'Of course,' he said.

Sophokles glanced at Nestor. 'I'll go with them,' he said. 'They all need medical care.'

Nestor was surprised. 'You were just hired as the tyrant's physician,' he said.

Sophokles shrugged. 'I feel responsible,' he said.

Satyrus looked at the Athenian, trying to read his soul.

'Let's go to dinner,' Melitta said.

Satyrus was struck again by the sheer bulk of Dionysius of Heraklea as he entered the man's hall. The tyrant filled the dais, and his couch was three times the width of every other couch, and he lay alone. He was grotesque, and his bristle of short blond hair made his head seem all the smaller. He looked like an ogre come to life.

He held the eye nonetheless, his white chiton immaculate, the gold wreath on his head brilliant in its Helios-like spray of leaves and tendrils that flickered like fire in the lamplight. Satyrus and Melitta led the way to the dais, arm in arm and walking with their heads high, and Satyrus was aware, even as he stared at the tyrant, that every other eye in the hall was on him or his sister.

The couches of the principal diners were drawn up in a circle. Where women had been invited, they sat in chairs beside their companions. The dinner was not an orgy but a feast, and when Satyrus managed to tear his eyes away from the tyrant, he saw that the couches of the inner circle were full of serious-looking men attended by women their own age – not hetairai.

Before they approached the circle, Satyrus turned to Philokles. 'Any special etiquette for tyrants?' he asked.

'Be polite,' Philokles answered. 'Don't make speeches about the freedom of the assembly.'

Theron choked a laugh, and then they were passing an empty couch and entering the clear space before the dais.

'Greetings, Prince Satyrus and Princess Melitta!' The tyrant raised himself on an elbow. 'Nestor, offer me a libation on the altar for the safety of our twins.'

Satyrus hadn't noticed that Nestor had somehow beaten them to the dining hall. The black man was seated behind the tyrant, and he rose, took a libation bowl and poured wine on a small altar set into the wall, with a statue of Dionysius in gold and ivory in a niche over the altar.

The tyrant nodded. 'The blessings of Dionysius stay with you. May the strength of our patron Herakles defend you.' He smiled, and it was a hard, dangerous grin for such a fat man. 'You are still wearing your sword, young man.'

Satyrus bowed deeply. 'I rejoice in your – your favour, Dionysius. I thank you for your hospitality, for the healing of your doctor, the safety of your roof and for your generosity. Even the clothes on my back I owe to you.' He bowed again, and his voice rose as his nerves betrayed him. 'But—' Too squeaky. 'But – twice, men have tried to kill us under your roof. I beg your forgiveness and your permission to wear this sword.'

'I missed the last part of that,' Dionysius said. He rolled heavily and the legs of his couch creaked. 'Nestor, what does the boy say?'

Nestor leaned down by the tyrant and whispered in his ear.

Dionysius nodded heavily. 'So be it. I am deeply sorry that these criminals have so abused my hospitality. Now sit and eat dinner. How is the slave girl?' He asked the last with a sudden quickening of his eyes.

'She will live,' Melitta said. 'She may be – marred.'

Dionysius's eyes roved over Melitta. 'I have a niece – Amastris – just your age. Would you sit with her?'

Melitta nodded her head gracefully. 'I would be delighted.'

Nestor made a sign, and a chair was moved. Melitta followed the chair to sit beside another girl her own age.

'You sit by me,' Dionysius said to Satyrus. He pointed to the couch on his left hand.

Satyrus went and lay on it. Philokles and Theron were escorted to other couches in the second circle.

As soon as the Tanaisians were in their places, Nestor clapped his hands and dancers entered. They danced the rites of spring as village girls danced them throughout the Euxine, if with more grace, and while they moved beautifully through the familiar figures, the first course was served on three-legged tables next to each couch.

'Nestor tells me you wish to abandon my hospitality,' Dionysius said. He was enormous, and he was elevated by the height of a man's lower leg. The combination made conversation awkward, as the tyrant's head was four feet above Satyrus's head.

'Lord, you know that the slave – Tenedos, the steward of Kinon – was at large in your citadel?' Satyrus craned his neck to see the tyrant's eyes.

'Young Satyrus, I know of every event in this castle. I know when a slave girl fucks – or does not fuck – a guest, and how much he tips her.' He put a morsel of food in his mouth and winked. 'Tenedos is now past worrying about, but he had many interesting points to make before he went to Hades.'

Satyrus nodded, the lesson going straight home to his heart. 'Did he betray his master?' he said carefully.

'Yes and no, young man. That is, he admitted that he was turned by this Stratokles, but he claimed – while in enormous pain – that it was the slave girl, Kallista, who was the driving force. Not he, of course.'

'Oh,' Satyrus said.

'Ahh, to be so young. A man will say anything under torture. Anything. It need not be the truth. Indeed, it seldom is.' The tyrant took a whole quail and dropped it in his mouth.

'What of the Athenian? If I may ask, lord?' Satyrus took a quail for himself when the platter was offered.

'Fled – days ago. By ship, I suspect. But he will have left other agents here, I have no doubt.' The fat man spat bird bones into his hand and dropped them into a bowl on his couch.

'How convenient for everyone,' Satyrus said.

'I regret that I must agree. In your place I would suspect that the tyrant Dionysius was complicit.' He smiled.

Satyrus sipped his wine bowl. 'The thought had crossed my mind,' he said. He tried to sound like a man of the world, but instead he heard a scared boy.

'But of course, if I wanted you dead, you'd be dead.' Dionysius winked again. 'Nestor could have gutted you both and had your meat served in a local shop at the crook of my finger. Or you could die of poison right now, from the wine in that cup. You didn't have it tasted. You'd never know. Or I could have you strangled in your sleep by my slaves. Really, there's no need to concern yourself with such things – you are so utterly in my power that it may be that I just can't make up my mind how to dispose of you.'

Satyrus forced himself to take a bite of food. He had no idea what it tasted like. His mind was not moving.

'The sword you wear is a nice conceit, but will it defend you from poison? Or even from a determined man with a sword? From my ill will, it offers no defence at all, and by wearing it, you accuse me of being a poor host. It is rude.' The tyrant rolled over on his couch, and from his position under the huge man, Satyrus could see the length of the thongs that held the mattress and how stretched they were.

'But you wished to make a statement. Perhaps you felt that you needed to get my attention. Boys do such things. They posture.' The tyrant smiled again. 'I posture too. When you are as old as I, and as fat, men will assume that as you are ugly, so you are evil. Don't you? *Kalos kalon*? The beautiful *is* the good. Eh, boy? And since I'm so ugly, I must be evil. I must rape virgins every night, and perhaps bathe in blood. Eh?' The man leaned over the edge of his couch. 'So when they call me evil, I posture a little. Understand, boy? Stupid, violent men often mistake goodness for weakness and see evil as strength. You look smart. Do you know whereof I speak?'

Satyrus had, in fact, got the drift. He raised his cup. 'I drink to the virtue of ugliness, lord,' he said, turning a pretty phrase. He'd held it in his mind since the tyrant had used the stock phrase *Kalos kalon*.

Dionysius sat up, and his couch protested. 'Nestor, did you hear that? The boy just paid me a genuine compliment!'

Nestor chuckled.

'Virtue of ugliness, indeed. Well said, young man. I think we may indeed be friends. Tell me what you want.' Dionysius snapped his fingers, and the second course was served. He watched the servers with much the same pride as Kinon had shown, and then a messenger distracted him.

'Lord, I want to – that is—' Satyrus stared at the tyrant. *What do I want?* he thought. Since the man was distracted, he looked around, and his eyes found Melitta's, sitting on an ivory-decorated chair to his right. Sitting next to her, with her face almost touching his sister's, was the Nereid from the other night, her black curls framing her face. She was telling his sister a story, and they were both laughing. Melitta caught his eye, and the other girl saw her attention waver and turned her head to look at him, and their eyes met.

Hers were green. All thought left his head. *So green.* A slave bent over his dining table.

The slave was holding out a solid silver ewer, and he should have asked if Satyrus wanted more wine. Instead, he opened his mouth, and the buzz of the diners, the ebb and flow of conversation, the drone of flies and the sound of the sea spoke like the voice of the god from his mouth.

'*That girl is what you want,*' said the slave. He raised the ewer.

'What did you say?' Satyrus asked.

'More wine, master?' the slave squeaked.

When Satyrus looked back, his sister and the Nereid were laughing together again. He looked at the slave. The boy was terrified. Well, slaves were often scared. He was learning a great deal about slaves.

He held up his wine cup. The boy raised the pitcher and poured, and Satyrus noted that the pitcher was nearly empty.

The boy spilled wine when his hands shook, just a few drops that fell harmlessly on the couch's cover.

'Never mind,' Satyrus said kindly. He dismissed the boy with a wave. He turned back to the tyrant. 'What I want, lord, is revenge,' he said. 'And the restoration of my city.'

'Revenge is utterly worthless, young man.' Dionysius sipped his wine. 'I hope you haven't already had a surfeit of tunny. The run this year is superb.'

The giant fish was carried past him by four sweating slaves, all grown men. When Satyrus glanced around, he realized that the boy who had just served him was the only young slave in the hall.

He was nowhere to be seen. 'I have a mind to make myself king of the Bosporus,' Satyrus said, and raised the wine cup to his lips. 'I had no such intention, but Eumeles – Heron – has forced this on me.'

Dionysius narrowed his eyes.

Satyrus put his wine cup down untasted. He'd just made the

connections. 'Lord, I think this wine is poisoned.'

Dionysius flinched as if struck. 'That is quite an accusation.' He motioned to Nestor, who came up.

'Take this cup and test it on someone. The boy thinks that it is poison.' The tyrant motioned him away. He turned back to Satyrus as if nothing untoward had happened. 'It is all very well, planning to be a king. That will require riches and armies. What do you want from me?' Dionysius's voice made it clear that neither riches nor armies would be forthcoming.

'I would like permission to leave, and an escort. I wish to reach my friend Diodorus the Athenian.' Satyrus watched Nestor until he vanished. He had a pounding headache, and he wondered if he had absently already had a sip of the wine. Or been poisoned earlier. He felt queasy.

'Done,' the tyrant said.

Silence fell over the hall. Nestor came in by another entrance with a file of soldiers. One of them was carrying a dead dog. Soldiers took station at every entrance.

Slaves suddenly moved like lightning, herded by other soldiers.

Nestor moved to the foot of the dais. He bent his head down and spoke to the tyrant, and the man started. Then he spoke rapidly.

'I apologize for the inconvenience,' Nestor announced. 'This dinner is ended and you are all guests of the tyrant for the night. Soldiers will escort you to rooms. When you are cleared, you will be escorted home. Again, we apologize for any inconvenience. Those responsible will be punished,' Nestor glanced around, 'with the utmost rigour.'

Diners looked pale. A woman burst into tears. Soldiers moved up to every couch and took the diners away. Satyrus saw two soldiers escort Theron from the hall, and another pair taking Philokles.

'Your wine was poisoned, young man. And there's a boy with his throat cut in the kitchen.' The tyrant shook his head. 'I *hate* that this has happened here. It makes me feel weak. It makes me *look* weak.' He shrugged, moving the whole mass of his flesh. 'Escort them to their rooms. Young man, you have brought me a great deal of trouble – but you have also identified for me a serious threat, and for that you have my thanks.' He gestured with his hand. Nestor moved to Satyrus's couch.

'My lord?' he said.

Satyrus rolled to his feet. Melitta came up next to him and together they bowed to the tyrant, who responded with a civil inclination of his head. 'You are excellent children,' he said. 'I hope that you live.'

Satyrus met the ogre's eye. 'I hope that I will always remember that beauty is not the only good,' he said.

He started to turn away, but he caught the smile that flashed over the tyrant's face. 'When you are ready to be a king, come to me,' Dionysius the tyrant said. 'I think I would be happy to be your ally.' With that, despite his bulk, he moved quickly, vanishing into his guards.

'Not bad,' Melitta said. 'I think you're starting to play the prince.'

'I'll have to live long enough to grow into the part,' he shot back, but then he grinned at her. 'Watch out, Lita. I could grow to like it.'

Nestor escorted them to the door. 'Draco!' he called out. Many of the diners were gathered outside, being searched with brusque efficiency by the tyrant's guard. There was a fair amount of silent outrage.

Draco ran up and saluted. 'Captain?'

'Take these two back to their rooms,' he said. 'I will make arrangements on your behalf. Be ready.' He spoke tersely and turned away.

Satyrus glanced at Melitta. She shook her head. 'He means, don't go to sleep,' she whispered.

'Right this way, lady,' the soldier said. When they were clear of the guests and the other soldiers, he led them by the servants' ways and the slaves' stair to their rooms. There were soldiers at every junction in the palace.

'This happens a little too often for me,' he said. 'Word to the wise – the guards saw a man going up the slaves' stairs about twenty minutes back. They shouted – should have just charged the fucker – and he got away.' The Macedonian shrugged. 'More poison? Going to bag that slave girl? Who the fuck knows? I've never seen the like of this, except at court at home.'

Satyrus paused at the door of his room, suddenly over-whelmed with an irrational – or perhaps wholly rational – fear of a dark room. 'Would you have someone search my room?' he asked.

Draco sighed. 'I'm not even on duty. Can the search of your room wait until morning?'

Satyrus whirled. 'No, it cannot. Listen – someone just tried to poison me. Earlier, someone had a go at my sister and man-aged to poison Kallista – er, her slave. My mother is probably dead in Pantecapaeum, I'm cut off from my friends and my patrimony, and I'm at the end of my tether and I want you to get your arse into that room and check it out, or get someone who will. Understand me?' His voice was shrill, and his tone was murderous, and he regretted the whole speech the moment it was out of his mouth.

Draco stiffened. 'Yes, my lord,' he said, woodenly. He sum-moned two more guardsmen, had a whispered conversation and then, with lamps in hand, they searched the room, ripped the coverings off the couch and searched them for needles, and summoned a pair of slaves to remake it. Then they did the same for Melitta, moving the snoring Kallista.

When they were done, Satyrus tried to make amends. 'I'm sorry,' he said.

Draco shot him a look of contempt. 'Just my *job*, my lord. I'll be on my way.'

Satyrus paused. 'Yes, it is, Draco. Sorry for the inconven-ience, but it *is* your job.'

Draco stalked off.

Philokles and Theron joined them in Melitta's room. They dropped their packs and sat on them. Then Philokles went with Satyrus to his room and they collected his gear and moved it to his sister's room.

Before they could get it all arranged, there was the rattle of armed soldiers in the colonnade, and Nestor appeared through the curtain.

He entered, followed by a slim figure wrapped to the head in cloaks. 'The tyrant himself is otherwise engaged,' Nestor said.

'He sent me to prove his determination on your behalf,' Amastris said, emerging from her wraps. She smiled hesitantly. 'And because I wanted to say goodbye. Nestor will escort you to the stables. Uncle wants you gone immediately – while he has the palace locked down and no one can speak of your flight. Then he intends to sell every slave in the palace. That boy – the one who served you – was one of ours.' Her eyes met Satyrus's, and she smiled at him. He had to lean against the wall. 'He shouldn't even have been in the room. He's not a server – just a cook's boy. But none of the slaves seem to know anything.' Her shrug told a great deal. 'So uncle is selling every one of them in the morning.'

'Ares!' Philokles said. 'Every slave in the palace?'

Nestor's face hardened. 'I'll find the man responsible. And we'll never get to the slaves while they're still on the staff.'

'The man responsible is the Athenian, Stratokles,' Satyrus said. 'And his agent, the slave Tenedos.'

Nestor shook his head. 'Stratokles has fled the city, and is a citizen of Athens. We have the house watched, but there is not much more we can do. It now appears that this slave, Tenedos, may have been his messenger to someone inside the palace.'

'Surely you can take action against him! Arrest him!' Satyrus blurted.

'Athens, young prince, does not take well to the prosecution of its ambassadors.' Nestor snapped his fingers, and a pair of soldiers brought a cauldron of stew. 'Or their murder. I have eaten from this pot. The wine is my own. Please eat.'

Satyrus didn't hesitate. He took a loaf of bread from one of the soldiers, picked up a bowl and began to eat. Melitta did the same. Philokles and Theron joined in.

Amastris took a bowl and joined them. She shared the room's only chair with Melitta, like sisters. 'My uncle says, "I smell Olympias and her pet, Cassander." Olympias serves dark powers. She loves poison.' She glanced at Melitta. 'We all fear Olympias. She has been a figure of fear to me since I was born.'

'Many of your soldiers are from Macedon,' Melitta said.

Nestor nodded. 'It will be looked into. You need to be gone from here before someone gets you.' He looked at Philokles. 'How long have *you* been with the twins?'

'All our lives,' Satyrus answered. 'He was my father's friend. You cannot possibly accuse him.'

Nestor shook his head. 'My lord, I accuse no one, but I must ask everyone. So you are the same man as figures in tales of Kineas? Good.' Nestor nodded at Philokles and turned back to Satyrus. 'I think that if he drank less, he'd be more trustworthy; but he seems a solid man.'

Philokles went red and then a blotched red and white.

Impervious to the Spartan's rage, Nestor glanced at Theron. 'How about this athlete? Theron?' Nestor pointed at him. 'How long have you known him?'

'He has been with us from the attack at Tanais,' Satyrus said. His voice was very low. He looked at Melitta.

'He would never betray us,' she said. 'He's had a hundred chances to kill us.'

'Nestor, why are these things happening?' Amastris spoke in a low voice, almost husky.

'Why, my lady?' Nestor shrugged. 'People play games for power. Olympias and her friend Cassander play them for the love of playing. Olympias is like a cat – she likes to hurt her prey. And they want to own us – and Sinope and the north shore, as well.' Nestor's mouth was a hard line. 'The last time Olympias stretched her talons out towards the north, your father cut them off,' he said to Satyrus. 'Zopryon was her lover.' He chuckled. 'Of course, everyone at the court of Macedon was her lover at one time or another,' he continued.

Satyrus was gazing at Amastris, who looked even more like a Nereid. She was gazing back, the pressure of her green eyes on his almost too intense to bear, like strong sunlight on a sunburn.

Satyrus wanted to touch her curls and see what kept them bound so close to each other.

She smiled at him. 'I like your sister,' she said, as if she had been his friend for millennia, and as if the two of them were alone in the room.

'Me too,' Satyrus said. He ruined the line with some weak giggles.

Nestor put a possessive hand on Amastris's shoulder. 'Amastris will rule here one day. Amastris, this handsome boy is a penniless exile, and you will *not* pay him the slightest attention. You are going to Ptolemy to find a husband – a powerful husband with a fleet.' He said these words with the amusement of a father.

'I know, *Captain*,' she replied. She smiled at Satyrus again.

'Look all you like, young man,' Nestor said. 'She is our greatest asset in this game of thieves, and she is not for you.'

'We're looking for a middle-aged tyrant with a good fleet. Syracusa, perhaps,' the Nereid said. 'I've been raised to it. I can name the rowing positions. I think I'd make a decent navarch.' She laughed and turned her grass-green gaze on Melitta. 'If your brother ever restores his fortune, you'll be in the same boat, Melitta. He'll marry you off to secure his coast.'

'Not if he wants to live through the night,' Melitta said. She reached over and ruffled her brother's hair and met Amastris's eyes. 'Your uncle is not what he appears,' she said.

'If he were what he appears,' Nestor said, 'he'd have eaten you for dinner tonight. But he regrets that someone has the power to show him weak. You two must be gone. The choices are by ship or by caravan. It is your life, young man – which will you choose?'

'I may be a foolish boy,' Satyrus said, 'but I think that if I can make it safely to my father's friend Diodorus, I will be safe. Many of the men I grew up with are among Diodorus's mercenaries.' Even as he spoke, Satyrus relived the last two weeks. He pursed his lips and looked at his sister.

'Will we ever be safe?' she asked, speaking the same thought that bounced around in his head.

Philokles was still silent with anger, hitting his wine cup hard.

Theron put a hand on the Spartan's shoulder. 'I think we're safer by land.'

Philokles shrugged. 'All I have chosen goes wrong,' he said. 'I'm just a drunk.'

Melitta went and stood in front of the Spartan. 'Is that how it is going to be, Philokles?' she asked. 'If you won't think, won't help and keep drinking wine, I'd just as soon leave you here.'

Theron shook his head violently, out of the Spartan's sight line.

Satyrus stepped in. 'Philokles, please help us. You saved our lives again and again the last few weeks. Get us to Diodorus.'

'Land,' Philokles said thickly. 'Let us ride.'

Satyrus turned to the captain of the guard. 'We will go by land. Now, if you will help us. We'll need a mule litter for the slave girl.'

Nestor nodded. 'All is ready, my lord.' He looked at Satyrus's leg, and meaningfully at Kallista, who was still pale and could barely eat.

'You are, all of you, injured,' he said. 'If my lord allows it, I think that you should take the doctor.'

Melitta shook her head. 'I don't like him.'

Philokles shrugged. 'I take your point – drunkard that I am. You think that we need his skills.'

Melitta made a noise and Philokles cut her off. 'Doctors do not grow on trees,' he said.

'May you be safe!' Amastris prayed.

'We will be safe when we have power,' Satyrus said.

'That is not the lesson that Philokles would teach, if he were sober.' Melitta struggled for composure. She looked at her new friend. 'Pardon me, Amastris. Sometimes, I remember that I have no home.'

The other girl gave her a quick hug.

When the hasty meal was over, Nestor summoned Amastris's maids to take her to her own wing of the palace. She hugged Melitta. 'Write to me in Alexandria,' she said. 'You have adventures! I marry some old man with a fleet.' She smiled. Then she frowned. 'Hestia protect you, I didn't mean that you *should* have adventures. Stay safe! Hestia keep you safe, and Artemis, who protects virgin girls.' She blushed, and hugged Melitta again. She was a year older than the twins, but Melitta was a head taller, and Satyrus was taller yet.

Satyrus reached out a hand to her – the bravest act of his life – and she took it. 'You – be safe,' she said, stammering a little, and blushing.

'And you, my lady,' Satyrus said. He kissed her hand, as he had seen Theron do with Kallista.

She giggled. 'My uncle would kill you,' she said, and followed her maids.

She left something hard in Satyrus's hand – a ring. It was quite a ring, made of gold with garnets around a big red stone carved with a tiny, perfect representation of a man with a club and a lion skin – Herakles. He looked from it to her – he'd never held anything so precious.

'Hermes protects travellers!' she called from the doorway. 'But Herakles triumphs!'

PART III

QUENCHING

9

316 BC

Stratokles lay on a couch in the shade of a flame tree and watched the sun set against the towering storm clouds to the north. His mind was on a thousand things, but the beauty of the sunset infected him, and he called for a tablet and a stylus. But all that came to him were snippets of other men's poems and tags of Menander. He laughed.

Lucius, lying on the other couch, coughed and shook his head. 'Not much to laugh about.'

'That's just where you are wrong,' Stratokles said. 'We're alive. Other men are dead, and we, my friend, are still alive.'

'Can't tell you how – how much I appreciate that you came back for me,' Lucius said. His tone conveyed more insult than flattery – his tone told Stratokles that he never expected, once wounded, that his employer would pick him up and fight his way out.

'What a cock-up, and no mistake,' Stratokles said. 'To be honest, I must be responsible, but I cannot see how. Anyway – I like you, Lucius. I'm tired of thugs. You're a gentleman.' He shrugged. 'Not sure why I went back for you, myself.'

Lucius started laughing. 'Oh, fuck, that hurts,' he said, and wheezed. 'So – what next?'

'We heal up. You'll be out a month – more, I expect. I'll be able to hobble about in a week, but it'll be a month before I can exercise.' He shrugged. 'Then back to Athens and fucking Demetrios of Phaleron, who will tell me how I could have done it all much, much better.'

'He's your boss?' Lucius asked.

'You are a fucking barbarian, anyone ever tell you that?' Stratokles laughed and snapped his fingers for wine. A Thracian girl with flame-red hair bustled out on to the terrace, poured his wine and vanished. 'Demetrios of Phaleron is the tyrant of

171

Athens. A scion of Phocion. Friend of Kineas, whose children we just so notably failed to murder.' He sighed. 'An extreme oligarch whose policies will overthrow two hundred years of democratic traditions in Athens.' He raised his wine to Lucius. 'My boss.'

'How does that work?' Lucius asked. 'I don't get much of your Greek politics, but I've read Aristotle, and I have ears. You're a democrat. If he's an oligarch, you're *not friends*.'

'Lucius, if I've learned one thing in my life, it's that in politics there are *no friends*.' Stratokles sighed. 'Look, there's no point in deposing Demetrios of Phaleron if that costs us alliance with Cassander and Athens ends up being sacked. Give the man his due – Demetrios of Phaleron is brilliant, ruthless, the best diplomat of the age. And a passable poet.'

'Poet?' Lucius asked. He took an appreciative sip of the wine. 'Makes my wound pound like the tide on the sea, but tastes like heaven.' He looked up. 'Who owns the redhead?'

'She came with the house.' Stratokles waved his hand. 'Ours for the use, I think.'

Lucius shook his head. 'You Greeks are so rich you don't know,' he said. 'Someday, someone's going to come and take all this away from you.'

'Someone did,' Stratokles said. 'His name was Alexander. And he took our liberty and our way of life and left us a bunch of mercenary wolves in place of a government.' Stratokles shrugged again, sipped wine and watched the red-haired girl return. 'I'll give my life, if I have to, to win my city back her liberty.' The red-haired girl was moving self-consciously, clearly aware of what the Italian wanted. Perhaps unsure of what to do about it.

'I hear a lot about your Alexander,' Lucius said. 'Most people say he was a god. We Latins don't believe in that crap.'

Stratokles raised an eyebrow. 'And you predict the future with the entrails of chickens?'

Lucius laughed. 'We learned that from you Greeks,' he said. 'Hey, girl? Know how to play a flute?'

*

172

Stratokles sat carefully at a writing table and two slaves brought eight-wick lamps for him. The Latin and the Thracian girl were making a fair amount of noise upstairs, which made Stratokles smile. The Latin was like a character in Menander – overblown, comic, larger than life – until he said something like *I've read Aristotle*.

Stratokles rubbed his hands together, sniffed the coriander on his fingers and thought, *It was worth the risk. I need a man I can trust – really trust. Lucius is the man.* He remembered the blood and the noise in the house in Heraklea, and his hand trembled just a little. Stratokles had fought in every battle of the Lamian War, and ten more actions – but fighting the monstrous Spartan in the dark had had an almost supernatural terror to it.

I did it, though.

He watched his hand until the trembling stopped. Then he flipped his wax tablets open and began to write.

Stratokles to Menander, Greetings!

It is too long since we strolled in the Academy or listened to the muses – or booed the chorus at the theatre!

Our mutual friend has sent me to virtual exile on the Euxine – a business trip that threatens to take me until the end of my life and perhaps a little longer. I have had many opportunities to observe the trials and triumphs of life, and I have to say that there have been many trials and few triumphs.

It seems to me that I have arranged for all the grain our friend will need, despite some business matters that did not go as planned. I would appreciate it if you would tell him from me that the first shipments of grain should arrive with this letter.

I also wish to note that some political matters have not fallen out as our mutual friend might have hoped, or expected. There is a rumour here that Heron, the ruler of Pantecapaeum, attacked Tanais, a little city on the Bay of Salmon, and destroyed it – but failed to catch its rulers.

Still, they are children, and many years must pass before they play any role in the grain trade!

In addition, it came to my notice while doing business here that Dionysius of Heraklea is much more powerful in the region than is commonly asserted in Athens, and Heron, for all his bluster, has no hope at all of seizing Heraklea or Sinope. That said, we might consider a slight change in policy. After direct observation of his business practices, I fear that our partner in Pantecapaeum may prove difficult and even dangerous. Heraklea, on the other hand, impressed me with efficiency and culture. And a great deal of available grain.

I further wish that our mutual friend might understand that our partner in Pantecapaeum and our friend in Thrace may not be friends for ever. I wish to have a free hand to decide where we may turn in such an event, but I will await advice. In the meantime, shipments of grain from Pantecapaeum, Heraklea and Sinope should all be arriving at the Piraeus in the next moon. Think of me as they send their cargoes ashore.

I sit under a beautiful moon, after a sunset of such splendour that I could wish for your stylus and your muse-led wits rather than my own. Write and tell me of what passes under the gaze of grey-eyed Athena.

He read through the tablet, struck out a bad phrase here and there, and rewrote his work twice. Then he took ink and papyrus and began to copy fair. He was so intent on his task that he didn't notice when Lucius came up behind him in the dark room.

'Mars, brother! You'll lose your sight.' Lucius's voice made Stratokles twitch, but his hand was steady, and his writing was beautiful.

The Latin bent over the table. 'You're either a scribe or a fucking aristo, Stratokles.'

Stratokles sat back and rolled his shoulders to loosen the muscle. 'Guess which.'

Lucius sat on a folding stool and handed the Athenian a

174

cup of wine. 'Is that *the* Menander? The playwright? Mars and Venus, brother, you are the friend I've always wanted. Look at this fucking house! Ours for the asking. You know Menander?' He winked. 'I could learn to like this.'

Stratokles couldn't help himself. 'We grew up together,' he said with a shrug, and put a finger to the injury on his nose. 'Hermes, my face hurts.' He laughed. 'I used to be accounted a handsome man.'

'Bah,' Lucius said. 'Now you look like a hero. Or a villain. A man of action. Not a Greek aristocratic pansy.' He was reading over Stratokles' shoulder. 'You didn't like Heron any more than I did, eh?'

Stratokles shook his head. 'I don't like people reading over my shoulder.'

'Pardon!' Lucius backed away.

Stratokles shook his head. 'No. no. Just as a matter of course. Much of what I write is – secret. I expect that eventually I'll share it all with you. But I'm not there yet.' He smiled to take the sting out. 'If you choose to stay with me. Anyway, no, I thought Heron was a brilliant fool – more of a danger to us than an ally. I want Demetrios of Phaleron to tell Cassander to ditch him.' He touched his nose again and winced.

'Are we giving up on putting the two children down, then?' Lucius asked. He was naked, and he smelled of lavender oil and cloves – a real improvement, Stratokles thought.

Stratokles shook his head. 'No. It's a foolish order, and probably an ignoble one – but I've done worse for Athens and I will again. We need Heron's grain. The children must die. I have other resources in place. I've already mobilized several.'

'They don't call you Greeks wily for nothing,' Lucius said. 'You have so many spies that you keep some just lying around for emergencies?'

Stratokles sighed. 'Yes.'

Lucius laughed. 'You need to get your sausage wet, friend. And get drunk. And live a little. I'll send you the redhead. She's open-minded.'

Stratokles shook his head. 'I'm not really so far gone that I need a barbarian to get me laid,' he said.

Lucius laughed, a full-chested roar that shook the tablets on the table. 'Mars and Venus, friend. You're a cool one, and no mistake.' He got up. 'If you don't want her—' He hobbled across the room, his wounded leg barely able to support his weight. But he stopped at the stairs. 'What you said – about secrets – you'll keep me on?'

'Absolutely,' Stratokles said.

'I'm yours,' Lucius said.

I know, Stratokles thought. But he didn't say it out loud. He just took a sip of wine and ran his eyes over his letter one more time.

10

They rode through the night and all through the next day, changing horses every hour and changing the mules on the litter twice. Nestor sent them with guides and a pair of soldiers – Philip and Draco, and Sophokles, the physician. He was a poor rider and a constant drain on their spirits, complaining at every turn of the road.

They crossed the plain south of the city, riding through long rows of farms kept by Mariandynoi helots. The farmers watched them from their fields, and once a woman sitting on a bench in front of her hovel spat as they rode by. Their guides were Mariandynoi. Satyrus wondered if either of the pair – Glaucus or Locris – felt the same way.

They crossed the Kales River around noon and immediately they were climbing into the mountains of Bithynia. The guides were stunned at their speed and began to join in complaints about the pace from Sophokles and Kallista. By the time the sun had begun to set, even the soldiers were complaining.

Melitta teased them. 'You conquered Persia?' she asked, riding up close. 'You must have walked.'

That kept them going another hour. They camped on a feeder stream of the Kales, with the whole valley of the river at their feet and the sea just on the edge of the horizon in the distance.

Philokles made the entire ride in silence. He dismounted without a word, took out an amphora of wine with some ceremony and emptied it while Theron glowered at him. Then he fell asleep.

The twins watched, hurt but unable to express themselves. After a while, ignored by the soldiers, they made up a bed, put Kallista into it and fell asleep themselves.

The next morning they were a mass of stiffness, aches and pains. Kallista was awake, and complaining, but Theron got them all in the saddle an hour after sunrise.

'Do you understand that if we're caught, we'll all be killed?' he said. 'Everyone get that through your skull – or your hangover,' he added with a glare for Philokles.

'No one could keep that pace you set yesterday,' Draco grumbled. 'Give us a rest.'

'Stay behind if you need rest,' Theron shot back. 'Leave the litter and ride. We have to move faster!'

They rode an hour before Kallista began puking. She lost her breakfast and proclaimed that she couldn't ride another stade. 'My thighs are bleeding!' she cried.

Theron rode up to her and pulled her off her horse. He put her across his saddle. 'Ride!' he ordered.

At the noontime halt, Draco offered Satyrus a bite of garlic sausage. 'Your tutor intends to ride at this pace all the way to Eumenes?' he asked.

Satyrus gave the Macedonian a tired grin, happy that the man had decided not to stay mad. 'My sister and I can keep this up for days. This is how we ride, on the sea of grass.'

Philip shook his head. 'I'd rather die,' he said. He shrugged. 'But I won't. Just you watch. I won't die.'

Kallista lay on the patchy mountain grass and sobbed. At the end of the halt, Theron picked her up like a sack of grain and put her across his lap to ride.

'Fucking hills is full of thieves,' Draco said, watching the hillsides around them as they rode.

'We're going too fast for thieves,' Philip said. He nodded at Theron. 'Athlete knows his business. At this speed, any bandit what sees us gets left in our dust.'

'We need a watch tonight,' Draco said. He drew his knees together, favouring his thighs and trying to sit back on his horse's haunches. 'Prince, you willing to take a trick? I hear how you're a swordsman.'

Satyrus looked away, unsure – as he always was with these men – whether he was being mocked or praised. 'I'll take a watch,' he said.

Draco pushed his gelding up next to Theron. 'Three watches? You and the Spartan, me and the boy, and Philip and the guides?' He looked at the Athenian doctor with thinly disguised contempt. 'And you, Sophokles? Can you fight?'

'I'd rather not,' the doctor said.

'That's fucking helpful. You helots – what about you?'

The guides, Locris and Glaucus, looked at each other. 'We're not allowed weapons, lord,' Locris said.

'Can you throw a javelin?' Draco asked.

Both men nodded, after some looking around.

'Sling?' Philokles asked. It was his first sensible word in a day.

Again, both helots looked at each other for some time. After a minute, Locris nodded. 'We can sling,' he said.

Draco and Philokles shared a look. Draco nodded back. 'Why don't you two boys make yourselves slings at dinner?' he said. 'And I'll give each of you a javelin and my warrant that you can carry it.'

'Thank you, lord,' Locris said to the Macedonian. Everyone was a lord to the helots.

At dinner, the two of them sat by the fire, unweaving a net bag for the twine and then making slings. They wove the fibres – braided them, really – so fast that Satyrus couldn't follow their motions.

Philokles watched him watching. 'In Sparta, a helot can make a weapon out of anything,' he said. 'The Spartiates keep disarming them, and the poor bastards never really give up.' He stroked his beard. 'Ten slingers will beat a hoplite every time.'

Satyrus wanted to say 'You're sober!' but he knew that would be the wrong thing to say. 'I haven't had a lesson in weeks,' he said, as if requesting a lesson from your tutor was an everyday thing.

Philokles gave him a tight smile. 'The last three weeks have been nothing *but* lessons, boy.'

Sophokles, the doctor, produced a wineskin. 'Here!' he said, offering the skin to Philokles. 'Have some wine!'

Philokles swatted the skin away. 'Rat piss.' He produced his own. 'Want some?' he asked. He looked dangerous; he thrust the skin at Satyrus like a swordsman.

Satyrus sat on his haunches, balancing his forearms on his knees. 'No,' he said. 'I don't want any wine. And I'd rather you didn't have any, either.' His voice broke as he said it. Philokles scared him when he was this way. 'Why do you have to be like this?'

'Wouldn't you like to know?' Philokles said, and started drinking.

The doctor watched the Spartan, his face full of anger. Later he offered wine to Melitta, and she glared at him. 'Keep your wine,' she said. Sophokles stalked off.

Still later, when they were all in their blankets, Philokles started to sing. Satyrus didn't know the tune, but it sounded martial, with a strong beat. The big man was by the fire, dancing, stomping his feet to the rhythm of the music that he sang. The postures of the dance looked like pankration, and then they looked like swordsmanship, and then they looked like marching. Philokles' dancing was beautiful, and he danced on, singing as his own accompaniment.

'Fucking Spartans,' Philip said.

'You people ought to do something about him,' Sophokles said.

Later, just before the Dog Star set, the Spartan sat suddenly, like an olive shaken from the tree, and burst into tears.

It was a long night.

'You look glum, brother,' Melitta said. She didn't look glum. Riding freed her, somehow, and she wore her freedom on her face when she had a horse to ride.

'Thinking of Harmone's golden sandals,' he said. 'She had four pairs. Now she's been sold. She was the head of the tyrant's wardrobe – a real job, doing something she liked. Where'll she go?'

Draco laughed. 'Any brothel will be happy to have her, lad. She loves the game.'

Satyrus shook his head with adolescent vehemence. 'She'll be a whore!'

'Aphrodite's tits, boy! Begging your sister's pardon, of course. But are you in love with her? She'll land on her feet.'

'Or her back,' Philip said with a leer.

'I think what my brother is saying,' Melitta said primly, 'is

180

that she might just possibly want more out of life than sweating under the likes of you.'

That reduced the two Macedonians to silence for twenty stades.

The Athenian doctor laughed, later. 'They've never considered the possibility that women might be human,' he said. 'Good for you!'

'Why does he applaud every time we fight among ourselves?' Satyrus asked his sister.

She laughed. 'You've been to Athens?' she asked.

Satyrus made a show of receiving a blow. 'Of course!' he said.

Just after the noon halt, they met a caravan coming the other way. Two Heraklean merchants with salt and alum and a consignment of lapis lazuli on forty donkeys made up the convoy, with ten paid guards, two of them wounded.

Theron stopped their group at a wide point in the twisting mountain trail and pulled them all to one side so that the donkeys could pass in single file.

'Have a fight?' Philokles called.

One of the merchants rode over. 'The next pass but one is full of bandits – old soldiers.' He looked at the group, and the two girls. 'Best ride back with us. They'll kill you for the women.'

Philokles loosened his sword in his scabbard. 'Have any wine to sell?' he asked aggressively.

The man shrank back a bit from this display. 'I might find you a skin,' he said. He thought that he was being threatened – it was obvious from the way he looked up at the hillsides.

Theron glared at Philokles. Philokles paid no attention. He paid a silver owl for a skin of wine, an unheard-of amount, and the merchant beamed with friendship. 'Drink it in good health!' he called.

Theron drew his sword while Philokles' attention was on the merchant, and cut the skin right out of Philokles' hand, leaving him holding the neck. The wine made a gurgling noise as it poured out into the dust.

'Get down and lick it, if that's what you want,' Theron said.

There was no warning. Philokles launched himself from the back of his mare on to the back of Theron's mare, and the two of them went down on the far side of the horses in a tangle of limbs. Philokles landed on top and got in two vicious blows at Theron's head, breaking his nose so that blood fountained and Satyrus's nose hurt in sympathy.

Satyrus edged his horse closer, but a Macedonian arm blocked him. 'Let 'em fight,' Draco said. 'The Spartan bastard has it coming. Besides, I want to see this.'

Theron, broken nose and all, gripped Philokles' arms and began to force the man off his chest. He managed to raise his own hips, an amazing feat of strength, and then he rolled and tumbled and suddenly he was free. Dust flew as if they were dogs fighting, and Satyrus saw Theron get a fist in Philokles' hair, and then there was a sickening thud as Philokles landed a heavy blow on the Corinthian's head.

'Ten gold darics on the Spartan,' Philip said.

'Shouldn't somebody stop this?' Sophokles asked. The doctor was amused.

The Macedonians ignored him. 'Done. You're an idiot.' Draco turned to Satyrus. 'Here – you're a prince. You hold the money.'

Theron was on his feet with the Spartan's hair in one hand. He'd taken three heavy blows and his face registered pain, but now he stepped in, grabbed a hand and suddenly, as if by magic, he had Philokles kneeling in the dust, one arm behind his back.

'Submit!' he ordered.

'Fuck yourself!' the Spartan spat.

'I'll break your arm,' Theron said, and put some pressure on the joint.

Philokles roared with rage and kicked back with his right foot. For all that he was off balance and in pain, it was a shrewd blow, but Theron had not competed at the Olympics for nothing – he loosed his hold, rotated his hip and avoided the blow and then replaced his hold, all as if giving a lesson. This time he jerked the Spartan's head up and his right arm down.

'Submit,' he said.

'Or what?' Philokles said. Despite the pain in his arm socket, he managed to roll his own hip and land an elbow in Theron's gut. He broke the hold and rolled away. When he rose, he could barely raise his right arm.

Melitta slipped off her horse. 'If you two don't stop, one of you will be too injured to fight bandits.' She planted her hands on her hips.

'If he will not submit, his drunken foolishness will kill all of us,' Theron said. 'Act like a man, Spartan. I'm not going all out, you fool of a Spartan. I could pull your arm right out. Shall I? Or do you have to pretend that you can take me?'

'All I hear is talk,' Philokles spat, and came forward.

There was a flash and a sound like a tree branch snapping in the wind, and then only Theron was standing. He was shaking his right hand back and forth. 'Apollo, lord of games!' he said. 'Fucking Spartans!'

Philokles lay unconscious in the dust. Sophokles dismounted in weary disgust and went to look at him, glaring at Theron all the while.

Locris and Glaucus had eyes as round as kraters.

The last guards from the caravan hurried away, exchanging money as they went and laughing nervously. Satyrus handed Draco all the money he had put in his hat.

It took both Macedonians and Theron to get the Spartan over his horse, and they made poor time until Philokles recovered consciousness. Satyrus watched him, and met his eye, and smiled.

Philokles winked.

Satyrus suppressed his urge to say something. Instead, after ten minutes had gone by, he raised a hand. 'Halt!' he said. He slipped down from his horse and, with some help from Philip, they got Philokles on his feet. He walked his horse for some time, without speaking, and then he climbed painfully on to the beast's back without using his right arm, and then he rode with his face in his horse's mane.

They were a silent crew until they made camp.

'Can you manage a watch?' Theron asked Philokles. Every head in the camp turned.

'Why don't you stand it with me?' Philokles asked.

'I will,' Theron responded.

Philokles looked around. 'I want the doctor on my watch,' he said. His tone said that he was looking for trouble.

'I don't stand watches,' Sophokles said. 'I need a clear head.'

'Fine,' Philokles said. 'I'll just kick you every few minutes.'

Satyrus wondered why Theron did nothing to interfere, but he didn't.

'I want to say something,' Satyrus said to his sister.

She shook her head emphatically. 'Theron has some idea of what he's doing. Let him do it.' She rubbed her chin. 'There's something going on – Philokles and Theron. And the doctor. I don't get it.'

'Philokles is up to something, and Theron is in on it,' Satyrus said. He didn't get it, either, and he went to sleep thinking about it.

It was Philokles who woke Satyrus for his watch. His blankets were warm, and his sister had been pressed comfortably against his back, and the mountain air, even in summer, had a bite to it. But he rose, took the offered spear and sat by the fire with Draco.

Draco nodded. 'You've done this before, lad?' he said.

'My mother made us stand watches on the sea of grass,' he said. 'I'll go and look at the horses.'

'Good lad,' the Macedonian said.

Three or four similar exchanges passed the whole of the watch, and then Satyrus was in his cloaks again, and asleep.

The next day they awoke to find that both of the guides were gone – fled or deserted, it was hard to know. They'd taken the javelins they'd been given and nothing else.

The two Macedonians were for riding after them. Philokles shook his head.

'How would we find them?' he asked. 'They were our guides. They'll know the tracks and the hillsides. We'll stick to the path.'

They rode down and down into a deep valley, where they halted for lunch. The two Macedonians were hyper alert, but nothing came at them. They ate standing by their horses, and after they had all switched to fresh, they rode on. Kallista moaned quietly. She was on her own pony now, and she looked so miserable that no one would mistake her for a beauty. The doctor watched the hillsides endlessly.

An hour from the valley, Draco rode up past Satyrus and pushed his horse close to Theron's. 'I just saw the flash of metal on the hillside,' he said. 'Right up above us.'

'I saw it too,' Philokles said. He turned to Theron. 'Since you're in charge, Corinthian, you can tell us – what are we doing?'

Theron looked at them. 'We're four competent fighting men and a boy who knows which end of the blade to hold – and a girl who can kill if she has to. If they're foolish enough to attack us, we kill them. Bandits are all cowards.'

Draco grunted. 'Not here they ain't, athlete. Here, they're like as not veterans of Arbela and Issus, or the fight between Athens and Macedon.'

'The one Macedon lost?' Sophokles asked. 'We call it the Lamian War.'

Even Melitta, who didn't like the doctor, was surprised by the venom in his voice.

Philokles tried to rotate his right arm in its socket and his face clouded with pain. 'Any more good ideas, Corinthian?'

Theron smiled at him. 'Since you're sober, why don't you tell *us* how to proceed, Philokles?'

Philokles was still. He held Theron's eye steadily, and after a pause that went on too long, he said, 'I would rather not.'

Theron looked around. 'I'll go first. As soon as they start shooting, we ride for it. We have fresh beasts and we can outdistance pursuit. If the twins would care to give us some archery, we'd be the better for it.'

Melitta grinned. 'I thought that you'd forgotten me.' She took her bow out of her gorytos.

'Put that away,' Philokles said. 'Don't let them know we're on to them. Draw when they come for us, not before. And Melitta – don't let yourself be taken. Understand? I've been pig-headed – I should have turned us back when we met the caravan.' He looked at the ground and then at Theron. 'Don't let the children be taken.'

'Speak for yourself,' Philip said. He sat straighter. 'Let's see how many we can put in the earth, eh?'

Draco nodded, but his lips were pursed.

Theron shook his head. 'If we go back, we're certain to die,' he said. 'If we get through the bandits—'

The doctor spoke up. His face was white. 'I don't think that this is well thought. What if there are very many of them? Let us go back. We can still take ship from Heraklea—'

Theron didn't even turn his head. 'We're not going back.'

'This is foolishness!' the Athenian said. 'Are you insane? We can ride back up the trail a day and go down the Gordian passes with a real caravan! Just turn back!' Spittle flew when he spoke.

'Enough talk.' Philokles looked at Theron.

Satyrus was *sure* that there was some exchange in that look.

Then the Spartan tucked his heels into his girth and prodded his gelding forward. 'I'll go first. My arm isn't worth a crap and I might as well eat the first spear.' He had the set look of a man committed to a course of action.

'We have armour,' Satyrus said.

Draco was dismissive. 'If we put it on they'll know we know they're there.'

Satyrus shook his head. 'We stop, and Melitta sneaks away to have a piss – in a way that can be seen from above. Get your cuirass on under your chlamys while you pretend to have a dump.'

Philip laughed and looked at Satyrus as if reappraising him. 'You may make a general yet, boy.' He ruffled Satyrus's hair.

Theron nodded. 'Halt!' he said. He turned to Melitta. A little too loudly, he said, 'Very well, *princess*. Go and relieve yourself.'

With a credible imitation of a shame-faced girl, Melitta climbed behind a rock to their left and they could hear her muttering to herself as she fumbled with her multiple chitons.

Satyrus had a small thorax of scales from the armour shop. He got off his horse on the downhill side, his heart pounding, and got to his pack animal with a minimum of fuss. His thorax was wrapped in goatskin. He unrolled it on the ground, put the skin back in the basket and pulled the thorax on. He laced it up the side himself, annoyed at the sound he made. Then he slipped his sword belt over the whole and pulled his cloak over it.

'This is insanity, boy.' Sophokles scrambled up. 'Call your sister over and we'll slip away. That Spartan is going to his death and taking us all with him.'

Satyrus shrugged twice under his armour, trying to get the chest to fit. It felt tight. He unwound one of the laces and redid it. He didn't know what to say to the older man, so he ignored him. He was afraid enough without help.

The man walked away.

The two Macedonians made a pretty good show of wagering on which of them could piss the farthest. Then they complained about how long women took, and then they argued over their wager until Philip threatened to piss on his partner.

Satyrus's brain finally realized that they were going to fight. It hit him between breaths, and his chest grew tighter, as if the armour was still laced too hard.

He met Philokles' eye.

'Scared, boy?' Philokles asked.

Satyrus chose nodding, as being better than squeaking.

'Me too,' Philokles said. He flashed a grin. 'Still, I won't kill anyone this way.' He winced as he got his left arm into the armour he had picked up. 'Pull it tight, boy,' he asked.

'That doctor is scared worse than me,' Satyrus said.

'Hmm,' Philokles answered.

Satyrus got Philokles into his armour while Kallista complained about her thighs, horses and the world. Satyrus didn't think it was an act. The doctor sat on his gelding, glaring around him as if every rock could vomit bandits.

And then Theron yelled at Melitta for being a weak-livered bitch, and she came out from behind her rock, and they were up and moving.

Satyrus could scarcely breathe. He tried to keep his right hand off his sword hilt and his left hand off his bow. The trail was steeper here and the sharp bends were so numerous that sightlines were less than a stade on each turn. There were no trees at all, just scrub and rock and summer meadow grass and more rock.

'Any time now,' Philip said, about one breath before an arrow hit Philokles between the shoulders.

The arrow didn't penetrate the bronze scale, and Philokles gave a shout and pressed his gelding into rapid motion.

Behind Satyrus, the doctor's horse panicked and he tried to turn the beast on the narrow road, blocking the track.

Satyrus looked all around him, saw an arrow coming in and flinched away, drawing his own bow. His horse leaped forward and he gave it its head, and the beast pushed right past Philokles and he was in the lead – not a position he wanted. Two arrows hit his horse – *thump-crump* – and the beast's legs collapsed, spilling Satyrus on to the scree of the trail so that he rolled clear of his dying horse and fell over the edge. He fell the length of his own body and all the wind was driven from his lungs as he hit. His head rang.

Time passed as he tried to focus his eyes. He could hear shouts on the trail above him, and then a clash of iron, or bronze. And then he had control of his lungs – and then, a few seconds later, control of his limbs. He was lying on a rock shelf a little wider than his body. He got to his feet and started collecting arrow shafts, as his fall had dumped the contents of his quiver. He grabbed ten or twelve and thrust them back into his gorytos, feeling the press of the fighting above him.

Melitta shouted something and he heard the buzz of an arrow.

He went to the end of the shelf and got a foot up on a projecting boulder, his head throbbing. As soon as he could look over the trail, he saw Theron standing over Philokles. He had his cloak over his arm and his sword in his fist, and a man lay in the trail. Philokles was clutching his knee in the gravel. Draco and Philip were back to back down the trail, with a knot of men around them, and Melitta sat between them, still mounted, shooting arrows.

Satyrus didn't think anyone had seen him. He pushed

himself over the edge of the trail and stood up, just a few horse-lengths from Theron. Then he nocked an arrow, forcing himself to go slowly, to get the nock on the string. He breathed in deeply, raised his bow, only then letting himself look at the desperate fight twenty feet away.

He chose one of Theron's opponents. The men were in armour, but Satyrus had all the time in the world to aim at the back of the man's thigh – an easy shot at twenty feet. The man's leg went out from under him immediately, and he rolled and fell.

They all had armour – Satyrus was just taking that in when Theron, freed from one opponent, feinted a cut and kicked his other opponent in the shield, so that the man went over backwards. Theron kicked the man between the legs and then finished him with a short thrust to his neck, already looking around.

Theron's other opponent made the mistake of thinking that Philokles was out of action. When he stepped across the Spartan to attack Theron's rear, Philokles' left hand locked on his ankle like a vice and Philokles scissored his feet up and grabbed the man's waist and pulled him down. Theron stepped back over the Spartan as if they had designed the whole move as a dance and cut the man's throat.

Satyrus had another arrow on his string. His sister shot and missed – an archer standing on the hillside. He ducked. But he didn't see Satyrus, and Satyrus could still see him. He shot on instinct, a little high, a little wide to the right for the breeze.

He watched his arrow fly, thrilled as it arced and vanished into the bandit's side. Satyrus saw it all, but he didn't see the archer who shot him. There was a blast of pain, like falling into cold water, and then he was out.

There was a slave market in Krateai, but it wasn't much, just a red mud-walled barrack with a heavy wooden door. The town only existed because the mountain roads divided here, the northern road going down the valleys to Gordia, while the southern road went past Manteneaon and then turned through the great pass into the plains of Anatolia, roasting in heat at this time of year. A small parcel of slaves – probably taken by thieves, claimed by no lesser being than the tyrant of Heraklea, or so the Macedonian factor said – was bound for Gordia.

Satyrus had a bruise on his side as big as his head, and the centre of it was livid and leaked pus where the scale armour had deflected the arrow's point – mostly. His ears still rang from time to time and twice he put down his heavy load to vomit, and the guards hit him with their canes and laughed at his feeble attempts to puke.

Melitta wanted to kill them – both of them. She was carrying the heaviest load of her life, a basket full of grain purchased with threats in a village lower down the pass. It was, in fact, about half the food that their little caravan had. And the water was running out. Springs were zealously guarded in these steep defiles, and the petty lords and bandit kings who ruled from their eyries charged heavily for each beaker of water.

But their new owner apparently had a soft heart. He stopped to get them water and a night's sleep, and bought a quantity of food. Then he offered his whole parcel for sale – Satyrus and Melitta, brother and sister, right on the edge of adulthood, and both startlingly attractive, both virgins – to a pair of Greek merchants. They also offered the other girl – also a beauty, you could tell, despite her pale face and her complaining. Satyrus was naked and had a bad bruise on his side and the girls were clothed, and men in the crowd shouted for both of the girls to be stripped. One of the soldiers in the caravan's escort used the stock of his riding whip to knock a heckler unconscious, and that was the end of the salacious catcalls.

Men bid – some bid high, for the twins – but the Greek merchants had cash and a seal from some great power down in the green valleys, and the men of the town glared lustfully at the girls – and the boy – as they were shackled and led away.

One of the two merchants was a Spartan by his way of talking. He was the worse for wine, even at the height of the sun, and he probably paid too much for the children, for his partner, a Boeotian, glared at him until their little cavalcade rode off down the south fork. No one thought to ask how the Greeks had happened to have so many horses, or why the merchant's caravan guards went with the Greeks.

'Was that necessary?' Melitta asked Theron after they had cleared all possible onlookers.

Theron was still calming Kallista. At some point she had gone from his enemy to his lover, and she had shared his blankets almost every night on the road since the fight with the bandits. She seemed as infatuated with him as he was with her – but even the pretence of a slave auction had driven her into a state not far from madness.

'Theron is not listening,' Satyrus said. His skin was burned a deep brown from days of riding and days of walking naked in a pack of slaves. His feet were harder than they'd ever been before, but the first day had been agony for him, and he still had an angry red mark on his left arm where the arrow had gone right through his bicep, and the wound in his side, while not life-threatening, hurt when he breathed heavily.

The soldiers had cooperated to make his journey as easy as possible, but the charade as slaves had been necessary to pass the town. He'd had to carry a load like a slave, and that had inflamed his side and put knots of pain deep into his back. The load had been as light as possible, but he couldn't be empty-handed without appearing different and negating the whole disguise.

He had muscles in his shoulders that he'd never had working in the gymnasium, and his chest was broader.

'I did not enjoy pretending to be a slave,' Melitta said. 'So – we're free. Did you worry that we might not ever get free, brother?'

'I worry about everything now,' he said. 'Yes, I wondered what would happen if bandits hit us again. We'd be slaves for ever.'

Philokles swayed on his horse. 'To some extent,' he said, 'we're all slaves.'

He had taken a cut in his leg in the fight and Theron had given him wine for the pain, and now he was drinking as hard or harder than before his fight with the Corinthian.

Satyrus was indignant. 'I didn't see you walking naked in the sun, *tutor*. I saw you drink wine in the shade, though!'

Their Athenian doctor laughed aloud, a nasty laugh. 'Ditch him,' he said. 'He's a drunk.'

That brought no reply, and they rode in silence while the sun sank.

There was an old Persian station house on the road just south of Geza, a tiny hamlet that had probably existed to serve the needs of the Great King's messengers. But a Macedonian veteran and his local wife kept the station house, and they camped in the yard and the woman fed them on beans and bread.

'We should fight,' Theron said, after dinner. He drank some water from the well and handed the dipper to Satyrus. 'You're bigger and stronger.'

Satyrus shrugged. 'Whatever,' he said.

Theron hit him. Not hard, but hard enough to hurt. 'That was the response of a child,' he said. 'I am your athletics coach. You are Satyrus of Tanais. Not a slave, and not an idiot. Act the part.'

Satyrus of Tanais sat for a moment in the mud by the well. He thought of thousands of replies – bitter, sarcastic, cutting, outrageous.

'You're right, of course,' he said after a pause.

'Good for you. Let's go.' They walked past some low scrub where the animal pens were, to a cropped lawn kept by goats, and stripped. Melitta followed them.

Satyrus hadn't fought anyone since he took the wound in his arm. He took his guard carefully, and the bigger man circled him, and Satyrus found himself viewing the fight from a very different perspective than he had the first time the two of them had faced off on the sand in Tanais. Most of all, he couldn't see it as a game any more. People could die in a fight. He knew that now.

Theron had a long reach, and he stepped in and grabbed with both hands. Satyrus blocked and kicked, and after a pair of exchanges, he was down in the grass, a recent contribution from the goats warm and liquid on his thigh, and his left side and shoulder screaming with pain.

'Don't be so cautious,' Theron said. 'Be confident.'

'Easy for you to say,' Satyrus grunted as he twisted around one of the Corinthian's long legs.

Theron tipped him and put him down while he was trying to dodge all those kicks.

He got up and tried again. This time he moved in close, trying to get inside his coach's reach. He tried to be confident and got a mouth full of grass for his efforts.

He got up and they began to circle again. He decided to go for a hold.

That ended quickly.

They went ten falls. Satyrus's new muscles served him well, in that he could continue, and for a blow or two he could match the bigger man. But experience told every time, and weight, and reach. And pain. His shoulder wound hurt all the time.

'Let's just practise some holds,' Theron said after the last fall. 'You are tiring, and we are boring your sister.'

So they stood in a line and practised guards, and Theron moved back and forth between them, making simple attacks so that his hands and feet could be blocked. When all three of them were breathing hard, he picked up his canteen from his clothes and handed it around.

'I never meant the two of you to remain on the road so long,' he said. 'But Draco was sure we were followed until we crossed the mountains. We should have gone south after Bithynia.'

Satyrus shrugged. 'We'll live,' he said, and a little happiness began to grow in his heart. He turned to his sister. 'We will live!'

They had barely spoken in days, and they shared a long embrace.

Melitta kissed him on the nose and turned to Theron. 'We have to stop Philokles from drinking,' she said. 'For good.'

Theron hung his head. 'He – he and I – it is hard to say this to a child. He thinks he failed you, and then – he feels I have spurned him for Kallista.' He looked at both of them. 'And there is more to this than meets your eyes. Trust me. And – trust Philokles.'

'I do,' Satyrus said.

'I can see that you have a plan,' Melitta said.

Theron wiped sweat off his face with his forearm. He paused a moment and said, 'Perhaps I have, at that.'

Melitta turned on her brother. 'Kallista wasn't for you, anyway. Why not Theron? And Philokles drinks because he is cursed, not because of a silly girl with big eyes.' She turned back to the Corinthian, and Satyrus thought that she was getting more and more like their mother.

'Tomorrow, as soon as we have ridden over the pass,' she said, 'we will get off our horses all together, and search all the baggage, and destroy every drop of wine in the packs.'

'That's a start,' Theron said. 'Until we reach a place that will sell wine.'

'One step at a time,' Melitta said.

'Sister, I love you extremely,' Satyrus said. He felt as if he was putting on his former self, and the last days were a skin that was falling away.

She hugged him again. 'I love it when you say things like that,' she said. She was serious, so he used the embrace to pin her and tickle her ribs until she boxed his ears.

Neither of them saw Theron grin.

The next day, the soldiers said that they'd seen bandits ahead. Theron stopped them beside the road where trees gave cover and sent Philokles with Draco forward to scout. Then the rest of them pulled every pack off every mount, opened all the baskets, collected all the wine and dumped it, until the last amphora but one leaked its red contents into the purple dust.

The Athenian sat on his horse and laughed his laugh at them. 'He's a wine-bibber!' he said. 'A cistern-ass! You'll never get it all.'

Satyrus ignored him and went back to searching. He was appalled to find how many jars of wine were secreted in the packs. Almost every armour pack had something. But he watched the Macedonian soldier, again amazed at the skill with which he searched.

Philip had an amphora to his mouth. He took a long pull and handed it to Satyrus. 'Last grape until we get the Spartan off the sauce,' he said.

Satyrus drank some and passed it to Melitta, who drank a little and handed the jar to Theron, who took a long pull and gave it to Kallista, who finished it.

'What about me?' the Athenian asked.

'You can have some when you start helping, *doctor*,' Philip said.

They loaded all the panniers and baskets and bundles, tied everything down and rode on.

The fun started when they made camp. When Philokles began his search, he at least pretended discretion, but then he went on with increasing desperation.

'It's all gone,' Melitta said. She walked up behind him, as he searched one of the armour baskets.

Philokles turned on her, his eyes wild.

'All gone, tutor. Every drop. It's two days' travel back to the last town and ten days forward. We all love you and we'll stand by you.' She offered her hand to him.

Satyrus watched with a lump in his throat. Theron and the Macedonians pretended to be doing something else. The doctor watched with the insolence of a man watching bad theatre.

Philokles made a grunting noise. After a few minutes it became sobbing. Then he was silent.

The silence lasted a day.

On the second night, Philokles got wine from somewhere, and he drank it. Then he was sick – violently sick. So sick that he puked his guts out.

The doctor looked him over, sprawled on his blankets. Fastidiously, he listened at the Spartan's chest and felt his neck and wrist. He pursed his lips and shook his head. 'Nothing I can do,' he said. 'When a man tries to kill himself with drink, he will.'

Theron glared at the Athenian and made Philokles drink salt water until he puked again. Then he sat with his arm around Philokles.

Nobody slept much.

The next day Philokles lay on the ground, barely breathing. The Macedonians walked around the camp, muttering, and Satyrus threw javelins and spent too much time squatting beside the Spartan.

'Is he actually trying to kill himself?' he asked Theron.

Kallista came and sat gracefully by them. 'I tried to kill myself once,' she said, in a matter-of-fact voice. She looked at the doctor. In an almost teasing voice, she said, 'And I almost died of poison, once.'

Theron looked at both of them, as if considering something.

Melitta came and sat by the slave girl. 'Where did he get wine?' she asked.

Theron shrugged. 'We missed something.'

Melitta looked at Satyrus, who shook his head. 'Philip and Draco went through every basket,' he said. 'I watched them. They've been trained to search.'

Sophokles came up, laid the back of his hand on the Spartan's cheek and shrugged. 'You missed something. I told you that you would.' Then he went and sat near Kallista. He laid two fingers lightly on her cheek, but she shook him off and he smiled at her.

Melitta watched Theron's face as he caught the physical exchange. He was angry.

Satyrus watched the three of them. There was something between the girl and the doctor. Theron was now the girl's lover. Satyrus rubbed his chin, and his wandering eyes found his sister's. Somewhere in the contact there was a spark of illumination.

'Of course,' Satyrus said, his eyes and his sisters locked in silent communication, 'we never searched your packs.' He raised his eyes from Melitta's and looked at Sophokles.

'I'm not denying that I have some wine,' Sophokles said. 'It's medicinal, and for my own consumption.'

Theron shot to his feet. When the Athenian attempted to move, one of Theron's long arms pinned him. 'Open his pack,' he said.

'I like the Spartan,' Kallista said. She seemed to be speaking to the air.

'I don't care who you like, slave,' the doctor said.

'I don't want him to die,' she said. 'Heal him.'

Satyrus opened the doctor's bedroll. The outer layer was a pair of goatskins. Inside were two chlamyses, with a cup, a very elegant leather bag, and a pair of amphorae wrapped in wolf skin. The amphorae were themselves beautiful – black, with red and white figures dancing.

'Keep your hands off those, boy!' the doctor said.

'Bring them here,' Theron said in a voice of bronze.

Satyrus obeyed.

Kallista looked at Melitta for a long time. Melitta met her gaze. Satyrus watched the two of them while he walked back, and felt disoriented. He was surrounded by secrets – even his sister had them. They were staring at each other.

The doctor was staring at Kallista. Then he looked up. 'Be careful with those,' he said. 'Chian wine – the best!' His voice had an odd inflection.

'Make him drink it,' Kallista said. Her voice had a dreamy quality to it.

'Shut up, slave girl,' the Athenian spat. 'This has gone far enough.'

Melitta shook her head. She had stopped staring at Kallista. 'Have you chosen your side, girl?' she asked.

The slave girl looked away.

'Now or never,' Melitta said.

Kallista looked at Satyrus. Satyrus understood it all in a moment of inspiration, as if Athena had whispered the whole plot in his ear. He drew his sword and stood by the slave girl. 'We can protect you,' he said.

Melitta gave him the look of a sister who is glad her brother has a brain. 'Choose!' she said imperiously.

Kallista hung her head so that her hair covered her face. 'He's no doctor. Not really.'

'You're a liar, whore,' the Athenian shot back.

'He kills for money.' Kallista's voice was calm.

'I don't have to listen to this filth,' Sophokles said. He began to squirm in Theron's grip.

'Kallista has chosen her side, traitor,' Melitta said. 'You tried to poison us, and her, and now you've poisoned Philokles.'

Sophokles looked around. 'Foolishness. You may be a princess, but you have the soft head of a woman. I saved her when she was poisoned, and—'

Theron tightened his grip, inspiration written on his face. 'The Spartan saved her,' he said carefully. 'You put on a show. I didn't see it at the time.' He nodded at the recumbent Spartan. 'He did. He saw through you, you bastard.'

'How long have you known?' Satyrus asked his sister.

'About two minutes,' she answered with a hard smile. 'Kallista told me with her eyes when you got the wine.'

'She's in on it too, then,' Draco said. He drew his sword.

'Yes,' Kallista said. She sighed. 'They offered me money and freedom.' She looked around.

'I meet the offer,' Melitta said proudly. 'You'll be free in days, Kallista.'

It was all too fast for Satyrus. He looked back and forth.

'You have no proof,' the doctor said. 'This is insane.'

'I don't need proof,' Draco said. 'Fuck, he must have been planted on the court. Who sent you, you ass-cunt?' His sword flashed as he hit the Athenian with the bronze hilt.

The doctor – if he was indeed a doctor – was unprepared for the leap to violence, and he went down clutching his head. Theron jumped him and pinned him again in a classic possession hold – head back, arm locked and near breaking.

'Stop,' Theron said. The doctor tried to struggle, and there was a burst of activity as he did something, but whatever his surge of wriggling meant, it failed to overcome Theron's impassive grip.

Satyrus and Melitta exchanged another glance. Satyrus got up. 'Would you like to live?' he asked.

The doctor couldn't even look up. 'Of course,' he said. If he was aiming for arrogance, he missed. He sounded worried – terrified.

Satyrus tried to look at Kallista. 'Save Philokles and I will let you live. Betray your employer and I will let you go.' He looked around. Theron nodded, and after a minute Draco shrugged.

'Fair enough, prince. But I can get it out of him anyway.'

Draco smiled with just half his mouth. 'Fucking traitor. Fucking Athenians, eh?'

'Too right, mate,' Philip said. He had a small, very elegant knife in his hand – steel, a slot of brilliant blue in the sun. 'Give me a minute – just a minute – and I'll see to it that we know all he has to tell.'

'Swear by Zeus Soter that you'll let me go!' Sophokles said.

'I swear by Zeus Soter that I will do nothing to harm you, and that, if you betray your employer, I will let you go free,' Satyrus said.

'Make your friends swear!' the Athenian said.

'I swear that I will order that you not be harmed.' He looked around. 'For one day.'

'I swear,' Theron said.

'I swear,' Melitta said.

'I swear by Zeus Soter that you *deserve* to die and I hope it comes to you soon,' Kallista said. 'But I swear not to harm you. Today!'

Philip and Draco shrugged at each other. 'Listen, prince. This is a big thing. If he betrayed our tyrant, his life is forfeit. It's not your place—'

Satyrus stood his ground. 'I understand you. But I'm here, and Dionysius of Heraklea is far away. A day's grace. That's all I swear to. He can have a day.'

Philip looked at Draco. 'I dunno—'

Draco nodded. 'We swear by Zeus Soter not to harm him for one day.'

Philokles gave a snort.

'There you have it, Athenian. Save him. Or die.'

The doctor took a ragged breath. 'In the leather satchel. There's a small black pot – that's it. Give him some with water.'

Satyrus mixed it himself while Theron kept the Athenian pinned.

'It won't work for an hour,' the doctor squawked. 'You going to pin me the whole time?' He shook his head. 'This whole thing is messed up. He should be dead. You should all be dead.'

No one bothered to answer him. Draco heated water and Satyrus added the orange powder at the doctor's directions. Then he spooned it into the Spartan's mouth.

'Now for your employer,' Draco said.

The Athenian shrugged. 'Stratokles – he hired me.' The man looked around. 'Now let me go.'

Melitta shook her head. 'Draco, how long has this man been at the tyrant's court?'

Draco shrugged. 'Two months? Since the Feast of Herakles, anyway.'

'How long has Stratokles been in Heraklea?' Satyrus asked, mostly just to show that he knew where his sister was going.

Philip glared. Draco glanced at the twins with open admiration. 'You two are good at this,' he said.

Sophokles looked disappointed. Satyrus almost had to admire his courage – he himself would be gibbering in terror at this point. But his hatred for the man grew. It was as if he was flaunting his contempt for them. 'Stratokles hired me,' he said, 'long before either of us came to Heraklea.'

Melitta spat, as Sakje did when showing contempt. 'You lie,' she said.

'You've all sworn your oaths,' the man said. 'So let me go. I've told you all that I have to tell.'

Satyrus tried to imitate Philokles' delivery. 'It's a pretty piece of sophistry,' he said, 'to pretend that after weeks of betrayal and multiple murder attempts, we could be in the wrong by breaking *your interpretation* of our oaths.' He shrugged. 'I admire you for trying, though,' he said.

Damn, that was good, right to the sarcasm.

'Stratokles,' the doctor insisted. 'That's all I know.'

'He knows more than that,' Kallista said.

'You're dead, you know that?' Sophokles said. 'You are fucking dead. All of you, really. Tyche preserved you this far – I've never been so unlucky in all my days as the last three weeks, and this drunk fuck on the ground somehow managed to keep me away from your food at every turn until I figured out that it wasn't all luck. So fuck yourself, Kallista. I know you know how. In fact, I might tell them what you did for me. Does Theron know how many of us you service?'

Theron turned at her, and she hid her face.

'Maybe that will serve you right, you faithless bitch,' Sophokles spat.

'He knows who employs him – us,' Kallista said. She sighed. 'I hate him. He scares me. I wish you would all kill him. But he knows.' She looked around, as if she expected the little valley to sprout enemies. 'He kills for Olympias. And yes – Theron, I've fucked him when he made me. I serviced them all, when ordered. I know.'

'You're dead,' Sophokles said again. 'I hope that you choke on the next dick you suck, harlot. *Porne*. Sperm bag.'

Theron was grunting with anger. His face was splotchy with rage, and his great hands clenched and unclenched.

Satyrus kicked the Athenian in the head. It was a hard kick, and he probably broke the man's jaw.

'That's for sowing poison with your mouth, traitor.' He stepped away. 'A man like you demeans all men.'

'Let's just waste him,' Draco said. He sounded happy to do it. His blue knife flashed.

Philip turned to Satyrus. 'Listen, lad,' he said. 'You can't play this game by the rules. Draco's right. Let's kill him.'

Sophokles suddenly realized that he'd gone too far. He could barely talk, but he managed. 'No – you swore. Listen to me – she's a fool! By saying that name, she's written all your death warrants and probably mine as well. We don't say that name. You swore. Let me go.' His mask of contemptuous bravery was gone.

It was very instructive for Satyrus, at a certain level. He was learning something about the game of ruling, and something about what bravery was. And evil, if that was the word.

'Don't do it,' Philokles whispered.

'What?' Satyrus asked. He looked at the Spartan, who was white as alum leather and whose eyes were rimmed in red. But they were open.

'Oath – gods.' Philokles' head, which had only been raised a fraction, sank back on to his blanket.

Satyrus turned to his sister. 'Lita?' he asked.

'Mama would gut him like a salmon,' she said in Sakje.

'Our father would let him go,' he answered.

After a moment, she nodded. 'Yes,' she said.

Satyrus stepped up close to the traitor. 'Listen,' he said. 'You think that you will have revenge on this girl, on me, on my sister.' He could see the man's rage, his helplessness, his intention to harm. The man had taken to killing because he was weak. Satyrus could see that.

It was very instructive.

Satyrus leaned close. 'I say – let the gods decide who lives. I give you, a proven oath-breaker, and your foul mistress, to the Furies.' He took a breath. His chest felt heavy, and there was something in the air. Moira. 'Give him a horse,' Satyrus said to the soldiers.

Draco looked uncomfortable. 'But—'

Theron nodded. His hands were trembling, but his voice was steady. 'Give him a horse. None of his kit.'

Minutes later, the Athenian galloped away.

They didn't move again the next day. Satyrus held the two Macedonians until the sun was as near to the height of the oath as he could. Then he let them go.

'You're close to Eumenes,' Draco said as he mounted. 'I can smell his Greek breath from here.' He reached down and clasped hands with Theron, and then Satyrus. 'You'll go far, boy – if the gods do as they ought.'

'In which case, we'll kill that Athenian bastard before to-morrow night,' Philip added. 'Travel well!'

The two Macedonians cantered away into the afternoon, and left the party poorer by a great deal of foul language and humour. Satyrus missed them immediately. But Philokles was better, if very quiet.

The next morning, Philokles was pale, but he could rise from his blankets, and after some sweating he managed to mount his horse. Two days later they were descending the mountains towards the great plains of the south. On the third day, the twins cornered Philokles while he loaded his packs in the morning.

'We've come to thank you,' Melitta said.

'And to beg you to stay with us,' Satyrus said. 'We're sorry we took so long to figure out what you were doing with the doctor.'

'I had to be sure,' Philokles said. He shook his head. 'I used to be very good at that game, children. I thought I could catch him and turn him, or catch him and use him to spot other trouble. We outsmarted each other.' He looked down. 'Wine doesn't help. I drank when I should have been sober, and I almost lost – everything.'

'Crap,' Melitta said. 'You saved us! Let's not have any sudden drama, master. Without you, we'd be poisoned.'

'I have humiliated myself. I am no use to you and I cannot possibly teach you after my – my—' The Spartan's voice cracked. Something like a sob escaped from him.

'Get on your horse and ride at my side,' Melitta said. 'I am Srayanka's daughter and Kineas's, and you swore to protect me. Please continue to do just that. No excuses.'

'That is just what I mean,' Philokles said, in something like his normal voice. 'You can order me like that because I have failed you so often. I cannot teach you ethics. I can only teach weakness.'

'I smell horseshit,' Melitta said. 'You protected us from the doctor.'

'Bah!' Philokles said, turning away. 'Drunkard's luck. I'm a fool. I cannot play this game any longer.'

'Stop!' Melitta called. 'Listen, Philokles. You have saved our lives fifty times. We owe you more than we can repay.' She shook her head. 'Get us to Diodorus and you may have your release, if you demand it.'

Philokles stood with his back to them. 'Very well,' he growled.

Satyrus looked at his sister as if he'd seen a ghost. 'You sure you know what you're doing?' he asked.

'No,' she said. 'I'm doing what I think Mum would do.' She put her head on his shoulder. 'What's *wrong* with people? Aphrodite and Ares, brother. Kallista acts as if fucking is the only way she can talk, Philokles drinks to forget things he had to do for *us*, Theron thinks that he's a failure because he didn't win the Olympics – the only ones who acted like adults were the soldiers, and they're a smug pair of thugs.'

Well put, sister. 'I think being an adult is harder than it looks,' Satyrus said.

Melitta stifled a giggle.

'Mind you,' Satyrus said, 'the hardest part still seems to be staying alive, and I think we've got that part licked.'

Melitta shook her head. 'Don't tempt the fates,' she said.

Four days later, they found Eumenes' army. Or rather, it found them. Just a few minutes after they completed the descent of the last range of hills into the plains of Karia, their group was surrounded by armoured horsemen.

'Aren't you kids a little far from home?' the officer asked. He had a red and grey beard sticking out from under a silver-mounted Thracian helmet, and a tiger-skin saddlecloth.

'Diodorus!' Melitta screeched. She flung her arms around his heavily armoured torso.

He flipped his cheekpieces open and tilted the helmet back on his head. 'What's happened?' he asked.

'Home's gone,' Satyrus said. 'Heron killed Mum.' Even now, two months on, his voice choked when he said it. 'Upazan took the valley.'

Diodorus looked as if he'd been punched, and after a moment, he wept. And the word spread among his patrol, and they heard shouts of rage, and men rode up to embrace the twins. A big blond man, almost as old as Diodorus, dismounted and drew his sword. He knelt in the dust and held the hilt out to Satyrus. 'Take my oath, lord,' he said.

Melitta dried her eyes on the back of her hand. 'Don't be silly, Hama. Diodorus is your captain.'

'Kineas was my chief,' Hama said. 'And then Srayanka. Now you.'

Andronicus the Gaul, grey at the temples and still lean, came and crushed her in an embrace, and Antigonus, still big and blond, gave her a Gaulish bow. He was Diodorus's *hyperetes*, and he had a fortune in gilded bronze armour on his back and rode a heavy Nisaean charger.

All of the dozens of other men she knew who came up and knelt, or grasped their knees, or touched their hands, looked prosperous. Carlus, the biggest man either of them had ever seen, slipped off his charger and came to kneel beside Hama. He, too presented his sword. The sword was hilted in silver and had a pommel of crystal. War had been kind to the hippeis of Tanais.

They weren't just weeping for Srayanka, either. Most of these men had had wives and children – even small fortunes – in Tanais, and now they were gone.

Diodorus shook his head. 'This won't be good for morale,' he said. 'Hades, twins, I wish I'd known you were coming with this sort of news.' He shook his head. 'I know it seems paltry beside the loss of your mother, but we have a battle – today, tomorrow, soon.' He pointed across the plain, where a dust cloud rolled north. 'Antigonus One-Eye, with Alexander's army.' Then he saw Philokles, sitting quietly with the baggage animals. He went over and embraced the Spartan. 'I missed you,' he said.

'I broke my oath,' Philokles said. 'I have killed.'

Diodorus shook his head, the stamp of his tears still plain on his face. 'You worry about the strangest things, brother.' He put his arms around the Spartan again, and unaccountably, Philokles began to weep, for the first time in days – weeks, even.

Melitta rode up close to her brother. 'It will all be better now,' she said. 'Just watch.'

Satyrus shook his head. He was looking at the dust to the north. 'This is going to be a big battle,' he said.

Melitta glanced from her beloved Philokles to the dust. 'So?' she asked.

Satyrus watched the dust, which seemed to be stuck in his mouth as well as his eyes. 'Off the griddle and into the fire,' he said quietly.

11

Eumenes' camp sprawled across several stades of scrub and red dirt, and the smell hit them while they were still a stade away – raw excrement, human and animal, from forty thousand people and twenty thousand animals, a hundred of them elephants. Tents of linen and hide stretched away in disorderly rows, intermixed with hasty shelters made from branches. Every tree on the plain was gone, cut by thousands of foragers from both sides to fuel thousands of fires. The smoke from the fires rose with the stench.

'That's the smell of war,' Diodorus said. 'Welcome to war, lad.'

'Antigonus's camp looks bigger,' Satyrus said.

'He has a bigger army. He has every Mede cavalryman in the east. Asia must be empty – he's got Bactrians! And Saka!' Diodorus watched the enemy camp. 'See the patrol going out? Those are Saka, with some Macedonians for stiffening.'

The enemy camp was so close that Satyrus could see the flash of gold from the Saka horses.

'Why are the Massagetae fighting for my enemies?' Melitta asked. 'Someone should speak to them.'

Diodorus shook his head. 'You are your mother's daughter, lass. Why don't you just ride over there – whoa! That was what passes for humour around here.' He had a hand across her chest. 'Honey bee, I'm taking you to my wife, and she's going to look after you. Greek maidens don't belong in army camps.'

'I am not a Greek maiden,' Melitta said. 'I am a Sakje maiden.'

Diodorus took a deep breath and looked at Philokles.

'They're growing up,' Philokles said. He spread his hands. 'I couldn't stop them.'

Diodorus gave his friend a look that indicated that he held the Spartan responsible. 'Let me get you children under cover,' he said.

Philokles rode up next to Diodorus. 'They've both killed,' he said. 'They've fought and stood their ground.'

Satyrus felt as if he might swell from the praise.

'They aren't children,' Philokles said.

Diodorus let out another breath. 'Very well. Satyrus, would you care to come with me?'

Satyrus nodded politely, and the cavalcade rode on.

They passed through two rings of sentries to enter the camp. The outer ring was cavalry, small groups of them spread wide apart, a few mounted and the rest standing by their horses. Closer in, spearmen stood in clumps where there was shade. Eumenes was being careful.

'Where are the elephants?' Satyrus asked.

'The opposite side of the camp from the enemy,' Diodorus replied. 'Antigonus made a grab for them last year – nasty trick. We only just stopped it. We can't put them with the horses – horses spook. So they have their own camp where it's safest.'

'May I see them later?' Satyrus asked.

'I'll take him, lord,' Hama said.

Diodorus nodded. 'Listen, twins. I'm a strategos here – a man of consequence. I love you both, but we're a day or two from the largest battle since Arbela and I won't have much time for you. Understand?'

'What's the battle about?' Satyrus asked.

Diodorus looked at him. 'You really want to know?'

Satyrus nodded. 'I know that Eumenes is one of the contenders for Alexander's empire, and Antigonus One-Eye is another. I know that Ptolemy is backing Eumenes because Antigonus is a bigger danger to Aegypt.'

'Then you know more than most of my cavalrymen,' Diodorus said. 'We're fighting for the treasury at Persepolis and the allegiance of the Persian nobles – winner take all. This is the Olympics, boy – the winner of this battle should be able to reconquer all Alexander took. Unless—'

'Unless?' Melitta asked.

'What am I, your war tutor? Unless the price is too high, and the battle wrecks both armies.' Diodorus squinted south, into the dust. 'Eumenes and Antigonus have each beaten the other. Eumenes is a superb general, but he forgets he's not a Homeric hero. Antigonus is not a superb general, but he tends to get the job done and his preparations are always excellent. Now – is that enough? I have several thousand men to see to.'

'Of course!' Melitta shot back. 'Do you think we're foolish?'

'I'll see to them,' a handsome blond man said. He made a barbarian bow from his saddle. He had a pair of gold lion fibulae and gold embroidery on his cloak and a sword that seemed to be made from a sheet of beaten gold. He was covered in dust.

'Crax!' Philokles said. 'It has been a long time!'

Crax bowed again, a broad smile dimpling his round Getae face.

'You look prosperous,' Philokles said.

'I like gold,' Crax said. He drew his sword and presented the hilt to Melitta. 'I was sword-sworn to your mother. Now I will swear to you – both of you.'

'That is a beautiful sword,' Satyrus said.

'You like it, lord? It is yours,' Crax said.

Philokles laid a hand on Satyrus's shoulder. 'Gift it back to him,' he whispered. 'If you are his lord, he *must* give you anything you ask.'

Melitta put her hands on either side of the sword hilt. 'You are our man and our knight,' she said, using the Sakje words.

Satyrus reversed the sword and handed it back. 'It pleases me for you to have this,' he said. 'It is one of the finest swords I've seen. As fine as Papa's.'

Crax took the sword back with pleasure. He turned to Diodorus. 'We waited all night, Strategos. We were not discovered – neither did the gods give us a challenge. We collected a dozen prisoners and returned by the secret way.'

Diodorus nodded. 'Get some rest. Crax commands my scouts.'

Melitta leaned forward. 'May I ask a question, Uncle?'

Diodorus nodded, although there were other men waiting for him under the awning of a striped tent. 'Go ahead,' he said.

'Where is Ataelus?' she asked.

'Off with Leon, searching the oceans for lost money. Perhaps in the Hesperides fetching golden apples. Not here, where I need him.' Diodorus slipped off his big charger, and a swarm of slaves took his horse and began to take off the tack. As soon as his feet hit the ground, men fighting for his attention surrounded him.

'Take them to Sappho,' Diodorus ordered. Then he was lost in his staff.

Crax kept them mounted with the wave of a hand. 'This is his command tent,' he said. 'He sleeps in our camp. Come!'

They rode off, unnoticed in the masses of soldiers, servants and slaves who filled the camp. They passed wide streets and narrow streets, stalls selling produce and wine and a hide-covered brothel whose occupants were as noisy as the animals in the street outside, much to Satyrus's embarrassment and his sister's amusement.

The camp was larger – and better populated – than most of the towns that passed for cities on the Euxine. Satyrus tried not to stare as they rode, although there was more to contemplate than you'd ever see in a town – there were no walls and no courtyards, so that every business was plied in the open. Boys squatted in front of tents, polishing bronze helmets or putting white clay on leather corslets to make them whiter. A sword-sharpener hawked his talents to a pair of Argyraspids, men in their fifties with shields faced in solid silver and inlaid with amber and ivory. Phrygian infantrymen stood in groups having just left an inspection, and a squadron of Lydian lancers cantered by, shouting and laughing. Their officer wore a garland of roses and he bowed to Melitta and then blew her a kiss. A porne knelt in the mud of a street, servicing a client while he dictated orders. A pair of dirty children sold sweets off a broad leaf.

The twins drank it in as if they had been starved. Philokles told an abbreviated version of their adventures to Crax, and introduced Theron, who seemed as stunned as the children at the spectacle around him.

The Getae man pointed to a magnificent pavilion in scarlet

and yellow that towered over every other tent in the central area. 'Banugul,' Crax said. 'Remember her?'

Philokles laughed. 'It's rather like muster day for old friends,' he said. Satyrus couldn't tell whether he was joking or not. But his attention drifted when Kallista threw back the shawl on her hair and immediately drew whistles and more vocal attention. She smiled on every admirer.

Theron watched her. 'Going into business?' he asked, his voice tense.

She pouted and flipped her shawl back over her head.

Philokles shook his head. 'You can't transform a porne into a wife overnight,' he said. 'And I believe that she is the slave of my mistress.'

Theron glared at the Spartan. 'Ahh, the philosopher is back,' he said. 'Perhaps you would like to give me some sage advice?'

'I would,' Philokles said. 'But you wouldn't take it. I scarcely ever take my advice myself – but that doesn't mean it isn't good.'

'Did you find all this wisdom in your amphora of wine?' Theron spat.

'There, and elsewhere,' Philokles returned, but the comment hurt him, Satyrus could tell. 'She will not do well with jealousy,' Philokles said.

'And you are an expert with women, I find!' Theron said. 'Really, it is a pleasure to have you sober!'

'Theron, shut up,' Melitta said. 'Philokles, please don't be offended. Theron is as happy to find you returned without your ill-daimon as we are. He has forgotten his place and will apologize. Theron, if you ever wish to lie with my serving maid again, you'll apologize.'

Theron shook his head. 'You are going to be a formidable woman, Melitta. Mistress. Philokles, I'm sorry.' He extended his hand.

The Spartan took it. 'As am I.'

Kallista glared at all of them from under her shawl. 'I was only playing,' she said.

Melitta nodded. 'Ask my permission next time,' she said. 'Your actions reflect on me.'

Satyrus watched it all with admiration, but while they were dismounting, he said, 'I thought that you were against slavery.'

'I am,' his sister agreed. 'But if you are going to do a thing, do it well. Kallista needs a mother. Since she doesn't have anyone but me, I'll do it as her owner.'

And then they were led into a tent with cool, dark panels of blue-green canvas.

Sappho – a family friend since they were born – reclined on a couch, fanned by a pair of children. She sat up as soon as they were escorted in.

'Children! I have wine and cakes for you. I heard that Srayanka is – dead. I'm sorry to be so blunt – my wits are astray and I'm an old woman.' She spoke at random, her arms wrapped around both of them.

Satyrus had forgotten her smell – a wonderful smell of incense and musk and flowers. No one in the world smelled like Sappho, and she was as beautiful at forty-five as she had been at twenty-five, her beauty the outward form of a hard-won happiness. Her shoulders were held high and her skin soft, her face lined with both laughter and pain, but more enhanced by the lines than aged, especially when she smiled. Her eyes were unchanged, large and liquid.

They both kissed her and allowed themselves to be held while slaves bustled around them, and then they were taken away to another tent to be bathed. Satyrus was mortified to be bathed by women, as if he was a child, but he was *clean* for the first time in thirty days. He found his riding boots and a fresh chiton on a stool and he put them on.

Melitta had beaten him to it, although she seemed embarrassed to be dressed in a long woman's chiton and gilded sandals. To Sappho, she said, 'I cannot ride like this. Please, domina – I am not a Greek woman.'

Sappho shook her head. 'You are while under my tent, my dear,' she said. 'There is likely to be a battle. Women dressed as men will be in danger.'

Melitta's brow furrowed. 'I can be raped to death as effectively in this kit as in my trousers,' she shot back.

'Where did you learn such things?' Sappho asked. 'War is awful – but no one is going to be raped to death here. Sold into slavery is more likely.' She raised an eyebrow. 'I would know.'

'From my mother,' Melitta answered. But she had lost the initiative. Sappho, who had endured the sack of Thebes, had survived rape and worse, and Melitta had no answer for her calm.

'If you wish to go riding,' Sappho agreed, 'I will see to it that you dress appropriately. In the meantime, you will be a Greek maiden for a while. And that slave of yours?' she said, reaching out a long white arm to point at Kallista. 'She is a hetaira, not a maidservant. Why do you have her? She's worth a few talents.'

'It is a long story, despoina,' Satyrus said. 'Melitta – inherited her from Kinon, Uncle Leon's factor in Heraklea. We promised to free her.'

Sappho crooked a finger at the beautiful girl – more beautiful still, now that her hair was clean and she had on a clean gown. 'Come here, my beauty. Can you dress hair?' she asked.

Kallista nodded.

'And perfumed oil? I imagine you know how to apply it?' she asked.

Kallista looked at the ground under her feet.

'Your mistress came into my tent looking like a cross between a barbarian warrior and a ragpicker. Do you have any excuse?' Sappho asked. She had the other girl's wrist between her fingers.

'Please, mistress! We were in disguise! People tried to kill us!' Kallista's voice was breathy.

'Hmm,' Sappho said. She looked at Melitta. 'I can give you a far better maidservant and have this one sold. She'd benefit herself – with that body and voice she'll be free before she's twenty.' Sappho's look at the girl was not unkind. 'You'll never purchase your freedom as a maid, dear.'

'We promised to free her,' Satyrus said. 'We owe her.'

Sappho nodded sharply. 'Very well. We'll discuss this later. Satyrus, you are to go with Crax to see the elephants. Melitta will stay with me. I see that I have a great deal to catch up on.'

'Despoina,' Satyrus said in his new-found voice, 'we are not children. Please, Aunt, don't be offended, but we've spent a month being chased and poisoned. We've killed men and seen – things.' He kept his voice steady by force of will. 'Melitta is not a child. Neither am I.'

Sappho reached out and took their hands in hers. 'I hear it in your voices, dears. But it is exactly because you are not children that I must be so careful, especially with your sister. She could be married – any day. And her reputation will matter to her.'

Melitta stamped her foot, which didn't do her case any good at all.

Satyrus, feeling like a traitor, slipped out of the complex of tents with a cleaner Crax by his side. 'It's not fair,' he said to Crax, and to Philokles, who was waiting by the horses, 'It's not fair,' he said again. 'She's always been allowed to ride and hunt. She's braver than I am!'

Philokles gave him a hard look. 'I doubt it, boy,' he said.

Crax shrugged. 'Greeks hate women,' he said. He shrugged again. 'I don't know why. Afraid, maybe.' He smiled. 'We'll break her out, lad. But listen. Lady Sappho – well, she's the only *wife* in this camp. There's some soiled flowers of various shades, but she's the only *wife*. She needs somebody to talk to. Hear me?'

Satyrus shrugged.

'Want to see some elephants?' Crax asked, vaulting on to his mare's back.

Satyrus banished thoughts of his sister. 'Yes!'

The elephants were huge. Not only were they the largest animals Satyrus had ever seen, they were many times larger than anything in his experience – horses and camels. They had long, wicked tusks that looked like curved white swords and they made noises that all but panicked his horse.

On the other hand, their eyes had a curious intelligence. 'Are they as smart as a horse?' he asked Crax.

'Fucked if I know,' the Getae replied. 'Let's ask a mahout. Hey – India-man!' he shouted at a wrinkled brown man sitting in the shade.

The elephant-keeper stood from his cross-legged squat with a foreign elegance and walked over. 'Master?' he asked.

'Are they intelligent?' Satyrus asked.

'Yes,' the man said, with an odd sing-song inflection to his Greek. 'Very smart. Smarter than horse or cow or dog. Smart like person.' He patted a big cow-elephant on the shoulder. 'Like person, they don't make war until man teach them.' He shrugged. 'Even then, they won't fight unless they have men on their backs.'

Hesitantly, Satyrus patted the heavy skin of the animal's shoulder. It was criss-crossed with scars. 'She has been in battle?' he asked.

'Since she was five years. Now she has fifteen years. Ten big fights and ten more.' The mahout beamed with pride – a sad pride, Satyrus thought. He spoke to her in another language – liquid and rather like a paean, Satyrus thought. She raised her head.

'I tell her – battle comes.' The India-man shrugged expressively. 'Men teach them war – but when they make war so much?' He shrugged again and smiled. 'Like a drunk man with wine? So is an elephant trained to war, and a battle.'

'War has the same effect on some men,' Philokles said.

'Yes!' the India-man said. 'Like elephants, man can be taught to love anything – even murder.'

'You're a strange one, for a soldier,' Crax said. He grinned at Philokles. 'Long-lost brother of yours?'

The India-man had a name, which proved to be something like Tavi, so Tavi was what they called him. They spent most of the afternoon roaming the elephant camp, meeting the beasts. None of them seemed very warlike, despite their size.

'Let them smell you,' Tavi said. 'Let them see you. Then they know you on the day of battle.'

Satyrus submitted to being smelled, and in some cases prodded, by elephants. He fed them nuts and grass, delighted by the manipulations of their trunks and the play of intelligence in their beady little eyes. 'I want to be a mahout,' he exclaimed with twelve-year-old enthusiasm.

Tavi put him up on the older cow, and he rode on the

beast's neck with the India-man behind him. He was allowed to carry the goad, and he tapped the old girl, called Grisna, on her shoulder and she turned obediently.

'This is power,' he said to Philokles and Crax when he had jumped down from the beast's neck.

'More proof, if any were needed, that war is the ultimate tyrant,' Philokles said. 'These beasts are as intelligent as men.' He shook his head. 'More intelligent, in that Tavi says they won't make war without men.'

Crax bit his lip. 'Always you say war is so wrong,' he said. 'Why? How do you stop an invader? How do you keep your freedom? By talk?'

Philokles made a clicking noise with his tongue and nodded to the Getae. 'That's the root of the matter, isn't it, Crax? You must train every man in the world out of his love for war at the same time – if you leave just one, he'll drag the rest of us back to Ares' bloody altar.'

Crax glanced around, as if looking for another speaker. 'So I'm right?' he asked.

Philokles looked at the elephants. 'Too right.' He turned away.

Dinner was a subdued affair, punctuated by Satyrus's excited descriptions of the elephants and of Tavi, the mahout, who had made a lasting impression on him and on Philokles. But Sappho was attentive to her husband, and Diodorus was far away. He would listen with a smile on his face to an elephant story and then his eyes would drift off the speaker and he would eat absently.

'Is it upon us?' Sappho asked, as the roast kid was cleared away.

'I'm sorry,' Diodorus said. 'I'm not happy with the arrangements for my wing. Excuse me for a moment.'

He rolled off his couch and went to the door of the tent and called one of his officers. They could all hear him speaking, and the brief replies, and then he was back. 'That's better,' Diodorus said when he returned.

'Will we fight tomorrow?' Philokles asked.

'Yes,' Diodorus said. 'Crax pulled in a dozen prisoners today, and Andronicus brought in as many yesterday. They all say the same thing. Antigonus will form his line of battle in the morning.'

Sappho bit her lip. But when she spoke, her voice was light. 'Then we must get you to sleep early, my dear. You'll be up in the dark.'

'You are the best soldier's wife in this army,' Diodorus said fondly.

'Faint praise indeed,' she returned. 'Considering that I'm the only wife around.'

'What of the children?' Philokles asked.

Diodorus shook his head. 'They'll stay in camp, of course. I expect that we'll fight on the plain to the north. They'll be safe enough here. Shall I find you a corslet, Philokles?'

'No, thanks. I've never accustomed myself to the idea of fighting on horseback, and I don't care to stand among strangers – Asiatic strangers, at that. I'll stay in camp with the children.'

Theron nodded. 'As will I, Strategos. Without offence, this is not my fight, and I have equipment only as a hoplite.'

Diodorus looked at the two of them and smiled. 'I could base one hell of a *taxeis* on you two,' he said. 'Theron, you're like a second Philokles. I'll bet you're a terror in the scrum.'

Theron shook his head. 'I've never done it,' he said. 'I've drilled with the ephebes, and I've fought men, but I've never stood my ground like my father at Chaeronea.'

Philokles smiled grimly. 'You haven't missed a thing,' he said.

Sappho's steward came in and bowed deeply. 'Master, there are more and more men waiting outside, asking for the strategos.'

Diodorus wiped his mouth. 'Excellent meal, my love. I must go and listen to Eumenes' fears and worries.'

'I remember him as a first-rate commander,' Philokles said.

'He is. But the Macedonians hate him for not being Macedonian. One of the reasons he hired me is to have a Greek officer on whom he can rely – but even that has made trouble. The Macedonians dislike me – all of us, really.'

'They haven't changed much, have they?' Philokles asked.

He and Diodorus both smiled, sharing some memory. Satyrus thought that it was like dining with the gods, to hear such things. They discussed the great Eumenes the Cardian as if he were just someone they knew, like a playmate!

Theron sat up on his couch. 'I heard some things I didn't much like today,' he said. 'About Greeks. About Eumenes.'

Diodorus looked around and lowered his voice. 'You notice that I came back to my own regiment to eat and sleep – that we have our own guards, and we're a little separated from the rest of the army? It's that bad, friends. If we lose tomorrow – if we even *look* as if we're losing, this army will disintegrate. The idiots in the Argyraspids would rather kill Eumenes because he's a Greek, than beat Antigonus who hates them.'

Sappho drank wine carefully, held her cup out to a slave to have it refilled and spoke slowly. 'You have never spoken so directly, husband,' she said. 'Should I make preparations?'

Diodorus rubbed his beard. 'It's never been so bad. I suspect that One-Eye is putting bribes into the Argyraspids but I can't figure out how he does it. I keep telling Eumenes to parade Banugul and her brat to quieten the hard-liners—'

'That's Banugul who claims to have been Alexander's mistress, and Herakles her son,' Sappho said, with a significant look at her husband. 'He's just your age, or a little younger, and the very image of Alexander.' She smiled, but her eyes did not smile. 'She herself is unchanged.' To the twins, she said, 'Banugul is the inveterate enemy of Olympias. Her son Herakles threatens everything Olympias aims at.' She shrugged. 'She should be your ally.'

Diodorus spoke over his wife as if she hadn't made a sound. 'But he won't. Says that he's not going to run his army through a child. Yes, Sappho. There's going to be trouble. In fact, I'm pushing us into a battle to see if we can beat One-Eye before the Macedonians assassinate my employer.' He shrugged. 'All in a day's work.'

Sappho summoned her steward. 'Eleutherius? Collect a string of horses and pack animals and have us packed and ready to move by first light. Leave the tents standing and all their contents. Just pack the clothes and bedding and what we'd need to live, eat and move fast.'

Diodorus got off his couch, leaned over his wife and kissed her. It was embarrassing for the other men in the room, because it was a lustful kiss, and it went on for too long. When he broke off, she slapped him lightly. 'I'm not a flute girl,' she said.

Diodorus kissed her again. 'No, you are the best staff officer in this camp. You just come with certain other benefits. I'm off. I may join you later and I may be up all night.' He glanced around the tent and lowered his voice. 'I've given the boys a rally point – in case of the worst. It's a stade behind the gully – the gully that's south of here. Philokles, you should get with Crax and see that you know the spot. May I rely on you to get the hippeis women and children there, if it all goes bad?'

Philokles was eyeing a wine cup. He rubbed his chin. 'Yes,' he said. 'That's a big responsibility.'

'You've handled bigger,' Diodorus said. He took a purple and dust-coloured Thracian cloak from a slave and swung it on to his shoulders.

'Go with the gods,' Philokles said.

Diodorus gave a sketchy salute and went out of the dining tent.

Sappho rolled off her couch. 'Bed – right now, children. We'll be up before the cock crows and in sensible clothes for riding.'

Satyrus looked at his sister. 'We're good at riding,' he said.

Melitta looked triumphant. 'I know it's wrong to hope we lose!' she said. 'But – I'm already stifled. I don't want to be a good Greek maiden. A *kore*.'

A few minutes later they were on their sleeping couches, listening to the bustle of a dozen slaves packing all around them. Each of them thought it would be hard to get to sleep, and then they did.

12

Satyrus saw the sunrise, already dressed and in boots, with his corslet under his cloak and a broad straw hat tossed back over his shoulder. It was a spectacular sunrise, pink and grey and red and gold, and he kept glancing at it while he helped Theron pack the two baggage mules they had brought all the way from Heraklea.

All around them in the semi-dark were men moving into the battle line about eight stades from the camp. The deployment was carefully organized, although Satyrus watched it critically, thinking how it might be done better. Men gathered at the heads of their camp streets by group, and then the groups were formed up in taxeis and moved off. The better-trained groups marched, with flute players playing and shield-bearers stepping as proudly as the phalangites in the ranks, but many – the Phrygians, the many Thracians and Lydians and Karians – simply wandered off after an officer or a nobleman that they knew. Staff officers, resplendent in bronze and iron, with big plumes of dyed horsehair, rode up and down the mobs of moving men, calling constantly. 'Artabarzes? Karian javelins? No! No! You're on the right wing, in the rough ground! No, sir, you must march this way!' and 'Philip? White Shields? Yes, sir. Centre of the line, with the Silver Shields on your right. Yes sir!'

When the baggage animals were ready and Sappho had ordered them all moved to the rear of the camp, the twins walked up to the head of their street to watch the grand parade of the army. They were just in time to watch the elephants come past, sixty enormous beasts that seemed to personify the power of war, each one festooned with red and gold blankets, with gold bands and bronze breastplates or headplates, their mahouts often as well armoured as generals.

'That's Tavi!' Satyrus cried, and began waving like mad.

The India-man, now looking like a brown Achilles in a

purple chiton and a scale corslet with alternating rows of gold and silver scales, raised his prod – itself a weapon – and saluted them. Behind him, a pair of Macedonians with long sarissas waved at the children.

On their street, the fourth troop of Diodorus's mercenaries – all the men who had had a night watch or other duties – were collecting and mounting, and as the elephants passed every man sprang to hold his horse's head. Their horses stamped and fidgeted until the last elephant walked slowly past.

Then Crax vaulted into the saddle and bellowed for the troop to mount. He looked down through the swirling dust at the twins. 'Stay safe,' he said. 'If it all goes to shit, rally behind the gully. Right?'

Satyrus nodded, and Crax gave a salute with his fist and the troop swung into line on the road, moving slowly at first, then faster, until they vanished into the rising cloud of dust. Every trooper saluted the twins as they rode past, and many of the Keltoi reached out and touched Melitta for luck.

'I want to watch the battle!' Satyrus said to Philokles.

'Me too!' Melitta said.

Philokles shook his head. 'Of course,' he said. He pointed at the bluff from where they had first seen the camp. He and Theron collected horses, and the four of them mounted.

'Where are you going?' Sappho asked. She was dressed in Persian trousers and a Sakje jacket, and her hair hung in braids.

'Please, Aunt, we want to see the battle!' Melitta said. 'Philokles will go up on the bluff with us.'

Sappho considered for a moment. 'I'm sending a slave with you. Targis! Go with Master Philokles and the children. Bring me word if anything untoward should happen.' She walked aside with Philokles. They spoke in low voices for a minute, and then Sappho was in Philokles' arms, weeping. Satyrus saw it, but he wasn't sure he'd really seen it, because a moment later she was issuing orders, the only sign of her tears a certain redness around her eyes. Philokles came back to them.

'Targis?' Philokles said politely. He was always polite to slaves. 'Come with us, please.'

Targis was a pale blond man with long legs. He looked like a runner. He nodded to his mistress and followed the group.

'I wonder what happened to Philip and Draco,' Satyrus asked.

Philokles raised an eyebrow. 'I doubt they could come to any harm,' he said.

'I miss them,' Satyrus said.

'You're starting to see that there's a world beyond yourself,' Philokles said.

They rode up the bluff at a trot, with Targis running hard behind them. The blond man ran easily, his arms pumping away. Theron admired his form. 'He's trained in a gymnasium,' Theron said.

When they stopped, Theron waved at the slave. 'You were an athlete?' he asked.

The slave averted his eyes. 'I was not born a slave,' he said.

'No one is born a slave,' Melitta said. 'Men make each other slaves.'

Philokles glanced at the girl. 'You show signs of real wisdom, girl! Where did you learn such things?'

Melitta blushed. 'From you, master,' she said.

'Bah!' Philokles said. 'I've never said anything as well put.'

Satyrus barely heard them. His attention was already fixed on the broad stretch of flat plain to the north and west, where both armies were forming, and he ignored the movement of men and horses on the bluff to focus on the armies beneath his feet.

At the bottom of the broad salt plain of the valley, there were skirmishers, *psiloi* and *peltastai*. None of them were visible as individuals, but the movement of so many men, even spread well apart, raised a salt dust that looked like dandelion fluff.

Behind the screen of his skirmishers, Eumenes' army was about half-formed, with the phalanx in the centre ready for action, their spears erect and the points glittering in the sun above the dust. The right-flank cavalry – where Diodorus had his command, subordinate to Philip, a Macedonian – were almost formed, and Satyrus could see that there were *prodromoi*

– the scouts – well out on the flank and armoured cavalry closer in to the phalanx.

On the left, however, closest to the camp, there was nothing short of chaos. A heavy curtain of sand rose high in the air, hiding Eumenes' best cavalry and his peltastai, who were forming to cover the flank of the phalanx where it would pass the rough ground of the valley floor, where heavy brush and an olive orchard interrupted the flat fields.

Across the valley, Antigonus One-Eye formed his best cavalry on his right, facing Eumenes' best cavalry, and they were already formed. His centre was wrecked, the phalanx in disarray and his left was in flux, lost in obscuring clouds. His far left – the part of his army that faced Diodorus – was reacting to the very visible fact that Diodorus's flank extended farther than his opponent's, and they were vulnerable.

Nothing seemed to happen quickly. At this distance they couldn't see individuals, and they couldn't hear anything but a vague roar, like a distant stream running over rocks.

'Why do they wait for each other to form?' Satyrus asked. 'Surely the first to form has a clear advantage?'

'Not a bad question, for a pup,' a harsh voice barked. Just to their right, almost unnoticed in their excitement at the panorama of war, a cavalcade had mounted the bluff. A swarthy man in a silvered breastplate and a matching helmet rode over. 'Neither commander will attack until he's sure of his own dispositions, and the longer we keep our men in line, the more shit we'll think of to fix. It can go on all day. War is nothing but a contest of mistakes, boy. The fewer you make, the more likely you are to win. I've failed to get my right wing in line, and I don't have my peltastai where I wanted them. And my opponent has fucked up the disposition of his elephants – he committed them to the line. Now's he's seen the error of his ways – I suspect his son had something to do with it.'

'Eumenes,' Philokles said. He was on his feet. Philokles gave a salute in the Spartan fashion.

'By all the gods, a Spartan. You have the better of me, sir.' Eumenes extended an arm, leaning down from the saddle.

Philokles took his hand and clasped it. 'Philokles – a friend

222

of your strategos Diodorus, and of Kineas, whom you fought in Bactria. These are his children.'

Eumenes grimaced. 'You could put them in with Herakles. We could start a nursery for orphans of great generals!' He looked down at them, imperious in purple and silver. 'What do you think, boy?'

'I think that you're hiding your elephants in that dust cloud,' Melitta said. 'And you're going to break the enemy in the centre.'

'I think Uncle Diodorus's flank extends well beyond his opponent's,' Satyrus piped up. 'And they're already scared.'

'Not bad,' Eumenes said, looking like a man who had all day to discuss his tactics with children. 'Not bad at all. But here's the question, boys and girls. He has more cavalry than I do. Yet – his battle line is shorter. *Where is the rest of the cavalry?* That is what I rode up here to see.'

Satyrus and Melitta exchanged a glance.

Eumenes went on, speaking mostly to himself. 'Battles happen because both generals think that they are in a superior position, and one of them is always wrong,' he said. 'Or because one of them is desperate. I'm not desperate. My phalanx is better and I have more elephants. One-Eye has more cavalry. It is his only advantage, beside the fact that he's a Macedonian and I'm a Greek.' He took a linen towel from his satchel and wiped his brow. 'So where the fuck is it?' he went on. 'If he's sent it out on the flanks – well, I may have crushed his centre before they arrive. No dust cloud. I guess they could be coming behind that range of hills to the west, but that's twenty stades.'

He pushed his towel back in his satchel. 'Well, Spartan, enjoy your view. Children, consider this a lesson.' Without another word, he waved at his entourage and galloped down the face of the bluff, raising a cloud of dust that took ten minutes to dispel and obscured their view of the battlefield.

Theron opened a basket and served a late breakfast of figs and dates. All of them enjoyed the rich fruits, and they were quite sticky before the dust cleared.

'So that was Eumenes the Cardian,' Satyrus said.

'In the life,' Philokles answered.

'What do you think he meant about this being a lesson?' Satyrus asked.

Philokles got the look that both twins associated with lessons. 'What did Eumenes say was the key to battle? Why do battles happen?'

Satyrus nodded seriously. 'Battles happen because both generals believe they are superior, and one of them is wrong,' he said.

Melitta jabbed him with an elbow.

'In this case, I believe that Eumenes has decided that his opponent is staking his battle on a flank march. Eumenes is staking his on his elephants.' Philokles pointed out at the field, where the curtain of dust was slowly subsiding. 'One of them is wrong.'

'Who?' Melitta asked.

'Ask Zeus,' Theron said. 'Look!'

Out on the plain, Eumenes' whole line had started forward. The apparent confusion of his left was now revealed as a ruse, with the whole force of his elephants guarding the left of his phalanx and walking boldly forward a stade or so behind the main line. On the right, Diodorus's cavalry was already well down the field and pressing on.

'But—' Satyrus was hopping up and down. 'But – nothing was happening!'

Philokles' voice sounded strange, almost as if he were drunk. 'Once a battle starts,' he said, 'it moves fairly fast.'

As they watched, both sides manoeuvred, pushing the last units into line or trying to straighten the more ragged divisions, but both sides had some forces in motion and any form of uniformity was shredded, except in the centres, where the phalanxes marched forward in order. They appeared about equal in size, and they were getting closer to each other – less than a stade apart now.

'This is the worst part for the men in the ranks,' Philokles said. 'When you can see that wall of spear points coming at you, you feel naked. Nothing but honour – and fear of the contempt of the gods and your friends – can keep your feet moving forward. Your heart races as if you're about to die. Perhaps you are.' He looked away. 'Poor bastards. May the gods stand with every one of them.'

'Look! Our men are winning!' Melitta cried. She was watching the cavalry on the right, where Diodorus was stationed.

'Ares!' Theron said. 'That was fast.'

Philokles shook his head. 'Either One-Eye has set a trap and Philip has fallen for it, or One-Eye has made an error.'

Satyrus caught the flash of sun on weapons to the far right. 'It *is* a trap. Oh, Uncle Diodorus!'

Even as the whole line – the rather thin line – in front of Diodorus buckled and fled, his prodromoi were struck in the flank by lancers coming over the low ridge to the east. But the contest was by no means one-sided, and just before the battle haze hid the action on the right from them, they saw a whole regiment of Diodorus's cavalry come out of the distant dust and fall on the ambushers, who were in turn the ambushed, while his main force continued straight on.

'What happened?' Satyrus asked.

Philokles stroked his beard for several minutes. 'I don't know,' he said. 'Cavalry fights are fast and confusing. It's like watching a pair of dogs go for the throat – until one lies dead, it is hard to guess who will win. But Diodorus has been at this for longer than you've been alive. I'd guess he walked into that with his eyes open.'

As Philokles spoke, the phalanxes in the centre moved so close to each other as to look like a single mass. And then both seemed to stop moving forward, but they both kept moving from the back. As a child, Satyrus had once watched two caterpillars collide on a narrow branch, their heads locked together while their rear legs kept moving, and the phalanxes were much the same. And then the noise carried to them, a strain of a paean and the crash as the two great bodies met.

'They both stood,' Philokles said.

'They were both moving,' Theron countered.

'That's not what I mean,' Philokles said testily. 'What I should have said is that neither broke before contact. It often happens that way, although no one likes to speak of it later.'

'Look!' Melitta said, grabbing her brother's shoulder and pulling at it.

Satyrus tore his eyes from the death struggle in the centre and the elephants marching stolidly up from the second line. Eumenes' left, the part with his elite cavalry, closest to camp, was about to be struck in the flank by a tidal wave of cavalry. Satyrus had missed their appearance. 'Where did they come from?' he asked.

Melitta shook her head. She was chewing her lips. 'They're going to sweep right over our cavalry,' she said.

'Right into the flank of the phalanx,' Theron said.

'It's not unlike watching the climax of a race,' Philokles said. 'Except that the contestants are dying.'

'Diodorus needs to turn into the flank of the enemy phalanx,' Satyrus added, after a tense silence.

Eumenes' elite cavalry were outnumbered, and their dislike of their employer showed in the haste of their retreat, so that his left wing collapsed in mere minutes. Bactrians and Medes surged forward, many units penetrating the line without having engaged at all.

Melitta was on her feet. 'They can't see the elephants!' she said.

Satyrus stood up with her. It *was* like cheering contestants at an athletic event. Thousands of enemy cavalrymen were pouring into the void left by the flight of Eumenes' left wing, but instead of hitting the flank of the phalanx, they were about to plunge over a very low ridge into Eumenes' elephant force. The low ridge was scarcely visible – Melitta was guessing that it must be there, because the Bactrians galloped straight at the elephants.

And on the farthest left, they could see a body of their own cavalry launch their own charge into the now-open flank of the enemy's Bactrians. Satyrus thought that it was remarkably like boxing – punch and counter-punch. The brave man who was leading the charge right in front of them was throwing a fairly feeble left, but in order to deal with it, the mass of Bactrians and Saka would have to change front and they would lose all the advantage of their position.

'See how the Medes are avoiding a second fight? When men have triumphed in battle, they are often just as finished with violence as men who have lost. So the Medes hesitate and look around for easier meat.'

Satyrus found that he'd eaten another fig without a memory of picking the fruit from the basket. Dust now hid everything all along the line. He put his cloak on the ground behind him and sat on it. He washed his hands from his canteen.

Nothing seemed to be happening, although the sounds of combat were now clearly audible, carried on a fresh breeze from the east. The Medes and Bactrians had vanished into the towering salt-dust clouds, and the battle line was hidden from end to end.

And then the Bactrians came bursting out of the edge of the cloud closest to the camp.

13

Philokles watched them for a long heartbeat, and then he grabbed the runner. 'Go to your mistress, as fast as you can run. Tell her that five thousand Asiatic cavalry are about to hit the camp. She may have ten minutes. She'll know what to do. Go!'

The young man was off down the hillside, his tanned limbs flashing in rhythm as he ran.

Philokles watched the Medes for ten more heartbeats. Then he turned to Theron and the twins.

'Eumenes' left is broken beyond saving, but the men who broke it have chosen to loot the camp rather than face the elephants.' He nodded. 'Very wise of them, actually. But in effect, it nullifies One-Eye's victory. Unless I miss my guess, that man down there – follow my hand – is Eumenes. He's trying to stem the rout.'

'Look at those cowards,' Theron said. Indeed, the cream of Eumenes' Macedonian cavalry were rallied off to the far left in an old river bed. Many of the units were formed up as if on parade, but they weren't moving forward.

'Difficult to tell the difference between cowardice and treason,' Philokles said. 'Is it our responsibility to tell Eumenes that his camp is attacked? Or even that his phalanx is still in the game?'

'What of your friend Diodorus?' Theron asked.

At their feet, a short column of horses and mules was already formed and moving south. 'Diodorus planned against this,' Philokles said. 'As did Sappho.' He shook his head. 'Diodorus needs to know that this has happened. Will you go, Theron?'

Theron looked at the maelstrom of churning salt dust and bronze. 'I don't even know who I'd be looking for,' he said. 'No. Not my game.'

'I'll go,' Satyrus said.

Philokles didn't even look at his student. He was looking

at the camp. 'I need to repay an old debt. You stay with the children. Diodorus is a big boy.'

'I'll go,' Satyrus said again.

Already, the word of the catastrophe was spreading and refugees were pouring out of the camp, heading south. To the north, the Bactrians were already in the horse lines, taking remounts. The Saka were riding to the east, coming around the tangle of tents that would impede their horses.

'What old debt?' Theron shouted. 'Ares, man, you can't go into *that*!'

'Banugul,' Philokles said quietly. The name didn't mean much to either of the twins.

'Mum used to talk about her,' Melitta said. 'You used her as an example once, of a woman of power.'

Philokles didn't take his eyes off the onrushing enemy. 'You really do listen to everything I say,' he said.

'Aunt Sappho said that she ought to be our ally,' Satyrus said.

'Your father saved her life once,' Philokles said, his eyes on another fight, far away in time and place. He reached up under his arm and loosened his sword in its scabbard. 'You children go with Theron. Down to the column and go to the rally point. I'm going to save a gilded harlot.'

The twins looked at each other. A message passed between them, but they mounted with Theron and started down the back of the bluff, both of them watching Philokles as he mounted and vanished over the camp-side crest.

'Is he insane?' Theron trotted ahead, muttering.

Satyrus turned to his sister. 'I'll ride to Eumenes,' he said quietly. 'And to Diodorus.'

She nodded. 'Good. I'll help Philokles.' She looked at his borrowed dun gelding. 'I wish you had a better horse.'

'Me too,' Satyrus said. They exchanged a smile, and he glanced at Theron and pulled his horse off to the left. On a dun horse, helmetless, with a dun-coloured cloak, Satyrus vanished in the dust as soon as he turned his horse. He was away, back up the slope of the bluff, until he had a view over the worst of the dust and down into the salt plain.

Eumenes' silvered helmet was a flash of white light, just a stade or so to the north. Satyrus pointed his gelding's head at the general and tapped his heels for speed, and they were away.

Melitta watched her brother turn his horse. She reached down and checked her bow case. Theron turned in his saddle. 'This way,' he called.

Melitta followed obediently for another minute, and then, as they entered the dust of Sappho's column, she shouted, 'Where's Satyrus?'

Theron turned in his saddle, retying his chlamys over his face against the dust. 'Where's he gone?' Theron asked. 'Ares!'

'He was right there,' Melitta said.

'Go to Sappho,' Theron said, turning his horse. 'Satyrus!' he bellowed.

Melitta didn't answer – she just rode towards where Theron was pointing until the dust swirled around her. Then she slipped her Sakje tunic off her shoulder so that her right arm and shoulder were bare and pulled Bion around in a short turn. Dust didn't bother her – she'd ridden in the drag position with the maidens and the boys on summer marches with the Assagatje. She wrapped a scarf over her mouth as she cantered back towards camp.

The dust was thick, and the Saka were close – she could see them shouting to each other just to the east. She waved her bow over her head at them and they shouted. Then they were gone in the dust.

She had a good idea where the enormous red and yellow tent stood, so she rode on instinct, trusting Bion to move carefully in a forest of tents and stakes and ropes. She didn't ride fast, but she took the straightest line she could find.

She terrified a great many camp followers, emerging from the curtain of dust. She looked like a Massagetae. Under her mask of dust and her head scarf, she smiled wickedly, gave a shriek of joy and terrified them a little more. It would only move them faster. That might save their lives.

Twice, Bion stumbled, catching a leg on a tent stake or a rope, but both times they recovered without a fall. 'Good boy,' she said in Sakje, patting his flanks. She was speaking Sakje and thinking in Sakje, and the Greek of the terrified women around her was almost incomprehensible to her. She felt Bion's weight change and she got up his neck for a jump – he was up and over, and she never knew what they'd just jumped. Then the gelding turned under her and she almost lost her seat, and they were cantering again.

She caught a flash of colour to her left, and then another, and beneath Bion's hooves she was looking at fruits. They were in the agora of the camp, and close to Banugul's tent.

Now, where is Philokles? she asked herself.

Satyrus rode easily, leaning well back as they slid down the face of the bluff and then shifting his weight forward as they got the hard ground of the valley under them. He let his horse have his head, and they were off at a gallop. Satyrus trusted his seat, so he used the gallop as a smooth platform to get his chlamys off his waist where he'd tied it and to wrap it around his head.

He had just got the length of wool around his face when he burst into a crowd of Bactrians. He knew them from their long burnooses and their trousers, and then he was through them, moving so fast that they had little chance to catch him. His heart raced and for the first time the foolishness of what he was attempting rose with his gorge to choke him.

I could die doing this, he thought. It was very different from being hunted by assassins – this was a risk he had incurred at his own will, and it felt stupid. *It's not even my battle!* some part of his mind shouted at him. *Too late now!* another part answered, and he came out of the protective wall of salt dust as if shot from a bow.

Instantly, he felt naked. There was a breeze here, and it had ripped the veil of salt asunder and left him riding alone with a thousand Bactrians in full view to the west, less than half a stade away. His bare legs proclaimed him a Greek and probably an enemy, and a dozen of them turned their horses and came for him with a series of shrill whoops.

Ahead he saw the body of men he was aiming for – Macedonian cavalry in white leather *spolades* and bronze helmets.

The man at their head had a silver helmet, but at this range it was obvious that he was *not* Eumenes. He was ten horse-lengths away, and he was shouting orders in a voice as young and shrill as Satyrus's own. His cloak was purple.

Satyrus got up on his knees, pressed his heels into his gelding's flank and raced for the narrowing gap between the Macedonian cavalry and the Bactrians. Behind him, a dozen Bactrians were down on their horse's necks, calling to one another in hot pursuit, but he was a lighter rider on a better mount. It occurred to him that he ought to shoot at them, but he didn't have the nerve to spare. He was too busy being one with his horse.

The young officer whirled around, and Satyrus passed him at javelin-toss. The pin on his purple cloak would have ransomed a small town.

In a flash he was through the gap, riding along a file of Macedonian troopers. Every head turned and some men pointed, and the Bactrians on the right started to turn, and more Bactrians, so close that they could almost touch him, turned their horses as he went by, and then he was past, out on the salt pan beyond, and the breeze was gone and he was back in the towering clouds of dust.

He galloped long enough to wind his mount, and then he curved carefully off to his right, slowing gradually and listening as hard as he could. He could hear fighting to the right, and his horse, though tired, was fidgeting hard. He couldn't imagine why she was so restive, but he curbed her hard while he got his wits about him.

He was lost on the battlefield, somewhere in the battle haze.

Melitta remembered the red and yellow tent as being at the south end of the agora, and she rode in that direction. The agora was already empty, except for rubbish and a dead child of six or seven with his throat cut.

That gave Melitta a shock. She looked at the little body too long, and then pushed on. Across the last food stalls, she could see the roof of the red and yellow tent. In front of it were a dozen horses. Men were shouting. And there was a rising sound of a panicked mob coming from the north. The Medes must be in the camp.

Suddenly the impulse to help Philokles rescue Banugul seemed foolish. How would she ever find him? How could she take on a dozen men? And she had no time – the wail of mass despair was right behind her.

'Were the fuck is she?' came a shout from the complex of tents clustered around the red and yellow. She knew that voice. That was the doctor – the false doctor, Sophokles.

'She ran!' another man said.

'Get her brat!'

'He's got a sword!'

Melitta was on the point of fleeing down the long avenue that ran back towards the gully when she heard Sophokles' voice, and the power of her brother's oath washed over her. She got her bow up, drew her akinakes and rode right up to the side wall of the great pavilion, Bion picking his way among the spiderweb of supporting stays. When she got there, she reached out and slit the walls of the tent from top to bottom so that they folded away on their supports, and then she was in the tent. She let the knife dangle from its wrist strap, nocked an arrow and watched a man chasing a boy a little younger than her brother – a bronze-haired boy with a sword. He turned and slashed at his attacker.

'Just kill him,' Sophokles shouted.

Melitta's first arrow hit Sophokles in the side just below his pointing arm. He never saw the shot and he went down in a heap and then her second arrow was in the man chasing the boy.

'Come with me!' she shouted at the boy. She dropped her bow into the gorytos at her waist and extended her left hand.

Her brother would have known what to do, but this boy just looked at her. 'Who are you?' he asked.

Sophokles was up again, holding his side. Her light bow hadn't put an arrow through his thorax. 'Who the fuck are you?' he said. He was two horse-lengths away.

'Up!' Melitta said to the boy. 'Now!'

'Do I have to do everything myself?' Sophokles said, stepping over the body of the other man. Two more men came into the tent at his shoulders. He scooped a spear off the floor.

He was distracted for a vital second when a third man pushed into the huge tent from the largest side corridor with a struggling woman in his arms. 'I have her!'

'Just kill her!' Sophokles called. 'Ares! Are you fools?'

Finally, after a hesitation that seemed to Melitta to last for aeons, the boy reached up and took her hand, his eyes fixed on the struggles of the woman. Bion moved under her, and she gave a heave and he was up, grabbing her waist and almost pulling her off Bion's back. Bion backed a step and another. She grabbed at her bow, her own dangling knife cutting the top of her thigh.

Sophokles cocked back his spear. 'That boy is not for you,' he said. 'Hand him over – I'll pay you gold. Gold! Understand?' He pointed at a gold armband he wore. 'Gold, you stupid barbarian.' Aside, he said, 'Fucking barbarians.'

'One-Eye said to *capture* the woman and her son,' a Macedonian accent said – one of the men behind the Athenian assassin. He was armoured like an officer, with fine gold bands on an iron cuirass. 'Do *not* kill her.'

Sophokles looked around like a man who has suffered one indignity too many. 'Fuck you, Macedonian,' he said. He whirled and plunged his spear into the neck of the officer, downing him instantly.

Melitta got her bow in her hand. She caught a flash of movement from the far doorway, and there was Philokles with a sword in his hand. He kicked a man in the back of the knee and the man went down with a curse.

Of course, Philokles had no idea who she was. He glanced at her and grabbed the woman on the ground. 'My son!' she shouted.

'I'm rescuing you, you stupid bitch,' Philokles said. At the word *rescue*, every head in the tent turned, and the action seemed to Melitta to speed up. Sophokles and Philokles recognized each other.

'Enter the drunk,' the assassin said.

'He's trying to kill them because he works for Olympias,' Philokles called out. 'Not for One-Eye. Kill him!'

'Hermes, you are a pest,' the false doctor said. He cocked back the spear he held and threw it.

Philokles managed in one athletic twist to let go of the woman, bump her with his hip hard enough to knock her flat and deflect the spear.

'Damn you!' Sophokles cursed. 'You have the luck of Tyche herself!' he said.

Melitta shot him in the back of the knee. It was the least armoured part of him that she thought she could hit, and the man had turned his back on her. Then, with the surge of elation that came with a really good shot, she backed her gelding out of the slit in the tent, wheeled her horse and rode.

Satyrus took too much time – a subjective eternity – to realize that his horse was thrashing like a mad thing because he was almost surrounded by elephants. They were in two long columns, each of twenty or more beasts, and he was *between* them, however he had managed that. There were men around him, on foot – skirmishers or psiloi or just men who had lost their way as he had – and none of them offered him any threat. He passed a Median peltastes in spotted trousers so close that the weary man's shoulder brushed his horse.

He got his horse under some semblance of control just as the elephants, obeying shouted commands, began to shamble from their deep files into an open line. His gelding broke into a panicked run, headed past the elephants and there were bellows of rage – elephantine rage, monster noises from legend in the dust that frightened him as thoroughly as they spooked his mount. He had no control of his charger, and the big gelding passed elephant after elephant before bursting through their line, so close to one great beast that Satyrus, had he been less afraid, might have touched the legs of the behemoth as he went by.

To his left, a pair of the animals were fighting, both creatures on their hind legs, tusks locked, blood weeping from their hides, the men on their backs clinging for their lives. As he watched, one serpentine trunk grasped a mahout, coiled around his arms and ripped him screaming from his perch on the head of the enemy elephant. Satyrus watched in horrified fascination as the man's body was dropped at the elephant's feet and meticulously trampled.

He galloped past and his fears changed from terror of the elephants to concern that his gelding had started to move heavily, starved of air, his flanks heaving and shuddering. Despite his panic, Satyrus got his mount clear of the last elephants and then pulled him in to let him breathe. Off to his right, he could see the flash of bronze and steel and hear, clear as a play, the desperate rage of another kind of monster – the two phalanxes grinding away at each other.

Satyrus's mind began to function for the first time since he escaped the Bactrians. He felt deeply ashamed at his own panic, but he knew that he had no hope of finding Eumenes in the dust.

On the other hand, Diodorus and the hippeis were just on the other side of the phalanx. The phalanx had sixteen thousand men – at the normal fighting depth, they were a thousand wide, or three thousand *podes* at battle order. Five stades.

Philokles had said that Diodorus needed to know about the camp.

He rode around the shoulder of the phalanx, pushing the poor gelding as hard as he dared. The horse was used up – the elephants had caused it more fatigue in five minutes of terror than the rest of the ride put together. But he was safe for the moment. He was riding down the back of the army, and he was surprised at how empty the battlefield was. A few bodies lay on the ground, and a few men cried out for water, but his charger's hoof beats hid the worst of the sounds, and he detoured around the biggest piles of bodies as best he could in the thick salt dust, which bit at his throat and his eyes. He was so thirsty he thought of plundering a corpse for its canteen.

It took him too much time to realize that he *had* a canteen. He cursed his own panic and got some water in his mouth, even as his mount stumbled from a canter to a slow trot. He could feel the change in the battle line here – he could no longer see the back of the phalanx, and the sound of the shouting to his left was more triumphant. He turned his weary horse towards the shouting, hoping he had ridden five stades. It was hard to measure time in the battle haze.

Ahead, in the white-grey clouds, there was a trumpet call – a familiar trumpet call. That was Andronicus with the silver trumpet of the hippeis.

Wasn't it?

At his feet, there were smiling men with crescent-shaped shields. They were loping forward and pointing, and they ignored him. He rode past them. Farther on he saw more peltastai, all moving forward, and he guessed that the enemy's flank was crumpling. The men he passed were drinking water, or shouting to each other, or plundering bodies. What they *weren't* doing was turning into the open flank of the enemy phalanx.

He thought about what Philokles had said about men who had won a fight being hesitant to enter a second fight. And he kept his horse moving, because he suspected that when the big gelding stopped, he wouldn't move again. They kept moving east, or what seemed in the haze to be east, roughly parallel to Eumenes' original battle line, as best he could tell in the heat and the haze.

Then there were no more infantrymen. He heard several trumpet calls, one of which might have been familiar. Satyrus couldn't see anything, and he couldn't hear anything except the sounds of the fighting behind him. So he turned his horse further to the left, hoping that Diodorus had continued to win on his flank, and thinking that he had heard the trumpet in that direction.

If Diodorus had lost the initial cavalry action, Satyrus reasoned, the peltastai would hardly have pushed so deep into the enemy's lines.

The sun was enough past noon that he began to become confident in directions – even with the haze, the sun was a hard, round, white disc in the sky, and he could reason out north and south, east and west. The phalanx fight was now west. Diodorus's trumpet was east and north.

Probably.

The longer Satyrus rode, the less certain he became. By the time his canteen was almost empty, he had again begun to wonder where he was. The solidity of the phalanx was long gone, the haze rose like a live thing, choking him and limiting his sight to a few horse-lengths, and the noise of the phalanx was so far away that he might have been off the battlefield.

The Median peltastes arose out of the dust like a mythological creature, stabbing with a javelin, trying to unhorse Satyrus. Satyrus took the first thrust in the centre of his abdomen where his cuirass was strongest and he lost his seat. His gelding stopped, kicked out weakly at the peltastes and stumbled a few steps forward. Then the horse came to a stop and with the slow inevitability of winter avalanche in the mountains, he fell. Satyrus kicked clear and rolled to his feet, tangled in his cloak. When he got up, his side was wet where his clay canteen had broken, and the peltastes was on him, stabbing twice with his javelin, fast as the strike of an adder. Satyrus stumbled back, stunned, with sweat and salt in his eyes. He got his right hand under his left armpit and drew his sword, and the Mede hesitated.

Satyrus wiped his eyes with his damp cloak. The Mede measured him and looked at the dying horse, stepped back and threw his javelin like a thunderbolt, but he miscast and it tumbled, and the shaft struck Satyrus a heavy blow on the tip of his left shoulder, and a lance of pain shot down his arm. Then the man turned to run and hesitated again.

Satyrus stepped forward, pulling his cloak over his left arm, and cut at the man before he could flee. The Mede jumped back, a look of panic on his face, and they both heard a trumpet, quite close.

Now that his horse wasn't moving, Satyrus could hear the sounds of fighting just to the north – horses and men. Somewhere nearby, a maddened steed gave a trumpet of rage. Somewhere else in the murk, men were wounded and screamed their pain, In a matter of heartbeats, the sound was all around him, and so were phantoms of battle, movements in the opaque curtain of salt.

The Mede came back at him, a knife held high in his right hand and his small shield of wicker and hide thrusting from the left.

Satyrus had time to think, *He has no training whatsoever.* It was a thought that gave him a feeling of calm and superiority, and he sidestepped and cut the man's knife hand at the wrist. He was too weak to cut through the bone, but the man's weapon went flying and the man fell to his knees, clutching his maimed hand like a mother with a sick child. In two beats of his heart, the Mede was transformed from a monster of violence to a helpless victim.

Satyrus left him. He stepped past, to the body of his horse, but there was nothing for him to take, and the feeling of success, of survival, left him as fast as it had come.

His breastplate weighed on his chest like an iron anvil, and he was soaked in sweat, and his mouth was dry as sand, and his head ached. His left shoulder hurt as it had after a fall from his horse as a child, and he was afraid to look at it to see if there was blood. And he was still lost.

His father had been famous for his ability to navigate a battlefield on sound alone.

Tears stung his eyes.

'I *will not cry*,' he said aloud, and started to walk forward, towards the sounds of combat. He kept his sword in his hand, more for the symbolism than for any use a sword would be to a dismounted man in a cavalry melee.

A riderless horse ran out of the curtain, eyes white with fear, and knocked him flat. He rolled from under the beast's hooves and there were horses all around him.

'Rally on me!' a voice shouted. 'Sound the rally!'

The trumpet rang out – a trumpet he had heard a thousand times as a child in Tanais, and he pushed to his feet, heedless of the hooves flying around him.

'Rally on me! Form a rhomboid! Phylarchs sound off!' Diodorus shouted.

The trumpet rang out again, a long call. The horses around Satyrus were jostling for position, every man struggling to get his mount to the right place in a haze of dust and a crowd of animals. Satyrus was crushed between two horses, and he ducked to get under a belly and got kicked in the back of his head by a rider.

'Hey!' he said. 'Hey, help!' The last came out more like a squeak. He was *that* close to finding his uncle and he was going to be trampled or crushed.

A spear point glittered wickedly in front of his face. 'Stand where you are,' Hama said.

'Hama, it's me!' he yelped back.

Hama reached out and grasped his wrist, sword and all, and hauled him up on his crupper. 'Men die on foot when horses are this thick,' the big Keltoi chief said. 'Little lord, what for fucking gods are you here?'

Satyrus got his leg over Hama's horse. 'I will not cry,' he said aloud. The relief was so great that his eyes filled and his throat hurt from more than salt dust.

The trumpet sounded again.

'Anyone have a clue where the fuck we are? Phylarchs, sound off!' Diodorus said.

'File one! Two men missing!'

'File two! All present!'

'File three! One man dead!'

'File four! Four men missing!'

'File five! All present!'

Hama shouted, 'File six! Two men missing! Lord Satyrus on my horse!' He pushed his own horse forward and men made way for him.

Off to the left, file seven and eight reported. Hama got his horse next to the hyperetes. Diodorus glanced at Hama. Satyrus opened his mouth and his uncle's hand came up like a blow, demanding silence.

'File nine! All present!'

'File ten! Three men missing!'

Diodorus nodded sharply. 'Thirteen are missing out of a hundred. That's bad.' He looked around. 'Anybody see Crax or Andronicus?'

'No, sir,' came a chorus of answers. The salt dust swirled.

'Dion – take file one off to the right. Don't go far – ten

horse-lengths a man. Return on one trumpet blast. See if you can find anybody. Paches – take file ten and do the same to the left. Go!'

He turned to Hama and Antigonus. 'Where the *fuck* are we?' Without waiting for an answer, he turned on Satyrus. 'What are you doing here, child?'

Satyrus took a breath and concentrated on having his voice level. 'I came with a message,' he said.

'What message?' Diodorus was all but kneeling on his horse's back, trying to see over the dust.

'But first, you are about five stades beyond the rightmost point of the enemy phalanx, Uncle. And all the peltastai have been driven off. I rode from there.'

Diodorus looked at him for a long breath. 'You are *sure*? Men's lives depend on this.'

Satyrus choked a little. 'No,' he said hesitantly. 'I'm not *sure*.'

Hama steadied him with a hug. 'But pretty sure, yes?'

Satyrus met his uncle's eyes. 'Pretty sure, Uncle.'

Diodorus nodded sharply. 'If you're right, I'll never doubt you again. Hama – get Paches back in and put him in front – we feel our way along the path Satyrus indicated. One troop of horse behind our *own* phalanx would panic them in this crap. One more trumpet call, hyperetes.' He took Satyrus from Hama. His hard grey eyes locked on Satyrus's eyes. 'Message?' he said. He held out his hand and a canteen was put in it.

'There are Saka and Bactrians in the camp,' Satyrus said. His uncle's beard was grey. It had once been red.

'Ares' *balls*, boy!' Diodorus looked around. 'I have a hundred men – less. What the fuck?'

A flash of gold, and Crax cantered out of the dust. 'You called,' he said, his armour flashing.

Diodorus laughed. 'Tyche is smiling!' he shouted, and there was an answering roar from the rank behind him. 'You have fourth troop?'

'Six missing,' Crax said, with a salute. 'I'll get them lined up with you.'

'Satyrus says we're on the flank of the phalanx, and that

it's *that way*. What do you think, Crax?' Diodorus handed the canteen to the Getae officer.

Crax took the flask, drank deeply and put the wooden stopper back. 'Sounds right to me,' Crax said with a wink at Satyrus – a wink that Satyrus appreciated. Suddenly there was a great weight on his shoulders – the burden of everyone's lives.

Crax was gone into the salt and Diodorus shouted, 'Remount! Anyone have a horse!'

A trooper that Satyrus didn't know pushed forward. 'Here, Strategos!'

Satyrus went straight from his uncle's crupper to the back of a dark bay with a beautiful animal-skin saddlecloth and silver mounts on the bridle.

'Thank you,' he said.

'You owe him for the horse, boy!' Diodorus said. 'And the tack!' He gave a wicked smile. Then he got his horse under him and motioned to Satyrus. 'Someone get him a spear and a helmet. Right up with me, boy. You're the guide. If we fight, get your animal in behind mine and keep your Ares-addled head down. Put that toy sword away. Now, which way?'

Satyrus found, to his immense joy, that he could *feel* which direction the phalanxes were. 'If they haven't moved,' he muttered. His heart raced and felt a very different fear from the fear of being torn to pieces by elephants. This was the fear of disappointing his friends – of being a child. He nudged his horse into motion. 'This way,' he said.

'March – walk!' Diodorus called, and the trumpet rang out.

Satyrus sat straighter. He was actually *leading* a troop of cavalry.

Men rode up to Diodorus and then rode away, and there were more trumpet calls and more orders. Satyrus, an arm-length from the man he called his uncle, understood that Diodorus was trying to get his two troops aligned while still searching the battlefield for his two missing troops.

'You know what you're doing, boy?' Diodorus asked after a few minutes' riding.

'Listen!' Satyrus said. He could hear a low roar to the front and right.

'Halt!' Diodorus shouted. 'No trumpet! Paches – get out there and tell me what you find – go a stade or two, no more!'

They were halted in a vast, rolling cloud of white and grey. There were bodies under their hooves, and as Satyrus watched, a pair of Thracian peltastai emerged from the white dust. They were so shocked that they stopped.

'Eumenes?' one asked. He gestured at the chaplet of roses he wore over his fox-hide cap.

Satyrus nodded. 'Eumenes!' he called.

By his shoulder, Crax rattled away in a barbarian tongue, and the two Thracians turned and ran off into the salt.

'I said we were about to charge,' Crax said. 'I've found some troopers from second troop, but they're lost. Maybe ten men.'

Diodorus took his helmet off. 'I fucking hate this. Somebody could smack us silly and we'd never know they were coming. This dust could hide *anything*.'

'Canteen's empty,' Crax said. He spat. 'Worst dust I've ever seen. Fucking *salt*.'

Paches came out of the swirl. 'Boy's dead on,' he said, with a salute towards Satyrus, whose heart filled with joy. 'Less than two stades – the back ranks of *their* phalanx. Nothing in our way,' the man continued, his voice rising with excitement.

Diodorus looked around. 'Well,' he said, pulling his helmet back on and tying the cheekpieces, 'This is where we all get to be heroes.' He looked at Satyrus. 'Get in the middle, boy, so I can get you home alive.' He turned his horse. 'Everyone get it? Into the *shieldless* flank. Don't fuck around. Get in deep and cause panic. Stay with me till you hear the trumpet. When they break, let someone else kill them – go *forward* to our lines. Understand? If you lose me, rally on the ravine. The camp is gone. READY?'

Two hundred parched throats found the energy to shout, *Yes!*

'March – walk! No trumpets!'

They were off. Now Satyrus was pushed back and back until he was in the sixth rank, the very centre of the rhomboid. He knew the drill, but it was different in the dust. He was between two complete strangers, but the one on his left turned a pair of bloodshot eyes from deep within a Thracian helmet. 'Nothing to worry about, kid!' he said. 'Safe as being home. First time?' he asked.

'Yes!' Satyrus shouted over the rising noise of their passage.

'Careful with that spear, then!' his new file-mate said. 'Don't hit Kalyx with it. He's not the forgiving kind.'

The other men laughed.

Half a stade passed very quickly.

'Paean!' said his uncle's voice. 'Make them hear you!'

The Paean of Apollo began with four beats of carefully measured rhythmic silence, and Andronicus beat his trumpet with a knife hilt – *crack, crack, crack, crack* – and the paean bloomed like a flower in the rising dust, an offering to a god who valued more than just slaughter.

Satyrus sang with them, and he was so moved his voice choked, and he felt as if he was one with all these men around him – one pair of arms and legs in a beast with a hundred arms and legs like the titan of legend.

They began to trot.

'Close up!' shouted the man on his right. Satyrus was embarrassed to see that he had lost ground. His horse responded beautifully, closing the gap in a few anxious heartbeats, and they were at a canter, the files a little spread from the speed, and then, in an instant, there were men all around him shouting, screams of terror and panic as if the gods had rendered every man witless. Satyrus couldn't see anything – there was no one to fight, and then, out of nowhere, a sarissa head slid past his knee, the sharp edges cutting his thigh where one enemy soldier, at least, had tried to change his front.

Then they were plunging through the enemy phalanx – Satyrus hoped that it was the *enemy* phalanx – among hundreds of men in heavy armour, but they were casting their sarissas to the ground and running or dying under the hooves. There were men on foot all around Satyrus and his horse had almost stopped.

He stabbed overarm with his spear at the first hand to try to seize his bridle. These men were desperate – and terrified. Most of them weren't even fighting back, just trying to push past him, but some either intended to die fighting or simply wanted his horse. A blow in the back nearly unseated him.

He punched back with his spear on reflex and almost lost his seat again as he failed to hit anything.

It looked to him as if the cavalry had lost all of its momentum and cohesion in the impact and now spilled out along the rear face of the phalanx, but the centre of the rhomboid had penetrated deeply – and Satyrus was in the part that had penetrated, lost in a sea of enemies.

For no reason he could discern, Satyrus was now a file-leader. He saw mounted men *behind* him. He managed to lock his knees on the dark bay's back and he obeyed his uncle and put his head down so that oncoming foes had only his helmet to attack – the best armoured part of him – and the charger responded by pushing forward through the press. Twice he reared his charger to clear the men in front, and the second time, she lost her footing on a corpse and they fell heavily. The horse rolled off, uninjured, and a spear-butt rammed into the earth inches from Satyrus's nose. He had lost his spear, but he got the sword out from under his arm, rolled to his feet, ignoring the pain from the old wound in his side, and parried the next blow, lifting the man's sarissa shaft high and stepping in under it as Philokles had taught. He cut out, almost blind, and his short sword bit into the man's hand and he screamed, and then Satyrus's file-partner, the man in the fancy Thracian helmet, spitted him on a spear. 'Get your horse!' he shouted.

The charger with the fancy tack was standing obediently just an arm-length away, and Satyrus swarmed up her side as if he was getting onboard a ship – she was a tall horse. The man in the Thracian helmet knocked another fleeing Macedonian flat, and then Satyrus was up, sword in hand, helmet askew but otherwise none the worse.

'Come on, lad,' Thracian helm called, and they were off into the dust. Then there were more horsemen, and more – men in blue plumes and cloaks – and then Satyrus had Crax at his shoulder.

And then there were other men – men with bright white shields – shouting and laughing and waving all around him. An officer was yelling for his men to open a file and let the cavalry through.

Satyrus reined in his charger and simply breathed. He was pressed up hard against the white shields, but they were grounding their spears, pushing the bronze butt-spikes into the salt sand.

'Ares,' a Macedonian voice said. 'Look at this child!'

Satyrus peered down at the dust-covered face. 'Eumenes?' he asked.

'Yeah,' the Macedonian panted. 'Yeah, Eumenes, kid. Who are you guys?'

'Hippeis of Tanais!' Crax roared by his side. Satyrus nodded proudly.

The man behind him slapped his back. 'Well done, little lord,' he said.

The trumpet sounded off in the dust.

'Fucking dust,' Hama said. The Keltoi had appeared as if by magic.

'Try being down in it, horse boy,' the Macedonian said. Then the white-caked face creased in a smile. 'Thanks, horse boys!'

Another Macedonian called out, 'First fucking Greeks I've ever liked – you saved our arses!'

They were moving again, because the Macedonians were shuffling to the side, opening a lane. Satyrus followed Hama, who was now, apparently, his file-leader. All the other men who should have been in between were gone.

'Hama?'

'Shush, lord,' was his reply. 'Listen for the trumpet!'

Melitta could see the length of the main avenue of the camp, and there were Saka coming in her direction. She hesitated as long as it took to push her bow deep in her gorytos, and then she was riding towards them at a smart trot, her male burden bouncing like a sack of potatoes.

'This is embarrassing,' he said.

'Don't talk,' she replied. 'Look terrified.'

She rode right at the lead group of Saka – four men and a

deeply tanned elder. She raised her whip and called one word in Saka.

'Mine!' she said, pointing at the boy over her shoulder. The elder smiled.

She rode past them without a challenge – she rode the length of the street without so much as a question. At the far end, the avenue was plugged with a roiling mass of Saka who couldn't decide what to loot first. She pushed forward, her boots rubbing against their boots.

'The red and yellow tent!!' she called. 'Gold and silver!' Her Sakje had the western accent, but that didn't bother anyone. She turned and pointed her whip. 'All the way through the market, cousins!'

'Thanks, little bride!' shouted a warrior with tattoos of dragons twined up his arms. Sauromatae warrior maidens were often called 'little brides' because in war they earned the right to choose their husbands. Voices laughed, but again no one raised a hand against her – much the opposite. Men moved their horses to let her pass, and she left the crush with nothing bruised but her feet. Once free of the press, she urged Bion to a trot and then a canter, and when she was beyond the rows of cook fires, dangerous pits in the murk, she gave the big gelding his head and his legs opened into a long gallop that ate the ground.

'It's like flying!' the boy at her back said. 'Are you really a Saka?'

'I'm Assagatje. My mother is the queen of the Assagatje. Of course, she's not really a queen. Sakje really don't ...' She was babbling. She cut herself off. He was very warm, pressed against her back, and calm, in a way she liked. Solid, like her brother. 'My mother is Srayanka,' she said.

'I'm Herakles,' he said. 'My mother is Banugul, and my father was a god.'

'Banugul?' she said. 'That's good. It's nice to know I rescued the right boy. Try to move your hips – it's easier on the horse.'

The gully was just beyond the bluff on her left – she could see the loom of the bluff passing her shoulder, and she began to swing the horse wide to the right to avoid the inevitable calamity. The ground changed and she slowed Bion and pulled his head ever further to the west as she felt the horse's weight change. She was riding right along the edge of the gully.

She was just picking her way south again when she was challenged.

'Who are you?' called a voice with more fear than authority.

She could see riders, and carts. 'Melitta of Tanais,' she called. 'With Herakles.'

Women gathered around her.

'What the fuck?' Crax croaked. The dust was not subsiding. They'd been an hour in one place, just a stade from where they'd shredded the enemy phalanx. For no reason that they understood, they were waiting near their starting position in the battle line of the early morning. Diodorus had ordered the halt and told men to dismount and other men to get out and scout, and then he'd left Crax in charge and ridden off with Hama. Stragglers wandered in, both their own and other mercenary cavalrymen who'd been in Diodorus's command, or Philip's, when the day began.

Dismounted men prowled the ground around them stripping the enemy dead of loot – and water. Other parties searched the salt flats for their dead, and buried them. A young trooper from Olbia went down with heat sickness and suddenly the phylarchs were everywhere, demanding that men empty their canteens.

Andronicus spoke up to Crax. 'The horses won't last much longer,' he said.

Satyrus wondered what his eyes looked like. All the men around him had the eyes of mourners – red-rimmed, red-creased, with red blood in the corners. The salt was vicious. He wiped his eyes on his arm again and felt the burn on his eyelids and his hands and winced.

'Did we win?' he asked the man next to him.

'We won, son. That doesn't mean the whole army won,' the man cackled. 'Got any water?'

'No,' Satyrus admitted.

'I do,' he said. 'Cleitus,' he said, extending an arm.

'Satyrus,' he answered, clasping the man's hand. He felt like a grown man.

The other man offered his water and Satyrus took a swig, and then another before he could stop himself. He handed it back. There was wine in the man's water – it tasted divine, as if Dionysus had blessed it himself.

'We've found most of our dead, and buried them,' he said. 'We didn't need to ask for a truce to do it, either. In my book, that's a victory.'

'We plundered their dead, too,' another man said.

'Here comes the strategos,' Crax called. 'Stand by your mount!'

Diodorus came up in a new cloud of salt. 'Call in the scouts, hyperetai. Satyrus, on me. Everyone not actually doing anything, get the fuck off your mount *now*.' He turned to Crax. 'Report!'

'Most of second troop is in, but not Eumenes,' Crax said. 'He vanished in the first melee. Otherwise, we've buried our dead.'

Diodorus shook his head. 'He's been with us since we started,' he said. 'Well, almost.' He looked around. 'Not finding his body is hard.'

Crax nodded. 'Since the first winter in Olbia,' he said. 'Maybe he'll turn up. Anyway, otherwise second is down seventeen. We're down nine, and first is down thirteen. Third is nowhere to be found, and I swept all the way back to where we hit the Medes in the first hour.' The Getae officer looked around. The hyperetai of all three troops were shepherding the dismounted men into a column, every man leading his horse. Beyond them, the phalanx was seething as if it was still in combat, and the settling salt dust revealed an angry agitation.

Crax pointed at the activity. 'This looks bad,' he said. 'How bad is it? Did we lose?'

'Rally point,' Diodorus said tersely. 'And we walk to save the horses. It's bad.'

Crax looked back again. Men in the phalanx were shaking their fists and cursing at each other. 'How bad?' he asked.

'The Macedonian fucks just handed Eumenes to One-Eye. Alive,' Diodorus said bitterly. 'I was too late to stop them, the treasonous cunts.'

There were shouts from the phalanx behind them, and then more shouts, and an ugly murmur.

'Just keep moving, boys,' Diodorus said. 'March!'

Crax shook his head. 'How can such men make their peace with the gods?' he asked.

Diodorus shook his head. 'Antigonus took our camp,' he said. 'The Argyraspids traded Eumenes for their loot from years past. Can you imagine?' He went on, 'If they'd stood their ground, we could have had it back at spear point in the morning. That army was *beaten*. Listen – every man in our phalanx knows that they've been robbed.'

Crax swore expressively in Getae.

Diodorus walked silently, and Satyrus kept his head down to avoid being sent away.

The column of troops set off. They were short of men, missing or dead, but they had also collected several dozen cavalry stragglers and Crax formed them into a fourth troop. Many of them protested against walking in the salt dust, and a few mounted their horses and rode away in disgust, refusing to accept discipline that they felt was foolish. The rest obeyed, obviously glad to have someone to follow, another lesson that was not lost on Satyrus, although he was now so tired that he couldn't remember what he had done or the order in which it had happened or whether he had been brave or cowardly, but only that he was alive.

Word of the betrayal of Eumenes the Cardian by his own officers began to filter down the column, so that men shook their heads or cursed.

The sun was well down in the sky, and Satyrus couldn't account for all the hours of the day.

Next to Satyrus, his uncle gathered his officers and issued orders as he walked.

'When we get to the gully, water the horses by troop, fast as you can. Crax, you cover us while we water. Then we retire past the gully in column till we find the girls, and camp. Every man grooms his mount before he sleeps – we'll fight again tomorrow. And we've lost all our remounts. This is what we have.'

'Lost our remounts!' Antigonus said. 'Zeus Soter, strategos. That's bad.'

'Worse than you think, brother,' Diodorus spat. 'Don't let anyone stop. Don't let anyone fall out. Use force if you have to – we can't spare a man, even the lost sheep back there. Understand?'

The hyperetai and the troop commanders all nodded, saluted and walked back to their places in the column, and a litany of 'Close up!' and 'Move your arse!' started to roll up and down the small column.

'Uncle Diodorus?' Satyrus asked quietly.

The strategos turned his head and raised one salt-crusted eyebrow.

'Did we win?' Satyrus asked.

Diodorus shook his head. 'I don't think we won *enough*,' he said.

The stream at the bottom of the gully flowed clear and bright despite the events of the day, and Satyrus and his new bay drank greedily. Satyrus washed his face and hands in the crisp water and found that the burns around his eyes were far worse than he'd expected, and he poured handfuls of water over his eyes until a Keltoi trooper pulled him firmly from the stream. He collected the reins of his mare and led her up the far bank of the watercourse.

'That horse looks like she has some life in her,' Diodorus said. He had a fig in his fist and was eating it. Between bites, he gave orders. 'Boy, take that nice horse and go and find the baggage. Should be less than a stade, over the ridge. Then double back and tell us where they are.'

Satyrus took two tries to get himself up on the big mare's back – his arms were too weak to vault. But he got up, and he pleased himself immensely by giving his uncle a salute. Then he pulled his broad felt *petasos* hat off his back where it had rested uselessly all day while his face burned raw and pulled it down over his eyes.

The water made a difference. He set his mare at the slope and she got up it with style, her haunches pushing powerfully as they climbed. He patted her neck. 'Good girl,' he said.

All her tack was mounted in silver, with silver belt ends and Saka-style buckles. The Greeks seldom used buckles, but they looked wonderful. And the leopard skin made him smile.

As soon as he emerged from the gully end he was in the midst of a horde of camp followers, and there were more all along the trade road going south, hundreds of women, some with children, many crying and more walking in a worse silence. They shied off the road as soon as they saw an armed man, except for a few too tired or too victimized to flinch.

A stade past the eastern end of the gully, he saw pickets – a dozen cavalrymen in three posts. He rode towards them, urging his mount into a canter. She responded easily, crossing the low scrub grass like the wind – the very wind that was dispersing the clouds of salt dust, so that for the first time in eight hours, the Plain of Gabiene was again visible.

Satyrus rode up the ridge to see Tasda, a Tanais-Kelt he'd known all his life, greeting him from the picket.

'Tasda!' he called, and his voice cracked. He clasped hands with the man, who removed his helmet.

'Your sister will rejoice,' Tasda said soberly. 'Keep going over the ridge. We have a laager.'

'Is Antigonus here?' Satyrus asked.

'And Eumenes – our Eumenes, that is. We're all that's left of our cavalry,' Tasda said soberly.

Satyrus grinned through his fatigue. 'Diodorus and the rest are right behind me!' he said, and all the pickets turned their heads, and Dercorix, another childhood acquaintance, came trotting over.

'The strategos lives?' he called.

'I'll be back,' Satyrus said, and turned his horse down the hill.

In a quarter of an hour, they were all together. The officers strained their voices and their authority to keep men from embracing their women and their comrades, and despite the trials of the day, the hippeis got enough eudaimonia from the discovery of their missing comrades to get their horses groomed and their tack stowed before they collapsed to lie sprawled on the ground and be fed by their equally exhausted slaves and followers.

Satyrus and Melitta embraced while Theron berated them.

They ignored him. 'I rescued this prince Herakles,' Melitta said proudly, indicating a blond boy smaller than Satyrus who stood behind her. 'The son of Iskander, no less!'

Satyrus grinned and hugged her again. 'I didn't manage anything so heroic,' he said. 'But I got to ride in a cavalry charge!' He looked around. 'Where's Philokles?'

Theron spat. 'Sitting with the women, basking in admiration,' he said. 'You are all insane.'

Satyrus couldn't stop smiling, although he found that he was sitting and couldn't get up. 'You came with us of your own free will,' he said.

Theron shook his head. 'So I did,' he said.

Melitta tugged his arm. 'Come and meet Herakles,' she said. 'I like him.'

Just for a moment, Satyrus was jealous. He had never heard his sister *like* anyone with such fervour. 'He can't be much if you had to rescue him,' Satyrus said.

Melitta gave him a look that indicated that he didn't know much. 'He was as smart as you,' she said. 'He didn't lose his head.'

Satyrus was mollified by the comparison. He hugged his sister again. 'Zeus, that was stupid, sister. What possessed us?'

'The oath, silly,' she replied. 'We swore, right? So every time we have the ability, we have to fight.'

They came to Herakles, standing alone and self-conscious. He was a tall boy, blond like his father, but gawky, his features too sharp and his shoulders too narrow to be the child of a god. Some of the Olbian veterans were watching him, a few staring openly. He was, after all, Alexander's son.

'I hate being stared at by common people,' Herakles said.

Satyrus felt an immediate contrariness for this awkward boy – an unfair dislike. He succumbed to it anyway, as he was tired and beginning to lose the daimon of war and to feel the collapse that followed. 'No common people here,' he said. 'That big man staring at you is Carlus. He was my father's bodyguard when he defeated your father at the Jaxartes River.'

'My father was *never* defeated,' Herakles responded hotly.

'Have you ever met anyone who was there?' Satyrus asked with lazy contempt. 'Shall we ask Diodorus? Hama?' He put a hand on the boy's shoulder.

'My father is a *god*!' Herakles said. 'You are just a decadent *Greek*.'

Something about the boy's defiance made Satyrus smile. 'Hey – Herakles. It's okay. We're alive and a lot of people aren't. Assassins didn't get us. Relax!'

Herakles looked around. 'Why won't my mother let me in the tent?' he asked. 'I hate it when she does this.'

Melitta rolled her eyes behind her new friend's back, and Satyrus shook his head. 'Let's go and get some *kykeon*,' he said, taking the boy by the shoulder and leading him away. Melitta shot him a look of thanks, and he shook his head.

It was odd, having a younger boy to support, because Satyrus's feeling of disorientation vanished when he had to lead the boy. He walked straight up to Crax, who was surrounded by soldiers, and asked where he should put his blanket roll and whether he and the boy could get some food, and Crax dealt with him as if he was any other soldier.

'Do I look like a hyperetes?' Crax said. Then he scratched his dusty blond beard and relented. 'Your baggage and your sister's is in first troop's row. There's wine and salt-fish stew at the head of every street.' He grinned. 'Your Aunt Sappho did well for us.'

Satyrus walked down the rows of blanket rolls and packs that littered the 'street' (there were no tents) of *his* troop. He felt like a man. He found his sister's red wool pack and then his own, opened his leather bag and removed the carefully wrapped gold cups. He also pulled out a wooden plate and a horn spoon.

'Let's eat,' he said, walking back towards the head of the camp.

All around him, men were eating and then going straight to

sleep in the evening sun. There was little talk and less laughter. Most men prayed, and many libations were poured in the white sand by men who had felt the hand of a god keeping them alive.

'Why are they so quiet?' Herakles asked suddenly. 'Soldiers are usually so – boisterous.'

Satyrus looked at the other boy and felt old. 'They fought a battle,' he said. 'You did too, or so my sister says.' He looked at Melitta, who was walking with them, being silent and a little gawky – not herself at all. 'Nobody feels like talking after a battle. Right?'

'I do,' Herakles said. 'I never get to talk to anybody,' he said. 'And I didn't get to *do* anything. Your sister rescued me.'

Melitta was starting to look uncomfortable. 'You helped,' she said. 'You didn't lose your nerve.'

'My father would have killed them all and laughed,' Herakles said miserably.

'You need food,' Satyrus said, trying to sound commanding. He scooped his wooden bowl full of kykeon, a rich porridge of soft cheese, barley meal and, in this case, wine. 'Eat!'

Philokles walked up to the fire, filled his bowl and sat down. 'Good evening,' he said formally.

'Good evening,' Satyrus replied. He was a little shy of the Spartan, aware that he was guilty of gross disobedience.

'The Lady Banugul is concerned for her son,' Philokles said. 'Herakles, you should go to her.'

'She told me to leave the tent,' Herakles said, between spoons of porridge.

'She has just been made a widow,' Philokles said. 'Your step-father—'

'I have no stepfather. My father is Alexander, the God. My mother should never touch another man.' Herakles spat the phrases as if he had learned them by rote.

Philokles took a deep breath. 'Young man, you are not my pupil. But if you were,' and he gave Satyrus a significant look, 'I would tell you that your father's godhood is neither here not there for *you* – that you are responsible only for your own acts, and need have no concern for your mother or your father. And condemning your mother to a life of celibacy is unfair.'

'Easy for you to say – you just want to fuck her like every other man.' Herakles turned his head away.

'I assure you that I have *no* interest in sex with your mother. And if you were my pupil, I would now proceed to beat you to obedience.' Philokles shot Satyrus a look, and Satyrus sighed.

'Why did you rescue her then?' Herakles asked. 'Men only do things for her for one reason – she says it herself!'

Philokles smiled – a look that neither Satyrus nor Melitta had seen in a long time. 'Once,' he said, 'your mother made a poor decision, and tried to kill Satyrus's father – and me.' He raised an eyebrow at Herakles. 'This is an adult explanation. Are you prepared to be an adult, young man?'

Herakles looked around – at Melitta, most of all. 'Yes,' he said.

'Your mother tried to kill us. Instead, we killed all her soldiers. Then, Satyrus's father gave her an escort and let her go. I wanted her killed.' Philokles sat back.

Herakles swallowed, hard.

'When time had passed, I saw how Kineas's – how Satyrus's father's mercy had been the right decision, for gods and men. And then I decided that if I, in my turn, could ever do her a service, then I would gain honour with the gods.' He nodded brusquely. 'In this way, I share in the honour of my friend, Satyrus's father. Understand?'

Melitta nodded. 'And you have,' she said.

'Yes,' Philokles said. 'Herakles, if you have finished that bowl, you should give it to Satyrus, so that he can eat, and I will take you to your mother.'

Herakles rose to his feet and handed Satyrus the bowl. 'Thanks,' he said.

'Come back and sit with us,' Melitta said.

Herakles smiled. 'Thanks, Lita,' he said.

Philokles was only gone for as long as it took him to walk to where Sappho's slaves had pitched a small tent for Banugul and back.

'Have you eaten?' Philokles asked Satyrus.

'Yes,' Satyrus said.

'Come with me,' Philokles said. He didn't say a word as they walked through the camp, until they came to a third troop mess where Theron sat stirring fish stew. Theron looked at Satyrus and then looked away.

'Well?' Philokles asked.

Satyrus hung his head. 'Master Theron, I come to beg your forgiveness for my bad behaviour.'

Theron nodded. 'Lad, I am going to offer you the same choice that a tutor once offered me. I know that your actions, and your sister's, saved lives. I also know that the gods must have worked extra hard to save you from death, and that I gave a year of my life in worry. You understand, boy?'

'Yes, Master Theron.'

'Good. Here is your choice. A beating, now, or I leave your service.' Theron stood up. He was *very* large.

Satyrus didn't hesitate. 'I'll have the beating,' he said, head up.

Both men nodded, obviously pleased. Theron had a switch, cut from poplar. He hit Satyrus ten times. It wasn't a particularly savage beating – Satyrus had had worse from Philokles – but neither was it symbolic. It hurt, and then it was over.

Afterwards, he lay down on his blankets – face down, because his whole back hurt – and Melitta cried a little.

'Why don't they beat me?' she said. 'It was my idea!'

Satyrus laughed through a sob. 'You're a girl,' he said.

'Stupid Greeks,' she said.

After a while, Theron came and massaged his back, and helped the twins put a pair of cavalry javelins up like an X with a third for a tent pole. 'You were both very brave today,' Theron said.

Despite the pain in his back, Satyrus went to sleep with a smile on his face.

14

In the morning, Satyrus was so stiff that he could only rise to his feet by grasping the pole of his impromptu tent, and even that caused his stomach muscles to protest. But he rose when ordered, stumbled out into the near dark and found his beautiful new horse. He made sure she was fed and walked her all the way back to the gully with the watering party before he got a handful of dried figs from his sister and a slice of honey cake from Sappho for breakfast. Melitta was astride Bion, eating her breakfast in the saddle, and casting a great many glances at the small tent where Banugul lay.

He repicketed his horse and sat with Hama and Dercorix to eat, sharing the honey cake with an appreciative audience.

'You have to pay Apollodorus for that horse,' Hama said. 'Or give it back and we'll find you a remount.'

Satyrus rubbed his chin, which felt weirdly itchy. 'I don't have any money,' he said.

Melitta came and sat with her back to his, handing out dates. 'We're not poor, brother. Diodorus will give you money.'

'That beast's worth a talent of silver,' Hama said.

'Poseidon!' Satyrus said. 'Really?'

'She's wearing a dozen mina of silver on her harness, boy.' He was watching something. 'There's trouble,' Hama said, pointing a tattooed arm at a clump of Saka sitting on their ponies across the gully. Two of them turned and rode away in a spurt of dust.

'Now?' Satyrus asked Hama. He looked around. 'Don't we need to do something about the Saka?'

The Keltoi man nodded. 'Not really, lord. No one wants more killing right now – and they have had a taste of bronze from our pickets. Now, no time like the present. Just acknowledge the debt, lad. That'll be enough.'

Satyrus wiped his sticky hands on his sister's barbarian trousers, arousing her indignation, but he skipped out of range and trotted off. She didn't follow, because Herakles came out of his mother's tent, wearing a shining white chiton and a diadem of gold.

Most of the hippeis had camped in the same order that they rode, so each file became a mess and sat around their own fire. Apollodorus was in third file of first troop. Satyrus found him drinking camomile tea.

'Is a talent fair?' Satyrus asked, walking up.

All the men in the mess group stood, as if he was an officer.

Apollodorus frowned. 'A talent of silver, lord?' He couldn't hold the frown. 'That'll have to do!'

'Herald coming in,' another trooper said, shovelling barley-porridge into a bowl. 'Can't be good news.' He handed the bowl to Satyrus. 'Barley, lad?'

It was *full* of honey, and Satyrus ate the whole bowl with more appetite than he thought he had, while the herald dismounted and exchanged words with Andronicus beyond the wagon laager.

'Clean your bowl, lord?' a woman asked.

The camp was almost besieged by women – not their own women, who were inside the laager, but hundreds of hungry refugees from yesterday's disaster, begging food for their children. Grim-faced pickets kept them outside the wagons, but many of the troopers handed out their scraps.

A few single men simply walked out of the gate and chose companions. They and their children changed status instantly, coming in past the pickets. Satyrus watched his uncle, who in turn was watching the process with a jaundiced eye. He shook his head, gathered a couple of handfuls of grass and wiped the bowl clean and handed it back to the owner. Then he walked over to Diodorus, who stood alone, looking thunderous. Satyrus wanted to continue being a soldier, not a boy. He hoped he'd be allowed to ride with the troop again.

'Good morning, Strategos,' Satyrus said.

Diodorus finished his wife's honey cake. 'Nice piece of work yesterday, boy,' he said, dusting his hands on his chiton.

'I told you *not* to get honey on that chiton,' Sappho called.

The strategos looked sheepish and stepped away from his wagon. 'We need to move,' he said. 'The refugees will get desperate tomorrow. Antigonus – the strategos, not our troop commander – has demanded a parley.' The hippeis seemed to get an unending amount of mirth out of the fact that they had both a Eumenes and an Antigonus among them.

Satyrus was delighted to be addressed in such an adult manner. It seemed to promise well. 'What will you do?' he asked.

Diodorus nodded. 'You and I will go and meet the great man,' he said, 'While Eumenes and Crax get our people out of here. You ready to move?'

Satyrus was wearing the same chiton as yesterday and no boots. 'May I have a few minutes, sir?' he asked, heart pumping hard.

'Five. No, three. Hurry.' Diodorus was already turning away to Crax, who looked clean, neat and golden.

Satyrus had missed some change in orders, because all around him men were tying up their kit, wrapping spare gear in cloaks and tying them in bundles, handing things to slaves. Satyrus's gear was the last in his area of the camp to be lying on the ground under the hasty shelter. He pulled it all down and tried to roll his cloak as tightly as he saw the soldiers doing, but his sister stopped him.

'Don't be silly,' she said. 'I'll get slaves to pack you. Get your corslet on and your boots.'

His Thracian boots were crusted in salt and dried hard, but he got them on, feeling the beating in his back and the fatigue in his abdomen. His corslet was soaked through with sweat and clammy. The cord that held his sword was almost broken and he tied it hurriedly and tossed the scabbard over his head and made sure it was in his armpit, and then he made himself trot to his mare, although he didn't want to trot anywhere. Melitta didn't look exhausted, and his uncle and Crax looked as fresh as the new day.

Of course, neither of them had been beaten by their tutors for disobedience.

It took him three attempts and some ungraceful squirming to get a leg over the mare's back. She stood for it, though, and he was up. Only then did he realize that he didn't have his petasos hat or his helmet.

'Zeus Soter,' he swore, and regretted his impiety. Too late to get his hat. He rode around the camp to the gate, pushed his horse through the crowd of women and children, and reined in by his uncle.

Melitta ran up, clutching his hat. He smiled at her. 'What would I do without you?' he asked.

'Get even redder,' she said. She clasped his hand, and then his uncle was up on a charger and they were riding, out of the gate, through the women, past the pickets and past the gully. Andronicus came with them, his trumpet on his hip, and twenty troopers led by Hama.

On the far side of the gully they saw the band of Saka. The chief motioned with his hand, as if beckoning the Tanais troopers to come across. The gesture might have been well meant, but it might also have been mocking.

'I'll go,' Satyrus said. 'I can talk to them.'

Hama grunted.

Diodorus sighed. 'Nothing less threatening than a twelve-year-old.'

Hama spat. 'They could kill him.'

Diodorus looked around. 'Carlus? Go with him. Do it, Satyrus. Our goal here is to waste as much time as possible.' Diodorus patted him on the shoulder.

Satyrus glanced at Hama and rode forward. He angled off to avoid the gully and then rode straight at the Saka, who came to meet them, surrounding them and calling shrilly to one another.

Carlus towered over him, right at his shoulder, his spear on its throwing loop.

'Whose band is this?' Satyrus called out in Sakje, and the man with the most gold reined in his pony and laughed.

'Astlan of the River Foxes,' he called.

'I am Satrax of the Cruel Hands,' Satyrus responded. 'My mother is Srayanka, who fought with your Queen Zarina against Iskander.'

Astlan raised his hand in greeting. 'Names of story,' he said.

'You do not look like a son of the people,' he said. He shrugged. 'But you talk the people's talk.'

'We intend to make parley with Antigonus,' Satyrus said. 'Will you let us pass?'

The Massagetae chief shrugged. 'You are no enemy of mine, son of Srayanka. Ride free.'

The Saka whooped and rode off in a thin veil of dust.

Satyrus rode up the ridge towards the bluff, Carlus at his shoulder. A couple of the Saka paced them, and a young woman waved at him.

'Greetings, cousin!' he shouted.

She grinned. 'Greetings, cousin!' she shouted back, and rode in closer. She had gold plaques on her tunic and gold in her hair and gold foil wrapped her braids. 'You are just a boy!' she said when she was closer. 'I thought you were a spear-maiden!'

Satyrus blushed with embarrassment, but she smiled again. Her eyes had an odd shape. 'I'm Darya of the Golden Horses,' she said. 'I killed a Greek yesterday! Yiee!'

'Satrax of the Cruel Hands,' he called to her. *I maimed a peasant and cut down some fleeing men who wanted my horse.*

She paced him up the ridge. 'Good hunting!' she called, and wheeled away, waving her bow. 'Nice fucking horse!'

My sister would have made her a friend for life, Satyrus thought. He sighed.

Carlus grunted. 'My shoulders are tight,' he said. 'I wait for the arrow in the back.' He gave Satyrus a gap-toothed grin. 'Like riding with your father, eh?'

At the top of the ridge were a dozen horsemen, and Satyrus was surprised to find that one of them was the young officer he'd outrun the day before.

'Hail, lord,' he said, slowing his mount. 'I come to speak for Diodorus of Tanais.'

The young man had a blond beard and bright blue eyes. 'I am Demetrios,' he said in a tone replete with self-importance. 'Bring your Diodorus to me.' He looked down the ridge. 'You seem friendly with my Saka. I'm surprised they did not eat you for breakfast.'

Satyrus kept his face as neutral as twelve years could manage. 'I will go and find my strategos.'

'Don't keep me waiting, boy,' Demetrios called. His breastplate and helmet were newly polished. His eyes were on the horse Satyrus was riding.

Satyrus bowed from the back of his mare and turned away.

'Where did you get that horse?' Demetrios shouted after him.

Satyrus affected not to hear and rode down the ridge and around the gully, passing back through the loose line of Massagetae. They paid him no attention at all, although Darya waved at him.

He cantered back to Diodorus and saluted. 'Demetrios awaits you at the top of the ridge.' Satyrus shook his head. 'I don't like it.'

'I don't like it either, lord,' Carlus said. 'He has a hundred men around him and he's a hothead boy. He didn't offer us laurel or olive or safe passage.'

'Demetrios is Antigonus's son,' Diodorus said. 'He honours us, in a backhanded way. And we're buying time.' He motioned over his shoulder, where a distant curl of dust indicated Sappho's wagons rolling out, heading south and east. They started forward around the gully, riding slowly, never faster than a walk.

'You know what happened last night?' Diodorus asked Satyrus.

Satyrus wondered if this was about his punishment. He looked at the strategos. 'No,' he said. Anything to keep his uncle talking.

'We didn't lose the battle yesterday. Antigonus lost his phalanx – heavy casualties. Our leader, Eumenes, rallied his beaten cavalry at the end of the day, and Antigonus retreated.' Diodorus's voice was grim, and he held his horse to a walk, although Demetrios was plainly visible on the skyline.

'So we won?' Satyrus asked.

'Listen, boy. Late afternoon, and Eumenes summoned all his commanders to meet him. Remember? I rode away?' Diodorus looked at him, and Satyrus could see the fatigue in his eyes.

'Yes,' Satyrus replied.

'As I rode up, the fucking Macedonians seized him. They tried to get me. *His own officers* betrayed him.' Diodorus's face was a mask. 'There are no rules any more, Satyrus. No honour. Zeus Soter, they call us mercenaries faithless.' He shook his head. 'So be ready for anything. Hear me?'

Satyrus wanted to ask why he'd been brought, but he decided to let it go.

Astlan and a pair of riders rode up, looked at them from a few horse-lengths and cantered easily away. They had bows in their hands, but no arrows on the string – yet.

Satyrus turned out of his uncle's small column and trotted over to Darya, feeling bold. He reached into his quiver and took out an arrow – one of his own red-shafted arrows fletched in heron feathers. 'Here,' he said.

She smiled. She had dimples and jet-black hair. She gave him one of her own arrows. The Massagetae of her band began to tease her, and she swatted another girl with her bow. Then she flashed a smile at Satyrus, who returned it with interest and cantered back to Carlus.

'I thought that I'd lost you for a moment,' Carlus said. 'Try not to do that again.'

'Give the boy some respect,' Diodorus said. 'His Sakje may be all that is keeping us from their arrows.'

Demetrios displayed his impatience by cantering down the hill away from his entourage. 'Can we get this done?' he said. 'My father offers you all your lives. You will take service with us. There, it's done. You, boy – that's my spare horse. Hand it over. She's a Nisaean!'

The silver-helmeted young man reached for Satyrus's reins.

Satyrus backed the mare away, leaving the blond officer grasping air. 'Spear-won!' he said, delighted with himself for remembering the right word at the right time.

'You lost, you stupid Greek. Give me my horse!' Demetrios became aware that he was surrounded by enemy cavalry. 'Touch me and you are all dead.'

Diodorus caught the enemy boy's bridle and turned his horse. 'You'll be worth a pretty penny,' he said. 'Ride for it!'

They thundered away, through the surprised Saka and across the ridge, past the gully. Satyrus didn't start breathing until they were within the circuit of their own pickets. Not an arrow flew their way.

Demetrios was all but raving. 'You are all dead men! You have broken your oaths! You fucking Greek mercenaries, you scum!'

His escort hadn't pursued them past the gully.

Diodorus handed the blond's reins to Hama. 'I couldn't resist. Listen, *boy*. We swore no oaths – you offered us no safe conduct. Your herald didn't have a staff. And you did not win the battle. Now – speak your piece. Then – maybe – I'll let you go back to your father.'

Demetrios didn't lack courage. He looked around him, as if assessing the situation. 'You're the boy who shot past us yesterday!' he said to Satyrus. He grinned, suddenly, and looked like the statue of a young Apollo. 'My father offers you wages. And demands the return of any booty you have taken. And the handing over of certain people. I am not to discuss this in public.' He looked around him.

Satyrus admired his coolness, because the golden boy was smiling as if he'd just been given a gift.

'Dad says I'm a hothead. I'll never live this down. You will let me go? He really will kill you. Look at the force he's putting together!' Demetrios pointed at the mass of cavalry already gathering on the ridge beyond the gully.

'What people?' Diodorus asked.

'Eumenes' widow and her bastard son,' Demetrios said. 'We will not mistreat her.'

Diodorus looked south along the valley. From the top of the ridge that had held their pickets all night, he could see that Sappho's wagons had made fifteen stades and were still rolling.

'The answer is no,' Diodorus said after a moment. 'No, we won't take service with your father and, no, we won't return any booty and, no, you cannot have Banugul. Although I wish you fucking had her already,' he said, shaking his head. 'As to being fucking Greeks, and mercenaries—'

'I was overwrought,' Demetrios said cheerfully. 'I have a temper.'

'Your father arranged with the Argyraspids to have my employer murdered, did he not?' Diodorus was watching as more Macedonian cavalry crested the far ridge.

'The mutinous troops killed Eumenes,' Demetrios said. 'What you say is a very serious accusation.'

'Go and tell your father that if he wants us, he can try and catch us,' Diodorus said. 'Now get off your horse.'

'This is my best horse,' Demetrios said.

'It is about to become *my* best horse,' Diodorus said. 'Think of it as the cost of a little lesson in war. You still have a great deal to learn. Next time you offer someone a truce, keep it.'

Demetrios dismounted. He turned to Satyrus. 'Who are you?' he asked.

'Satyrus, son of Kineas,' he said.

Demetrios gave him a good-natured smile, and tossed him his silver helmet. 'You might as well have this to go with the horse. That way, I'll know you next time!' He grinned, turned away and started to jog across the grass to the north.

'There goes fifty talents of gold,' Hama said bitterly. 'We got a horse!'

Diodorus led them back south, towards the vanishing column of dust. 'Antigonus One-Eye would follow us to the ends of the earth to rescue his son,' he said. 'I hope it won't be worth his while to pursue us otherwise.'

'They really murdered Eumenes?' Crax asked.

'Someone did. I saw them grab him yesterday – Argyraspids and some cavalry officers.' Diodorus shook his head. 'He deserved better.'

'Where in Hades do we go now?' asked Eumenes the Olbian, who rode up from the head of his troop. 'Hello, young Satyrus.' He reached out for the silver helmet that Satyrus was still holding. 'That's quite a piece of kit.'

Satyrus hugged him.

Eumenes eyed the helmet. 'Well, I'd be careful where I wore it,' he said, laughing. 'Young Apollo over there will probably want it back.'

'He said something of the sort,' Satyrus admitted.

Diodorus looked around. 'Has this outfit lost any semblance of discipline? You people have troops to command, I believe?'

'Where are we going?' Crax asked. 'Tanais is gone, and Eumenes the Cardian is dead. We're out of employers!'

Diodorus gave them a tight smile. 'Aegypt,' he said. 'Down the hills to the Euphrates, up the Euphrates until we can cut across the desert to the Jordan, and down the Jordan to Alexandria.'

Crax shook his head. 'That's five thousand stades!' he said. 'By Hermes, Strategos, we don't have remounts, we don't have food, and we're surrounded by enemies. We don't have a bronze obol amongst us!'

'Twenty days should see us to Ptolemy's outposts,' Diodorus said. 'We'll buy remounts – or take them. Look, I have the first one under my hand.'

'We couldn't buy a donkey,' Crax said.

'Remember how One-Eye was asking for our loot back?' Diodorus asked, smirking at Eumenes.

Crax grinned. 'That was a good one. What loot?'

'The loot I got,' Eumenes said. 'While you folks were gallivanting around the battlefield, I lifted One-Eye's treasury.' He shrugged at Crax's disbelieving look. 'All Tyche, brother. I got lost in the salt haze, and I tripped over these packhorses.'

They all laughed, and Satyrus, now one of them, laughed too.

When they rejoined the column, they found Banugul sitting on a white Nisaean with her son on a black mare. She looked like a queen, her pale-skinned beauty scarcely aged. She wore a considerable amount of carefully applied cosmetics, more than Satyrus had ever seen on a free woman, and she had a cloth-of-gold scarf tied over her hair. Her purple-blue eyes sparkled under the shawl, and she was obviously angry.

Herakles looked deeply unhappy.

Diodorus rode up in a swirl of dust and embraced his Sappho. 'Beautiful job,' he said.

She gave him a lopsided grin. 'Men,' she said. 'Birth a baby and they've nothing to say. But get a column moving—'

'I wish to go to One-Eye,' Banugul said.

Diodorus gawked at her. 'What? He tried to kill you yesterday.'

She shook her head. 'I am not going to Aegypt with a column of mercenaries,' she said. Her tone softened. 'There are many men here with no reason to love me, or Alexander's son, either, Diodorus. I will never forget that Philokles saved me, nor that Kineas's daughter saved my son. But I am the satrap of Hyrkania, and Antigonus One-Eye is now my lord. I will go and make obeisance to him.'

Sappho laughed.

Banugul glared at her.

Diodorus rubbed his chin. 'He asked for you and the boy, right enough,' the strategos said. 'He might just kill you.'

Banugul smiled. It was an easy smile, a light smile, and it undid fifteen years of ageing and rendered her Aphrodite-like. 'He will not kill me. He needs my father, and my brothers, and my son will give him legitimacy.'

'I want to be a king,' Herakles said suddenly. 'Not a pawn.'

'Your father started as a pawn,' Banugul said. And then, in a kinder way, she said, 'Your turn will come.'

'I want to stay with Satyrus and Melitta,' he said.

Satyrus rode over to the boy and clasped his hand, as men do. 'We will be friends,' he said.

Diodorus looked at Sappho, and then at Eumenes. The young Olbian gave a slight nod. So did Sappho.

'You'd be doing us a favour, and no mistake, lady,' Diodorus acknowledged. 'If you were to – to go to him, One-Eye might just let us go.' He looked at the northern horizon. 'But we've got Hades' own jump on the bastard. I think we can outrun him.'

Banugul smiled her Aphrodite smile again. 'So many brave men. But not today.'

Diodorus exchanged one more look with his wife. 'Fine. I'll send a herald.'

Banugul nodded. 'By leaving you, I return the favour that Philokles – and Kineas – did me.'

Sappho turned her head away. Satyrus could tell that his aunt didn't like the beautiful queen.

Melitta came up the column, already covered in dust from riding around, visiting. Apparently unaware of her condition, she rode into the command group. 'Herakles is leaving?' she asked.

'Yes,' Sappho answered. 'Say your goodbyes. His mother feels she'll do better with our enemies. The men who just murdered her husband.'

Banugul's head shot around, and her glare had the power of a thousand courtly confrontations, and Sappho met it full on.

'Better for all of us, really,' Diodorus was heard to mutter. 'Hama? Take a file from first troop, and Andronicus as your herald.'

Melitta embraced a startled Herakles, who then hugged her back with sudden fervour. She kissed him, which got a grunt of disapproval from his mother. Sappho exchanged her frown for a smile – anything that displeased the blonde Persian woman pleased her.

'I won't forget you!' Herakles called, as he rode away. Satyrus waved to him, and then pressed his heels to his mount, galloped up by the other boy, and handed him a javelin – one of his own, a nice heavy one.

'Now you're armed,' he said. Then he made himself say something personal. 'Remember what Philokles said yesterday. Don't try to be your father. Just be yourself.'

Herakles gripped his hand so hard it hurt, and Satyrus was shocked to see tears in the boy's eyes.

They clasped hands again, and Herakles rode away.

When Satyrus rode back to his uncle, the strategos was frowning at the dust raised by Banugul's party. 'I should have sent more of an escort.'

'You should have sent her *alone*,' Sappho said.

'You are *not helping*,' Diodorus said through clenched teeth.

Satyrus rode away from them, back along the column to his sister, who cried for a little, very quietly.

'I really liked him,' she said.

Satyrus didn't have much of an idea what to say, so he gave her a quick and clumsy hug from horseback and they rode on without speaking. Silence was the order of the day, and a lot of glances back past the dust of the column.

'They're all worried about the escort,' Satyrus said. He'd just worked it out. 'If Antigonus murdered Eumenes the Cardian, he could do anything, including murdering Banugul.'

His sister sobbed.

'What did I say?' he asked the gods.

'Just the fucking obvious! You are *so* useless.' Melitta's voice trembled.

Crax went out with the prodromoi to find a campsite and still there was no sign of Hama or the escort. Crax returned long after Melitta's tears had dried, and she and her brother were reconciled, and still there was no news. They made camp – a cold and hasty camp, which consisted mostly of picketing horses and unrolling blankets and cloaks. The mountains rose all around them, and it was cold, and in the last light of the late summer evening, it began to rain. Melitta pressed hard against her brother's back.

'I really liked him,' she said. 'Herakles, I mean.'

'I know who you mean,' Satyrus said.

'Of course you did,' Theron said kindly, from the other side of the sleeping pile. 'He was a nice enough boy, for the son of a god.'

'Go to sleep,' Philokles ordered.

They all slept fitfully, the intermittent rain and the cold making real sleep impossible. Melitta shivered and Satyrus's hips were hurting from sleeping on the ground. He pulled his Thracian cloak over his face to keep the rain off of it and managed to slip away.

He smelled the lion skin first, and then he saw the club.

'You have done well,' said a voice deep enough to raise the hairs on the back of his neck.

Satyrus snapped awake with the scent of wet cat fur in his nostrils. He lay awake a long time, listening to his heart race and to Theron's snores, until the reality of the dream slipped into the next one, and he relaxed, and slept.

*

They were all stiffer, and older, in the morning, and the horses were tired. But just after first light, when the sentries were calling men to wake, a young trooper rode in, weary but obviously full of news, and went to the cluster of tents that stood in the centre of the camp. By the time Satyrus was sharing a bowl of yogurt and honey with his sister, the news was spreading from fire to fire, and the sound of laughter could suddenly be heard, and fatigue began to fall away.

Philokles came over, having been to Diodorus's tent. 'Melitta? One-Eye welcomed Banugul as a queen, with open arms, and his escort hailed Herakles as the son of Alexander.' He smiled at her.

She nodded. 'Excuse me,' she said, slipping away a little.

'That's good to hear,' Satyrus said, just to say something.

Philokles and Theron both nodded.

'One-Eye sent Diodorus a safe-conduct,' Philokles added.

'Zeus Soter!' Theron said. 'So we're going to live?'

'Eventually he's going to discover that we have his pay chest,' Philokles said.

Not much later, the whole escort came in, with another dozen troopers who had been accounted dead. They were stripped of their armour, but they were mounted, and glad to be released. Most of them had been taken prisoner while wandering lost in the dust cloud.

Diodorus, finished with other business, strode up. 'You don't have to live like soldiers. You know that you can all stay with us,' he said. 'We have an empty tent,' he added, pointing at the tent where Banugul had stayed. It wasn't meant to be funny, but for some reason it made all the men around the fire roar with laughter.

Satyrus looked at his tutor. Philokles nodded. 'I think it is time my charges learned to live like soldiers,' he said.

Diodorus smiled. 'Well,' he said, looking at the horizon, 'they'll have all the way to Aegypt to learn it.'

They all laughed together, glad to be alive, and their laughter rose to heaven like a sacrifice, and just for a moment, Satyrus could smell lion skin.

PART IV

GRINDING

15

'I have no intention of fighting One-Eye if I can help it,' Cassander said. He was dressed in a magnificent purple chlamys over a chiton that would have looked rich on a king. 'Fighting One-Eye is foolish. He eliminated Eumenes, and now he's on top – but he's vulnerable. I want One-Eye to fight Ptolemy while I take Ptolemy's soldiers away from him.'

Cassander was visiting Athens, in state. He came with an extensive entourage that taxed the best efforts of Demetrios of Phaleron and all his political allies to support him. As Menander joked, it was as if the man ate gold.

They were gathered in Demetrios's house – a palace in all but name. Cassander was surrounded by Macedonians, but there were other Greeks in his train, and important allies, like Eumeles of Pantecapaeum.

Demetrios of Phaleron had brought his own allies – the men he trusted to run Athens, and then men whose gold helped keep Cassander fed.

Stratokles lay full length on a *kline* and fingered his beard – more salt than pepper in it now – and exchanged a glance with the only men in the room that he trusted, the scarred mercenary who called himself Iphicrates, and his own lieutenant, the big Italian called Lucius.

'How will you persuade Antigonus to attack Ptolemy?' Philip son of Amyntas asked. He was just the sort of fool who asked such questions – indeed, Stratokles counted on him to ask such questions. He was not the only officer in the room to wonder – every Macedonian officer wondered the same. And Stratokles wondered if Cassander, the murdering regent, the ally of Athens, the rapist of Greece, was finally losing his touch.

'Never you mind,' Cassander said. His chuckle was syrupy,

almost flirtatious. 'Antigonus and I go back,' he said, with a wicked smile. 'He's old. And his son is a fool. I can control them.' Coming from the man who had assassinated Olympias, Alexander's mother, *and* her principal rivals, the statement didn't seem to hold the *hubris* it might have held from a lesser – or greater – man. Cassander was no fool on the battlefield – but in the world of politics and assassination, he was the master.

'I think that you underestimate Ptolemy,' Demetrios said.

'Perhaps,' Cassander smiled. 'But I doubt it. A man with a reputation for plain-dealing, called "Farm Boy" by his troops, is hardly a candidate for survival in this world.'

Stratokles couldn't help himself. 'He's done pretty well so far,' he said.

Cassander turned and looked at him. Always an unsettling experience. Most men flinched from the physical reality of Stratokles' face, but not Cassander.

'With my ally's permission, you seem perfect to go to Aegypt on my behalf, my duplicitous darling. As Athens's ambassador, craving freedom from tyranny.' Cassander smiled, because the Greek city-states and their prating about freedom made him laugh. 'But anyone with a brain at Ptolemy's court will see that you are from me. Tell him I'm desperate. Get him to fill his ships with his Macedonian regulars and send them to me. I'll strip him of real soldiers and then Antigonus can have him and Aegypt too.'

Stratokles rubbed his beard. His eyes went to Menander's, and the playwright nodded slightly.

'A simple enough piece of deception. I can do it,' Stratokles said. 'But I'm not sure ...' he added, prepared to make an honest summation of his hesitancy, largely based on how many enemies he had made in the Athenian factions. 'I'm not known here as "Stratokles the Informer" out of the love of my fellow citizens.'

Athens, the things I do for you.

'Do it?' Cassander laughed. 'My dear viper, you can do it and make the Farm Boy like the taste of the poison, I have no doubt.' He looked at Demetrios. 'Can you spare me your snake?'

'But if Antigonus has the revenues of Aegypt, he'll be invincible!' said Diognes, Demetrios's lover – the handsomest man in Greece.

Demetrios of Phaleron had hard grey eyes – the eyes of Athena, men said. He ignored the beautiful young man on his couch and his eyes flicked from Cassander to Stratokles. 'I can spare him. But I doubt your wisdom in this, Cassander.'

Better you than me, Demetrios, Stratokles said to himself. He, too, thought it a fool's errand. But as usual, Cassander was the one driving the chariot, and Athens was only along for the ride.

'Diogenes, my dear, beautiful and rather empty-headed boy, this is why you are an ornament at parties and I'm the regent of Macedon. If Antigonus takes Aegypt, he'll use more of his precious Macedonians to garrison it. That's all that matters – don't you see? Soldiers – real soldiers. They come from Macedon. Our only export, but just now, the most valuable export in the world. No one but a Macedonian can hold a sarissa and fight. No infantry in the world can beat us.' He smiled at them, uncaring that he'd just offended every Greek in the room. 'We'll take Ptolemy's veterans as our tax. And next year, we'll use them to break Antigonus One-Eye. Or perhaps Lysimachos. It hardly matters – once I have the phalanxes, I can go where I want.' The regent raised his heavily lidded eyes from the pretty Athenian and they dropped on Stratokles as if his glance had real weight. 'You, my viper, are the tool I need to move this particular rock.'

Stratokles thought that it was a bad sign that the Macedonians were starting to believe their own propaganda. It was less than ten years since the hoplites of Athens had broken a Macedonian phalanx. He caught the eye of his friend Iphicrates, whose face was mottled red and white with anger. It was his turn to shake his head, even though any outburst would have been supported by every Athenian present. Even Menander, a notoriously unmilitary man, was offended.

The insult from the regent – viper, a term no man could bear – was almost a compliment from Cassander. *Athens, the crap I take for you*, Stratokles thought. *When the time comes, I'll bury these arrogant barbarians in their own guts.*

Eumeles – everyone called him Heron, the so-called king of the Bosporus, pushed forward past the Macedonians. 'Ptolemy still harbours my enemies,' he said.

Cassander glanced at Stratokles with a grimace that was hidden from the Euxine's tyrant. He made a motion with his hand, as if to say 'What can I do?'

The regent of Macedon rolled over to look at Eumeles. 'And no grain will reach my enemies? Your word on it?'

Eumeles bowed. 'My word on it.' He glanced at Stratokles. 'But I'd like the – ahem – unfinished business wrapped up.'

Cassander nodded. 'That's right. Stratokles – the two children. Olympias wanted them dead – Heron here wants them dead – and you missed them. Eh? Don't miss them again. Understand?'

Stratokles shrugged. 'Heron over there – *he* wanted them dead. And Olympias made it her business. But it's no part of an embassy to murder brats.' He looked to Demetrios of Phaleron for guidance. Demetrios had been a follower of Phocion's – as had the children's father, Kineas. Although Stratokles had no real love for Demetrios, he was an Athenian.

Demetrios's hard grey eyes narrowed. He took a breath to speak, and then shook his head and took a drink of wine.

Cassander pursed his lips. It was always dangerous to confront Cassander on any subject, and Demetrios, the most powerful man in the room save Cassander, had refused.

We must be pretty desperate, Stratokles thought. 'Very well,' he said. 'I'll try and put the children down before I leave. But not until then. If my hand is seen, I'll be expelled or worse.'

'Then don't be caught,' Cassander said. Then he relented. 'I see your point. Hire someone to do it and make sure my hands can't be seen.' He smiled. 'How about your doctor? He's been useful before.'

Cassander's golden good looks and his eyes, heavily lidded like an opium-eater's, were all deceptive. *He's a good deal uglier than me,* Stratokles thought. *I think it's time we changed horses,* he thought to himself.

Later, in a private room, he made the same point to Menander.

'I agree,' the poet admitted. 'But Demetrios says we need him right now. Things are bad. Succeed in this Aegyptian thing, and perhaps we'll get a breathing space.'

Stratokles took a deep breath and rubbed his nose. 'I hate him enough to consider tyrannicide.' At his friend's startled look, he said, 'Not our tyrant, Menander – I mean Cassander.'

But he packed his bags for Alexandria, nonetheless.

He took the time to send a letter to the doctor in Athens, offering the man a place in his embassy and providing, in addition, a list of members of the assembly of that city and their various transgressions, and he brought Lucius to run his bodyguard. He had many enemies, and the judicious use of force would be required.

He changed the emphasis of his reporting system, so that reports from Alexandria took priority. He listened to a great many reports from spies before he sailed away in his own trireme for Alexandria, the newest city in the world.

Stratokles' informants were capable men and women. He paid informers from the Euxine to the Pillars of Herakles to provide him information. So when the new city rolled up at the edge of the horizon, he knew where Leon lived, and who lived with him; he knew the names of Leon's ships and the names of his factors. This was routine information, because Leon and Stratokles had brushed up against each other in the pursuit of their own interests – sometimes in conflict, sometimes in alliance – for ten years.

And he knew that Ptolemy had an Aegyptian mistress and he knew that Amastris, the daughter of Dionysius of Heraklea, was due to return to Alexandria any day – the richest heiress in the Hellenic world, from a city vital to Athens's interests. He knew that the court was looking to hire a doctor for the palace.

He even knew that Sophokles the Athenian, standing at his side, had been bribed by Cassander to watch him. The thought made Stratokles smile at the smooth-faced man at his side.

'You always worry me when you are so palpably amused,' the doctor said. He reached down and rubbed the scar on his knee.

Stratokles smiled and slapped him on the back. 'Plenty of work for you in Alexandria, my friend,' he said.

'My pleasure,' Sophokles said.

16

The sand of the palaestra was cool on his cheek, but he shifted his weight and rotated his shoulders and his trainer rolled off him and backpedalled swiftly, regaining his feet in the motion.

Satyrus rose a little more slowly, with his hands up and his arms well extended. There was some scattered applause from other men who had stopped training to watch.

'That used to get you every time,' Theron said. He smiled. 'Of course, you didn't always have shoulders like an ox.'

Satyrus was three years older and heavier, taller and wider, a young man in peak physical condition with long, dark hair and shoulders as wide as many Alexandrian doors.

But he still hadn't beaten Theron.

They circled, and more men gathered to watch. They were army officers and senior courtiers, Macedonians, most of them, although a few were Greeks. They knew a good fight when they saw one, and some quiet wagers began.

Satyrus spun on his right foot, raised his left a fraction and faked a blow at Theron's face with his left hand.

Theron caught his jab and went to hold the arm, and Satyrus had to abandon his feint combination and backpedal to avoid the humiliation of giving his opponent an easy win. He felt the skin abrade as he ripped his left hand free.

Theron stepped in, following up his advantage, and shot his right fist out, catching Satyrus on the ribs – a bruising blow, but it was only pain. The younger man moved his hips to the right – the same way he'd spun out of the last two holds – and then went left.

Theron was caught by the move, and Satyrus managed to land a weak left jab to his coach's head as he moved, and then he did it again, faking a third sliding step and then kicking out with his right foot at Theron's left ankle. His blow went in, and the Corinthian rolled with the pain, put his weight on his good

281

right foot and shot a fist at Satyrus, catching him high on the side of the head and rocking him back before losing his balance to the left and stumbling.

Both of them backed away, and every man in the gymnasium breathed as one, and a few cheered. The betting thickened. In Athens, betting on two gentlemen citizens in a public gymnasium would have been bad form, but Alexandria was a different city. A different world.

Theron circled warily, favouring his left foot.

Satyrus thought that he was lying. Faking injury was part of the massive repertory of tricks that a good pankrationist had to master, and Theron did it well.

Given that his left foot is fine, what should I do? Satyrus thought. He wiped sweat from his eyes and fought a temptation to attack just to cut the tension. He had landed several good blows – the leg kick would have put most of his friends down on the sand.

Theron feinted and Satyrus stepped back, declining the engagement, and both of them went back to circling.

Satyrus considered a feint based on the false assumption that Theron's foot was hurt. In a few heartbeats, he assessed the possible blows and holds and chose two simple, obvious moves – a faked kick at the same ankle should draw Theron into committing on the very foot he pretended was injured. After that weight change, he would step in for a grapple.

No sooner had he seen the combination than he allowed his body to flow into the routine, not a sudden attack but a graceful sway of a body feint followed by the 'real' blow – no more real than Theron's fake injury, a low sweep with his right foot against his opponents 'weak' left leg.

Theron obliged him by putting his weight on the 'injured' leg and striking like lightning.

Satyrus was quick too, and he took Theron's blow on the point of his shoulder. The pain was a spike of lightning in his skull, but he was under much of it, and he butted his head straight into Theron's jaw and then stepped on the man's left instep and just *barely* avoided the instinctive planting of his left knee in his coach's crotch, a killing blow combination that they practised for war but not for the palaestra.

In that hesitation, Theron's left arm wrapped around his neck, pinning his head to the Corinthian's chest. The second he felt the pressure, Satyrus pushed with the full strength of both legs, attacking into the hold and spilling the Corinthian backwards as he himself twisted to avoid the hold.

Both of them rolled as they hit the sand and there was a flurry of prone holds and blows and then both of them, scrambling like wounded crabs, rolled apart and got slowly to their feet.

Applause – hearty, this time. At least a hundred men.

Satyrus made himself smile. He'd had the fight there, just for a second, and somehow he'd missed his shot and now his confidence was ebbing and his coach was rising, blood leaking from a big gash on his thigh but otherwise unimpaired.

'Lord Ptolemy!' came the shout. Men scurried to get out of the ruler's way, and many – not all – bowed.

'Stop that!' Ptolemy called. 'Don't stop the pankration! Hades! Is that Theron?'

He had a white chiton trimmed in purple and a diadem in his hair. He was one of the ugliest men in the room, with a nose like the prow of a ship and a forehead that rose into a naked egg of baldness.

Satyrus liked him. He clamped down on his fears and willed himself back into the fight.

Theron was smiling. He stepped in and launched his usual strong right. Emboldened by the king's appearance, Satyrus didn't step back. Instead, he tried the same trick that Theron had used earlier in the bout – he reached out to trap the Corinthian's blow.

'They've been at it five minutes and not a single fall,' a courtier said.

'You should have seen—'

'Hush!' the king said.

Theron was not surprised by his attempted trap. He *let* his pupil grasp the arm and then he reached out with his other arm and grabbed Satyrus's right shoulder, half-rotated him on impetus and tripped him over an outflung leg.

283

But Satyrus still had the arm. As he went down he tightened his hold – virtually the same attack he'd tried as a much lighter twelve-year-old.

Theron tried to spin with the hold and Satyrus tried to keep his feet. Both of them failed, and down they both went, to a dogfight on the sand. They fell too close for either man, and Satyrus got an elbow in the face that blinded him and a foot in the gut that took his wind, and then he rolled clear. He'd landed at least one hard shot himself in the scrum. He got to his feet on training alone.

Theron was slower, rising with his right arm cradled in his left. But he shook his head to clear it and got his hands up to guard.

Satyrus exerted every mina of his will to raise his arms into the guard, but his left arm didn't want to obey. It didn't hurt – it just wouldn't move. He shook his head and the room swayed. Nonetheless, he had enough grasp of the fight to see that Theron was as rocked as he, and he stepped forward to try a right overhand blow to end the fight.

'Stop!' the king said.

The men roared.

Satyrus rocked a little, frozen on the edge of his blow.

'You are both on the verge of serious injury, and I need every man,' the regent of Aegypt said. He grinned his farmer's grin. 'It was beautiful, though.'

'Who wins?' called one of the many Philips, an officer in the Foot Companions. 'We have bets!'

Ptolemy looked at both of them for some beats of Satyrus's heart. 'Draw!' bellowed the lord of Aegypt, and the crowd roared again.

Ptolemy came and clasped hands with the contestants before they went off to the baths. He and Theron exchanged a smile – Theron occasionally trained him. Then Ptolemy turned to Satyrus. 'You are a very promising young man,' he said.

That set tongues wagging throughout the court. Satyrus's 'family', his 'uncles' Diodorus and Leon and Philokles, were important men.

Ptolemy's words suggested to Satyrus that his turn was

coming, and his heart soared. He clasped the lord's arm and beamed. 'At your service, lord,' he said.

Afterwards, after the hot bath and the cold bath and the massage, they went out together with a crowd of Satyrus's friends, down the steps of the public gymnasium in a tide of adulation.

'You may yet defeat me,' Theron said with a grin. 'I doubt it, but I begin to think it is possible.'

Satyrus shook his head. 'I had a moment today ...' He shrugged. His neck hurt, and his left eye would have a bruise like badly applied henna in an hour or so. 'I still have a lot to learn.'

'Music to my ears, boy!' Theron said.

'A cup of wine with you, master?' Satyrus asked.

'No. Go and drink with your cronies, boy.' Theron put a giant arm around him and gave him a squeeze. 'Your uncle Leon is home tonight. His ship is already in with the light-house. And when he's home you'll be worked like a dog, and no more playing with flute girls.'

Leon had taken Satyrus on a dozen voyages. Satyrus had rowed, he had served as a marine and he had served as a super-cargo, counting amphorae. Leon believed that boys needed to work. This summer, he had sailed twice as helmsman – under instruction, of course. Satyrus loved girls and wine, but so far, the greatest love of his life was the sea.

Satyrus grinned, already being tugged away by his friends. 'I'll be there. And I'll sacrifice to Poseidon for his safe return.'

'See that you have a safe return, boy!' Theron called over the crowd, and then they were away, crossing the great agora where the four districts met.

'You don't believe all that shit, do you, Satyrus?' Dionysius asked. Dionysius was a year older, the son of a Macedonian in Ptolemy's service. He was handsome, well bred and intelligent, and he could quote most of the plays of Aristophanes and every new work by Menander. 'Propitiating the gods? That's for peasants.'

Satyrus wasn't in the mood for a philosophical quarrel – the more so as Dionysius, for all his airs, wasn't nearly as well educated as Philokles. 'My tutor says that respect for the gods cannot ever be wrong,' he said.

'You're such a prude,' Dionysius said. 'If you didn't have a beautiful body, no one would speak to you.'

Satyrus had learned enough from his sister to sense that Dionysius was unhappy at having Satyrus at centre stage because of his near-triumph in the gymnasium.

'Well fought, youngster!' called Timarchus, one of the Macedonian cavalry officers. And Eumenes, far above him on the steps, waved. Satyrus waved back.

'So much attention from a lot of washed-up old soldiers!' Dionysius said.

'They were my father's friends. And mine,' Satyrus said.

'You look a lot less like a prig with a flute girl's lips locked around your cock,' Dionysius said. Some of the young men laughed – Satyrus's somewhat Spartan ethics made some of the young men uncomfortable, and they loved to be reminded that he was as human as they – but Abraham, a smaller boy with rich, dark curls and a wrestler's build, leaped to his defence.

'You're a godless lot,' Abraham said. 'You'll pay, mark my words!' He laughed as he said it, because it was one of his father's favourite remarks.

Satyrus blushed and pulled his chlamys – a very light garment indeed, in Alexandria – over his shoulder. 'Nonetheless,' he said to all his friends, 'I'm going to the Temple of Poseidon.'

'Bah! No temple girls to ogle, no wine shops to trash, no actors. What's the point? I'll go to Cimon's and wait.' Cimon's was their current addiction, a house that stood on the edge of a number of districts, both physical and legal. It was a private house that served wine all day. The wine was served in the form of an ongoing symposium – where a great many women, and not a few men, disported with the patrons. The house stood on the long spit of land where Ptolemy was building the lighthouse, and it had a remarkable view out over the sea. The inscription over the lintel said that it was 'A house of a thousand breezes', which Dionysius translated as 'The house of a thousand blow jobs' at every opportunity, to Cimon's apparent delight.

The owner, Cimon, was a former slave who had risen to

prominence running a brothel. Satyrus knew that he was one of Leon's men, and that Leon owned the tavern at several removes. He went to Cimon's because he knew it was safe. Whereas Dionysius went there because he thought it was dangerous. Satyrus wondered how Dionysius would deal with a storm at sea or a fight. Despite the young man's pretty-boy airs, Satyrus suspected that he had a serious backbone.

'I'll meet you at Cimon's, then,' Satyrus said.

'I'll save you a flute girl,' Dionysius said. 'Her cunny will taste of salt, like the sea – perhaps you could make your sacrifice to Poseidon inside it?'

Satyrus blushed again and smiled. Abraham swatted the Macedonian. 'You jest too much about pious things,' he said, and this time he was almost serious.

The other young men were divided evenly between the two favourites and their differing errands.

Theodorus laughed. 'No contest,' he said. 'If I go to the Temple of Poseidon with Satyrus, my father will shit himself with happiness. If I'm caught at Cimon's again, I'll get the *opson* and dissipation lecture and you won't see me for a week. Poppy?' he said, and a small boy-slave came up to him. 'Poppy, run and tell Pater that I'm on my way to the temple of Poseidon to sacrifice. Get him to provide some cash.'

The other young men laughed. Xenophon, Coenus's son and Satyrus's best friend, shook his head. 'None of you will live for ever in Elysium,' he said.

'You'll lose interest in religion when your pimples clear,' Dionysius said. He mimed picking at one. 'Perhaps they are a gift from the gods?'

Xenophon stepped up close to the Macedonian. 'Fuck you, boy-lover. Ass-cunt.'

'Ooh,' Dionysius said. 'Very religious.' He waved, slipping languorously out of Xenophon's grasp. 'Another time, darling. And I only love boys with beautiful skin – Satyrus, for instance.'

Satyrus felt the flush even as the Macedonian went off into the crowd with a dozen howling youths.

'I want to kill him,' Xenophon said. His face was splotched red and white with fury.

'Stop acting like a child,' Abraham said. 'You let him get at you far too easily. You have pimples. Big deal! I'm a Jew, Satyrus's father is dead – it's all grist for Dionysius's mill.' The dark-haired young man gave a practised shrug. 'To be honest, Xenophon, he doesn't even mean harm, and he is always surprised at the strength of your reactions.'

'My father says that when a man offends you, you fight,' Xenophon said.

'My father says that when a man blasphemes, I should kill him,' Abraham said. He raised an eyebrow.

Xenophon allowed his rage to evaporate under the other boy's humour. He shook his head ruefully.

'Can we go to the temple now?' Satyrus asked. 'Abraham's right, Xeno. Dionysius is like that to everyone. You just need to roll with it, like a blow on the palaestra.'

'Easy for you to say,' Xeno spat. 'You have *beautiful skin.*'

'Temple of Poseidon,' Satyrus said, like a battlefield command, and he started walking.

From the steps of the temple, he could see Leon's dark-hulled ship with its deep-gored golden sail. The ship was hard to miss, with vermilion paint on the rails and vermilion oars flashing in the sun, so close to the temple as he weathered the point that Satyrus could hear the chant of the oar master and see Leon himself standing by the rail. Satyrus had often imagined commanding the *Golden Lotus* – he'd made two voyages in her, one just to Cyprus, the other the length of the sea to the coast of Gaul, serving under the helmsman, Peleus – one of the heroes of Satyrus's adolescent pantheon.

'Uncle Leon!' he shouted across half a stade of water.

Leon, closer to the call of the timoneer and the creak of the oars, didn't hear him as the beautiful ship swept on. Even as she passed the temple, her deckhands were getting the sail down and the whole rowing crew was settling on to their benches for the last pull into the harbour.

'Uncle Leon!' he called, and his friends took up the cry. Their combined efforts got the black man's attention, and Leon waved. Leon had been up the Aegean to the Euxine, seeing old friends and avoiding enemies. He had been all the way to Heraklea, or perhaps Sinope. Trade was hard – all the contestants in the Great War had fleets, and every side had authorized pirates to seize shipping in their names. Athens, Rhodos and Alexandria still tried to keep trade going – all three cities required trade to flourish.

Behind his uncle's flagship came a dozen merchant ships and then the triangular sails of heavy triremes – six of them. Leon was rich, even by the standards of Alexandria, and when he put together a convoy, only a fleet could take his ships.

'Look at that,' Xeno said. 'My father says that when I'm sixteen, I can go with Leon as a marine.'

Satyrus smiled. He had already gone as a marine and hoped to go again soon – as a helmsman. The thought was never far from his mind.

But there was a rumour in the villa that Leon was going to take them *home*. 'I loved being a marine,' Satyrus said. 'I'd love to do it again to get to sea. Even as an oarsman.'

Abraham chuckled. 'Rumour is that you, sir, are a prince. Lord Ptolemy isn't likely to let you ship out again as a marine. Xeno here – well-born Geeks are an obol a dozen.'

Satyrus shrugged. 'Not an obol a dozen – if they were, Ptolemy wouldn't be so desperate to get settlers from Greece.'

Abraham tugged his beard. 'Well argued,' he said. One of his most endearing qualities was that he was open to reasoned argument and he conceded gracefully. The young Jewish man stopped at the edge of the temple precinct. 'I'll abide by Jehovah's precepts and keep my body clear of your idolatry,' he said. His smile took the sting from his words.

Satyrus nodded. Alexandria was home to twenty religions and hundreds of heresies, all of which fascinated his sister. Most citizens had learned to accept other religions, even if they were not entirely respected. Abraham's people were monotheists, with a few exceptions and a complex set of beliefs about a feminine embodiment of wisdom – Sophia – and they didn't hold with temples and statues. *Not much difference from Socrates,* Satyrus thought.

'Enjoy the view,' Satyrus said, and went inside, Xeno at his heels and Theodorus close behind. Just as they found a priest, Theodorus's little slave caught up with him and handed him a purse.

'Gentlemen, we're in funds!' Theodorus said. 'Shall we have a ram?'

'That would be noble,' Xeno said with enthusiasm.

Satyrus reached into the breast of his chiton and extracted his purse. 'I couldn't cover my half,' he said.

'Don't be foolish, Satyrus. My pater is paying.' Theodorus turned to the priest and said, 'We'd like to sacrifice a white ram for the safe return of Lord Leon. You can just see his *Golden Lotus* rounding the point.'

The young priest bowed. 'Certainly, sir.' The priesthoods at the new Temple of Poseidon were easy to acquire, and most of the priests were social climbers. This one was no different. He looked them all over and decided that Theodorus, the one with the purse and the silk chlamys, must be the one in charge. 'Let me choose you a fitting animal.' He bowed again.

Satyrus winced. 'He represents the *god*. Surely he ought to have a little more spirit.'

Xeno nodded, and Theodorus laughed. 'You two deserve each other. Listen, lads. If he was *anybody* he'd have been at the gymnasium. Do you know him? No. My money is that like all the other priests, his mother's a local girl and he's trying to make his way – by being as oily as possible. All the Gyptos are greasy.'

The priest came back leading a white ram – a very attractive animal. 'My lord?' he said to Theodorus.

'My friend is actually making the sacrifice,' Theodorus said dismissively. 'I am merely attending.'

Satyrus took the halter of the animal and led it up to the altar. The ram began to buck and shake as he smelled the blood, but Satyrus's arm was too strong for him, and Satyrus got the lead rope through the ring on the altar before the young animal could set his feet to pull. Satyrus wrapped the rope twice around his left arm, drew his sword – disdaining the offer of the priest's dagger – and pulled *hard* on the rope, cinching the rein tight against the bolt so that the ram was stretched out almost on tiptoe. In one blur of movement he slashed the animal's throat and then pivoted away from the gush of blood. The priest came up and put a bowl to catch it.

'That was well done,' Theodorus said. 'Would you teach me? My father ...'

Satyrus grinned, although both of his shoulder joints hurt from the fight. He turned to the priest and handed him a silver coin. 'A second sacrifice is never amiss, is it?' He winked, and the young priest bowed.

'A goat, lord?'

'Yes,' Satyrus said. He stepped off with the young priest. 'What's your name?' he asked.

'Namastis,' the man said. He was a couple of years older than Satyrus, and his beard was wispy. 'Namastis, lord.'

'Listen, Namastis,' Satyrus said. His sister was better at his sort of thing, but he could hear Theodorus's comments playing over and over in his head. 'You're as good a man as any of us – and the priest of a great god. Greek men *never* call each other my lord. Priests are famous for their disdain.' Satyrus smiled. 'I appreciate your lack of disdain, but you should *never* call us lords.'

Namastis narrowed his eyes, unsure if he was being mocked.

Satyrus met his eye and held it.

'Very well,' Namastis said. 'I'll find you a goat, shall I?'

'Exactly!' Satyrus said. 'I'm Satyrus,' he said, extending his hand.

The other man took it. He tried a cautious smile. His hand was limp.

'Now squeeze,' Satyrus said. Egyptians never got the Greek hand clasp.

The squeeze was cautious, but Satyrus smiled and nodded.

'Zeus Pater, Satyrus, must you make friends with every half-caste in the city? Is your house full of stray cats?' Theodorus asked.

Satyrus grinned at him. 'Yes,' he said. 'Now, do you want to learn this, or not?'

Namastis came back with a goat – a healthy specimen with a

plain brown coat. Then he set to work with his knife, butchering the first sacrifice. 'Will you take the meat?' he asked.

After a glance at Theodorus, Satyrus shook his head. 'No. Keep it.' He looked back at Theodorus. 'It's all in your left hand, Theo. The animals know what happens at the altar. They can smell it, right?'

'Too right,' Theodorus said, shaking his head. 'At the feast of Apollo, I had to sacrifice a heifer for my family. I fucked it up. Completely. My father's still not really speaking to me.'

'A heifer is tough,' Satyrus said in sympathy. 'And a little more upper-arm strength wouldn't kill you. Can you carry the weight of a shield?'

'Who cares?' Theodorus asked. 'Pater has people to do that for us.'

Satyrus raised an eyebrow but said nothing. 'Very well. Here's my trick. I pass the lead through the ringbolt with my right hand. Then I take it with my left and draw my sword with my right – all one move – and pull and cut.' He pulled the goat's head hard against the ringbolt but only tapped the animal with his hilt.

'That's how my father taught me,' Xenophon added. 'Always use your own weapon. It adds dignity to the animal's death and keeps your quick draw in training.'

Theodorus shook his head. 'It's like hanging out with Achilles and Patroclus,' he said. He stepped up and made to take the lead from Satyrus, but Satyrus stripped the lead out of the ringbolt. He stepped away, dragging the goat. Well clear of the altar, he pulled his sword belt over his head. 'Try this. See how it hangs.'

Xeno shot him a look as Theodorus pulled the belt on. It was clear that the rich young man had never worn a sword.

Satyrus stepped up behind him and tugged the hilt until it was under Theodorus's arm, right under his armpit. 'Draw it,' he said.

Satyrus still carried the short blade he'd got in the Gabiene campaign, and Theodorus drew it easily, but Satyrus caught his wrist.

'Tip the scabbard *up*, so that the hilt is *down* and then pull.

See? That will work no matter what size sword you carry.' Satyrus released the other young man's wrist.

Theodorus shook his head. 'You take all this as seriously as my father,' he said. 'If I started wearing a sword, Dionysius would mock me.'

Satyrus considered a number of responses. While he was thinking, Xenophon beat him to it. 'So only wear a sword on feast days,' he said. 'Practise in private.'

Satyrus looked at the two of them, realizing that his friends didn't always think the same way as he did. 'Or you could just ignore Dionysius,' he said. He could tell from their reactions that while his views on drawing a sword were valuable, his views on Dionysius were not so.

Theodorus drew the sword, tilting the scabbard each time in a manner that Satyrus found theatrical, but it worked.

'Ready?' Satyrus said, handing Theodorus the rein.

The goat immediately began scrabbling with his hind feet. Namastis looked up from butchering the ram. Theodorus dragged the goat up the steps and put the rein through the ringbolt right-handed, but when he switched the rein to his left he gave the animal too much slack and the goat ripped the rein right out of the bolt and ran.

Xenophon stopped the animal within a few feet of the altar, caught the lead and brought it back to Theodorus. He couldn't hide his grin. 'It's all in the hand switch,' he said.

'All in the sword draw, all in the hand switch – I need more muscle,' Theodorus said. 'This is like spending an afternoon with my father, when he has time for me.'

'No – we'll go to Cimon's when *we're* done,' Satyrus said, and got a smile from his friend. 'Come on – try again.' He knew instinctively that he needed to get Theodorus to succeed.

He caught a smell of burning hair from another altar, and then his spine prickled as he smelled wet cat fur – close. Satyrus looked around, feeling the presence of his god.

Xeno ignored him and handed the other young man the rein. 'Through the ring, step in like a lunge, pull, cut,' Xenophon said. He was about to say more – something like *I was six when I learned this* – but Satyrus kept him quiet with a look.

Theodorus was hesitant in his approach to the altar, and he managed to slip on a step and lose the rein. Satyrus stepped on it, his sandal slapping on the marble floor. He smiled at Theo, who took the rein back. He had to drag the goat up all three of the altar steps. His eyes were on his friends.

'Keep your eyes on the animal – all the time,' Satyrus said. 'Start concentrating on where you'll place the cut, and think of your prayer. I think today you should pray to give a good sacrifice!'

Namastis was watching, his eyes narrow.

Theodorus passed the hemp rope from his right to his left. Too fast, he pulled on the rein and the goat stumbled – the luck of the gods – and its head came up against the bolt. Theodorus swept the sword out, nicking his ear in the process, and cut – a little too hard, but accurately enough. Blood fountained, catching him across the legs and the lower folds of his chiton.

'I did it!' he said. He didn't seem to care that he was drenched in hot blood. There was more flowing down his face from where he'd over-drawn the sword. Satyrus was prepared to glare at Xeno if he mocked him, but Coenus's son smiled. 'Well done, Theodorus,' he said.

'Yes, well done,' Satyrus said.

'I can't wait to tell my father,' Theo said. 'Thanks! I'm going to do another.'

'Namastis?' Satyrus said.

'I only have a small goat left,' Namastis said. There was a twinkle in his eye.

'That'll have to do,' Theo said with some relief.

Satyrus gave Namastis a secret smile, having found that the priest had a brain.

His second animal, a little smaller, was better yet, and he didn't need the hand of the god to get the kid up the steps. This time he made a better job of stepping clear of the jet of blood.

'You two are the best,' Theodorus announced. 'Namastis, is it? I'll mention you to my father.'

'How many animals do you pagans plan to kill?' Abraham asked from the base of the steps.

Namastis came up close to Satyrus. 'Do you truly believe?'

he asked. 'Do you truly pray when the stroke goes home?'

Satyrus nodded. 'I do,' he said. He turned aside so that the half-Aegyptian priest couldn't see his friends. 'I am a devotee of Herakles. I feel him at my shoulder. I have seen him in dreams.'

Namastis grinned like the Aegyptian hyena god. 'You make my heart rejoice, Satyrus,' he said seriously. 'Sometimes I think that all Greeks are atheists, or posturing fools.'

'But you are Greek yourself,' Satyrus said.

The other man gave a grim smile. 'Too greasy to be all Greek,' he said, mimicking Theodorus.

'I'm sorry you heard that,' Satyrus said. He offered his hand to the priest, who clasped it.

'Grip,' he said.

Namastis gave a weak pulse of a squeeze, and Satyrus sighed. 'Better,' he said.

Theodorus washed himself in the public fountain. He managed to tell three different passers-by that he had been sacrificing at the temple. Then he sent his slave to fetch a clean chiton and a new chlamys. 'Be sure my mother sees that it is blood!' he called, standing naked. 'From sacrifice!' He turned to the other three. 'Is it right to go straight from the temple to Cimon's?' he asked, suddenly inspired by religion.

'Why would it be wrong?' Satyrus asked. 'Poseidon does not disdain wine, nor good company.'

Xenophon hung back. He gave a shy smile. 'I should go home,' he said.

Satyrus knew the trouble, so he said nothing, but Theodorus shook his head. 'For what, nap time?' For a youth who had been worried by impiety a moment before, he was suddenly lecherous. 'You can have a nap at Cimon's – with a nicer set of pillows on your couch!'

Xenophon turned salmon pink under his tan. 'Can't afford it,' he muttered. Coenus had lost everything when the Sauromatae and the men of Pantecapaeum took the kingdom of the Tanais. He had survived a bad wound to rejoin his friends and now served as a phylarch in Diodorus's hippeis. But he was no longer a rich man.

Theodorus shook his head. 'On me, Xeno,' he said. 'The least I can do, really. Listen,' he said, and he put an arm around the other two boys and kissed Abraham on the cheek by way of apology. 'Listen. Will you guys teach me to fight? Pankration? And the sword?'

'Your father can afford the best pankration tutor in the city,' Satyrus said.

Theodorus shook his head. 'No – Theron is yours. Besides, if I ask my father, he'll want to watch.' He shook his head. 'It's hard to explain.'

'Sure,' Xenophon said. 'I've got your back, Theo.'

Theodorus glowed. 'Listen – if you teach me all this hero stuff, I'll see to it that you drink and fuck like a gentleman. Deal?'

Xenophon looked at Satyrus, who shrugged and nodded. It was quite a fair deal – Xenophon was excellent in all the warrior skills, a better spearman than Satyrus and already being watched for the Olympic Games as a boxer.

'Deal,' Xenophon said. 'Do I get control of your diet, too?'

Melitta sat in the shade of the old town's largest acacia tree. The priestess was a little younger than the tree, but not much.

'Hathor does not need the worship of a Greek girl,' she said.

Melitta bowed silently, her hands clasped. 'I come seeking only wisdom,' she said.

The priestess nodded and glanced at Philokles, who sat quietly, wrapped in just a chlamys. Egyptian women coming to pray for love or for children glanced at him. The nudity of Greek men never failed to amaze the natives of the oldest land. One young matron, probably younger than Melitta, tittered to her friend and stared at the Spartan, but she got no reaction from him.

Instead, he sighed and opened a purse. Reaching inside, he took out a number of silver coins and offered them to the priestess.

'Of course, in return for proper respect, Hathor will teach all who come before her,' the priestess said. 'Are you a virgin?'

Melitta flicked a glance at her tutor. 'No,' she said.

'Good,' the priestess said. She smiled. 'Greeks can be such prudes.'

Philokles coloured slightly.

When they had taken their leave, Philokles fetched his staff from where he had placed it against the temple wall and glared at her. 'You are not a virgin?' he asked.

She shrugged. 'No woman can go to Hathor a virgin,' she said. 'My servants told me as much.'

'So you went and lay with a slave boy? You could be *pregnant*. You will never *marry*.' Philokles was biting his words, swaying slightly as he walked – drunk, and now angry. 'You dishonour—'

'Oh, Philokles,' Melitta said. 'For the love of all the gods, be quiet. *When* have I had the chance to get a man in my bed? Really? I lied. How will that old priestess ever know, do you think? Will she put a finger between my legs? Eh?'

'Don't be gross,' Philokles said. His relief was obvious.

'I am *not* a Greek girl! I am a Sakje, even here in the desert, and I will lie with whoever I please, and neither you nor my brother will gainsay me!' She was going to go on about what age her mother had first copulated, but she held her tongue. Philokles was dangerous when drunk.

'How many priests will I have to pay off so that you can explore divinity, child?' Philokles asked.

'Wasn't it you who proposed that I should explore all the religions of the Delta?' she asked. Her cork-soled sandals were getting to be too small. Everything was too small – her chitons risked scandal and her legs were too long and she was so obviously a girl that it took a major conspiracy of her uncle Diodorus and her uncle Coenus and her brother to get her time to ride in private, which was *unfair*. She visited temples because it was a pastime allowed to women, and it let her be out on the street, walking, in the heat and the sun and the flies. Today they had walked twenty stades to reach the old temple of Hathor, and now they would walk twenty stades back to the new city.

'Don't be cross, Philokles,' she said.

He walked along next to her, trailing fumes of wine and garlic.

'It's boring! I have a brain! I have a body! I'd give *anything* to be a boy and spend an afternoon at Cimon's drinking wine, hearing the news and getting my precious dick sucked.'

'Melitta!' Philokles snapped.

'It's not fair! Satyrus gets *everything*.' She walked along more quickly, snuffling away a tear.

She could hear the thump of his staff as it hit the road behind her.

'You were given too much liberty when you were young,' Philokles said.

'Donkey piss! And to think that I tell other girls that you are the smartest man in Alexandria! Donkey piss, Philokles. Let me go back to the sea of grass! Sakje doesn't even have a word for *virgin*. But they have twenty words for smoking hemp, which you have forbidden me.' She had the bit in her teeth.

Philokles stared straight ahead. 'Only slaves smoke hemp. It is unseemly.'

'Slaves drink lots of wine, too.' She stood and faced him in the road, and a two-wheeled donkey cart laden with rice from the Delta side of the port bumped past her, just missing her outflung elbow. 'Let me have your wineskin. I'll drink as much as you – no more.'

Philokles shook his head. 'We have had this discussion before. And you are drawing a great many stares.'

Melitta blew out a great breath. 'Men,' she said to the hundreds of passers-by. Then she turned and walked on.

'Are you calm enough for some news?' Philokles asked some time later.

'Yes,' she said, her good humour restored by the sight of a troop of Aegyptian acrobats performing by a beer-house.

'Your uncle Leon will be back today,' he said.

'Kallista told me as much when I awoke,' she said. 'You'll have to do better than that.'

Philokles smiled. 'That girl has – sources of information.'

'She can get blood from a stone, and no mistake,' Melitta said with great satisfaction.

'Your uncle ran up the coast to the Euxine to see how the ground lies,' Philokles said. 'We hear that Heron is losing his grip on Pantecapaeum – and Ataelus has made great strides in the east.' He grinned at his charge. 'Ataelus has spent *years* harrying the Sauromatae and raiding Heron. If there is any resistance to Heron's usurpation, it's because Ataelus keeps it alive. We all owe Ataelus.' He was silent, and then he said, 'And Leon will be bringing Amastris back from Heraklea.'

'Oh!' She clapped her hands together. 'Will she still be in love with my brother?'

Philokles appeared stung. 'Amastris of Heraklea is in love with your brother?'

Melitta looked stricken. 'Oh,' she said. 'I shouldn't have mentioned it. Wait! That means we're going back!' Melitta said, and clapped her hands together. 'No more Alexandria? Back to Tanais?'

Philokles looked around. 'This is not to be shouted on a public thoroughfare, girl – but I won't have you make a mistake that can warp your life because you don't know what's in the wind. Leon and Diodorus and I – we see a time coming when it would be worth trying.'

Melitta clapped her hands together again, stepped in and kissed the Spartan. 'I knew you were the best. I must have armour!' She pointed at her breasts. 'My old corslet won't even cover my chest.'

'I can't imagine how hard it must be to fight with those things,' Philokles said, waving vaguely at her chest. 'But you do it well enough.' Philokles still gave her lessons in private, as did her brother. Theron had reverted to the Greek code – that no girl needed to know pankration.

'I wish that someone would attack us,' Melitta said, looking around. 'A beautiful girl like me, and an old man like you – why don't these people see us as easy meat?'

Philokles rolled his eyes.

Melitta continued, 'A pity about Olympias and her assassins?' She grinned. 'They would have attacked us!'

Philokles shook his head. 'She lost us in the desert. And now she's dead.'

'Good riddance,' Melitta said with a shake of her head. 'She's one we didn't need to use the oath against. Or perhaps I should say that Artemis got her before I could.'

'Olympias had so many enemies that the gods needed no tool to bring her down.' Philokles shrugged. 'Already nostalgic for the brave old days of age twelve and a half?' he asked.

'I used to *do* things,' she said, in reply. 'Now I just lie around watching my breasts grow.'

Philokles relented. 'Listen, honey bee. When your uncle Leon is home, you'll hear. But if Antigonus makes his summer campaign in Macedon, we'll hire two thousand infantry and sail for Tanais.'

Melitta stepped up close to him, and her eyes bored into his although he was a head taller. 'Promise me by all the gods that I'm going,' she said.

Philokles met her gaze without flinching. 'You are going,' he said.

She threw her arms around him in the middle of the road. Heads turned. Philokles blushed.

'May I tell Satyrus?' she asked.

'Best to wait. Leon will be home tonight.' Philokles started to walk again. 'I don't like all the company your brother keeps.'

Melitta was quick to spring to her brother's defence. 'Who? You can't object to Xenophon?'

'Never in life, my dear. No, nor Abraham, for all that his father is a zealot. But Theodorus's father would sell his mother for gain or social prestige, and that Dionysius—' Philokles bit off his words.

Melitta had a different use for Dionysius, who, for all of his effete airs, had a beautiful body that he seldom hid and a wicked sense of humour. 'Dionysius wrote a poem about my breasts,' Melitta said.

Philokles quickened his pace. 'I know. So does every man in the city.'

Melitta stuck her tongue out. 'So? They're right here. Every-one can see them. Why not read a poem about them?' She bounced along, almost skipping, despite forty stades of walk-ing. 'What about that beautiful boy – Herakles?' Just saying the name gave her a little tingle. 'If my brother can have Amastris, perhaps I can have Herakles.'

'Honey bee, Banugul is the last woman on earth that you want as a mother-in-law. All she wants is to make her son King of Kings.' Philokles stopped to get a pebble out of his sandal. 'Need I remind you that they are with Antigonus? Banugul is no doubt busy scheming.'

'And yet you saved her, Master Philokles.' Suddenly the bouncing gait was gone, and she eyed him appraisingly.

'*We* saved her, my dear. And I did it, as did you, because the gods told us. Yes?' Philokles raised an eyebrow.

'I remember,' she said.

When Philokles was in the mood to teach Satyrus lessons, he liked to say that the Greeks were used to colonization and cleruchy, rapid settlement and rapid building. Athens had dropped forts everywhere when she was queen of the seas, and Miletus had spread colonies the way a profligate spreads bastards. Greeks could move to a place, build a temple or two, run up some houses with the regularity of a marching camp, and before the architect could say 'Parian Marble', there was a new city. Or so the Spartan said.

But Alexandria represented city-founding on an unprecedented scale, as if someone had desired to create a new Athens or a new Corinth. Some said that it was the will of the God-King Alexander, and others that it was the solid administration of Ptolemy and the fifteen thousand talents of silver he drew from the treasury of Aegypt every year. Philosophers – and there was no shortage of them – gathered in the agora, or in the shade of the new library, so far just a pile of materials and some gardens – and debated the virtues and vices of mixing religions and races, of trade, of kingship.

But a new city lacks traditions and in their absence often creates new habits. In Athens or Corinth, men from the highest classes never drank in wine shops. They worked from their homes, held business meetings in their homes, threw parties, wild or decorous, in their homes. Virtue and vice were practised in the confines of the home. Satyrus had experienced it, had visited Athens repeatedly until Demetrios of Phaleron became the de-facto tyrant of Athens and Kineas's son was one of the casualties of his regime. In Athens, where Satyrus owned a house, he might give a party – or he might go to a party. But if he were seen to buy wine or flute girls for his own use alone, he would be mocked. And the thought of going to a wine shop would be enough to label him a *thetes*, a low-class free man, and not a gentleman.

Philokles theorized that in Athens, the will of the people in the assembly – even under a tyrant – had the effect of minimizing private display of wealth. If you showed that you had too much, the people would vote that you should give an expensive entertainment or maintain a trireme or something equally ruinous.

Alexandria had a king, not an assembly, despite the fact that Ptolemy had not yet assumed the title or the formal honours of a king. The thousand richest men in the city competed to demonstrate the extent of their wealth and the beauty of their lives. Many competed in an old, Athenian way – by raising monuments, even by maintaining a trireme for the service of King Ptolemy. Uncle Leon was one of these. He maintained a squadron. His money had laid the foundation of the Temple of Poseidon. He was always in the public service.

Other men, however, used their money in different ways – to keep beautiful mistresses, to give lavish parties on a scale unknown in Athens, to dress in silks brought overland from Serica, a hundred thousand stades, or in the finest wools from Bactria, dyed in the most elaborate colours from Tyre and Asia.

Philokles despised all this display and often spoke against it, and he said that the outcome was places like Cimon's, because if men had clothes worth twenty talents of silver, they needed a place to wear them – and that the kind of man who spent twenty talents on a chiton was not the kind of man to maintain the perfection of his body in the gymnasium or the perfection of his mind in the agora.

Philokles said that in Sparta or Athens – two cities often presented as contrasts, but Satyrus's Spartan tutor said they had more in common with each other than either had with Alexandria – a man went to the gymnasium and to the agora to show that his body was ready to serve the state in war, and his mind ready to serve the state in peace. Satyrus loved it when Philokles spoke in such a fashion, and he could quote the Spartan at length, and he often thought about his words when he walked.

Even when he walked to Cimon's.

Cimon's stood among a row of hastily built private houses backing on the sea. The low bluff on which they were built allowed the owners to catch the sea breeze after the rest of the city had lost it, and the houses had been built in the first flush of the city's wealth, back in the decade after the founding.

But fashions change. When Ptolemy began building the royal palace complex, the western end of the city became unfashionable, the home of warehouses and workers. A few wealthy Macedonians hung on, but most moved, if only to be close to the seat of power. Many of them had never finished their houses, and few of them had ever been landscaped or had gardens planted, so that the neighbourhood appeared ruinous, as if a conquering army had swept through, stealing mulberry bushes.

But Cimon's was an island of green. The first owner had gardened himself, importing plants from the interior of Africa and from all over the sea. When he died and Cimon the public slave purchased his property, Cimon had purchased the gardeners with the land. Inside, the former owner had arranged for expert painters to render scenes from the *Iliad* and *Odyssey*, from Alexander's conquests, and from the tales of the gods in brilliant gesso work, so that a bored patron might feel as if he watched the siege of Troy – or, in some rooms, the rape of Helen.

Satyrus understood the philosophical reasons why Cimon's was bad for him and bad for the city, but he loved the place – the quiet green alcoves, the hard-edged mirth of the pornai and the flute girls, the acrobats and the broiled tuna and the art, the gossip and the fights.

'What can I get the hero of the hour?' asked Thrassylus, the former slave who acted as the steward of the house. You could always gauge your status in a heartbeat with Thrassylus, and the oiled Phrygian seemed to know every nuance of gossip from every quarter. 'Ptolemy clasped your hand? And sacrificing for your uncle? What splendid piety, young master. Wine?' A Spartan cup was put in Satyrus's hand – other cups went to Abraham, Xeno and Theo – and wine was poured from a silver pitcher while they all sat in the entrance hall. Two children, a boy and a girl – twins, he could see – washed his feet.

'Aren't they adorable?' Thrassylus said. 'I bought them today.'

The girl washed his hands. She had a serious expression on her face and her tongue showed between her teeth. 'Yes,' Satyrus said, with his usual unease about slaves.

'Kline?' Thrassylus asked, referring to the long couches on which well-off Greeks reclined to eat and drink. 'I have the whole of the seaward garden open, young master.'

Satyrus nodded, and his party was escorted past the two main rooms, where dozens of young men, and a few past youth, cavorted with each other and with the house's numerous offerings.

'May we have Phiale, Thrassylus?' Satyrus asked. Phiale was a genuine hetaira, a free woman who sometimes acted as an escort and sometimes as a hostess. In addition to her beauty – a particular, square-jawed beauty that was not the typical fare among hetairai – she played the kithara and sang, often composing mocking songs to tease her clients.

Phiale had consented a year before to deprive Satyrus of his virginity. Satyrus suspected that his uncle had paid her for the service, as she was very choosy about her clients, and ever since she had treated him with warmth and a certain reserve – as if she was a distant cousin, he had joked to Abraham.

'I will see if she is at leisure,' Thrassylus said with a bow. 'She is with us this afternoon.'

Abraham laughed. 'She's a little over our heads, don't you think?' he asked.

Xeno beamed. He liked Phiale, and she didn't make him uncomfortable the way the pornai and the flute girls did, an aspect of his friend that Satyrus understood perfectly.

Theo, on the other hand, pouted. 'I want a flute girl to play my flute,' he said. 'Phiale drives them all away.'

Satyrus allowed a boy to take his sandals and his chlamys and he reclined, arranging his chiton as well as he could. He didn't *love* Phiale – she was, after all, a hetaira – but he didn't want to let her down. Or perhaps he really did seek to impress her. He sighed and arranged his chiton again.

He met Abraham's raised eyebrow and laughed.

'You Greeks,' Abraham said. 'She's old enough to be your mother!'

'I heard that, Samaritan!' Phiale said. She was laughing, and she slapped Abraham on the shoulder and sat on the edge of his kline.

'I'm no Samaritan—' Abraham began, and then threw his head back and laughed. 'You are the wonder of the city, madam! You even know how to tease a Jew!'

'I can do more than tease a Jew,' she said, leaning over him, somewhere between seduction and threat. 'I can flirt with one!'

Abraham mimed panic and terror. 'Ahh! Ahh!' he cried, clearly delighted at the attention.

The other young men laughed. 'Flirt with me!' Theodorus pleaded.

'No, no! You're all bad boys. I'm with another party and I just came to visit the hero. You went three falls with Theron and came up in a draw? That must have been beautiful to watch, Satyrus?'

Just the way she used his name made him feel older, stronger and more handsome.

'My party are all cursing that they missed the fight. One of them – a stranger – asked if you were by any chance from the north – from the Euxine? I said that I thought you were from Athens – dear me, Satyrus, I find myself shockingly under-informed about you,' she said. She put a hand on the side of his face – a lovely touch, personal and intimate and warm. 'And your uncle is home tonight,' she asked.

'We sacrificed for him,' Theo said.

Satyrus winced a little at his friend's adolescent self-importance. 'We saw his ships from the temple, and we saw him standing with the helmsman on the *Golden Lotus*.' It was the first time that Phiale had ever asked him a direct question, and her manner seemed – odd.

'I will send him a basket of flowers with a note to Nihmu,' Phiale said. Many wives would resent a basket of flowers from a hetaira, but Nihmu was different.

She stretched her long legs, flexing the toes, and then shot to her feet like an acrobat. 'I really can't stay.'

Satyrus was bold enough to place a hand lightly on her side – not possessively, not holding on, but not hesitant either. 'Might you come back and sing for us?'

Phiale made an actor's bow. 'I might,' she said, 'if I don't find a dozen flute girls already playing your instruments,' and she winked at Theodorus, who blushed.

She walked off, drawing every eye in the garden, and was re-placed by a pair of laughing wine attendants. 'We'll be invisible now,' said the elder, a dark-haired Aegyptian with full breasts and a face that was nearly round. 'Nobody wants to flirt with a wine girl after Phiale saunters by.'

'Much less give us a tip,' said the younger, a Cypriot who was as sylphlike as a Nereid. 'How is a girl to buy her freedom?' she asked rhetorically, sucking a fingertip. 'Wine, anyone?'

The boys laughed, patted, drank wine and ogled as a troop of acrobats pirouetted, a pair of Africans did a war dance that impressed Satyrus, and a single olive-coloured girl danced alone with a spear in a way that caused all the young men to consider the green arbours at the back of the garden.

Theodorus winked at his companions. 'I don't want to offend Phiale's delicate sensibility,' he said, 'so I'm going to oil my lamp-wick in private.'

Xeno blushed. Abraham laughed.

'Was that good?' Theo said, pausing. 'Really? I got it off one of my father's slaves.'

'It's not as dumb as some of the phrases I hear,' Abraham said. 'Go and find a sausage-eater!'

Theo nearly choked with laughter and hurried away.

A group of middle-aged men came in, stopped by Satyrus's couch and paid their compliments. They were all men Satyrus knew – officers who served with Diodorus. Panion, a taxeis commander and a rising star, let his eyes wander over Satyrus's body until the young man was uncomfortable.

'Come and see the drill of the Foot Companions,' Panion said. 'I hear that Lord Ptolemy made much of you.'

Satyrus felt the heat rising on his face. Panion was the leader of the 'Macedon' faction – the men who felt that mere Greeks and Jews must be kept in their place. But he had never hidden his admiration for Satyrus.

Satyrus thanked all the men politely. As a younger man, he rose and attended them to their own couches before returning to his own, flushed with praise and the embarrassment of Panion's obvious advances. Macedonians didn't flirt – that was a flute-girl saying, but one with a great deal of truth to it.

Slaves appeared and dusted his kline, scraping away bread-crumbs and cheese.

'I should go home,' Satyrus said.

'Not until I sing for you,' Phiale said, appearing suddenly and dropping on his couch.

Satyrus immediately brightened. 'I thought that you were – busy.'

'Silly boy.' She touched his face again. 'You're not really a boy, are you, Satyrus?' Her hand stroked down his arm, her thumb following the line of his muscle, and his groin stirred.

'Half and half,' he admitted. Her eyes were as big as cups. Her lips had minute ridges and were so rich in colour that they were almost brown. Her nipples were the same – he could remember them.

Vividly.

'May I sing something of my own?' she asked.

The three young men all nodded.

She stood up and faced them, and then sang – no build-up with Phiale. Her arms spread as she sang, a simple, unaccompanied song of a girl whose love had gone off to Troy and who wanted to follow him or die.

When she was done, they were quiet a minute. The whole

garden was quiet, and then all the circles of couches began to applaud, sometimes with men standing up by them.

'You didn't sing for *us*,' a young man said. He didn't sound angry, just bored. 'Should I have paid more?'

Satyrus knew him. Everyone did. Gorgias was the youngest rich man with his own fortune in the city – the death of his father and uncle had left him a massive amount of wealth and no adult supervision. Philokles used him as an example of dissolution because he ran to fat and disdained philosophy. His friends were always older men who he used and was used by.

He had a soldier with him, a bigger man with a red line all down one side of his body from his jaw to his right knee, and another man that Satyrus couldn't quite see though the crowd, a shorter man of perhaps forty years.

'I might have paid for more than a song,' said a barbarian voice, with an Athenian accent. The big man gave Phiale a wry smile. 'I don't pinch every obol, either.' He laughed. 'When a man is as old as I am, he prizes a song. And a singer.'

Satyrus couldn't really see past Phiale's hips from his couch, but he could see by the set of her back that she was unhappy.

'In Alexandria,' Phiale said, 'we don't discuss the prices a hetaira might charge. If you have to discuss them, you can't afford her.' She gave the men a hard smile. 'But I owed my friend a song for his exploits, and I always pay my debts. Being, as you must understand, a free woman and capable of choosing my clients.' She laughed lightly, but Satyrus thought that she was nervous. He'd never seen her like this. She also clapped her hands – a girl's signal that she needed the house to intervene.

The big foreigner frowned, obviously offended. 'All prostitutes like to be called hetairai,' he said. 'But the only difference is the price.' He said the last in a tone of contempt, a man who was used to getting his way and didn't like being mocked in public by a mere woman. 'They both look the same when their lips are around my dick,' he said, and several men nearby laughed.

Satyrus swung his legs over the far side of his couch and stood up. In the same motion he reclaimed his sword from the peg where it hung from its cord. Now he could see the shorter man. He had only seen him two or three times, but he knew him in a glance. The Athenian. Stratokles.

'This isn't your fight, boy,' the big foreigner said. He put a hand on Satyrus's chest. 'Just an uppity girl who needs—'

'Watch it!' Stratokles called. His attention had been divided between Xenophon and Phiale, and he hadn't seen Satyrus past Phiale's hips. He saw him now.

Satyrus put one hand on the mercenary's shoulder, gently, as if ready to remonstrate. One of Theron's lessons about fighting was that when your life was on the line, there were no rules, no manners and no requirement for announcing your intentions, and Satyrus's adventures at the age of twelve had convinced him of the truth of the Corinthian's assertions. So he didn't posture or shout or work himself up like a young man. He reversed his hold and turned the scarred man under him, rotating his arm in the socket and making him scream with pain.

Even as he struck, body running on trained responses from the palaestra, Satyrus's mind ran on like a philosopher's automaton. *Stratokles,* he thought. *What in Hades is he doing in Alexandria?* Satyrus's head was flooded by the daimon of combat, and he had to concentrate on the strength of the foreigner. He went down clutching Satyrus's arm and growling, and Satyrus reckoned him tough enough that he paused to spend a full-weight kick to his head. That took him out of the fight. Then Satyrus drew his sword.

Stratokles was, for once in his life, caught unprepared. He leaped back, trying to get his chlamys off his shoulder and into his hand and producing a sword from under his arm. 'Grown up quite a bit, haven't you?' he said. And then, 'I didn't recognize you. You planning to kill me in cold blood?' he asked, backing away.

Satyrus stepped across the fallen soldier, undeterred. 'Call the watch!' he shouted at the patrons. 'He's a murderer!' In the distance, Thrassylus was approaching with two big slaves, but he would be too late to save Stratokles. He started into a simple combination, a feint to the head, and suddenly Phiale caught at his arm. 'Satyrus, stop!' she said.

The Athenian used the pause as his opponent was pinned

by the hetaira to cut at Satyrus's legs. Satyrus, with nowhere to retreat, managed a clumsy parry that allowed the Athenian's sword to clip his shin – and Phiale's. She screamed and went down, her hands on her leg.

Clear of Phiale's obstruction, Satyrus leaped to attack the Athenian. Their swords rang together – edge to edge – and sparks flew. Satyrus was stronger – but not faster. He almost lost fingers on the next exchange – only a clumsy, desperate parry with his cloak saved his hand.

Sword fighting without armour was merely pankration with a blade. It was something on which Satyrus prided himself. He growled and stepped forward. Stratokles changed his guard, raising his sword hand slightly, and Satyrus pounced, wrapping his cloak-clad hand around the Athenian's sword in a carefully timed grab.

The Athenian stepped in and grabbed *his* sword.

Satyrus headbutted the other man, catching him under the chin and rocking him back.

At the same time, Stratokles swung back with his blow, minimizing it, and punched with his cloaked hand up between them, catching Satyrus's shoulder and knocking him back. The Athenian fell.

Satyrus planted his feet on either side of the downed man and cut at Stratokles' head, but despite the blow to his head, the Athenian wasn't done yet. Their blades rang together, and Satyrus grabbed his opponent's sword hand at the pommel – a dangerous move that Theron had made him practise a thousand times. He ripped the blade from the Athenian's hand just at Stratokles landed a heavy left, this time to the side of his ankle, which made him stumble back. Stratokles gasped for air, grabbing at a couch and getting to his feet. Then Satyrus stepped in to finish him.

'By Apollo! He's unarmed!' Abraham caught at his left hand.

Stratokles raised his hands. 'Ho, young Herakles!' he croaked, and stepped back again. 'If you cut me down unarmed, even your bloody uncle can't save you.'

The man's grin was so offensive that Satyrus ripped himself

free of Abraham's restraint and punched the pommel of his sword into the man's forehead, laying him flat in one blow, choking on the tiled floor.

Phiale's cry – 'He's the Athenian ambassador!' – stopped the descent of his back cut into the man's neck.

Gorgias stood aside, and then slowly subsided on to a kline. 'Oh, Zeus!' he said. 'All my guests are dead!'

'Let's get you out of here,' Abraham said. 'That was – ill-considered, my friend.' He shrugged. 'But spectacular to watch.'

As the soldier shook and mewled on the floor, Satyrus looked at Phiale, trying to discern if this had been – what had it been? An assassination attempt? They happened every day, in Alexandria.

She *had* tried to pin his arms.

'He tried to kill me and my sister when we were children,' Satyrus said. It sounded pretty weak, with two men bleeding on the tiles.

'He's the ambassador of Athens!' Phiale said again. 'He brought the king a message from *Cassander*! They are *allies*! Are you insane?'

Abraham had his arm. 'Argue later,' he said.

Xenophon already had their cloaks at the door. Fights were not uncommon at Cimon's, but the two rich foreigners lying prostrate on the marble floor were attracting a great deal of attention.

Satyrus looked back again at Phiale, who was looking at the men on the floor and who then lifted her eyes.

What did he see there? Confusion? Or complicity?

'Argue later,' Abraham said again. 'Come.'

The garden was starting to return to life – noisy, shouting life – as they hurried down the steps.

'Let's run,' Abraham urged.

'What are we running from?' Satyrus asked. He was already moving at an easy lope.

'I don't know,' Abraham said.

Satyrus ran in through the business gate, past the sailors and into the courtyard.

Uncle Leon was by the fountain, issuing unpacking orders to a phalanx of slaves and servants and retainers and some sailors who had carried his most precious cargoes up from the warehouses.

Theron had an armful of Serican silk hangings and looked as if he was afraid to move.

'I just half-killed the new Athenian ambassador,' Satyrus said. 'Welcome home, Uncle Leon!'

Leon wasn't tall, but he had piercing eyes of dark brown and his brown skin was perfectly tanned to an even leather colour. He looked like a dark-skinned god – a mature Apollo.

Abraham, coming in behind him, bowed his head respectfully to one of the city's richest men, and Xeno looked sheepish.

'I heard you were sacrificing for my return,' Leon said. He took Satyrus in a hug. 'We don't usually sacrifice ambassadors.' Then he caught sight of the other young men. 'Is this serious?' he said. 'Every time I come home, you have something stupendous to announce, don't you?'

'It's Stratokles!' Satyrus panted. 'Remember him? From Heraklea?'

'Oh!' Leon said.

'Fuck,' Theron said. He was still holding the silk. 'Did you kill him?'

'Kill who?' Philokles asked. He pushed his way past the crowd of young men at the entrance to the garden courtyard, and Melitta came with him, ignoring Xeno's sudden blushes of confusion as she rubbed against his back.

Satyrus filed that little scene away for further consideration.

'The new Athenian ambassador to the court of Ptolemy is your former nemesis, Stratokles,' Leon said, having taken in the whole sweep of the problem with his usual acuity. 'Why didn't anyone tell me?' he asked, looking at his factor, Pasion.

Pasion bowed. 'It was in the morning's reports,' he said sheepishly. 'I missed the importance of the fact.'

'Too late to unspill the wine,' Philokles said. 'Demetrios of Athens let that cur be his ambassador?'

'Put a suit against him,' Leon said. 'I'm sure we can make a deal with him. He's a man of business.'

Philokles pulled his *himation* closer. 'I'll do it this instant.'

'Exactly.' Leon nodded. 'Go!'

Philokles, despite three years of heavy drinking and endless agora debates, could still move quickly when required. He was out of the gate before Leon was done thinking out the next step.

'Tell us what happened,' Leon said.

Satyrus related the incident, with some hesitant description of Phiale's role.

'You put two grown men down,' Theron asked. 'Then you let them live.'

'Thank the gods he did!' Leon said. He rubbed his chin and his shoulders slumped. 'Killing an ambassador would make any political career here impossible.'

Theron stood his ground. 'Being dead is worse. Listen, Satyrus. The next time you have an enemy under the edge of your kopis, push the blade home. Then he's dead and your story is the only one in the law courts.'

Leon shook his head. 'That's evil advice to give a boy, Theron. *Always leave your opponents dead.*'

Melitta came and put her arms around her brother. 'You have all the luck,' she said. 'I was just wishing for assassins.'

'Careful what you wish for,' Theron said.

'This alliance with Cassander means a lot to our Ptolemy,' Leon said. He tugged his short beard. 'I think you are best out of the city, lad. Pasion, summon Peleus the helmsman to keep his crew in hand – one night on the waterfront, and on duty by sunrise in the morning. Move!' He turned to look at Theron. 'I have a hundred pieces of news for all our friends,' he said. 'I'll try and get through it all at dinner.'

One of the many ways in which Satyrus's 'uncles' differed from other men was the manner in which they lived. Leon and Diodorus were both rich men, yet they had built their houses together – so close together that they shared doors and gardens. Nihmu, Leon's Sakje wife, and Sappho shared women's quarters. Theron, Philokles and Coenus all lived in the same houses, and the establishment, four times the size of most houses, was run on military lines, with common meals and a certain regular discipline.

The other thing that set them apart from other men of property was that Leon, Philokles, Coenus, Satyrus, Diodorus, Theron and the women, Sappho, Melitta and Nihmu, all took dinner together with Leon's upper servants in a manner not unlike the Spartan mess system, except that the food was superb and women ate with men. These communal dinners had been a feature of life in Tanais before its fall, and Leon had transferred the system to Alexandria. Diodorus added some of his officers – Eumenes was almost always with them for dinner, and Crax – and Leon added his senior helmsmen and his business friends and the tribal leaders he used to keep his caravans moving, when they came. Philokles brought philosophers and divines from the agora and the temples, and Coenus added an occasional barracks-mate, and once the king himself, who knew Coenus of old. Dinners were sprawling affairs of twenty or thirty klines, food, wine and debate.

Dinner was where they all came together – especially now that Leon was back.

'Don't leave the house,' Leon said to Satyrus. 'You boys were there?' he said to Xenophon.

'Yes, sir,' Xenophon said.

'You had best stay, then. Until I know more.' Leon nodded to Abraham and called to a slave. 'Run and tell Ben Zion that I have his son at my house for dinner as a guest, and that I will send a message home with him.'

The slave nodded. 'Ben Zion. Son for dinner. Message later.'

'Good,' Leon said. 'Go.'

Pasion came back from his last errand. 'Both men are alive,' he said.

Leon nodded. 'Close the gates. No admittance without my express permission. Ask Crax for Hama's file as guards on the gates.'

'We aren't overreacting, are we?' Theron asked.

'I wasn't there, Theron. I've tangled with Stratokles – and done deals with him – and I find he has a tendency to focus very hard on success. If memory serves, he tried to kill both of Kineas's children.' Leon raised an eyebrow. 'He *stormed a private house* in Heraklea. Yes?'

Theron bowed his head. 'Point taken.' He looked at Satyrus. 'See? You should have killed him, Satyrus.'

Satyrus felt himself growing angry. 'I—'

'We took an oath!' Melitta said.

This criticism was the last straw. 'That's not fair!' he said. 'Stratokles is the ambassador of Athens! That makes his person sacred! And when exactly did Stratokles get included? Are we killing every flunky, or just the people who ordered Mama's death?'

Melitta bit her lip. 'I—' she began.

'Don't turn into Medea,' Satyrus said. He squeezed her hand.

'Sorry, Satyr.' She knelt and touched the blood on his leg. 'You're wounded.'

Theron raised an eyebrow.

'He's good,' Satyrus said. 'You know, I'm pretty sure that putting down two trained fighters would be cause for praise in most households.'

Leon stared off into space, rubbing his short beard. 'Perhaps,' he said.

Satyrus looked around, chewed back an angry response and crossed his arms.

He stood silent and angry as Leon dispatched messengers to various quarters and sat in his garden, saying little, and his silence was more ominous than his orders.

Nihmu and Sappho came from the women's quarters and sent everyone off to the baths before dinner. By the time that Satyrus, feeling disoriented in his own home, had towelled off, he could see Hama setting a pair of armoured cavalrymen at the front gate – men of Olbia or Tanais, absolutely loyal. That settled him.

Nonetheless, he hung his sword over his chiton.

A servant came in through the curtain at his door and bowed. 'Leon asks that you dress in your best, lord,' the man intoned. 'I am to help you.'

Off came the sword and the chiton. Satyrus opened the chest under the window and poked through the folded wool there, looking for his favourite – a plain white wool chiton with a minute stripe of Tyrian Purple. He found it as much by feel as by sight – the wool was superb.

'How about this?' he asked the servant.

'Certainly, sir,' the servant replied. This time he was oiled, his hair carefully arranged and the chiton adjusted so that every fold fell as if it had been sculpted by Praxiteles, closed by a girdle made of gold cord.

Satyrus added a knife that hung around his neck from a cord, vanishing into the folds of the chiton. The servant made a face. 'Hardly required, sir,' he said.

Satyrus was always annoyed by talkative servants. 'I'll be the judge of that,' he said, and sat to have his best sandals put on his feet. When he was shod, he nodded. 'Thanks,' he said to the servant.

'Yes, sir,' the servant replied, and retreated through the door.

Not for the first time, Satyrus wished he had a servant or a slave of his own – a comrade. Someone who would understand his own needs. All of Leon's freedmen treated him like a child.

Caught up in all that was the thought that he had treated Phiale badly. He sat at a table in the courtyard and scribbled a note, searching for a nice bit of poetry to use to express himself, but finding none. So he wrote:

That man is my enemy, and has been for years. I am sorry that you were injured in our squabble. If I can be of any assistance, please send to me.

He sealed it with his Herakles ring and sent it with a slave.

It occurred to him as he walked down the cool marble halls towards the garden that he hadn't asked *why* he was dressed like a prince.

Melitta was still lying naked on her day-bed, trying to will herself to calm and coolness in the evening breeze, when a senior woman servant came to her chamber. 'I am to ask you to dress your best,' the old woman said, with a smile. 'You have an invitation from the palace.'

Kallista, also naked, rose from the balcony and clapped her hands. 'Amastris! It must be! I heard that Master Leon brought her home.'

Melitta smiled. 'Thanks, Dorcus! I'll be ready.'

Dorcus turned to Kallista. 'It wouldn't be amiss to pack a wrap for morning,' she said, laying a finger along her nose. 'The palace messenger suggested that the Lady Amastris might wish to entertain our mistress overnight.'

'Dorcus? Be a dear and tell the steward that I'll be out for dinner. And does Uncle Leon know? Oh – it's his homecoming. Perhaps—' She paused. 'Amastris is going to use me to see my brother, isn't she?' Melitta asked the older woman.

Dorcus shook her head slightly. She was a woman of consequence in the household, and Melitta knew that every rumour came to her ears. 'Master Leon has an invitation of his own,' she said. 'As does your brother – from the king himself. If the princess wishes to see your brother, she will have to scheme very quickly indeed. Dress well, young mistress.' She paused. 'Given the – *incident* – this afternoon, all may not go as the princess imagines. Understand me, despoina?'

Kallista didn't need a second admonition. She had Melitta's best Greek gown laid out on the bed – wool so fine as to be transparent, carefully oiled to a fine finish, the colour a dark purple-blue with gold stripes. There were also the Artemis brooches that Kinon had given her three years ago, and a dagger, and a wicked bronze pin in her hair, the knobbed grip hidden by an enormous pearl that matched the strings that held her long black tresses.

Kallista slipped long, dangling gold earrings into her ears and clasped a necklace at her throat. Her hands rested on her mistress's shoulders. 'You are beautiful,' she said. She held up a silver mirror so that Melitta could admire herself.

'Not as beautiful as you,' Melitta said. Her slave was like an avatar of Aphrodite – in fact, some men called her that very title. Melitta had been offered sums of up to twenty talents of silver for her slave's favours.

'Hmm,' Kallista said. She put her head down next to Melitta's, so that the two were side by side in the mirror. 'Dark and fair. You are more the image of Hera or Artemis. A colder beauty – but no less beautiful.'

'Flatterer,' Melitta said. She poked Kallista in the side and made the other girl squeal.

'Not with you,' Kallista giggled. 'Every man's head will turn when we walk in the palace. Hah! I feel like a cat among mice when I go there.'

'Freedom has not made you modest,' Melitta said.

Kallista lowered her eyes in a parody of virginal modesty. 'Has it not, my mistress?'

'How was Amyntas?' Melitta asked. Amyntas was one of Ptolemy's Macedonian officers. He was supposed to command the phalanx, and he was a famous soldier, but he spent little time on his duties. He had offered Kallista ten talents of silver for a single night.

'Adequate,' Kallista said with a shrug. 'For the money.'

'No transports of joy?' Melitta asked.

'I can buy all the transports I wish for ten talents of silver, mistress.' Kallista smiled.

'You make love sound so – mercenary!' Melitta complained.

'Mistress, I'm a hetaira!' The older woman shrugged. 'Men started mounting me when I was eleven. There's never been a great deal of *romance* involved.' She stroked Melitta's shoulders. 'It will be different for you – I'll see to that. A boy your own age – a beautiful boy.'

Melitta smiled. 'Your lips to Aphrodite's ear,' she said. She rose to her feet, complete from her gilded sandals to the tiny touch of rouge on the tops of her ears and the long tendril of black hair that seemed to have artlessly escaped her diadem – one of Kallista's best contrivances. 'Mind you, dressed like this, I might as well be a hetaira!'

Obligingly, Kallista walked to her household altar – to Aphrodite of Cyprus, like most hetairai – and knelt. She fingered the ivory statue and spoke quietly to it as if the statue were the goddess herself, and then kissed it and put it back in its place.

'Shall we?' she said.

Melitta walked to the door.

Leon was waiting in the foyer. 'We are expected at the palace,' he said. Even as he spoke, Philokles came from the garden with Coenus, talking about hunting, at his side. Diodorus came in the main gate. He was in armour, and Philokles was wearing a plain white chiton and the long himation of a scholar. Coenus and Leon were dressed well, although their clothes were more befitting merchants than leading aristocrats.

Leon addressed them all together.

'Satyrus and I have been ordered to attend the king. Melitta has been invited to visit the princess of Heraklea.' He looked around at them. 'After today's events, we can't be too careful.'

'Surely you don't expect that Ptolemy will do anything foolish,' Philokles said.

Leon raised an eyebrow. 'I wish to ensure that he does not,' he said. 'So I would like you gentlemen to accompany us.'

Philokles rubbed his jaw. 'Do I need a sword?' he asked.

'If it comes to that, there'll be no saving us,' Leon said.

Diodorus nodded. 'Let's get this over with then,' he said. 'I'd like to see Sappho before the day is over. Hello there, Satyr. Lita, you look like – like a particularly seductive nymph. And to think that I watched you being born!'

Coenus rolled his eyes. 'In my day, young lady, you would never have been allowed out like that. Aren't you even going to cover your hair?'

Kallista muffled a squeak of outrage. Melitta put a hand on her companion's wrist. 'Troy has fallen, Uncle,' she said with a smile. 'Penelope is cold in her grave. In the modern era, young women of good family are allowed out of their houses.'

Coenus made a noise between a grunt and a laugh.

Leon waved them all out through the garden and on to the street like a dog herding sheep.

'Goodness,' Kallista murmured. 'Are we going to *walk*?'

If Leon heard her, he gave no sign. He strode off and eight torch holders arranged themselves around the party. Satyrus knew them immediately – although masquerading as house slaves in simple chitons, they were all soldiers, troopers from Eumenes' squadron.

They walked along the streets, only one such group among dozens, although Melitta and Kallista drew attention like a new vendor in the agora. Satyrus watched the crowds as they walked, annoyed that his best sandals might be stained by the rubbish in the street while simultaneously fascinated by the scenes around him, as he always was in the city. Women waited at public fountains with jars for water on their heads or hips. Men stood in the cool evening air and grumbled, heckled and bartered, or discussed the new city's politics. Criminal factions eyed each other from opposing street corners. Couples mooned in dark corners or fought in tenements, and a late caravan of camels from the Red Sea stood in a long row on the central avenue, liberally decorating the clean sand of the street with droppings as they waited for slaves to unload the incense of the southern Arabian kingdoms.

Their torch-bearers watched everything and their eyes went everywhere. The man closest to Satyrus was the giant, Carlus, and Satyrus wondered how anyone could take him for a slave. His eyes were moving, appraising, watching. He looked up at the rooftops and down in the doorways.

'See anything, Carlus?' Satyrus asked by way of conversation.

The big Keltoi shrugged. 'No,' he said. 'Lots of bad men, but they don't want us.' He glared at a beardless Aegyptian on a street corner, who stood with his arms crossed over his chest. He was small, and light, and young, but he met Carlus's stare with cool indifference. 'I'd love to come down here with some of the boys and clean up,' he said. 'Forced loans, prostitution, extortion, arson – these scum do it all.'

Satyrus looked at the Aegyptian as he passed him. The young man didn't even raise an eyebrow. 'Are you sure?' he asked.

Carlus grunted.

Leon's villa was comparatively close to the new library and the palace precincts, and it dawned on Satyrus that Leon was parading his group through the most public thoroughfares for a reason. After half an hour's walk they climbed the low hill that led to the palace gates, still under construction. As far as Satyrus could see, the palace was in a permanent state of construction.

Bored Macedonians greeted Leon, gave perfunctory salutes to Diodorus and ogled Melitta and Kallista, their comments loud enough that Satyrus became offended on his sister's behalf.

'Soldiers,' Leon said, putting a hand on Satyrus's shoulder. 'Calm yourself.'

Slaves led them from the gate to the main hall, and female slaves came and took Melitta and Kallista away. Greek women might walk the streets and even sometimes attend a party, but at the palace many of the old ways were preserved, and women were received in women's rooms. Satyrus kissed his sister on the cheek while Amastris's personal attendant waited patiently, her shawl over her head. He had a sudden premonition – as if an icy hand had rubbed his back.

'Watch yourself, sister,' he whispered.

She looked back at him and squeezed his hand. 'And you, brother.'

Then the women were gone and they were walking up the steps of the central *megaron*. Ptolemy's Greek steward was waiting for them, and he bowed. 'Lord Ptolemy wishes to greet you in private,' he said. 'Please follow me. Your torch-bearers can wait.' He snapped his fingers and a pair of slaves emerged from the portico and gestured to the torch-bearers.

'I understood that we were to have an audience,' Leon said.

'Lord Ptolemy wishes to speak to you in private,' the steward insisted.

Leon looked around and then nodded. 'Very well,' he said. He turned to follow the steward. The Greek shook his head. 'Just you and Master Satyrus,' he said. 'My regrets to these gentlemen.'

Philokles snorted. 'Gabines, take us to Ptolemy, and stop pontificating.'

The Greek steward looked more closely at Philokles. He gave a short and rather discontented bow. 'Master Philokles. I didn't see you. Philosophers are always welcome in our lord's presence.'

Diodorus and Coenus pressed closer in the gathering gloom. 'Perhaps you shouldn't have been so quick to send the torches away, Gabines. Now, take us to the king,' Diodorus said.

Gabines looked around, as if expecting help.

Satyrus checked to make sure that he had his knife. It was absurd to feel physically threatened in the palace, but he was on edge, walking as if he expected ambush, and he noted that Diodorus and Coenus were the same, starting at shadows. Philokles, on the other hand, pulled his chlamys back over his head and walked with the calm of a priest.

They walked down the back of the megaron and across the central courtyard to the royal residence. Reliefs of Alexander's victories decorated every surface on the exterior, meticulously painted so that the horses seemed to ride out from the walls, and on the peristyle were ships under oars. Satyrus stared and stared – even Leon's villa had nothing like this for sheer display.

Leon wasn't looking at art, but at the guards. He motioned with his chin where more Macedonian guards waited on the portico, and yet more inside.

'He's got half of the Foot Companions on duty,' Diodorus said. 'Something is wrong.'

Leon shrugged. 'We already knew that something was wrong,' he said. He climbed the steps, nodded at the guards and entered.

Satyrus followed him up the steps. He noticed that the colonnade was full of men, and he saw the white glimmerings of the new quilted linen armour that the guards wore. His shoulders prickled as he passed them, and then he was in the residence, directly under the fresco of Herakles that filled the entryway arch. Up on the ceiling the gods sparkled, their faces adorned with real jewels as they seemed to watch both living men and the deeds of the demi-god. The floor was five colours of marble inlaid in a complex pattern that baffled the eye. At the centre of the arch, Herakles was carried by chariot into the heavens to become a god.

'Your majesty? Master Leon of Tanais, his nephew Prince Satyrus, Master Philokles the Spartan and Strategos Diodorus, as well as Phylarch Coenus of Olbia to see you.' The steward gave a deep and very un-Greek bow and, as he said their names, led them into the main hall, a sort of roofed garden in the middle of the building. Up on the ceiling, gods disported. A burly Apollo forced his favours on a not very unwilling nymph, while smiling over her shoulder at – Athena?

It looked blasphemous to Satyrus. And very beautiful.

'Leon? You brought an army to visit me?' Ptolemy was running to fat, and his high forehead and straight nose made him so ugly he was almost handsome. He rose from a heavy chair of lemonwood and ivory to clasp the Numidian's hand.

It was not the tone of a king about to murder one of his richest subjects. Satyrus felt the blood retreat from his face, and his pulse slowed.

'We all thought it wisest to come together,' Diodorus said.

'Meaning that you feared my reaction to this young scapegrace's attack on the Athenian ambassador. And well you might. Boy, what in Hades or Earth or the Heavens above moved you to attack the Athenian ambassador?'

Satyrus looked at Leon and received a nod of approbation. So he told the truth. 'He has tried to murder me before – and my sister. I want to kill him. Despite this, Lord Ptolemy, I took no action against him. His man attacked me, and I dealt with him.' He bowed his head. 'I am conscious of the religious obligations of a man towards a herald or an ambassador.'

Ptolemy smiled. His wide eyes appeared guileless when he smiled, giving him that look of pleased surprise that had earned him the nickname Farm Boy. Those who knew him well knew that the look was utterly deceptive.

'In other words, you are the outraged innocent and he is a viper at my breast?' the king asked.

Leon stepped in front of his nephew. 'Yes, lord. That is exactly so.'

Ptolemy fingered his chin and sat back down in his chair. 'Seats and wine for my guests. I'm not some fucking Persian, to keep them all standing for awe of me. Boy, you've put me in a spot and no mistake. I *need* Cassander. I *need* Athens. Stratokles is the price I pay for it, and he brought me news. I need him!' He glared at Leon. 'You and this Athenian have a history. Don't deny it – Gabines is a competent spymaster and I know things.'

Leon remained closest to the king when stools were brought. 'Is it nothing to you, Lord Ptolemy, that I have finished my summer cruise, and that I, too, have news?'

'Credit me with a little sense, Leon. I invited you here. No one has been arrested.' Ptolemy pointed at a side table with a wine cooler on it and closed his fist. At the signal, a squad of slaves appeared and began to pour wine.

Leon took a *phiale* from the side table and poured a libation. 'To Hermes, god of merchants and wayfarers and thieves,' he said. It was a curious gesture – the host usually poured the libation. Satyrus thought that his uncle was telling the king something. He just didn't know what it was.

'Since you are all three of them,' the king said with a smile.

Leon shrugged. 'Heraklea is buzzing with rumours of war,' he said. 'Antigonus is planning a campaign against Cassander and he's put his son in charge of an expedition – somewhere. No one knows where the golden boy is going. He had already marched when I left the coast.' He looked around. 'And his fleet is at sea, and we don't know where it is going. Rumour is he's going to lay siege to Rhodos.'

Ptolemy nodded. 'Exactly what Stratokles says.' He cocked his head to one side. 'Cassander has asked me to send him an army.'

'Don't do it, lord,' Diodorus said.

Ptolemy glanced at the red-haired man. 'Wily Odysseus, why not?'

'Call me what you will, lord. Cassander has the whole of Macedon to recruit. If we send him our best, he'll buy them as well – with farms at home, if nothing else – and we'll never have them back. We're far from the source of manpower, and he's close. Let him raise his own levies. And perhaps send us some!' He looked around. 'We're recruiting infantry from the Aegean and Asia and soon we'll be reduced to Aegyptians.'

Ptolemy nodded. 'I may send him some ships,' he said. 'But I regret to say that I have summoned you to forbid your expedition into the Euxine, Leon.'

Leon nodded slowly. 'I had your promise, lord.' He glanced at Satyrus.

Satyrus held himself still. No one had told him anything directly, but he had felt the expedition must be close – Philokles had dropped hints.

He wasn't sure whether he was angry or relieved.

Ptolemy put his chin in his hand and nodded. 'Circumstances change. Eumeles and his kingdom are allies of Cassander. I can't afford to have you making trouble there just now. I need to know that Antigonus and his army are going to Europe and not coming here. Then I'll let you go – with my blessing, which will have a very tangible effect. You and your nephew ruling the northern grain trade would be of the utmost value to us – to Aegypt and to our allies in Rhodos. But not this year.'

Leon gave a faint shrug. 'Very well, lord.'

'I'm sorry, Leon, I need better than that. Your oath, and your nephew's, that you will obey me in this.' Ptolemy's voice hardened for the first time, and suddenly he wasn't a genial old duffer. He was absolute ruler of Aegypt, even if he didn't call himself pharaoh yet. Yet.

Diodorus – one of Ptolemy's most valued men – nodded, the closest to a sign of submission that an Athenian aristocrat ever made to anyone. He glanced at the guards. 'Lord, you know us,' he said.

Ptolemy nodded.

'You know that we – Coenus, me, Leon, Philokles and a few others – follow the Pythagorean code.' He spoke forcefully, if quietly. Satyrus leaned forward, because all his life he had heard from his tutor about Pythagoreans, and it had never occurred to him that his tutor and his mentors were all initiates.

Ptolemy gave a half-smile. 'I know it.'

'We do not lightly take oaths, lord. In fact, we avoid them, as binding man too close to the gods. But if you require our oath, we will keep it. For ever. Is that what you want?' Satyrus had never heard Diodorus sound so passionate.

'Yes,' Ptolemy said. 'Get on with it.'

Leon took a deep breath. 'Very well, lord. I swear by Hermes, and by Poseidon, Lord of Horses, by Zeus, father of the gods, and all the gods, to obey you in this. My hand will not fall on Eumeles this year – though he betrayed my friendship and murdered Satyrus's mother, though his hands are stained in innocent blood to the wrists, though the Furies rip at me every night until he is put in the earth—'

'Enough!' the king cried, rising from his seat. 'Enough. I know that you have reason to hate him. I have reason to demand your oath. And you, boy?'

Satyrus stepped forward. 'I have sworn to the gods to kill every man and woman who ordered the death of my mother,' he said. 'The laws of the gods protect Stratokles, and now you, my king, order me to preserve Eumeles. Can you order me to break my oath to the gods?'

Ptolemy nodded. 'I carry the burden of every oath I ask my subjects to carry,' he said. 'Obey!'

Satyrus took a deep breath. 'By Zeus the Saviour and Athena, grey-eyed goddess of wisdom, I swear to wait one year in my vengeance against Heron, who calls himself Eumeles,' he said. 'By Herakles my patron, I swear not to take the life of Stratokles for one year.'

Ptolemy raised an eyebrow at Leon. 'One year? Is the boy attempting to bargain with his lord?'

Satyrus made himself meet Ptolemy's heavy gaze. 'Lord, yesterday I didn't even know that there was to be such an expedition. I can wait a year. If the year passes, perhaps I can wait another year.' Satyrus felt the grey-eyed goddess at his shoulder, guiding his words. 'Perhaps we can renew the oath like a truce.'

'Philokles, you have nurtured a rhetorician!' the king said.

'Satyrus has grown to manhood at this court,' Philokles said. He sipped his wine. 'And the essence of the teaching of Pythagoras has apparently slipped into his blood.' The Spartan gave Satyrus a smile that made Satyrus feel as light as air.

'There's more,' Leon said. 'You wouldn't have summoned us merely to prevent the expedition.'

'You mistake me, Leon,' Ptolemy said. He held out his cup for more wine. 'Or perhaps you don't. Yes, there is more. I am going to exile young Satyrus for a few months. To placate the Athenian.'

'Good gods!' Leon said. He shot to his feet, and his anger

rolled off him in waves. 'You get my oath and then exile my boy!'

Ptolemy gave a grim smile. 'Got it in one. Send him to sea, Leon. Later, I will of course allow my erring young prince to return.' He shrugged. 'I'm sorry, Satyrus. But I need the Athenians right now, and I need Cassander sweet – and bearing the brunt of One-Eye's attack.' He shrugged. 'It's a hard thing, ruling. I suspect that Stratokles the Viper intends to kill your charges.' Ptolemy shrugged, and grinned. 'If I exile you, and you take your sister – well, he can hardly complain, and he's unlikely to find a way to kill you, either. Everyone's equally unhappy.' Ptolemy looked around. 'I don't intend to let him kill these children, but neither, frankly, will I imperil an alliance that I need – that Aegypt needs – to preserve two teenagers, however wonderful.'

Coenus stood up. 'Listen to me, Ptolemy. You call yourself lord of Aegypt – I remember you as a page, and as a battalion officer. Is that what you learned about loyalty and command? What is this, Hephaestion's style? You know what they say about you in the army? That Antigonus will take us any time he wants, because he's a *real* Macedonian. Understands duty and honour and loyalty to his own.' The big man shrugged. 'Half the men in the city saw what happened today at Cimon's. You know yourself that the boy is guiltless. When you exile him, it's another sign you won't protect your own.'

'Watch yourself, old man,' Ptolemy said.

Diodorus stretched his legs in front of him. 'I remember a campfire in Bactria,' he said dreamily. 'You owe us, O King. And we're your friends.'

Ptolemy nodded. 'Yes!' he said. 'Yes, I *do* think that you men are my friends. And so I believe that I can ask this of you – I call you in private and I ask for this exile, so that I can preserve appearances. And so you can preserve the boy's life – I'm not a fool, Leon. I told you that I know that this Stratokles will try for the boy – and the girl, too. Because Cassander's stupid ally needs them dead.'

Leon raised his face, and the scowl dropped from his dark features. 'Oh – are you *asking*, lord?'

Ptolemy's face underwent a remarkable set of changes – anger, puzzlement, amusement, laughter. 'I've been playing at royalty too long,' he said. 'Yes, I'm asking. If you decline, I'll find another answer.'

'Ah!' Leon said. 'That's another thing entirely. If you ask,' he glanced at Satyrus, 'as a favour, then we will of course do it for you.'

Ptolemy nodded. 'As for the army,' he said to Coenus, 'I know that they are discontented. What can I do? Send them to fight in Nubia? Pay them better?'

'Make them feel noble,' Coenus said. 'They want to be heroes, not bodyguards.'

Ptolemy sighed. 'Do they even remember how fucking miserable life in Macedon was?' he asked. 'Or the campaigns in Bactria? Zeus Soter, that was Hades risen to fill the middle world. Tartarus incarnate.'

Leon rose to his feet. 'Lord, it occurs to me that I can send a cargo to Rhodos as early as tomorrow. They are our allies, and they are virtually under siege – every mina of grain will count. It will do us no harm to see if Demetrios has laid siege to Rhodos – or Tyre. Or gone elsewhere – and what armament he has. I must go and make my preparations.' He glanced at Coenus. 'Is Xeno ready to ship out?'

Coenus smiled. 'Now there's at least one man happy in all this!'

Ptolemy rose and clasped hands all around. 'I'm glad you all came to put me in my place,' he growled. He turned to Coenus. 'How bad are the Macedonians, Coenus?'

Coenus drained his wine and handed the cup to a slave. 'Do I look like an informer, Ptolemy? Eh?' Satyrus thought that the gentleman-trooper had to be one of just a handful of men who called Lord Ptolemy by name *all the time*. Then the Megaran's face changed, softened, and he shook his head. 'No, but listen. They don't hate you – some still love you. But the word in the ranks is that any contest with Antigonus is a foregone conclusion. I've heard men in the Foot Companions say that the phalangites won't fight – they'll just stand ten yards apart and watch.' Coenus shook his head again. 'Of the officers – there's rot there, but you know it as well as I.'

Ptolemy drained a cup of wine. 'Gabines?'

The steward hurried forward from behind the throne. 'It is much as he says, lord.' Gabines looked apologetic. 'I could bring you witnesses.'

'I have all the witnesses I need standing in front of me. Leon, listen to me – you and a dozen like you are the pillars that support this city. Understand me – and tell your friends, the Nabataeans and the Jews and all the other merchants. We cannot afford to fight. I *know* my army has rot all the way to the officer cadre. I know it! And that means that I have to rely on guile to keep Cassander and Antigonus off me.'

Philokles raised an eyebrow. He raised a hand to speak, opened his mouth and fell silent – his lips moving like a fish. It was rare for Philokles to behave so, but such was his power at court that the king waited, and on the second attempt, Philokles managed to speak.

'It seems to me that it is time to try an alternate source of manpower,' Philokles said.

Ptolemy nodded. 'What do you suggest? Spartans?'

Philokles frowned. 'Aegyptians. A citizen levy, like the hoplites of any Greek city.'

Ptolemy scratched under his chin, eyes on his guards, some of whom couldn't stop themselves from mutters as the idea was broached. 'They make awful soldiers,' he said.

'They once conquered the world, or so I understand,' Philokles said. 'Besides, I rather intended to suggest the citizens of this city – Greeks and Hellenes. And Nabataeans and Jews and native Aegyptians and the whole polyglot crew. You have been generous in granting citizenship – now is the time to see if these people are citizens in fact or only in name.'

'By the gods, Philokles, listening to you is like having an ephor of my very own. Who will command this mongrel mob?' Ptolemy asked.

Silence fell over the room. Ptolemy's eyes met Satyrus's, and the young man couldn't look away. It was odd, to have the eye of the ruler and want to be out from under it. *Why is he looking at me?*

'The Macedonian army has a nice tradition,' Ptolemy said. 'The author of a "great idea" is considered to have volunteered to lead. Why don't *you* raise this city levy, Spartan? I know you are the hoplomachos of all spear-fighters in the city. You can train them to be Spartans!'

Philokles got red in the face. 'You mock me,' he said.

'Careful there, Spartan. You Pythagoreans are supposed to avoid anger.' Ptolemy grinned. 'But I do *not* mock you. It's a fine idea – and I can afford it. Money we have. Find me a taxeis of locals and I'll arm them. If nothing else, it offers me—' He hesitated, and then smiled. 'Options.' Lord Ptolemy didn't describe what his options might be.

Philokles nodded and pursed his lips. Satyrus knew him so well that he could feel the oncoming rebuke. The skin over the Spartan's nostrils grew white, and the philosopher's grip on the staff he usually carried grew white-knuckled. And then his face softened, and he gave a faint smile.

'Very well,' Philokles said. 'I accept.'

'Good. Gentlemen, for all that you are the very foundation of my rule in Aegypt, it is late, and I have had too much wine.' Ptolemy rose.

Leon and Satyrus bowed gracefully. Diodorus, Philokles and Coenus nodded and clasped Ptolemy's hands like the old friends they were, whatever his power.

'My chair is always filled for any of you. Even the boy. Listen, boy – I saw you fight Theron today. I liked what I saw. Go away for a while and I'll have you back in style. Here's my hand on it.' Satyrus took the king's hand. Then Ptolemy smiled around at all of them like a conspirator and vanished into a screen of soldiers, and they withdrew.

'It seems to me that for all your complaints, you got exactly what you wanted,' Philokles said quietly to Leon.

'You're the dangerous one,' Leon said. 'A taxeis of locals? Suddenly you're going to have political power. And enemies. Welcome to *my* world.'

'I expect I will,' Philokles said. 'Should that deter me from an action that will help to balance the disaffection of the Macedonians and will render all of us safer? Stratokles is here, Leon. In this city. We need to gather our friends.'

Outside in the darkness, they all gulped lungfuls of smoky Alexandrian air. Satyrus was old enough to realize that they had all been as scared as he.

'Where will we go?' Satyrus asked. 'Rhodos, really?'

'We?' Leon asked. 'You will take the cargo as my navarch. You'll have excellent officers who you will listen to as if they were your uncles. You can sell a cargo and buy one, I hope?'

Satyrus's heart swelled to fill his chest. 'I'll be navarch *my-self*?' he asked.

Diodorus slapped him on the shoulder. 'You keep telling us you're a man,' he said.

A slave approached from the shadow of the megaron, guiding a woman with a shawl over her head. 'Lord Satyrus,' she called quietly.

Before his uncles could restrain him, Satyrus responded, 'Here!'

The young woman took his hand. 'Your sister intends to stay the night,' she said in a whisper, 'and requests that you visit her for a moment before you go.'

Leon shook his head. 'I'm afraid that I cannot allow my niece to spend the night in the palace,' he said. 'She has urgent duties to which she must attend.'

The young woman's face was white as tawed leather under the shawl. 'Oh – oh dear!' she said. 'Then you must come with me, lords.'

She led the way to the women's quarters.

'Where are my torch-bearers?' Leon asked the palace slave.

'I don't know, lord. I'll find them and meet you on the portico of the women's wing.' The slave turned and ran.

The women's palace was well lit, and sounds of laughter and music carried out into the night. A kithara was being played – two kitharas. And Melitta was singing with Kallista. Satyrus grinned.

'This wasn't supposed to happen this way!' said the young

woman at his side. She caught at his hand. 'Come with me,' she said.

Her hand was remarkably smooth and soft for a slave. He looked at her, and in the increased light of the portico, he realized that she was Amastris – the princess of Heraklea. His Nereid. He had seen her dozens of times at court. They had shared long glances. But he hadn't touched her hand since – well, since he was a supplicant at her uncle's court.

'Amastris!' he said.

'Shh!' she said. 'My beautiful plan is in ruins. I wanted to see you.' She smiled, her lips red in the torchlight. She glanced past him, where Leon was sending a slave in to fetch Melitta. 'I thought that your sister would stay for a few days. I've been on a ship for three weeks and trapped in my uncle's politics for the summer.'

'You wanted to see me?' Satyrus breathed. He leaned a little closer.

'There's a rumour in the women's quarters that you are to be exiled.' Amastris was standing very close to him, in the darkness of the columns. 'Oh, I feel like a fool.'

Satyrus knew with his usual sense of doom that in three days or so he'd think of the words he should have said.

'I have to go in,' Amastris said. 'I'm sorry that ...'

Satyrus felt his breath catch and cursed his cowardice – his knees were weak. His *elbows* felt weak. But he reached out anyway and caught her to him. Amazed that years of training in pankration should have prepared him so badly for this vital grasp.

He missed her shoulders in the dark and his right hand brushed her waist. She turned towards him, just the way an opponent would turn to get inside the reach of his long arms. He felt her hands on his upper arms, the press of her breasts against his chest. His own breath rasped in and out and his heart pummelled the inside of his ribcage like a dangerous opponent trying to fight its way out. As he lowered his mouth on hers – her hands locked behind his neck like a triumphant wrestler; her mouth, her lips, soft as lotus flowers and yet tough and pliant; his lips on her teeth, and their tentative opening, like the gates of a garden, and the ecstasy of the softness of her tongue – the dispassionate part of his mind noted that his composure was far more affected than it had been while fighting Stratokles. His heart was going like a galloping horse.

Then he stopped thinking, and lost himself in her.

'Satyrus!' Leon said in a voice of command. 'Find him!'

Amastris was out of his embrace before his heart could beat again, her fingers brushing down his arm as she fled, and then she was gone into the dark.

'Here, sir,' Satyrus called, emerging from the darkness of the colonnade.

'Kissing a slave girl!' Carlus growled approvingly. 'I saw her!' The torch-bearers were coming up out of the darkness.

'Satyrus!' Leon said. 'We have enough troubles without you assaulting palace slave girls. By all the gods – keep that thing under your chiton.'

Diodorus laughed.

Melitta came to the door and embraced another girl – Satyrus strained to see if it was Amastris – and came outside. 'Uncle, I was to spend the night!' she said, in a tone that came close to a whine.

'Come, my dear,' Philokles said, putting an arm around her. 'We're sorry—'

'Oh, Hades and Persephone, it's true, then! Satyrus is to be exiled!' Melitta looked around for him and then drew him into a hug. She whirled on Leon, who was arranging the torch-bearers. 'I'm going with him!'

'Yes, you are,' Leon said.

That left Melitta speechless. While she stood staring, Kallista emerged from the women's quarters and threw her chlamys over her head. The torch-bearers closed around them and they walked for the main gate. Gabines, Ptolemy's steward, met them on the way.

'Sometimes a man has to take sides,' Gabines said without preamble. 'You are all in danger. Now. Tonight. Men – I will not say who – informed Stratokles as soon as you were summoned. Understand? And there's a faction – you know them as well as I – of Macedonians here who would love to see you *all* dead.' He looked around. 'I think you are all the king's friends. I've doubled the king's guard and I'm sending three groups out of the gates to confuse them. Now go!'

Philokles stepped out of the group and took Gabines by the arm. They spoke in private, rapidly, the way commanders speak on a battlefield. Then both of them nodded sharply, in obvious agreement even in the torchlight, and Gabines hurried away.

The guard was being changed, and they took several minutes to get clear of the construction platforms and the smell of masonry, minutes that Coenus, Diodorus and Leon spent in whispered consultation with Philokles, who then took a weapon from one of the torch-bearers and walked off into the night, and another pair of torch-bearers doused their lights and ran off into the night with instructions from Diodorus. The gate guards watched this with some alarm, and Satyrus noted that one of them also left the guard post at a run.

Diodorus barked an order and they were out on the darkened streets.

They were well out on the Posideion when Philokles reappeared at a run, his chlamys wrapped around him. He made a gesture and Carlus raised his torch and swung it through a broad arc. 'We are being followed,' Philokles said, breathing hard. There was a line of blood on his hip. 'Be ready.' He looked at Satyrus and shook his head. 'I'm old and fat, boy!'

Melitta didn't turn her head. 'Carlus,' she said to the man behind her, 'I'm unarmed.'

The big barbarian – scarcely a barbarian after fifteen years speaking Greek, but his size still stood out – reached under his armpit and produced a blade as long as a man's foot. The blade sparkled in the torchlight. 'One of my favourites,' he said.

Melitta took the blade and slipped it under her cloak.

They turned suddenly off the Posideion into an alley that ran behind the great houses and temples, and the whole group moved faster – and then Diodorus had Satyrus by the shoulder and turned him south, away from their route. Carlus had Melitta right behind them, and the rest of the torch-bearers continued on as if nothing had happened. The twins were swept along by the big Keltoi and Diodorus, down the narrow gap between two courtyard walls and into a back gate. Satyrus had a dim recollection of having visited this house by daylight – buying spices with Leon – and he saw an Arab man standing in the courtyard, wearing a white wool robe.

'Thanks, Pica,' Diodorus said.

'I see nothing, friend,' the Nabataean replied. He laughed.

Then they went out of the front gate and found themselves down by the docks. They were almost opposite Leon's private wharf.

'Now we need some luck,' Diodorus said. They ran from warehouse to warehouse along the waterfront.

'This is living!' Melitta crowed.

Satyrus saw men moving just one alley to the north, and a shrill whistle sounded.

'Hermes,' Diodorus said. 'He's hired every cut-throat in the city.'

'Uhh,' Carlus grunted. 'I could go and thin the herd.'

'Do it. We're going for the *Lotus* – Leon says there ought to be six boat-keepers aboard.'

'Uhh,' Carlus said. 'I find my own way.' And then he was gone.

They dashed across the open road to the gate of Leon's wharf. 'Open up!' Diodorus called.

Nothing.

Running feet behind them and a whistle like the cry of a falcon.

'Open up! In Leon's name!' Diodorus cried. He had his sword in his hand – a wicked kopis with a long, heavy blade. He banged the backbone of the weapon on the gate, and started to look up along the wall, searching for a place to climb. Satyrus was several seconds ahead of him, up and over the wall and then drawing his own weapon.

The rush of feet grew louder – bare feet, mostly. And then there was a sound like an axe hitting soft wood, or like an oar slapping water in the hands of an inexperienced oarsman – and another, the same. And then a third, and this time the sound was accompanied by a shrill scream that cut across the night like fabric being ripped asunder.

Satyrus got the gate open and looked out past Diodorus as the man pushed in. Carlus – no one else was that big – was killing men silently. The victims were not so silent, but there were more whistles after the scream.

'Sorry, lord,' said a voice at his elbow, the house porter. 'It sounds like murder!'

'Get the gate shut. Help me.' Melitta and Satyrus helped the porter shove the gate, and it made a clang as it latched. They were in Leon's precinct.

'Is there a boat party on the *Lotus*?' Diodorus asked.

'No – that is, yes, lord.' The man got the beam back across the gate. 'Alarm, lord?'

Diodorus nodded. 'Better have it,' he said.

The man at the gate was short, broad and had the slightly stooped look of the professional oarsman. He picked up a billet of wood and started to hit an iron bell. 'Alarm!' he called.

Diodorus took the twins by the shoulders.

Melitta was still facing the gate, unwilling to be dragged towards the ship. 'What about Kallista? Or Carlus? By Athena, Diodorus!'

'They are in a great deal less danger for *not* being with you, my dear. Well, not Carlus. I think he has sacrificed himself. Be brave, girl. This is the real thing.' Diodorus paused to tighten his sandals. 'Stupid things. Never wear *anything* you can't fight in.'

'I don't want to *run*,' she said.

'Then you'll die.' Diodorus had no more patience. 'Listen to me, girl. In a minute, a dozen paid thugs are going to come over that wall on ropes. They'll kill everyone here. We're getting on a boat and getting out. Understand? The moment to stand and fight will come another day.'

Melitta was silent. 'What about the men who are here?' she asked.

Diodorus started to run. 'Figure it out,' he called as he dragged her towards the looming bulk of the *Golden Lotus*. Satyrus followed them, sword naked in his hand.

He hailed the deck from the pier, and the watch was awake. 'What news?' called an Athenian voice.

'Leon told me to ask for Diokles!' Diodorus said.

'Here, mate! What do you need?' Diokles was apparently the man coming down the plank.

'We need the boat under the stern and two men to row us around to Lord Leon's. Right now. And there'll be armed men coming over the wall any moment.' Diodorus punctuated his speech with glances over his shoulder.

Diokles didn't hesitate. He grabbed a rope and pulled and in moments they were in a light boat – lovingly painted in red and blue, a display piece that nonetheless had serviceable oars. He pushed four men into the boat. 'Kleitos, row them round to Leon's – I'm going to cut the hawsers and pole off. Robbers won't swim to get to the *Lotus*, and if they do,' the man's teeth shown white in the dark, 'I'll just gaff 'em like fish.'

'Save the slaves,' Diodorus said.

'Sure!' Diokles laughed. 'They brought the wine.' And then they were rowing, four pairs of arms pulling hard so that the low boat shot across the harbour.

Listen as they would, they heard no sounds of fighting behind them. Diokles shouted and the slaves and workers on the night shift ran aboard the *Lotus* as if drilled to it, and then – nothing.

The row home was uneventful, and then they were going up the water-steps to the back of Leon's villa and into the dining hall, where Nihmu and Sappho and many of the household's older servants were already dining.

Satyrus seated himself on a couch and untied his sandals. His feet were filthy. Her mouth had tasted of youth – very different from Phiale's cinnamon and clove. Despite the nearness of death – or because of it – Amastris was at the surface of his thoughts.

'She found you, didn't she?' Melitta asked, lying carefully on the couch they shared. She was careful of the covering, because her beautiful chiton had a long smear of something that looked to be tar and another even worse. 'I can smell her scent even now. And you look as if you've been struck by lightning – or Aphrodite.'

Kallista came up beside him and made a show of picking up his sandals. Even as she did so, she dropped an oyster shell in his lap. A scrap of papyrus curled out of the corner of the shell, and Satyrus rolled on to the couch while scooping it up. 'Thanks, Lista!' he said. 'You made it back!'

'Always happy to help the goddess,' Kallista said primly, and then flashed him a smile. 'We've been back half an hour.' And then, soberly, 'Master Philokles killed a man. I saw it. And Master Coenus killed another.'

Leon was outlining the terms of Satyrus's exile to his wife. Satyrus glanced down at the papyrus.

All it said was *Stay safe and return.*

Satyrus was grinning like a fool.

Nihmu met his eyes and smiled. 'You look very happy for a boy who has just been attacked on the streets and exiled,' she said.

Satyrus attempted to modify his expression.

'You'll have to send her a response,' Melitta said. She poked him in the soft flesh over his hip so that he writhed in ticklish agony. 'Kallista can carry it while we pack.'

'No, I can't,' Kallista said. 'Perhaps tomorrow. Master Leon says no slave is to leave the compound for any reason until further orders.'

'What can I tell her, anyway?' Satyrus asked. In a breath, he began to see the complications of kissing Ptolemy's ward, the daughter of the Euxine's most powerful tyrant. Men had tried to kill him in the city he'd come to think of as his own. He felt disoriented, as if the world had slipped off its axis.

'Tell her you love her?' Melitta said, and poked him again.

'I'm to go as a marine!' Xeno called from an adjoining couch. 'Who cares if you're exiled! You'll be a navarch! We'll fight pirates!'

'I'm going too,' Melitta said.

Xeno's smile was rapturous. 'We'll protect you, despoina,' he said. Then his face fell as he realized how badly this comment had gone down. Satyrus rolled over and saw his sister's anger.

'I don't want to be protected, you overgrown *boy!*' Melitta spat. 'If you had as many brains as you have pimples, you'd understand!'

Crushed, Xeno rolled on his couch and faced the other way, the flush on his face spreading right across his back.

'By Artemis, goddess of virgins, may I kill a pirate before that snot-faced boy!' Melitta proclaimed.

Nihmu leaned over towards the younger people. 'You wish to go as an archer, perhaps? My husband could set a new fashion!' She smiled her enigmatic smile. As a girl, Nihmu had been an oracle among the Scythians on the sea of grass. Her oracular powers had left her a serious young woman with a head for figures, and she had married Leon after his second expedition to the east. 'Amazon crews? Eh?' she asked.

Nihmu, as the only other Sakje woman, was Melitta's special friend, a bridge between the world of Alexandria and the sea of grass. Melitta laughed. 'Why can't I?' she asked. 'Once at sea, who would know?'

'The other archers,' Leon called from his couch. 'Take this seriously, friends. We are at war as of now.'

Melitta stood up and raised her wine cup. 'We were always at war, Uncle Leon. We just forgot.'

Sappho shook her head, as if denying this assertion, but Philokles, coming in with his whole midriff wrapped in linen, nodded. 'She's right,' he said. 'Life *is* war.'

'Spare us the Heraklitus,' Sappho said.

'Where are we going, Uncle?' Satyrus asked. To have kissed Amastris and be going as a navarch all in one day seemed unbearable joy, despite everything, and thoughts of revenge on his mother's murderers slipped farther away.

'*We* aren't going anywhere, lad,' Leon said. 'You will take *Golden Lotus* up to Rhodos and drop a cargo of grain they need desperately. Then, if the helmsman agrees, you will go north around Lesvos to Methymna and across to Smyrna, drop some hides and some odds and ends and pick up a cargo of dye. And then home on the wind. Three weeks if you are quick – a month at the outside. By then, I predict that the king will be your friend again.'

Melitta was consuming broiled squid at a rate that made Satyrus dizzy. 'We have to pack!' she said.

'What if he is not our friend then?' Satyrus asked. *What if the king learns that I've kissed his ward?*

Diodorus finished drinking a bowl of soup. He rubbed a hairy forearm across his mouth and Sappho made a gesture of resignation. 'Then we'll have *Hyacinth* meet you in the outer harbour and you can take her to Cyrene!' He laughed and reached across his wife for wine. She scowled. He looked around. 'Listen, friends. We've grown soft. Now we go back to being hard. We, here, have a month to do Stratokles all the harm we can. We need to destroy him and his power base in this city. That goes for every servant – every slave. If you see one of the Athenian's slaves getting water, beat him – or her. Understand?'

The servants in the hall nodded – some looked eager, and others looked scared.

'You make mighty free with my people and my triremes, brother,' Leon said to Diodorus, but then he shrugged. 'That is, of course, what we'll do – keep the twins moving until the problem is solved, and fight Stratokles in the shadows.' He shrugged apologetically to his wife. 'It will be hard here. And the Macedonian party won't just stand by.'

Satyrus ate some bread and fish sauce. 'But Philokles will come with us,' he said. And then he understood. 'Won't he?' he added, sounding weak even to himself.

Philokles shook his head. 'Time for you to fly on your own, lad,' he said.

'Theron?' Satyrus asked.

Theron, lying with Philokles, raised his head and shook it. 'Philokles and I are apparently raising an army to defend you, my prince,' he said.

Satyrus recalled that earlier that day he had dreamed of commanding the *Golden Lotus*.

Lamplight, and Melitta standing by his bed. 'Carlus came in!' she said. 'Alive – but wounded. Philokles is with him.'

Satyrus rolled to his feet with the ease of practice and

followed his sister down the dark corridor and out across the courtyard between the two houses. He could sleep-walk the route to Philokles' rooms.

Carlus took up the whole of Philokles' oversized sleeping couch and still his lower legs dangled off the end.

'I must have sent a dozen of them to hell,' he said in his thick accent. 'And they broke, but there were more, and more. Fifty.' The big Keltoi shook his head weakly. 'Zeus Soter, I was afraid, and then – they left me. Gone, like a herd of deer running in the woods.'

'They weren't paid enough to go chest to chest with you, Titan,' Philokles said. 'If it makes you feel better, I think we'll be going into those neighbourhoods you wanted to clean. Soon.'

'Uhh,' the Keltoi grunted, and fell asleep.

'Will he live?' Satyrus asked.

'Look at the muscle on that chest!' Philokles said, shaking his head. 'Yes – none of these dagger blows got through his muscle. Those were brave and desperate men, Satyrus. Contempt for your opponents is always a waste of time. Imagine facing Carlus in the dark. Two men got close enough to mark him. Imagine.'

'He's passed out,' Melitta said.

'Poppy – he's so full of it he should bleed poppy juice,' Philokles said. 'So we all made it home. That makes me feel better – there was a moment in the dark when I thought we were all going down. Ares, I'm not as young as I used to be.'

'I wish you were coming with us,' Melitta said.

'Me too,' Satyrus said. He found that he was holding his sister's hand.

Philokles got up, wincing and favouring his left side. 'Listen,' he said, putting a hand on each of their shoulders. 'Pythagoras teaches that there are four seasons to life as there are four seasons to the world – spring, when you are a child, and summer, in the full bloom of adulthood – then autumn, when a man reaches his full power and a woman's beauty fades, and winter, when we age towards death. Yes?'

'Yes,' the twins chorused.

'I pronounce that you have passed from spring into summer,' Philokles said. 'Melitta, you are a woman, and Satyrus, you are a man. What is the first lesson?'

Together, the twins spoke, almost one voice. 'To your friends do good, and to your enemies, harm.'

'That is the lesson,' Philokles said. 'See that you live it.'

It was still dark when they were rowed aboard the *Golden Lotus*, which had been brought around from the yard and stood just off the beach, her oarsmen keeping her steady against the predawn breeze. Melitta went up the side, and then Satyrus swung his leg over and dropped to the deck amidships.

Peleus the Rhodian, Leon's helmsman, stood with his legs apart, braced against the roll of the deck. 'Welcome aboard, *Navarch*,' he said. He put special emphasis on the word, but it wasn't mockery – quite.

'Peleus!' Satyrus said. He clasped the older man's arm, and his clasp was returned. He stepped back. 'This is my sister, Melitta.'

'Despoina,' Peleus said, and turned his back on her, grasping Satyrus by the arm. 'Let's get the *Lotus* clear of the land, and then we'll have time for girls and orders and all the crap that the land brings, eh? First time out in command? Feel any butterflies, boy?'

'Yes!' Satyrus admitted. He looked at Melitta, who had the look of a woman withholding judgment – Peleus's comment hadn't escaped her. He had to make Peleus, whose dislike of women at sea was legendary, accept his sister's presence. He had to make his sister – well, toe the line.

'Banish the butterflies,' Peleus said. 'Oars, there. Do ye hear me!'

A chorus of affirmatives, and the Rhodian turned to Satyrus. 'Ready for sea, sir,' he said.

Satyrus had been to sea since he was nine years old, but his heart was beating as if he was in mortal combat. He took a breath, and made his voice steady. 'Carry on,' he said, as if it was nothing to command a warship at sea.

Like wings, the oars rose together and dipped, and suddenly

they were in motion, as close to flying as Satyrus was ever likely to achieve.

Two stades away across the port of Alexandria, a scarred man leaned on the rail of a trireme, head swathed in bandages, watching under his hands as the familiar shape of the *Golden Lotus* gathered way as the first fingers of dawn stretched across the sky.

'There they are,' said Iphicrates. 'Kineas's brats,' he growled.

The Latin, Lucius, shrugged. 'Frankly, boss, I think the gods love 'em. I think we should just let 'em go and good riddance.'

'I couldn't agree more,' Stratokles said. 'Despite which, I want you to find them at sea and kill them. It is probably better this way,' he said after a moment's hesitation. 'Last night was too bloody and too obvious, and sooner or later, that fat parasite Gabines will know we did it.'

'Fucking public service,' Lucius said. 'The sheer number of street thugs who died last night has got to make this city a better place to live.' He laughed.

Iphicrates shook his head. 'We should have had them last night. And Diodorus and fucking Leon into the bargain.'

'They were on to us from the start of the evening, gentlemen,' Stratokles said. 'I don't like losing a contest any more than the next man, but it is a pleasure to be up against men of worth. You'll have to be on your toes, Iphicrates. *Golden Lotus* is the toughest ship in these waters, or so I'm told.'

The scarred Athenian mercenary stretched and shook his head. 'I've been fighting at sea since I was twelve, Stratokles. And I've taken a few Rhodians in my time, and they are *never* easy. But if I have a clean chance, I'll take 'em. The new engines will give me an edge they can't be ready for.'

'Engines?' Lucius asked. He had quite a bit of intellect, but most of it was reserved for war.

'Like big bows, with ratchets to hold 'em cocked. Shoot a bolt the size of a sarissa. Goes right through a trireme's hull.'

'Despite which,' Stratokles added, 'your first duty to me is information. I need to know what One-Eye is up to on the coast of Syria – and Cyprus. And what Rhodos is doing. *Golden Lotus* is bound for Rhodos. Need I say more?'

'No, sir,' Iphicrates said.

'Go get them then,' Stratokles said, and slapped the mercenary on the back. 'I'll take care of business here. I've fomented a fair amount of treason,' he said. 'Macedonians are the most perfidious race on the face of Gaia. And they call Greeks treacherous.' He laughed. Then he turned back to Iphicrates and put a hand on his arm. 'Don't loiter out there. I know you have piracy in your blood, but I need your reports – and I need to know I have a way out of here. When Gabines starts to follow up on the tags I've left – I can't help it! He's going to be after me like a pig on slops. And Leon will strike back after last night – count on it.'

'Hurry out, take the *Lotus*, check Rhodos and Syria, hurry back. Anything else?' Iphicrates shook his head. 'Tall order and no mistake.'

'That's why I'm sending the best,' Stratokles said.

17

Two hundred miles north-north-east of Alexandria, and the helmsman, Peleus, had made a perfect landfall at Salamis of Cyprus, the island's beaches just a heat shimmer while the headland temple to Aphrodite Lophos shone in the sun.

'Peleus, you are the very prince of navigators,' Satyrus said. He had the steering oar under his arm.

Peleus was not looking ahead at all, but watching the wake. The *Golden Lotus* was a *triemiolia*, a three-and-a-half-er that carried an extra half bank of oars and a permanent sail deck and the crew to manage her sails even in a fight. Pirates loved the smaller version, the *hemiolia* and so did the Rhodians, the best sailors in the world. *Golden Lotus* was Rhodian-built, and Peleus was Rhodian-born, a seaman from the age of six. His current age was unknown, but his beard was white and every sailor in Alexandria treated him with respect.

'When you talk, there's a notch in the wake,' the helmsman said.

With the grim determination of youth, Satyrus gripped the steering oar.

'Never had a boy your age train to be a helmsman,' Peleus said. But he had half a smile when he said it, and the curl of his lips suggested that maybe – just maybe – Satyrus *was* the exception. 'If I tell you to steer north by east, what's the first headland you'll see?'

Satyrus looked back at the wake. 'Open sea until we see Mount Olympus of Cyprus rising on the port oar bank,' he said.

Peleus nodded. 'Maybe,' he said. 'It's the right answer. But what's wrong with the order?'

Satyrus hated questions like this. He stared out at the blinding white of the distant temple. 'I don't know,' he said after a gut-wrenching interval.

'That's a fair-enough answer and no mistake,' Peleus

answered. 'It's true, boy – you don't know, and you can't. Here's the answer – we're too far in with the land to keep the sea breeze, so our lads would have to row every inch of the way.' He was watching the land. 'I aim to make for Thronoi for the night – the beach there is soft white sand and the villagers will bring us food for a little cash. I used to have a boy there.' He gave a smile that creased the long scar down his face.

'What happened?' Satyrus asked. He was in love, and so wanted to hear about the loves of others.

'He grew up and got married to some girl,' Peleus said gruffly. 'Mind your helm, boy. There's a notch in the wake.' He looked behind him, across the water and almost straight into the sun. 'We have companions.'

Satyrus looked back until he saw the dark smudges, right on the edge of the horizon and almost invisible in the sun dazzle. 'I see them,' he said.

Peleus grunted.

Thronoi stood well back from the sea – no unwalled village could afford to be too close to the water – and the first men to approach carried spears and javelins, but they knew *Golden Lotus* and they knew Peleus, and before the sun became a red ball in the west, the crew was cooking goats and lobsters on the beach, drinking local wine and discussing their chances with the navarch's beautiful sister, who excited comment even wrapped from head to toe in a chlamys big enough for Philokles. She had pleaded to be allowed to ship as an archer, but Peleus had put his foot down, and she was merely a Greek lady of means with her maid. The oarsmen couldn't see her as anything but a beautiful mascot. They competed for her glance, and Peleus had told Satyrus that he'd never seen such powerful rowing in all his days at sea.

'Every ship needs a beautiful woman,' Peleus allowed, standing at Satyrus's elbow. Like every other man on the beach, he was watching Melitta. She was standing apart, watching some archers shoot at a mark. Satyrus knew she had her bow in her baggage, and he also knew she could outshoot most of these men. Her posture was defiant. Her maid stood behind her, muttering. Dorcus was the middle-aged free-woman Leon had sent in place of Kallista, whose sea-sickness was as legendary as her beauty. Dorcus's beauty lay in her practical application of the back of her hand.

'That friend of yours is going to break his face staring at her,' Peleus said, pointing at Xeno. Coenus's son was stripping off his cuirass, but his eyes were on Melitta.

Satyrus shook his head. 'What do I do?' he asked.

Peleus pursed his lips. 'She's Artemis's avatar, boy,' Peleus said with a pious glance towards the temple of Artemis's heavenly rival, Aphrodite. 'Nothing you can do but hope that she doesn't tear anyone apart.'

They slept in watches. They did everything in watches, because all the major states hired pirates to pad out their navies, and piracy was the biggest business in the Aegean that summer. Satyrus slept alone, because he was the navarch, technically in command, with a tent of his own. Melitta slept on the other side of the tent with Dorcus.

He awoke with the sun, noted that his sister was absent from her bed, cursed the stiffness in his shoulders from sleeping on sand and threw himself into the ocean as the sun rose and swam down the beach and back. From the water he couldn't see the sentries, but he could see his sister swimming on the other side of the headland.

'I thought I saw the flash of oars,' she called out to him.

Naked, he climbed out of the water and climbed the cool rocks of the headland to the sentry post.

Both of the sentries were sound asleep. It was understandable, as they'd had three days at sea and too much rowing, but it was unforgivable too. Dawn was the time that pirates attacked.

Satyrus looked off into the rising sun with his hand up to shade his eyes while he was still considering how to waken the two offenders. He saw the flash of low sun on oar blades to the north beyond the headland at Korkish. Twenty stades at the most.

His heart rate surged.

'Alarm!' he called. Melitta took up the cry and ran down the line of sleeping oarsmen, ignoring her own nudity to kick each man and shrill the alarm as she ran. 'Alarm!'

Peleus was out of his sheepskins and bounding up the rocks like a much younger man. Satyrus watched the distant flash of oars – afraid that he had it wrong, and equally afraid that he was correct.

The beach was full of movement. This was a veteran, and well-paid, crew. The oars were already going back aboard. The marines were forming on the beach, led by their captain, Karpos. He watched Melitta run by with an appreciative glance while checking his men's readiness. Xeno stood in the front rank, his aspis on his shoulder and a pair of heavy javelins in his hand.

Behind the marines, the archers formed. There were only half a dozen of them, with Scythian bows and quivers that held two dozen arrows and some surprises, as well.

Peleus kicked one of the half-asleep sentries in the crotch. 'Fear the evening, Agathon!' he spat at the other one. 'I'll have the hide off you, you whore's cunt-washing.' He looked under his hand and turned back. 'Dead right, boy. Coming out of the eye of the wind at dawn – no honest sailorman would do such a thing.' He looked at the beach. 'Fight or run?'

Satyrus wasn't sure his opinion was even being asked, but curiosity got the better of him. 'Surely we could just wait for them on the beach. The men of the town would stand with us.'

Peleus nodded. 'Yes – but we'd lose the *Lotus*. If we were lucky they'd just beak her and leave her to sink. More likely they'd board her over the bow and row her away. Hard to hold a boat on a beach. Not impossible.' He shrugged. 'Thanks to you, we've got the jump on 'em. I think we should run.'

'Run?' Satyrus asked. 'Can't we take them?'

Peleus curled the corners of his lips down. 'Listen, Navarch – this is your call. Your uncle put you in charge of the *Lotus* and that makes it your decision. But we're *merchants*. We have a full cargo and your sister, too. And fighting pirates is soldiers' work.' The old helmsman pointed at the beach. 'How many of them are you ready to lose so that you can have a hack at some pirates? And what happens to your sister if we lose?' The man frowned. 'Or you, for that matter.'

'Point taken, helmsman. We'll run.' Was it cowardice that Satyrus felt better already?

'Good lad. You may yet make a sailor.' Peleus sprang off the rocks like a man in his prime and started bellowing at the oarsmen.

Xenophon already had his armour on, and Melitta had her gorytos out of her deck baggage and an Aegyptian corslet of white quilted linen and a small Pylos helmet on her hair. 'Pirates?' she asked, her eyes gleaming.

'Put that away!' Satyrus said.

Xenophon's grin was just the same. 'Let her fight!' he said from the ranks. 'She's a better shot than Timoleon!'

'We're running,' Satyrus said.

'We're what?' Melitta asked. 'Are you joking?' She went from elated to angry in a heartbeat.

'Running.' Satyrus shrugged. 'We're merchants, Lita. We're running.'

He hated the looks on his sister's face and on Xenophon's.

'This is Amastris's noble warrior?' Melitta asked him. 'How will you tell this story to her? Eh, brother?'

'Lita, mind your manners.' Satyrus turned away, because Peleus was calling to him.

Melitta wouldn't let up. She followed him down the beach. 'Peleus told you that you couldn't risk me, right? Fuck that, brother. Let's get 'em! Think about the ones they've sold into slavery – think about whoever they catch tomorrow – all on our heads.' She glared at him. 'You're afraid I'll be raped? *Fuck* that. You're as pretty as I am.'

'No!' Satyrus said, a little too loudly.

'Are you *afraid*, brother?' she shot back, and she said it so loud that every man left on the beach could hear her.

'Fuck off, sister. We're running!' Satyrus was up the plank in three long strides.

Peleus pulled Melitta up behind him and then kept her hand pinned in his. 'If you were a man, I'd beat your fucking head against the steering post,' he said. His face was red. 'Dare to question the officers?' he asked with murderous quiet.

Angry men did not intimidate Melitta. 'Only when they make bad decisions, Peleus. Those are *pirates*. We should *kill them*.'

'You may yet get your wish,' Peleus said. 'If you want to impress me, you're going about it the wrong way, *girl*. Now get to your station. *Not with the archers, missy!*' She went sullenly to the amidships awning with Dorcus, glaring at every man in sight.

'You should discipline her,' Peleus said.

'You first,' Satyrus said, and drew a quick half-smile. And then the half-deckers and the sailing crew were pushing on the stern and the *Lotus* hissed down the last of the shingle and her stern bumped the beach again, causing a little restrained chaos among the rowers for two strokes, and then they were clear of the beach, and *Lotus*'s bow was cutting the breakers, the bow-ram showing copper-red on the rise in the red morning sun.

'Left one of the cauldrons,' the sailing master said, pointing at the beach.

'We'll get it next time. If we live. Poseidon, stand with us,' Peleus said, and he tipped a phiale of red wine into the sea.

The pirates came around the last point – two black ships crammed with men. Both were the size of the *Golden Lotus*, one a trireme of the old Athenian pattern and the other a heavy Phoenician, and as soon as they saw their prey afloat they sprang forward, their oar masters calling for the fighting stroke and getting it with a speed that showed that these crews knew their business.

'Nope,' Peleus said, looking astern. 'We don't want a piece of that, boy. Steady on that tiller. We're heavier with our cargo, and they've got weed and those hulls haven't seen a drying shed in years. This'll be close.'

'Should you be at the tiller, helmsman?' Satyrus asked.

Peleus shook his head with his half-smile. 'No. You can handle it.' The old man rubbed his beard for several breaths and then pointed aloft. 'Get me the boatsail, you bastards,' he called, and the deck crew sprang to their stations – they already had the sail spread on the deck. Satyrus couldn't help but notice that Agathon had led the men in putting the sail out – trying to make up for his lapse.

Satyrus felt the change under his hand before they had the whole sail aloft – *Lotus*'s stern rose as the boatsail pressed her ram-bow deeper in the waves, but she also sprang forward. Steering became easier as speed increased – a big ship like *Lotus* went straight very easily at speed.

They'd cleared the beach with just the lower bank manned, but now Peleus ordered all the banks manned, and they pulled easily, supporting the sailing speed and adding to it. Then the helmsman came back to the stern and stood with his thumb covering the enemy.

'Just even,' he said. 'Just want to tell you, Navarch – if we dump the hides, we'll run away from them in an hour.'

Satyrus shook his head. 'Would you?'

Peleus scratched his beard. 'Probably not. Not yet, anyway.'

'Fair enough,' Satyrus said. 'No, we'll—'

There was a crash from aft and a spear the size of a boatsail mast shot by the stern. Satyrus ducked – he couldn't help himself.

'Shit,' Peleus said. 'One of those new-fangled engines. Where the *fuck* do a pair of Cypriot bum-boys get an Ares engine?'

They lost ground because the rowers were as confused as Satyrus. The black ships gained steadily, and then the engine fired again. This time, Satyrus had the time to see the whole flight of the lance – it vanished in the waves well to starboard of the stern.

'Now I'd dump the hides,' Peleus said. 'If he gets a bargepole into our rowers, we're dead.' He was watching the sea. 'Good time for a chance Rhodian patrol,' he said under his breath. 'Usually a ship out this way. Or off the beach round the point. It was my station, once.'

Satyrus felt curiously light. He shook his head. 'Poseidon stand with us,' he said. 'We can do it.' Akrotirion promontory was close, just a dozen stades away on the starboard bow, and Satyrus knew that the moment they weathered the point they'd have deep water in the bay and a wind change.

One of the engines fired with a wooden crash that was audible over the water and the lance flew true, straight on for the *Lotus* but aimed too high, so that the whole shaft passed down the main deck, missed the mast and vanished ahead of them.

'Get me Timoleon,' Peleus called. In seconds, the archer-captain was standing with them. Peleus waved astern. 'Can you hit the men on the engine?'

Timoleon shook his head. 'Only if Apollo draws my bow,' he said, but without any further complaints, he took a shaft from his belt and drew it until the bronze head was on his fingers before he loosed.

Satyrus lost the flight in the rising sun, but Peleus shook his head. 'Well short.'

The engine in the bow of the Phoenician fired, but the bolt went short, fired at the wrong moment as the bow swung with the waves. They were coming in with the shore at a rapid pace as both sides tried to weather the point as close as possible.

'Put the starboard oars right in the surf, boy!' Peleus said. 'There's more water there than you think. Shave it close!' To the archer, he said, 'Try again.'

This time, Timoleon waited for the height of the rise of the waves under the stern and he drew so far that the head almost dropped off his thumb before he loosed. Again, Satyrus couldn't follow the flight of the arrow.

'Better,' Peleus said.

'Shoot these,' Melitta said. She ignored Peleus's look of anger. 'Sakje flight arrows. Cane shafts. Allow for the wind – they don't weigh anything and they'll blow around.'

Timoleon picked one up – a hand-breadth longer than his longest arrow, made of swamp cane with iron needle points. 'Nasty,' he said. He grinned at Melitta. 'Thanks, despoina.'

Melitta smiled at him. 'Poison,' she said.

Timoleon's hand froze in the process of reaching for the point. 'Fucking Scythians,' he said respectfully and drew the shaft across his thumb. He pulled the shaft to the head and loosed at the top of the roll.

Even Satyrus saw the eddy of disturbance in the bow of the pirate. 'Good shot!' he shouted.

Timoleon beamed. 'Apollo held my hand,' he said. 'Never shot so far in all my life.' He nodded to Melitta. 'Thanks, despoina. Care to have a go?'

She shrugged. 'I could never get an arrow that far,' she admitted.

The lighter of the pirates now thrust ahead, but they didn't fire their engine. As the promontory grew to fill the horizon, their own archers fired, and with the sea breeze behind them, their arrows carried easily. One oarsmen was pinked, the broad bronze head of the arrow slicing his back.

Timoleon returned fire, but he used up Melitta's supply of cane arrows without scoring another hit, each arrow blown to the right or left as if made of feathers. Melitta watched with a look Satyrus knew well – a look that said that she could have done better.

'Let me have a shot,' she said, when Timoleon was down to her last cane arrow.

'Be my guest,' he said.

She got up on the very tip of the stern platform, balanced a moment, lifted her bow, drew and shot in one fluid motion.

Her arrow vanished into the nearer trireme's rowers, a little high to get the crew of the Ares engine, but she was rewarded with a thin scream, and then a rising shriek.

She clapped her hands in delight. Timoleon slapped her on the back.

The Phoenician's engine fired, the bolt ripping along the port oar banks with a noise like tearing linen. It hit several oar shafts, bounded about inside the loom of oars and then fell into the sea without breaking anything.

Satyrus's hand on the steering oar was like iron. He didn't feel fatigue, and he was not particularly aware of the missile exchange. He watched his wake and adjusted his course, cheating the bow towards the open sea and allowing the incoming waves to push his hull a little further towards the promontory.

Just so, he thought, and held his course. He was in another place in his mind – a place where *being the helmsman* drove out room for any other fear.

Melitta slipped down the stem, followed by Timoleon.

Peleus watched her with pursed lips, but when she was gone amidships, he said, 'She bought us a ship's length there.'

They weathered Akrotirion promontory as close as they dared, the starboard oars in the surf, with the black hulls half a dozen stades behind. Every pair of eyes on the *Lotus* that were above deck level strained for the Bay of Kition in hopes of seeing a couple of Rhodian warships riding at anchor.

The pirates lost a stade because the big Phoenician wouldn't come in as close to the beach. They made a dog-leg out to sea and Satyrus breathed a little easier, *almost* sure that he could beat them in a dead sprint.

And then all that careful helm work was by the board, because sure enough, there *was* a Rhodian three-er riding high, her crew still at breakfast on the beach. Rhodos was a free port, independent of the wars of Alexander's successors, but she protected Ptolemy's trade because that suited her own interests, and the three-er in the harbour deterred the pirates instantly. Even as the Rhodian crews raced aboard, the pirates were already running for the open sea, their Ares engines silent.

The rowers on board the *Golden Lotus* cheered.

The Rhodian skipper came aboard with his trierarch and his helmsman, and Peleus hugged him, a handsome man with skin like old leather and hair so blond as to be almost white. His trierarch was like a reverse image of his captain, pale skin and black hair, and the helmsman was as black as a Nubian – an exotic trio, from the most famous navy in the world.

'Peleus, I knew the *Lotus* as soon as she rounded the point. And Juba here says she's moving mighty fast, eh? And I watched your rowers,' he pointed at the tired men on the benches, 'and we all yelled alarm together!'

'And we were still too late, by Poseidon!' the pale man said. He was the youngest of the three, and his face was burned red and he wore a purple chiton like a king's.

'This is my navarch. He's Satyrus.' Peleus motioned, and Satyrus stepped forward on the deck and smiled. 'Leon's nephew.'

'Any ward of Leon is a friend of Rhodos,' the Nubian said.

He offered his hand, and Satyrus clasped it. 'I'm Juba. The boy who can't stand the touch of Helios is Orestes, and our fearless leader is Actis. Aren't you a little young for a navarch?'

Peleus pursed his lips. 'He was at the helm as we came around the point,' he said.

Juba gave Satyrus a long look. 'Not bad, old man. Is he serious, or another aristocrat?'

Peleus shrugged. 'I don't know yet,' he said.

They shared dinner with the Rhodians, and breakfast, and then they were away, rowing hard along the south coast of Cyprus until the wind was fair for Rhodos. They touched at Xanthos, and all the news was bad – Antigonus One-Eye had his fleet at Miletus, and Rhodos was all but closed. The Rhodian navy was bold, but it was small.

Peleus sat across from Satyrus at a benched table in a wine shop on the waterfront in Xanthos, so close to the *Lotus* that her standing rigging cast a net of shadows in the setting sun. A slave rose on her toes to light the oil lamps along the back of the wine shop. Peleus watched her without interest.

'The wind is fair for Rhodos,' he said. 'If it doesn't change, I'd say we crew her at the first blush of dawn and have a go. *Lotus* will be faster than anything they have at sea.' As he spoke, he touched the wood of the table and then made a sign to avert ill luck.

Melitta came down the board from the ship wearing a decent woman's chiton. The wine shop slave shook her head. 'No women!' she said.

Melitta raised an eyebrow and went and sat with her brother.

The slave followed her over. 'Please, mistress! No women. It is the law of the town. Only slave women in the brothels and wine shops. The watch will arrest us both.'

Melitta sighed. She and Satyrus exchanged a look, and Melitta rose and walked back up the plank to the stern of the *Lotus* and vanished into the hull. She reappeared as a somewhat androgynous archer in a Pylos cap, and the slave submitted for a few bronze obols.

'I hate Asia,' Melitta said.

Peleus raised an eyebrow. 'Athens would be worse, despoina,' he said.

'What's the verdict?' Melitta asked.

'Peleus thinks we should try for Rhodos,' Satyrus said.

Melitta drank some of his wine. 'I knew you weren't a coward,' she said. The comment was tossed off, not meant to wound, but Satyrus felt his temper flare. He turned away.

Peleus sighed. 'Ladybird, fleeing pirates is not cowardice, and frankly your whoring after a little glory is going to get people killed. You act like a boy – a particularly stupid boy. This is the sea. We have different rules here. We follow Poseidon, not Athena and not Ares. The sea can kill you any time it wants. You think a battle is a wonderful thing? A test of your courage? Try a storm at sea, despoina. I've seen a hundred – aye, and another hundred fights.'

Melitta nodded. 'So much of your store of courage is used up,' she said with half a smile. 'Mine isn't.'

Peleus's face drained of blood. 'You risk angering me,' he said slowly.

'That's a risk I can stand,' Melitta said.

Satyrus sighed. 'Shut up, Melitta. You're being a fool. Last time I looked, it's *me* who's the young man – I should be the hothead and you should be the voice of reason.' He made her smile, and turned to Peleus. 'Ignore her – my sister has to be braver than Achilles all the time. It's the problem of having to represent all of the female half of the race.'

Xenophon appeared at the bow and sprang ashore in a fresh chiton and a light chlamys. 'Well?' he asked.

'Rhodos,' Satyrus said. 'First light. Any objection?'

'You're touchy tonight,' Xenophon said and shook his head. 'May I sit next to your sister?'

'You mean that archer there? Be my guest. Give him a good hard shove as you sit down. That's from me.' Xenophon obeyed, Melitta yelped and Satyrus laughed.

Peleus wasn't mollified. 'I don't like being made fun of by children,' he said directly across the table to Melitta. 'Leon says you ship with us – it's a mistake. You have no discipline and no

356

obedience and you'll let us down. If I see you get a man killed, I'll throw you over the side. Understood, *girl*?' Then he turned back. 'I'll sleep aboard and have orders for the men to come aboard with the sun. Anything else?'

'No, Peleus,' Satyrus said. He rose with the Rhodian and followed him out of the wine shop into the dark. 'She means no harm. She wants your respect.'

'If she were a man – a *boy* – I'd have spanked her bloody, the ignorant pup.' Peleus shrugged. 'She's a fine shot. That doesn't make her special. Women have no business at sea. I'll have a hold on my temper tomorrow. But I want her sent home from Rhodos. Not on my ship.'

He stomped off.

Satyrus sighed. He went back through the bead curtain to the wine shop, just in time to see Xenophon's head jerk away from Melitta's.

He jumped as if he'd been stung.

They both looked guilty – his sister's skin was red as the setting sun. He sat across from them, framing his comment, but he wasn't sure. Had they been kissing?

Was it his business?

Satyrus was used to his sister being the calm one, the steady one and the brave one. Something had changed – suddenly he was the calm one.

She leaned forward, eyes bright. 'Well?' she asked. Her tone was aggressive.

Satyrus made himself smile. 'I'm for my cloak and whatever insects share it with me,' he said. 'At least I'm not lying by a smoky fire on an open beach. Peleus intends to sail with the first brush of dawn's fingers.'

They're holding hands under the table. Apollo, is this my buisness? Satyrus sat back, his head against the greasy wooden partition that separated this shack from the next one, and suddenly swung his sandalled foot up between his sister and his best friend, so that his foot caught – hands.

'Melitta, go to your bed,' he said.

She shrugged, her face suddenly splotchy with anger. 'Why? You can't make me.'

357

'If I reveal you as a woman, I can have you held at a temple – for the rest of your life, you stupid *fool*. What's got into you? And Xenophon – you going to marry my sister? Eh? Better talk to me about it, *friend*. Because if I see either of you touch the other again before Rhodos, blood will flow. My promise on it.'

'I am *not* your chattel!' Melitta spat.

Heads were turning.

Satyrus took a deep breath. 'No,' he said. 'You are not. But neither am I yours, Lita. I have the responsibility – not you. For the ship, for the cargo and for your virginity. When you have the responsibility, do as you please. When you have taken charge, have I obeyed you?'

Xenophon sat silently while the siblings glared. Melitta put her hand in her mouth and bit her palm until it bled. It was an ugly thing to watch.

Then Melitta shook her head. 'You obeyed,' she said sullenly. Then she burst into tears and fled to the ship.

'I'm sorry, Satyrus,' Xeno said. 'I – I love her. I think I always have.'

Satyrus shook his head. 'Not on this boat, understand me? There is no love on this boat. She's a passenger, and you are a marine.'

'I'll try.' Xenophon's tone carried no conviction.

Satyrus summoned up his best imitation of Philokles. 'Don't try,' he said, rather enjoying using the line he dreaded most from his tutor. 'Just do it.'

Then, alone, he sipped the last of his wine and watched the waterfront. His best friend, his helmsman and his sister were all equally angry.

Alone in the dark, he grinned and finished his wine.

When the red ball of the sun was fully above the eastern horizon, they were well out from Xanthos, running almost due west as if fleeing the chariot of Apollo. Sunset found them on the same heading, running straight into the sun. The headland of Rhodos, the city itself, shone like a beacon in the sun, and the head of the statue of Apollo on the headland burned as if the very god was crowned in sacred fire.

Behind them, in the gathering murk of evening, a pair of shadows were visible, hull-up and almost hidden by the coast of Asia, but revealed by their sails.

Peleus watched them under his hand. 'Same two bastards,' he said. 'That's not right. We're not worth that much effort. That big fuck is down from Tyre – he ought to have stayed on the east coast of Cyprus.'

Satyrus was trying to keep the wake as straight as an arrow's flight, so he answered with a grunt.

'Ships on the port bow,' came a cry from forward – a high-pitched cry. Melitta.

Peleus looked around and then ran down the central decking, ducked under the mainsail and vanished from Satyrus's view. Satyrus saw a flash, and then another. The pirates were starting to row as the breeze lessoned. They'd be making distance.

Peleus came back, moving so fast that his bare feet slapped on the smooth deck. 'Not Rhodian,' he said tersely. 'Give me the helm.'

'I'm giving you the helm,' Satyrus said formally, and he waited until Peleus's hands were on the steering oar before he let go. 'You have the helm.'

'I have the helm,' Peleus said.

'There's a Lesbian freighter just clear of the headland,' Peleus said, swinging them a few points to the north. 'I'm going to turn away from those ships I don't know – who may be blockading Macedonians, or may not – and offer the pirates behind us, if they are pirates, a nice fat Lesbian merchant.'

Satyrus ran forward to watch. The ships off to the south and west were just a line of marks against the sea – black hulls and no sails – but the flash of their oars as they rowed was rhythmic and predatory. Four – five – six ships. A column of ships.

To the north, a big round-hulled merchant under sail made to cross their path, broad-reaching on the wind and trying to hold a course as far west of south as he could get out of his sails. Satyrus watched him for a moment and then ducked back under the mainsail and ran back along the deck.

'Those are warships to the south,' he said.

'Aye,' Peleus said. 'That they are.'

The two dark shapes behind them began to gain in resolution as they rowed harder.

Peleus watched them as the distance closed. 'Poseidon's mighty dick, those *are* our friends with the machines,' he said, his voice now certain. 'How can that *be*?'

Satyrus didn't have an answer for him. 'What should I do?' he asked.

Peleus swung his lips from side to side, pursed and unpursed them, and looked aft again. 'Pray?' he said. He smiled, and swung the tiller a fraction more. 'Man the top-deck oars,' he called.

The oar master sounded a bronze drum once, and then called 'Ready!' Most of the rowers were in position. On a ship with fewer than two hundred men, news travelled fast.

'Ten stades and we're safe,' Peleus said out loud. He cheated his helm another fraction to the north. 'Oar master, give us a touch of speed.'

The oar master started to call the beat, and the upper-deck oarsmen gave way with a will, rowing carefully so that the drag of their oars wouldn't fight the last push of the breeze.

'Sail down on my command,' Satyrus sang out, and got a nod from Peleus, and the deck master had them all lined up, with Agathon handling a rope despite the stripes on his back – he'd been punished in Xanthos that morning, beaten with a rope.

The breeze was failing them as they came in with the land. It was a matter of judgment as to when the oars were of use, and then again when the sails became a liability – the sort of fine judgment that could make all the difference in the world.

'Lower decks ready,' the oar master called.

'Mainsail down,' Satyrus called at a nod from Peleus.

The deck crew released lines at the rail and the sail folded to the deck in a gleam of red. The pirates – if the dark hulls were pirates – were coming up fast. Their bows shone clear – the Phoenician had a pair of eyes painted above his ram.

Something flashed astern, out of the sun, and splashed into the sea well astern, and then there was the sound of a distant thud.

'There they are,' Peleus said. 'Same fucking ships.' He pulled the steering oar a little farther to the north, so that their course lay opposite to that of the Lesbian merchantman on the southern tack.

'All oars!' he roared. 'Best speed, boys!'

Off to the south, the warship squadron was at full speed now, but Peleus had fooled them by steering farther to the north of his course every stade. They were coming on in a column, led by the two heaviest ships, and despite having the advantage of the tide and fuller galleries of rowers, they weren't gaining ground. But there they were, like breakers or a lee shore, a threat that couldn't be ignored.

'Macedonians. Some Corinthians, and maybe an Asiatic,' Peleus said. 'Antigonus's fleet.' He shook his head. 'You can't see it, but we're already past them. They'll give up in a minute – they'd better, or we're in a lot more trouble.'

The bolt-thrower astern fired again, and the bolt skipped over the waves to pass them before it sank.

'Poseidon, I hate those things,' Peleus swore. 'A new calf smoking on your altar, Wave-Treader, if you will see me safe into Rhodos.'

One more time, as they heard the protests of the Lesbian, Peleus moved the steering oar and pushed the bow north, so that they were now on the opposite tack to the merchant ship, almost at right angles to their initial course, and the two pirates astern had to fetch their wake to make distance. They were no longer losing the race, and the angry merchant ship, which had to turn south to avoid collision with the madmen aboard the *Lotus*, called insults as they shot by.

'And will the pirates take the easy prey?' Peleus asked. 'And how *dare* they come so close to Rhodos?'

Satyrus shook his head.

Sure enough, away to the south and west, the military squadron had abandoned their chase. Dark was coming on, and they needed a beach.

'Look at that!' Peleus said.

Astern, the two pirates ignored the merchant ship, which actually passed *between* them with another chorus of insults.

'They've been paid well,' Peleus said. 'Ready to take the helm?'

Satyrus walked over. 'Ready to take the helm,' he said, and took the oar into his hands. The living ship moved under his grip.

'You have the helm,' Peleus said.

'I have the helm,' Satyrus said.

'On my word, we're turning ninety degrees off our course and running for the harbour.' Peleus left him and ran forward, calling to the oar master.

Satyrus grinned, suddenly understanding. Because the Macedonian squadron was pulling for its night beach, they'd opened a different road into the harbour – in effect, the *Lotus* would *pursue* them – and the pirates would once again have lost ground. Too much ground this time to overtake.

'Everyone together – steering oar keep her steady, and the oar banks will turn us. Ready? All ready? On my command,' Peleus shouted. Heads came up as all the bench leaders showed that they understood.

The ship rowed another stroke north. Peleus was watching the pirates. Satyrus didn't even turn his head. That was Peleus's job now.

'Hard to port!' Peleus roared.

Instantly, the oar master translated the order into rowing orders. In three heartbeats, the port oar banks were backing water, the steering oar bit deep, and every sailor and deckhand on the half-deck ran to the starboard side and threw themselves outboard, and forward the marines and archers did the same. Satyrus, eyes on the bow, saw his sister and Dorcus throw themselves on the outboard lines like deck-crewmen. Every bit would count.

The *Lotus* turned from north to west in twice her own length and raced on, her way virtually undiminished.

Aft, the predators couldn't even get their engine to bear. They rowed on for precious seconds as their prey jigged like a rabbit chased by dogs, and then they took too long to make the turn – the heavier Phoenician trireme took so long to make the manoeuvre that she was almost a stade north of her prey and lost several stades in distance.

The big Phoenician chose to lose more ground and fire his machine again. It was his last throw – it cost more time and more manoeuvres.

'Lie down!' Peleus shouted, and got his back against the stem. He looked stricken as he realized that Satyrus was standing up with nowhere to hide – a long-stretched moment as Satyrus saw the bolt leap from the engine in the last of the sun, but it passed harmlessly off to the south, mistimed, and the older man straightened up with a wry look for his own worries.

As the last fingers of the sun reached across the wine-dark sea, *Lotus* shot past the headland at ramming speed and into the outer harbour, the pirates already turning away in their wake. Down on the beach below the Temple of Apollo, a small crowd of onlookers cheered them as Peleus ordered the rowers to crash-stop the ship, putting their oars into the water against her momentum.

Peleus rubbed his back and straightened. 'All's well that ends well,' he said. He shook his head. 'Too damned close for an old man.'

'I never saw your trick coming – neither did the pirates!' Satyrus said.

Peleus just shook his head. 'Your sister's right,' he said. 'My nerve ain't what she used to be.'

They unloaded a hidden cargo of finer things – amulets, engraved seal stones and super-fine Aegyptian linen – and the real cargo, Aegyptian emmer wheat. Leon's factor had already arranged buyers for every item, and Satyrus, as the navarch, received a small bundle of papyrus notations indicating the value of the cargo and the final sale. Not an obol changed hands – the money stayed on paper, where pirates couldn't seize it.

'Athenian tanned hides to Smyrna,' Satyrus said.

'Already loading,' the factor said smugly. 'Glad you know your business, boy, but we know ours. Nestor the Gaul is factor in Smyrna. Land him the hides and he'll have a load of stuff for you to carry back to Aegypt. Wool and oil, that's my guess.'

The short man smiled for the first time. 'He must love you, boy. Trusted you with the *Lotus*.'

Satyrus smiled in confusion and let that comment go.

Peleus took him from the factor's office to the Rhodian navy's offices by the Temple of Poseidon, just above the ship sheds. 'Every officer is supposed to report in,' Peleus said. 'If you plan to stay in this business, you'll do well to be one of them.'

Satyrus went up the steps with Peleus. By the time they were abreast of the courtyard of the temple, a dozen scarred veterans had greeted Peleus with the utmost respect. They went in through a row of painted wooden columns and joined a dozen men in weather-worn chitons and oil-smeared cloaks gathered around a pair of older men on wooden stools.

'Peleus!' said the oldest, a gnarled man with a beard as white as the snow on Olympus. 'I heard a report you were inbound.'

'Here I am. This young scapegrace is Leon's nephew, Satyrus. A passable excuse for a navarch. Satyrus, the two old men are Timaeus and Panther. They command the fleet this year.' Peleus walked around, clasping hands with the men his own age.

'That's Satyrus, son of Kineas of Athens? Eh, boy?' Panther looked like his namesake, with a shock of white-grey hair un-thinned by age, fierce eyebrows and a mighty beard that failed to hide the furnace that burned behind his eyes. 'When are you going to rid us of that poxed whore Eumeles? Eh, boy?'

Satyrus cleared his throat. 'My sister would have killed him already,' he said. 'I'm giving it some thought.'

'Lord of stallions, I can hear his balls clanking together from here!' Panther said. He turned to Peleus. 'We were just talking about your pirates. After you came in, guess what they did?'

Peleus shrugged. 'Hauled their wind and rowed north?'

Satyrus smiled. 'May I guess, sir?'

Panther growled. 'Have a go, boy.'

'They sailed south and coasted along, looking at Antigonus's fleet,' he said.

Timaeus narrowed his eyes. He looked at Panther, and Panther grunted.

364

Peleus smiled. 'Smart lad,' he said. 'So, why?'

'They aren't pirates,' Satyrus said. 'Or rather, they aren't *just* pirates. They're out to get Melitta and me – for Stratokles and Athens. Maybe as part of a wider deal.' He shrugged. 'Stratokles the Informer is just the sort of man to have a safe-conduct from his own opponents. And to want to spy on them.' He shrugged. 'Give the man his due – he's good at what he does.'

'Athens has no great love for Cassander, and that's a fact.' Panther looked around. To Peleus he said, 'When Antigonus comes at us, will Ptolemy back us?'

Peleus nodded. 'He has to. He's building a fleet. It's not a fleet the way you or I would have a fleet, but it's better than nothing.'

Timaeus grunted. 'Part of One-Eye's fleet is on our beaches, blockading us.' He rubbed his chin, eyes on the floor.

Satyrus looked down and realized that he was standing on a chart of the Inner Sea. His sandals were on the coast of Rhodos, with Helios's rays detailed in gold, and Smyrna was two steps away. 'The rest have vanished,' Panther said, pointing vaguely at the coast of Asia.

'For all I know, Demetrios took them straight into Alexandria to burn the place. He's a bold one.' Timaeus shook his head. 'We put all our cruisers to sea to avoid blockade, and then they made their move, and we're blind.'

'Our harbour is empty, if you didn't notice. We don't have any more ships to send as scouts. Your lading says you are bound for Smyrna. Will you scout the coast of Palestine on your way back?' Panther spoke urgently to Peleus. 'Our need is great.'

Peleus looked at Satyrus. 'It's his call to make, gentlemen. Palestine is well off our course. And we couldn't get the news back here.'

'You could get word to our station on Cyprus. Peleus, we're hard-pressed. And we're on the *same side*.' Timaeus rose from his chair.

Peleus shrugged. 'I'm as Rhodian as the rose, Timaeus. But I serve an Alexandrian and I'm an honest servant. Last year *you* sent ships to serve Antigonus One-Eye.'

Panther shrugged. 'It was expedient. You know who we prefer.'

'Welcome to the Olympic Games of politics, boy,' Peleus said to Satyrus.

Satyrus stepped forward. 'Will you find a merchant to take Lord Leon's hides across to Smyrna?'

Timaeus nodded. 'We can do that.' He shrugged. 'Eventually.'

'So we'll pick up some luxuries to pay the oarsmen and ship empty for the Palestinian coast,' Satyrus said.

Peleus nodded. 'And we'll *fly*.'

'That pair of wolves will be on you as soon as you leave harbour,' Panther said.

Peleus nodded. 'They *almost* caught us when we were fully laden,' he said. 'Unless the gods will our doom, empty, we'll be over the horizon before they can get in range with their infernal engines.'

Satyrus took a deep breath. 'We need three days,' he said. 'The crew needs a rest.'

'Fair enough,' Timaeus said. 'Perhaps one of our cruisers will come in and we won't need you at all.'

Satyrus turned to Peleus. 'And my sister stays aboard,' he said.

Peleus shrugged. 'Done,' he said.

A day of debauch and a day of rest, and the *Golden Lotus*'s crew mustered on the beach, surly or smiling depending on their natures. Many of them had acquired companions, most of them temporary, and a few of them had gained or lost possessions – Satyrus could see a younger oarsman with what appeared to be a cloth-of-gold chlamys wrapped around his shoulders, standing next to an older man with his head between his knees who appeared to be completely naked. But none were late, or absent, and every man of them had his rowing cushion, whatever the state of his dress.

Peleus stood up, wearing a bronze breastplate and carrying a helmet. 'This is a war voyage,' he shouted. 'Anyone want to sit it out? I have a pair of javelins for every man and I'll add an owl to everyone's pay. But we won't ship much of a cargo and that means no shares.'

Kyros, the oar captain, spoke up. 'What about captures?'

Peleus nodded. 'Right enough. But we're scouting an enemy coast, boys. Not much time to make a capture. If we do, shares by the custom of Rhodos.'

Kyros nodded and went back to squatting on his haunches.

Peleus turned to Satyrus. 'That's what passes for a council among men who use the sea,' he said. 'We've got the tide.'

Satyrus nodded. 'Let's use it then.'

The two wolves were aware as soon as the *Golden Lotus* passed the Temple of Apollo and left the inner harbour. Peleus watched them under his hand as they threw their oars aboard and then pushed their sterns down the beach. But they didn't have the wind and their rowers were slow to respond and the *Lotus* drew away effortlessly.

'Good riddance,' Peleus said, staring under his hand. 'Heavy metal in their bows and no mistake. I won't be sorry to see the last of them.'

The last they saw of them were their masts slipping away under the horizon as the coast of Asia came up on the port bow.

Satyrus could see the first of the tell-tale headlands that would lead him into Xanthos. 'I guess we're not going into Xanthos,' he said.

Peleus shook his head. 'Beautiful day, crew hard as old wood. Let's use this fine west wind while it blows and see if we can make the beaches of Pamphylia. If the weather holds,' he said, and made a horn sign with his hand, 'we might coast into Paphos on Cyprus, and we'll never see those cocksuckers again.'

Kyros took a dipper of water from the butt amidships and raised an eyebrow at the helmsman. 'I won't mention that to the boys, I guess.'

Peleus barked a harsh laugh. 'Maybe when the moon rises.' He glanced at Satyrus. 'It'd be something to tell your grand-children, that you went from Rhodos to Paphos in a day's

367

rowing.' He came and stood by Satyrus for ten strokes of the oars, and then they felt the true west wind at their backs.

Peleus gave one of his rare smiles. He turned to the deck master. 'Hoist the mainmast, Kalos. Get the cloth on her.'

'Mainmast and mainsail, aye,' Kalos answered. Short, hairy and scarred, his name spoke for what he was *not* – beautiful. He was perhaps the ugliest man Satyrus had ever seen, Stratokles included, but he had a sense of humour, and often claimed that he had been an avatar of Aphrodite in a former life and was paying the price now.

Of course, he was also a highly skilled seaman. In less time than it took to pull an oar a hundred times, the mainmast was up and roped home, and the mainsail was drawing, taut as a board and round as a cheese.

'Navarch,' Peleus said gruffly, 'if you'll have my advice, I'd say that we could make the run to Paphos.'

Satyrus nodded a few times, considering. 'Then carry on,' Satyrus said.

'It's only that it is open water all the way. No landfalls and no refuge.' Peleus raised a shaggy eyebrow.

'For one day? Are we sailors or not?' Satyrus asked rhetorically. 'What's the heading?'

'Years since I did it.' Peleus squinted at the sun and the sky. 'South and east. No – more south. I like that. Hold that course.' He looked at the wake for long enough that Satyrus thought he might have changed his mind. 'Deep-water sailing is where we find out if you can mind your helm or not,' he said. 'No landmarks. No seamarks. Your wake is straight, or he ain't. Hear me, lad?'

Satyrus was growing weary of a life that seemed to consist of nothing but an endless series of tests – but he bit back on his first answer and managed a grin. 'Do my best,' he said.

'Notch in your wake when you talk,' Peleus said.

When the sun was high in the sky, Melitta walked down the raised deck between the rowers. Most of them were sitting comfortably, and a dozen of them were busy rigging a long awning on the port side against the sun, while the sailors did the climbing.

Wherever she walked, silence followed, and stares, and some quiet comments. Life on shipboard had brought home to Melitta how very *stupid* men were. Her body was capable of ending argument, discussion, religious affirmation – really, it was a wonder that men managed to do any work at all.

Whereas, by contrast, there were naked men all around her, and none of them moved her by so much as an iota. Some had fine bodies – her brother, for instance, or old Peleus, in his way. Xenophon, if you ignored the pimples on his face, had the physique of Herakles. The marine captain was exercising naked, gleaming with oil and obviously trying to attract her attention. It was a fine body, but, as Melitta had already commented to Dorcus, there wasn't much inside it.

She swept her Ionic chiton under her with one arm and gathered her chlamys with the other before sinking on to a bale of sheepskins that acted as the stern-seat for the helmsman's visitors.

'I'm tired of being stared at,' Melitta said to her brother.

'I'm tired of being tested. Trade you!' Satyrus said with a wry smile.

'Deal!' she said, and spat in her hand. They shook without his unwrapping his arms from the steering oar.

'Now you've put a notch in my wake,' he said.

She laughed. 'You're pretending to be a sailor while I pretend to be a Greek woman,' she said. 'When do we get to stop pretending?'

Satyrus watched the horizon over the stern for a long minute. 'I remember when I thought that you were so much older than me,' he said. 'Now I think maybe I've passed you – for a while. Because I learned something last year, and I learned it again after I kissed Amastris.'

'You kissed Amastris? Not some slave girl in her clothes?' Melitta leaned forward.

'Was she chewing cinnamon just before she summoned me?' Satyrus asked.

Melitta gave an enigmatic smile. 'So – you kissed her. Was it beautiful?'

Satyrus sighed. 'It *was* beautiful, Lita. That's what I mean.

It wasn't like kissing Phiale at all. Kissing Phiale made my member stiff. Kissing Amastris made *me* soften.'

'You're killing me. My brother has a poetic soul? While I'm left with all this chaff?' She waved around her at the men on deck. Then, seeing that Peleus was coming up the central deck, she leaned close. 'Tell me what you learned.'

'We're *always* pretending.' He looked at her, eye to eye, so close that he could see the flecks of colour in her iris, and she could see her own reflection in his. She could feel his breath on her face. 'I pretend to be brave when I'm afraid. I pretend to be interested in sex when I'm interested in impressing my peers, I pretend to be religious when I go to temple. I pretend to be obedient when I steer the ship.'

She cast a glance at Peleus and he grabbed her arm. 'Listen, Melitta. Because that's what every ephebe knows. But what I know is that the pretending *becomes the reality*.'

Melitta looked at him as if she'd never seen him before. 'But—' She made a face. 'Satyrus, why can't you be like this all the time?'

Satyrus furrowed his eyebrows. 'What?'

Melitta raised her arms as if supplicating the gods. 'At sea, you are – as wise as Philokles. As subtle as Diodorus. On land, you're often – well, my not-quite-a-man brother.'

'Thanks. I think,' Satyrus said. After a second, he shrugged. 'I don't know. At sea I'm in command – at least this trip. Command – well, it's like a dose of cold water when you're asleep. And I keep seeing people do things I know that I do. Xeno does stuff that makes me tremble, and so help me—' He laughed, and Melitta joined him.

'If you two was sailors, I'd expect a mutiny,' Peleus said. He spared Melitta a smile. 'May I offer the despoina an apology for my rude ways when we was running from pirates?'

Melitta gave him the full weight of her smile – eyes flashing, teeth, a hand sweeping back her hair. If these were all the weapons she had to use as a 'Greek' woman, she'd wield them ruthlessly. 'Were you rude, helmsman? I thought that you were doing your duty.' She swept by him down the deck, heading for her own awning with Dorcus under the boatsail mast.

She heard his grunt as she moved away, and smiled again in satisfaction. They weren't her weapons of choice, but they did cut.

Well past midday, and the sea rose, blue and blue, out to the rim of the horizon's bowl. The sun rode the sky above them, heading west, and the handful of fleecy clouds were more ornament than threat.

'Nothing more frightening except a storm,' Kalos muttered. He squatted in the stern, out of the wind. He kept his eyes forward, as if he didn't want to see the empty rim of the bowl, unmarked by even the hint of land in any direction.

'Don't be a woman,' Peleus said. 'The boys do as you do.'

'I hate not seeing a coast,' Kalos said. He got to his feet, stretched like a big, ugly cat and glided forward, light on his feet and unaffected by the roll.

'I hate it too,' Peleus said. He gave Satyrus his secret smile. 'But cutting across the empty sea is what makes us better sailors, lad. And you have to look like you know your way – like there's a path of gold hammered into the surface of the water for you and only you.'

Satyrus thought of his advice to his sister. 'I pretend I'm not afraid all the time,' he said.

'We have a name for that, lad,' Peleus said, slapping his shoulder. 'We call that *courage*.'

'Do you know where we are?' Satyrus asked.

Peleus looked around. 'No,' he said. 'But give or take a thousand stades, we're west of Cyprus. I draw some hope from that bank of low cloud that just came up under the bow. See it?'

Satyrus stretched his neck to see under the mainsail. 'I think I do.'

'I'll go forward and look – slowly, so it doesn't look bad. Notch in your wake, lad.' Peleus went forward, adjusting sheets and cursing the oarsmen, most of whom hadn't touched an oar since mid-morning and were so much human cargo.

Satyrus watched him go and stood looking at his sister and thinking of Amastris. Thinking that, like the flower of the

371

lotus, Amastris was probably something that would be bad for him in the long run. What if he endangered their chance at revenge? At having their own kingdom? In his mind's eye he could see Ataelus – just to name one man – the small Sakje had been with his mother when she died. He'd escaped to raise his clan in revolt, and he had worked tirelessly at rallying the former coalition of the Eastern Assagatje to fight against the Sauromatae and against Eumeles, supported by Leon. Or Lykeles, who spoke against Heron every day in the assembly in Olbia.

What if he incurred her father's real displeasure? Or Ptolemy's?

He watched his wake. Life, he thought, is too complicated. He enjoyed being a helmsman. He enjoyed the simple, yet endless, task – he enjoyed the trust and the responsibility and the palpable success at the end of the day. If you piloted a ship well, it *came to port*. Task complete. Kingship seemed to be much worse.

His thoughts wandered off to the moment when she slipped into his arms, the surrender of her mouth, the quickness of her tongue—

'Planning to sail back to Rhodos, lad?' Peleus said. He pointed at the long curve of the wake.

'Oh – ugh!' Satyrus brought the ship back on course with a perceptible turn that made heads come up all along the deck. He was irrationally angry – at himself, at Peleus – at always being tested. Again.

'Girl?' Peleus asked.

'Yes,' Satyrus answered, almost inaudibly.

'Don't think about any of that when you're at the helm. Mind you, you've been at it without relief for a watch and a half. I'll take the helm.'

'I'm fine,' Satyrus said.

'No, you ain't. I'll take the helm, navarch. If you please.' Peleus was suddenly very formal.

Satyrus stood straight and managed to get the oar into the helmsman's hand, despite the shame of his burning face. 'You have the helm.'

'I have the helm. Go and lie down and dream of your girl, boy. You earned a rest – don't fret.'

Despite this last admonition, Satyrus knew that he'd made an error – a bad error, one that in a normal young man would have been punished by a blow or worse. He walked to the awning in silence, and the deck crew made way for him as if he was injured. Sailors were very perceptive to social ills – they had to be, living so close – and he'd seen before how a man who had been punished was treated with consideration that verged on tenderness.

Now that same blanket surrounded him, and he hated that he had failed them. He collapsed on a cushion of straw next to his sister. 'Don't say anything,' he said.

She raised an eyebrow but said nothing, and after a long bout of recrimination, he managed to fall asleep.

Evening came – a beautiful evening. Satyrus woke to find his head pillowed in his sister's lap, with the first star – Aphrodite – just rising above the ship's side. 'You were tired,' his sister said.

'Hermes! I've slept for hours!' Satyrus bounced up and found that his whole body was sore, and that his mouth was dry and he was cold.

Kyros came aft and passed him a water skin. 'Drink,' he said. 'You got too much sun today. Old bastard left you too long at the oar. He's got no skin left to burn – just hide.'

The water skin no sooner touched his lips than he drained it right down to the evil-tasting swill in the bottom, where the resin and the goat hair and the water made a disgusting brew. He spat over the side and Kyros laughed.

'Get some more, navarch. You're sun-sick and no mistake. Cold yet?' he asked.

Satyrus nodded guiltily.

'Wrap up. You'll be colder tonight. Glad you slept. Good pillow, I expect,' he said with a sidelong glance at Melitta.

Satyrus climbed down past the oarsmen in the bilge, which stank of piss and worse, where amphorae of clean water stood point down in the sand of the ballast. He lifted the open one clear of the bilge and filled the leather bucket and then refilled the oar master's skin, punishing himself with the task. With the bucket he refilled the butt on deck so other men could drink, and then he passed the skin back to the oar master. Only when the whole smelly job was done did he present himself to the helmsman.

'Sun-sick, I hear,' Peleus said.

'Yes, sir,' Satyrus answered.

'You don't call me sir, lad. You're the navarch. I left you too long at the oar, and that's no mistake. I'm a fool. Mind you, you stood there like a fool without asking to be relieved.' He shrugged. 'You'll live. I can smell the land – can ye smell it?'

Satyrus took a deep breath. 'No, but I see the gulls.'

'Right you are, and land birds before the sun sets. Now comes the hard part – where on Poseidon's liquid plain are we, eh? Because we'll want a beach as soon as we can get one – fresh water, and a place to cook in the morning. The boys can only slurp kykeon so many times before they rise up and murder me.' He nodded, as if talking with a third party.

'You want me to take the helm?' Satyrus asked.

'No. Into the bow and watch the horizon. Landfall any time, now. Bring me word.'

'I could climb the mainmast,' Satyrus asked. He was gushing in his eagerness to be forgiven.

'Only in an emergency,' Peleus said. 'Makes the whole ship lean. A nice trick on a merchantman – not on a trireme, eh? Into the bow.'

'Aye!' Satyrus headed forward, scooping his heavier Thracian cloak as he went past his sister. Most of the men on deck were naked, but Satyrus was chilled to the bone, and yet the last rays of the sun seemed to flay him when he emerged under the mainsail into the bow.

Behind him, he heard Peleus order Kyros to begin clearing away the oar decks, as the wind that had carried them all day was now dying away to a breeze. In the bow, the low clouds of mid-afternoon were now well up in the sky and catching the sun in a wall of pink and red.

Satyrus had to look at them and away twice before he was

sure. Then he ran back along the central deck between the top-deck rowers, dropping his cloak in his rush aft. 'Land! Right on the bow, no points off.'

Peleus took the news as if he had never known a moment's doubt. He nodded. 'Ready to take the helm, Navarch?' he asked.

Satyrus put a hand on the oar. 'I have the helm.'

'You have the helm,' Peleus said, and slipped from the stern to move forward. He vanished under the sail. Kyros came up with Kalos in tow. Satyrus nodded. 'Land,' he said.

Both men looked relieved. Kalos stopped when Kyros turned away. 'Sorry to be so scared,' he said. 'Your first time at the steering oar across the blue water – we could end in Hades, understand?' Then he slapped Satyrus's bare back, making him cringe and notching the wake. 'But you didn't!' he said, and went back to organizing the lowering of the mainmast.

Melitta brought him his cloak while Peleus watched forward. He pulled it on gratefully, feeling more like an old man on a winter night than was fair. 'Everyone says I have sun-sickness,' he said.

'You're as red as Tyrean wool,' she answered. 'You mind your oar and Dorcus will rub some oil into your skin.'

Together, she and her maid rubbed a mixture of olive oil and wool oil into his skin and he felt better – warmer, and less as if his skin would be flayed off by morning. 'Thanks, sister,' he said.

'Now who's all grown up?' she asked. 'I have the sense to stay out of the sun. He was testing you.'

'I failed,' Satyrus said bitterly.

'You're an idiot,' Melitta answered fondly. She stood with him in companionable silence until Peleus joined them, and then she slipped away.

'The Rock of Akkamas is just under our ram,' Peleus said, appearing from under the mainsail. 'Your course may be as erratic as a newborn lamb, but you are Poseidon's son, lad. We're bang on course – so fine that we'll weather the headland to the north and have the north coast and the west wind tomorrow.' Louder, he turned and addressed the sailors and oarsmen in the waist of the ship. 'Perfect landfall. Thirty stades of light rowing and the white sands of Likkia will be under our stern.'

With a quiet cheer, the oarsmen settled into their benches with a will. Before the moon was full on the swell, they were turning the ship just off the beach, the long hull broadside-on to the whispering surf, and then the rowers reversed their directions and the *Lotus* backed up the beach until the curving stern kissed the shining sand and they were safe.

Satyrus slept late the next morning, and hid his face from the sun as they set out, and Dorcus rubbed him down twice that day as the west wind carried them down the north coast of Cyprus, with Peleus pointing out the promontories and the best beaches, where a helmsman could slip ashore for an unlicensed cargo of copper, where the food was cheap. They landed for the night at Ourannia with a rested crew and Peleus paid for meat. The oarsmen had a feast.

'Tomorrow we cross over to the coast of Lebanon,' Peleus said. 'Pirates everywhere, Privateers, rovers, so-called merchants, and maybe, just maybe, advance squadrons of One-Eye's fleet. I want our lads in peak shape. *You* want them in peak shape.'

'I didn't see a ship today,' Satyrus said.

'You were asleep all afternoon, lad. And I was glad to see it. Sun-sick is a hard way to go. But you missed the three big Phoenicians – deep laden – heading west. With an escort.'

Satyrus thought it over for a moment. 'So anyone chasing us—'

'Will get a nice little report. That's right. And the Rhodian cruiser wasn't on his station off Makaria. That's not good.' Peleus rubbed his nose. 'We're cruising a sea that's too empty by half.' He shrugged. 'Anyway, we'll sleep late again and have the last of the west wind across to the shore of Asia. Then the weather will change.' He rubbed his beard.

18

In the morning, the worst of Satyrus's sun-sickness was off him. He took the steering oar as they cleared the beach at Ourannia and turned the bow back to the east, into the rising sun. Kyros brought him a broad straw hat, like a cavalryman would wear. 'You're a hippeis,' he quipped. 'A girl was selling them on the beach.'

Satyrus smiled. 'I'll buy it from you,' he said.

'See how it has a good linen cord so it won't blow off?' Kyros said. 'Nah, boy, that's for you from the oarsmen. Luck is luck. All that dicking about with the oar and you landed us on the Rock of Akkamas like a whore in Piraeus lands on a sailor's cock.' Kyros smiled. Over his shoulder, Kalos leered. 'Boys think you're lucky, Navarch.'

'And you paid the price in sun-sickness,' Kalos said. He pointed at the hat. A tiny silver trident was pinned to the crown. 'Deck crew threw that in – pilgrim badge.' He smiled. 'So you stay lucky.'

So Satyrus wore the hat.

'What are you smiling at?' Melitta asked, coming into the stern.

'How smart people are, even when they seem ordinary, or slow, or just plain dumb.' He shrugged. 'Sometimes I wonder if I ever fool anyone.'

She nodded, and stood there, watched by a hundred eyes, as the stades flowed away under the keel.

The sun was setting and Peleus announced that their landfall was twenty stades north of Hydatos Potomai on the north coast of Syria. That night they pulled down the coast under oars until Peleus and Kyros both liked a beach and landed by moonlight, sending the marines and a dozen deckhands in the boat to land and search the sands and the hillside beyond. The *Lotus* waited on their word.

Satyrus had shipped as a marine and he'd done the drill for

camping on a hostile beach, but he'd never done it for real, and he felt his heart pound while he watched their white corslets in the moonlight.

Melitta quietly strung her bow.

They were all poised, riding their anchor and with the top-deck rowers giving the occasional stroke to keep her steady, bow-on to the open ocean in case she needed to run. There were lookouts all along the hull and a man up the mast, watching the moonlit open ocean where the sky was still salmon pink.

A long whistle from the beach. All Peleus had to do was nod – Satyrus could land the ship himself.

'Ready on the oars. Backstroke on my command. Give way, all.'

The *Lotus* slipped in, grounded her stern and the oarsmen were over the side as fast as they could, every man racing for the lines as he hit the beach, simultaneously lightening the ship and helping haul him farther up the beach until Satyrus called 'Hold and belay' and looked at Peleus.

'Not bad,' the Rhodian commented. Then, very quietly, he said, 'There's something wrong.'

Satyrus had assumed it was his own fears rising in his throat. 'Yes,' he said. He stood straighter, made himself be alert. 'Something smells wrong,' he said with sudden realization. He looked at Peleus in the moonlight. 'Smell.'

'Death,' Peleus said. He nodded and walked to the side. 'Karpos? I need you to scout north. Smell it? Something died.'

'We all smell it, Peleus,' Karpos called back. Then he was off at a run, with a pair of marines behind him. The archers went south.

Fires were lit and food cooked – cauldrons of heavy stew with yesterday's lamb. In an hour they were wrapped in their cloaks, the marines all together in the middle and a double watch on the promontories that rose like towers at either end of the beach.

The Dog Star was high when Satyrus awoke to find Karpos kneeling in the sand next to Peleus. He got out of his cloaks and knelt next to them in the moonlight.

'This isn't for everyone, lad. Go ahead, Karpos – tell him what you saw.'

'Ships. A fight.' Karpos shook his head. 'Breeze fooled us. The next beach south is covered in corpses, and a hull turtled in the swell, breaking up.' He shook his head. 'Rhodian cruiser. She took a ram amidships, but only after she wasted a Macedonian trireme. Three or four hundred corpses.' Karpos sank on to the sand.

'Shit,' Satyrus said, without meaning to.

Peleus rubbed his chin. 'Sleep while you can. So – old Panther isn't as foolish as I thought. Some of One-Eye's fleet is on this coast – and they attacked a Rhodian to keep that news a secret.'

'We should sail with the first finger of dawn,' Satyrus said.

'That's the truth, lad.' Peleus lay his head back down. 'So sleep while you can.'

Karpos got up. 'Why not run now?' he asked.

Peleus didn't answer. So Satyrus did. 'What if we have to fight?' he said. 'We need fresh rowers.'

Karpos nodded. 'I won't sleep – coming across that in the dark – fuck me.' He turned away. 'Ever seen a battlefield in the dark, lad?'

'Yes, I have,' Satyrus said.

'Too bad for you, then,' Karpos said. And he lay down, rolled in his chlamys and pretended to sleep.

The next Satyrus knew, Kyros was clasping his shoulder, still a little tender from the sunburn. It was dark as Tartarus, and the oar master was pulling him to his feet. 'You're to launch us,' he said. 'Master Peleus is climbing the headland.'

He swallowed some hot wine and some porridge and then he was standing in the stern and the ship was sliding down the beach into the waves. His sister was standing in the bow, a heavy cloak over her, and Satyrus knew her well enough to know that she was wearing armour under that cloak and not a chiton. He heard rumours around him in the first blush of light – that the lookouts had seen a squadron pass in the dark, that there were fires on the next headland.

The stern was free – he felt the change in weight. 'A sea!'

he shouted and the last oarsmen and all the sailors came up the side, almost swimming, while the fore-top-deck rowers gave him enough way to keep the bow on to the waves.

'All oars,' he called. 'Cruising speed. Give way, all!' He waved at the oar master the way Peleus did, and his chant started up, and they were clear of the beach in the time it took for an early gull to circle them once and give a cry.

The light boat came off the headland before they'd pulled their oars a dozen more times, and once they were out of the surf, Satyrus had his oarsmen rest, the shafts crossed amidships, while the boat came alongside and Peleus leaped up the side. Kalos, pulling the light boat, brought it up under the stern, caught a rope and tied off before swimming aboard.

Peleus was naked. He shivered as he came into the stern, and Satyrus handed him his Thracian cloak.

'Thanks, lad,' he said. He shook his head and lowered his voice. 'We should do well enough,' he said. 'Wind's from the north. We'll sail until we have to weather the big headlands. There's a big force somewhere on this coast – Aristion's *Rose* was a tough nut and she wouldn't have stayed to fight unless she was trapped.' He shook his head. 'I'm shaken, boy. In Rhodos, we say we can outrun everything we can't fight and outfight anything that we can't outrun. But *Rose's* become a turtle on that beach – you'll see her in a little while – and young Aristion's so much fish bait.'

'How long ago?'

'Two days, or three. Long enough for the corpses to rise.' Peleus shook his head. 'What is One-Eye doing on this coast? I thought he was going after Cassander.'

Satyrus shrugged. 'That's what he wanted us to think, maybe. And maybe Stratokles wanted Ptolemy to think the same.'

'Nasty thought, lad. If that's the case – why then, he's going to have a go at Aegypt. Could already be over.'

'I worried about that last night.' Satyrus shook his head. 'And other things.'

'You're a worrier, and that's a fact. Make you a good helmsman. Except that your steering oar will be a sceptre, won't it, lad? This is just an adventure for you, eh? Timaeus told me who you are. Sort of knew all along, of course. Anyway, you could be a helmsman.' Peleus sounded rueful.

'Why – thanks!'

'In a few years,' Peleus said, with a glint.

Early afternoon. Laodikea's beaches shining to the east in the hazy sun and the wind rising to a scream and then falling away to a fitful breeze that somehow failed to clear the haze.

An Athenian grain merchant, sails flapping, barely making headway. He was a huge ship, with something like a full load, heading south along the coast.

'Lay me alongside,' Peleus said. That was the only order he issued, and the oar master and the sailing master did the rest. The merchant ship needed wind to run away, and the wind was not cooperating.

Rising and falling on the swell, grappled to the Athenian, Satyrus waited with the archers all on their toes, eager to shoot, and all the marines away on the giant merchant ship with Peleus. And then the boat came back, the marines all shaking their heads, and finally Peleus coming up the side, his chiton soaked through from climbing the side of the grain ship.

'Grain for Demetrios,' he said, shaking his head. 'Grain for his fleet. He assumed we were Rhodians. Surrendered. I told him not to be silly – we're not at war.' Peleus shrugged. 'We can't tow that behemoth. I'd like to let him go.'

Satyrus stared up at the towering sides of the great ship. 'I see your point. Won't he report us?'

'Only as a friendly merchant ship that paid him a ship visit. And he gave me a chestful of information.' Peleus stripped his chiton over his head and pulled another from the leather bag he kept under the sternpost.

Satyrus waited, as did Kyros and Karpos. The marine captain had his cuirass open to catch any air that happened to brush past him, and his Attic helmet was tilted back on his head.

'Demetrios, One-Eye's golden son, has two hundred ships of war on the beaches south of here. He's got half his father's army, and they're on the march, heading east into Nabataea.' Peleus nodded into the silence. 'It's a money raid. He's going to rape the Nabataeans for gold and use it to finance the war in the west against Cassander. See?'

Satyrus waited patiently – not an easy feat for a sixteen-year-old. But he wanted to let the grown men speak first. In case he was wrong.

'So we're done,' Karpos said. 'Slip away to seaward and we can be in the Bay of Kyrios tomorrow afternoon and find the Rhodian cruiser. Make our report.' He slapped his hands together and sailed one away over the horizon of the other. 'And home.'

Kyros shook his head. 'It's clear you're not a Rhodian, Karpos my lad. No Rhodian captain will take a report like that. We need to see this fleet.'

Peleus nodded. ''Fraid so, Karpos.'

Karpos shrugged. 'Let's get at it, then.'

Satyrus stepped forward. 'They're not raising the money for the war on Cassander,' he said.

The other three turned to look at him.

'It's all a deception. Listen – I grew up with this. Stratokles came to get troops out of Ptolemy. Now there's an army in Nabataea and the *whole* of One-Eye's fleet is two days' sail from Aegypt. The target is Aegypt. Cassander has made a deal with One-Eye.' Satyrus looked around at them, conscious that he had pounded his fist into his palm in his eagerness to convey his conviction.

Peleus rubbed his beard. 'Not saying I believe you, lad – but not saying I don't. It could be that way – aye, and that makes the risk all the worse if we're wrong.'

Karpos pursed his lips, spat and then said, 'I may not be a fucking Rhodian, but I can tell you that what we need is a prisoner. A good one – somebody who knows this crap.'

'How do you propose we get one?' Peleus asked.

Karpos glanced at the towering sides of the grain ship. Due to the fitful wind, the grain ship was still less than a rope's length away.

Peleus rubbed his chin. 'I gave my word,' he said.

'We're not pirates,' Satyrus said, 'and we're no worse off than we were this morning. Down the coast, on the lookout. If we can find a prisoner, fine. Otherwise, the moment we see the ships on the beach, we're away for Cyprus. And then straight across the great blue to Alexandria. I'm happy to help Rhodos – but it's Ptolemy who needs this information.'

'I think—' Peleus began.

Satyrus nodded pleasantly and cut the older man off. 'Happy to listen to your council, helmsman. In private.'

Peleus looked stung, but only for a moment. Then he gave a grim smile. 'Well – you're the navarch, right enough.'

As if to confirm their decision, the wind came up – first two strong gusts that laid them over, and then a long, hard blow from the north that swept the Athenian away. He had bigger yards and a stronger hull. *Golden Lotus* had to brail her boatsail, strike the mainsail and row to keep her direction, and the merchant ship was gone over the horizon in an hour.

'Storm coming,' Peleus said. He had the steering oar. 'And wind change.'

True to his word, half an hour later and their sails were hanging limp again. It was all Satyrus could do to stay awake. He was trying to decide how long he could sweep this hostile coast before he had to turn back north or out to sea just to find a beach for the night that would be safe.

Mid-afternoon, and they were cruising the coast of Lebanon north of Tyre – a coast so empty of shipping that it was as if the gods had swept the seas clean. They were coasting on their boatsail, the oarsmen resting under awnings, the water gurgling down the side with just enough way on the *Lotus* to give the steering oar a bite on the water.

Peleus was cursing, almost without ceasing. Every new headland and every bay they passed without seeing a merchant ship or even a fishing smack brought new invective.

'As soon as we open Laodikea,' Satyrus said, finally forcing himself to decide, 'we turn west into the open sea.'

'What's the matter?' Melitta asked, as they ate new bread and goat's cheese at midday.

'The longer we don't see anything, the worse it looks all the way around,' Satyrus translated. 'The bigger the sweep was, the bigger the fleet that's here. And the longer it endures, the longer ago it got here, and that's bad too.' He looked out to sea. 'If we could find a ship to take, we'd get a prisoner and be *gone*. Right? We don't want to find One-Eye's fleet ourselves. We want to *hear about it*.'

She nodded, obviously craving some excitement and not in complete agreement.

'Melitta, listen to me. Alexandria may already be blockaded – perhaps under siege. There may have been a battle. See? It's that bad.' Satyrus shook his head.

'Why don't we run down the coast and help? Tell them what's happening?' she asked.

'Because we don't *know*,' Satyrus said. 'We can guess. But until we see a hundred triremes, or find someone who has, we're just making stuff up to scare ourselves.'

Melitta nodded while she watched the water. 'Mama used to talk about scouting just this way,' she said.

'I was listening,' Satyrus said. He was watching Laodikea Head. Beyond, the great beach ran for a hundred stades, but he wouldn't see it for half an hour, and the light was changing as afternoon gave way to golden evening. He needed sea room if there was to be a blow – better yet, he needed a safe beach. He rubbed his chin in unconscious imitation of Peleus. The breeze was dying to nothing. Time to have the oars out.

'Ships! Ships on the horizon to starboard!' came the call from the mast, where the sail hung almost still.

Satyrus came awake without being aware that he'd been napping. He looked aft, and then over the side to the west and saw one on the horizon – and then another.

He nudged Peleus and pointed.

Peleus grunted. He opened his mouth to speak and the bow lookout gave a cry like a man drowning.

'Poseidon – the beach is full of ships!' he shouted after a sputter.

Peleus had the oar, so Satyrus ran forward, past his sister still wrapped in her cloak, to where he could see. Once there he didn't wait for advice from his helmsman. 'Kalos, get the mainmast *down*. Rig for fighting.'

He ran back the length of the ship. 'Fleet. Fills the beach. You'll see yourself in two shakes of a lamb's tail.'

Peleus nodded. 'Look west,' he said.

The two nicks in the horizon were defining themselves – a heavy trireme and a lighter one.

'Ares and Aphrodite,' Satyrus swore.

Just then the north wind gave a gust and then backed.

'Good order, getting the mainmast down,' Peleus went on, 'because the north wind is about to be a south wind, and then we're going to have to fight. At least, we'll fight until all those Macedonian cruisers see us, and then we're all fish bait.' He leaned close. 'Don't let your sister be captured, lad. Do it yourself it you have to.'

Satyrus swallowed. But his eyes were on the hundreds of hulls on the golden beach – unmoving.

Peleus shook his head. 'With your permission, Satyrus, I'm going to release the lower decks and row with just the top deck until the pirates are firm on our wake.'

Satyrus nodded. 'Look who's standing off the bay,' he said. He pointed at the big Athenian grain freighter off riding out in the deep water of the bay, just fifteen stades down the coast.

'No difference to us, boy,' Peleus said.

'Does Laodikea have a harbour?' Satyrus asked.

'Open beach,' Peleus answered. 'If we're going to lighten ship, now's the time.'

With a rattle and thump that Satyrus had come to dread, the engine fired. But the two pirates were well astern and the changing wind was blowing across their path. The bolt never became visible.

They rowed two stades, Peleus taking them as close in to the headland as possible in a belated attempt to remain invisible to the Macedonians on the beach.

Satyrus nodded. 'Straight across the beach,' he said. 'If they can't get a boat in the water, we're clear.'

He spoke as much to hearten the deck crew in earshot as anything else. The changing wind favoured the deep hull of the heavier Phoenician galley, who was pulling away from his lighter brother ship.

The second bolt flew as if it came from the hand of Zeus and struck their sternpost square on, an impact that could be felt throughout the ship.

'Poseidon, we're sunk!' the oar master said.

Peleus punched the man hard enough to make him writhe in pain. 'Don't be an ass!' he said. 'A hundred of those spears won't hurt us, as long as they hit the works. It's rowers they can kill!' He went astern and climbed the rail with an axe and cut the lance free. 'Nice piece of bronze,' he said. 'Now, about dumping some weight?'

'Do pirates read Thucydides, do you think?' Satyrus asked. His eyes were on the merchant ahead.

'I doubt there's a man in those ships who can read a word, lad,' Peleus said. 'Something on your mind?'

'Have *you* read Thucydides?' Satyrus said.

Peleus shook his head. 'Ancient history. Can't say as I have. What'd he do?'

Satyrus felt his stomach turn over in fear, and he made himself smile. 'I have an idea,' he said.

There were hordes of Macedonians on the shore and as Satyrus watched he saw oarsmen forming in long lines by the sterns of a dozen triremes – and worse, a heavy quinquereme, the biggest warship on the beach.

Satyrus prayed to Herakles.

God of heroes, he prayed, *now I will roll the bones with fate. Stand by me.*

The Athenian merchants were also watching, standing on the high stern of their ship. Some of their crewmen were already ashore, and others were lying on pallets of straw on the deck, cheering as if they were watching a race.

From their shouts, Satyrus could tell that they thought the end was near. The *Lotus* was dumping what little cargo he had in the outer roadstead, and he shot ahead, but throwing his cargo overboard took time and effort and men off the benches and he couldn't keep the pace. The *Lotus* began to labour, his rowers apparently exhausted and ill-trained – or perhaps their morale had collapsed. The pirates increased their efforts, sure of their prey. And their engine of war fired bolts the size of a sarissa. Two of them stuck in the stern of the fleeing galley.

Satyrus was up on the half-deck with the sailors, while Peleus steered as close as he could.

'I want it to come down in one go,' he said for the third time, because sailors could be stubborn. 'Make it look like the boatsail mast went. *Can you do it?*'

His sister was right behind him, trying to get his attention. He ignored her.

'Like enough,' said an Aegyptian mate with a thick accent. 'Like we was winged, eh?'

Satyrus nodded. 'Just so,' he said. He glanced aft, prayed to Poseidon and tried not to flinch as the next bolt sank four inches into the planking of the stern. He looked forward, judging the distance, and aft.

'Next one. Can you do it?'

The sailors all shrugged and looked uninterested, and Satyrus couldn't decide whether to scream or cry. To starboard, the Athenian merchant ship, a giant tub with high sides and a towering mainmast, stood alone in the deep water just half a stade off the beach. He rode so high out of the water, even with a full load of grain, that his bulk screened three-quarters of the beach from sight.

Now that Satyrus's orders were given, the whole idea seemed absurd. His throat was so tight that he didn't think he could speak. But he smelled the damp lion skin, and suddenly he felt as if he'd been filled with ambrosia.

'What the hell are we doing, brother?' Melitta asked.

Peleus was ordering the archers and marines into the bow, which seemed to be against all reason, as they were almost at long bow shot over the stern.

'Let me take some long shots,' Melitta said. 'Maybe I can kill some crewmen on that machine.' She had her bow in her hand.

'We're going about, Lita,' Satyrus said. 'We're going to fight, the way you wanted.' He couldn't manage to be angry, and he hugged her briefly. 'Get your armour on and join the archers.'

Peleus glared.

Satyrus shrugged. 'Wait until you see her shoot,' he said, by way of apology.

She hugged him back fiercely. 'Don't be captured,' she said.

'Nor you,' he said, and then he could see the men on the enemy bow cranking at their machine, the arms of the bow coming back.

Melitta was leaping down from the half-deck into the bow.

'Ready!' Satyrus called out. His nerves receded – mostly. Another part of him said they had enough of a lead to run the bow up the beach and leap clear – and surrender to the Macedonians.

He couldn't imagine going back to his uncle without the *Golden Lotus*. Was that cowardice, too?

'Steady!' Peleus called. 'Every man on deck – hard in on the port rail. *Now, you whores!*'

At Peleus's command, all the men on deck without other orders ran to the port-side rail, tilting the ship an awkward angle to port.

Less than a stade aft, the engine fired and the bolt, aimed high, ripped across the deck at head height. The oar master died instantly; his head exploded like a ripe melon so that his brains showered the half-deck rowers and one of his eyes smacked Satyrus in the cheek and splatted on the deck at his feet. Satyrus gave a squeak of pure fear and stumbled back.

The boatsail fell in a rush of heavy linen that filled the deck so that Satyrus was covered, swathed as if in a burial sheet, and the boat seemed to steer wildly, the stern shooting out to the port side and the heavy bow pivoting as the helmsman seemed to have lost control of his vessel. Satyrus grasped at the heavy linen, swimming through it in increasing desperation. There was a man screaming, and then he was free of the cloth, and they were screened from the rush of the pirates by the high side of the merchantman towering above them as they turned and turned, their deck crew stiffening the ship by leaning far out on the port side while their rowers pulled or backed at Peleus's direct command, because the oar master was a headless corpse whose blood continued to be a spreading stain on the boatsail.

'Pull, port! Drag, starboard! Half-deck, racing speed!' Peleus called and Satyrus was out of the cloth and jumping on to the steering platform.

'Take the helm, boy!' Peleus said. 'It's your plan!'

'Where are you going?' Satyrus asked. In the bow, he could see his sister nocking an arrow. His palm slapped the steering oar and he spoke automatically. 'I have the helm,' he said.

'You have the helm,' Peleus responded. He grinned. 'We need an oar master.' He jumped for the platform amidships. Before he was up on the half-deck, he called, 'Give way, all!' And then, his voice swelling in power, 'Ramming speed!'

Satyrus had never, in his wildest dreams of heroism, imagined steering a ship in combat. This was the art for which helmsmen got the highest pay.

'Right between them, boy!' Peleus shouted. 'Don't get fancy – fuck them in the oars!'

That made it through his fear-addled brain. An oar-rake. He took a moment to breathe – really breathe, all the way in and all the way out. One glance at his wake and then he steadied down.

They had turned all the way, like a hairpin, around the Athenian merchant ship, their whole manoeuvre screened from the two pirates by the grain ship's high sides.

The bow swung clear of the merchantman. Using the big hull for cover, and even as a fulcrum, the *Lotus* had turned all the way around, losing very little of her speed, and now, with all banks pulling with the expertise that Leon paid for, they shot out from the merchant's stern like one of the bolts fired by the enemy's machine.

The two pirates were abreast, close to their prey and eager to cut off escape. The apparent success of the last bolt had made them cocky – a ship steering wild, with her oars all over the place was no threat to anyone.

In heartbeats, the situation was transformed, and the big hemitrieres emerged from the stern of the grain ship less than a stade from them. Their combined speeds of closing left the pirates only heartbeats to react.

'Oars in!' Peleus roared, and all along the decks, the oarsmen grabbed their oars and hauled them inboard, sometimes fouling each other, sometimes injuring themselves, desperate to get the oars clear of the imminent collision. They practised this. The oars began to come in, all eighteen feet of oak coming across the benches until the handles rested under the opposite thwart.

Satyrus stood straight, a wild grin plastered on his face, the smell of cat fur streaming off the wind, and he flicked the steering oar as he had seen Peleus do, so that *Lotus*'s bronze beak kicked a few feet to the starboard side without a major change of direction, and then their own archers fired, all together, his sister's body leaning into the shot like the goddess herself – she nocked and shot, nocked—

He flicked the oar back and *Lotus*'s bow moved and crashed into the oar box of the top deck of the older Athenian boat, so that *Lotus*'s heavy cat-head ripped the light outrigger right off the side of the smaller boat, and oarsmen screamed as they were snuffed out by thousands of pounds of wood and metal driven by three hundred arms. Inside their hull, their own shattered oars ripped them to death, the sharp fragments of the wood lashing like spears in the hands of giants, shards of hardwood filling the hull, the ends in the water driven up and up into the decks, breaking bones and slashing skin, while the ram crushed the outer hull and the men who had been rowing there a moment before.

Lotus passed between her enemies, and left the former Athenian hull a drifting wreck while she caught many of the Phoenician's oars in the water. The heavy-hulled Phoenician didn't take the damage that the Athenian did, but he was labouring, and before his oar master could make corrections he was turning because his starboard oars were undamaged. They could hear the oar master screaming, even as Peleus rose to his feet.

'Oars out!' he roared. 'Blood in the water and silver in our hands, boys!' and the oars shot out of the ports like the legs of a live monster as the *Lotus* continued to coast, on and on, her momentum almost unchecked by the oar-rake down the side of the opposing ships.

Melitta, graceful as an acrobat, leaped up on the port-side

gunwale, balanced a heartbeat and shot the Phoenician oar master as he roared orders. Satyrus saw the other deck officers on the stricken ship staring, their mouths open, as his sister jumped down, avoiding with athletic contempt the shafts aimed at her.

'On my mark!' Peleus called. 'Port side give way! Starboard side to reverse your benches! Ready about! Pull, you bastards! Pull for hearth and home!' He raised his stick and hit the mast. 'Pull!'

Like the legs of an enormous water bug, the oars dipped and pulled, each side pulling in opposite directions, and the deck tilted absurdly. Satyrus could see that the archers in the bow had stopped shooting and were hanging on to avoid being tipped over the side.

The heavy Phoenician was wallowing in the beach swell, his rowers paralysed with fear, their oar master dead with a Sakje barb in his voice box. Peleus looked down at Satyrus as the ram seemed to cross the beach. They were turning so fast that Satyrus was afraid that they might capsize, and even as he watched, the marines and the archers began to pull themselves outboard to stiffen the ship, led by Xenophon, who jumped fearlessly for the outrigger as if unaware that a missed jump meant drowning in his armour. But Satyrus could again feel the change as soon as his friend's weight went outboard of the rail, and again as other marines joined in – they were above the waterline and outside the hull, and still the bow came round – the Phoenician was almost broadside-on to them now, the two ships parallel. If the archers had stayed in the bow, they could have fired again, but all of them, even his sister, were hanging off the port-side rail, and still *Lotus*'s head came around, and the beach swell caught the Phoenician again and pushed her bow back. Men were trying to get her around, but no one seemed to be in charge.

Peleus waved to get his attention. 'You going for the kill, boy?' he shouted.

Satyrus nodded, his eyes fixed on the enemy ship.

'Marines, get back in the bow!' Peleus shouted. 'We need to get the bow down – and clear. Prepare to back-water on my command, all decks!'

Satyrus wrapped both arms around the steering oar against the shock and watched his sister roll inboard like a sea nymph and bounce to her feet, racing for the bows and scattering arrows from her upturned quiver.

And then the bow began to slide across the Phoenician, and Peleus called the stroke – the whole ship rocked as the starboard-side oarsmen reversed their benches, and he had to put his breastbone against the oar to keep it steady, and then the first stroke fell like a hundred axes and the bow leaped forward and down as the marines dropped to the fighting deck, and the rowers, led by Peleus, began to sing the Paean.

Melitta was right in the bow, pressed flat against Xenophon, crushing him against the breastwork of the bow, where all fifteen of them were crammed in a little wooden box to weight the ram and be ready to board. Suddenly she had another view of the fight she had lusted for since the day began – because over the scaled bronze of Xeno's shoulder piece she could see the white faces of the panicked foe, and dead men, and shark's fins already cutting the water. The men in the Phoenician knew they were dead. And for the first time, death was real to Melitta – their deaths, and thus her own – and her throat filled with bile.

Karpos, the marine captain, raised his head from his forearms. 'When we hit,' he said calmly, 'you archers shoot, and the rest of you don't fucking move until we know whether the ram is stuck or not. I don't want any of you left behind when we pull our bronze dick out of that fucker. Got me?' he asked, his voice as rough as gravel, and then he was down, an arrow right through his armour. Melitta froze in the moment of nocking an arrow.

'Lock up!' Xenophon bellowed. The marines got their heads down and the archers pressed on top of them and Melitta put her cheek on the smooth bronze of Xeno's shoulder piece, trying not to vomit because blood was spitting out of Karpos on her legs. The Paean rose to drown his cries, driving all thoughts from her mind – sweat in her eyes, hot moisture on her legs, an arrow almost forgotten in her fingers.

The longest, loudest crash she had ever heard – the ship seemed to stop dead under her and the pressure on her gut was intense as she crushed Xenophon beneath her, bounced and slammed into the wooden partition at her back.

'Archers!' Xeno's voice cracked as he yelled again, higher pitched but still firm, 'Archers!'

Melitta nocked without any conscious thought, and her bow arm swept the deck until she saw a man in armour trying to cross the deck. *Loose.*

The arrow went into his shield and she had another on her string. The man next to her shot, and his arrow went into the shield, and then there was another man in armour – their own ship still pushing forward, their ram under the other ship's spine, so that instead of holing her they were tipping the heavy Phoenician over, driving her starboard gunwale under the water. Every armed man on the pirate was surging for their bow.

'Stroke!' roared Peleus and Satyrus together.

'Fuck, fuck, fuck,' Xeno said, and Melitta leaned past him and shot the first armoured man just a few fingers below his shield, and he sank slowly to one knee, the arrow buried in his thigh, and then flopped into the water.

Xeno looked back over the half-deck. And then his eyes met Melitta's. 'Repel boarders!' he yelled, looking at her. 'Don't move a fucking foot off this deck!' he roared at an older marine.

The marine grinned back, leaned forward and hurled a javelin at the first enemy to reach across. The enemy deck was tipping fast, and water was rushing to fill the Phoenician – he was tilted at a wicked angle and there was no hope for him, and the marine's javelin, a heavy, old-fashioned *lonche*, went through the pirate's bronze-faced shield and through the bones of his arm – he bellowed and fell into the sea, but there were a dozen men behind him.

Javelins flew both ways – a volley and a counter volley, and then the fighting deck was full of men. Melitta backed away and away again, using her arrows like a Sakje, shooting men in the face and groin when they were close enough to touch Xeno, who fought from behind his heavy aspis and covered her. She lost track – shot, and shot, and saw Xeno take a heavy blow to his helmet. She shot his opponent between the cheekpieces of his ornate Thracian helmet and reached for her next arrow to find that she had none.

There was a scream – rage and triumph and horror – and when she flicked a glance to see what had happened, she saw the enemy trireme turn turtle right over their ram, his other rail falling on their ram with a heavy thud and a hollow sound like a temple bell, so that they rocked deep, men falling flat, but she kept her feet. Xeno fell backwards into her and the last attackers, desperate men, surged forward and she was pinned against the back rail of the fighting platform. She went for her akinakes, got her hand on the horn of the hilt and knew that it was too late as the pirate's axe went back – a heavy bronze axe that her helmet would never turn – but she pulled the knife anyway. It seemed slow, and the axe paused as Xeno rose into its path, got a hand on the haft and butted the axe-man in the face with the bronze of his helmet. Then he fell into the space at her feet, his body across Karpos's – she had her knife out and tried to stand, and then a spearhead flashed past her and caught the axe-man in the throat, and suddenly – there was no more fighting.

Her brother was balanced on the rail behind her, weaponless, and Peleus stood below him with an axe of his own.

'Good throw, boy,' Peleus said. His voice was hoarser than usual, but otherwise he seemed calm. Then he crumpled like an animal at sacrifice, and she could see the arrow that transfixed his lungs front to back.

Her brother pitched forward on to the enemy dead. 'Xeno!' he cried.

Xeno got his head up. 'Oh,' he said. He was bleeding.

Melitta looked back at the oarsmen, who were cheering as they backed water. 'Satyrus!' she yelled into his ears. 'You're the navarch. Peleus is down!'

Satyrus hadn't seen. He stood up, whirled, his face crumpling as he saw his hero lying on the deck in a pool of lung-bright blood. He fought a strong desire to sit on the deck and go to sleep. He sucked in a breath.

'See to the wounded. You there,' he pointed at a marine, 'don't kill their wounded. I want prisoners. Understand?'

'Yes, sir!' The marine looked ready to fall over, but he stood up.

Satyrus leaped the rail and ran down the amidships deck. 'I need an oar master,' he shouted. 'Who's the man?'

The oarsmen were not used to having their opinions asked. Even as they rowed, heads turned and the stroke suffered. Satyrus didn't know the oarsmen as well as a real navarch should. But he knew Kleitos, who, though young, was often sent off in the light boat. Kleitos had rowed with him that night in Alexandria two weeks ago, which now felt like another world.

'Kleitos!' he called. He pulled the man's arm, then pushed a deckhand on to the bench. 'You are the oar master.'

'Me?' the young man asked. His jaw worked silently, his eyes wide.

'I want to turn to starboard in our own length – all the way around. The way Peleus and Kyros did it.' Satyrus looked out over the stern – plenty of room now. Backing water for fifty strokes had them well clear of both wrecks.

The lighter Athenian trireme was limping away, only a dozen oars going on her port side, and she was turning involuntarily out to sea.

'Starboard oars,' Kleitos said.

'Louder!' Satyrus said.

'Starboard oars!' Kleitos shouted. He had good lungs, when he used them. 'Back-water on my mark!'

'They're already backing, lad,' Kalos said. The deck master was standing by Kleitos.

'Portside oars, switch your benches!' the man called. His voice was tentative, and many of the oarsmen looked at Kalos before obeying.

Satyrus winced – he'd made a bad choice. Kleitos was not ready for the job – but Satyrus didn't have another oar master under his hand.

The ship tilted as ninety men shifted their weight and reversed the way they sat. 'Port side, give way on my mark! Give way, all!' Kleitos seemed to be getting the knack of it, although his orders came a little too fast and the execution was slow.

It didn't matter, because the Athenian galley hadn't made a stade since they started their turn.

Satyrus ran aft, to where a deckhand held the steering oar, petrified with responsibility. 'I have the helm,' he said. 'Go and see to Master Peleus.'

The sailor ran off, bare feet slapping the deck.

'Master Kalos!' Satyrus called. 'I'll do my best to lay us alongside that Athenian. I intend to come up from her stern and take her. You will prepare the deck crew to board her. You will go aboard with all our marines and all our deck crew and get her boatsail on her. Is that clear?'

Kalos's grin filled his ugly face and showed all his missing teeth. 'You're going to *take* her? Aye, Navarch!'

With the sails down, Satyrus could see the whole run of his deck. Xenophon was standing, and there were three prisoners stripped of their armour being bound to the mast. Peleus lay in his own blood with two deckhands standing ineffectually above him.

'Master Xenophon!' Satyrus called. His voice was cracking every shout. He wanted to sit down and rest, but they were not done yet.

Xenophon's bare feet slapped the deck as he ran to the stern. 'Sir!'

'Take all the marines who can fight and support Master Kalos in boarding the Athenian.' Satyrus corrected his course even as Kleitos ordered the starboard side rowers to pull forward again. They were around – perhaps the ugliest manoeuvre in the *Golden Lotus*'s history, but they were around. Satyrus leaned forward. 'Xeno, can you do it? Secure that ship? Kill their oarsmen if it comes to that? Do I need to put another man in charge?'

'Try me,' Xeno said. He grinned. 'I got us through the boarding party!'

'So you did.' They embraced, spontaneously, a certain hard joy flowing between them. And then Xeno turned away and started calling for 'his' marines. And Satyrus felt better.

Suddenly he stood up, aware that his shoulders had been hunched since he'd thrown the spear.

'Right then,' he said to himself. 'Lita!' he called, and his sister ran down the central deck. He had some time in hand – perhaps a hundred heartbeats until he would have to give the next order. He was flying on the daimon that came to men in war and sport – so full of it that his hands shook and his knees trembled, but his head was clear and the world seemed to slow. Melitta sprinted to his side. 'Sir!' she said. She smiled when she said it.

'You and Dorcus are the closest I have to doctors. See to the arrow in Peleus's lungs – and the other wounded.' Quietly, he said, 'See that he goes easy if that's what it takes, Lita.'

Melitta's nose was pinched in an unaccustomed way, and she had a tendril of snot across part of her face and blood on her forehead. She used her sleeve to wipe her face. 'I'll do it,' she said, and turned away, shouting for Dorcus.

Satyrus still had time in hand and he turned to watch the Macedonians.

The quinquereme was in the surf with her oarsmen aboard, and two triremes were coming off the beach, but the wind was rising – from the south and west – and the helmsmen were being careful. Satyrus felt that he had time in hand – still. Just ahead and to port, the Athenian wallowed in the growing swell, oarsmen beating the water ineffectually.

'Master Kalos, get me that boatsail rigged before you go off,' he said. 'Slow the stroke, oar master.' He felt very much in control. He looked at the sky, and back at the beach.

The sailors got the boatsail rigged, the stain of Kyros's blood like a blossom in the centre of the sail. The moment it filled, the *Golden Lotus* leaped forward like a warhorse changing gaits, a smooth acceleration that made some of the sailors grin with pleasure, while aboard the Athenian trireme, men pointed over the rail at them in panic.

Satyrus put a second sailor on to help steer, because at this speed she could veer wildly, and he kept four of the sailors back from the boarding party to manage the sail.

'Oars in!' Satyrus roared.

The Athenian turned away, yawing wide at the last minute, but Satyrus had seen the helmsman move his hands and he was on the Athenian's stern, his ram under the Athenian's port side in a few heartbeats, and the Athenian's rowers panicked, fleeing their benches to avoid the second oar rake, and in the confusion Xenophon leaped across the narrowing gap alone on to the enemy deck. He landed, rose to his feet and knocked the enemy helmsman unconscious in one continuous motion and then faced the enemy trierarch. Grapples flew from all along the *Lotus*'s deck and the sailors were over the side, flooding the enemy rowing deck.

Just a few feet away, the enemy trierarch and Xenophon faced off. Xenophon made a simple fake and then cut overarm at the top of the Athenian's shield. His opponent took the blow on his shield and pushed forward, knocking Xenophon to the deck effortlessly. He towered over the prostrate young man and raised his spear.

Melitta shot. Her arrow rose on the breeze, a shot that had to pass the length of the ships, past ropes and rigging and hulls and rails, and fell from its apogee as if guided by Athena's hand to bury itself in the mercenary's thigh, a handspan above his greave. The man fell to one knee, and Xeno was up.

The mercenary parried, parried again, using his spear with desperate skill. He tried to rise to his feet and failed, fell in his own blood, and *still* managed to block Xenophon's death stroke. He rolled over – red blood from his thigh wound dripping from his fine bronze cuirass – and got back up on one knee. Xenophon stepped back and saluted him, and the mercenary laughed and returned the salute – then turned it into a cut.

Xenophon parried, but now he had a long red line on his sword arm.

During the pause, Kalos had stepped up behind the Athenian with a deck maul. After the salutes were done, Kalos struck, hitting the Athenian hard in the side of the head. The man went down.

Satyrus was able to breathe again, and under his breath he offered a prayer to Athena and to Herakles for preserving

398

Xenophon, who, for all his skill, was clearly outmatched.

After the Athenian trierarch went down, the Athenian ship offered no fight at all. The swell was increasing, out away from the beach, and it was all their port-side oarsmen could do to keep them bow-on to the waves, which were twice the height they'd been ten minutes before.

Satyrus dropped back and then put his ram under the Athenian's stern with a far more threatening *crash* than he had intended – but he got it done, and the rest of the marines and sailors were across in a single long peal of thunder.

'Follow me, and may Poseidon send we make it,' Satyrus called. 'Try and keep their navarch alive!'

Kalos waved and Satyrus could hear him bellowing orders, could see the Athenian marines being disarmed in the bow, Xeno with his helmet off, pouring water on a wound. He ranged alongside with the wind in his brailed-up boatsail alone and his archers covered the decks. There was no more resistance.

Kalos had the Athenian boatsail mast up before the waves turned to whitecaps, and then he was scudding away. The Athenian trireme was damaged, but with the wind now directly astern, she went well enough, and Kalos had time to reorganize the rowers – captives, now.

Satyrus watched the quinquereme come off the beach and start to pull into the waves.

Two unemployed oarsmen brought Peleus to sit in the stern. He was as white as new-scraped parchment and blood dribbled from his mouth, but he was alive. Melitta and Dorcus had washed him and cut the arrow shaft at the wound so that he could rest against things. The fact that the shaft hadn't been withdrawn told Satyrus everything.

'Master Peleus.' Satyrus sat on his heels, holding the oar, trying to hear the helmsman as his lips moved.

Peleus raised his head. 'Beautiful,' he said. Then he said, 'Need to get on the beach. Now!'

'If you were hale, master, we could have a go at the big ship.' Satyrus found that his cheeks were wet. 'What do you mean, on the beach?'

'Storm,' Peleus said.

Satyrus looked out to sea and knew that the helmsman was right.

'Fucking beautiful,' Peleus said. He had himself up on an elbow, and he could just see over the stern. 'Two to one, under the eyes of the enemy!' He laughed, and the laugh turned to a gurgle and a spray of blood. Peleus's eyes caught Satyrus's, and the younger man could see that the older was going – could all but see his shade pulling free of his body.

'Storm coming,' Peleus said. Then, with enormous effort, 'Tell Rhodos!'

He slumped then, and Satyrus thought he was gone. He turned to watch over his stern. The storm was coming from the sea, moving so fast that he could see the bow-shaped front and feel the drop in temperature. Out to seaward, there was a line, like a line of fog, but Satyrus knew it was a squall line.

Landward, the quinquereme had already abandoned the chase. He was backing into the heavy surf even as they rounded Laodikea Head and the beach full of Macedonian ships vanished around the point.

They were sailing fast – so fast that a moment's inattention caused the hull to tremble like a dog on a leash and sway. They were overhauling the captured Athenian hand over fist now that they had the sail well set.

They passed within an oar's length and sailed on, the edge of the storm carrying them as fast as a galley dared to sail. They cleared the rocks north of Laodikea Head and then the next bay to the north in minutes.

'I'm going for it,' Satyrus said. He was speaking to Peleus, whose eyes still had life in them. There was no one else to talk to – Kleitos was busy with his new responsibilities and Melitta was forward with the archers. 'I'm going to try to beach right here and make it through the night.'

Peleus nodded, startling him. 'Good boy,' he said.

Satyrus hadn't been at sea his whole life, but he'd seen storms. He prayed that this one would follow the usual pattern – a lull just before the front came in.

'Master Kleitos!' he called.

Kleitos came up.

'I intend to beach us, stern first, on the next beach – see her?' Satyrus pointed over the starboard bow, and Kleitos looked blank.

'When I order the boatsail down, you must have all the oarsmen ready – one quarter circle turn to port and then back oars for their lives.' Satyrus mimed the manoeuvre with his hands.

Kleitos nodded, but his eyes showed no understanding.

'Repeat it to me,' Satyrus urged.

'When you drop the boatsail, quarter turn to seaward and back him into the surf,' Kleitos said. He didn't sound as if he believed it.

'Pass that word to every man. No relying on orders at the last minute. Got me?'

'Aye, Navarch!' Kleitos's eyes were dull – he was already exhausted by the effort of command.

Satyrus grabbed an oarsman. 'What's your name, man?'

'Diokles, lord.'

Satyrus started, recognizing the man from the night in Alexandria.

'Diokles, can you take the steering oar?' Satyrus had seen Diokles with Peleus often enough – if they were friends, the man had to be competent. He'd been in charge of the watch.

Diokles reached out and took the heavy oar. 'I have the helm,' he said. His voice was thick, foreign and raspy. He looked down at Peleus, who gave a very short nod.

Heartbeats until they were in the surf. So much to do. 'You have the helm!' Satyrus said, and went forward. He found the four sailors.

'On my command, bring the boatsail down. Down flat – understand – nothing to catch the wind.' Too much information – he could see it on their faces.

'We know our business, Navarch,' the oldest said. He gave a lopsided smile. 'No worries, lad,' he whispered hoarsely.

He went back aft, found that Diokles had been cheating the bow in towards the beach – a nice job of steering.

They had a great deal of way on them – in fact, Satyrus wasn't sure but that this was the fastest he'd ever moved in his life. Satyrus watched the shore – so close – and took a deep breath. He glanced at the Athenian galley. Did they have a chance of duplicating his motions?

They were both angling towards the beach. Just short of the breakers – the rising, increasingly angry breakers – Satyrus ordered *Golden Lotus* parallel to the beach, waiting for the lull. Praying for it. The squall line was ten stades away and coming like a cavalry charge.

A flaw in the wind – the sail cracked and swayed.

'Drop the boatsail!' he called. Then he watched as Diokles leaned his whole weight on the steering oar, and Satyrus stood amidships, willing the bow to turn out to sea, to get head-on to the swell.

Poseidon, let us live! Drop the wind!

The rowers' response was as crisp as could be. They turned the quarter circle in the time it took for two breakers to roll under their stern, so much pressure on the backing oars that Satyrus could see the shafts bend under the strain; and then they were backing water, oars dragging on the gravel of the beach, and the stern was carried high and came down with a heavy thump.

The whole manoeuvre was near perfect – but now the trials of the day showed. The *Lotus* had almost no deck crew to leap ashore and steady the stern, and the sea pounded the bow relentlessly. Kleitos called a stroke on his own initiative, so that the bow oars that could still bite steadied the ship. Sternwards oarsmen started to leap over the sides, which lightened the ship so that he drove higher up the beach and the bow caught a wave and almost swept in – but there were just enough oars in the water and just enough strong backs in the surf to drag the hull a few feet higher, and then a few more. The ship was diagonal across the grain of the beach – but now the hull was empty, and before the next breaker could seize the ram and push it in to break his back, two hundred men and two women were pulling and the whole black-tarred hull shot up the beach half his length. It wasn't pretty – in fact, the whole manoeuvre swirled at the edge of confusion, chaos and failure – but then the *Lotus* was on the sand and upright, and there was a strong cheer.

The Athenian wasn't so lucky. He made his turn with style, and his oarsmen knew their lives depended on their rowing, and Kalos had redistributed rowers and oars to get men on both sides, but their backing-water was clumsy and the Athenian ship came in on the crest of a heavy breaker just as the storm hit. A wave broke over the bow, pushing it up the beach, out of control. Exhaustion and broken spirit cost them precious seconds as the rowers lost their stroke and the ship flooded amidships.

But Kalos had friends ashore. He had the deck crew. They had ropes over the side before the trireme could broach, and the two hundred men ashore were not willing to lose their prize to Poseidon when they were so close, and they pulled, and pulled again, hauling the damaged ship ashore and out of the clutches of the storm. The ship fell over on its side, spilling the water it had taken and dumping rowers in the surf, but the howling wind gave the stern a push and the next wave lifted the bow as Kalos roared 'heave' like Poseidon come to life, and the balance changed. The Athenian hull groaned, but he went up the beach the length of a horse – and again on the next wave, as the last of the oarsmen scrambled out. And once more, lifting the ram clear of the waves, three hundred men pulling together, drenched by the lashing rain.

And then they sank to their haunches on the wet sand. They were ashore, and alive.

Satyrus lay panting on the rain-slick sand, a rope end still clutched in his hands. He was ready to go to sleep, but a crisp voice in his head said, *Not through yet, boy.* He forced himself to his feet and walked to where Peleus lay. The helmsman had died during the last manoeuvre. Satyrus closed his eyes and whispered a prayer.

Then he stood up and pulled his cloak around him in the rain. 'Master Xenophon?' he called. 'Secure the prisoners. Let's get a sail up in the lee of—' He looked around. There was no lee. They were on a beach that swept from horizon to horizon, and only the towering cliffs a few stades inland promised any cover at all.

Melitta took his arm. 'There are caves,' she said, pointing.

'Sail up to cover the cave entrance. Melitta will take you there. Injured men under cover first.' The orders flowed out of him like water from a spring. As if Peleus was giving them.

Kalos was calling his men to action.

Kleitos was kneeling in the sand, shaking his head. Diokles gave Satyrus a look, punctuated by lightning, and Satyrus nodded.

'All right, you lot!' Diokles shouted.

Satyrus stayed upright until the last men were in the caves. The sand underfoot was dry, and the fires of driftwood were roaring, and it was all he could do to speak . His cloak was heavy with water and the wind howled, and if the surf came up any higher, they would lose the trireme – and he couldn't do anything about it. He wanted to keep on moving, keep on commanding, because now that he had time to think, all he wanted to do was weep.

He stood there alone in the storm, water streaming off his face and his sodden chlamys. Lightning pulsed and flashed, and thunder roared louder than a hundred rams hitting a hundred hulls.

Kalos came up to him. 'Inside, sir!' he shouted over the wind and the thunder. He pulled Satyrus by the arm, and they went through the flapping boatsail that covered the cave's entrance and suddenly it was warm. Satyrus stumbled and almost fell. The whole cave was full of men – lying so close that they looked like the amphorae that a merchant ship carried as cargo. The fire – not the first this cave had known – and the heat of more than three hundred bodies made Satyrus shed his cloak.

'Try this, lad,' Kalos said.

Diokles came up and pushed a heavy black-ware mug into his hands. It was too dark to see what was in it, so Satyrus took a sip – kykeon, full of cheese and wine. The wine went through him like an electric shock. The taste of honey and the tartness of the wine were the finest things he'd ever had.

'Finish it,' Diokles said in his raspy voice. He smiled briefly, and then, as if that smile took too much effort, his face went blank again.

Satyrus slumped into an open space near the cave mouth. He fell asleep with the mug still warm in his hand.

Farther down the cave, Melitta was entwined with Xenophon, wrapped around him for warmth and for the emotional protection of his familiar body. She wanted to sleep, but her thoughts ran around and around her head the way an exhausted child will run around and around. Screaming.

She saw her brother come into the cave, and she knew in the flicker of firelight what he would look like when he was thirty – or perhaps fifty.

'You saved my life,' Xenophon said out of the darkness. His voice sounded different, and he didn't make it like a flat statement, but as if he was trying to make out a puzzle.

'You saved mine, too,' she said. She shrugged.

'But – it was single combat,' Xeno said. 'He was better than I.'

Melitta wriggled, seeking to get a stone out from under her hip.

He misinterpreted her wriggle, and wriggled back.

'No, it wasn't,' Melitta said. 'You had to face the helmsman – he was in armour – and the mercenary and perhaps half a dozen sailors. So it was a general action. I shot because it was my duty to shoot.'

'It was a wonderful shot,' Xeno said. This time it was he who shrugged, and she who thought that it was a wriggle, and she wriggled back. 'I was lying on my back, waiting for death – so like Homer! And I saw the arrow go into his thigh just above my head, and I thought – Melitta shot that!'

This was the praise that Melitta wanted. It had been the best shot of her life. 'I killed a few men today,' she said, somewhere between bragging and sobbing. Unsure what to make of those deaths. Feeling mortal herself.

'Me too,' Xenophon said. He rolled over to face her.

In a moment, she rolled over too.

And at some point when most of the oarsmen were snoring, their wriggles of discomfort and embraces of support changed rhythm, and became something else. It wasn't the romantic idyll that Melitta had imagined, with her buttocks trapped against a stone and three hundred possible witnesses – and yet, it was.

'We shouldn't do this,' Xenophon said, when it was far too late to change their minds.

PART V

POLISHING

19

312 BC

The Athenian trireme had seen action, and his expensive Phoenician consort was missing, but he was rowing strongly as he passed the foundations to the new lighthouse and his owner might have been forgiven for feeling a twinge of pride. He'd watched for that ship for two weeks, and there he was, one more piece falling into place.

Stratokles leaned on the stone wall that edged his rented garden, fondling the scar tissue at the end of his shortened nose as he watched the familiar Athenian shape fold his oars to meet the harbour boat. He nodded, well pleased – the ship had been at sea long enough to temper the oarsmen, and now they responded like professionals. Then, calling to his slaves, he dressed in a plain chlamys, called for Lucius and his guards, and headed for the waterfront.

I need some luck. The problem with spying – with almost all forms of subterfuge – is that it was hard to trust anyone, and harder to find the person who could be trusted and still be clever enough to carry out orders. His guard captain, Lucius, was a capable fighter – but not a thinker. Or not the kind of thinker who could compete with Leon and Diodorus.

I need news. He needed to know that the Olbian boy was *dead.* He'd seen this sort of thing before – where a minor issue in a plan began to develop a life of its own. Satyrus had become such an issue. Stratokles shook his head, because the children were such a side issue.

I need Iphicrates. Stratokles had spent long days negotiating with Macedonians – hard men who despised Ptolemy only a little more than they despised Cassander or Antigonus One-Eye. They despised Stratokles utterly, and they didn't always hide their contempt. *Iphicrates can deal with them. I shouldn't even have met them.* Even as he walked, Stratokles made a gesture with his hand – a sort of peasant gesture to avert evil, but in his lexicon it meant that he was conscious of having made a mistake.

I hate Macedonians. Iphicrates might be sullen and secretive, but he was a brilliant fighter and a man who the Macedonians would accept as a negotiator – fools and thugs every one. And he needed Iphicrates to fight back against Leon and his minions.

That black bastard has everything, Stratokles thought. *Good subordinates, time, money – fuck him. I'm smarter, and I'll pull this thing off with my bare hands if I have to.*

Stratokles had endured a month of humiliations as his household servants were hounded and beaten, his slaves stolen, his house vandalized. A punitive raid by Leon's mercenaries had all but destroyed one of the criminal associations he had hired, and now only a handful of desperate men would take his coin.

Don't go soft, short-nose, he told himself.

The endless friction of the job was getting to him, and he stopped on the wharf to take a deep breath and look around him. He was close – very close – to suborning Ptolemy's senior officers. No time for self-pity now. His plan – and the future of Athens – needed him to keep a steady hand on the tiller. And it wasn't all doom and gloom. Despite growing frictions between Cassander and Ptolemy, he had lulled the court with his tales of a summer campaign against Cassander by One-Eye and managed to convince the lord of Aegypt to ship a full taxeis of his veterans away to Macedonia, and he had demanded, and gained, a declaration of independence for the city-states of old Greece, a political statement that would muddy the waters at home and help Athens in fifty different ways. Demetrios of Phaleron would smile in delight, the oligarchic bastard.

Athens, I will yet free you! he thought. Then he grinned. Out loud, he said, 'Athens, I will free you. If I have to sacrifice every one of these bastards to do it.' That made him feel better.

It was time to repay Cassander for two years of slights and indignities – time to play his hand for himself and Athens. Cassander was losing his touch, and he wasn't going to be the winning side. Stratokles needed Athens to be on the winning side – powerful on the winning side – to get what he needed and make Athens free.

So he had begun – carefully – to exchange letters with Antigonus One-Eye, ensuring himself a soft and feathered nest when he jumped – when Athens jumped. He would take a satrapy – preferably Phrygia. Phrygia would make a useful springboard for Athens, a capable ally, a market for goods. And he had an eye on the perfect wife for the Satrap of Phrygia. A fine child, the only heir of the Euxine's second or third most powerful city. Amastris of Heraklea. All he needed was one last brilliant thrust and a little astute kidnapping – in most ways, an easier mission than playing all three corners between Cassander, One-Eye and Ptolemy.

The mutiny of the Macedonians – that would paralyze Ptolemy whether the doctor was successful or not. *Always have a second line of plans,* Stratokles thought while fingering his beard. *And a third line if you can manage it.*

Then he'd board that ship and leave, before Ptolemy discovered how thoroughly he had been bought and sold. The Athenian grinned and thought again of his employee, the doctor. If Cassander was paying the doctor, Stratokles thought that he might do well to avoid the man, even if he had been the doctor's patron. Because soon enough, Cassander would realize that Stratokles had changed horses, and then the doctor would come after him.

And then it came to him – the master stroke that would sweep the board. He actually stopped walking in the middle of the Posideion and stood still as the wonder of the idea filled him.

Short-nose, you're the smartest bastard in all the circle of the world.

Stratokles beat his own ship to the piers and spent an uncomfortable ten minutes waiting around for the trireme to come alongside. He couldn't afford to draw the attention of the guards at this point – he didn't mind if people associated his ship with the death of the Olbian boy, but he didn't want the link too plain. He felt the frustration of a man on the edge of a great success, who has to depend on the whims of Fate.

But the guards on the piers were busy checking bills of lading, or collecting bribes from merchants. None spared him a glance.

Finally, the Athenian trireme turned in for the pier. Her oars shot in – a beautiful manoeuvre – and she coasted along, just barely moving, so that her helmsman only had to make a single turn to spend the last of her momentum.

Stratokles didn't know that voice. He froze. The Athenian trireme embraced the pier like an old friend with scarcely a sound. Iphicrates had never handled the ship with such – elegance. Or without a lot of swearing ...

'Something's wrong,' Stratokles said to his guards. He walked quickly to the sternward edge of the pier. 'Iphicrates?' he called. 'Show yourself!'

He waited a moment as marines put a plank over the gunwale. 'Back to your places!' he called.

'Best let me go first,' Lucius said.

Stratokles shook his head. 'No,' he said. 'I need to know what's going on. If Iphicrates is hurt ...' He shook his head. 'Fuck this.' He leaped on to the plank. 'Who's in command here?'

Momentum carried him two steps up the stern after the shock of recognition struck him. Those were *not* his officers standing in the stern. He reached for his sword. And *that boy*—

He leaped back on to the docks, rolled without tangling his cloak and came to his feet.

'Secure that man! Xenophon!' the boy barked.

Stratokles owed his life to the fact that the men on his ship – *his ship!* – were as stunned as he. He gathered his guards and ran, and the marines didn't get another sight of him.

All the way back to his house, Stratokles tried to see how this could have happened and what the ramifications were. The loss of his ship was a serious blow – that ship meant mobility and freedom and a last bolt-hole if things went spectacularly wrong.

Just short of his gate, Stratokles shook his head as if he'd been in a conversation with another man. He put his hand out and stopped his guards.

'Lucius – wait.' Stratokles pointed at the house. 'We don't know that's safe.' He rubbed his chin. 'No – they can't have got word here yet – have to move fast. Get all the slaves, all the chests and the cash. Load it on the slaves. Fast as you can. Go!'

Lucius was a man used to obeying, and he leaped into action, barking orders at the other guards, most of them Keltoi or Iberians.

In less than an hour, they stripped Stratokles' residence of cash and belongings, made a train of his slaves and some hastily hired porters, and vanished to his bolt-hole – that is, to one of his bolt-holes.

Stratokles fought for calm acceptance, but he was angry. 'What the fuck could have happened?' he asked Lucius. 'More important, what do I do now?'

Lucius shrugged. 'Anything that got old Iphicrates ...' he muttered, and shrugged. 'We've got horses. Let's head out across the desert. You said yourself that most of your damage was done and that Gabines was on to you.'

Stratokles stood still in the street, breathing hard. But then he shook his head. 'No,' he said. 'No – we won't cut and run. Not yet. I'm *this close* to burying Ptolemy for ever. I'll stand my ground, for now.'

Lucius shook his head. 'Well, I'm with you, then,' he said. 'Let's get this done.'

When he was standing in the courtyard of his safe house, a shit-hole taverna he'd purchased in the unfashionable south-east quarter, he breathed easier despite the stink of the tannery next door.

Think it through, he said to himself.

Terrified slaves put bales of his goods down in the courtyard. Stratokles snapped his fingers, and two of his guards stepped forward.

'Pay them well,' Stratokles said. The expense was ruinous, but he couldn't afford the betrayal of a slave at this point.

A young Gaulish woman with a yellow bruise that covered

the left side of her face turned and bolted, fearing something in his voice and guessing incorrectly. She ran out of the courtyard, a six-year-old child at her side. Two of his best went off in pursuit.

'Athena!' Stratokles protested to the heavens. 'Zeus Soter! I intended no impiety!' He stopped imploring the heavens, as it scared the slaves. To Lucius, he said, 'See to it we have no more runners.'

The rest of the slaves huddled together, as if by closeness they could achieve protection against the swords, like the sheep in the tannery. Lucius's men herded them into their new quarters and put a bar across their door.

Before the shadows grew longer, the smaller of his guards returned from the chase with a smug look on his face and a head in a sack – a head with blond braids.

'And the child?' Stratokles asked.

The man looked around. 'Never saw a child,' he said.

Stratokles shook his head. 'She had a child.'

The man blinked. 'Never saw a child,' he said. 'Maybe Dolgu saw the brat.'

Stratokles stifled his annoyance. 'Fine. Send Dolgu to me when he returns. In the meantime, go and buy me two new slaves in the market and get this courtyard cleaned. And arrange to send this note to the doctor. The usual way.' The doctor was comfortably ensconced at the palace, and would only communicate via codes.

He had a new plan – it lacked the endless vistas of beauty of the former plan, but it would serve. Its simplicity was its beauty.

He would continue to foment the mutiny. That was too easy. Cassander wanted the Macedonians in Macedon, and they all wanted to go home. No need for deep planning there. The new wrinkle was that he would use his tools to kill *Ptolemy*. And then, when Antigonus strolled into the ensuing chaos, Stratokles would use him to free Athens.

'You want me to take the boys and have a go at Leon's men?' Lucius asked. The big Italian was eating an apple.

'No,' Stratokles said. 'No, Leon's a sideshow. The children

are a sideshow. If the doctor can get them, well and good, but I'm done with such stuff. We work the Macedonians, and then we decamp.'

Lucius finished his apple, right down to the seeds. 'For what it's worth, I agree. We can't fight everyone.'

'That's just what I think,' Stratokles said.

20

'You have a prisoner?' Leon said. 'Where?'

'Welcome home,' Nihmu said. She smiled sleepily.

Diodorus came through the adjoining house door with a sword in his hand. 'In the name of all the gods,' he said, and then he lowered the sword.

Coenus was right behind him. 'Satyrus!' He grinned. Then, carefully, like a man who fears to speak a bad thing lest it become true, 'Is my – is everyone well?'

'Xenophon is standing in the courtyard with a file of marines. And one of Stratokles' people, wrapped in a rug.' Satyrus grinned. He couldn't help it. Then, sobered, he nodded to Leon. 'Peleus is dead.'

Leon threw a chlamys over his naked shoulders while Sappho ordered torches and lamps lit. 'I don't suppose you could have warned us you were coming? And you're still under exile, young man.' He gave Satyrus a hug. 'So – you've taken a ship on the sea and lost me the best helmsman on Poseidon's blue waters. I assume there's a story?'

Philokles appeared from the darkness of the doorway. 'Coenus, your son is outside with a rug on his shoulder,' he said.

Satyrus smiled at Philokles and then looked at the man again. The change was profound, for having been gone just a month. The Spartan had lost weight. He moved differently. He stepped up and put his arms around Satyrus. 'I missed you, boy,' he said.

Theron came in from Diodorus's house, pulling a chiton over his head. 'I should have known that it was you,' he said by way of greeting. 'Do you know what hour it is?' But he, too, had to give Satyrus a crushing hug.

All together, they went out into Leon's broad courtyard, where six marines stood easily with their shields resting on the ground and their spears planted, butt-spike first, in the gravel. When they saw Leon they all stood straighter.

Xenophon put his burden carefully on the ground and bowed. 'Sir?' he said.

Leon crossed his arms. 'Let's hear the story,' he said.

Satyrus started telling it. Servants brought wine while he talked, and he was on his second cup by the time he got to the fight off Syria and the long night of the storm. 'The next morning, Demetrios could have had us with ten children and a sling,' he said. He shrugged and handed the wine cup to Xenophon, who took a slug and gave a belch. 'We slept late and all the guards went to sleep – three hundred of us in a cave, with the ships out on the beach like a signal.' He shrugged. 'But the gods protected us, or Demetrios is a fool.' He motioned at the rug. 'None of the prisoners know much – they worked for this Athenian mercenary; they had orders to find us and take us. This one seemed to be in command. Kalos hit him hard, and he's been comatose for days. He needs a doctor.'

Philokles motioned to Xenophon. 'Rolling an injured man in a rug is not actually a way to heal him. Let's see him.'

Xeno placed his burden on the ground. 'He was a fine fighter. I'd like him to live.' Together with Philokles, he unrolled the rug.

Philokles gazed at the unconscious man in the torchlight for a long moment. 'Well, well,' he said.

Diodorus stooped over the man and then stood up. 'Look what the cat dragged in,' he said.

'I thought he was dead,' Coenus added. 'Hera protect us all. Put him in my room.'

'We need a doctor,' Philokles said. 'This is beyond me.'

Leon looked puzzled. 'I don't know him.' He turned to his steward. 'Fetch us—'

Diodorus shook his head. 'Wait. Clear the courtyard.' He turned around. 'Trust me. Get everyone out of here. Marines – to the kitchens. Get yourself some wine.' He looked back at Leon and made a sign. '*Friends only*,' he said.

'Xeno can stay,' Coenus said.

'And the twins,' Sappho said.

Satyrus thought that he was on the edge of some great secret.

All his life he'd seen them act like this – as if some sacred bond called them all together.

'Demetrios is in Nabataea,' Melitta said, out of the air, 'and none of his ship commanders had the balls to come out after us.' She reached out and took the wine cup from Xenophon. They glanced at each other for a moment – too long a moment, as far as Satyrus was concerned. *What in Hades?* Then she looked at Diodorus. 'Who is he?'

'Nabataea?' Leon asked. He was standing like a man about to run a race. 'Let me make sure I understand this. Demetrios son of One-Eye is on the beaches of Syria with two hundred ships, and his army is in Nabataea – and you can prove these things?'

Melitta was being embraced by all of her uncles, and she was in Sappho's embrace when she said, 'Prove it? We have two hundred witnesses, if Leon's oarsmen can be trusted.'

Leon and Philokles could be seen to exchange a long look.

Philokles shook his head in answer to some unvoiced question from Leon. 'We need to go to Ptolemy right *now*. Every heartbeat counts.'

'What about the Athenian?' Leon asked. He was rubbing his beard. 'Who is he?'

'He's Leosthenes,' Philokles replied in a low voice. 'He led the revolt of the mercenaries against Alexander. And helped beat Antipater in the Lamian War.'

'He's dead!' Leon said. Then, in a whisper, 'Is he one of us?'

Philokles shook his head.

Diodorus disagreed. 'He was too political to take the oath – but he was a friend of Kineas. A fickle man – I heard that he survived the Lamian War and changed his name, but I'm still surprised.'

'What the hell was he doing working for *Stratokles*?' Coenus asked.

Diodorus shook his head. 'I can only guess that when Cassander took Athens five years back, Leosthenes went with what he thought was the lesser of the evils. Say what you like about Stratokles, gentlemen – he's a loyal Athenian.'

'We chose Ptolemy,' Coenus said, nodding.

Sappho bent over the prone man. 'We could ask him when he recovers. In the meantime, leaving him to lie on the stones of our courtyard is unlikely to save him.'

'We almost had Stratokles on the docks,' Satyrus said. He didn't really understand who the unconscious man was, but he thought that they needed to know the whole story.

That took more explanation.

When they were done barking questions at him, Philokles rubbed his chin. 'Stratokles will bolt,' he said.

'Into a hole,' Diodorus said.

'Regardless, this is the moment to crush his influence at court and sting the Macedonian faction into action,' Leon said.

'Except that we could be fighting Demetrios any moment,' Coenus said.

'Where's the *Lotus*, lad?' Leon asked Satyrus.

'South coast of Crete. She ought to be homeward bound by now,' Satyrus said. 'I thought that I could surprise – well, everyone – if I came in the prize. And Peleus's last wish was that the Rhodians be informed.'

Leon nodded. 'Fair enough. I'll order that Athenian trireme into the yards – not a bad hull, if a little knocked about – and get to sea myself in *Hyacinth*. I'm for the coast of Syria.'

'I'll come with you!' Satyrus said.

Philokles shook his head. 'No,' he said. 'I have work for you here.'

'I'm in exile!' Satyrus said.

'We need to go to Ptolemy anyway,' Philokles said.

'Are we done plotting?' Sappho asked. She waved at the slaves peering out of the door. 'Come along, my dears. Gently with the poor man.'

'We have to keep him a secret!' Diodorus hissed.

Nihmu gave him a raised eyebrow, and his wife poked him in the side as she went by. 'Keep who a secret, dear?' she asked.

'We need to go to Ptolemy now,' Philokles said. 'Or it's all rumour in the morning. Tonight we'll have his whole attention.'

'Grumpy attention,' Diodorus put in.

Philokles frowned, his face like an actor's mask in the torchlight. 'We've heard about all this for a month, but no firm evidence, and always Stratokles whispering to Ptolemy that it's all a feint.' He raised an eyebrow and looked at Satyrus. 'We have even started training the new phalanx.'

'Satyrus is still in exile,' Leon muttered, as if just remembering the fact.

'Now,' Philokles said. 'We have to go now.'

'Herakles' deified tit,' Ptolemy growled. 'This had better be good.'

Leon shuffled. Satyrus had never seen his uncle so nervous, and it suddenly struck him that this was no easy triumph. If Leon was frightened, then there was something about which Satyrus should be frightened.

The ruler of Aegypt was wearing a chiton of transparent wool that showed far too much of his ageing body. He had a garland of drooping grape leaves around his head. But his gaze was steady. 'You, boy?' he asked, looking straight at Satyrus. 'Gentlemen, I thought that we had an agreement.'

Philokles stood forward. 'I think you had best hear this story yourself. Then judge us.'

Ptolemy nodded. 'On your head be it. Who tells the tale?'

Leon shuffled, and Satyrus started forward, but Philokles held his ground. 'We sent Satyrus to sea. Stratokles of Athens sent ships to follow him.' Philokles was a trained orator, and his arm came up and his stance changed subtly, and his diction became slower and clearer. He dropped his voice, and the hall became quieter, and men leaned forward to hear him speak. 'Satyrus took the *Golden Lotus* to Cyprus, and Stratokles' ships followed him there. He fled to Rhodos, and the pirates followed him. Rhodos is under blockade by One-Eye's fleet. That's news – but what follows is worse. Satyrus saw the fleet of young Demetrios on the beaches of Syria. Two hundred ships of war and as many transports.'

Even the guards behind the throne made a noise.

'Silence!' Ptolemy roared. He had been standing. Now he

sat on the pear wood and ivory chair that he used for informal receptions. He held out his hand and a slave put a silver goblet into it. 'How do you know that these ships belonged to the Athenian ambassador?' Ptolemy asked. 'For a month many voices have told me that One-Eye was coming here – always the same voices, I'll add. Now you have found hard evidence?'

Satyrus didn't want to be stopped. 'Lord, we fought and took the Athenian's galley. Anyone in this room will know it in the harbour. If that is not evidence enough, we have his sailing master and his marines and his oarsmen, too.' Since the room was still silent, he said, 'Everywhere my ship went, he followed me.'

Ptolemy's eyes widened. He nodded. 'You wouldn't lie to me, boy?' he asked with deep cynicism.

'I swear it on my father's grave and on – on the lion skin of Herakles, my patron.' Satyrus wondered what had moved him to say that – the god at his shoulder, he hoped.

Ptolemy turned to his guards. 'Get me the Athenian,' he said. 'Let's see what he has to say for himself.'

Diodorus stood forth. 'I'll bet you a silver owl to an obol that he's gone – bag and baggage and slaves.'

Philokles began to fidget, and Leon grimaced and stood his ground.

It was a long half-hour. Diodorus yawned, over and over.

'Stop that!' Ptolemy insisted, yawning himself. He laughed when he said it, and the tension dropped a little.

A pair of guards came back into the megaron and whispered to Gabines, who whispered in Ptolemy's ear.

'So,' Ptolemy said. He rubbed his chin. 'He's gone. Just as you predicted – unless you did him in yourself. Don't tell me you ain't capable of it, Odysseus.' Ptolemy was looking at Diodorus, who nodded.

'I am,' Diodorus said. 'But I haven't.'

'Fuck,' Ptolemy said. It wasn't very regal. He looked around the room. 'Clear the room,' he said to Gabines. 'They stay, and you, and Seleucus.'

'Seleucus?' Satyrus whispered to Leon.

'Another player in Alexander's funeral games,' Leon

whispered. 'He lost his army at Babylon fighting Antigonus, and he came here and offered his sword to Ptolemy.'

The man called Seleucus went and stood on the raised platform by Ptolemy's chair. A pair of the Cavalry Companions – the *Hetairoi*, Ptolemy's most trusted troops – came in from the barracks and stood by the chair. Satyrus knew both of them – men Diodorus liked.

'So,' Ptolemy said. He looked around. 'Demetrios *is* coming. Gentlemen, we're not in good shape.'

No one said anything to deny this assertion.

'Gabines, how reliable are my Macedonian troops?' Ptolemy asked.

'I wouldn't risk a field battle,' Gabines replied. 'Although – if I may be so bold, lord – it is Demetrios, an unknown youth, not old One-Eye in person. He would be a far greater threat, both as a general and as a figurehead.'

Seleucus nodded. He was a short man with the legs of a cavalryman and the speech of a Macedonian noble. 'One-Eye has the king – that is, young Herakles – and Cassander has the other, unless he's murdered him. Most of your Macedonians wouldn't face Herakles or Alexander IV in battle – but young Demetrios has neither of the kings.

'How many troops will Demetrios have?' Ptolemy asked.

'Twenty thousand infantry, forty elephants,' Seleucus answered. 'Good cavalry.'

'So if we could make our infantry fight, we could outmatch him,' Ptolemy said. He looked at Diodorus. 'You're awfully quiet, for you.'

Diodorus yawned again. 'I'm just old, Ptolemy. But it seems to me that if we launch our army at Demetrios, we roll the dice. If we sit here in Alexandria, he rolls the dice.'

Seleucus nodded. 'I agree.'

'The disappearance of Stratokles will panic the extremists in the Macedonian faction,' Gabines said. 'Expect defections.'

Ptolemy shook his head as if to clear it. 'Cassander was double-dealing me? I still find that hard to stomach. If I go down, Antigonus and his golden child get Aegypt. How on earth can that profit Cassander?'

Seleucus shrugged. 'I don't waste time worrying too much what a man like Cassander thinks,' he said. 'Demetrios is here, now. If we can keep your army together, he may make a mistake. How do we keep the army together?'

Diodorus looked at Philokles. 'By pretending nothing has happened, except the news that Demetrios is marching here. That by itself should drown all other noise in the agora.'

'Where is Leon?' Ptolemy asked.

'Putting to sea to keep watch on Demetrios's fleet,' Philokles said.

Ptolemy nodded sharply, and stood. 'You, boy,' he said, pointing at Satyrus. 'Keep your head down. Understand me, boy?'

'I have work for him, with the phalanx,' Philokles said.

Ptolemy nodded. 'I can accept that.' He looked around. 'No talk of this, anyone. If Stratokles surfaces, we deal with it. Otherwise, let the plotters plot, eh? When any of them is ready to defect, I wish to know.'

Gabines nodded.

Ptolemy looked around. 'Well then. I suppose we'll try to fight this golden boy and his forty elephants. Athena of the victories, be with us!' He turned to Seleucus. 'Ready to march in ten days. Pass the word. And see how they react.'

Diodorus saluted, as did Coenus.

Satyrus slept for a whole day, and then the reaction hit him. The killing – the fighting – left him feeling nothing, and then it left him feeling like a stranger. His body seemed strange. His thoughts, or lack of them, seemed strange. The accomplishment of commanding a ship seemed a small thing – the death of Peleus loomed large.

His sister came and went. She babbled about riding and said something about Xeno, as if her infatuation for his best friend needed to be discussed. He listened to her without hearing a word, said what he hoped were the right things in return and she went away.

The third morning, he felt no better. So he drank some wine and that seemed to help. He just kept reliving his decisions

– when to turn the ship, when to fight. He saw too many ways he could have done it. Spur-of-the-moment improvization was revealed as boyish bravado.

His sister came and he listened to her, and then drank more wine, and that helped too. Kallista came, closed the curtain at his door and kissed him.

He stiffened immediately, and she caught his erection with a practised hand. 'Have your attention?' she asked.

'Mmm?' he answered. She was not melting into his arms.

'Philokles has been around several times asking for you, and everyone in this house is girding for war, and you are sulking like Achilles.' She relinquished her hold on his body and he pawed at her, and she shrugged him off with a laugh and walked out through his curtain, leaving him feeling like a *boy*.

He sat on the floor, depressed and ashamed of all his many weaknesses, and then he found another amphora of wine.

And then Philokles came.

'Stand up,' Philokles said. He was taller than usual, at least viewed from the floor. He'd added muscle to his chest and his paunch was almost gone.

Satyrus obeyed. 'I'm a little drunk,' he slurred. 'You'll understan', I'm sure.'

'There's work to be done,' Philokles said. His voice was kind.

Satyrus couldn't meet Philokles' eye. 'I – am – sorry.'

'Because you slobbered at Kallista? Or because you got Peleus killed?' Philokles was clean and sober. 'Most men would grab Kallista's tits if they could, and any man worth his stones would have to think hard after he ordered men to their deaths. That's good. However, your time for such thoughts is over. Stop wallowing. Get up. The world's going to hell and we have work to do.'

'You're the philosopher, Philokles! And the hoplomachos, the best spear in Alexandria. And I'm just a boy.' There, it was said. He felt better, and took a little wine.

Philokles went and sat on the bed. He had military sandals on and a chitoniskos, the undergarment to armour. He was dressed for war. He rubbed his chin and then nodded. 'I'm here to get you moving and bring you out of this. It's tempting to tell you a couple of lies and get your heart beating again.' He shrugged and raised an eyebrow. 'But you're a man, not a child.'

'Twenty men died. Peleus and nineteen others. I want—' Satyrus bit his lip. 'I did not do much of the fighting,' he said.

'You want to be forgiven?' Philokles' face was the mask of Ares. 'There is no forgiveness, Satyrus. None. Just the next task. You are as brave as you need to be and your fears about your courage are foolish,' Philokles said. 'But you can prove yourself brave, if you like. Come and stand your ground with me in the phalanx. Beside me. In the front rank.'

Satyrus nodded. 'Yes!' he said, willing to try. He drew a breath. 'Very well,' he said. It came out pretty well. 'So that's the next task?'

'I took that for granted, as you don't appear an ingrate and you are a citizen. It will mean that you won't ride with the hippeis. Frankly, you're not a trained cavalryman. And it will help me keep you hidden. I believe that Stratokles will hunt you. And the factions – it'll be open fighting soon, anyway. But you have friends – dozens of friends. Young men who go to the gymnasium, fight on the palaestra, run the races. I want them.'

'You want them? Are you the commander?' Satyrus thought that Philokles would make a very good commander.

'Hmm. I am the real commander, alongside a dozen old mercenaries. Right now, some of the Macedonian faction have managed to put a man over me. *I need your friends.* I need two ranks of spirited, brave, athletic young men. You have a week.' Philokles smiled. 'Some of them will die,' he said.

Satyrus took a deep breath. 'How many?'

Philokles sneered. 'How many will die? Ask a prophet.'

'How many do you need?' Satyrus shot back.

Philokles rubbed his chin and deflated. 'A hundred, more or less.'

Satyrus laughed. 'That's every prosperous Hellene in Alexandria. The whole young set at Cimon's!'

Philokles nodded. 'I rather expected you to start at the gymnasium.'

Satyrus took a deep breath. 'Leon's marines?'

Philokles nodded. 'Ours as soon as they return. They're watching the approaches at sea. That's where I expect to get my file-closers.'

Satyrus, interested, reached into a cedar trunk for his own chitoniskos. 'Sailors?'

Philokles scratched his cheek. He didn't look at all like the mask of Ares. 'What are you, some kind of democrat?'

'You have Aegyptians, right?' Satyrus took a sponge from a basin and tried to clean himself. He was still partly drunk, but he felt that if he stopped moving he would fall back into the pit.

Philokles shrugged. 'Some sailors. But right now, every ship with a fighting ram is at sea, watching for One-Eye or his son.'

Satyrus brushed his hair roughly, forcing the horsehair brush through his own as if to punish his transgressions. He put on short Thracian boots and a cloak, put a straw hat on his head and picked up a hunting spear.

'First,' he said, 'I need to apologize to Kallista.'

Philokles nodded. 'That might be a virtuous act,' he said. 'We drill all day at the sea wall. Not that we accomplish much. The Aegyptians have had all the war spirit beaten from them. They go through the motions like slaves.' Philokles came and suddenly embraced Satyrus. Then he stepped back with his hands on the younger man's shoulders. 'Fighting in the phalanx is messy,' he said. 'Everything depends on the first two ranks. Everything.'

Satyrus nodded. 'I'll be there?'

'Right next to me. Can you keep my spear side safe?' Philokles stepped away.

'You trained me, Spartan.' Satyrus grinned. The expression used muscles in his face he hadn't used in days.

'See you don't embarrass me, then,' the Spartan said.

Satyrus walked into his sister's rooms, announced by Dorcus. He embraced his sister and apologized all at once. 'I didn't listen to a word you said,' he pronounced. She looked terrible – pale and worried – but she smiled for him.

'I'm your sister, stupid. I don't need apologies.' She hugged him nonetheless.

Satyrus kissed her, and they leaned their foreheads against each other for a moment. 'Thanks to the gods,' Melitta said. 'I really thought you were gone. The veritable black pit of despair.'

'Part of me is still there,' he said quietly. 'But Philokles gave me something to do. Acting is so much easier than thinking.' He hoped that didn't sound too bitter.

'Actions have consequences,' she said. Her eyes flicked away.

'I keep learning that,' he said. She was hurting, too – he could see it, but he couldn't imagine what it was about. 'I'm off to Cimon's to recruit an army.'

'A drunk, lecherous army?' she said, brightly. 'Nice of Philokles to find something for *you*. I'll just sit here and weave or something.'

'You're not a lot better off than I am,' Satyrus said.

'No, I'm not,' Melitta said. 'And now that you're back from the land of the dead, I may just go there. Come and talk to me? Promise?'

'I'd be happy to help,' Satyrus said in a whisper, and then louder, 'Where's Kallista?' He already smelled her perfume.

'Right here,' said the avatar of Aphrodite. Dressed in white and perfumed, she was almost too much to look at. She offered him an embrace, but he took one of her hands, pressed it to his forehead and bowed.

'My apologies, Kallista. I was weak. And behaved badly.'

'Hah!' Kallista drew him into an embrace. 'Men!' She smiled and gave him a very unsisterly kiss. 'One of these days, young man.'

He flushed. But she embraced him again, and then gently pushed him away. He found that he had an oyster shell in his hand.

'I should go,' he said hurriedly, fooling no one.

'Go then,' his sister said. Something going on there – she looked caged, almost desperate, and he owed her. 'What's wrong?' he asked.

'Nothing!' she said. 'Get out of my rooms before you burst!'

Relieved, he went. Only when he was outside in the courtyard did he think of her look at Xeno and how close the two of them had become on board ship. But then his whole mind went to the oyster shell in his hand.

The message inside the shell said, *Lord Ptolemy speaks highly of you and your sister, and I will soon be moved to invite her to visit. The man who brings her might receive a reward.*

He went out of the courtyard singing a hymn to Aphrodite.

The fear of pregnancy stalked Melitta's sleep and her every waking hour. The loss of her virginity troubled her very little – Sakje girls did as they pleased, and she laughed at the posturing of Greek women. But the consequence loomed, and she listened to the music of her body with the avidity of a newcomer to the world of the body, and it carried tales.

Every rumbling of her stomach frightened her. Every itch, every feeling in her genitals, every change in her skin. A chance comment in the market – *your hair is richer today, my lady* – sent her into depression.

Her lover – Xeno – was worse than useless, vacillating between fear and wonder at what he had done and a strong desire to do it again. And she had a hard time recapturing any of the feeling of the ship about him. In Alexandria, he seemed a strong boy with a tan, and she feared that his obvious looks would give them away, and that the consequences would rule their lives.

She wasn't going to marry Xeno. She was going to be queen of the Assagatje.

While her brother was still drinking himself into courage after coming back – *such a fuss for so little* – Xeno went away again when the *Hyacinth* went to sea to watch for the enemy fleet, and she was left in peace, until her brother walked out with a foolish oyster shell in his fist and Kallista turned to her.

'Are you pregnant?' she asked in a matter-of-fact voice. She did wait until Dorcus was clear of the room.

In a matter of minutes, she told everything. She wept in Kallista's arms until the hetaira made clucking noises.

'Not the lover I'd have chosen for you, but Hades, at least he's clean and your own age. By your own will?'

Melitta had to smile at that. 'I did all the work,' she said.

Kallista shook her head. 'I can imagine. Boys – all the same. Was it fun?'

Melitta shrugged. 'Yes – no. Yes. It was. Didn't hurt at all. None of that. But so little for so much *worry*!'

Kallista made a face. 'Don't say too much of that, honey bee. Men hate that.' She frowned. 'I wish I could tell you that you were safe, but I don't know. How many days?'

'Seventeen,' Melitta said promptly – the whole scroll of her fears rolled into that one number.

Kallista nodded. 'We course at the same time, so that means nothing. You should see blood in a week – Aphrodite, you did this at the wrong time, girl. Did I teach you nothing? Early or late in the month and you can make mistakes.'

'And if I don't?' Melitta asked. She had hoped – hoped against hope – that when she told Kallista, the hetaira would *know* and calm all her fears.

'Then you have a baby. There's no need to borrow trouble by discussing all that now. That's for a month from now – maybe more. Girls miss their courses – I still do, sometimes. Late, early, nothing – it's like philosophy, honey – it never has the answer you need.'

'I'm *afraid*.'

Kallista smiled. 'Nothing to fear. Are you some streetwalker, or a slave in a rough house? Go and tell Sappho and Nihmu. Today. Get it done. People here *love you*. You understand me, girl? They even *love me*, and it took me time to get that – but you are the lady of this house.'

'Sappho will throw me out,' Melitta cried.

'Sappho was a hetaira!' Kallista said. 'And she's been a better mother to *me* than my mother ever was. Get your head out of your arse – or wherever it is – and tell Sappho. Do you love him?'

'No,' Melitta said in a small voice.

Kallista laughed. 'That's a mercy.'

Satyrus went to Abraham's house first because Cimon's was something he couldn't face alone. Or because he missed the man – Xeno had turned very strange these last few weeks, and seeing Abraham seemed like a return to a better time. A safer time. Whereas Xeno now lived in a world of war. And Xeno was probably in love with his sister.

His stomach turned over, and he was standing in a public street, the intersection of two great avenues constructed by the conqueror to allow the breezes to move freely through his chosen city. He leaned against a building.

'Master?' asked the slave who'd come out with him. Young, smooth-faced and useless.

'What's your name, lad?' Satyrus asked.

'Cyrus,' the boy said, sullenly. Again, Satyrus thought that he wanted a servant he could trust. Someone of his own. 'It's nothing,' Satyrus said. He rubbed his brow. Then he turned on to the Alexandrion and walked along it, passing the temples and the near-palaces of the Macedonian upper class. Many of them were poorer than Uncle Leon, and few of them had the political or military power of Uncle Diodorus, but they lived lives of the most reckless ostentation, because (apparently) that is how they lived in Macedon. Then past the Posideion, with its merchant houses and their public and private wharves. More and more of Abraham's fellow Hebrews were moving into the Posideion, which had a certain logic to it, as two-thirds of the lots were empty and most of the new arrivals from Palestine were merchants.

Ben Zion had one of the larger houses, a utilitarian building on the Greek pattern with little outward decoration. Like the man himself. Ben Zion tolerated Leon, but the man was reputed to be a Hebrew zealot and he dressed in the plainest of tunics and always wore elements of his Canaanish or Israelite tribal clothing, as if disdaining the Hellenic world in which he lived.

Satyrus had only met him twice – both on errands to fetch Abraham from his lair. Like this one.

Avoiding a man lying dead in the central gutter, and fastidiously wrinkling his nose as a specialist butcher disposed of the unclean parts of an animal, watched by a Hebrew priest, into the very same gutter, Satyrus moved past them, smiled at a knife sharpener because the man was doing such a careful job, and caught a glimpse of a pair of eyes looking out from behind a curtain in the exedra of Ben Zion's house.

Satyrus smiled to himself, because for all the black clouds in his mood, he was still moved by those eyes – a pair of eyes he was quite sure he would never attach to a voice or a body. Hebrew women lived in even more seclusion than Greek women.

The street door to the courtyard was open, and labourers – a mix of races – were standing with their backs against the courtyard wall, panting. There was a heavy crate on the marble-chipped ground, and Ben Zion stood with his hands on his hips, a heavy wool robe over his vaguely Hellenic tunic.

'No visiting during working hours,' Ben Zion barked, catching sight of him.

Satyrus recoiled; then, forcing a smile, he stepped forward. 'I need your son, sir. Public business.'

Ben Zion had a heavy beard like many older Greek men, and he ran his fingers through it, both hands – a foreign gesture. 'Public business?' he asked.

'You are a citizen?' Satyrus asked in his best helmsman voice.

Ben Zion actually smiled. Recognition lit his dour face. 'Yes, young nephew of my partner Leon. I am a citizen.'

Satyrus bowed. 'Your son is a citizen?'

Ben Zion nodded.

'I call on your son to serve in the phalanx, with panoply and arms, against the common foe, in defence of the city.' Satyrus ground the butt of his hunting spear against the marble chips.

'I hope you'll have better spears than that,' Ben Zion said. 'Leon said you would come. So. And so. Benjamin – fetch my son.' He motioned at one of the labourers. 'May I show you a wonder, young warrior? Or do thoughts of armour fill your head to the exclusion of everything?'

Satyrus didn't know why people didn't like Ben Zion. He

was, in some Hebrew way, *just* like Diodorus and Leon. 'I'd be delighted,' Satyrus said.

Seeing the wonder seemed to involve stripping his chlamys and helping the labourers raise the crate off the marble chips – 'God send it not be damaged. Fools!' – and carrying it, the heaviest load Satyrus had ever put his shoulder to, around the corner and deeper into the house.

'Ahh! Softly! God witness that I have done all I can to get this precious thing into my house! You there, Master Satyrus, you have strong arms – see to it that you have a light touch, as well! Mind the loom!'

A thousand imprecations, some in Greek, and many others in a language that Satyrus didn't understand, except that it had to be Hebrew. Past a kitchen, whose smells made Satyrus want to eat. He was now carrying the crate with the help of one other man, passing through arched doorways too narrow to admit more hands, and he was unable to do more than walk and carry. He was sweating like an Olympic athlete in the final stade, and the wooden supports by which the heavy thing was carried were beginning to creak and bend.

'Just on top of this – here – hold it up! Up! Now down – slowly – perfect, my children, perfect!' Ben Zion actually clapped his hands. 'Get the crate off, you lot. Master Satyrus, you are ever welcome in my house – you are as strong as my strongest servant, and I might not have got this done without you.'

Satyrus stood up, for the first time seeing where he was – a handsome round room, quite large, with the feeling of a temple. Scrolls in pigeonholes as far as the eye could see, and the crate now rested on an elegant dark stone plinth against a tiled wall. Satyrus rubbed his back, looking around – the ceiling was like the vault of heaven, the first mosaic he'd ever seen. 'When did my uncle say I was coming?' he asked, to indicate that he was not altogether foolish.

'Ah. Today, of course. What can I say, young master? When one has the repute of a famous Hellenic athlete, a poor trader must make what use can be made, yes?' Ben Zion handed him a steaming cup. '*Qua-veh*. An acquired taste. Nabataean. I have sent a note to your uncle that my sources from Nabataea say

432

that One-Eye's son invaded them, looking for tribute money, and suffered for it.'

Satyrus nodded at his carrying partner, an enormous man who wore the same tribal marks as Ben Zion. The man nodded back – comrades in fatigue and accomplishment. Then he sipped from the cup and almost spat – the stuff was bitter.

'Put some honey in it,' Abraham said from behind him. 'I see my father got his money's worth out of your visit.' He sounded a little contemptuous. It was a tone that Satyrus would never have taken with Leon, but Ben Zion merely smiled.

'Honey is Abraham's answer to everything – eh? Greeks will love Jews if only we add a little honey?' Ben Zion shrugged. Nonetheless, he helped Satyrus himself, using a heavy horn spoon to add honey. A woman appeared with a tray – an attractive young woman, unveiled, who smiled right into Satyrus's eyes as if they were old friends.

'Miriam! Up the stairs this instant and no more of your sluttish ways!' Ben Zion was angry. 'How dare you?'

'That's my sister,' Abraham murmured. 'Drink your qua-veh and look imperturbable.'

Satyrus cast a smile at the retreating Miriam, who seemed unbowed by her father's anger. A female voice was raised from the exedra – Miriam's mother, Satyrus had no doubt. He didn't understand a word of Hebrew, but he would have bet a dozen silver owls that the words 'what will the neighbours think' had just been shouted.

Ben Zion turned back with a shrug that seemed at odds with his display of rage – all an act? 'My daughter. The apple of my eye. Beautiful – is she not? Come, be frank, Hellene. Esther, Ruth, Hannah – all fine girls. But Miriam is like Sophia incarnate.'

'Except for the lack of wisdom,' Abraham whispered.

'Bah! I heard that. Listen, my atheist scapegrace, this Hellene has come to my poor shop to require your service in the phalanx of the city. Eh?' He looked at Satyrus.

Abraham grinned like a fool. 'Really? I thought I'd have to beg to join. Very humiliating, for our people. Asked to join? Totally different. I would be *delighted* to serve.'

'Delighted enough to find ten more like you?' Satyrus asked. 'Who can furnish their own panoply to Philokles' standards?'

'Ah! Armourers will grow rich all over the city!' Ben Zion said. Both hands tangled in his beard. 'How lucky that Leon and I own most of them.' He nodded. 'It is as my son says, young master. We hate to beg – but invited? I doubt you'll find fewer than fifty.'

'Philokles in command? That's a frightening thought.' Abraham laughed.

Satyrus smiled, and then frowned. 'You could die,' he said suddenly, unsure how to approach the matter. 'This is real.'

Ben Zion nodded curtly. 'War causes death? In Greece, this may be news. In Israel, we already know what war does.' He nodded to his son. 'See to it that you do us honour.'

Abraham nodded. He bowed respectfully to his father. 'I will.'

'I know,' Ben Zion said. He turned away suddenly. 'Your Hellene friend should see this, since it is the triumph of our two peoples, working together.' He had turned away to hide emotion, and Abraham busied himself with the cups, leaving an embarrassed Satyrus to fend for himself.

He and the giant Hebrew lifted the crate straight up, over their heads, and then carefully off the gleaming bronze that lay beneath. Before the box was clear of the thing, Satyrus had an idea what it was.

'A machine!' he said, in awe.

'More than a machine,' Ben Zion said. Indeed, it looked like two great tablets of bronze – but on the backs, there were hundreds of gears and cogs and several different handles that could be pulled. The sheer complexity of it boggled the mind.

'What does it do?' Satyrus asked.

Ben Zion shook his head. 'It calculates all the festivals and holy days,' he said. 'See the stars? See the moon? Do you know your astronomy?'

'Well enough to handle a boat,' Satyrus said.

Ben Zion paid him the compliment of a glance of respect. 'That is an accomplishment for a boy your age. You Greeks are not as ignorant as some peoples. So what star is that?'

'I assume this is Orion's Belt,' Satyrus said, and then they were exchanging star positions and turning levers. A button was pressed, and the calculator whirred, gears moving inside gears, and then the dials moved.

'By Zeus and all the gods,' Satyrus said enthusiastically. 'It's more than just a festival calculator, isn't it? It can predict *where the stars will be*. A great navigator—'

Ben Zion's face darkened. 'By the god, and only the god,' he said softly. 'This is a holy place.'

Satyrus bowed. 'I mean no profanity, lord. Many Greeks, too, think there is but one god, of many aspects.'

'And many Jews think their one god has at least two, or even three aspects,' Abraham shot in, before his father could reply. 'I think we should go and recruit more men, Satyrus. While you and my father are still friends.'

In the courtyard, Ben Zion bowed stiffly. 'I meant no bad feeling to arise,' he said.

Satyrus, still a little scared of the older Hebrew, bowed formally. 'None has. I thank you for your hospitality. And the sheer marvels of your machine. Who built it?'

'Many men – and a few women – had hands in it. Aristotle of Athens divined that the calendar wheels must needs have the same number of cogs as there were days in the calendar. A Pythagorean in Italy worked out the elliptical wheel.'

'Elliptical wheel?' Satyrus knew his geometry, but he had no idea what was being described.

'Another time, Satyrus the curious. I find your company surprisingly erudite for a young barbarian idolater, and would welcome your return.' Ben Zion bowed.

Satyrus returned the bow. 'Everyone is someone's barbarian idolater,' he said. 'And thanks for the qua-veh.'

'I shall send a bag to your house. Have a care of my son. He's the best of the lot.' Ben Zion bowed again.

Abraham coloured as they went out of the gate, accompanied by Satyrus's worthless slave. Ten courtyards further down the avenue, Abraham peeled off his wool robe and flung it to the slave, now another bearded Hellene to outward appearance.

'That's the best thing my father has ever said of me,' he said, in wonder.

'I liked him!' Satyrus said.

'You stood up to him. He likes that – right up until religion enters the picture. Then he doesn't like it. But you did well. And I'm sorry for Miriam. There's nothing sluttish about her, but she's starved for life the way a drowning man starves for air. She claims she'll go and serve as a hetaira to escape my mother, and sometimes, in her naivety, I fear she will.' Abraham looked around. 'Where are we going?'

'Cimon's.' Satyrus wondered if he could do several people a favour at once. 'Would your father let Miriam see my sister?'

Abraham raised an eyebrow. 'Your sister is not exactly a byword for genteel behaviour,' he said. 'But she is the same age and she and Miriam would probably start their own phalanx together.' He nodded. 'I'll try it on my mother. I should have thought of it myself. You liked her?'

'I scarcely saw her,' Satyrus said. Not quite the truth. He'd seldom seen anyone he so instantly liked. Like Amastris.

Queens and Jews, Satyrus thought to himself. I really have to find a nice Greek girl somewhere.

With Abraham to guide him, they made three more stops at Hebrew houses where Abraham was welcomed in a way that suggested that he was a man of more worth than Satyrus, a Hellene, had guessed. And young men sprang to follow him, and their fathers guaranteed their panoplies, so that by the time they arrived at Cimon's they had twenty young men behind them and the porter gawked.

'I can't seat all these!' he said. But he smiled, seeing a great evening and a pile of silver.

'May I see Thrassylus?' Satyrus asked the porter, and the great man was sent for and arrived in heartbeats.

'Master Satyrus?' he asked.

'Thrassylus, Antigonus One-Eye and his golden son are coming with a mighty army to burn fair Alexandria to the ground,' Satyrus declaimed. 'I need to address your patrons from the stage.'

Thrassylus bowed. 'Your uncle had already mentioned something of the sort,' he said. 'The stage awaits.'

Satyrus walked in, followed by two files of Jewish men, most of whom were quite familiar with Cimon's. He walked straight up the steps to the wooden stage, where musicians and other performers were commonplace. He stood on the stage and drew his sword, and silence fell over the whole tiled room, punctuate by a buzz of gossip.

'Demetrios the Golden is two weeks' march away,' he said. 'Every man in this room is a citizen. Demetrios means to destroy all we have – all we hold dear. Our temples, our hearths, our homes. Demetrios will sell our women into slavery and we will be sent to foreign places – if we preserve our own freedom.' Satyrus had thought his speech out carefully, like the orator he wanted to be. So now he pointed at Abraham and the men seated around him. 'The Jews will fight. They know freedom – and they know slavery. Look at them – twenty of the richest boys in this town, and they will go to be the front rank of the new phalanx.' Satyrus raised his sword. 'Greeks? Macedonians? Hellenes? Are we the worse men? The greater cowards? I will go! I will go with the new phalanx. And you? Anyone out there?'

One young man had the courage to stand up. 'But I'm a Macedonian!' he said. He was Amyntas, son of Philip Enhedrion, household officer at the palace. What he meant was that if he was going to fight, his father would find him a place with the other pure-blood Macedonians. 'And – aren't you exiled?'

Satyrus shook his head, sword still held out. 'Bullshit, Amyntas. You are no more Macedonian than Abraham. You, sir, are Alexandrian. Now, get off your arse and fight for our city!' In his head, he considered that coming to Cimon's perhaps wasn't the best way to keep the low profile that Lord Ptolemy had required of him.

Theodorus was sharing his couch with a flute girl, and he suddenly rose up, a little drunk and flushed. 'My father will kill me. Don't we have an army to do this, Satyrus?'

Satyrus was still holding out the sword, steady, unwavering, like a male Athena. The sword said, symbolically, that he was judging them. And they were reacting as if they feared his judgment.

'Defend yourself, Theo. This is our hour. This is when we stand up for the city that nurtured us. I've only been here three years, but this is my home, and when I see the foundations of the lighthouse from the deck of the *Golden Lotus* I know that this is the place that I will defend. Who will stand with me?'

Theo sneered. 'Who commands this phalanx? Is this the foreign phalanx that my father laughs at on his way to the sea wall?' Young men were stirring on their couches.

'Foreign? If your Macedonian father means that the rank and file were born *here*, then he has the right of it. We will be the front rank of the *Phalanx of Aegypt*. Philokles the Spartan will lead us and train us. But you – every man here – you train at the gymnasium. You can afford the fullest panoply – better than any mercenary and better trained than some Pellan farm boy who has never wrestled a fall. Stand up! Flex those muscles! Show your elders that we aren't soft!' Satyrus spoke to the room in general, but his eyes were on Dionysius the Beautiful, who flirted with him and wrote verses about his sister's breasts.

Theo stood up. He was swaying. 'My father will kill me,' he said. 'Can I come and live at your house?' But when his hands were steady, he said, 'I will serve.'

'Fuck, I'll serve too,' Amyntas said, and stood by his couch.

Dionysius, the handsomest young man in Alexandria, and one of the richest, smiled – and stood. 'If I'm willing to put my body between Demetrios and this city,' he said, 'then the rest of you should be with me.' He smiled wickedly. 'You all have so much less to lose.'

Dionysius was the deciding vote, if it had been an assembly. Suddenly all the young men were standing, and the older ones – most of them already soldiers, looked around, muttering. Some applauded, but others looked angry. Satyrus did a quick count and found that he had eighty-six adherents.

He took them as a mob to the parade ground, the keener boys attempting to march and failing utterly. He handed them over to Philokles, who kept a straight face and made the Spartan salute.

'I need Theo and Dio and Abraham,' he said. 'For recruiting.'

'Carry on,' said the voice of Ares. Then Philokles grabbed his shoulder. 'I take it that every patron of Cimon's saw you?'

'Yes,' Satyrus said, defiantly. 'I told you I was going there.'

'You are a man now, and not a boy. But if they saw you, they will start adding things together. Understand?'

Satyrus nodded. 'I understand. I'm at risk.'

'Good lad. Watch yourself. Your uncles are probably all starting at shadows.'

21

Theo knew the richest boys...

Theo knew the richest boys. Dio knew the handsomest boys and the athletes and musicians. Abraham knew the Jews, and some of the Nabataean metics and other Arabs. They went as a group of four from door to door, portico to portico, palace to warehouse.

They gathered a hundred and forty more young men, one and two at a time. It took days, precious days, and every armourer in Alexandria had orders for the finest armour, the lightest corslets with the best iron and bronze scales.

It was curious work that left Satyrus exhausted at the end of the day, full of minor triumphs and equally minor snubs and rebuffs – doors closed to him that he'd always imagined opened, a share of curses, but worst of all, the bored refusal of the rich – men who mocked him for his recruiting campaign, and men who questioned his sanity.

Croseus the Megaran, for instance, waited only to be told the magnitude of the threat before ordering his best things packed and taking one of his own ships for Corinth. 'I owe this city nothing,' he said. 'Neither do you. Stop being foolish – you will not get my son to stand in the ranks. That's for slaves and fools – poor men who have to do such things. Men like us don't fight. Leon won't be in your precious phalanx, I'll wager.'

'No, sir,' Satyrus said.

'See? Childhood fantasies. Myths. Like thinking that Alexander was actually a god.' Croseus shook his head.

'Master Leon will serve with the cavalry,' Satyrus said.

'Take your foolery and your rudeness and get out of my warehouse,' Croseus said.

Again, he found his Macedonian friends vanishing like startled gazelles in a hunt down the Delta. Not all of them – Theo's father was delighted to see his son in the ranks – but others spoke, quietly or openly, with derision, of the city and of

Ptolemy. It was one of these meetings that showed that the war of the factions had reached explosive proportions.

Sitalkes was a young man that Satyrus knew from pankration. His father was an officer in the Foot Companions, a captain of ten files, who shared the name Alexander with most of the Macedonian men of his generation. Sitalkes stood in his own courtyard, enthusiastically nodding as Dionysius and Satyrus gave him the whole recruiting speech – and then his father came through the courtyard gates.

'Well, well,' he drawled. 'Boy, are these your friends? Please introduce me, unless we don't use such polite conventions any more.'

Sitalkes bowed. 'Pater, this is Abraham, son of Isaac Ben Zion. This is Satyrus, son of Kineas of Athens. Dionysius, son of Eteocles; Theo, son of Apollion. All of them—'

Whatever all of them did together was not something in which his father took much interest.

'You're *Satyrus*? The famous *Satyrus*?' The Macedonian officer nodded. He made a motion. Then he stopped and swallowed. 'Well!' He looked around his courtyard. 'Hold on a minute, boys. I'm eager to hear Satyrus's proposals, as is every citizen, I'm sure.' The man's heavy teasing had the same smell as his breath – red wine and garlic. He snapped his fingers and wine was brought, and he sent the wine slave away, but Satyrus noticed that the slave went and spoke to one of the Macedonian soldiers who loitered around the gate. The soldier put his shield against the wall and sprinted off down the street.

'Wine?' the officer asked.

Sitalkes appeared stricken. He tried to speak and then shook his head.

'No wine? Perhaps you are too young to have a head for it. I hear you are a pankrationist. Go inside, boy,' Alexander ordered his son.

'No wine, thank you,' Satyrus said. 'I'm trying to convince Sitalkes to join the Phalanx of Aegypt.'

Alexander smiled – a false smile that made Satyrus's guts roll over. 'We'll consider it,' he said.

Abraham was already by the gate. Theo was on his feet,

having caught on that something was not right. Dionysius sneered. 'Macedonian debates must be like Macedonian flirting.'

'Come away, Dio,' Satyrus said.

'No, stay,' the officer said. 'I love punishing unruly children.' And when Satyrus dragged Dionysius away, the officer roared, 'Close the gate!'

Abraham was ahead of the Macedonian gate guard all the way – he got his back against the gate, and he was bigger. And when the man went to grapple, Abraham gave him an elbow in the temple and down he went.

The officer thrust Dionysius from behind. 'Go, then,' he said. 'Get your foreign arse out of *my house* and don't come here again.' Then he laughed, and even the laugh was surly. 'I imagine you'll get all the chastisement you have coming to you, *Greek*.'

Satyrus swept up the Macedonian shield by the gate and got it on his arm. 'Run!' he shouted.

Cyrus, his slave, needed no further admonition. Theo bolted through the gate, and Dionysius, seeing the gate guard put his hand on his sword, hesitated, and Abraham shoved him.

The gate guard tried to knock Theo down and Satyrus caught the man's shoulder on the shield and turned it, then kicked out under the shield and knocked the man sprawling, and he was out of the gate.

'What in all Tartarus does that madman think he's doing?' Dionysius asked when they stopped at the next corner.

'He sent a man,' Abraham said between gulps of air. They began to walk as they all gasped for breath and then Theo laughed. 'What an idiot!' he said. 'Our fathers will bury him in court.'

Abraham shook his head. 'He didn't seem very worried about court. Listen – he sent a man!'

'I saw it,' Satyrus said. He was trying to think ahead. 'We should go home by a different route, then we—'

'My father will order him arrested,' Dionysius insisted.

'I don't think …' Abraham said, and then Cyrus, who was walking next to Satyrus, leaned forward to point at something on a roof and took an arrow in the neck. The boy dropped like

442

a sack of flour, the main artery in his neck severed, his blood splashing like a badly sacrificed bull's.

Satyrus looked around. 'Cover,' he yelled, and jumped under the overhang of the exedra of the nearest building.

Abraham copied him and Dionysius had the reactions of an athlete, but Theo had never been in real danger before and he froze in the middle of the street. There was the rush of feet behind them, and Theo cried out and went down. Satyrus saw the man who killed him – a mangy footpad who carefully put his sword in Theo's eye as the boy thrashed on the ground.

'Herakles!' Satyrus yelled. Even as he shouted the god's name as a war cry, he knew that Theo was dead. He threw himself forward at Theo's killer in a muddle of conflicting thoughts – terror and a desire for revenge, expiation, some vague thought that with a shield he could cover everyone's retreat. That was his thought as he got his feet on either side of his friend's corpse and punched the bronze rim of his shield into the mangy footpad's face. The man had no shield – all he could do was step back.

One. Two.

Just as he was taught, Satyrus stepped forward and drew his sword, then cut the man down with the back cut, the edge of his sword right in the man's neck, and then Satyrus spun, ready for the next man, as an arrow thudded into the shield where his back had been seconds before.

The other two murderers ran.

Satyrus could see the archer up on the roof of the nearest house. The man wore Persian clothes, all in the dullest of colours, and he had a Sakje bow. He aimed carefully – the oddest feeling, Satyrus thought, to be so carefully singled out for death – and shot.

Satyrus moved the shield and ducked, and the arrow clanged against the rim. With a full-size aspis, he'd have been immune. With the smaller Macedonian shield, he had to react like a snake.

The man raised his bow again. Abraham was calling for help, shouting at the top of his lungs for the watch, and Theo was still dead between his feet.

Thump. The man was shooting for his head. Relentlessly. Satyrus felt an irrational desire to stand his ground and not flee back to the exedra – after all, fleeing the first time had killed Theo. And perhaps dying would solve it all – all the endless complexity.

Thump. He just barely caught that one – shot for his knees. His shield arm had no interest in death.

There were calls from the watch – a dozen armoured men running full tilt down the Alexandrion.

The archer shook his head in frustration, cursed and vanished across the roof line.

Listless, angry at himself and the world, Satyrus was interrogated by the officer of the watch – a Macedonian, of course – and then again by Theron when his coach arrived to take him from the clutches of the law, and again by Sappho when he arrived at home.

'You're lucky the watch officer was an honest man,' Sappho said. 'Or you'd be dead.'

Satyrus sat looking at his hands. He had blood under his nails. Theo was still dead.

'They fucking killed him,' Satyrus whispered.

Diodorus came in, resplendent in a bronze breastplate and a gilt helmet with a white horsehair crest and a pair of exotic blue plumes on either side of his head like ram's horns. He had a dark blue cloak embroidered in gold laurel leaves, and the hilt of his long kopis was solid gold. He looked like a king, or a very great man. 'Satyrus, there's no time for revenge. How did Theo die?'

Satyrus was aware that somewhere, four troops of elite cavalry were training without their hipparch. He shook his head, and the anger choked him. 'Thugs. Two-obol thugs. One of them got him, thinking he was me.' He all but spat in disgust.

'Ares and Aphrodite!' Diodorus said, pulling off his helmet. 'His father is going to wreck what's left of the pro-Ptolemy faction.'

Sappho rose gracefully, put a hand on her husband's golden armour and shoved. 'Get out of my rooms,' she said softly.

'Come back when you have the temper for it. He's been through a great deal, Dio – you are not helping.'

Diodorus grew as red as a piece of Tyrian wool – but he walked out through the door.

Satyrus ran after him. 'No – I can do this,' he said. 'They were thugs – an assassination attempt, organized on the fly. We visited Sitalkes – a friend of mine from the gymnasium. I could tell his father was – turned. Already a traitor. Call it what you will. He wanted to kill us himself.'

Diodorus put a hand on his shoulder. 'It's not your fault.'

'I know it's not my fucking fault!' Satyrus shouted. 'I want this done! Over! Before they get you or Melitta or Sappho or the lot of us!'

A slave handed him a cold cloth without being asked, and Satyrus put the cloth to his face. With his eyes closed, he could see Cyrus's body lying half in and half out of the gutter, the blood running out of his neck and swirling away with the bilge water and the urine and the faeces – and Theo's blood creeping along behind. And then another stream from the almost-severed neck of the man he'd killed.

Theron came back with Philokles and Diodorus, now out of his armour and with an ancient *mastos* cup full of wine. 'Sorry, lad,' he said. 'And you, wife. My apologies.'

Sappho nodded. 'Very well.'

'We need to know what happened, lad,' Philokles said.

Satyrus had the force of will to make himself recover, to avoid the indulgence in passions that marked a weak man – or marked him any further. He didn't sob. He told his story as best he could – again.

'Theo's father has two other sons, but he's ready to go to war personally on this matter. He's got a reward out for this Persian archer.' Diodorus shook his head. 'This is a bad time for Leon to be away.'

Philokles was interested in other matters. 'You did *not* kill Theo, Satyrus. Listen to me, lad. Your illogic is overwhelming and very much a piece with your age. The assassins *intended* his death. It was their actions—'

'Don't treat me like a *child*!' Satyrus said. 'The assassins

445

intended *my* death. I failed to read the signals – clear as trumpets on a summer day! And then, when the attack started, I didn't help Theo – the youngest of us, and the least trained. And what of Cyrus? Doesn't Leon teach us that slaves are men, too? Cyrus is just as dead as Theo – and his blood was just the same colour. Come to think of it, Theo's killer bled the same – when I put him down. I'm sick of it. I'm no good at it and it goes on and on and the bodies just pile up. How many of my friends will die? Some fighting Stratokles, some fighting One-Eye – more to make me king of the Bosporus, perhaps! Fuck it! It's just violence, on and on, bloody slaughter to the end of the world!'

Silence greeted his outburst. Theron winced. Diodorus shrugged and turned away, anger obvious on his face. Sappho wore an odd and somewhat enigmatic look.

Philokles actually smiled. 'You are growing up,' he said. 'Some men never do. We tell children nice tales so they'll learn – lies that often have truth in them. Fables. Some men cling to those lies all their lives, Satyrus. Lies about how one nation or city or race is better than another that justify killing, death, war.' He sat straight. 'Nothing makes killing *right*. If you wish to live a life of pure righteousness, I think you must turn your back on killing – on violence. On raising your voice when angry, on hurting others to accomplish a goal.'

Satyrus made a noise, and Philokles raised a hand, forestalling him. 'Killing is always wrong. But many other things are also wrong – oppression, theft, tyranny, arson, rapine, on and on, the catalogue of human wrongs. When you turn your back on killing and violence, you also surrender the ability to prevent wrongs to others, because in this world, we stop oppression when we stand firm in our ranks with the bronze.' He gave an odd smile. 'You know what amuses me, Satyrus? What I just told you is what the elders taught in Sparta. I have spent a lifetime reading and listening and studying and hating war, and what it makes me become – and all I can say is that life is a choice, an endless series of choices. Men can choose to think or not to think. They can choose to lead or to follow. To trust or not to trust. You may choose not to take life – even not to fight. That choice is *not cowardice*. But that choice has consequences. Or you can choose to kill – and that choice, too, has consequences. When the blood fills your lungs and the darkness comes down, all you have is what you did – who you were, what you stood for.'

'So what's the *answer*?' Satyrus asked. 'How do I ... ?' He couldn't even enunciate his question. *How can I stop seeing the corpses? How do I avoid the consequences?*

'Shall I just give you an answer, lad?' Philokles got to his feet. 'Or can you take the truth like a man? *There is no answer.* You do what you can, and sometimes what you have to. So – if I am to be your judge, putting your steel in that man-killer was no sin before gods or men. Nor can any man hold you responsible for young Theo – not even his father, whose grief is formidable.' Philokles put his hand on Satyrus's shoulder, and Satyrus didn't shake it off, and Theron, who had been silent because Philokles had said everything he had to say, came over and embraced Satyrus.

Diodorus grunted. 'I'm glad to know that my life is immoral, Spartan. What a fine thing philosophy must be!' He shrugged. 'But the immediate problem is that Stratokles, or somebody like him, is out there trying to kill the twins. Satyrus – no leaving the house, except with one of us. Understand?'

'No,' Satyrus said. He looked around at these men – these heroes. 'No. If I'm a man – I can do this. You can't nursemaid me. I can stay alive. I think I proved it today.'

Philokles nodded. 'He has a point,' he conceded.

The evening breeze whispered through the palm trees and the Mediterranean surf hissed against the gravel of the beach behind the main wing of Leon's house, and the north wind carried the smell of the sea – rotting fish and kelp and salt, a smell that could sink to a miasma or rise to a wonderful scent of openness, blue waves and freedom.

Satyrus had a porch off his rooms that opened on the sea, and tonight he felt the need of it. He took a cup of wine from a slave and walked out into the breeze. Out here, in the dark, the sound of the sea was much louder.

'When we first came here, I used to sit just like this and listen to the sea,' Melitta said from a chair. 'I used to imagine that the water coming up the beach was the same water that had passed out of the Tanais.'

Satyrus sipped some wine. 'I still think the same thing,' he said. 'All the time.'

Melitta got out of her chair. 'After the sea fight off Syria, I lay with Xenophon. It's not his fault, it's mine. I'm sorry. I told Sappho – I didn't want you to hear it second-hand.'

Satyrus digested this in silence.

'Say something!' Melitta said.

'Theo is dead,' he said. 'Killed by men sent to kill me. I left him standing in the street. *I didn't do it – I just let it happen.*'

'It's not all about you,' Melitta said.

'No,' Satyrus agreed, and drank more wine. 'I'm learning that.'

'I'm sorry about Theo. What did his father say?' Melitta asked.

'Nothing. He was frightened. *Frightened!* What is this city coming to?' Satyrus took a breath and drank more wine. 'Why Xenophon, though? I mean, he's my best friend, you've spent my whole adult life teasing him and telling me about his short-comings, and he's enough of a gentleman to feel – things. You won't marry him, I assume?' Satyrus wished he sounded a little more adult.

Melitta was silent. Then she said, 'I don't plan to marry anyone among the Hellenes, Satyrus.'

'Going to go to the sea of grass without me, Lita?' Satyrus knew that he'd had too much wine.

'If I have to,' Melitta said. 'I want to be a queen, not a girl.'

Satyrus shook his head. 'That's just where we differ, sister. I'd like very much *not* to be a king.'

'You wallow a lot, you know that? It's not all about you! You didn't kill Theo. You didn't kill your precious Peleus. Sometimes you make me want to punch you.' Melitta shook her head. 'You get everything I want – and you don't even like it!'

'After this campaign—' Satyrus began, but Melitta cut in savagely.

'After this campaign? After we sail to Rhodos? After we make war on Antigonus One-Eye? How long do I have to wait?' Now they were shouting at each other.

Satyrus raised his hands, spilling some wine in his frustration. 'What's so bad?'

'What's so bad? How did you spend the day? Recruiting? To save the city from Demetrios and his one-eyed father? Was it frustrating? Did useless merchants turn you down? Fighting for your life against assassins? Lost a friend?' She was shouting now. 'I *sat at home and wove some wool.*'

He was silent.

'In my spare time I worried that I was pregnant,' she muttered. 'I want to go and fight Demetrios. I want to ride free, or be a helmsman, or recruit young men to fight. But most of all I want the attention of the men and women worth a conversation. Tonight, I confessed my transgression to Sappho. Do you know what she said? *Best not tell Satyrus until the battle is fought.* Philokles treats me like a *girl*. Why? Because I have breasts and my body can make a baby! Why doesn't somebody recruit me? Demetrios is going to have forty elephants and we don't even have *one*, and by Apollo, I may be the best archer in this city. What are we doing about raising a corps of archers?'

'Maiden archers?' Satyrus said, looking to win a smile and failing utterly.

'Is the loss of my virginity painful to you, brother? Was our family honour strapped between my thighs?' Melitta swelled with rage.

Satyrus shook his head. 'Stupid joke. Sorry, Lita.' He made himself reach for her, refusing to be cowed by her anger and believe that she really aimed her darts at him, and she was in his arms, her head on his shoulder, and at the speed of their embrace they stopped being at odds.

Melitta rocked back and forth for a little while, and Satyrus watched the stars behind her head blur with his own unshed tears and then return to normal.

She stepped back. 'I know it's not your fault. But suddenly

everyone in this house is treating you like a *man*. Whereas I get to be a perpetual *child*.'

'I can't get you a corps of archers, maiden or not,' Satyrus said. 'But when Leon lands his marines, I know a ship that could easily land one more archer. But Lita – this isn't a fair battle. We're the trapped dogs – Demetrios has everything his way.'

Melitta raised her chin. 'I was there when we took two pirate galleys,' she said.

'True enough,' Satyrus said, and kissed the top of her head. 'Why Xenophon? He's so nice – he's going to follow you like a dog for the rest of your life.'

She shrugged. 'Hard to describe, really. He knew that I had saved his life – thanked me for it. Comrade to comrade, even though he had fought like Achilles and I was a mere girl.' She shrugged again. 'And I saw – things. The same things – gods, you know as well as I. I was *dead* when your spear put that man down. I felt *dead*. And then – I was alive.' She hung her head. 'I don't care a fig for my virginity, brother. But I agree that actions have consequences, and I insist that Xeno should not pay the price – the bride price or any other price.'

Satyrus slugged back his wine. When they were children, they had fought – and then one big hug and it was over. Tonight, he felt the loss of that simplicity, because she was closed to him on some level, and because *no*, he had not really forgiven her. But his failure to forgive her weighed on him, like a failed sacrifice.

She felt his hesitation. She stared at him.

He stared back. Once, they had been eye to eye. Now he was half a head taller.

'Will you really help me get away?' she asked.

'Yes,' he said. He imagined her lying dead, trampled by an elephant as he had seen back in the great battle on the salt plains. He shook his head – too much wine. 'Fuck it, Lita. Yes, you have as much right to lie with a man as I do to lie with a woman. I, too, have spent too much time with Hellenes.' He smiled bitterly. 'It's going to be hard to talk to Xeno.'

'Imagine how I feel,' Melitta said. She rose on her toes and kissed his cheek. 'Thanks,' she said, and went back inside. She turned back and smiled. 'I have a rendezvous for you. With Amastris. I was going to throw it in your face if you played high and mighty with me.' She shook her head. 'Which you didn't. So I feel like a fool.' She reached in her bosom and pulled out an oyster shell. 'Tomorrow night,' she said.

The slip of papyrus leaf had two lines from Menander, and Satyrus smiled, because the lines named the hour to anyone who had seen the play.

'By the steps of the Temple of Poseidon,' Melitta said. 'Do you love her?'

Satyrus looked at his sandals. 'Yes,' he mumbled. And yet …

'Don't be foolish, brother. Don't get caught. I don't think – I shouldn't say this! I don't think you're Amastris's first boy, man, what have you.' She shrugged, clearly unhappy at having said what she had said.

'What?' Satyrus asked. 'But—'

'I'm sure it is different for men,' Melitta said. 'Listen – don't go. It's not worth the risk.'

'This from my sister who wants me to smuggle her into the archer corps to fight elephants?' he said.

She smiled. 'That's a hit and no mistake, brother. Very well – go if you must. But she won't show. Not the first time. The first time will just be a test of your devotion, I'm her friend – I know these things.' She turned and slipped away, leaving him with an oyster shell and a feeling of confusion.

The next morning, the wind still carried the sting of the sea in its tail, and it blew hard enough to cool the sweat on two thousand backs and breasts as they drilled without shade. Panion, the commander of the Foot Companions, stood at the head of the taxeis with Philokles and Theron and half a dozen Macedonian officers.

'They're absurd,' Panion said, loudly enough to carry into the first three ranks. 'Children and slaves. One-Eye's veterans will go through them the way his elephants will push through our cavalry.'

His Macedonian officers laughed ruefully or disdainfully,

depending on their faction. Philokles said something softly, and Panion shrugged. 'Work as hard as you like, Spartan. I'll put them in the second line, or somewhere where their flight won't cost us much. Perhaps we can use them to carry baggage?' He laughed, and the six Macedonians laughed again.

Philokles fingered his beard. 'I need more sarissas,' he said. 'We don't have enough.'

'Ptolemy sent too much equipment off to Cassander,' Panion said with a shrug. 'Make do with what you have. After all,' he said cheerfully, 'if Ptolemy's kingdom relies on this lot, we're doomed.'

Philokles said something quiet, and Panion shook his head. 'I think you forget your place. I am a *Macedonian*. Your people once had a certain reputation for war, I'll allow. But I assure you, sir, that no amount of drill will make these slaves into soldiers, and that I don't give a flying fuck for their morale.' Panion looked around him and spat in contempt.

Later, he and his staff reappeared as Philokles forced the phalanx through another wheeling movement – badly executed, like every wheel.

This time, the Macedonian went along the first two ranks. He called every Macedonian out of the ranks. He stopped at Satyrus.

'You?' he said. Then, when he'd recovered his confusion, he gave Satyrus a smile. 'You don't belong here, with this rabble,' he said. 'Come with me.'

Satyrus could see Amyntas shuffling nervously among the young Macedonians. 'What rabble?' Satyrus said.

'Aegyptians.' Panion shrugged. 'Good for farm work.'

'Seems to work to train Macedonians,' Satyrus said.

'Yes,' Panion said. 'But they're men, not slaves. These boys are Macedonians.'

Satyrus wiped the sweat from his eyes. 'Not a one of them was born in Macedon, sir,' he said, meeting the commander's eyes. 'I recruited them here in Alexandria. For *this* phalanx.'

Panion narrowed his eyes. 'Another uppity Greek,' he said. 'Very well – swelter on, boy. Revel in your remaining hours.' Then, louder, 'You Macedonians, come with me.'

When Panion was gone, Philokles continued to drill the men, and as the shadows lengthened, he tried to provide the physical training that would allow Aegyptians to go up against men in the peak of fitness. They weren't weak – many of them had fine bodies and heavy muscles from labour – but Philokles walked around, urging them to lift greater weights or run farther.

The men were listless – worse than usual – and when the sun touched the rim of the world, Philokles dismissed them, obviously keeping his temper in check. Satyrus fell in next to the Spartan as they walked back in the last light of evening.

'Half of them won't come back,' Philokles said after they had walked a stade. 'That fool, that posturing ninny. I should have put my sword up his arse on the spot.'

'Philokles!' Satyrus said. 'Master, I have never heard you speak in this manner.' He managed a grin, his first since Theo died. It had occurred to him that Panion might have had something to do with that death. 'You are not always a philosopher.'

'Do you know what the Macedonian officers discuss?' Philokles said. 'Putting on a good show. Fighting long enough to get the best possible terms from Demetrios. Remember what happened to Eumenes? When part of his precious Macedonians decided not to fight. It's happening here, lad. Another week or two and our taxeis would be worth something, too. They shape well – better than many Greeks. Strong backs, these Aegyptians. But Panion just told them that they are slaves to him.' Philokles spat. 'Six weeks' work, for nothing. And he took half of the cream of your boys. Every one of those Macedonian boys knew which end of a spear to wield.'

'We still have the Greeks and the Jews,' Satyrus said.

Philokles gave half a smile and put a hand on his former student's shoulder. 'So we do,' he said. 'I don't think they're enough, and I think that we need ranks and ranks of strong, faithful and courageous Aegyptians behind us, or it won't matter. But I should swallow my own medicine and deal with these troubles when they present themselves. What do we do for sarissas?'

Theron leaned in. 'For now, the first three ranks can use their hoplite equipment – all the Hellene ephebes have them, and even the Jews came with heavy spears.'

Philokles agreed. 'Shorter spears in front is not a way to build the confidence of your front ranks, lad. Do you know what it is like to face a Macedonian taxeis? Unless they're disordered, every file has six or eight spearheads sticking out in front. They move, just from the natural movement of the men carrying them – like the ripple of grass in the wind. Hard to face. Terrifying.'

'You told me yourself that with an aspis and discipline, you had no problem penetrating the wall of spears.' Satyrus had heard the tale of the fight at the fords of the Borysthenes a dozen times or more, from different men. He knew that Philokles and the elite men of two Euxine cities had held, and then beaten, a Macedonian phalanx.

Philokles made a face. 'Veterans should know better than to tell such tales. We were lucky – and brave. There were good men in that taxeis – hard men, and men in the very peak of athletic training. I had ten Olympians.' He looked out to sea, his spear-butt making a rhythm as he tapped it on the paving stones. 'I was a younger man myself. Look at me! It has taken me six weeks just to get the lard off my stomach. Fifteen years ago, I'd have had muscles like your cuirass – like you have, wrestler.' He pointed at Theron, who wore his chitoniskos off one shoulder, showing the near-perfect musculature of his torso.

'We have Theron. He's an Olympian.' Satyrus was interested by the fact that he was now cheering up Philokles, a complete reversal from the day before.

'Ahh, Theron,' Philokles said. They were at Diodorus's gate, which was the closer of the two properties to the drill field. 'Three days until we march. Where are you heading, young man?'

'A nap,' Satyrus said. 'I have this magnificent physique to maintain.'

Theron slapped him on the back.

'Don't forget to appear at the gymnasium,' Philokles said.

'Read something before bed. I have never had a child of my own, lad, but when you speak of having a nap, I suspect that you have somewhere to go tonight. Hmm?'

Blushing, Satyrus hung his head, a complex rush of embarrassments flooding him.

'Remember what Diodorus said. I do not, note, order you to obey his stricture – only to understand that disobedience will have consequences, for you and for others. Understand me?'

Satyrus wasn't sure that he did understand, but he nodded anyway, gave a ridiculous smile and then bowed and retreated to his room, where he spent half an hour inspecting his tutor's comment from any number of angles.

Moonlight would have helped both his mood and the physical difficulty of moving around, but the moon was dark and the stars weren't much help as a thin haze made the night as black as a priest's cloak. Satyrus clutched his chlamys tighter and moved carefully back and forth at the base of the steps to the Temple of Poseidon. Deep in the temple precincts there was light – and the soft sound of voices – but out at the edge of the steps there was just a vague glow and the voices sounded like a haunting, and he was afraid. It was foolish for him to have come. He saw assassins in every movement.

Satyrus was beginning to feel a fool. He walked back and forth again, listening for any sign of another person – above him, or perhaps a boat out in the harbour? But he heard nothing but the cry of a late-night gull and somewhere, far off down the curve of the bay, two voices raised in angry confrontation.

He looked at the sky. If there had been stars – the right stars – he could have told the time. The dark sky mocked his ignorance, and the night seemed to move along far more slowly. Satyrus sat on a step, feeling some lingering warmth from the heat of the day. For the thousandth time he thought of Amastris, and then of Melitta, and then of the marvellous machine in Abraham's house – not that these thoughts were connected, but only that one followed another, and served to keep other thoughts at bay – just thinking that unlocked them like Pandora's cursed box, and then he was seeing Theo with the dirk in his eye, and then the Sauromatae girl he had killed, and then he shivered.

Why would Amastris leave him waiting? He rose to his feet and walked over to the sea wall. The two voices down the coast were gone. He could hear a kithara playing.

'My lord?' came a voice from the top of the steps.

Satyrus jumped. 'Yes?' he answered.

'I have a message, I think,' the voice said.

Satyrus couldn't see anything – the god might have been addressing him directly. That seemed unlikely, so Satyrus climbed the steps. He was careful, and he found that he had drawn his sword without thinking.

'I am here,' Namastis said. Closer, Satyrus could recognize the Greco-Aegyptian by the sound of his consonants.

'So am I,' Satyrus said. Now he could see the priest outlined by the pale luminescence of the white marble portico and the brightly coloured statues that glittered with gold even on the darkest night. 'Good evening, Master Namastis.'

'So!' Namastis said. He sounded amused, a far cry from his daytime subservience. 'I am asked to perform a task for the palace by a priest of Hathor, and look – I'm running an errand for a Greek.' He reached out and placed an oyster shell in Satyrus's hand.

'I can't very well read it in the dark,' Satyrus said.

Namastis made a tapping noise and then a scuffing, as if he was carrying a staff and tapping his sandals. 'I can light a torch in the outer sanctuary,' he said. 'Come.'

Satyrus climbed up to the portico behind the blackness that was the priest's cloak against the white of the steps, and then he paused in the incense-redolent interior. He didn't know his way and the priest vanished.

He wondered if this was an ambush. He was behaving like an idiot – in more ways than one. And Namastis – was it just coincidence? How would Amastris know of their connection? Satyrus grasped the hilt of his sword, and just then he heard a strong grunt as the Aegyptian blew hard on a spark, and in seconds a resin-impregnated torch burst into flame, with the heady smell of burning pitch.

The scenes of the temple interior sprang to life in the flickering light of one torch, but Satyrus glanced around, his head turning like a falcon's or a hunting owl's.

He sheathed his sword and his hand fell away from the hilt. He was, quite literally, starting at shadows.

He went over to the priest and stood with the torchlight at his right shoulder while he opened the shell and read the note.

Apologies.

Satyrus shrugged. 'Let that be a lesson to me,' he said.

The priest shook his head, saying nothing. Then he paused. 'I could offer you a cup of wine,' he said. 'We're not supposed to,' he added, in a tone that suggested that this rule was not widely obeyed.

Satyrus shook his head. 'No, thanks,' he said. 'I have been enough of a foolish boy for ten nights. I need to get some sleep before Philokles has me on the drill field in the morning.'

Namastis peered at him as if his eyes were weak. 'You are with the Spartan? In the Phalanx of Aegypt?' he asked. 'I hear news of you every day.' He smiled hesitantly.

Satyrus shrugged. 'If it is still there in the morning,' he answered.

Namastis nodded. 'Yes. The Macedonians didn't want to arm any mere *native* and now they seek to drive them all away.'

Satyrus had to laugh. 'I don't think it's an organized plot, friend,' he said. 'Macedonian arrogance is sufficient. Panion came today and in one speech undid four weeks of Philokles' work. And your countrymen aren't the world's best soldiers, either. Lots of obedience and not much spirit.'

Namastis rubbed his bare chin. 'Would a priest of Poseidon be welcome in your phalanx, lord?' he asked. 'Satyrus?' he said.

Satyrus shrugged. 'My father had priests in his phalanx. In Greek cities, many priests serve in the ranks just like other men.' He made a face. 'I have no idea what the tradition is here.'

'Then I will come tomorrow,' Namastis said.

*

457

As Philokles had predicted, fewer than half of the Aegyptians returned to the ranks the next day, and those that came were surly and often stood immobile instead of exercising.

'Why did you come, if not to work?' Philokles asked one. The man carefully grounded his pike and walked off.

'Look at the bright side,' Dionysius said. 'Now we have enough sarissas.' He shrugged. Dionysius was the least affected by the death of Theo. He'd never liked the boy and didn't even pretend to mourn him.

Satyrus was working with the young men, practising with the hoplite arms most of them had – heavy shields, a handspan larger than the Macedonian shields and much deeper, so that they protected the whole body; shorter spears with heavy heads and long bronze butt-spikes, like those carried by Leon's marines. They were practising a marine tactic – one that Philokles admired – a short burst of a charge from just three paces out from the enemy line. On board ship, this was all the deck space any marine *ever* had for a charge. On the battlefield, Satyrus reckoned, those three paces represented the length of the enemy sarissas.

He had bargepoles affixed to two-wheel carts so that the spears stood out two spans past the poles of the yokes. A line of these carts represented the enemy, and again and again the young men practised flinging themselves forward three steps, stooping low and shields held at an acute, uncomfortable angle – *slam* into the face of the carts, hopefully avoiding the tips of the bargepoles. And pushing the carts back.

Every fourth or fifth time, they managed it, and the carts rocked back. The other times, they tripped and fell, or someone got a bargepole in the head or lost his grip or the pace – ugly accidents, and reminders of what would happen when there were veteran killers at the other end of the bargepoles.

It was after one such disaster, with Theron berating a gaggle of Jews as if they were slaves and not the sons of four of the city's richest citizens, when Satyrus saw that all the Aegyptians were standing still, refusing any further orders. It was a curious form of rebellion – the phalanx was voluntary, and any of them might have grounded their pikes like the first rebel and walked away.

'Uh-oh,' Abraham muttered. He pushed the helmet back

on his head so that his arming cap showed white against his tawny skin.

'Why are we working so hard, if all the Gyptos are going to quit?' Dionysius asked. He took a pull from his elegant black canteen and then handed it around. It had straight unwatered wine.

Satyrus drank some anyway. 'If Philokles were here, he'd say that if they mutiny, that's their decision and not ours about defending our city.'

Dionysius looked far more capable than he usually did. He raised an eyebrow. 'That's a nice argument for the schoolroom, dear. But for a man who's considering facing a line of spears, it doesn't seem to me to carry much *weight*.'

Philokles was standing with his hands on his hips. His face was red, as if he was about to give way to anger. The Aegyptians moved as if a breeze was passing over a field of their own emmer, and a sigh escaped from their ranks, which were none too even.

And then a file of men in dark cloaks came on to the parade ground from the west, towards the temple district. Most of them – but not all – were of mixed birth. A few were marked by their features and their distinctive linen garments as Aegyptian priests. There were more than twenty of them, and they came to a dignified halt behind Philokles.

Namastis stepped out from the gaggle of priests. 'Lord Philokles? The temple district sends its tithe of men who are citizens to serve.'

Another sigh escaped from the men in the ranks.

Philokles returned the priest's bow. 'Twenty willing men delight me, but the favour of the gods would delight us all.'

An older man wearing the curious long garment favoured by servants of the older Aegyptian gods stepped forth. 'I may not serve under arms,' he said. 'But if I might address your men, you might find them better soldiers.'

Philokles frowned, and then stepped out of the command spot at the head of the square. 'Be my guest, priest,' he said politely. He walked over to where Theron and Satyrus were standing. 'Can't hurt us,' he said with a shrug. 'Perhaps he'll help. I know him – Temple of Osiris. A fine speaker.'

Theron shook his head. 'Strange, like all barbarians. Priests who won't fight?'

Satyrus furrowed his brow. 'You told me that in Corinth the priests of Aphrodite didn't fight, but pimped for their priest-esses who sold their bodies.'

Theron rubbed his nose and had the grace to look embar-rassed. 'Um – that's true.'

Philokles and Satyrus exchanged glances, even as the older priest of Osiris raised his arms and began to speak.

Some of the men in the ranks looked inattentive, bored or even angry to be addressed by the priest – but a great many more listened as if receiving the words of the great gods them-selves, and some fell to their knees until the priest was done speaking. One by one, five priests addressed them in Aegyptian. Then all five gave a benediction in Greek and in Aegyptian, and they went off to the side, where a stand of date palms offered some shade.

The priests of the Greek gods also offered benedictions, but when they were done, Namastis clapped his hands and slaves brought them shields and linen armour like the Aegyptians wore, and good Greek Pylos helmets straight from the forges.

Philokles looked around. 'Harmless,' he said. He rolled his shoulders as if taking the weight of his responsibility back. 'Might even do some good.'

It had done some good. If the natives had ever intended mutiny – and none of the Hellenes knew them or their language well enough to know – they meant no mutiny now. Most of them began to drill with something like enthusiasm, and despite the fact that they were a thousand men short of their required size since the day before, Philokles led them through exercise after exercise with something like enthusiasm himself, and Dionysius shook his head in admiration at their first successful wheel all the way through a circle – a difficult manoeuvre even for professionals. Of course it was easier with half the men, but the *spirit* of the whole was different – profoundly different.

When the sun touched the horizon, Satyrus sought out the priest of Poseidon. 'What did you do?' he said.

Namastis shook his head. 'I did very little. It had already been discussed – but meeting you last night stiffened my spine.'

'What did the priest of Osiris say? It was like magic!' Satyrus said.

'Yes!' Namastis replied. He glanced at Philokles. 'He told them to act like men. That the eyes of the entire lower kingdom were on them. That they, and they alone, stood between the old gods and destruction.'

Satyrus shook his head. 'Well, he's a fine old fellow.'

'Don't patronize me, Greek.' Namastis looked far more imposing in a linen corslet and a helmet than in his robes. 'And don't patronize him.'

Satyrus bit back an adolescent retort and nodded. 'I won't.'

Namastis shook his head. 'It's hard not to be touchy when you are half-caste. Listen – he also told them that Philokles is the very avatar of the war god – at least for now.'

'My tutor?' Satyrus laughed, but then he stopped. A great many scenes passed before his eyes in a few heartbeats. 'That's not altogether far from the mark,' he said.

Namastis glanced over Satyrus's shoulder to where a knot of fashionable young men waited for their friend but were too polite to break in on the two of them – or too disdainful of the Gypto. 'You Hellenes are great fools,' Namastis said. 'He wasn't speaking in allegory, Satyrus. He meant that Philokles is the very avatar of the god of war. Here. Now.' The priest picked up his spear and swung it carefully erect. The full length of the pike made any sudden movement perilous.

A prickle at the back of Satyrus's neck, and then the smell of a wet lion skin, and then nothing – a sort of absence of sense.

'You *are* god-touched,' Namastis said reverently. 'I forget Hellenes are not all fools. My apologies, lord.'

'Satyrus, not lord,' Satyrus said, offering his hand.

Namastis took it, and clenched it hard – too hard, but a good try. 'Men are hunting you,' he said suddenly.

'I know,' Satyrus said. He actually smiled, like the hero in an epic, although his smile was more self-mockery than dismissal of danger.

'No Aegyptian will help them,' Namastis said. 'That much I guarantee you. But the Macedonian faction intends your death. They have hired men. That is all we know.'

Satyrus favoured the hand all the way back to Leon's villa by the sea.

No more oyster shells came, and no fights with his sister, who was gone – visiting Amastris herself, or so Dorcus claimed. Satyrus went to sleep picturing elements of the drill.

And in the morning, the ranks were full. Two thousand Aegyptians, half-castes and Hellenes stood together in the ranks. Their armour was a patchwork, and their spears and sarissas were four different lengths, and most men had neither body armour nor cloaks – but the ranks were full.

Philokles asked the priest of Osiris and the priest of Zeus to address the men. Each offered a brief prayer. And then, when the priest of Zeus had intoned the hymn to the rise of day, Philokles gestured to Abraham.

'We have no priest of your god, son of Ben Zion,' Philokles said. 'Can you sing a hymn or some such? This taxeis will use every shred of divinity on offer.'

Abraham nodded. He was in the front rank, beyond Dionysius whose beauty included the kind of fitness that caused Philokles to put him in the front. He shuffled forward past Dionysius – no easy task with an aspis – and stood in front. In a deep voice he began a hymn – Hebrew, of course. Fifty voices picked it up. Some sang softly, as if embarrassed, and some carefully, as if forcing the words from their memories. But they sounded well enough, and they smiled self-consciously when finished – just as the Aegyptians and the Hellenes had done.

'If all the gods are satisfied, we need to do a great deal of work,' Philokles shouted.

For the first time, his words were greeted with the sort of spontaneous cheer he expected from good troops.

At supper, back at Leon's, Philokles shook his head. 'We were down,' he said. 'Now? I see a glimmer of that fickle creature, hope.'

Theron grunted and ate another helping of quail. 'When do

462

we march?' he asked. 'And will we carry the baggage?'

Philokles shrugged. 'I can't believe the delays. Ptolemy hasn't even decided on a strategy yet – he vacillates, so I'm told, between offence and defence, and he has twelve thousand slaves rebuilding the forts along the coast. And six thousand being gathered to support the army. We won't carry the baggage – but if we have a defensive campaign, these men will melt away, priests or no priests. And if the campaign flares into sudden battle before marching makes them hard – again, I dread it.' But after these words, he brightened. 'But I tell you, gentlemen – philosopher that I am, something changed today. I felt it. I, too, will go to my task with a lighter heart.' Philokles looked at Diodorus. 'When do we march, Strategos?'

Diodorus was lying with Sappho. He looked up. 'When Ptolemy is ready. When the storm breaks. When the Macedonian faction makes their move.' He spread his hands. 'Or the day after tomorrow. Is your taxeis worthy to stand in the line?'

'No,' Philokles said. 'But give me twenty days of marching, and I might speak otherwise.'

Diodorus shook his head. 'Ptolemy has all but given up. If Leon returned, we might act. All day long, Panion and the Macedonians of his ilk pour poison in his ears. I'm not sure that we're any better off for Stratokles being off the board.'

'If he is off the board,' Philokles said. 'The attack on Satyrus—'

'Might just have been the work of the Macedonians,' Diodorus said.

'Too well planned. Footpads. Stratokles.' Philokles flexed his muscles, reassured that they were returning. 'Trust me, Diodorus. I know what the man does. I did the same once.'

'For my part,' Satyrus said, 'I'd *rather* go and fight Demetrios than be afraid of going out of this house.'

'Ptolemy is afraid they'll sell him,' Diodorus said. 'Like Eumenes.' He finished his wine and lay on his back next to Sappho, shaking his head. 'Macedonians.'

A slave came in and whispered to Sappho, and she rolled over.

'Coenus sends that our guest is awake,' she said.

It took a moment for that information to penetrate the gloom of the dining hall.

'Gods,' Philokles said. And headed for the door.

Leosthenes returned to full consciousness without transition, Apollo having granted him life, or so it seemed to Satyrus. The scarred man lay on Coenus's spare couch and smiled at the men in the room.

'Friends,' he said.

Coenus held his hand. 'How did you come to serve that scum?'

Leosthenes shook his head. 'Stratokles? For all his failings, he is a patriot for Athens. I am an Athenian.'

Philokles shook his head. 'No wonder the Macedonians own us all, Leosthenes, if a man like you will serve a man like Stratokles because he is a *patriot*. He is a traitor twenty times over. And he's trying to kill Satyrus – that's *Kineas's son*.'

'Save your breath,' Leosthenes said. 'I will not defend him or Cassander either. I'm glad I have been taken by friends. And I tried to kill Kineas once myself – don't try that argument on me. Nor will I betray the men who served with me, either.' He managed a thin smile and shook his head. 'Stratokles thinks he's the smartest man in the world.'

Leosthenes was sinking again. Diodorus went and bent over him. 'Listen, Leosthenes – your precious Stratokles is getting ready to betray Cassander, I can smell it. What does that make him? We need to know where he is!'

Leosthenes shook his head. 'Glad to be taken by friends,' he said, and subsided into unconsciousness.

'Apollo!' Diodorus swore. 'Of all the useless fools to follow – and a man like Leosthenes, too!'

'It is because men like Stratokles can attract men like Leosthenes that they are dangerous. Coenus, he must be watched. We cannot have him go back to Stratokles now.' Philokles took a deep breath and met Diodorus's eye.

'If he went back, we could follow him,' Diodorus said.

Philokles shook his head. 'There are limits to the duplicity a man can practise and not be tainted,' he said. 'I have been past those limits and I will never go past them again.'

Diodorus nodded. 'I thought you'd say something like that. Athena send we march before long – the sooner we're out of this city and doing some honest fighting, the better for everyone.'

In the morning, Leon was back, and the house was full of sailors, and Satyrus found that despite his sister's problems, he had no trouble embracing Xeno like a long-lost brother.

'Demetrios has his army in Syria,' Leon said. 'He's building up supplies in Palestine and then he'll come for us. If he hadn't had his cavalry beaten up in Nabataea, he'd be here now and we'd be wrecked. As it is, we've hope.'

In whispers, Xeno related how the *Lotus* had ghosted up the Palestinian coast and seized a message boat.

'I'm off for the palace,' Leon said. 'Diodorus?'

The hipparch drank off his morning beer. 'I'm with you, brother. Listen – I take it he's coming by land?'

'Best I can tell,' Leon affirmed. 'How's Ptolemy?'

'Panicking,' Diodorus said, and then their voices vanished into the courtyard.

One hundred professional marines had a profound effect on the Phalanx of Aegypt, as they provided file-closers for every file and the drill smartened up immediately. And forty sailors joined them, most of them upper-deck professionals who owned some armour.

One of the sailors was Diokles. He attached himself to Satyrus as soon as he came on the parade square, displacing the Greek boy who stood in the second rank behind Satyrus with a polite nod and a gruff 'On your way, then.' The Greek, who'd been a little too shy of pushing forward for Satyrus, seemed happy to be moved to a place that was slightly less exposed.

Satyrus rammed his butt-spike into the sand and turned. 'Good to see you, by all the gods!' he said. He was surprised by the warmth of his own reaction.

So was Diokles, but he was visibly pleased. His hand clasp was firm. 'Thought I'd try my hand at being a gent,' he said with a smile. 'Your uncle Leon asked me to look after you,' he said.

'Really!' Satyrus said.

'Fighting-wise,' Diokles said. 'What did you think?'

'Shut up and listen!' Philokles bellowed, and they were back to drill. They faced to their spear side and they faced to their shield side, they changed grips on their spears and raised and lowered their shields, they marched to the sound of pipes and halted to the shrill blasts of a whistle. In the afternoon, a man was killed when they practised a full-out charge and he got a butt-spike in the face from an incorrectly lowered pike. Anyone who was not sobered by that death was affected when the Spartan stood them in ranks in the setting sun and marched them past the corpse.

Even Satyrus, whose body was at the peak of training, was ready to drop.

'We march the day after tomorrow!' Philokles roared. His voice carried easily – one of the reasons men trained in the arts of rhetoric. 'Phylarchs will attend me for instructions on what kit your men need to have. Water bottles! Hide or clay or bronze, I don't give a shit, but every man *must* have a water bottle. A spare cloak! Understand? The Macedonians will have shield-bearers to carry their kit. Most of us *won't*. That means we have to march light. Again – phylarchs will attend me. Very well – fall out by ranks and stack your sarissas. Carry on!'

Theron, who acted as Philokles' second, began falling out the ranks. This process prevented the men from tangling the long pikes and becoming injured while being dismissed – a real difficulty. Philokles gathered the three hundred men who led files, closed files or led half-files – sixteen men to the file – and read off for them a list of basic equipment every man had to have: wool stockings, heavy sandals, a water bottle, a spare cloak, net bags for forage and a scrip or pack for gear, and other things.

Satyrus and Abraham and many of the other phylarchs carried hinged wax tablets for notes, and they pulled out their styluses and copied the lists, but not all the phylarchs could write.

'I'll post it at the temples,' Satyrus said.

Theron, who had overseen the dismissal of the phalanx, shot him a grateful smile. 'That'll save a lot of crap, Satyrus, and no mistake. Make sure the priests know it, too – then men can ask for it.'

Abraham nodded. 'I'll take a copy for my father. He can see to it that a dozen copies go around the market.'

'Some men in my file may be too poor to afford all this,' one of the marines commented. 'They seem like good lads, but half of them don't even have sandals.'

Philokles shrugged. 'I have to try,' he said.

Abraham raised his hand. 'Sir, I think that many of the merchants would help equip men – from pride – if they were asked.'

Philokles laughed. 'Well, lad, you seem to have volunteered. Figure out a way to discover which men can't pay, and get them kit. Pick four men to help you.'

Abraham shook his head at Satyrus. 'Me and my big mouth,' he said, but he looked more happy than chagrinned. 'Busy?'

'I have to cover the temples,' Satyrus said.

Dionysius raised his hands in mock resignation. Then he smiled wickedly. 'Cimon's should donate!' he said. 'Perhaps we could have the words "House of a thousand blow jobs" embroidered on our armour.'

Abraham put a casual elbow in Dio's side and then caught him. 'That's enough from you. You *can* write, I assume? You're not just a pretty face?'

Dio made a moue. 'All I ever *wanted* was to be a pretty face,' he said. In fact, his face was red from sun and had the strange burn of a man who had been on parade all day in a helmet.

Satyrus took Diokles because the man was to hand and seemed determined to shadow him anyway. 'Can you write?' he asked.

Diokles nodded. 'Sure – hey, maybe not my place, but Hades – ain't we supposed to go straight back to your uncle's?'

Satyrus shook his head. 'Yes and no. Yes, we are – but this has to be done. Look, it's just a run to the temples.' He undid the wire that bound his tablets and handed a copy to Diokles.

'Take this to every temple on the south side. Make sure it is copied fair and that you find some priest who has read it.'

'You sound like a navarch I knew once,' Diokles said. He looked at the Alexandrion suspiciously, but it was late afternoon and the streets were full of men and women of every stratum – hardly a threatening crowd. 'All right, sir. Give it here. Where do I find you?'

'Temple of Poseidon, last one before the sea wall. On the steps.' Satyrus wanted to be off the street as much as Diokles wanted him off, so he put his head down and hurried through the errand, passing the list at every temple and watching as a clerk or an under-priest or an acolyte copied the list, bouncing up and down as he waited, watching the crowds from the relative invulnerability of many-stepped porticos.

The Temple of Poseidon was last, and he didn't see Namastis, which made sense as the young priest had drilled all day. But the priest who copied the list was thorough and interested, able to memorize without effort, and Satyrus found himself standing on the steps watching the crowds. There was no sign of Diokles – and then he saw the man, well down the street, crossing from the Temple of Athena to the Temple of Demeter.

The shrine of Herakles beckoned to him from across the avenue. He had the time.

Satyrus crossed the street as quickly as possible and went up the steps, ignoring some acquaintance who called his name. He gave his list to an acolyte to be copied and then stepped into the precinct of the temple, searched his bag for a silver coin and found one, and made a hasty but exact sacrifice under the gilt statue of the master pankrationist, left arm stretched forward, right arm back and holding a sword, the lion skin of shining gold covering his back. He felt nothing untoward, except that the eyes of the statue seemed to be upon him, and he dedicated his sacrifice to the dead boy, Cyrus – Theo would have his own sacrifices. Satyrus thought of the young man's eagerness to learn to sacrifice – it seemed as if that was so long ago, and he found that tears were running down his face.

Then he was back out of the precinct, and he went down the steps in a sombre mood.

'Master Satyrus!' called a voice, close at hand.

Satyrus felt that something was *wrong*. He felt as if the god had put a hand on his shoulder and turned him – indeed, he spun on the steps and stumbled when his right foot slipped off the marble step, and his side absorbed an impact – his ribs burned with fire. Only as the knife was withdrawn did he understand that he had been attacked.

'Hades!' a familiar voice cursed, and Satyrus got his hand on the attacker's elbow. They struggled for the knife, and they exchanged blows – Satyrus took a blinding blow from the top of his opponent's head and returned one with his fingers to his opponent's eyes, and then the man broke his hold in exchange for the loss of the knife and bolted down the steps.

Satyrus was bleeding from his side. He put a hand to it, and it came away covered with blood, and he felt queasy.

Diokles appeared at his side. 'I see him!' he said.

Satyrus managed to get to his feet. 'Follow him!' he said. 'See where he goes!'

Diokles hesitated. 'But—' he said.

'I'll be safe in the temple,' Satyrus said. Suiting the action to the word, he dragged himself up the steps, leaving a trail of blood.

Diokles hesitated another moment and then raced away.

Satyrus was helped by many hands. In the end they carried him into the precinct and laid him on a bench. His side hurt, but the doctor who appeared in moments shook his head.

'You're a lucky lad,' he said. 'Skidded off your ribs. It'll hurt for some days, but the bruise'll be worse than the cut.' He wrapped Satyrus in the temple's linen, and Hama came with four files of cavalry to escort him home.

Hama was silent all the way home. Satyrus assumed that somehow he was going to be blamed, but he had drawn the wrong conclusion.

'You're hurt!' Sappho said, when he came into the court-yard.

Diokles had managed to follow the would-be killer into the tannery district before he lost the man, and he stood in the middle of a dozen of Diodorus's cavalrymen, describing

469

the district while Eumenes of Olbia wrote his directions on a tablet.

'I recognized his voice,' Satyrus said. 'Remember Sophokles?'

Philokles smiled ruefully. 'Who could forget?' He narrowed his eyes. 'Really? Here?'

'Yes,' Satyrus said.

'Don't tell me!' Sappho put a hand to her throat. 'Where's Melitta?' She sent for Dorcus.

'Speaking of armour,' Diodorus said. He shrugged. 'This was supposed to be a dramatic moment, but I think my thunder has been stolen somewhat.'

Dorcus returned. 'In the bath, my lady,' she said, grim-faced.

Sappho took a deep breath and let it out. Then another.

Diodorus embraced his wife. 'I think we have to let Satyrus go his own way,' he said.

Sappho raised her head. 'Very well,' she said. 'How badly hurt are you, my dear? I assume that if you were dying, some-one would have told me.'

Satyrus managed a smile. 'It shocked me when it happened, but I assure you I've had worse in the palaestra.'

Eumenes stepped forward and saluted. 'Strategos? With fifty men, I think I could find him.'

'Hold that thought,' Diodorus said. 'Stay by me. I need to consult with Leon and with Philokles before I send a troop of cavalry into the streets, even for Stratokles.'

Satyrus hadn't seen Eumenes in weeks, and he shook hands with the youngest of his father's friends. 'The gods keep you well,' he said.

Eumenes grinned. 'The gods need some help with you!' he answered.

Diodorus stepped in. 'I have a small surprise for you, Satyrus.' He shrugged. 'I hope that you like it.' He led them all in from the courtyard.

In the main room there was an armour stand, and atop it was the helmet of silver that Demetrios had given Satyrus three years before. Now, under it, was a full-sized cuirass of tawed leather and alternating rows of silver and gilt-bronze scales –

every scale a small disk, so that the whole looked like the scales on a fish. There was a gilt and silver vambrace for the sword arm and a pair of rich greaves.

'I wish that Melitta had as good,' Satyrus said. 'Oh, that's beautiful, Uncle. Who made it? Hephaistos?'

'Much like,' Diodorus agreed, pleased that his gift was so well received.

Philokles came in, still in armour, and glanced at the display. 'Goodness, Achilles is going to fight right next to me. Young man, see that you don't blind me.' He turned to Diodorus and Eumenes. 'So?'

'Leon's man followed the assassin,' Diodorus said.

'I think I can find him,' Eumenes said. 'I need fifty men.'

Philokles shook his head. 'This whole city is right on the edge of a violent explosion,' he said. 'The news isn't public, but two of our senior officers have fled to Demetrios – this morning. And just now, Ptolemy announced that he will march. We'll set off tomorrow – the Phalanx of Aegypt at the rear.' He smiled grimly. 'If we send ten files of cavalry into the market, the war will start right here.'

Diodorus nodded. 'I agree. What do we do?'

Philokles looked at Satyrus. 'We ask our Aegyptian friends to find them for us. The tannery district is almost entirely native. The native populace is so disaffected with the Macedonians tonight that they may rise against Ptolemy himself – foolish as that would be, that's where they are. Satyrus? Any ideas?'

Satyrus was looking longingly at his new armour. 'Namastis – the priest of Poseidon. He'll help. I wish I knew where to find him, but the temple is the place to start.'

Accompanied by Diokles and a dozen cavalry troopers whose military gear was inadequately disguised by borrowed civilian cloaks, Satyrus went to the Temple of Poseidon.

Namastis greeted him from the top of the steps, as if they'd made an appointment. 'I heard what happened!' the Aegyptian said.

'That's what I'm hoping you'll help with,' Satyrus said. 'Listen – my uncles say our city is on the edge of civil war – Aegyptians against Macedonians.'

Namastis's face closed. 'I wouldn't know anything about that, lord.'

'Satyrus! Call me Satyrus, by the gods! By Poseidon Earth-shaker, priest, this is about our city! Your city and my city! Men are manipulating the thetes. Alexandria cannot stand without Lord Ptolemy. He is *not* the enemy. The enemy is Antigonus One-Eye and his army – if they come here, they will *sack the city* no matter what promises he makes.'

Namastis nodded. 'I know that. But desperate men make poor choices.'

Satyrus shook his head. 'These men who attacked me—'

'Who are they? And why? No man of Aegypt would do it. I have let it be known – that is to say, it is known that you are a friend.' Namastis looked deeply disturbed by his slip.

Satyrus ignored it. 'They serve One-Eye. Understand?'

The priest shook his head. 'No, I do not understand. Explain it to me.'

Satyrus had to smile. 'To be honest, I'm not positive that I understand myself. One-Eye is enemies with Cassander, the regent of Macedon – yes? But it appears that they have a secret agreement – to give Aegypt to One-Eye.'

'Yes – that's a common enough rumour. Why kill you?' Namastis asked.

Satyrus shrugged. 'I'm an old enemy,' he said. 'My father and mother left me a claim to be king of the Bosporus.'

'The king of the grain trade!' Namastis nodded. 'Ahh! But then, you are no more an Alexandrian than the Macedonians!'

'What – do I seem to you to be an ingrate? A barbarian? I am a *citizen*. No matter what my birth. Don't be as bad as the Macedonians, priest. So what if I was born somewhere else?'

Namastis grinned – the first honest display of emotion that Satyrus had seen him show. 'So,' he said. 'And so. How can this poor and unworthy priest help you, King of the Grain Trade?'

Satyrus explained it to him. The priest listened carefully, and then nodded.

'There are men who stand close to you all day,' he said. 'And you don't know their names, or where they live. But they will spend the night searching on your behalf. Does that tell you something?'

'It tells me that I should learn their names,' Satyrus said.

Namastis grunted. 'That would be a start,' he said. He produced an oyster shell from under his robes. 'I'm not sure that I should give you this, given what you have told me. Except that now I understand why the lady of Heraklea has to do with an upstart Alexandrian gentleman.'

Satyrus snatched the oyster shell, the conflicting emotions of the last one banished.

'I am to say, *tonight*.' Namastis raised an eyebrow. 'I won't ask if you will go.'

Satyrus took a deep breath. 'That's right, friend,' he said. 'Don't ask.'

At the base of the steps he looked out over the sea wall and thought about his sister. *Why can't you be like this all the time?* she'd asked at sea. He nodded and made the sign of Poseidon.

Eloping wasn't as difficult as it might have been for another girl. First, Melitta wasn't afraid of the world outside Sappho's women's quarters. She knew the streets and she had clothes in which she did *not* look like a rich Greek girl. Second, she had weapons and a strong desire to use them. Third, she had somewhere to go. Xeno had offered to meet her and be her escort, but that's not what she wanted.

She dropped off her balcony on to the beach and froze as she heard movement to her left. Barefoot in the sand, she moved slowly and carefully back into the shadow of the house, at the same time drawing her Sakje akinakes.

She saw her brother drop to the sand from his own balcony and she almost laughed aloud – but she couldn't be *sure* that they were on the same side when it came to her running away. She wondered where he was going, and then she caught a glint of gold. He was well dressed. *Amastris.*

She gave the superior smile of the sister, crouched down on her haunches and waited for him to vanish up the beach. When he was gone, his footsteps lost in the noise of drunken sailors, she picked up her armour and the leather wallet that held the rest of her boy's clothes, and ran off along the strand, past the beached squadrons of Ptolemy's fleet until she reached some lower and thus less opulent houses, where she cut inland. She leaned against a stable to clean her feet before pushing them into Thracian boots. Other expeditions in boy's clothes had taught her that her hands and feet gave her away more than her breasts – carefully bound and now almost flat under her Sakje jacket.

Just short of the northern agora, she stopped, straightened her clothes and began to walk purposefully, like a man in a hurry. Not like a girl running away.

The agora was busy, despite the darkness, and she wanted to linger. There were torches everywhere and the heady odour of burning pitch filled the air along with the reek of patchouli and the smell of burning garlic and unwashed people. She wanted to be part of *everything*.

The night market was a strange world where the thieves and the pornai and the beggars ruled, where soldiers were customers and slaves paid to be entertained. In some ways, it was the daytime world stood on its head, as Menander had so rightly observed. Menander was sometimes a denizen of the night market himself, and his plays were full of night-market expressions.

She bought a skewer of meat – probably rats or mice – from a girl no older than five, who took the money with the concentration a young child gives to an adult task, while her mother serviced a noisy soldier in the booth behind her.

'I couldn't – I had to come,' Xeno said beside her, and she looked up into his eyes.

'You found me in the night market? You must be part dog!' she said. She ought to have been angry, but instead she squeezed his hand.

They wandered from stall to stall, paid a blind singer with a kithara for his songs and watched a troupe of slave acrobats perform for free what their master charged heavily for them to perform at a symposium or a private house.

'The archer-captain is sitting over there with his mates, drinking wine and telling lies,' Xeno said with a smile. 'I told him a bit about you – not about you being a girl, of course. About how you were small and you can shoot.'

She kissed him on the nose, as she had seen boys do with their men, even in public. 'I take back all those things I say about you behind your back,' she said.

Xeno winced. There was some fear in him, some hesitation, and it annoyed her.

'Let's go and meet this captain,' she said.

They wandered across the agora, avoiding a deadly brawl so sudden and explosive that Xeno was splattered in blood and Melitta found that she had her akinakes in her fist before she thought to draw it.

'This your little archer, Master Xenophon?' asked a deep voice, while Xeno was still wiping the blood off his face. He was looking at the body as if he'd recognize the victim any moment, but he turned.

'Captain Idomeneus!' he said. 'My friend—'

'Bion,' Melitta said, offering her hand to clasp the archer's. He was a Cretan by his accent, and he looked like a caricature of Hephaestos – his face was handsome enough, but he was short and wide, with powerful arms and short legs. Indeed, he only topped her by a couple of fingers.

She must have looked at him too long, because he gave a fierce grin. 'Like what you see, boy? My dick is short and broad, too. Hah!' He had a mastos cup in his hand, and he drank wine from it. 'No offence, boy. You can shoot?'

'Anything,' Melitta said. 'I've been shooting since I was four years old. I can hit a target seven times out of ten at half a stade. I can—'

'You can string a bow? Avoid bragging, boy, it's too fucking easy for me to test you tomorrow. What kind of bow do you have? Let me see it.' He didn't seem drunk, but a whole life spent with Philokles had taught her that some men could operate efficiently through a haze of wine.

She took her bow from its gorytos and handed it over.

He whistled. 'Sakje? Maybe you ain't so full of shit, boy. It's your size. Made for you?'

She nodded. 'Yes,' she said.

475

'You Sakje, boy?' he asked. 'People going to come looking for you?' There was something in his tone that she liked – a firmness that showed his command skills. So she told him the truth.

'I have family here,' she said. 'They might look for me. Even if they find me, I doubt they'll make a fuss.'

'Rich kid?' Idomeneus asked.

Melitta shrugged. 'What do you think?' she asked, trying to roughen her voice and sound tough.

The Cretan grabbed her by the ear and pulled her face close to a torch. She flinched, grabbed his hand in a pankration hold and rotated his arm, using the hand as purchase.

'Whoa!' the Cretan called. 'Hold!'

She let him go. He rubbed his shoulder. 'I think you speak like a boy who had a tutor,' he said. 'I don't want to waste my time visiting magistrates and archons. And,' he shrugged, his eyes flashing in the torchlight, 'if I didn't know better, I might wonder if you were a girl. Not that I particularly give a shit, you understand. Just that if an outraged father or brother kills me, I'll haunt you. You as good as that bow says you are?'

'Yes,' Melitta said.

The Cretan shrugged. 'Okay. I'm desperate, which this young animal has no doubt told you. We need archers the way a man in the desert needs water. You're on. If your father comes for you, though, I'll hand you over in a heartbeat. Understand me, *boy*?'

Melitta stood straighter. 'Yes, sir!'

'Pluton, none of my boys call me "sir".' Idomeneus grinned, his teeth glinting in the torchlight. 'Can I buy you two a cup of wine to seal the bargain?'

Melitta wanted to accept, but Xeno shook his head. 'I thought I'd go to the slave auction,' he said.

Melitta flinched. 'You know how Uncle—' She reconsidered her sentence. 'What do *you* want with a slave?' she asked.

Idomeneus gave her a steady look. Xeno glanced around nervously. 'I want a shield-bearer,' he said. 'I have all my share from the ship. All the rich boys have a shield-bearer.'

'A fool and his money,' the Cretan muttered. 'Listen, boys –

never buy anything at the night auction. Half those poor bastards were just kidnapped off the street, and the other half are shills who follow you home just to help their allies rob your house.'

'I can't afford anything at the day market,' Xeno said. He was avoiding Melitta's glares.

'Go without,' the archer-captain said, with all the firmness of age and experience. 'Oh, fine. I'll go with you – otherwise you'll both end up on the block. Argon?' he called, and another Cretan stepped away from a big fire, downed the wine in a cheap clay cup and handed it to another man.

'With you, humpback. Who's this boy?' Argon was taller and handsomer and didn't look very bright.

'Bion – just joined. We're going to the night auction. Come and cover my arse.' Idomeneus grinned and the two men slapped each other's backs.

The four of them made their way to the auction, where a deep throng of onlookers – many of them slaves themselves – gathered to bid on the dregs of the dregs of the city of Alexandria. Melitta was disgusted by the whole process – she shared her uncle's views on every aspect of the trade. Most of the people on auction were hopeless – the kind you saw on the fringe of the agora in the daytime, begging and stealing, many scarcely capable of speech. They were scrawny, ill fed, most had few teeth and all flinched whenever a free man came too close. The only healthy, normal-looking specimens were children, and their version of normality was abject terror at being sold. One boy sobbed incessantly.

What kind of parent sells her child? Melitta asked in her head, but the answer was plain before her, as two of the children were auctioned off by a toothless bastard with an evil smile. The two children he sold were bruised and silent, watching the torch-lit crowd with all the interest of dead souls watching the living.

Melitta found that her right thumb was rubbing the hilt of her long knife. She wanted to kill the man.

The next lot was a single boy, the one who kept sobbing. Under his dirt and his scrunched, unhappy face he was healthy, blond and larger than most of the other children.

Xeno was shifting nervously, aware, like most boyfriends, that he had annoyed his lover, and unable to think of a way to make it right without giving up his precious project of buying a slave.

Melitta could read him so easily that it hurt her – hurt her opinion of him. But without weighing the morality of her actions, she smiled up at him. 'Buy that boy,' she said. 'He looks strong enough.'

'My aspis is taller than that kid!' Xeno said, but he looked at the boy again. 'He's whimpering.'

'Zeus Soter, he's big, and in a few years he'll be strong. Besides, he's just the sort a certain uncle of ours tries to rescue. Don't be a git, Xeno.' Melitta tried to whisper, but the crowd was hooting for the next lot to be stripped – two whores being sold for debt.

Idomeneus caught something of what she said, because he leaned in. 'That boy? He looks all right. I'll go and look him over.' The Cretan shrugged. 'Boy that size is like having a kid, though. Have to teach him everything – but if he lives, a good investment.'

The crowd was so anxious to see the pornai that the hawker was having trouble getting bids on the blond child.

'I fucking *hate* seeing kids sold,' Argon said. He spat at the man who had sold the two children, now standing at arm's length from them counting his silver coins. The man felt the moisture and whirled in anger.

Argon didn't move. 'Fuck yourself, clod.'

The clod flinched and backed away. Argon was a big man.

Melitta nodded. 'I wanted to kill him,' she said.

'Really?' Argon asked. 'Want to?'

Melitta realized then that she was in a different world – that Argon meant just what he said.

'Three silver owls,' Idomeneus said. 'Argon, don't make trouble. Bion, did you stir him up, the stupid lout? Argon, take a deep breath and *back off*.' The Cretan shook his head. 'He's the kind of man who makes other people call us *Cretans*.'

Xeno handed the officer three big silver coins, and Idomeneus made them vanish. 'Never flourish money like that at night,' he said. 'You boys should get some training in real life. Anyway, boy's yours.' He reached out and took a leash from the hawker. Xeno took it and pulled, but the boy didn't move, and the crowd was howling for the prostitutes to be stripped.

Melitta put her arm around the boy's shoulder. 'Come on, boy,' she said.

He sobbed and hunkered down.

Idomeneus picked him up as if he was made of feathers. 'Let's go somewhere bright and quiet and look at what you bought,' he said. 'Camp.'

Satyrus dropped from his balcony to the beach with a minimum of fuss, except for the pain in his side over his ribs, which burned anew as he hung from his fingers for a moment. Then he gathered the bundle he'd thrown from the balcony moments before and sprinted off down the beach, the sound of his feet covered by the shouts of the men and women on the beach.

The *Golden Lotus* was stern-first on the beach between the *Hyacinth* and the *Bow of Apollo*, her bow awash, ready for action in minutes, and her crew were drinking and enjoying the company of hundreds of Alexandria's waterfront whores, who had turned the beach into an outdoor market, with wine and food and other delights for the thousands of oarsmen from Ptolemy's fleet.

Satyrus had no difficulty slipping through them in a plain cloak, ignoring a few offers of companionship and his own sense of what he *ought* to be doing, and seizing hold of the rope that led to the ship's boat, moored alongside the oar box. He pulled off his boots and climbed aboard, loosed the rope and rowed away.

Satyrus rowed across the harbour in the light of a new moon, the upside-down crescent that the Sakje and the Aegyptians both called the 'maiden with her legs spread'. Whatever powers Sophokles and Stratokles possessed, Satyrus didn't think they could track him across the harbour.

He rowed right past the guard post at the palace without a challenge – not the first time – and coasted silently into the tiny harbour, scarcely larger than a courtyard, where Ptolemy's own barge loaded and unloaded. What he was doing was insane, but he was smiling, for the first time in days.

Her directions were specific – he was to come to the gate. Amastris had no way of knowing that the front gate full of Macedonian guards was the last place he wanted to be. He moored his boat at the trade dock and climbed the ladder to the pier, which was empty. Ptolemy had problems of his own – he was not going to fill his palace full of Foot Companions the night before he marched. Satyrus had bet on it, and his bet was coming up.

At the top of the ladder, he stripped off his chiton and pulled on the dun chlamys of a palace slave. Slaves seldom wore a chiton. He looked longingly at his sword, and then tossed it on top of his chiton. One thing no slave ever had was a weapon. Barefoot like a slave, he stole into the palace.

No one challenged him. There were slaves in every corridor, but they ignored him, although he got enough glances to see that many of them knew he was not one of them. Neither, however, did they seem inclined to betray him.

He passed through the court and the megaron, carrying a wine pitcher he found on a chest, and then he went out of the main entry under the wall painting of Zeus. He left the wine pitcher in the entryway and walked with his head bowed across the great courtyard towards the main gate.

The gate guard tonight were Cavalry Companions – the ruler's own Hetairoi, and thus men he could have trusted. Many of them were friends of Diodorus, and although most were Macedonians, their fates were so tied to the house of Ptolemy that they would never betray him – or, by extension, Satyrus. He sighed for all his extra effort, and in between the beginning and end of that sigh, he spotted a slender shadow amidst the pillars and scaffolding of the new gate.

A man on guard laughed bitterly.

'Or we'll all die,' he said, and his words carried clearly across the night.

Satyrus moved as quietly as if he were hunting ibex in the south, or deer on the Tanais. Twice, his bare feet touched gravel and he had to move yet more carefully – and then he was in the shadow of the new portico. In crawling under the edge of the scaffold, he managed to get sand under his bandage.

Nonetheless, he was able to come up to the pillars without being discovered, and he reached out just as she turned.

'Don't scream,' he said.

She opened her mouth, put a hand on his chest and then put her mouth up to his. 'You came!' she breathed.

Her kiss was everything he remembered, and nothing,no shred of conscious thought, entered his head for many heartbeats. She kissed him for so long that he breathed the air from her lungs, and she took it back from him, and then she leaned back against the pillar as if all the strength was gone from her legs.

'You are *naked*,' she said.

'I am pretending to be a slave,' he answered. 'Besides, my nudity shows my physique, and my physique shows that I am ready to do my duty as a citizen.' Gods – he was parroting Philokles in the middle of kissing Amastris.

'It shows more than that,' she said. She ran a finger down his chest. 'How did you get here?' she asked, but her tongue didn't let him answer, and her hand closed over his manhood, and she laughed into his kiss, a low laugh full of promise. Then, before things got out of her control, she took him by the hand and led him back, away from the gate, screened by the line of scaffolding, until they slipped by a pair of torch-bearers and under the columns of the main wing of the palace.

'This is where you first kissed me,' she said. That seemed to demand certain actions, and then they were moving again. Just the sight of her gold-sandalled feet seemed the most erotic thing he'd ever seen, and he followed her in a daze until they emerged from the line of pillars.

'The gardens,' she said, as they passed between the gateposts of entwined roses.

An odd, observant part of his mind noted that she knew the gardens very well, as she led him past the maze to an arbour adorned with a statue of a nymph – possibly Thetis of the glistening breasts.

'I never thought that you would actually come,' she said into his ear, and then licked it.

Satyrus picked her up and carried her to the bench.

'Put me down!' she said, but her voice was soft.

Satyrus pulled the golden pin that held the shoulder of her dress and began to kiss down her neck, over her shoulder, and without pause up the curve of her breast, even as he sat carefully on the bench. Training was good for many things.

'Oh!' she said. 'Satyrus – no. Oh, I never thought that you would come.'

'No?' he asked, raising his head.

Her eyes sparkled in the near dark, reflecting distant torchlight like a thousand stars. 'No,' she breathed. 'Not that sort of no. Or perhaps – I don't know. Oh, my dear.'

He straightened.

She drew him down for a kiss, and wriggled off his lap on to the bench. 'Where's my pin?' she asked.

He produced it, and she carefully thrust it through her gown without repinning her shoulder, and then she turned back to him. 'I don't want to lose anything,' she said, her eyes as big and deep as night itself. Then she unpinned the other shoulder and put the pin in the same place, and turned to him with a smile that took his breath away. 'Now,' she said. 'Gold pins do not grow on trees.'

The sun streaked the horizon as he rowed back, his mind buzzing, his shoulders curiously tired.

'Make it possible for Ptolemy to give us to each other,' Amastris had said. That phrase filled his head, and he rowed across the harbour at a speed that might have won a race.

The beach was silent, except for the snores of the oarsmen and their companions. A pair of women bathed in the sea as he rowed up, and one of them rose out of the water. 'Aphrodite,' she called. 'Coming out of the sea just for you!'

Satyrus laughed. 'I have nothing left to give that lovely goddess,' he said, and both the girls laughed. 'Nor have we,' they called.

His good humour lasted until he climbed into his room, where Philokles sat by his empty bed.

'Where the *fuck* have you been?' the Spartan asked. And

without listening to an explanation, Philokles said, 'We were attacked last night.' He shrugged. 'I thought you were taken. Dead.'

'I'm sorry,' Satyrus said.

'Dorcus is dead. Nihmu has a knife wound in her shoulder. Three men – in through the women's quarters.' The Spartan shook his head. 'Gods – so you were gone all night – and Melitta too, unless her note is forged. She says she has eloped with the god of war, so Stratokles failed by the will of the gods.'

Satyrus ducked out of his room and down the hall, scattering servants. He went into Sappho's wing, past the guard. 'Auntie?' he called.

Sappho emerged in a Persian robe, slapped him and then embraced him. 'You were with a girl!' she said. 'Is this what we taught you? You smell of sex. You little *fool*!' she said, but she hugged him all the tighter.

Satyrus wondered why he ever thought that he could get away with anything.

'That's quite the expensive scent,' Kallista said from behind Sappho. 'Were you with Phiale, by any chance? Why didn't we think of that?'

He shook his head. 'I'm so sorry!' he said.

'Now, if we could recover your sister, I could stop worrying,' Sappho said.

Melitta lay under the stars, her two men's cloaks crossed over her and her legs entwined with Xeno's. His new boy lay on the other side, full of soup, asleep.

The boy was a sadder case than Melitta had guessed – mother dead, father dead – killed by their own *owner*. Melitta thought about the boy's story, trying to piece together a six-year-old's account of his life. Something rang – something was trying to fit with the rest of her head, like a piece in a mosaic.

Xeno was too adoring, and in some ways his adoration was more difficult than anything, but she had shot ten bullseyes out of ten at fifty paces by torchlight, and even the archer-captain of the *toxotai* was impressed with her – him. She had a place among the archers who were training to face Demetrios's elephants. Xeno's adoration seemed a small price to pay.

Melitta wondered what her brother was doing. In her rush to get free of the smothering confines of Leon's house, she hadn't thought about what it would be like to be separated from him, despite his many failings. He was, after all, her twin. Where had he gone?

Xeno was already snoring. She smiled at him – the bulk of him so familiar and so unfamiliar – and smiled at the thought that none of the other soldiers considered that there was anything remarkable in their sharing blankets and cloaks. She wondered how long she could keep up her role as a man.

As long as she could.

22

The army of Aegypt was supposed to begin to march with the dawn. Their departure was marked with riots and protests in addition to all the usual difficulties, and the sun crossed the height of the sky before the cavalry had marched. The baggage train of wagons, carts, donkeys and porters filled the road before the first squadron departed, and there were more and more non-combatants with every unit. The feeling in the column was ugly, and the feeling in the streets of the city was worse.

The Foot Companions were rumoured to have mutinied in their barracks, but they did march – sixteen files deep, with shield-bearers sandwiched between the files of soldiers, so that the men walked unencumbered while their slaves carried their armour, their weapons and their food. Unlike the cavalry, many of whom had worn their best for the departure, partly to make a show and partly to overawe the populace, the Foot Companions disdained to do the same. They walked off in dusty red chitons, grumbling. There were gaps in their ranks, and rumour said that some men had deserted, or worse.

The other taxeis also marched, each body with two thousand men formed four deep in huge long files, followed by carts and slaves. Only lucky men in these less prestigious formations had a shield-bearer. Again, there were gaps – files where a man or two were missing. Rumours swept the column that there was a plot against Ptolemy – that the Macedonians would rise and murder him – that Aegyptians would murder him – wilder and wilder stuff.

The Phalanx of Aegypt continued to drill on their parade near the sea. At the head of the parade was their equipment. Every man had a bundle to carry, carefully tied, and the phylarchs worked their way down their files, inspecting every man's campaign gear before passing their files on to the captains who inspected them again. When they were inspected and passed, which took until noon, with the poorer men scurrying to the market and back for last-minute donations, they stacked their gear at the head of the square and did drill until the shadows began to gather, and then Diodorus appeared.

'The strategos of the rearguard!' Philokles said.

'The very same,' Diodorus replied, saluting. 'We wouldn't even make it to a campsite tonight, my friend,' he said, pointing at the bundles. 'Can your men camp here? On the parade?'

Philokles shrugged. 'I expected nothing less,' he said.

Satyrus stepped up by Diodorus's leg. 'All day we've heard rumours,' he said. He was light-headed with lack of sleep. 'What's happening?'

'The mutineers have gathered,' Diodorus said, but his eyes were on Philokles and not his nephew. 'As we discussed, eh, brother?'

Philokles gave a strange half-smile. 'Just as we planned.' He saluted and then waved at Rafik, his trumpeter, who came at a run. He turned to Satyrus. 'Lad, get Abraham and tell him to send for the food we discussed. Rafik, sound "Phylarchs to the front".' The call rang out, and then Philokles bellowed, 'On me!'

Satyrus found himself teaching a strange mix of men how to cook over an open fire. Most were city dwellers with no more knowledge of how to cook than they had of how to sleep comfortably on the bare ground. As he discussed the best mix of cheese and barley in the wine and water, the merits of an egg dropped in the mess, and the taste of the result with a hundred new mess cooks, he also gathered that the men were on edge – excited, too. Something was in the wind.

When the sun's long rays welcomed the evening, he found Philokles standing at his elbow, eating a bowl of barley soup and chewing on a piece of fish. 'Not bad, Phylarch. Your men eat well.'

Satyrus grinned. 'Don't look at me. Diokles brought spices – pepper! Who brings pepper to war?'

'Me,' Diokles said. 'Bread and olive oil, Strategos?'

Philokles pressed close to his student. 'Diodorus has sent Eumenes into the southern quarter with guides that Namastis

provided,' he said. 'In an hour we'll know one way or another.'
He kept his voice low. 'Your sister – gods only know how
– sent a note with a slave boy to Leon. The slave boy told us
where Stratokles is – he and all the Macedonians who are bent
on mutiny have gathered together. They probably mean to attack the palace.' He looked around, ate a mouthful of soup and
then, seeing the confusion on Satyrus's face, raised an eyebrow.
'It's Stratokles, lad!'

Satyrus nodded, fatigue forgotten. 'May I come?' he asked.

'If the quarry is all in one place – if our information is
right – we'll strike tonight. I mean to use some of our men
– Aegyptians and Hellenes together.'

Diokles grinned. 'Blood 'em a little? That's the spirit.'

'So that's why we stayed behind!' Satyrus said.

'Hmm. More of an effect than a cause, lad. Good soup. Pick
three men and join me at the head of the square in an hour
– swords and shields only.'

'Yes, sir!'

It was full dark by the time they were in the southern quarter. The
moon provided some light, and there were guides – Aegyptians,
often men from the phalanx that Satyrus recognized. More than
a few of them took his hand and shook it, or pressed it to their
lips. He didn't understand why he had their devotion – but he
did. That had a taste more bitter than sweet.

The tannery stank – the smell was so bad that men sneezed
and spat.

'Silence!' Philokles whispered. 'Wait until you smell the
dead on a battlefield!' He had Xeno with him, and Xeno was
holding a small child by the hand.

Satyrus clasped hands with his friend. 'Who's the kid?'

'I bought a shield-bearer,' Xeno said. He looked pained. 'He
knew how to find that Athenian. Tyche.'

The boy was trembling. Satyrus knelt down next to the boy.
'What's your name?' he asked.

The blond boy turned his head away and hid in the folds of
Xeno's chitoniskos.

'Satyrus, your sister is serving as an archer,' Xeno said.

'Sappho will kill her,' Satyrus said. He shrugged. Every time he looked at the head of the alley, his stomach turned over, and the daimon of combat was starting to sing in his ears, and his hands shook. Satyrus had no idea what his tutor's plan was. He led his file where he was told, to the back gate of a warehouse, where he saw Hama, an under-officer of Diodorus's hippeis, waiting with another armoured man.

Hama touched his brow when he recognized Satyrus. 'Lord,' he whispered.

'What are we doing?' Satyrus asked, because Philokles had vanished into the moonlit dark, Xeno and the child trailing along.

Hama shrugged. 'When the trumpet sounds, we charge that gate,' Hama said. He shrugged again. 'Diodorus says – prisoners.' Hama showed Satyrus that he had a Persian horseman's mace. 'So I brought this.'

The night was full of men. Satyrus thought that Philokles must have brought half the phalanx, with the other half acting as guides – Ares and Aphrodite, as Diodorus liked to say. With the dismounted cavalrymen, there were two thousand soldiers waiting in the dark.

Philokles reappeared with his trumpeter, the Nabataean youth called Rafik. Xeno and the child were gone.

'What are all these men for?' Satyrus asked.

'I'm using a hammer to crack an egg,' Philokles said. 'It's a good strategy to use, if you have the option. Put another way, more is more.'

Satyrus was going to ask another question, but Philokles put out his hand. 'Steady – we're going before they see us. Ready?'

Satyrus nodded.

Philokles raised his hand, and Rafik put the trumpet to his lips.

Satyrus ran for the gate with Hama. Behind them, a dozen phalangites with a log jogged along, and Satyrus felt foolish as he stepped clear to allow the ram to hit the gate. It blew open as if Zeus had struck it with a thunderbolt.

The courtyard was full of men – dozens of men, perhaps hundreds, some in armour, all with weapons. They might have been formidable, except that they were under attack from *thousands* of men coming out of the dark, and they were taken completely by surprise.

That didn't affect Satyrus, who was the third man through the back gate. The first was Philokles, who had a shield, a huge Greek aspis, and a club, and the second was Hama with his mace. Each felled a man, and then Satyrus was facing a panicked Macedonian who was screaming – not that Satyrus was listening. He punched his shield into the man and knocked him down, then headed for the building.

He fought a second man just heartbeats later – turning the man away from Philokles and then stabbing him in the chest as he tried to fight. Most of the men were trying to surrender, but the phalangites had their blood up and they were breaking heads.

Satyrus hesitated, shouting at men he knew to spare the men surrendering, and Hama stepped in front of him and burst open the main door with his shoulder and got an arrow in his shield, but this didn't slow Hama by a pace – he put the shield up and pressed forward, virtually blind, his speed a wicked surprise to the man behind the door. Then he stopped, quick as a cat, and cut *under* his shield, breaking knees and shins.

Satyrus followed Hama through the door. An arrow whispered evilly by his face and then he was facing a rush from a side room – despite his strength, he was shoved back against a wall, and then the man who slipped past him screamed as one of Satyrus's Aegyptian rear-rankers spitted him on his long knife.

'Thanks!' Satyrus said.

The man grinned and shook his head. 'I'm with you, lord!' he said. Then Diokles pushed forward past the Aegyptian.

'Lost you in the press,' Diokles said.

They entered the side room, some kind of wine shop, and two more men rushed them from behind the trestle tables that marked the landlord's portion of the shop. One man had an axe, but he hesitated when Satyrus faked a cut at his head, and then he was dead. The other man fell to his knees.

Diokles killed him anyway, running the sharp point of his kopis into the man's neck.

At the back of the shop were stairs up to the exedra, or so Satyrus assumed. The front door of the shop burst open, and there was Diodorus in full armour.

'It's me!' Satyrus shouted.

'Hold!' Diodorus bellowed. He came in, and a dozen troopers came in behind him. Satyrus knew most of them.

Now or never. Easy enough to hesitate and let them go first – Diodorus or Eumenes, perhaps, or Diokles or his nameless Aegyptian file-partner. Fuck that. 'Follow me!' Satyrus yelled, and went for the stairs. He roared, and his fear fell away. Inside, he laughed with triumph.

There was an archer on the stairs. Satyrus got his shield up and felt the blow as the arrow went into his shield, popping through the bronze face and the papyrus leaves and the poplar wood to prick his arm. He roared again, banished the flood tide of fear and his legs powered him up. He thrust his shield into the archer and his sword under it, over it, everywhere until the blood flew and the man fell – a nameless stranger, not the Athenian doctor who he saw in nightmares but some poor mercenary, toppling off the stairs with his guts spilling free like an anchor chain. Then he turned as a knife glanced off his scale cuirass.

'I surrender!' said the man who had just failed to kill him.

Satyrus held his swing. The man backed away, dropping the knife. 'I surrender!' he said and ran back through the door.

'Satyrus!' Eumenes of Olbia called from the base of the steps. 'Wait, boy!'

The man who had just surrendered fell backwards against him, pleading. 'Please!' he begged. 'Help!' he squeaked.

Phalangites and cavalrymen had used ladders to storm the exedra and were killing every man they found.

'Stop that!' Satyrus said. 'Prisoners!' he roared in his best storm-at-sea voice.

Men glanced at him, and the madness left their eyes.

Diodorus was shaking his head. 'We have a *hundred* prisoners,' he said. 'Ares and Aphrodite. Macedonians – what in all the shades of Tartarus were they doing here?'

Philokles shook his head. 'I can guess, brother. But we do *not* have the men we came for.'

Satyrus pushed the prisoner from the head of the stairs forward. 'Gone an hour ago,' he said. 'Pure ill luck. And his whole fucking household and all his guards.'

'Lord,' the terrified mercenary said. 'Lord, he left to – arrange – that is – to kill Lord Ptolemy!'

'Zeus Soter!' Diodorus said.

Theron and Eumenes began shedding their armour without comment, and Satyrus joined them. 'Running?' he asked, and both nodded.

'All the athletes!' Satyrus shouted, and the cry was taken up, and Dio came, and a dozen other young men. They stripped to their chitoniskoi, threw their sword belts over their shoulders and they were off.

They ran in a pack through the darkened streets – their own men slowed them for many blocks, as the thousands Philokles had employed hampered them, curious for news and at one post insistent that they prove themselves – good men, obeying orders, who cost them precious minutes until a hippeis officer verified them and they were off again.

They ran like sprinters up to the palace gate and found no guard there, just a pair of dead slaves.

'Where in Hades do we go?' Eumenes asked.

Satyrus was familiar enough with the palace. He led the whole group across the courtyard to the entry to the megaron – where a pair of cavalry Hetairoi barred the way with bare steel.

'Stratokles seeks to murder Lord Ptolemy!' Theron yelled. His words echoed around the rows of columns and the courtyard and the garden. The two cavalrymen faced them, clearly prepared to fight.

'Hold, hold! I know that voice!' shouted a Greek from within the megaron, and then Gabines came through the archway with more guards.

Eumenes, as the senior officer, stepped forward. 'Lord,' he said, 'I am one of Lord Diodorus's officers. We have just taken a hundred of the mutineers – more, I think.'

'Praise the gods!' Gabines said.

'We are told that Stratokles the Athenian means to kill Lord Ptolemy,' Eumenes said.

'We know,' Gabines answered wearily. 'You are too late. He has already failed.'

'Thank the gods,' Satyrus said, and behind him, his companions gave a loyal cheer.

'*You* may not thank the gods,' Gabines said, looking at Satyrus. 'Lord Ptolemy left today, in secret, disguised as a trooper. He is safe.' Gabines shook his head. 'But Stratokles the traitor has taken the Lady Amastris.'

PART VI

FLEXING THE BLADE

23

Stratokles rode easily, most of his attention concentrated on controlling his craving for water. The rest of his attention fell on his captive, who rode calmly, her head up, and occasionally favoured him with a smile.

Her smiles disconcerted him.

Around him rode the best of his hired killers, Lucius at their head, and beyond, just a few stades unless he had utterly missed his mark, lay the army of Demetrios the Golden, son of Antigonus One-Eye – the youngest and handsomest of the contestants in the wars that men called 'God-like Alexander's Funeral Games'.

Stratokles straightened his back, trying to erase layers of fatigue and a dozen hours in the saddle, and trying to arrange his thoughts to prepare for the interview to come. He had *failed* (so far) to kill Ptolemy. Best not to dwell on that.

Hermes, god of spies, his mouth was dry.

'How long did you plan my abduction?' the princess asked. She smiled and dropped her eyes, the very model of feminine dignity.

Stratokles shrugged. 'It was on the fly, my lady,' he admitted. He rubbed the stump of his nose. *Why,* he asked himself, *did I say that? Surely a more elaborate fiction would have won more prizes than that single bare fact.*

'So, having failed to kill the regent of Aegypt, you thought that I might do as second best?' she asked as if deeply interested in the inner workings of his mind.

He straightened his back again and cursed inwardly at his own lack of discipline – his craving for her good opinion. 'Lady, it is my intention to barter my services to Antigonus for a satrapy. Phrygia lacks a lord. You would make an effective ally – even a consort. Or so I reasoned.'

'My, my,' she said. They rode in silence for more than a stade, and she began to fall behind. She pulled her shawl over her face and rode with her face covered, and he alternated thinking about that face and about his desire for water.

Then she pushed her horse to a faster walk and nudged the weary animal back to a position next to Stratokles, and he felt his heart rise with foolish happiness when she did. 'Because my father is the tyrant of Heraklea, you mean? Or because you observed some quality in *me* that would make – how did you put it? – an *effective ally*?'

Stratokles considered answers from the offensive to the flattering, but again, despite years of practice, he found that his mouth was spitting out the truth. 'Your father and his city, of course. Although,' he said with a bow, 'now that I have your measure, despoina, I know that I *underestimated* your qualities.'

'Oh, fairly spoken!' she laughed, throwing her head back – no falsity at all. 'For a man as careful and as wily as you to admit that you underestimated me is quite a compliment.'

That made him smile. When had he ever smiled this many times in an hour? 'You take my meaning exactly, lady.' As they rode, he found himself telling this lady the truth, if for no other reason than that she asked, and seemed content to ask, riding by his side and talking as if he were an old and trusted advisor. It made him feel foolish. And old.

They were laughing together by the time they reached the first cavalry pickets. 'It's like speaking to Pericles,' Lady Amastris said. Stratokles glowed.

'You tried to kill old Ptolemy?' Demetrios asked. He was sitting on a plain wood camp stool in the midst of a circle of his companions, but the simplicity ended there. His golden hair and his matching golden breastplate contrasted with the leopard skin he wore in place of a cloak, and his feet were encased in magnificent open-toed boots of tooled and gilt leather. Indeed, he looked like an image of one of the heroes – Theseus, Herakles or a burly Achilles.

Stratokles had seen him before, but never been confronted with all his charm and charisma face to face.

'Yes, lord,' Stratokles said.

'Well, high marks for the attempt, but I'd rather defeat him myself. Hand to hand, if I can do it. That's the stuff that myth is made of, Athenian.' Demetrios's youth shone from him like light from a lamp.

Stratokles was still struggling with his shoulders, both of which wanted to slump down, lower and lower, until he lay on the ground and slept. He'd had a hard week. And he disliked how the golden boy's eyes slid off him. It was a reaction men had always had to his ugliness. Cassander didn't do it. Cassander could at least meet his eye. 'You will certainly master Ptolemy, my lord – in combat or any other way, but those that love you will do their best to ease your path,' he said. Pericles couldn't have put it better.

In the privacy of his thoughts, Stratokles was already doubting his commitment to this arrogant pup.

Perdikkas, son of Bion, one of Demetrios's young officers, with curly hair and an equally curling lip that promised arrogance, snapped his fingers. 'What of the Macedonian officers?' he demanded.

Stratokles shrugged. 'I arranged for the leaders of the mutiny to meet, and I made sure that they were armed in preparation for the attack on Ptolemy. In any event, they didn't come. My fault? Perhaps. Perhaps they got cold feet.'

'We hear a rumour that they were massacred,' Demetrios said. His eyes no longer rested on Stratokles. He was assessing the qualities of the young woman who sat quietly behind Stratokles, swathed in wool, one demure ankle and foot the only clue to her age and vitality.

Stratokles felt more than protective towards the girl. He stepped forward to draw the commander's eyes. 'I doubt it. Wouldn't you spread such a rumour if you feared a mutiny, lord?'

'Is ugliness like a disease, that can be caught?' Demetrios asked, and all his companions laughed. 'I'm sure that you've done me good service, Athenian, but it wearies me to look at you. What did you bring me? Is that a present? Briseis, brought to my tent?'

Stratokles couldn't resist. 'Briseis was *taken* from Achilles, lord.'

'Nothing more fitting, then, although I have a hard time casting you as Achilles. Let's see you, girl.' Demetrios rose from his throne.

'She is the daughter of the tyrant of Heraklea. She is a modest girl.' Stratokles moved swiftly to her side.

She moved back, to put Stratokles between her and Demetrios. No other action could have tugged so firmly at the shreds of Stratokles' sense of honour – a tattered garment, but one with more body to it than he himself might have expected.

Demetrios found himself reaching out towards Stratokles. Men behind him put their hands on their sword hilts. 'Don't be foolish, ugly man,' the golden boy said.

Just give him the girl. Stratokles' political sense, a daimon finely honed from a generation of Athenian politics with a voice of its own, told him that he could have anything he wanted with this golden boy – if he gave him the girl. *Or better yet,* the voice suggested, *the more you struggle before giving this new master the girl, the better this new master will value her – and her giver.*

For the first time in some years, Stratokles ignored the dispassionate daimon that ruled him on affairs of state. His flexible wit sprang to his aid.

'I'm no fool,' he said calmly. 'And neither are you, lord, to offend the tyrant of Heraklea when your father depends on his ports and his shipping.'

'She has the ankles of Aphrodite!' Demetrios said. He put his hands on his hips. 'I don't give a fig for the tyrant of Heraklea.'

'I imagine that you've used the Aphrodite tag before,' Stratokles replied.

Amastris laughed at his elbow, and he felt like the king of the world. Then she allowed the folds of her himation to fall back off her head, and she stepped forward. 'You may care nothing for my father,' she said, and she smiled at Demetrios, 'but I promise you that he will have a care for me.' The sun of her smile overwhelmed her words, and Demetrios clapped his hands together.

'Have her conducted to a tent – throw the occupants in the sand. See to it that she wants for nothing.' Demetrios bowed low. 'Let me rescue you from this toad.'

Amastris turned the sun of her smile on Stratokles. She shook her head. 'He is my toad,' she said. 'I trust him, and I do not know you.'

Something hot boiled up in Stratokles' heart. His face flushed, and his nose hurt.

'I will protect you,' he said thickly – the wrong words, he knew, and said the wrong way. He didn't care.

She flipped her himation back over her head, but her eyes remained on his. He hadn't noticed how dispassionate they were before. 'Yes,' she said. 'You will.'

Her smile was visible only at the corners of her eyes, but it was for him. It was a long time since he had seen eyes do that – for him. It made him wince.

Then she stepped back. His guards surrounded her.

'We will be pleased to occupy any tent you see fit to give us,' Stratokles said.

'No, toad. She is mine. I'll see to it that you are paid a talent or two for your betrayals, but she is mine. Perhaps I'll add to your reward for bringing her. Really, she makes the conquest of this strip of sand almost worthwhile.' Demetrios laughed, and all the companions laughed with him. 'Aphrodite, goddess of love, you didn't imagine that she found you anything but horrible? The man who abducted her? Have you ever looked in a mirror? While I, the golden one, chosen of the gods, will save her from your venomous clutches.' Demetrios laughed. 'She's moist for me now, toad.'

That last made all the companions roar with laughter.

Stratokles had the strength to smile. He stood straight. *I am the hero of this piece,* he thought. *Not you, boy. Me. The toad.* 'This is not how your father deals with men, lord,' Stratokles said above the laughter. 'Schoolboy insults insult only school-boys.'

Demetrios turned suddenly, his eyes narrow. 'You dare to

tell me what my father would or wouldn't do? You call me a boy?' His companions fell silent.

'Your father offered me the satrapy of Phrygia. I have done my best to honour my part of the bargain and I still have agents in place. Now,' slowly, carefully, as if the words were dragged from him, 'now you call me names and take from me my ward and offer me a few talents of silver?' Stratokles shrugged. 'Kill me, lord. For if you don't, I will tell your father that you are a fool.'

'My father—' Demetrios began. Then he stopped, as if listening to someone speak. Demetrios stood like a statue, staring off above his friend Paesander's head, and then he turned back.

'You are right to upbraid me, sir.' The alteration in Demetrios was so total that Stratokles, still in the grip of his own acting, felt that he had to step back before the power of the gods. Demetrios bowed to the Athenian. 'It was ill of me to call you names – although you must confess that you will never model for Ganymede.'

Some of the companions laughed, but the laugh was nervous, because Demetrios's voice sounded *odd*.

Stratokles inclined his head in a token of agreement. 'I have never bragged about my looks. Nor have I ever sought to model myself on Ganymede,' he said, pointing the barb at the handsomest of Demetrios's companions, a beautiful boy who stood next to Paesander. 'Although I gather that some do.'

Demetrios laughed. 'There's more to you than that ugly face,' he acknowledged. 'We are on the edge of battle – the battle that will give us Aegypt. Then we shall reward all of our faithful soldiers. It was wrong of us to speak in terms of a few paltry pieces of silver. Please accept our apologies.' Demetrios bowed, and Stratokles had to fight the urge to forgive him out of hand.

That is power, he thought.

'And the girl?' he asked.

Demetrios smiled. 'Let it be as she wishes.'

Stratokles led her away, with Demetrios's friend Paesander as a messenger. The daimon hectored him that he had fallen prey to a pretty girl.

24

The pursuit of Stratokles didn't last out the night. Midnight had come and gone before they found the means he had used to leave the city – a boat waiting off the palace – and his head start was sufficient to guarantee his success.

'He'll run to Demetrios,' Philokles told Satyrus.

The young man was dry-eyed – tired, wrung out and incapable of further emotion. Subsequent days did little to raise his spirits. They marched from the city into the desert, and the next five days were hard – stretches of bright desert punctuated by Delta towns and river crossings, so that a man could be parched with heat and an hour later nearly drowned. The mosquitoes were the worst that Satyrus had ever known, descending on the army in clouds that were visible from a stade away.

'What do they eat when there aren't any Jews?' Abraham asked.

'Mules,' Dionysius answered. 'The taste is much the same.'

Satyrus marched along in silence, sometimes lost in dark fantasies of the torments Amastris must now be suffering, and again, tormenting himself with his own inability to rescue her. Few things are more calculated to indicate to a young man just how small his role is than marching in the endless dust cloud and bugs of an army column that fills the road from morning until night – one tiny cog in the great bronze machine of war.

At night they camped on flat ground by branches of the Nile and drank muddy water that left silt in their canteens. Every morning, Satyrus made himself roll out of his cloaks and go around the circle of fires, helping one mess group start their fire, finding an axe for another and reminding a third how to cook in clay without cracking the pots.

All in all, the cooking was getting better, if only because the Phalanx of Aegypt was beginning to acquire followers. Every village seemed to have girls and very young men who wanted to go *anywhere*, if only to leave the eternal drudgery of the land. On the river, a girl was accounted a woman when she was twelve, and *old* when she was a grandmother of twenty-five or so. Most of them were dead when they were thirty. Satyrus had heard these things, but now he marched through it, and every morning there were more peasants at his campfires, cooking the food – and eating it. And the files of shield-bearers began to fill in, so that the phalanx looked more like the Foot Companions.

On the third day, Philokles walked up and down the ranks, ordering men to carry their own kit. 'Let them carry the cook pots!' Philokles roared. 'Carry your own weapons! You spent the summer earning the privilege – don't sell it for a little rest!'

The fourth morning and already Amastris was like a distant dream. Satyrus had fallen asleep with Abraham, and he awoke to find his friend shivering. Satyrus was shivering too, but he knew what to do – he was up in a flash, and threw his chlamys over the other man, and then ran along the Thermoutiakos, a stream of the Nile, and then around the camp until he was warm.

Well upstream, he came across a pair of marines he knew and Diokles, leading a goat.

'Where'd that come from?' Satyrus asked.

'We found it, didn't we?' one of the marines answered. 'Wandering, like.'

Diokles wouldn't meet his eye. 'Didn't actually belong to anyone,' he said.

Satyrus rubbed at the beginning of a beard that was forming on his jaw. 'You know what Philokles says about theft.'

'Wasn't theft,' Diokles insisted.

'Wandering about, like,' the marine said.

The other marine was silent.

'I know where you can find your sister,' Diokles offered suddenly.

If he intended to distract his officer, he certainly succeeded. 'You do?' Satyrus asked.

'I'll catch up with you,' Diokles said, waving at the marines. Then he turned back the way he had come. 'She's in the archer camp. All the sailors and marines know it – you won't send her back?'

'Hades, no!' Satyrus said.

They walked half a stade, to where a dozen young men were shooting bows at baled forage for the cavalry. 'She got us the goat,' Diokles admitted.

'Really?' Satyrus asked.

'Do you really want to know?' Diokles answered. 'You'll find her. I'll see you in camp.'

Satyrus jogged over to the men shooting at the bales. It wasn't that hard to pick out his sister, if you knew where to look. He came up and swatted her on the backside, the way soldiers in armour often did to each other.

Melitta whirled. 'You bastard!' she growled.

He laughed. They embraced.

'You're insane!' Satyrus said.

'No more than you, brother,' she said. 'Any word about Amastris?'

Satyrus sat on his haunches in the sand – a new talent for a world with no chairs. 'No word at all. Stratokles took her and sailed away.'

'He won't bother her,' Melitta said. 'She's too clever.' After a moment, she said 'much too clever' in a way that suggested that all that cleverness wasn't entirely admirable.

'I'm afraid for her.' Satyrus frowned. 'I know how stupid this sounds, but – I want to rescue her.'

'That's not stupid, brother – if it was me, I'd fucking well expect you to come and save me.' She laughed in her throat, a deeper sound than she'd ever made at home.

'Nice swearing,' Satyrus said.

'I get lots of practice,' Melitta said.

'I have to go back and make sure the breakfast gets cooked,' Satyrus said, and saw Xenophon coming up, his whole demeanour sheepish. 'Now I know where you sleep,' he said with more venom than he meant.

Xenophon wouldn't meet his eye, and Satyrus was sorry to find that he didn't care much.

'I'll walk back with you,' Xenophon said. He and Melitta exchanged a significant look.

'No,' Satyrus said. 'You have your armour on and I'm going to run. See you soon. What do you call yourself?'

'Bion, like my horse.' She flashed him her best smile and he returned it. Then he waved, nodded to Xeno so as not to seem rude and ran off for his camp.

An hour later, his belly full of under-roast goat, he was marching again.

They marched through Natho and Boubastis, picking up more followers and meeting carefully assembled grain barges that supplied the army and kept the looting of the peasants down to manageable limits. At Boubastis, Philokles caught an Aegyptian and a Hellene stealing cattle from an outlying farm and he brought both men into camp at spear point.

'What will you do with them?' Diodorus asked. He and Eumenes rode in while the sun was still bright enough for work. A barge was unloading bales of wood for fires – there wasn't enough wood in the desert to build a raft for an ant, as the Aegyptians said.

Satyrus listened attentively, because the camp was buzzing with rumour about what the Spartan had planned.

'I intend to hold an assembly of the taxeis tonight. What else should I do?' Philokles asked.

Diodorus laughed. 'Most of your men aren't Greek, Philokles.'

Philokles shrugged. 'So you say. When it comes to a desire for justice, and a desire to have each man have his say – who is not a Greek? You want me to kill these men out of hand, as an example?'

'I do,' Diodorus nodded. 'That's exactly what I want.'

Philokles shook his head. 'You'd need a different commander for this group, then, Strategos.'

Dinner was good, because the barges were less than a stade away and there was plenty of food and plenty of fuel. Just five days into the march, the Phalanx of Aegypt was harder and more capable than they had been in the near riot of leaving the city. They could cook, and sleep, and eat, and pack, and march, without much fuss. But the assembly was a new adventure, and a dangerous one, because there was death in it.

The Hellenes knew what was expected, and so all the men gathered in a great circle in the crisp night air. Above them, the whole curtain of the heavens seemed to be on display, the stars burning with distant fire. Every man was there, even those who had the mosquito fever or the runs that seemed to come with too much Nile water – at least for Greeks.

'Soldiers!' Philokles' voice was as loud as any priest's. 'These men have disobeyed my orders and the orders of the army. In Sparta, in Athens, in Macedon, these men would forfeit their lives. But only,' his voice grew over the murmur of the men, 'only if the assembly of their regiment approved it. Who will step forward and speak for the army, prosecuting these men for their crime?'

Philokles' eyes pressed on Satyrus. Into the silence he stepped. 'I will prosecute,' Satyrus said.

Philokles looked around. 'Who will speak for these men?'

The two culprits grinned around at their comrades, and were surprised to find many serious faces looking back at them. Finally Abraham stepped into the silence. 'I will defend,' he said.

Satyrus looked at him, surprised that his friend would oppose him, but then he shrugged, understanding that Abraham no more wanted to defend them than he wanted to speak against them. This was duty.

The evidence was brief and damning, offered as it was by the phalanx commander.

Satyrus asked a number of questions to make their guilt clear, and then shrugged. He had read every case ever pleaded in Athens – he could quote Isocrates, for instance – but this didn't seem the place for such flights of rhetoric. 'If we rob the peasants,' he asked the silent men of the phalanx, 'why should they help us? And what are we but enemies, no different from those who come to conquer?'

His words went home – he could see them, like an arrow launched from a distance that, after a delay, strikes the target. He bowed his head to Philokles and stood aside.

Abraham stood forth. 'I am not a Greek,' he said. 'But in this I think that the Greeks are right – that a man should be judged according to the will of his comrades. Because his comrades are best fitted to judge the crime.' Abraham turned so that he was addressing the Aegyptians, who filled one half of the circle. 'I ask all of you – who has not eaten stolen meat in the last week? Who has not lifted a bottle of honey beer? Let that man vote that these miscreants be killed. For myself, I am no hypocrite. My friend has told us why we hurt our own cause when we steal, and I hear him. I will not eat another stolen goat. But until the taste of that stolen food is gone from my lips, I will not condemn another to death.'

Philokles was suppressing a smile when he stepped past the two advocates. 'Well said by both.' He looked around. Fifteen hundred men stood in near perfect silence.

'Remember this moment,' Philokles said to the assembly. 'This is the moment that you began to be soldiers.' He looked around with approval, and still they were silent. 'So – you are all goat-eaters. How then should I punish them? Even their advocate did not trouble to claim them guiltless.'

Namastis stepped forward from among the Aegyptians. 'Will you punish both alike?' he asked.

Philokles put his hands on his hips. 'What do you think?' he asked. 'Don't anger me, priest.'

Namastis shook his head. 'Old ways die hard,' he said. 'If you seek to punish both alike,' he said, 'let them carry pots with the peasants until it is your pleasure to return them to the ranks.'

A sound like a sigh escaped from the men gathered in the dark.

'Whoa!' said the guilty Hellene, a marine from the *Hyacinth*.

'Silence!' Philokles said. 'Any dissenting opinion?'

Another murmur, like wind passing through a field of barley – but no man stepped forward.

Philokles nodded sharply. 'Theron, pick the two best shield-bearers and swear them in to the phalanx. These men may carry their kit. If either of you desert, you will earn the punishment of death. Serve, and you may be restored.' Philokles raised his voice. 'Do you agree, men of Alexandria?'

They roared – a shout that filled the night.

The eighth day found them at Peleusiakos, where mountains of wheat and cisterns of fresh water awaited them with barges of firewood and tens of thousands of bales of fresh fodder for the cavalry. Twelve thousand public slaves laboured at fresh earthworks in the brutal sun, raising platforms of logs and sand and fill brought from the Sinai and even from the river. The ramparts rose four times the height of a man and the platforms carried Ares engines that could throw a spear three stades or a rock the same. To the north lay the sea, and to the south the deadly marshes, which offered no hope to an army. Even with the breeze from the sea, the stink of the swamp mud over-whelmed the smell of horse and camel and the filth of men.

Satyrus marched with the rest of his phalanx into a prebuilt camp and handed his kit to a slave to be cleaned. They had *tents*. Of course, the interior of the linen tent was airless, white hot and brilliantly lit, so that no man could sleep there in the daylight – but the extent of Ptolemy's preplanning was stagger-ing. Satyrus put his shield against his section of the wall and put his spear in a rack set for that purpose.

Later, after a dinner cooked by public slaves with enough mutton to quieten the loudest grumbles, Satyrus stood on the parapet with his uncles and their officers, Andronicus the hyperetes of the hippeis of exiles, Crax and Eumenes, all look-ing out over the Sinai and the road to Gaza.

'We're not doomed at all,' Philokles said. 'I've underesti-mated our Farm Boy.'

Diodorus laughed. 'Just as you were meant to. Mind you, if the Macedonians had managed to get their mutiny together, we'd never have got here. But look at it! Every man in the army is going to look around at the walls and the camp, the tents, the spiked pits – and the stores! And every man is going to say the same thing.'

'Ptolemy can hold this with slaves,' Philokles said. 'With mice.'

'Something like that,' Diodorus said. He had wine in a canteen, and he handed it around.

Satyrus was cowed in the face of so many veterans, but he mustered his courage. 'So,' he said, 'when will we fight?'

Diodorus laughed and slapped Satyrus on the shoulder. 'That's the great thing, lad. We'll *never* have to fight. Demetrios is a child, but he's not a fool. He'll take one look at this and cut a deal. Then he'll turn around and march home.'

'So no one wins,' Satyrus said. 'And Amastris remains with the traitor.'

Diodorus shook his head, but Eumenes, who was younger and perhaps understood Satyrus better, cut in. 'That's not true, Satyrus. First, *we win*. All we sought to do was defend Aegypt. We win. That's an important concept for a soldier to understand. Second,' he shrugged, 'I know it's not the stuff of Homer, but even now, I suspect that Amastris's uncles and father and every other lord on the Euxine and quite a variety of other busybodies will be speaking for her. And when the golden boy looks at these walls and puts his tail between his legs, well …' Eumenes looked at the other officers, and all three of the older men smiled.

'Well – what?' Satyrus asked, torn between annoyance at being treated like a boy and the knowledge that, to these men, he was one. 'What, Eumenes?'

'He'll probably make a treaty just to get his men fed,' Philokles said. 'Amastris will go on the table to buy some of that grain.'

Satyrus spat in disgust.

Diodorus flexed his shoulders under his cuirass. 'I want to get this bronze off my back. Satyrus, I share your disgust. You look very like your father when you're annoyed.'

Philokles put an arm around his shoulders. 'He is growing to be like his father.'

'So's his sister,' Diodorus said, and they all laughed, even Satyrus.

It was almost a week before they saw the scouts of the enemy, and another week before Demetrios brought up his infantry.

The cavalry went out of the works and skirmished. The hippeis of Tanais rode forth and brought back prisoners – Sakje and Medes – and Seleucus, Ptolemy's new second in command, won a cavalry battle somewhere to the south and east on the Nabataean road. The pikemen of the phalanxes played no part in any of this. Most of them sat in camp. But the Phalanx of Aegypt drilled all day, every day. They marched up and down the roads, and they charged across broken ground and open ground and they dug on the walls when ordered, because Philokles refused to give them a rest.

They worked harder than anyone but the slaves.

Melitta watched them march by, sitting on the great earthwork wall with her legs hanging over the edge to catch the breeze – legs which drew no notice at all in a camp so full of available peasant girls that no one gave her a second look. That thought made her smile. Beneath her feet, Xeno and Satyrus and all the young men she knew – there was Dionysius, his hair plastered to his head under a filthy linen skull cap, making a sarcastic comment to his file partner, she could see it on his face – the lot of them marched by. They were singing the Paean to Apollo to keep in step and they sang it well enough to move her.

'Bion? Bion!'

Officer. She pulled her legs under her and swung off the parapet to drop to the hard-packed gravel of the sentry walk. 'Phylarch!' she called in her low voice.

Idomeneus was a Cretan, like most expert archers. He wore quilted armour and carried a massive bow and Melitta suspected that the spade-bearded mercenary knew she was a girl and didn't care. She saluted him as she'd been taught.

'Listen up, lad. I'm to take my best hundred archers – we'll ride double with some of the horse-boys and try a little ambush. There's likely to be some plunder. What do you say?'

'I'll get my kit,' Melitta said.

'Whoa, horsey. Sunset, at the camp of the Exiles.' He grinned. 'Professionals. They won't leave us to die, I think.'

Melitta hoped her face didn't register her reaction. 'Exiles' is what Ptolemy's army called Diodorus's hippeis from Tanais. Those were her people – they'd know her.

Too late to back out. 'I'll be there,' she said.

She accepted the derision of her peers with grace when she appeared on parade in Persian trousers she'd bought from a slave. Like most of them, she had a big straw hat the size of an aspis and under it she wrapped her head in linen against the sun. There wasn't much of Melitta, daughter of Kineas, to be seen.

The hundred picked toxotai didn't so much march as stroll across the camp. Good archers were specialists – like craftsmen – and they didn't have the kind of discipline that the men in the phalanxes needed. In fact, they derided the phalangites as often as they could.

Cavalry were a different matter. Cavalrymen often had a social distinction, and they considered all infantrymen to be beneath their notice. Melitta, as the child of the Sakje, shared their disdain, and it was odd to receive the cutting edge of it from men she knew.

'Pluton, they smell!' Crax laughed. He trotted his horse along the length of the toxotai, his charger actually brushing Melitta. He stopped and leaned over by Idomeneus. 'This is the best you could do? They look like dwarves, Ido!'

Crax actually pointed at Melitta. 'That one can't be more than twelve.'

Her captain didn't get angry. Instead, he pointed at 'Bion'. 'Fall out,' he said. 'String your bow.'

Crax laughed. 'Well, at least he's strong enough to get it bent. Say – that's a Sakje bow, lad.'

Melitta had the string on with the practice of years. Without waiting for an order, she put an arrow on her string, chose a target – a javelin target across the Exiles' parade square, a good half a stade away – and loosed. The arrow rose, drifted a little on the evening breeze and struck the target squarely, so that the wooden shield moved and the *thunk* echoed.

'Hmm,' Diodorus said. 'That lad looks familiar to me, Crax.' Diodorus had a dun-coloured cloak over a plain leather cuirass and two spears in his fist.

Crax reached down and slapped Idomeneus. 'I take it all back, Cretan. They're all Apollo's own children. At least they won't burden the horses!'

After a quick inspection, ten of them were sent to fill all the water bottles, a task Melitta always drew because she was clearly one of the youngest. Then they paraded with the hippeis, and every archer was assigned to a rider.

Bion was assigned to a Macedonian deserter she didn't know well – although she did know him – but just as she prepared to climb on to his mount, Carlus trotted his gigantic charger along the line.

'Captain says I take the boy,' Carlus said.

The Macedonian shrugged. 'He's the lightest, that's for sure. Not sorry to ride without him, though. They've all got lice.' He turned his horse and moved back along the file.

Carlus lifted Bion with one hand. 'Hands around my waist, lad,' he said.

Carlus smelled of male sweat and horse – not a bad smell at all, but—

'Your uncle says that if you want to go with the army, you should be with us,' Carlus said. His voice was level. 'We can keep you alive.'

'I can keep alive. I have comrades who I value,' she said. And she knew that life in the camp of the Exiles would not be *real* like life with the toxotai. She was gaining a reputation as an archer and as someone to be taken seriously, at knucklebones or even boxing. With the hippeis, she'd be known for what she was. Kind glances and helpful hands and some laughter behind her back.

Carlus shrugged. 'Everyone needs to make their own way,' he allowed.

The moon was bright, and the desert empty, and they rode fast – the kind of speed that Medes and Sakje practised, and few Greeks could manage. Every man had two horses, or even three, and they changed every hour.

It was exhilarating to go so fast across the moon-swept landscape, with such comrades. The sense of purpose was remarkable and heady. The hippeis were exactly as silent as required – loud when they felt secure, silent as a necropolis when they began to close on the enemy camp – and the toxotai were infected by their absolute conviction that they would win. At the second halt for a horse change, Idomeneus grinned at her. 'Someday I'd like to train archers this well,' he said.

'They've been together twenty years,' Bion replied, and then realized she had blundered. 'At least, that's what the big barbarian I'm with said.'

Idomeneus nodded. 'Still,' he whispered.

'You kids done chatting?' Crax asked. He was already mounted and he extended a hand to the Cretan. 'I hope we're not keeping you up too late. The party is just about to start.'

No one bothered to tell Bion the plan until they halted a final time, just after the moon had set. Carlus was pointing at the ground.

'What do I do?' she asked.

Carlus's grin was ghastly in the moonlight. 'Dig a hole and climb in. We'll draw them to you at first light. When you hear the trumpet, start shooting.' He shrugged. 'Not my plan.'

She rolled off the broad back of Carlus's elephantine horse and gathered her small pack. She did not, of course, have a pick or a shovel. All around her she could see other archers with the same difficulty.

They scraped shallow pits with their hands and some, who had helmets, used them, while Idomeneus walked up and down, cursing and demanding that they dig faster. By the time the very first rays of dawn turned the eastern sky pink, she was lying in the cool sand with her cloak over her and a few hastily gathered blades of swamp grass over her cloak. It wasn't much. To her right she could see another Cretan, Argon, with his rump sticking up because he was a lazy sod and couldn't be bothered to dig hard.

Why am I here? Melitta asked herself in the privacy of her hole. She'd been warm enough while working, but now the sand was soaking the warmth out of her and she didn't have her cloak around her and she was cold and none of this made any sense. The cavalry had ridden away.

She must have fallen asleep, despite everything, because suddenly there was movement around her and the sky was very bright indeed. She raised her head and saw dust, felt the hoof beats of horses, many horses at a gallop.

'Wait for it!' Idomeneus called. He was standing in the shadow of a big rock. 'String your bows!'

A hundred capes wriggled and the sand seemed to roll like the sea as the toxotai strung their bows lying flat. Even the desert generated too much moisture to leave a bow strung overnight.

To Bion, it seemed as if the galloping horses were right on top of them, and still Idomeneus didn't call and the trumpet didn't sound. Louder and louder – impossibly loud. And terrifying.

'Stand up!' the Cretan called.

Eumenes was right in front of her, two horse-lengths away, and even as she stood, his horse passed between her and Argon, his head turned to watch the rear and his cloak streaming behind him.

She put a heavy arrow on her bow as she noted that there were dozens – no, hundreds – of horses, but only a few of them had riders.

They stole a horse herd, she thought. It made her smile – such a Sakje thing.

The riderless horses raised quite a dust cloud. She wrapped her linen wimple over her mouth and tilted her straw hat down to block the sun. Now she could see almost a stade, and there were two big bodies of cavalry.

The enemy. This was different from anything she'd ever done – different from fighting pirates. She found that she was grinning like a fool. She looked around – she could hit at this range, but she wasn't sure she was allowed to shoot.

Just half a stade away were *hundreds* of enemy cavalry. And they were coming *fast*.

A heavy Cretan arrow leaped into the air – Argon, damn him – and it swept high before stooping like a hawk and falling just short of the lead company.

'You fucking idiot! Do you want to eat horseshit tonight,

you useless turd?' Idomeneus was not yelling – but he was right there. 'Wait for the trumpet!' More quietly, 'Ares, what a fuck-face.'

The enemy were so close that they *must* see the archers – but they continued to canter along, making the earth rumble. Melitta was shaking the way she had before telling Aunt Sappho that she'd lain with Xeno – where was Xeno, anyway? And whose plan was this?

The trumpet rang.

Bion loosed without thought, then watched as another arrow was dragged from the quiver and nocked, red fletch upward – bow up, full draw, four fingers over the mass of horsemen, loose, third arrow …

The lead company burst under the volleys of arrows. The first arrows hit them in a tight clump, most of them falling from high and hitting the unprotected hindquarters of the horses, so that the animals screamed and fell, or rolled, or stood and fought the air, bellowing their agony with noises that made Melitta's Sakje stomach roll over with discomfort that killing mere men never caused her. The effect on the company to her front was total – where there had been a hundred cavalrymen, there was a dust cloud and the screams of the dying. Nothing came out of the cloud but a single riderless horse and even as she watched, the third volley of arrows vanished into the rising sand to a thin chorus of new screams.

The second and third enemy companies didn't hesitate. They swept wide, going for the flanks of the archers, having changed from pursuers to desperate men within three flights of arrows. The men on Bion's side of the engagement had long beards and Persian dress, they rode good horses and moved fast. Their captain wore rippling golden scale mail and had a henna-dyed beard. Bion shot him from the saddle – a pretty shot even at close range – before he could react to the new threat coming at his own flank: serried troops of the Exiles coming over the low sand and mud ridges to the north and south.

Leaderless, his men were still focused on the archers flaying their front when the Exiles ripped into their flanks, heralded by a point-blank volley of heavy javelins that could knock a horse flat.

Even so, determined men – bearded easterners who had grown up fighting Sakje on the frontier and knew a disaster when they saw one – didn't hesitate. One group went straight for Melitta. She nodded, even as she fitted another arrow to the string – fingers suddenly clumsy, a spasm of fear even while part of her mind was above the whole battle, thinking things through—

Their leader knew he'd be safer going *through* the ambush than turning tail. A good leader.

They were going to make it to her position and she couldn't stop them and nobody else could either.

She loosed – hit or miss, she didn't know, because she threw herself flat and rolled in a ball as the Medes went over her, their sabres reaching for her. *That* was her moment of fear – blind and waiting to be pinned to the ground like a pig in the agora, but then they were past and Argon was making a shrill whistling noise. She looked around – dust, no more – and ran to the Cretan, who lay in his too-shallow pit with blood under his elbows and his back arched in pain.

His throat was cut – just barely cut, the extreme reach of a Mede's sword – and he gave up as she watched, his body ceasing to struggle, his rump sinking into the hole he had dug for himself. His head turned and he saw her. His mouth moved – no sound. She never knew what he tried to say because a blow to her side suddenly knocked her flat.

Her left arm and side rang with pain but she wasn't dead. Her hair was full of sand. She spat – got a foot under her.

The Mede had a sword like a Sakje akinakes, long and narrow, and he got a hand on the javelin he'd thrown at her while she rose to her feet.

He hesitated when he saw her trousered legs, and she got her sword out from under her arm before he could finish her off. She didn't hesitate – she put a hand up against the heavy javelin, missed her grab and stepped in anyway, swung the sword with the whole weight of her body behind it. He got his akinakes up to parry but her blow sheered down the blade and cut into his fingers and hand from brutal momentum.

He froze in pain.

She swung hard, cutting so deep into his neck that her sword stuck, and he flopped in the bloody sand, still alive, arms reaching for her. He got a hand on her leg and she kicked, slammed her fist into his face – blood from the neck wound splashing over both of them – got the sword free from his muscle and bone and cut again and again and again and again until the sword flew from her fingers from exhaustion to land a horse-length away in the sand.

She knelt by the body, empty of anything. Later she got up and fetched her weapons, drank some water and walked off down the line to where the other survivors gathered around Idomeneus.

'Argon's dead,' she said.

Carlus rode by her. 'I can't find her!' he roared, and a dozen hippeis rode back the way she had come into the battle haze. The archers watched wearily, uncaring as to what the fuss was. Melitta didn't care much herself, so she walked boldly across the sand to Diodorus.

'I'm right here,' she said.

Diodorus looked down at her and his dust-caked face creased in a smile. 'You look like your father sometimes,' he said. He pointed at Andronicus and gave him some visual cue that caused the Gaul to blow a complex trumpet call, and all the Exiles began to rally. Several Exiles waved at her, and Eumenes pointed her out to Crax and Carlus, who shook their heads.

Carlus rode over. 'You scared me, missy!'

Melitta spurned the hand he offered her to mount. 'Bodies to loot,' she said. 'And I suspect there are horses for everyone, Big Guy. And if you call me missy again in public, I'll gut you.'

Carlus grinned as if he'd just won a contest, but his voice sounded gruff. 'You and what army, archer?' He spat. And worked to hide his grin.

Melitta walked off into the sand, and she made herself pull rings from fingers. There was some good armour and a lot of decent swords – not that she needed either. After the first minutes, she couldn't bear the sounds the wounded horses made, and the sight of the men – in particular, the sight of men she liked ignoring other men dying in agony at their feet while they stripped their bodies – sickened her. So she pulled a handsome saddle blanket from the corpse of a horse and a rider fallen together, and she took the bridle and bit from henna-beard, who she'd dropped herself, and then she walked all the way to the horse herd, well clear of the carnage, and cut out a pretty mare, tall and dark with four white feet. She put the tack on, dealt with the mare's unease with the smells and the whole situation, and got herself mounted, kit bundle, bow and all. And she had a few gold darics to wow the boys in camp.

Idomeneus found her waiting with her horse. 'You won't leave me for these centaurs, will you?' he asked. 'I shouldn't have put you at the end of the line in your first fight – but you shoot faster than most of the others. Was it bad, kid?'

She wanted to say something witty, the way Satyrus did – always brave, always ready with a quip. Finally, she said, 'I didn't throw up.'

Idomeneus nodded. His lips were as pinched as she felt hers must be. 'You saw Argon go down?'

She shook her head. 'Medes got him in the charge. We all hit the sand – he didn't get flat enough.'

Idomeneus nodded again. 'Help me get him on a horse then,' the Cretan said. 'He's been with me five years – least I can do is put him in the ground.'

They recovered all their dead, and Crax and Eumenes gathered armour and built a trophy and left it sticking out of the sand, a taunt at the whole army of Demetrios, whose tents were just visible ten stades away on the horizon. When they rode off, with plunder and prisoners and two hundred new horses, the trophy glittered behind them under the new sun until they crested the big ridge south of the walls, and then they were home.

25

Demetrios didn't make a treaty. After two weeks of staring at the impregnable works of Peleusiakos, losing cavalry fights and watching his plans for conquest unravel, Demetrios decamped in the night, leaving his fires burning, and retreated across the Sinai along eight hundred stades of coast road.

The morning after he vanished, Ptolemy's army was awakened by trumpets. From the door of his tent, Satyrus could see the cavalry in the next camp rolling their blankets and putting their bronze kettles in old linen bags.

'They're moving!' Satyrus shouted at Abraham, who was still in the blankets with Basis, an Aegyptian girl he'd adopted.

Philokles came up, already in armour and carrying his shield and spear. 'Shield-bearers, get packed. March in one hour! Satyrus, see to it that every man has food in his belly and more in his pack.'

Satyrus saluted, but he caught his tutor's arm. 'What is it?' he asked.

Philokles nodded in satisfaction. 'One-Eye's golden child has made a mistake, lad. And now we're going to chase *him*.'

'I don't understand,' Satyrus said. 'You said no battle.'

'I was wrong,' Philokles said. 'If we catch him short of his depot at Gaza, he'll have to fight. I never thought Ptolemy had the balls.' The Spartan made a face. 'No – that's wrong. Like Demetrios, I *forgot* that Ptolemy had the balls.'

Satyrus stood in the sand west of Gaza on the coast, looking at the thousand pinpoints of fire that marked the army of Demetrios.

'His army is huge!' Dionysius said.

Abraham stood with Xeno and Dionysius and a circle of their friends and file-mates. They had now been in the field long enough that there were friendships starting across the Hellene–Aegyptian divide – enough friendships and strong enough that Namastis would share wine with Diokles and Dionysius.

'I thought we weren't going to have a battle,' Abraham said wryly. He handed some really bad Aegyptian beer around. They were six days out from the stockpiles at Peleusiakos, and there wasn't much of anything.

'According to Philokles, Demetrios might have avoided battle if two things hadn't worked against him.' Satyrus felt very all-knowing. He was the only man in the phalanx who had information every evening, straight from the command staff, and it did a lot to reinforce his reputation. 'The first was Seleucus, who stayed on his southern flank and harried him, so that every man he had lost in the sands of Nabataea came back to haunt him. My uncles have fought his cavalry three times and put up a trophy every time.' He grinned, thinking of what Eumenes had told him about a certain fight in the sand.

'Horse-boys,' Dionysius said, but he lacked his usual venom.

Xeno took a swig of the beer, spat and pretended to crouch, as if in terror at the taste. 'Ares, I'd rather drink water,' he said. 'Listen, mock the horse-boys all you want, friends. You'll be happy enough to have them around if it comes to a fight.'

'Listen to the old sweat!' Abraham mocked. But he smiled, and Xeno smiled back.

Satyrus, full of information to impart, tried to be patient while he waited for silence. 'Listen!' he said. 'Philokles says that the worst of it is his own pride, so that even when his father's advisors told him to take the elephants and the best of his infantry and race for his depot he refused.'

'He's close,' Dionysius said. He drank the beer and made a face. 'Ares and Aphrodite, this is horse piss! No, listen! I'm serious!'

'He would know,' Xeno shot in, and roared with laughter. He didn't get to score against Dionysius often.

'Try this, then,' said a low voice, and Satyrus found a wine-skin pressed into his hand. He turned to see his sister's eyes – Bion, he reminded himself. He gave her a hug.

'Who's that?' Dionysius said. 'Aphrodite's insatiable cunny,

519

gentlemen, our Satyrus has himself a *boy*. A boy in barbarian trousers! Satyrus, how could you? When you had me?'

There was a brief silence, and then Abraham slapped his thighs and roared with laughter, and so did all the men by the fire – even Namastis, who was not usually loud in his demonstrations, had to hold his gut. Xeno, Satyrus and Bion stood silent while half a dozen young men squirmed. Dionysius actually went to the ground. 'Your face!' Dionysius managed. 'Your—'

Abraham stumbled over to Satyrus and put his hand on his arm. 'God – you look fit to kill us. Joke, friend.' His eyes flicked over Bion and in a stage whisper, he said, '*We know.*' And then he sputtered a few times and subsided.

Satyrus found that he was smiling. So was Xeno. After a while, Bion smiled too. 'Fuck the lot of you,' he said in his low voice.

'Don't go leaving angry,' Dionysius called. 'Or if you do, leave the wine.'

That got another round of laughter, until voices from behind them ordered them to pipe down.

Half a skin of wine later, Dionysius declaimed his hymn to the breasts of an unknown avatar of Aphrodite. Bion drank wine indifferently, and when Dionysius lay down on his cloak, he found a snake – harmless, Bion assured him several anxious moments later.

Philokles and Theron came to drink the last of the wine. Theron gave Bion a long look but said nothing. Philokles produced his Spartan cup and filled it. 'Who among you poured a libation?' he said.

That silenced them.

'What a thankless bunch of recruits you are. The noisiest men in the camp, and no libation?' He poured a good half of his cup into the sand. 'I offer this wine to all the gods – but most of all to Grey-Eyed Athena to keep us safe, and to that god most men never name – gentle Hades, take only the old and leave the young to enjoy their youth.'

'That's a chilly health, Strategos,' Dionysius said.

Philokles shook his head. 'Men will die tomorrow. Men you

know. You may be dead yourselves. Lack of sleep could kill you as dead as an enemy arrow, lads. I doubt that ten of you could get any ill from one skin of wine, but I think it's time to get in your cloaks and sleep.'

'Still,' Theron put in, after taking his sip of wine, 'I'd rather hear my front rank laughing their arses off the night before a fight, than pissing in their beer.'

Philokles smiled. 'Anyone afraid?'

Satyrus managed a smile, and a nervous silence greeted Philokles, who laughed.

'You're all lousy liars,' Philokles said. 'But brave ones!'

Theron put an arm around his shoulders. 'Know what, Satyrus? This will be my first fight. In a phalanx. I'm so scared I can't get to sleep.' He raised his cup.

Philokles took the cup from his hand and drained it. 'This will be my eleventh fight in a phalanx on a big field.' He looked around at the younger men, and they looked at him, the very image of the warrior. 'I'm as scared as any of you – more, because I know what I face tomorrow. But listen – no philosophy here, lads, just the straight bronze, as we say in Sparta. Keep your spot in the line and get through their pikes as fast as you can, and we'll be fine. We're really quite good. Tomorrow, you'll see how good we are.'

'Will we win, Philokles?' Dionysius asked.

Philokles scratched his head like a farmer. 'Lad, I don't know. We ought to lose. Ptolemy is taking a mighty risk. There are still men in this army – Macedonians – who *want us to lose*. So the Greeks and the Aegyptians have to fight extra hard. See? Now go to bed.'

And they did.

PART VII

THE CONTEST

26

Stratokles had plenty of time to be disgusted with himself.

The worst of it was that he had been wrong. He, the great political philosopher, had backed the wrong horse as surely as Demosthenes had with Alexander. It wasn't that Demetrios the Golden was incompetent. He was ruthless and he had strokes of brilliance, and his will was strong. It was simply that he was too young and too inflexible to command an army. His own brilliance and beauty clouded his judgment. He assumed himself to be a child of the gods and behaved accordingly. And even when events proved him wrong, he couldn't be seen to change his mind.

Stratokles watched as the golden boy's strategy unravelled, and he shook his head quietly. He didn't need spies to tell him how badly their cavalry was losing the foraging war – he saw the wounded, the empty saddles, the disgust of the Saka and Mede nobles.

On the other hand, his networks – his carefully paid webs of informers and messengers – hung together, and he had at least two reports a day on the treason of Ptolemy's Macedonians. The Foot Companions – the elite of Ptolemy's army – would change sides as soon as the fighting started. The deal was done. When they changed sides, every Macedonian on the field would know who the winner was – and the golden boy would owe his throne to a wily Athenian and his web of informers.

'If he was a wrestler,' Stratokles commented to his one-time kidnap victim, 'Demetrios would be at the edge of the sand, with one foot on the line, down two falls to one.'

'Hmm,' Amastris said. 'Why did you bring me here?'

'I thought more highly of the boy and his father than either deserves,' Stratokles answered. Having begun on a path of scrupulous honesty, he didn't deviate. 'It might be said that I erred.'

Amastris nodded. 'Except?'

Stratokles spread his palms. 'Ah, despoina, there are some things even you are not yet ready to hear. You have other loyalties. Let us say that I have the means to save the golden boy from his folly.'

'And thus render him deeper in your debt than would have been the case if he had been as competent as you imagined him to be.' Amastris settled on to her cushions and smiled at him. She had no problems looking at his face.

'You are a superb student,' he said, and she glowed at his praise.

Stratokles had always devised plans in layers, so that when one layer failed, he had a reserve – sometimes two or three. He looked at his new student of statecraft, and he thought lovingly of his new reserve.

In Demetrios's camp palace – a set of tents as big as Xerxes' captured tents in Athens – he had a young hostage. A glowering, handsome boy who claimed to have had Alexander himself for a father. Herakles.

In Macedon, Herakles was a rumour. Now that Stratokles had laid eyes on him, it was hard not to plot. Difficult to keep himself from imagining what he could accomplish for Athens – for the world – if he had Alexander's heir and this brilliant girl.

He looked at her again and knew that she was not for him. But neither was the satrapy of Phrygia. Suddenly it seemed like a limited ambition – a wasted life. He didn't need to be lord of a rich province. Instead, he could stand behind the throne of the earth, the trusted advisor, the hands – gentle hands – on the reins of state. Athens would be the richest city in the world, and he would have a statue in bronze on the Acropolis.

'You have seen the man that calls himself Herakles?' Stratokles said to his student.

She allowed herself a smile. 'Yes.'

'He is the son of Alexander. He may well prove to be the most important player on this board.' Stratokles stroked his beard.

'He's younger than my Satyrus, and has no experience of

anything but being a hostage.' Amastris waved for a cup of wine.

'His experience is not the issue,' Stratokles said. 'His blood is the issue.'

'Ahh!' she replied.

'A child of yours by him – Alexander's grandson – could guarantee the future of Heraklea for ever,' Stratokles said carefully.

She didn't blush. Instead, she smiled demurely and shook her head. 'Or make my city a target for every adventurer with an army,' she said. 'And my child. And me.'

'Ahh!' Stratokles responded, and they both laughed.

Nonetheless, he sent for his Lucius, and gave him some exacting instructions.

So – while Stratokles had plenty of time to be disgusted with himself, he was not. He was too busy plotting.

27

Satyrus rose with the first of the light, feeling as if he hadn't slept at all, bitten by insects and with his left hip sore from sleeping on the ground. His guts churned, and every time he looked out over the sand towards Gaza, they flipped again.

He went out beyond the horse lines and did his business, but it didn't help. Before the sun was another handspan higher in the sky, his guts churned again and he felt as if he had the same trots they'd all had camping on the Nile. When he stood still, he shook.

After a while, he ran. It wasn't a decision – he just dropped his chitoniskos on his pack and ran off, naked except for his sandals. He ran a stade, and then another, along the 'streets' where men lay in rows, some awake, facing the dawn, and others snoring in bliss or simply in exhaustion. He ran until he passed the sentries to the west, where the road led towards Aegypt. And then he turned and ran back. Without disturbing Basis or Abraham, he used pumice to polish the scales of his cuirass, and then he buffed the silver on his helmet until it shone like the moon.

Like thousands of other men, he went down to the beach and swam in the cool dawn. Far down the beach towards Gaza, he could see thousands of other men performing the same ritual.

He went back to his pack and took out his best red chitoniskos, and then he put on his armour – all of it, even the greaves, which he had only worn for parades. Then he walked around the Phalanx of Aegypt, feeling hollow, and made sure all the men ate a good meal.

Melitta was up with the dawn, having lain with Xeno and regretted it somehow – not the act itself, but the surrender. The *triteness* of sex before battle. Xeno was going to face battle with a thousand friends, and he was *scared*. She understood. She was scared herself.

She and her people were facing the elephants.

Archers, javelin men, all of the peltastai – they were out on the sand, digging pits and putting stakes in the bottom. Ptolemy's greatest fear was the power of Demetrios's elephants – fifty of the monsters, where Ptolemy didn't have a single one. So the light troops went out in the new dawn, each attended by a handful of slaves, and they dug. This time they had tools. Ptolemy prepared for things like this.

She dug and dug. She thought of Argon and his too-shallow hole, and she dug more.

She was soaked in sweat by the time yet more slaves came with food, and she got out of her hole and ate, slurping cool water from a clay cup and then eating mutton soup so fast that barley streamed down her chiton. She regretted every minute that she'd stayed awake the night before, but she found, as the sun rose and the colour of the world changed, that she didn't have to be worried about being pregnant.

That was for tomorrow.

Today, she had elephants.

Both armies threw out clouds of skirmishers first. Demetrios, with all of Asia in his father's hip pocket, put out several thousand peasants with javelins and the occasional sling or bow.

Satyrus watched them. He had his shield on his foot and his spear in his hand, but most of his file was still donning armour or finishing a bowl of soup. Rafik stood with Philokles at the head of the parade, the trumpet still on his hip.

Food was not helping. Satyrus felt that if he let go a fart, his breakfast would stream down his legs with the last of his courage. He gritted his teeth.

Abraham came up, put his shield face-down on the ground and raised an arm. 'Buckle my cuirass?' he asked.

'Sure?' Satyrus said. 'Where's Basis?'

'Praying,' Abraham said.

Satyrus got the buckle done. 'Hold my spear?' he asked. 'I have to piss, again.' He ran off to the edge of the parade and ran back, still feeling as if his guts would leak out, picked up his shield, took his spear from Abraham and tried to stand tall.

Rafik blew the trumpet. Satyrus felt his knees lose their strength. He wondered how men who were condemned to death felt. He hated his weakness, but the weakness was real.

'Priests!' Philokles called.

One by one, the serving priests came to the head of the parade. All along the line, men sacrificed – a hundred animals died in as many seconds.

Satyrus was surprised – through the fog of his fear – to find that the Phalanx of Aegypt was next to the Foot Companions. The Macedonian foot-guards were just a few paces to the right of his file, silent except for the occasional order. The men in the ranks had their armour on, but their sarissas were being carried by servants.

Their priest cut the throat of a young heifer.

Out on the sand in front of them, men died – javelin men and archers and naked men throwing rocks, four stades from the line of priests. The battle had started.

The enemy light troops were terrible – like slaves driven forward with a whip. In fact, for all Melitta knew, they *were* driven forward with a whip. All of Idomeneus's toxotai were together – a better-armoured band than they had been before the ambush – spread at two-pace intervals over several hundred paces of ground. Aegyptian peltastai with small shields and heavy javelins moved through them to face the hordes of Demetrios's peasants, and the fighting – such as it was – didn't last long before the peasants ran.

Idomeneus came by and offered her an apple. She smiled at him and took it.

'I love apples,' she said.

Another band of psiloi came out of the rising dust and hurled rocks at the peltastai, who charged and drove them off, but this time a few of the peltastai were left to bleed in the sand.

She could feel the earth pounding under her feet before she saw them. They were *immense*. Too big to be real. They moved with an un-horse-like gait, and they were slow – but they were coming.

Ahead of them came a fresh wave of psiloi – men with light

armour and round bucklers who seemed to have some spirit.

'Stand your ground!' the Aegyptian officer yelled. His voice was not reassuring.

She found that she'd finished her apple. She dropped the core and kicked sand over it without thinking.

'About to be our turn, I think,' Idomeneus said. 'Luck, Bion. Shoot straight.'

'Same to you, pal,' she said. And then she strung her bow.

Satyrus could see the light troops, as far as his eyes could see – several thousand men. Their movement raised a curtain of dust, but it was nothing like what it would be later in the day, and *nothing* like it had been at Gabiene. Just the thought of the fight on the salt flats made him take a sip from his canteen.

'The army is going to move forward,' Philokles called. 'Be ready.'

This far out, there was no marching. When the trumpet sounded, men lifted their shields and trudged forward in open order, their servants still carrying canteens and food – some men in other taxeis were still making their servants carry their shields. The movement sounded like thunder and the ground moved as sixteen thousand pikemen and their servants and shield-bearers – almost thirty thousand men, and not a few women – walked forward. The polemarchs and the phylarchs watched attentively, and men at the flanks of formations roared at each other, because crowding or bowing at this point could disorder the whole line which had been formed so carefully.

Satyrus saw humps moving opposite him. *Elephants.* He stumbled and forced himself to stand upright. *Ares. Ares, god of war, do not let me be a coward.*

Curiously, the elephants had a steadying effect on Satyrus, most of all because he knew that his sister had to face them and he wanted her safe. Thinking of other people was a strange relief from fear, but it was real – as if fear was something selfish.

Aha.

Satyrus smiled. He turned and looked at the pale faces of his companions. Philokles was still ahead of the phalanx, as was Theron on the opposite flank.

'Watch your spacing, Aegypt!' Satyrus called. He forced a smile at the front rank. 'They're only elephants, gentlemen!'

Fifty paces forward, and then a hundred, and then another hundred. The elephants were two stades away – less – and he could feel it when they moved. In less than a minute, the great brown and grey creatures would be among the Ptolemaic skirmishers – and his sister would be facing the monsters.

'Halt!' the trumpets called.

'Fall out the shield-bearers!' Philokles called.

This is it.

Abraham reached over, shield and all, and they embraced. Satyrus reached past Abraham to clasp arms with Dionysius and then with Xeno. Xeno held on to his arm. 'I'm sorry,' he said. Behind him, his boy flashed a shy smile and turned to leave the ranks.

Satyrus grinned and hugged him. 'Tell me later!' he said, and his grin wasn't faked.

All around him, as the servants cleared the files, men clasped hands. Satyrus got a quick squeeze from Diokles and another from Namastis, a kiss from Dionysius, and then the files were clear.

'Half files, close to the front!' Philokles called. The same order could be heard from the Foot Companions, who were just to their right.

Namastis marched his half-file forward to fill the opening left by the shield-bearers. Now the phalanx was eight deep but much closer in order. Behind Satyrus, Diokles and the rest of the file shuffled forward to form the close-order battle formation.

Satyrus could see Panion, the commander of the Foot Companions, striding across the sand towards Philokles. His body betrayed rage.

'You are crowding my files with your fucking slaves,' Panion said. 'Double your files again and give me room.'

'Your men must have drifted on the march,' Philokles said. 'We're matched with the White Shields on our left.' He shrugged. 'Open out to the right.'

Panion spat. 'I've had enough of you, Greek. You and

your corps of baggage-handlers don't belong in the line. I told Ptolemy you'd lose him the battle. Now you're on *my* flank. And you know what? You and your pack of dogs? Cowards!'

'Go back to your taxeis,' Philokles said. 'We are in the same army. I do not question your courage – have the courtesy to do the same.'

Panion spat. 'Listen to you!' He turned to face the Phalanx of Aegypt. 'Most of you will be dead in an hour! You don't even have to stand in the line! Your so-called polemarch demanded that you stand in the battle line. Run along home, now, Gyptos!'

The Phalanx of Aegypt shuffled. Panion laughed contemptuously. 'Dogs pretending to be men,' he said.

'Turn and face me,' Philokles said.

Panion turned.

'Listen, Macedonians!' Philokles roared, and his voice carried a stade. 'I am a man of Sparta. When we charge the enemy, see who flinches. No man in our ranks has a friend across the lines, Macedonians. No man there will offer a single one of our men mercy.' He walked up to Panion, and stood a half a hand taller. 'Foot Companions! Your officer is *bought and paid for by the enemy.*' Philokles pulled his cloak back off his shoulder.

'You lie—' Panion began, and he raised his spear.

'Let the gods say who lies!' Philokles roared. Panion struck, but Philokles' arm moved as fast as a thunderbolt and his spear slammed into Panion's helmet and the man went down.

Philokles *laughed.*

Satyrus was an arm's length from the nearest Macedonian file. They were roiling with fury.

'Macedonians!' came a roar from behind Satyrus. He turned to see Ptolemy and Seleucus on horseback, brilliantly armoured and surrounded by Hetairoi. 'Macedonians! The enemy is Demetrios, who we will destroy in a few hours. The enemy is not next to you in line. The next man who speaks against another is a traitor – mark my words.' He looked down at Panion, who was rising from the dust.

'Fucker—' Panion said, with something incomprehensible.

'Prove the charge unfounded on the field,' said the lord

of Aegypt. He pointed at the commander of his foot-guards. 'Myself,' he said, just loudly enough that the front rank of both taxeis could hear. 'Myself, I think you probably are a fucking traitor, Panion. Die well and I'll see to your widow. Try to screw me, and I'll put my mercenaries right into your shieldless flank and you will *all die* whether I win or not.' The lord of Aegypt waved his arm at ranks and ranks of Diodorus's Exiles, who stood by their horses on the flank of the Foot Companions.

Then the lord of Aegypt waved, and most men cheered – not the Foot Companions – and Philokles stood and faced them. He clasped hands with Philokles and rode away, leaving Panion in the sand.

Behind him, the elephants were closing on the toxotai.

'Men of Alexandria,' Philokles said. He paused, and even Panion's men fell silent. 'Yesterday, or two weeks ago, or a year ago, you were different men. You lived a different life. Some of you are rich men, and some are poor. Some of you stole, and others drank wine. Somewhere in these ranks is a man who killed for money. Another carried bricks. Some of you are Greek, and some are Aegyptian. A few of you are even Macedonian.' He paused, and men laughed.

'Today, no one cares how you lived. All that men will ever say of you is how you fought here, and how you *died*. Are you in debt? Desperate? The gods hate you?' His voice rose to fill the air, as if a god was speaking – the voice of Ares come to earth. 'Stand your ground today and die if you must, and all men will *ever* say of you is that *you served the city*. You will go with the heroes – your name will adorn a shrine. Be better than you were. *Serve the city.* Stand in your ranks and push when I call you. Remember that you will have *no mercy* at the hands of the men across the sand. Not a one of you will be spared.'

He raised his spear over his head. 'When I call, every man must push forward *one more step*. Understand?'

'Yes!' they roared.

'Remember, every one of you! There is nothing but this day and this hour. Show your gods who you really are.' He lowered his spear and walked to his place in the line, pulling his helmet down and fastening the cheekpieces.

'Not your usual take on philosophy,' Satyrus said, when his tutor took his place.

Philokles stood straight. 'Wisdom has a different look from the front rank,' he said to Satyrus, with a smile that showed under his cheekpieces. 'Prepare to march!' he roared.

The Aegyptian peltastai stood their ground longer than Melitta had expected. Just in front of her pit, they closed their ranks and counter-charged the enemy psiloi, running the bronze-shielded men back among their elephants. Then they lost their nerve and retreated, and their officers couldn't hold them after a man was caught by an elephant and spitted on her sword-tipped tusks. The animal shook the dying man and he *split open*.

The peltastai ran back half a stade. Melitta stopped watching them. She had targets.

She loosed a dozen arrows at the leading elephants before she knew that her shafts were having no effect. The lead elephant had so many arrows sticking out of her back that it looked as if she'd sprouted some scraggly feathers, but the beast continued her leisurely stroll forward, still tossing the remnants of the peltastes on the twin swords around her mouth.

None of the other archers were doing any better.

'We're fucked,' she muttered, drawing and loosing again.

Their arrows had cleared the last of the enemy psiloi, so that the monsters strode down the field in a long line with no infantry covering them, but that seemed to be a very minor flaw as the line plodded across the sand towards her pit.

If they go through us, they go into the face of the phalanx, she thought. *And we lose.*

Next to her, a pair of Greek archers called to each other as they lofted arrows high. 'Their skin must be thinner somewhere,' called Laertes, the oldest man among the toxotai.

The beasts were now so close that the archers could try to aim for softer parts – also close enough for flight to seem like an option. She drew to her eyebrow and loosed – to see her bronze-headed barb *bounce* off the lead elephant's head.

For the first time she realized that there were *men* on the backs of the behemoths. Without thinking, she shot one – the range was just a few horse-lengths – and for the first time in fifteen shafts she saw a target go down, the man clutching his armpit as he fell from the beast's back.

She thought of the elephants in Eumenes the Cardian's army, and how their mahout said that they were only deadly as long as there were men on their backs.

The lead cow elephant turned her head, as if curious as to what had happened.

Melitta shot two arrows as fast as she'd ever shot in her life. The first missed – right over the top of the cow, who was so close that Melitta was shooting *up* to aim at all. The second hit the other spearman on the elephant's back, sticking in his shield but not, apparently, doing any harm.

She looked around her and realized that the toxotai were running. She was the last archer shooting. She turned and ran herself.

Satyrus pulled his helmet down and tied the chinstrap one-handed even as they marched forward. Flute players sounded the step, and Satyrus glanced right and left, his heart filled by the sight. As far as his eye could see, their ranks were moving. The centre was slow, and the mass of the phalanx bowed, but he could see now that the line of his own phalanx – all the army of Aegypt together – was longer than the enemy line.

Off to the right, the cavalry was moving. Off to the left, just a stade away, Satyrus could see Diodorus sitting alone on his charger at the head of the Exiles. He seemed to be eating a sausage.

Right in front of him, the elephants had broken the line of peltastai and toxotai. His gut clenched, his chest muscles trembled and he had to make himself stand taller. *Elephants.*

Melitta ran twenty paces and stopped – in part, because Idomeneus was standing there, putting an arrow to his bow, and in part because she had to see what happened when the monsters hit the pits.

'Stop running!' Idomeneus yelled. 'There's nowhere to go!' He shot.

Forty paces away, the lead cow shuddered as her front feet slid out from under her. In seconds she had slipped most of the way into the hole – head first, and her head cap of bronze pushed the stake flat and it did her no harm. She bellowed, gathered her hindquarters and scrabbled out of the pit, shaking her head.

Too shallow. Melitta shot. Her arrow struck in a great fore-foot.

But something was wrong with the beast, because she stopped. She rolled her head, looking right and left, as arrows pricked her. Her snake-like trunk touched the prone form of the man who'd come off her head when she'd stepped into the pit – he didn't move. Melitta almost had pity as the great beast tried to move her driver.

Her driver. *Her driver.*

'Shoot the drivers!' Melitta shouted. Her voice broke – it was the most feminine shout on the field – but it carried, and she didn't care. 'Shoot the drivers!'

Idomeneus took up the shout. 'Drivers!' he said, pulling his great bow to his ear and punching a finger-thick shaft into the mahout of the next beast in line. The man threw up his hands and fell back, and the beast, riderless, stopped.

'Be ready!' Philokles roared beside him.

Satyrus felt his arse clench, felt his guts turn and turn again. Three times now, his fear had fallen away, and every time it came back.

Elephants.

He looked at the front rank, and it was bending because the Foot Companions weren't keeping up. 'Dress up, phylarchs!' he shouted. Really Philokles' job, but he had his attention on the trumpets and the battle in the front. 'Theron!' Theron was a hundred paces distant – a hopeless distance on a battlefield. 'Theron! Step up!' he called, and other voices repeated it – the front rank flexed, and there was Theron, waving his spear and pushing forward. The file-followers struggled to close up from behind. A pikeman fell and the whole body of men rippled and someone cried out in pain. 'Close up!' Philokles bellowed.

Satyrus tore his eyes off the recovery of the middle ranks – he was drifting left because he'd turned his head. 'Watch your spacing!' Namastis growled. A deserved rebuke.

And then, through the limited vision of his close-faced helmet, he saw that the elephants had *stopped*. 'Look!' he said to Namastis. 'Look!'

The monsters were in the line of pits. Almost half managed to walk right through without touching the obstacles, but they didn't exploit their success – they had a curious morale of their own, and when the archers began to clear the crews off the backs of the animals in the pits, the whole elephant advance broke down.

Idomeneus was the first man to run forward and Melitta loved him for it. Stripped of their psiloi, the elephants were vulnerable once they stopped. The archers ran in among them in their open formation and began massacring the crews. It wasn't even a fight – the men on the backs of the huge beasts had no reply to make to the hundreds of shafts aimed at them, and a few even tried to surrender.

No prisoners were taken. The archers slaughtered the crews in a paroxysm of fear and rage, and then the beasts began to turn away, the masses of sharp shafts and the point-blank shots beginning to scare them, and suddenly they were running – *away*.

'Halt!' sang the trumpets.

'Halt!' echoed the officers.

The phalanx ground to a halt. All along the line, officers raced up and down ordering the line to dress. The front was disordered everywhere, and the Foot Companions were almost a full phalanx-depth to the rear.

'If they hit us now, we're wrecked,' Philokles said to Satyrus. 'Gods!' He ran off along the front of the phalanx, ordering men to dress the line.

The White Shields took up the cry first, and in a heartbeat, all discipline was forgotten. 'The elephants run!' men shouted, and the front ranks, the men who would have had to face the brutes first, all but danced.

Philokles roared for silence. Ptolemy appeared from the right and rode down the front rank. 'Look at that, boys!' he called. 'Every man of you owes our light troops a cup of the best! By Herakles!' Ptolemy halted in the centre of the White Shields. He seemed to be addressing the whole line. 'Ours to win, boys! Right here! Right now! *Remember who you are!*'

The White Shields roared, and so did the Phalanx of Aegypt, but Satyrus thought that the other cheers were muted. He hoped it was just his fears.

Philokles reached past Namastis. 'Don't point,' he said. 'It's not all good.'

Over to the left, the cavalry fight wasn't going well for any-one – but suddenly, in a flaw in the battle haze, the whole line of the phalanx could see forty more elephants waiting.

'Ares,' Satyrus cursed. His heart sank. Again. So he made himself turn his head. 'Drink water,' he yelled.

Philokles was nodding. 'We have to break the phalanx in front of us before Demetrios throws those elephants into us,' he said. 'That just became the battle.' He drank and spat. 'When I fall, you take command.'

'When you fall?' Satyrus asked.

Philokles gave him a brilliant smile – the kind of smile his tutor scarcely ever smiled. Then the Spartan ran out of the ranks towards Ptolemy. He grabbed at his bridle, and they could see Ptolemy nod and signal to the trumpeters, and the signal for the advance rang out before Philokles was back in the ranks.

Ptolemy turned his horse and rode away towards the cavalry fight on the left. Way off to the right, Satyrus saw Diodorus. He wasn't eating sausage any more, but he hadn't moved.

The Foot Companions were *still* not in their place.

Philokles jumped out of the front rank, held his spear across their chests and roared 'Dress the line' so loudly that Satyrus flinched, helmet and all.

'Prepare to execute the marine drill!' he called. He ran along the front rank, heedless of the javelins that were starting to fall, until he reached Theron, and then he sprinted back, fast as an athlete despite age and wine and armour.

'Spears – up!' came the order. They were less than a stade

from the enemy. A handful of brave or stupid psiloi still stood between the two mighty phalanxes, but they were scattering, running for the flanks. Satyrus watched the last of their own archers running off to the right to get around the killing ground.

Now that he could see the enemy phalanx, he could see that it looked bad – there were ripples and gaps where he assumed the elephants had burst back through, and officers were dressing the ranks.

Half a stade, and he could see the enemy move – they had their ranks dressed – they shivered as if the phalanx was a single, living organism and the whole thing leaned forward as the enemy began their advance, and suddenly everything happened at twice the speed.

The length of a sprint – he could see the emblems on their shields.

'Spears – down!' came the command – by trumpet, repeated by word of mouth. And the sarissas came down. In the Phalanx of Aegypt, the men in front had the shorter spears, and they lifted them over their heads in unison – a sight that literally banished fear, as training took over and Satyrus got his shoulder firmly under the rim of his aspis.

'Sing the Paean!' Philokles called, and the Alexandrians started the call to Apollo. The song carried him forward a hundred paces – literally buoyed him up – but at its end, in step and facing the foe, he still had ten horse-lengths of terror to face.

Ten horse-lengths, and he was confronted by a wall of spears that filled his mind as Amastris's body had filled it, so that nothing and no one could take his eyes away from the lethal glitter of twelve thousand pike points.

The White Shields were *slowing down*. Ares—

'Eyes front!' Philokles roared. 'Ready, Alexandria!'

The taxeis growled.

Five horse-lengths. The thicket of steel was pointed right at his throat – his head – too thick to penetrate. Thick enough to walk on.

It was *impossible* that a man could face so much iron and live.

His legs carried him forward.

'Charge!' Philokles' voice and Rafik's trumpet sounded together, and the front rank responded like trained beasts – left shoulder *down*, spear *down*, head *down*.

Spears rang against his aspis, reaching for his guts, again and again, and he bulled forward, legs pushing, blow to his helmet, *step* forward, another blow and another with enough weight to shift him sideways so that he stumbled, but he pushed, *he pushed*, nothing but the power of his legs and the weight of a dozen spear shafts on his aspis tilted almost flat like a table, and he *pushed* – Diokles' shield pushing him forward – through! UP and PUSH and he rammed his spear straight ahead, felt the weight of Diokles pushing him another half pace forward. THROUGH!

To this right, Philokles roared like a bull and his spear hit a man's helmet just over the nasal and burst it in a spray of blood and the man fell back and Philokles pushed—

Suddenly, as if his wits had been restored, Satyrus saw the fight for what it was, and in one smooth motion he killed a phalangite – not the man in front of him, but the man in front of Abraham whose shield was open, and then he placed his big shield against the enemy's and *pushed* and Abraham pushed forward into the new space, on his own or carried forward by his file, and now he took the file-follower by surprise and simply knocked him down, and Satyrus rammed his spear over his shield, once, twice, three times – connected with something – again and again. Glance at Philokles, cover his shoulder – and then his opponent was *down* and Satyrus was forward a step. Rafik's man was uncovered to his right, and his spear was there, scoring a clean hit on the man's helmet. His point didn't penetrate but the man's head snapped back and he stumbled and Rafik stepped on the man and went forward and Rafik's file-follower put his butt-spike through the man's chest. Satyrus's opponent roared, pushed his shield and Diokles killed him over Satyrus's shoulder and Satyrus leaped forward to cover Philokles, who had put another man down and was moving forward again. The men behind the man facing Philokles were flinching away.

Now Satyrus was chest to chest with another man. His opponent dropped his sarissa and ripped his sword from the scabbard and Satyrus felt the wash of the man's onion breath on his face and *he* was pushed back and the ranks locked – Abraham grunting, and Namastis shouting in Aegyptian.

Satyrus's spear broke in his hands, trapped against a shield. He swung the butt-spike like a mace and scored against the tip of the big Macedonian's shoulder where his shield didn't cover it, and then his body moved as if he was making a sacrifice – hand up, grab the hilt under his armpit, sword drawn, down, over, the feint – back cut. The Macedonian missed his parry, his kopis over-committed, and his wrist bones parted as Satyrus's blade cut through his arm and glanced off the faceplate on the other man's Thracian helmet. The blood from his severed hand sprayed and blinded Satyrus, and he flinched, stumbled – but forward, because Diokles shoved him and then stabbed at his next opponent over his head, saving his life. A sword scraped along Satyrus's helmet and he lost a piece of his left ear, although he didn't feel it.

'One more step!' the voice of the war god said. 'Now!'

The whole Phalanx of Aegypt planted and *pushed*. The Macedonian phalanx shuddered, and then, as if, having given one step, they could give another, they fell back.

And now the Aegyptians caught fire. Maybe they'd never believed. Or maybe they'd just hoped – but in those seconds, those heartbeats, the same message went out to every man in the taxeis.

We are the better men.

'Alexandria!' Namastis called. He was the first, Satyrus thought, but then everyone was shouting.

Then there was no battle cry that any one man could discern but a roar, a roar of rage and triumph and fear – the bronze-lunged voice of Ares – and the enemy phalanx gave another step, another. Something had broken at the back and the spears were dropping, and suddenly there was—

Nothing. Scattered men stood confused in front of Satyrus, the enemies too foolish to have broken, and Satyrus killed one without thinking, stepping up to the man and cutting – one, two, three, as fast as thought.

'Ares,' Philokles said. He sounded weak. 'Satyrus! We're *not done*. Rally them. Rafik, sound the rally!'

Satyrus looked back. He couldn't see anything behind him but his own men, but to the side, there were still enemies – some so close that he could hear the orders their officers shouted.

The notes of the rally sounded. Philokles was leaning on his spear. Satyrus thought that he was just breathing hard, but then he saw that there was blood all down the Spartan's legs – pouring away from under his bronze breastplate.

'I'll go for Theron,' Satyrus said.

'No time,' Philokles said. His knees went, and he slid down his spear, but he didn't turn his head. 'Right into their flank – *now, boy, before they recover.*' His arm shot out, pointing at the uncovered flank of the enemy phalanx, and Philokles fell just that way, his face to the enemy, his arm pointing the path to victory.

And Satyrus did not flinch. He stepped across Philokles, the same way he'd stepped across the deck of the *Golden Lotus*, as if he'd done it all his life – although the man he loved best in all the world lay in the sand at his feet.

Diokles snapped forward to fill his place.

'We will wheel the taxeis to the left!' Satyrus called. 'On my command!'

Through the cheekpieces of his helmet, it sounded remarkably like Philokles' voice, right down to the Laconian drawl. 'March!' he roared.

The taxeis pivoted on Theron, the left-most man – unless he, too, was dead. This was the manoeuvre they had so often done wrong – this was where the centre of the line would fold, eager men going too fast, terrified men going too slow.

Halfway around. All the time to consider how much like sailing a trireme it was to command a phalanx. All the time to watch the men opposite him. They were turning, but men at the back were already giving way, running for their lives past their file-closers. There was no hope for a phalanx taken in the flank.

The taxeis of Alexandria pivoted well enough. The centre buckled at the end – someone tripped, a man got a butt-spike in the head and the spears were still down, not erect. Too close for that.

Too late to worry. 'Three-step charge!' Satyrus called.

Rafik sounded it.

Only half the files responded. The centre was a wreck, just from two men going down and the spears of their files flying in all directions. Theron's end of the line never heard the command, or if they did they didn't respond.

It didn't matter. Because the fifty files that did respond covered the distance to the enemy at the run, and their shields deflected the handful of sarissas that opposed them, and then their spears were into the flank of the enemy, and the enemy regiment collapsed and ran like a herd of panicked cattle – two thousand men turned into a mob in a matter of heartbeats. Satyrus, the rightmost man of his line, never reached an enemy – by the time he'd crossed the space, they were gone.

They were gone, and the White Shields were unblocked. They had started to cheer. However late they had come into the fight, they were moving – wheeling to the left, just as the Alexandrians had done.

Philemon, the polemarch of the White Shields, was calling to Theron, and Theron came running across the face of the victorious Alexandrians. 'Drink water!' Satyrus called. No one left the ranks to pursue the fleeing Macedonians. Instead, a few men cheered, the rest simply stopped. Like exhausted runners at the end of a race.

'Philokles?' Theron asked. His nose was broken under his helmet, and blood covered his breastplate. He had blood on his hands.

'Down,' Satyrus said.

'Philemon wants us to march to the right to make space for him,' Theron said. 'I'll take your orders,' he continued.

'Good,' Satyrus said. He stood straight. He wanted to laugh at the notion that the taxeis of half-soldiers from Alexandria were being asked to face to the right and advance by files – a hard enough manoeuvre on the parade square – on a battlefield.

He did what he'd seen Philokles do. He ran all the way down the front rank, repeating the command – again and again. He waited precious seconds, the polemarch of the White Shields yelling from further to the left. He ignored him, waiting for the phylarchs to pass the word back. Then he sprinted to Rafik, cursing his greaves. They were eating his ankles.

'Face to the spear side!' he ordered. 'March!'

As one – almost as one, because he watched Dionysius face the shield side and then pivot on his heel – the Phalanx of Aegypt faced to the right and marched off – one hundred, two hundred paces deeper into the enemy lines.

From here, on the front right of the phalanx, Satyrus could see all the way to the cavalry fight on the left – could see the forty-elephant reserve.

'Theron,' he shouted. Satyrus pulled his helmet off. 'Face to the shield side! Restore your files! Dress!'

They knew the facing order was coming and they did it like professionals, and then the ranks dressed. Next to them, the White Shields wheeled up into the new line, while to their front, the next enemy phalanx began to shirk and flutter and men on the flanks realized what was coming.

Theron appeared from the dust as if by the hand of some god. 'Polemarch?' he asked.

'Go and find Philokles. Save him if you can.' Satyrus had his war voice on – no quaver of emotion. *Why can't you be like this all the time?* Melitta had asked him once. He wondered where she was and if she was alive.

'I'm the left phylarch—'

'If we don't flinch from the contest, nothing on earth or in the heavens can save the army of Demetrios,' Satyrus said. He pointed to where, before they were even charged, the centre phalanx of the enemy was melting away, throwing down their sarissas. Even the sudden arrival of the reserve elephants might not save Demetrios now. His centre was lost.

Satyrus looked back to where the Foot Companions waited in the sand, unblooded, less than a stade away.

Theron needed no second urging. He turned and ran off

towards the site of the first fight. Around Satyrus, all his men had canteens at their lips.

Satyrus sprinted out to the ranks and found the White Shield polemarch.

'My men need a minute,' he said. 'I'm going to go shame the Foot Companions into joining the line.'

Philemon had a helmet shaped like a lion's head. He tipped it back on his head and glared at the Foot Companions. 'They're supposed to be our *best*,' he said. He shrugged. 'We won't beat the elephants without them.'

Satyrus saluted the older man and ran back across the sand – just a stade, the same distance as a hoplitodromos, the race in armour at the Olympics. A stade had never seemed so long.

The Macedonians stood in neat ranks, their plumes undisturbed by a breeze. Panion was nowhere to be seen.

Satyrus pulled his helmet off his head. 'Do you want men to say that we won this battle while you *watched*?' he shouted. 'Or are we better men than you?'

He spat, turned on his heel and ran back to his own taxeis. When he reached his place in the ranks, he was so tired that his knees shook.

'The Foot Companions are wheeling into line,' Diokles said.

Satyrus pulled his helmet back down, got his aspis back on his shoulder – a shoulder that hurt as if it had been burned – and raised his spear.

'Alexandria!' he shouted, and fifteen hundred men roared.

And then they were moving forward, the White Shields strong on their flank, the Foot Companions on their other side, and Satyrus could all but see Nike holding her wreath over the end of the enemy line.

Melitta and the rest of the toxotai finished their battle when the elephants broke. When the phalanxes started forward in earnest, the light troops ran in all directions, and Melitta wasn't ashamed to run with them. They ran so far to get around the flank of the Foot Companions that she was severely winded.

They all were. It beat being dead. She knelt on the ground, breathing so hard that she almost retched.

'Look at that,' Idomeneus wheezed. She followed his gaze.

The Foot Companions had slowed to a walk, and the Phalanx of Aegypt moved away from them.

Idomeneus spat. 'Fuckers been bought,' he said, sitting back on his heels. 'We beat the elephants for *nothing*.'

And then they watched as the Phalanx of Aegypt charged home. Dust rose, and the sound of a thousand cooks beating a thousand copper pots. *Satyrus. Xeno.* The Foot Companions halted just short of contact with their opponents.

Watching the rear ranks, Melitta had no idea what she was seeing. Idomeneus walked off and started collecting archers, and then she saw that her uncle Diodorus was sitting on his charger just a dozen horse-lengths to the right, watching the other side of the field and then watching the dust cloud where the phalanxes had engaged.

There was a roar – something had happened – and she saw the rear of the Aegyptian taxeis ripple as if a breeze had stirred wheat on a summer day, and then they roared again.

She felt the shadow and looked up. Diodorus loomed over her.

'You fought the elephants,' he said.

'We did,' she said with pride.

Diodorus pointed at the back of the phalanx. The Foot Companions were moving forward now, as if they could no longer resist the attraction of the enemy. 'Philokles has just given us the chance to win the battle,' Diodorus said with quiet satisfaction.

'What?' Melitta asked.

Diodorus turned and looked across the field, where squadrons of enemy cavalry sat motionless. He raised his arm. 'See that cavalry? They outnumber me. And they aren't coming forward.' He gave her half a smile. 'I'm just supposed to keep them in check – but I *think* that Philokles has just broken golden boy's centre. I think I may just go and widen the hole. Care to come?' He grinned. 'Let's go and show Macedon why we're the best.'

Melitta sprang to her feet, fatigue forgotten. 'Of course!'

Diodorus waved to Crax, who trotted up with a cavalry mount. 'Ah, the mysterious archer,' Crax said when he handed her the reins. He grinned at her. 'Some people think they can fool other people,' he said.

Melitta was briefly abashed. 'I just wanted to—'

'Save it for Sappho,' Diodorus said. 'Myself, I wouldn't keep Kineas's daughter off a battlefield any more than Kineas's son. Second squadron, third rank. Go and find your place, Now.'

Melitta saluted and followed Crax. She waved to Idomeneus, who shook his head and then waved back.

Behind her, the Phalanx of Aegypt surged forward. She caught the movement, and Diodorus nodded. 'Just as I thought,' he said. 'Ready to move, hippeis!'

The enemy's centre taxeis never fought – they just melted away, the rearmost men running first, so that the whole regiment seemed to unravel like moth-eaten fur in a strong wind. Satyrus halted when the White Shields halted. He was amused to see the Foot Companions close up on his right at the double. He wondered if the bastards had even seen any fighting. But they were *there* and now they were committed.

Then the whole right of the army, formed at a ninety-degree angle from their original line, swept from right to left, and the rest of the enemy centre collapsed. The enemy's easternmost phalanxes were heavily engaged against Ptolemy's *loyal* Macedonians and they had no chance to run and many were cut down and more of them surrendered rather than be butchered from the open flank.

Satyrus had no idea what the cavalry were doing, but the infantry battle was over, and the enemy's infantry were *gone*, destroyed or surrendered or run. His taxeis was now in the centre of the canted line, facing a wall of dust and whirling sand. All he wanted to do was walk back and find Philokles, but he knew his duty and when the line halted he ran down the front rank, all the way to the left, where he found the polemarch of the White Shields.

'Now what?' Satyrus demanded.

The polemarch had a purple shield with inlaid ivory. He looked like Achilles come back to earth, but when he took his helmet off, he was bald as polished marble. 'Fucked if I know, son,' he said. 'You in command of those Aegyptians, right? Those boys are *on fire*.' He grinned. 'Not that we did too badly ourselves. And I'm *so pleased* that our Foot Companions chose to join the dance. Where's your big Spartan?'

'Wounded,' Satyrus said. He got his canteen to his lips – no easy feat in armour – and drank deeply.

'Hope he makes it. Don't know. Never been in a battle like this. Never seen the enemy phalanx so badly broken. It must be over – what can they do?' He shrugged. 'What have they got left to fight with?'

Just then, some of the Macedonian file-leaders started to shout, and Satyrus turned to look.

Demetrios's other forty elephants were shambling out of the battle haze.

Diodorus had the hippeis – the Exiles – and six other squadrons of mercenary cavalry. From the third rank, Melitta couldn't see much, but she thought that they were all going forward together. They rode forward at a walk, and when she knelt on her borrowed charger's back, she could see over the left squadron to the phalanx.

They moved and then halted, then moved at a walk again – and then halted. She drank water and waited.

'You look bored,' Carlus said from two ranks ahead. He laughed his big laugh.

Tanu, the Thracian who was just ahead of her, turned and joined in the laugh. 'Don't be in such a hurry to fight!' he said. 'Pay's just the same!'

'I can't see!' Melitta said.

'The cavalry in front of us are unsteady,' Carlus said. 'Their whole centre is gone.' The big man shook his head. 'Never seen anything like it, and I've been in a few fights.'

Diodorus cantered over to Crax at the head of her troop.

'Melitta, front and centre,' he called.

She rode out, sure that she was about to be sent to the rear for all his protestations. But he waved her forward impatiently.

'You know this Amastris?' he asked.

'Yes,' she said.

'Good. Stay with me. I'm going to have a go at breaking right through into his camp. If we make it through that cavalry, I don't think there's anything to stop us – and then, my dear girl, we'll all be rich.' Diodorus smiled and his beard, which was mostly grey, glinted with red.

'Well,' she said, 'we are mercenaries. But shouldn't we be finishing off those infantrymen?' She waved at the thousands of broken pikemen who were racing, weaponless, for the safety of the fortified town of Gaza.

Diodorus shook his head. 'No,' he said. He grinned. 'If you kill them, who will you use to retake Tanais? What we need is the money to pay them.' His grin grew broader, and Crax's grin and Eumenes' grin echoed his. 'And there it is – Demetrios's camp. Let's go and get it, shall we?' He gave orders and turned back to her. 'Stay right at my stirrup,' he said. 'Your friend the princess ought to be close to golden boy's tent. We need to get to her before all of Ptolemy's other cavalry.'

He turned and backed his horse until he was facing his squadrons. 'Over there,' he cried, his voice carrying easily, 'are all the riches of Asia. All you have to do is take them!' They were the words of Miltiades at Marathon, and the Exiles roared their approval.

They went from walk to trot, and then from trot to canter, the files opening uncontrollably the farther they moved, but the enemy did not await their onset. Rearguard squadrons who had stayed together this long fell apart when they saw themselves charged. No one stayed to fight a lost battle – especially against the same cavalrymen who had harried them for weeks out in the desert.

Crax dropped off five files to round up prisoners – mostly men whose horses were so poor that they couldn't outrun their pursuit. And then the whole line was rumbling up the long, gentle slope towards the fortified town of Gaza.

The gates were open.

28

The elephants came on undaunted by the long lines of pike-men – forty elephants against eight thousand men. Satyrus ran back down the front rank to his own men. Sandwiched in the centre of the line, his men had nowhere to go to escape the beasts. He knew what Alexander's phalanxes had done against elephants.

'Drop files! Listen, Aegypt! I'm going to count off the front rank by *five files*. I want those files to make a Spartan march – around to the rear and then halt. Make lanes through the phalanx!' Some men, like Xeno and Abraham, looked as if they understood, while others, like Dionysius, looked blank. Satyrus began to run down the rank. 'One, two, three – four, five! All of you – countermarch to the rear! Go!'

The men he touched – most of them he tagged by hitting their shields quite hard with his butt-spike to make *sure* they knew they were the ones he meant – turned and began to force their way back between the files – and their file-followers followed them, pushing and shoving where they had to, turning their shields side-on to the ranks to make space. It was ugly – it looked as if his whole phalanx had collapsed. Satyrus turned and looked back at the elephants, who were close.

'Herakles, stand by me,' Satyrus said aloud. 'Front rank! File-leaders, look to your spacing! Make it solid!' He used his spear as a baton, dressing the front rank.

Xeno shook his helmeted head so that his plume bobbed up and down. 'We have holes in our ranks!'

'The beasts will go down the lanes!' Satyrus shouted. 'Then we attack them!'

He turned back to look at the elephants. Half a stade.

'Stand fast, Alexandria! When I shout the name of Herakles, every man turn towards the nearest elephant and attack! Kill the riders!' He spared a glance for the White Shields, who were carrying out the same manoeuvre, making lanes, in a much more professional manner.

The elephants were so large that they filled the horizon, so close that he could see their tiny eyes, so loud that their footsteps caused the earth to tremble. Dust rose behind them like smoke from the forge of Hephaistos. Satyrus found that his hands were shaking on his spear haft.

The elephants sped up, their heavy bodies moving with grace, their massive feet crashing more rapidly against the earth, and Satyrus was frozen for a moment, and then he raced for his place in the front rank, knees soft as wet bread. He made himself stand straight, turned and faced the charge of the monsters. The idea of making lanes in his spear block seemed beyond absurd.

All those years ago, Tavi had said that the beasts wouldn't fight without a man on their back. Satyrus gripped that idea the way a drowning man grips a floating spar.

'Spears – *down!*' someone bellowed. At a remove, he realized that *he* had shouted the order. His body was running on its own.

The taxeis responded like one man, the spears flashing as the ranks lifted their weapons and put them in position – as if the mass of an elephant wouldn't snap the shafts like kindling.

Just beyond the reach of his spear, he saw the nearest behemoth turn slightly and race into the opening between Abraham's file and Xeno's, two pike-lengths away. The beast was already slowing, but it ran into the lane as if the driver had given the order.

Satyrus couldn't see any of the other beasts, but he could see the vermilion paint on the flank of the beast that had gone by and smell its strange stink. He could all but hear Philokles telling him that sometimes the leader had to show the way.

He shivered with fear, and filled his lungs, and even over the stink of the great monsters he smelled the wet-cat smell of the god at his shoulder. 'Herakles!' he trumpeted. He raised his spear and turned, stepping out of the ranks – suicide in an infantry fight, but now he was two files away from the elephant, and fear or no fear, this was something he had to *lead*.

He raced across the empty ground of the front and turned down the alley of the missing files, coming up on the beast from behind, its ridiculous tail swaying as it walked. The men on its back were terrified – their terror steadied him – both were thrusting pikes down at the Aegyptian phalangites, most of whom thrust back hesitantly.

'Herakles!' Satyrus called. He was within reach of the thing's leg. His spear was plenty long enough. He ran alongside the beast for three paces, pivoted on his left foot and punched *up* with his spear, right into the mahout's side. The man turned, too late, and his scream was lost in the thunder of the elephants and the phalanx roared as he fell from his perch.

The beast stopped. It made a sound – a horrible sound, the same sound that Satyrus would have liked to have made when he saw the blood pouring out of Philokles, rage and sorrow and mourning compounded.

Abraham's spear plucked the Macedonian pikeman from the beast's back and the man fell into the phalanx, screaming as he died on a dozen spears. The Aegyptian taxeis turned into a mob tearing at the men on the elephants, and in some places the beasts rioted, killing a dozen men in a few seconds. One animal threw an Alexandrian Jew so high in the air that his fall injured as many men as the elephant's rage had. Another animal pinned a man under one huge foot and used her trunk to pull the dead man apart, but everywhere the crews were being butchered at close quarters. The files who had retreated to form the gaps came charging back down the alleys without orders, without any intention but to join their comrades and kill, and even the horrors of the death wreaked by the monsters couldn't slow the inevitable conclusion as a thousand men fought ten elephants.

The elephant closest to Satyrus gave another hideous cry and then slumped, almost unmoving.

All around him, the sounds of fighting died away. Most of the elephants had broken free of the phalanx, and now, their crews gone, they ran away over the plain, but three of the elephants were trapped in the press of bodies and they simply stood, waiting for their fates.

Abraham caught at Satyrus's spear arm as he prepared to kill the beast. 'Stop!'

Satyrus turned his helmeted head. 'What?'

'Stop!' Abraham said. He pulled his helmet off, his long hair falling in a sweat-caked mass. 'They're ours! We've *captured* them!'

In seconds his cry was taken up, and as long as Satyrus lived, he would remember that cry, and the thousands of Alexandrian hands reaching out, not to kill, but just to touch the great beasts.

'The elephants are ours!'

The Exiles went through the crowds at the gate like a scythe through the stalks of wheat on an autumn day when the wheat is dry and the stalks are brittle. Then they passed under the great gate of the camp and into the narrow streets behind the gate.

Melitta followed Diodorus as they entered the town. There was no real defence, just panicked men running from horsemen who seldom stopped to cut them down. Then they were through the town and into the tented camp, and Melitta could see the enemy horsemen and many of the infantry already streaming away from the back of the camp – a complete rout, the enemy already abandoning their own camp, their wives, their treasure.

'Follow me!' Diodorus roared. He pointed his charger's head at the complex of tents in the centre, like a palace built of canvas, with a magnificent central structure of Tyrian purple. 'Exiles, follow me!'

Melitta had been all but born to the saddle but she still found Diodorus difficult to follow. He rode over obstacles, jumping tent ropes like a centaur, his officer's cloak streaming away behind him. Melitta rode around obstacles that Diodorus jumped, but she stayed with him, and Crax and Eumenes and both of their troops followed, their faded blue cloaks marking them as friends.

So far, they had the camp to themselves.

'Ares and Aphrodite!' Diodorus shouted as he rode under the

gate of the command area. It had its own temple to Nike, its own fountains. Behind him, the handful of guards surrendered to the Exiles. More poured in behind him.

Rows of gilded bronze statues decorated every entryway, and a bath of silver stood in the middle of the court. Diodorus let his horse drink from it.

'What an idiot,' Diodorus said. 'Eumenes! File-leaders at the door of every tent. Four files in the gate and *every fucking coin gets shared*. Understand, lads?'

Eumenes' men didn't wait for orders – they were off their horses and moving to protect their posts as soon as they heard the hipparch. Eumenes took more files out of the gate to surround the tent complex.

'Take it all!' Diodorus bellowed. The Exiles roared. To Melitta, he said, 'This beats glory any time.'

'We have to find Amastris!' Melitta shouted.

But Amastris was one woman, and here was reward for years of fighting – here was the treasure of an enemy army, and most men knew that this was the hoard that would pay for their return.

Leon rode into the courtyard. He saluted Diodorus. 'Third troop is sweeping the officers' lines and fourth is off to cull the horse herd.' He nodded. 'I see that we're the first ones here.'

Uncle Leon had a line of blood along his lip. 'You're hurt!' Melitta said.

'Look who it is!' Leon said. He didn't smile.

'We need to find Amastris. Everyone is looting!' Melitta shouted at her uncles. Behind Leon, Coenus was directing a crowd of eager men with crowbars.

Melitta shrank away.

'Ptolemy's flank was getting the worst of it, last I saw,' Leon said to Diodorus over her head. 'Won't do us any good if the Farm Boy dies while we're looting.'

Diodorus shook his head. 'Demetrios was over there with all his best cavalry,' he said. He pulled off his helmet. 'Ptolemy can handle it. If he can't win with both his left and his centre victorious, we were doomed from the first.'

'Eumenes looted the enemy camp at Gabiene, and you still

lost.' Leon was watching the dust to the east. 'Let me take the mercenaries—'

'You think that you could get them out of an enemy camp once the looting starts?' Diodorus looked around. 'Ptolemy's good, Leon. Coenus, forget the marble! Apollo's golden balls, that man will stop to look at art.'

Leon looked around. 'If you're sure, there may be some items amidst all this vulgarity that I want.'

Melitta looked back and forth. 'We need to find Amastris!' she shouted.

'Look sharp there!' Diodorus yelled when a knot of mercenaries tried to push past one of his files. 'This is ours, comrade. Push off!'

Leon saluted. 'On your head be it, brother,' he said. He ignored Melitta, clasped hands with Diodorus and rode off.

It was ugly, and there were things that Melitta didn't want to watch – rape, brutal killing without mercy – but not as much as she would have seen if the camp had been defended. The Exiles hadn't lost a man, and their blood wasn't up – and their discipline held. They found the treasury, took prisoners who seemed to be worth ransom and formed caravans of their loot before the rest of the army was in the camp.

Melitta watched it, sickened, and she watched the remnants of the beaten army flood away over the back gates and the back walls and on to the sand.

Just beyond the cordon of Exiles, she watched a line of men raping a woman – the victim didn't even scream. Tanu, the Thracian in her file, caught her eye and shook his head. 'Don't watch, lass,' he said.

'We should clear 'em out,' Carlus said.

'Ain't harming us none,' Tanu said. He shrugged. 'I could use a piece of that,' he said.

Melitta straightened her spine. 'My friend is out in that somewhere,' she said. 'I need some men who will watch my back while I find her.' She kneed her horse forward, until she was in front of the pickets. 'Who will follow me?'

'Lord Eumenes put us here,' Tanu said.

'Making trouble, girl?' Coenus said. 'You – Hama! And

Carlus. And Tanu, damn your black heart. Get your arse in the saddle.' He looked up at Melitta. 'Well?'

Melitta moved her gorytos and put the hilt of her akinakes in easy reach. 'Stratokles is no fool,' she said. 'Diodorus is too busy looting to care, and Uncle Leon is too angry to listen to me.'

Coenus nodded. 'I wonder why, girl?'

Melitta dismissed Leon with a flick of her hand. 'But Stratokles would have run as soon as he knew the battle was lost. He's gone and he's got Amastris with him – I know it.'

It wasn't her best rhetoric – Satyrus would have been better at this – but something in her tone went home, both to the men like Carlus who knew her and to Coenus. He nodded and waved at the man holding his charger.

'All right, I'm with you, lady. Looting is not for gentlemen.' Coenus raised an eyebrow. 'Besides, I'm done.'

The elephants were running, and a handful of terrified but elated volunteers were 'guarding' their three captures, led by Namastis – now a phylarch.

Satyrus was reforming his taxeis. The White Shields were streaming away to the north, all discipline gone – having survived the elephants, they were hunting fugitives. The Aegyptians were different, unsure of what to do with their victory.

Satyrus formed them, his stomach roiling at the losses and the gaps. Where was Xenophon? Where was Dionysius? Where was Diokles? There were so many holes in the front ranks that he had to use every one of the young men he'd recruited as a phylarch, and then he had to promote a dozen of Leon's marines.

He rallied them facing the enemy camp. To his left, there was still fighting – scattered bands of cavalry, enemy and friendly, appeared out of the battle haze. It was past noon. Satyrus drank water and tried to find someone to give him orders.

On his right, the Foot Companions rallied. The elephants had hurt them. Satyrus could look to his right and see familiar faces – Amyntas was now in the front rank, just a few men away. Satyrus waved and Amyntas waved back.

The motion seemed to embolden the Foot Companions' left phylarch. He turned on his heel and saluted. 'Any orders, Polemarch?' he asked.

Satyrus made a choking noise. He turned and spat. 'What did you ask?' he choked out.

The Macedonian shrugged despite his bronze breastplate. 'Quite a few officers failed to survive first contact,' the man said. He pulled off his helmet and offered his arm to clasp. 'Philip, son of Philip.'

'Satyrus, son of Kineas,' Satyrus said. 'I have no idea what to do now.'

Philip laughed. 'Fuck, are you sure you're an officer?' he asked.

Hoof beats.

Purple cloaks and dun cloaks moving in the dust to his front.

'Cavalry on our flank!' came the shouts from the left. Satyrus had to see for himself. He stepped out of the ranks. 'Philip, hold this line,' he ordered. 'Abraham! Take command of the right file! Rafik, on me!'

The Nabataean followed him out of the ranks and he ran, the rubbing of his greaves tearing at the blood-caked sores on his ankles as he ran across the front of his taxeis.

'Cavalry!' his comrades shouted. Theron wasn't there to command the left, but Apollodorus, one of Leon's marines, had ordered the flank files to face to their shields and down spears, covering the flank of the taxeis – a smart man. Satyrus stopped level with him.

'There they are,' Apollodorus said. He pointed into the haze of dust where Satyrus could just see movement.

Satyrus reached up and tilted his silver helmet back on his head. The cheekpieces hinged up, and he could breathe – and see.

The enemy cavalry was coming forward cautiously. They offered him no threat at all – his files were steady and Apollodorus had already made them secure. 'Well done, marine,' Satyrus said.

'Thank you, sir!' the marine answered woodenly. As if he

were a real officer. 'Looks to me like they crushed our right while we crushed theirs,' he added.

The leader of the enemy cavalry was encased in golden armour, and he had a golden helmet. He rode forward slowly, and then a trumpet sounded and his men halted.

Behind him and to the left, another trumpet sounded. Men pointed.

Satyrus flexed his back under his scale corslet and fought exhaustion. The man in the golden armour had to be Demetrios.

Gold Helm rode forward boldly. In a few heartbeats he covered the ground, and he pulled up just short of Satyrus.

'That's my helmet,' he said.

'Come and take it,' Satyrus said. Not his best line ever, but not bad. He managed a smile.

'I thought that you might be my infantry,' Demetrios said, conversationally. 'I seem to have lost.'

'We destroyed your infantry,' Satyrus said.

Demetrios nodded. 'Shall we fight? Single combat? You look like a hero to me.'

Satyrus's tired smile flashed into a grin. Demetrios's charm was like a force of nature. For just a heartbeat, he *wanted* to fight the magnificent enemy in hand-to-hand combat.

'Delighted,' Satyrus said. 'If you'll dismount?'

There were trumpets sounding behind the left flank, and Demetrios's troopers were starting to shuffle.

'No, I don't think I'd better,' Demetrios said. He smiled, as if Satyrus had scored a point. 'Pity – I think we might be a match, and I'd like to have something to show for today.'

Satyrus stepped out of the ranks so that he wouldn't seem afraid. 'Another time, perhaps?' he shouted. Men in the ranks were calling out.

Demetrios reared his charger and saluted – the Olympic salute. 'Next time then, hero.' He turned his horse and rode away.

'Hero?' Satyrus said.

Apollodorus was grinning.

He was still grinning when Ptolemy rode through the dust. 'Young Satyrus,' he said. 'I think we've won. Why are your men so far from your place in the line? What news?'

Satyrus shook his head. 'We've won, lord.'

Ptolemy grinned, his ugly face transformed. 'I thought we might have, at that. Seleucus saved my arse in the dust, and things seemed to get better. So – the boys stayed loyal!'

'All the ones who matter,' Satyrus said, and there was a thin cheer.

As official news of victory spread, the men of the Aegyptian taxeis collapsed like curtains cut from their rods. Men knelt in the dust, or even lay down. And then someone began a hymn – the Aegyptian hymn to Osiris. Most of the men knew it, even the Greeks – and the haunting melody was taken up.

'Zeus Soter, boy,' Ptolemy said. There were tears on his cheeks, and he slid from his mount.

Drawn by the singing, more men rode out of the haze. The dust cloud itself began to thin.

'Ares!' Seleucus shouted. 'The right-flank cavalry is already in their camp!' He seemed to see the infantrymen for the first time. 'Well fought, soldiers! No one will call *this* a cavalry battle.'

Ptolemy clasped Satyrus's hand. 'Where's your tutor, boy? Your polemarch?'

Satyrus's heart seemed to stop, because he hadn't given Philokles a thought in what seemed like hours. 'Down, sir,' he said. 'I'm in command.'

Ptolemy's grip tightened. 'Good man,' he said. He *embraced* Satyrus. 'I knew you were a young man of talent.' Then he looked up at Seleucus. 'Round up anyone who can still ride. We're going to press the pursuit.'

Seleucus laughed. 'No, lord. We're going to loot the camp. The men have already made that decision. But I'll offer a reward for the elephants.'

'We have half a dozen,' Satyrus said. He bowed to Ptolemy, and when the great man had remounted and ridden away, he felt as if he had to lie down in the sand. He felt like collapsing, but instead he turned and walked back to Abraham. 'Take the men back to camp. Do *not* let them join in the looting. I'm going to find Philokles.' Satyrus looked at his men, who looked more like a defeated army than a victorious one. The

Foot Companions weren't much different. 'Get men to bury the dead. And find our wounded. Send for the shield-bearers.'

Abraham nodded.

Satyrus walked off, alone.

As they rode out of the cordon, the scene turned to one of debauched violence that made the night market appear to be safe and orderly and the looting of the Exiles a model of decorum. Men drank anything they could find and behaved like animals for no reason or every reason, and Melitta stayed close to her own, riding behind Coenus as he kept to the centre of the great avenues of the tent camp. Twice, Hama and Carlus killed other men from their own army.

'This is horrible,' Melitta said.

'This is the river in which we swim,' Coenus said. He spat. 'Most men are little better than animals.' As if to make his point, an orange glow lit them. Behind them, the town had caught fire. It burned, and Melitta heard the screams of the trapped villagers. Ptolemy's army laughed as they screamed, and butchered those who ran. Macedonians from Ptolemy's army killed the Macedonian wounded of Demetrios's army.

They rode clear of the camp, past the horse herds and into the tail of the enemy rout.

Coenus reined in. 'This is insane, girl!'

Melitta rode straight past him. She knew she could find Stratokles. Amastris wasn't her real goal any more – although images of the rape of the woman in the camp filled her head when she thought of her friend. She rode faster, pressing past frightened camp followers and wounded soldiers. At her shoulder rode half a dozen of her father's best men – and no one turned to face them.

Philokles lay wrapped in his cloak, his head in Theron's lap. He had Theron's chiton wrapped around his groin, and Theron's chiton was Spartan red. Theron was weeping.

Satyrus ran the last few strides with a sob and threw himself on the ground. 'Philokles!' he said.

His tutor's eyes met his, and he grasped the man's hand. 'You broke them!' he said.

Theron's voice was thick and hoarse. 'He doesn't care about that!' he choked.

'I tried to be a moral man,' Philokles said softly. 'But I died killing other men.'

'You are a hero!' Satyrus said through his tears. 'You are too hard on yourself!'

'I love you,' Philokles said so softly that Satyrus had to put his head down to listen. 'Tell Melitta I loved her.'

Satyrus nodded. 'Yes,' he said, suddenly ashamed. 'We love you. All the time.'

Philokles made a noise in his throat. 'Just so,' he whispered. He took a deep breath. 'Examine your life. Love your sister. Be true.' He looked at Theron for a moment, and then he slumped a little, tried to move his hips and gave a short scream.

Blood poured over the ground so fast that Satyrus's feet were drowned in it.

'Kineas!' Philokles said. His eyes went to the sky.

And there, on the edge of dark, Melitta saw the satyr's profile by the light of the burning town – Stratokles. He was wearing a cloak, mounted on a fine mare, and his cut nose revealed him. Even in the dark, Melitta could see that he had Amastris mounted in front of him.

She grabbed at Coenus. 'Stratokles!' she called. 'There he is!'

Coenus turned his horse. It took him a long moment to see what she saw, and then he was riding at the Athenian.

Stratokles heard the hoof beats and turned his horse. He had his guards, and they turned with him.

'Stratokles!' Coenus called.

Melitta put an arrow on her bow.

The Athenian actually smiled. He lowered his sword. 'Gods, my luck has held! Listen! I surrender!' His grin broadened. 'A man of honour, in all this rout!'

Coenus slowed his mount to a walk and his men moved to surround the Athenian's companions. 'Drop your sword,' Coenus said.

Stratokles shook his head. 'Let's have an understanding,' he said, exchanging a look with one of his companions. 'I have someone very valuable here. And I know things – things very important to your Ptolemy. Understand?'

'I understand you killed my mother,' Melitta shouted.

Stratokles turned his head. 'Like fuck I did, honey. One of Eumeles' guardsmen did that – after she cut off my nose.' He shook his head, annoyed. 'Nothing personal about it, girl. Just politics.' Stratokles whispered something to his captive and she squirmed. 'Give me a safe conduct and I'll give you the girl,' he said.

Melitta found that it wasn't that hard, even after a long day, to keep her bow at full draw, but Amastris's movements were spoiling her aim. 'Look at me, Stratokles,' she said.

He didn't look at her. He touched his booted heels to his horse's sides, and the mare backed up. 'I don't think you'll shoot through the tyrant's daughter to get me,' he said. To Coenus, he added, 'I'm perfectly willing to surrender, just not to be murdered.'

'No need to surrender,' Lucius said in his low voice from behind them. 'Sorry I'm late, boss.'

'I have your life in my hand, Stratokles,' Melitta said.

Lucius had a blade at Hama's throat. 'Lady, look around you. I have ten men to your six.' He shook his head. 'And you can't keep that arrow drawn all night.'

Coenus laughed grimly. 'You don't know her. Stratokles, call off your dog and I'll call off mine.'

Stratokles nodded. 'Done. Amastris is going with you. Lucius, did you get the other one?'

Lucius grunted. 'Of course.'

Stratokles laughed. Around them, there was fighting, and the sound of a camel screaming filled the night. 'Time we all went our separate ways.'

Coenus glared at Melitta. 'Put up!' he said.

'He killed my mother!' Melitta said. 'I want him dead. You are all fools if you think that my life is worth my oath and my revenge. I don't mind dying!'

Coenus's arm touched hers and she lowered her arrow. She

saw Stratokles motion at his man, and the big Italian let his sword fall away from Hama's throat.

Stratokles tipped the princess on to the sand. 'See? I keep my part of the bargain,' he said. He bowed from the saddle. 'Princess? I hope we meet again.'

Amastris picked herself up. 'I've learned a great deal from you, sir,' she said.

Stratokles laughed. 'I won't even charge you for it.'

Stratokles turned his horse, nimbler now with just one rider, and rode for it. His men followed him.

Melitta shook her head. 'You have a lot to answer for,' she said to Coenus.

Coenus shrugged. 'You'll thank me yet,' he said.

One of Lucius's men spat as they slowed. There was no pursuit.

'All that loot and nothing to show for it,' he complained.

Stratokles was tired, but the encounter in the sand had filled him with fire and he laughed again. 'Nothing?' he asked. 'We have Alexander's son.' He pointed at the huddled figure of Herakles, bundled in Lucius's arms.

Men whistled softly.

Stratokles led the way up the coast, riding like a conqueror.

29

'I rather liked him,' Amastris said.

Melitta didn't answer. With Coenus and Hama, she and her escort trotted across the battlefield at the edge of night. There were beasts out already – vultures and worse creatures feasted on the dead. Melitta saw elephants being herded by frightened men, and hordes of Macedonian prisoners – thousands of captured pikemen from the shattered centre. She rode past them.

'What are you thinking?' Amastris asked.

Melitta said nothing, only pressed her charger harder. She had a feeling Moira was lying heavily on her. That feeling pressed harder the faster she rode, until she saw a circle of men standing in the last light. They were the only men on the battlefield who were not looting, except for some slaves already busy burying the dead.

They parted for her horse, and there was her brother.

Alive. She breathed in and out.

Philokles.

'He's dead,' Satyrus said. He looked old, even in the ruddy light of the burning town. 'He said goodbye to you.'

Melitta fell into her brother's arms.

'Xeno asked for you, but you weren't here,' Satyrus said.

'Amastris needed to be rescued. I – failed to kill Stratokles.' It was like telling Sappho how she had spent her day. Satyrus's expression was *wrong*.

Behind her, Coenus choked and gave a great cry.

'No!' Melitta said. But she didn't need to look at the cloak-wrapped body next to Philokles to know who it was. Xenophon's death was stamped on her brother's face for ever – the death of his youth. She could see it with the same inevitability that she could see that she carried the dead boy's child.

'We never—' Satyrus said, and then he turned his face away. 'It's not about me,' he said bitterly.

'What are you all doing?' Amastris asked. 'Satyrus? Is that you?'

Satyrus stepped away from his sister and took his love in his arms. 'Amastris!' he said.

Amastris kissed him and looked around. 'I'm sorry for them,' Amastris said softly. 'But Ptolemy won, love. You won.'

'Not tonight,' Satyrus said. He looked up at the sound of hoof beats, and saw the Exiles coming with a baggage train of loot and captured slaves. And then Diodorus was there, and Leon, and other men who loved Philokles and Xenophon.

EPILOGUE

The army of Aegypt gathered its heroic dead for return to Aegypt. Ptolemy collected his looters and his army and thrust north, scattering Demetrios but failing to catch him, and came back to Gaza rich in loot and plunder and leaving Palestine a flaming disaster behind him.

Satyrus and Melitta, like most of the survivors of the battle, spent a day unable to move, and then were pressed into duties – burying the dead. Hauling food.

There were never enough slaves, after a battle. And the danger of renewed conflict was, at first, very real. Demetrios saved most of his cavalry. His patrols began to prowl the shore north of Gaza.

Weeks passed. Ptolemy took his cavalry on a deep raid into Palestine, and cities opened their gates to him. Diodorus rode at his side, and the loot was legendary. But finally, Ptolemy turned for home, and the Phalanx of Aegypt led the march, fourteen hundred veterans. When they entered Alexandria, they sang the Paean, and the crowds cheered them as they cheered no other troops, and Namastis embraced Diokles and Amyntas and Satyrus and Abraham when they were dismissed as if they were all brothers.

And fathers and mothers wept for the dead.

But the war, and the world, marched on.

Alexander's funeral games had cost a few thousand more lives. But there was still no shortage of contestants.

A week after they returned to Alexandria, Leon sent Satyrus to the slave market with twenty talents of pure gold and Diokles and Abraham as his lieutenants. 'Buy the best of the Macedonian prisoners,' Leon said.

'What for?' Melitta asked. Everything made her grumpy now – Sappho's displeasure and Coenus's too-careful attention.

'They'll be the core of our infantry,' Leon said. 'Next

summer. When we sail for the Euxine.'

That made even Melitta smile, and she waved at Satyrus as he left for the slave pens, accompanied by his friends and some hired guards because of the money.

The captive phalangites looked terrible – underfed, hopeless. They didn't look like soldiers. Most didn't even raise their eyes as Satyrus walked among them, and they stank.

'We want these?' Satyrus asked Diokles, who still favoured his right shoulder and rubbed it a great deal.

'There's a sight for sore eyes,' said a familiar voice.

Satyrus turned his head, and there was Draco, and Philip his partner.

Satyrus grabbed the slave factor. 'I'll take that pair,' he said.

'That's our boy,' Draco said. He managed a smile. 'Zeus Soter, lad. I thought we were dead men, and no mistake.'

'Dead and dead,' Philip managed. He looked as if he was dead.

Despite their filth, Satyrus hugged them.

'What's the game, then?' Philip asked, eyeing the gold.

'I want two thousand of the best,' Satyrus said. 'Help me choose them.'

'What for?' Draco asked. 'Ares' dick, lad, that's more gold than I've ever seen except Persepolis.'

'I'm raising an army.' Satyrus grinned. 'With my sister.'

'Well, lad, the best are mostly dead,' Draco said. 'At Arbela and Jaxartes and Gabiene and a dozen other fields across the world.' He took a deep breath. 'Free men? You'll buy us free?'

'Of course,' Satyrus said.

'All right then,' Draco said, and the fire returned to his voice. Just like that. He straightened up, and began to point at men who were lying in their own filth. 'Party is over, boys,' he shouted. 'We're going to be free. This here is Satyrus, and he's our strategos.'

The Macedonians shuffled to their feet.

Satyrus watched, and was afraid. 'Philokles used to call war the ultimate tyrant,' he said.

Abraham nodded. 'Tyrant indeed.'

HISTORICAL NOTE

Writing a novel – several novels, I hope – about the wars of the Diadochi, or Successors, is a difficult game for an amateur historian to play. There are many, many players, and many sides, and frankly, none of them are 'good'. From the first, I had to make certain decisions, and most of them had to do with limiting the cast of characters to a size that the reader could assimilate without insulting anyone's intelligence. Antigonus One-Eye and his older son Demetrios deserve novels of their own – as do Cassander, and Eumenes and Ptolemy and Seleucus – and Olympia and the rest. Every one of them could be portrayed as the 'hero' and the others as villains.

If you feel that you need a scorecard, consider visiting my website at www.hippeis.com where you can at least review the biographies of some of the main players. Wikipedia has full biographies on most of the players in the period, as well.

From a standpoint of purely military history, I've made some decisions that knowledgeable readers may find odd. For example, I no longer believe in the 'linothorax' or linen breastplate, and I've written it out of the novels. Nor do I believe that the Macedonian pike system – the sarissa armed phalanx – was really any 'better' than the old Greek hoplite system. In fact, I suspect it was worse – as the experience of early modern warfare suggests that the longer your pikes are, the less you trust your troops. Macedonian farm boys were not hoplites – they lacked the whole societal and cultural support system that created the hoplite. They were decisive in their day – but as to whether they were 'better' than the earlier system – well, as with much of military change, it was a cultural change, not really a technological one. Or so it seems to me.

Elephants were not tanks, nor were they a magical victory tool. They could be very effective, or utterly ineffective. I've tried to show both situations.

The same can be said of horse-archery. On open ground,

with endless remounts and a limitless arrow supply, a horse-archer army must have been a nightmare. But a few hundred horse-archers on the vast expanse of a Successor battlefield might only have been a nuisance.

Ultimately, though, I don't believe in 'military' history. War is about economics, religion, art, society – war is inseparable from culture. You could not – in this period – train an Egyptian peasant to be a horse-archer without changing his way of life and his economy, his social status, perhaps his religion. Questions about military technology – 'Why didn't Alexander create an army of [insert technological wonder here]?' – ignore the constraints imposed by the realities of the day – the culture of Macedon, which carried, it seems to me, the seeds of its own destruction from the first.

And then there is the problem of sources. In as much as we know *anything* about the world of the Diadochi, we owe that knowledge to a few authors, none of whom is actually contemporary. I used Diodorus Siculus throughout the writing of the *Tyrant* books – in most cases I prefer him to Arrian or Polybius, and in many cases he's the sole source. I also admit to using (joyously!) any material that Plutarch could provide, even though I fully realize his moralizing ways.

For anyone who wants to get a quick lesson in the difficulties of the sources for the period, I recommend visiting the website www.livius.org. The articles on the sources will, I hope, go a long way to demonstrating how little we know about Alexander and his successors.

Of course, as I'm a novelist and not an historian, sometimes the loopholes in the evidence – or even the vast gaps – are the very space in which my characters operate. Sometimes, a lack of knowledge is what creates the appeal. Either way, I hope that I have created a believable version of the world after Alexander's death. I hope that you enjoy this book, and the three – or four – to follow.

And as usual, I'm always happy to hear your comments – and even your criticisms – at the Online Agora on www.hippeis.com. See you there, I hope!

AUTHOR'S NOTE

I am an author, not a linguist – a novelist, and not fully an historian. Despite this caveat, I do the best I can to research everything from clothing to phalanx formations as I go – and sometimes I disagree with the accepted wisdom of either academe or the armchair generals who write colorful coffee table books on these subjects. An excellent example would be the 'linothorax' or linen body armour of the Greek and Macedonian warriors. I don't believe there ever was a 'linothorax' in the periods about which I write, and you'll never find one here. If you want to learn more about *why* the 'linothorax' may be a figment of the modern imagination, I recommend that you visit my website at www.hippeis.com.

That said, all the usual caveats apply. Many professional and amateur historians read these books and help me with criticism – thanks! But ultimately, the errors are mine. I read Greek – slowly and with a pile of books at my elbow – and I make my own decisions as to what Pausanias says, or Arrian. And ultimately, errors are my fault. If you find a historical error – please let me know!

One thing I have tried to avoid is altering history as we know it to suit a timetable or plotline. The history of the Wars of the Successors is difficult enough without my altering it ...

In addition, as you write about a period you love (and I have fallen pretty hard for this one) you learn more. Once I learn more, words may change or change their usage. As an example, in *Tyrant* I used Xenophon's *Cavalry Commander* as my guide to almost everything. Xenophon calls the ideal weapon a *machaira*. Subsequent study has revealed that Greeks were pretty lax about their sword nomenclature (actually, everyone is, except martial arts enthusiasts) and so Kineas's Aegyptian *machaira* was probably called a *kopis*. So in the second book, I call it a *kopis* without apology. Other words may change – certainly, my notion of the internal mechanics of the *hoplite phalanx* have changed. The more you learn …

ACKNOWLEDGEMENTS

I'm always sorry to finish an historical novel, because writing them is the best job in the world and researching them is more fun than anything I can imagine. I approach every historical era with a basket full of questions – How did they eat? What did they wear? How does that weapon work? This time, my questions have driven me to start recreating the period. The world's Classical re-enactors have been an enormous resource to me while writing, both with details of costume and armour and food, and as a fountain of inspiration. In that regard I'd like to thank Craig Sitch and Cheryl Fuhlbohm of Manning Imperial, who make some of the finest recreations of material culture from Classical antiquity in the world (www.manningimperial. com), as well as Joe Piela of Lonely Mountain Forge for helping recreate equipment on tight schedules. I'd also like to thank Paul McDonnell-Staff, Paul Bardunias, and Giannis Kadoglou for their depth of knowledge and constant willingness to answer questions – as well as the members of various ancient Greek re-enactment societies all over the world, from Spain to Australia. The Melbourne and Sydney Ancients have been especially forthcoming with permission to use their photos, and many re-enactors in Greece and the UK and elsewhere have been tireless in their support. Thanks most of all to the members of my own group, Hoplologia and the Taxeis Plataea, for being the guinea-pigs on a great deal of material culture and martial-arts experimentation. *On to Marathon!*

Speaking of re-enactors, my friend Steven Sandford draws the maps for these books, and he deserves a special word of thanks.

Speaking of friends, I owe a debt of gratitude to Christine Szego, who provides daily criticism and support from her store, Bakka Phoenix, in Toronto. Thanks, Christine!

Kineas and his world began with my desire to write a book that would allow me to discuss the serious issues of war and politics that are around all of us today. I was returning to school and returning to my first love – Classical history. I am also an unashamed fan of Patrick O'Brian, and I wanted to write a series with depth and length that would allow me to explore the whole period, with the relationships that define men, and women, in war – not just one snippet. The combination – Classical history, the philosophy of war, and the ethics of the world of arête – gave rise to the volume you hold in your hand.

Along the way, I met Prof. Wallace and Prof. Young, both very learned men with long association to the University of Toronto. Professor Wallace answered any question that I asked him, providing me with sources and sources and sources, introducing me to the labyrinthine wonders of Diodorus Siculus, and finally, to T. Cuyler Young. Cuyler was kind enough to start my education on the Persian Empire of Alexander's day, and to discuss the possibility that Alexander was not infallible, or even close to it. I wish to give my profoundest thanks and gratitude to these two men for their help in re-creating the world of fourth century BC Greece, and the theory of Alexander's campaigns that underpins this series of novels. Any brilliant scholarship is theirs, and any errors of scholarship are certainly mine. I will never forget the pleasure of sitting in Prof. Wallace's office, nor in Cuyler's living room, eating chocolate cake and debating the myth of Alexander's invincibility. Both men have passed on now, since this book was written – but none of the Kineas books would have been the same without them. They were great men, and great academics – the kind of scholars who keep civilization alive.

I'd also like to thank the staff of the University of Toronto's Classics department for their support, and for reviving my dormant interest in Classical Greek, as well as the staffs of the University of Toronto and the Toronto Metro Reference Library for their dedication and interest. Libraries matter!

I now have a website, the product of much work and creativity. For that I owe Rebecca Jordan – please visit it. The address is at the bottom of this.

I'd like to thank my old friends Matt Heppe and Robert

Sulentic for their support in reading the novel, commenting on it, and helping me avoid anachronisms. Both men have encyclopedaeic knowledge of Classical and Hellenistic military history and, again, any errors are mine. I have added two new readers – Aurora Simmons and Jenny Carrier; both re-enactors, both well read, and both capable of telling me when I've got the whole thing wrong.

In addition, I owe eight years of thanks to Tim Waller, the world's finest copy-editor. And a few pints!

I couldn't have approached so many Greek texts without the Perseus Project. This online resource, sponsored by Tufts University, gives online access to almost all classical texts in Greek and in English. Without it I would still be working on the second line of *Medea*, never mind the *Iliad* or the *Hymn to Demeter*.

I owe a debt of thanks to my excellent editor, Bill Massey, at Orion, for giving these books constant attention and a great deal of much needed flattery, for his good humor in the face of authorial dicta, and for his support at every stage. I'd also like to thank Shelley Power, my agent, for her unflagging efforts on my behalf, and for many excellent dinners, the most recent of which, at the world's only Ancient Greek restaurant, Archeon Gefsis in Athens, resulted in some hasty culinary re-writing. Thanks, Shelley!

Finally, I would like to thank the muses of the Luna Café, who serve both coffee and good humor, and without whom there would certainly not have been a book. And all my thanks – a lifetime of them – for my wife Sarah.

If you have any questions or you wish to see more or participate (want to be a hoplite at Marathon?) please come and visit www.hippeis.com.

Christian Cameron
Toronto, 2009